SABER'S INSTINCT

SABER'S INSTINCT

LAURA NAPOLI

Saber's Instinct

This is a work of fiction. All the characters and events portrayed in this book are fictional, and any resemblance to real people or incidents is purely coincidental.

First Printing, 2024

Paperback ISBN: 979-8-9871949-8-0

EBook ISBN: 979-8-9871949-9-7

Heating Cats Pawblishing, LLC

https://heatingcats.com

This book was supposed to be dedicated to my Aunt due to a spicy chapter or three, but those particular chapters have been moved to the next book. Sorry, you'll have to wait to find out if I have any shame or not, not that there's really any question there. I don't. Still, thank you for your feedback and support, and I hope you like the changes. Grumble, grumble. Yes, that chapter needed work, and you and Mom were both right. Grumble, grumble. Yes, I'm still grumbling about it, even if I'm happier with the results. Grumble.

Instead, this book is dedicated to anyone who has ever had to fight through the same challenges Marsee does in this book. You are not a monster. I see your struggles, and I am so very proud of you. Keep fighting to live, if not for yourself, then for others. For you are loved, you matter, and you would be missed.

xoxo

CONTENTS

CHAPTER 1

Jer: Escaped

Jer pinned his ears flat to his skull and gasped as his tail stuck straight out in instant terror. "What do you mean Rip Current escaped?!"

His brother Marcus stared at his tablet as he continued to read. "Tamarin returned to her post after a short nap to relieve Thatcher but found both her and the pilot who relieved her unconscious and locked in the cell. She's notified the other guards but hasn't been able to reach or locate Avery."

"Ancient Gods! Marsee!" Flipping out his tablet, Jer scanned for messages from his daughter but didn't find anything since earlier that morning when she'd sent them the information about Snapper Fish. Frowning, he tried calling her, but she didn't pick up. He tried Clear Seas and Temperate next, but they didn't answer either.

"They're not answering, Marcus. I don't like it. Have Tamarin secure a ship and meet us here. Contact Lowell. Maybe she can find them." He grabbed the back of his scruff, torn with indecision. Every fiber of his being wanted to go after Marsee, but it was far more important that they figure out who else was involved and secure any evidence before Rip destroyed it. Taking a deep breath, he forced the beast inside him to wait while Marcus spoke with the Tech.

"They're together," Lowell said. "I'm sending you the coordinates now. It's half an hour old at least, and I'm not getting a current ping."

Marcus's tablet dinged with the message. "It looks like they're still at the Habitat."

Jer pursed his lips in a worried frown. "That doesn't explain why they're not answering. Avery's equipment should work anywhere on the planet."

"Yes, it does," Marcus replied, his voice far more calm than Jer felt. "They stripped out everything they could to prepare for demolition. There's not a lot of existing infrastructure out where they are, and it's going to take days to restore everything."

"Lowell, monitor their positions and let us know immediately if they leave the Habitat or if you get a current ping," Jer called out.

"Yes, sir."

"Has Ellie's tablet moved at all since this morning?" Marcus asked.

"No, sir."

Marcus signed off and stared at the house, one claw tapping on his tablet as he thought. "As soon as Tamarin shows up, we'll head to the Habitat. Let's see what we can find here while we wait." Marcus turned to Sampson. "Wait here for Tamarin."

Jer turned back to face the building and the locked door. Days of pent-up anger boiled over. Unable to control his fury any longer, he braced himself, digging his claws into cracks in the stone floor, and hit the door with everything he had. What turned out to be a rather flimsy door exploded open, with splinters of the door and frame floating off everywhere.

Oops, Jer thought, not the least bit contrite about damaging the door or worried about the paperwork he'd have to fill out later.

Marcus said nothing as he swam up next to him. They both peered inside, tense and ready for an attack, but none came. What they found instead was a small family room, empty save for a few hanging nets and a medium-sized monitor that hung on the far wall. Half a dozen pictures hung on another wall, most of a young female Water Sprite. A single sickly-looking plant drooped by the far window.

They entered and slowly made their way further into the house, cautiously checking each room as they went. Several rooms later, they found a middle-aged Sprite floating in what appeared to be a child's bedroom. The Sprite faced away from the door, looking out a tiny oval-shaped window, and held what appeared to be a picture frame in his hand. Toys were stored in several bulging nets surrounding a neatly organized collection of bookshelves. Something felt wrong about the space, but he wasn't sure what. Taking a deep breath, he realized the water smelled stale, almost stagnant, as if no one had been in the room for a long time.

It's far too neat for a child's room, he thought. *Has something happened to her?*

"Snapper Fish?" Marcus asked, bringing Jer's attention back to the Sprite, who hadn't shifted from the window.

The Sprite's gills fluttered as he took a deep breath, but he didn't move or turn around to face them. "I wondered when you'd show up," he said in fluent Saber. "I take it Rip turned me in?"

"No. We tracked Ellie's tablet here," Jer replied. "You're under arrest for theft, kidnapping, and assault with intent to kill."

He tensed, expecting Snapper Fish to attack, but again, nothing happened.

"I know you won't believe me, but I didn't kill the Senior Guild Master or hurt your daughter. They were both in the suite when I left. That was all Rip's doing. He took my daughter, too. Months ago. I haven't been able to figure out where he's hiding her, but I'll tell you everything I know. I fully deserve whatever punishment you give me, and I won't fight it, but please! Find her if you can."

He glanced at Marcus with a raised brow. "Rip Current escaped."

Snapper Fish spun around, horror and fear flashing across his skin. "Bottomless depths! He's going to kill her! Please! You have to save her!"

Jer's instinct activated, startled by Snapper Fish's sudden movement. "Your daughter?" Jer asked to clarify as he shut his instinct off and calmed his breathing.

"Yes, and yours if he gets the chance. Stormy too. He goes after anyone who gets in his way."

"Do you have any idea where he might go or where your daughter might be?" Marcus asked.

"There are two locations I'd check first. There's a secret room in his home back in the East Sea district, but I haven't figured out how to enter his home without him knowing. After he was arrested, I figured his house was under guard, so I haven't tried, but my guess is out by the new shipyard. He goes out there almost every day, but I can't get anywhere close to it due to the patrols."

Snapper Fish's eyes shifted to glance behind them.

Jer spun around, braced for an attack, but relaxed when he recognized Tamarin. Impressed at how quickly she'd arrived, he turned back around. "Show us where this room is."

Snapper Fish nodded and started to swim forward, but Tamarin bolted between them.

"Stop! Don't move!" she ordered.

Practically faster than Jer could follow, she unclipped and held up a shock collar in one paw and a stunner in another. Snapper nodded again, so she tossed over the shock collar, which he locked on without a fuss. Once in place, she swam over, confirmed it was secure, and took the picture frame, which she examined before handing it over to him. Jer glanced at it, confirming it was the same child in the other pictures, and handed it off to Marcus.

Tamarin motioned with her stunner for Snapper to head out.

They followed close behind, stopping only to collect Ellie's tablet. A small Water Sprite Honor Guard ship now floated outside the residence, leaving ripples in the water as the engines held it in place. Once Tamarin confirmed that no one had entered the ship while they were inside, she motioned Snapper Fish on board. Sampson was already strapped into the pilot's net, waiting for them.

While Marcus secured the picture and Ellie's tablet in one of the evidence lockers, Jer guarded Tamarin as she secured Snapper Fish in a safety harness before climbing into his own. "These nets are impossible," he muttered under his breath. Tamarin swam over to assist before climbing into hers. Marcus, having far more experience than he did with the Water Sprite's safety equipment, had no difficulty adjusting his.

"Where to, sir?" Sampson asked when he was finally situated.

He wanted to head to Marsee, but finding this secret room and securing Snapper Fish needed to happen first. There weren't any guards at Rip's home because they didn't know who they could trust in the local Honor Guard, and there was a fairly decent chance Rip would head there first to destroy any evidence. He gave Sampson the location, praying he was making the right decision, and they took off.

Along the way, they questioned Snapper but ended up with more questions than answers. What concerned him the most was that they now had confirmation that Marsee's account was compromised.

Fifteen minutes later, they landed in front of Rip Current's primary residence. He'd never been to Rip's home before, and like many traditional Water Sprite homes, it was built into the side of a small mountain, but unlike any of the others he'd been in, or Rip's residence in Council Platform, the interior was massive, ornate, and furnished with mastery-level artwork. It made his own home seem like a hovel in comparison and far exceeded what Rip should have been able to afford with his rank. While being on the Council had some benefits, like having access to a private shuttle and an additional furnished residence in their world's council city, in every other way, their compensation was tied to the minimum rate paid to someone who couldn't work. It was how they balanced the influence and power their rank gave them, but this wasn't just a home. It was a palace and so massive that Jer wondered how he even managed to maintain it. They'd struggled to maintain Myra's family compound over the years, even with cleaning bots.

Snapper Fish led them down a long hallway decorated with flowering plants and carvings that were strategically placed to work with a floor-to-ceiling mural that was so lifelike that Jer found it difficult to believe he was inside. Eventually, they came to Rip's office, which he would have completely missed, as the door was expertly hidden in the mural. Snapper hit a switch, and the door opened, revealing a fairly standard, if ornate, office. A carved desk sat facing the door in a position of power, with a painting of Rip hung above it. Flanking the painting was a floor-to-ceiling bookcase, which held a collection he knew Marsee would drool over. Monitors hung on the other walls, and a medium-sized table with seating nets hung around it was tucked into one corner. In the other corner was a life-sized free-standing statue of a female Water Sprite.

Tamarin had her stunner out, and he had his instinct on, ready for an attack as they entered, but the room was empty. Snapper swam over to the statue and placed both hands on the side of the Sprite, and a moment later, he heard a soft click. He spun as a motion caught his attention and watched as an entire section of the built-in bookcase shifted and slid open behind Rip's desk.

From his vantage point, the hidden room appeared to be at least twice the size of Rip's office, with another large desk against one wall and floor-to-ceiling cabinets along the others. Several tables filled the interior with a wide variety of unknown but very expensive-looking tech.

Tamarin cautiously swam forward to confirm the room was empty and safe for them to enter but frowned at whatever she saw before swimming back out and over to guard Snapper Fish again.

Marcus swam in first and took a deep breath before swimming off.

Jer frowned as he flipped off his instinct yet again and followed after, wondering what he was going to find. He sighed when he saw what it was: a stasis chamber with a large male Water Sprite floating inside. Next to it were three other empty stasis chambers. The wall behind them, hidden from view of Rip's outer office, had a row of restraints ending in shock collars. Stains on the wall and the faint scent of blood and fecal matter left little to the imagination.

Marcus was already on his tablet calling in a trauma ship, so he swam over to the desk and started opening drawers. The first he found stuffed full of letters. He picked one up and read a little of it, frowned at what he read, and set it aside to check the other drawers. The second drawer had more letters, but the third had a small ornate book, which turned out to be a handwritten journal in Water Sprite. Flipping to the last entry, he started reading.

Marcus hung up with the Trauma Center and started rifling through one of the massive filing cabinets, but only a few moments later, he started growling.

Jer's head shot up, hackles raised, and instinct on, once again bracing for an attack. When he realized Marcus was growling at whatever he was reading, Jer flicked his instinct off but pursed his lips with concern. He couldn't remember the last time his mentor lost control with others around enough to actually growl. "What is it?"

Rather than answering, Marcus swam over and handed him a folder.

He raised a brow and took the file with trepidation. It didn't take him long to start growling, too. He flipped past dozens of surveillance images of Marsee in what should have been private and secure locations. Most appeared to have been taken after the trial, but a few went back years. Flipping past those, he found Marsee's reports to the Council, including her report on psychosis, Kendra's investigation into Marsee's flag on her medical record, and her school and guild record. Every incident of recorded hunter's instinct was highlighted, including the report from her childhood when she'd been in a fight with a classmate. He flipped past that and found what appeared to be part of a private journal. Even though he felt guilty for invading her privacy, he kept reading, then swallowed hard with guilt as she detailed how much his words had hurt her when he'd tested her, not that he didn't already know, but somehow, it was far worse seeing it in writing.

No wonder he knew how to manipulate her, he thought bitterly and handed the folder back with a heavy sigh.

"There's a folder for half the Council at least and hundreds of other guild masters and seniors." Marcus nodded towards the book in Jer's hand. "What did you find?"

"Rip's journal and a pile of letters," he replied and returned to reading. A moment later, he let out another sigh.

"Now what?" Marcus asked.

"I think that's Rip's brother, Gentle Current. Gentle found out what Rip was planning, confronted him, and Rip killed him when he threatened to report it." He handed the journal over to Marcus so he could read it for himself.

Marcus sighed, flipped the journal closed, and started opening other drawers. More letters filled the next two drawers, but Marcus gasped when he opened the last one.

He couldn't see in the drawer from where he was, so he shifted over to peer down and swallowed hard at what he saw. The only thing in the drawer was a small stasis unit containing another one of Ellie's claws, or at least that's what he assumed, as it was about the same size as the others and still had a small tuft of black fur attached.

A minute later, the trauma ship healers swam in and started scanning the body. "I'm sorry, sir. He's dead, and based on his injuries, it's unlikely we'll be able to revive him."

Jer nodded. "I figured as much. Can you tell me who he is?" He needed confirmation.

"Yes, sir. Gentle Current," the healer replied.

Marcus pointed to the open drawer. "We found a claw, too. Can you tell me who it belonged to?"

The healer swam over and scanned the claw. "Senior Guild Master Khihar," she said a moment later.

"What about any of...that." Marcus waved his paw in the general direction of the stains on the wall.

"Sorry, sir. It's too degraded to get a positive match."

Marcus turned towards him with a frown. "Come on, Jer. Let's secure Snapper Fish and check out the shipyard before Marsee heads there herself. We can come back to this mess later."

Jer nodded and motioned for the healers to take the body. He waited until everyone else was out before closing up the room, and as he swam out after the others, he noticed Marcus still had the journal and folder with him. An agonizing fifteen minutes later, they landed back at the council building and escorted Snapper Fish down to a cell. Honor Guard Thatcher and the pilot they'd sent to help guard Rip floated outside one of the cells, waiting for them.

Thatcher hit the switch on the door as they approached, and Snapper Fish swam in without issue. Jer locked the door behind him.

"Are you two okay?" Marcus asked.

"Yes, sir," Thatcher replied. "The healers cleared us a few minutes ago."

"What happened? Jer asked.

"He knocked me out as I went through the door to bring him his noon meal and then shocked Carl before he could call for help. I'm sorry, sir."

"How did he get the shock collar off?" Marcus asked.

"I don't know, sir. We're still trying to determine that."

Jer sighed but shrugged. "There's little you can do against their natural defenses. Did anyone see him leave the building?"

"No one has come forward, but he stunned several people on the way out the back door. Thankfully, no one appears to be seriously injured."

"Why wasn't he under surveillance by Command?" It took everything he had not to growl at the guards. Even if he had escaped his cell, they should have been able to stop him before he left the building.

"He was, sir," Tamarin replied, her tone flat.

Jer frowned at the implications.

"I want whoever was watching arrested," Marcus ordered.

"Already done, sir," Tamarin said, nodding to a cell across the hall.

Marcus's tablet dinged, and he frowned as he checked it. "Lowell says their tablets just appeared at the new shipyard."

"Has anyone been able to reach Avery?" Jer asked.

"No, sir," Thatcher replied with a slight frown of worry. "Last I heard, we can't even get a ping on his coms device. I've been trying to reach him every five minutes."

Jer pulled out his tablet to try calling Marsee again, but Tamarin stopped him. He looked up at the guard with a frown.

"Her account's compromised. If Avery's turned off his comms unit on purpose and they're not answering their calls, then it's either because a call would be deadly or it's a trap."

Marcus nodded. "Agreed. Tamarin, you're with us."

Jer bolted out of the council building as fast as he could swim and back onto the ship with Marcus and Tamarin right behind him. A minute later, Jer's tablet rang with a call from Marsee. He stared at the tablet and shook, not daring to answer it. "Sampson, can this ship go any faster?"

"Yes, sir. Hold on." Sampson did something, and the ship punched forward, pressing Jer into his harness. The straps dug painfully into his skin with the force. He silenced his tablet and clipped it to his carry harness but shook with fear when the tablet vibrated with another call.

Several agonizing minutes later, they approached the platform, and two Sea Patrol ships challenged them.

Marcus raised a paw to stop Sampson before he could reply. "Don't tell them we're on board. I don't know if they're involved with Rip or just following orders."

Sampson's clearance was more than high enough to grant him access to the site, but Jer frowned as they approached Clear Seas' shuttle to land. He could see both Clear Seas and Temperate inside.

He bolted out of the ship the moment it landed.

Clear Seas spotted him and bolted out of his ship with Temperate right behind.

"Where's Marsee?"

"I don't know," Clear Seas replied, flashing worry and apology. "I've been trying to get ahold of you. The Sea Patrol isn't letting me leave the shuttle. Marsee left with Avery and Stormy maybe fifteen or twenty minutes ago. Why?"

"Rip Current escaped. We can't get ahold of Avery, and Marsee's tablet has been compromised."

Marcus held up his tablet to show a map with a dot on it. "Lowell says this is her current location."

"I know where that is," Clear Seas said after looking at the map. "Follow me."

After ordering Sampson to wait with the ship in case she returned, they grabbed drones from their ship and bolted after Clear Seas, pushing the drones as fast as they would go. On the way, Marcus gave Clear Seas a quick rundown of what they knew.

They were approaching the entrance to a small canyon when Tamarin called out to stop them. "Look, there's Avery!"

Jer squinted in the direction she pointed, not seeing anything at first, and then flicked his ears back in surprise. Hidden behind a tangled clump of seaweed, Jer saw the barest hint of Avery's tawny fur. *How under the three moons did she spot that?* he wondered as they approached. They found Avery unconscious but still breathing, along with a Sprite he didn't recognize.

"That's the Master Builder," Clear Seas said. "Tamarin, Temperate, there should be a healer at the build site. Get them medical care and call for backup."

"Are you sure, sir?" Tamarin asked. "You'll need assistance if Rip is here."

"Yes. Protect Temperate. If anything happens to us, he'll be the next target," Clear Seas ordered.

Tamarin glanced at Marcus for authorization. While he was a Senior Councilor, Clear Seas didn't have authority over Tamarin when her own Senior Councilor was present, and it was unlikely that Tamarin knew they'd cleared Clear Seas of involvement that morning.

Marcus pursed his lips briefly but nodded his agreement.

Tamarin hefted Avery over her shoulder while Temperate grabbed the Water Sprite by his harness and took off.

He watched them for a second, praying they weren't making a mistake, and turned to make his way into the canyon, expecting Rip to attack at any moment. Clear Seas and Marcus flanked him on either side.

A minute later, Jer's heart froze with fear as the horrifying sounds of Marsee's screams echoed off the canyon walls. He didn't think he'd ever heard a more horrible sound in his life, but it was even worse when it suddenly stopped.

CHAPTER 2

Marsee: Stalemate

"Hello, Little Kitten," Rip Current rasped. "It's so lovely to see you again." His voice dripped with sarcasm as a wicked grin slowly formed on his face.

Marsee flinched with remembered pain, triggered by his words and the harsh sound of his voice. She couldn't move, couldn't think, and she was sure her heart stopped beating as overwhelming fear froze her solid.

"What? No hello, Little Kitten? I'm *so* disappointed. After all the time we spent together? And here I thought we were such good friends." He placed his webbed hands over his heart as if he was crushed and started swimming slowly towards her.

Snap out of it! her instinct hissed at her.

She jumped, focused, and let her instinct free.

That's my girl. Now we kill him. Her instinct growled deep and low inside her, and she began looking for weaknesses. In the dark, Rip had taken on horrifying dimensions, but in daylight, the reality was even worse. He was easily twice her size, far faster than she was in the water, and could kill her with a single touch, but at least she could see him now.

Can we make it to the drone? she asked her instinct.

No, he's too close. We need to gain some distance and get away from the wall.

"AVERY! HELP!" she yelled as she shifted to the side and started backing away, hoping her guard was still within hearing distance.

Humor bubbled across Rip's skin as he tossed her drone away from them. "Oh, your *little kitten* of a guard won't be coming to your rescue any time soon. I made sure of that."

She growled through the pain and fear his words caused and shifted again, moving away from the canyon wall. If she could make it to where her drone now floated, she might be able to outrun him. That would leave Stormy unprotected, but if Rip chased after her, it might give Stormy enough time to escape and swim for help.

Rip continued to approach but kept the same distance between them, too far for her to attack but far too close for her liking.

Remember what we decided. Keep our distance. Don't let him get ahold of us. Burn the shocks off in small increments. Swipe, but don't grab. If he's already shocked Avery, then he won't be fully charged, so he can't kill us. Fight through the pain. He's not going to expect that.

"What did you do with the others?" she asked, hoping to distract him and give her more time.

"Who, the rodent you call your sister?" He waved a hand dismissively. "Oh, she's probably dead by now."

"No, they found her. Your little plot failed there. Turns out more people care for her than hate her. I was referring to Petra and all the protesters you made disappear."

"Them?" He shrugged. "I needed someone to practice on. Shame they didn't all make it." He made an arch of lightning crackle between his fingertips. "How else would I know how to make someone scream for hours without killing them?" He swam closer. "As for Petra, well, I certainly couldn't let *her* live, not after she killed your mentor and kidnapped you on her mother's orders. Now, could I? Really, you should be thanking me there. You had such sketchy friends."

She glared at him, trying to tell if he was lying about Petra. She wouldn't put it past him to have killed her. "If that's the case, what did you do with their bodies?"

"Oh, my little kitten. You're sadly mistaken if you think I'm going to tell you that, even if I do intend to kill you."

She flinched again but ignored it as hope bloomed in her heart. If he wasn't telling her what he did with the bodies, there was a chance they were still alive. "If you're going to kill me, why not tell me the rest of your plan? It would be a shame not to be able to share it with someone." She kept backing away as he continued to inch forward.

"I guess that's my burden to bear. Isn't it, my feisty little kitten." Without warning, he exploded forward.

She spun to the side, expecting him to attack the moment he said little kitten again, and tried to swim out of the way, but she wasn't even remotely fast enough to out-swim him. He reached out and grabbed her shoulder as he swam by. Pain radiated through her as she twisted out of his grasp, but it was surprisingly tolerable, not the agony of the shock in the cave. She spun back around and swiped at an opening he left in his side, making sure to hit with just the very tips of her claws. It was only a shallow scratch along his gills, but she didn't get shocked.

Her instinct cheered with their unexpected success. *Yes! Again!*

Why didn't his first shock knock me out? He grabbed my shoulder, she wondered, as she frantically backed away, trying to put as much distance as she could between them. Rip just as unexpectedly stopped to check at his side, his skin flashing a mix of anger, pain, and surprise that she'd managed to land a blow, however small.

No, he grabbed the cloak. It must have protected us. Use it against him. Keep the cloak between us. Drain him out and then attack when he's weak.

Rip turned his attention back to her, his face contorted in rage.

"Is that all you've got left?" she taunted. "I expected so much more from you. I guess when you get old, you must not recharge as quickly."

He flashed his anger and bolted towards her again, as she'd hoped he would.

She tucked herself inside the cloak, making sure she made contact with the cape between them, not her bare skin, easily pushing through the pain of his charge. Taking a chance, she ducked under the cape as she spun and swiped deeper at his gills, hoping that if she could make it hard for him to breathe, it would make him easier to kill. Her blow landed, slicing his side.

He roared and hissed with pain as his skin flashed bright red with fury.

Again, she didn't get shocked when she made contact with her claws, and she realized that area must be vulnerable. She swiped at him again, but he swam away from her reach before stopping again to check his side. She turned and swam with everything she had while he was distracted and surprisingly made it to her drone. Flipping it over, she turned it on and bolted away. Without warning, she found herself yanked back hard, not fifty feet later. The clasps on the cloak dug painfully into her neck, and she struggled to spin around and fight back as he pulled her away from the drone.

"Let's see how well you do without your little cape. You don't deserve this anyway," he snarled and yanked it off her, snapping the buckles. Now free, she spun and swiped at him again, aiming for his face this time, but he blocked it, grabbed her paw before she could pull it away, and started pumping her full of electricity. Her muscles spasmed as pain rippled through her, but she refused to give him the satisfaction of her screams.

Fight through it! her instinct screamed.

She gritted her teeth, forcing her body to move, and landed a blow across his face with her injured paw before he managed to grab that one, too. Not giving up, she pulled her back legs up to gut him, but he weaved his tentacles around her feet, pinning them down and away from his body. She twisted and thrashed as she struggled to break free, but he was far stronger than she was. She snapped at his face with her teeth, but she was too far away.

A tentacle wound its way up her back and wrapped around her neck. He pulled her head back and squeezed until she stopped fighting. The moment she did, he relaxed his grip just enough so she could breathe and stopped shocking her.

"I'm honestly impressed, Little Kitten. Few ever manage to fight back." Before she could regain her breathing enough to come up with a retort, he weaved his fingers through the holes in her mesh cast and flexed her paw back, snapping the cast as easily as if it were nothing more than a twig. The bones in her barely healed paw crunched and popped, and he grinned wickedly as her screams tore free.

"You have such a beautiful voice, my little kitten." His two remaining tentacles reached up and brushed along her sides, making her writhe with pain. "Intoxicating," he whispered. "I could listen to it for hours, but sadly, I think it's time for you to die now. Slowly, of course."

The charge running through her intensified, coming from every point of contact he had with her. She couldn't move, couldn't even think. All she could do was scream.

"Farewell, Little Kitten. Say hello to your father when you see him in the bottomless depths of the great beyond because once I'm done here, he's next."

The edges of her world started to fade and dim around her, and she stopped fighting, welcoming the end and praying that it would come quickly, yet every second felt like an eternity. Her world had mostly faded to darkness, save for the wicked grin on Rip's face that reveled in her pain and impending death, when a bright flash of red caught her attention.

No! she thought as Stormy flew out of the small cave in the wall.

Rip started to turn, having seen her expression change.

She tried fighting back again to distract Rip, and while she couldn't do more than a weak struggle in his grasp, it worked.

He refocused his attention on her, and he chuckled. "Nice try, Little Kitten."

Moments later, Stormy barreled into Rip. He wrapped his tiny arms and tentacles around Rip's neck and back and shocked him with everything he had. He was too small and young to do any real damage, but Rip roared with pain and flashed his fury.

Tossing her aside, he reached up, grabbed one of Stormy's little arms, and pulled him off his back. "Oh look, a two-for-one special," Rip sneered as he started shocking Stormy instead.

Stormy cried out in pain as the electricity caused his skin to ripple in waves of sickening colors.

She floated where Rip had tossed her, struggling to make her twitching muscles move through the pain, gasping for breath with lungs that didn't want to work.

Give me full control! her instinct demanded.

She gave herself over to her instinct, every last little bit. She merged with the beast inside her, nearly feral with rage at everything he had done to her and was now doing to her friend. The pain made them angry instead of weak, and they charged, teeth bared and claws out. He tried to stop her, but they welcomed the pain of his shocks, willing to die if that meant stopping him and saving their friend. They wrapped their arms around their prey, dug their claws deeply into his backside, and grabbed his throat in their mouth, drooling with the anticipation of the kill.

She wrestled control back from her instinct and stopped before her teeth broke through his skin.

No! Bite! Kill him! her instinct screamed and tried to force her to act.

No! We need him alive to find the others. Soon, she promised.

It backed off, waiting.

"LET HIM GO," she growled at Rip, her voice muffled by his neck, which was firmly wedged between her sharp teeth, but it was clear enough.

Rip was caught. If he moved, she would bite his head off and rip him to shreds. If he shocked her, the electricity would cause her to clench her jaw and kill him. He tossed Stormy away from them. Stormy floated, unmoving, and she growled, trying to decide what to do. She couldn't hold on to Rip and help Stormy. He was still breathing, which was something at least, but if she killed Rip, they lost all chance of finding the others.

Rip tried to move his arms up to pull her mouth off his neck, but she growled a warning and tightened her bite ever so slightly. "Move, and I bite," she hissed.

"Now what?" Rip asked. "You could let me go and help your little friend. He could be dying after all."

"Or, I could kill you and then help him," she snarled.

"You could, but you won't, and we both know it. If you were going to, you would have already. You don't have it in you. Killing me might mean you lose control of the monster inside you. You're close, aren't you? Besides, you need me alive. How else will you find the others?"

"She might not kill you, but I will!" her father snarled from off to her side. She turned her head and saw her father, uncle, and Clear Seas swimming fast towards them.

Clear Seas bolted to his son and gave him a gentle shake, "Stormy, wake up! Stormy!"

Stormy didn't respond.

"Go get him help. We've got this," her father ordered.

Clear Seas didn't hesitate. He grabbed his son and bolted back the way they'd come.

"Marsee, are you hurt?" her uncle asked.

Her broken paw throbbed, and every muscle in her body ached and twitched from lingering electricity, but her instinct was managing the pain. She shook her head no, and to her immense pleasure, Rip cried out in pain as her teeth pierced his skin. Her instinct drooled with the taste of his blood, and she struggled to control it, to not finish ripping his throat out like it wanted. Like *she* wanted.

Not yet! she growled at both herself and her instinct. *For now, we make him fear us. He made us suffer for days. We can wait a few minutes to kill him.*

Yes, you're right. He should pay for what he did to us.

They growled, low and deep in their throat, and to their immense pleasure, they could actually taste his fear. That was so unexpected that it momentarily distracted them from their revenge as they savored the taste. **_Delectable,_** her instinct drooled and then tried to decide if it tasted better than chocolate chip cookies.

Her uncle swam over so that Rip could see him. "Rip Current, you've been found guilty of the murder of your brother, Gentle Current, by your own written confession, along with the attempted murders of Senior Guild Master Khihar, Translator Chenzira, and Stormy Seas. You have also been found guilty of colluding in the kidnapping of Little Flower, GrandFather, and Hope Chenzira and attempting to frame both Senior Councilor Clear Seas and Guild Master Nardal for those actions. The sentence is death, to be carried out by the end of this day."

Oh good. We can kill him now, her instinct purred and tried to clamp down.

Not yet, she told it, although a big part of her wanted to give in, and her control was slipping because of it. She tasted more blood.

"You can't do that!" Rip cried. "I demand a trial!"

The scent of his fear bloomed in her mind, glorious, delectable, and better than anything she'd ever smelled or tasted before. She allowed herself to lick as her mouth drooled, and he shuddered, which made the beast inside her purr.

"You need me alive. As Marsee pointed out, you still don't know where the others are. If you let me live, I'll tell you where they are."

"No trial is necessary. It's a unanimous decision by the Senior Council of all three species affected. Besides, we're pretty sure the others are all dead," her father stated with a bland expression. If she didn't know him so well, she'd have thought he was bored with the whole situation. "Marsee, do you want to kill him, or shall I?"

Marsee growled, unable to speak with how much she wanted to kill him, and relaxed her control on her instinct. It purred with anticipation.

In response, her father let out a wicked grin and tilted his head in a single nod. "You may proceed."

She curled one of the claws embedded into his back and purred as Rip writhed and screamed in her fatal embrace. He grabbed at her face to try and peel her jaws off his neck. She increased pressure on his neck and growled a warning. He stopped, but she tasted blood again, and it was all she could do to contain herself.

"Please! They're not all dead! I swear! Let me go, and I'll show you where they are!"

Marsee slowly curled a second claw, then a third, and then a fourth.

A whimper of pain escaped his control. "Please! They're in the cave!"

She stopped.

What are you waiting for? her instinct asked.

To see if he's telling the truth. Once they're safe, then I'll kill him. If he doesn't bleed out first. Don't worry. I have no intentions of letting him live, no matter what the others say.

Ahh, I can be patient a bit longer, it replied.

"What cave?" her father asked.

When Rip didn't immediately respond, she tore her paw free from Rip's back and pointed. "It's over there by those bushes. Not sure you'll fit," she mumbled through her clenched jaw.

Rip screamed in pain, and the water around her filled with his blood before she wrapped her arm back around him. They drooled, and she nearly lost all semblance of control.

Slowly. We kill him slowly, she reminded herself and her instinct.

Her father swam over, looking for the cave.

"To your left," she called out.

He shifted, found it, and tried to fit through, but as she expected, he was too big.

"I'll be right back. I'm going to find someone who can fit," he said and took off back towards the platform.

They floated there waiting. Her jaw and neck were starting to cramp, but it was nothing compared to what Rip had put them through, and she spent her time trying to decide how she would kill him. She wanted it to last as long as possible.

Her uncle kept his attention focused on her, but she ignored him.

"Focus, Marsee," he signed after shifting around to better look into her eyes. "You're wobbling too much."

She checked but felt perfectly in control outside of her own desire to make Rip suffer and die a horrible, painful death, although she wished her father would hurry up so she could start.

"Do you need me to take over?" he signed.

Her instinct growled in response, and she shook her head, making Rip scream with pain. Rip was their prey.

"Then you need to focus harder, Marsee. You can do this. I believe in you."

She huffed with annoyance but pulled her instinct back just enough to make her uncle nod.

Her father returned a few minutes later with Clear Seas and Temperate and showed them where the cave was.

Temperate lit up his skin and floated through, as he was the smallest of the two. A minute later, he returned, exiting through the drilled hole. "I saw at least a dozen people, but the cage they're in goes further than I could access, so there could be more. I couldn't tell if they were all alive or not. We'll need tools to cut them out." He swam off before either her father or uncle could question him further.

"Where are the others?" her father demanded.

"That's all of them. I swear," Rip cried out.

"Over fifty people are missing. Where are the others?" her father demanded again. When he didn't answer, her father nodded to her.

Marsee started digging her claws back in.

Rip screamed and writhed until all of her claws were embedded down to the quick. "They're Leviathan food, just like your whole family should be!"

Rage made her shake with fury. Her control slipped as her instinct demanded revenge for the harm Rip had caused her and her family, and she did nothing to stop it. She no longer cared if she lost herself to her instinct. All that mattered was that he had to die, slowly, painfully, and before he could hurt anyone else ever again.

She felt herself merge fully with her instinct until nothing of her remained but a pure feral rage and the overwhelming desire to kill.

CHAPTER 3

Marsee: Ripped Apart

They shook their prey roughly several times, hard enough to make it scream but not kill it. Not yet. They wanted it to suffer first. A chuffing sound they'd never made before, halfway between a growl and a purr, built inside them. They began slowly raking their claws across its back as it continued to scream and writhe in their grasp. They didn't even feel the pain in their broken paw anymore. After several passes across their prey's back, they brought their hind paws up and gutted it just as slowly, its screams music to their tortured ears.

It tried to shock them, but they hardly felt it. It was nothing compared to what they'd been through before.

They wondered briefly if they were just used to it now or if it was out of charge. They shrugged. It didn't matter either way. It was as good as dead now. Blood pooled around them, making swirling patterns in the water, sweet and delicious, nearly as good as the smell of its fear.

It took advantage of her momentary distraction and reached up and grabbed her mask in one last desperate attempt to escape.

Her instinct reacted immediately to the threat, and they shook their prey again with a growl, biting down hard, and she felt the sudden pop as its neck snapped. Its screaming stopped instantly. They shook it again to be sure it was dead but continued to claw and tear at it, wanting it torn to shreds until nothing was left.

There was so much blood now that they were finding it hard to breathe, but they didn't care. The murky water shifted, and someone appeared. She didn't recognize him, but her instinct did and warned her of the threat. *Watch out!*

They pinned their ears and growled at him to back away. **"MINE!"**

"He's dead, Marsee," he signed. "It's over. He can't hurt you anymore."

Her instinct growled. *It's a trick. He wants to steal our prey.*

"We caught it. It's ours!" They backed away, dragging their prey with them, then dropped it, preparing to fight for it. He moved closer, and they roared at him in warning.

"Yes, you did. I'm very proud of you. Your prey is dead. It can't hurt you anymore. It's time to turn off your instinct. You're stronger than your instinct. Fight it. Take control again. Come back to me."

He lies, her instinct growled. *You are your instinct, and I am you. There is nothing but us. It's a trick. He wants us weak so he can steal our prey.*

He moved closer again. "I love you, Marsee. You're my daughter. Please come back to me."

They hissed and spat at him. **"You lie. You're trying to steal our prey! It's ours, not yours. Go away!"**

"No, Marsee. I don't want your prey. I only want you back. You can do this. You're so very close. I believe in you," he signed and moved closer. "I love you."

How could he love us if he's trying to steal our prey? she wondered.

He doesn't. It's a trick. He's trying to get close enough to steal it or hurt us again. Remember how he attacked us before? He's a threat. We should attack before he gets any closer.

He had hurt them, she remembered. They had fought, and she had beaten him once and knew she could do it again, but she didn't want to fight. She just wanted to tear her prey into tiny little pieces until there was nothing left of it. She hunched protectively over her prey, growling, then grabbed it in her mouth and dragged it further away from him. When she was a good distance away, she dropped it again. She growled at him, so angry that she could barely remember how to form words, and she felt her instinct preparing to defend them.

"You hurt us. We let you live before. We won't this time. Come any closer, and we'll attack!"

"I'm so very sorry about that. I was only trying to protect you from your instinct," he signed. "I didn't want you to lose control and hurt your sister or her cub."

Her instinct hissed, furious at his words. *Lies! Hope is our cub, not hers. He took her away from us, too. You don't need protection from me. I would never hurt our cub. I protected and kept us alive when our prey tried to kill us, and I saved Stormy.*

Fury built inside her at the memory of how he'd taken their cub from them. **"Our cub!"** they spat.

Her father blinked but nodded, "My mistake, your cub. Rip Current is dead. Come back to me so we can go see your cub and your sister. Rip hurt them too, and they need you."

Marsee blinked as her desire to see her sister and cub began to override her desire for vengeance. She missed them and needed to know they were safe. She needed to rub her scent all over them, mark them as hers, and protect them.

"You told me just a few hours ago that your father was only trying to test you to make sure you were safe to be around your sister and cub and to help you overcome your guilt at not being fast enough to help her," someone else signed.

Had I? She struggled to remember. *That feels right, but why don't I remember?*

He's lying too, her instinct hissed. ***Don't you remember what he did to us? He wanted to take our cubs from us, too!***

She growled at Clear Seas, suddenly remembering who he was and what he'd done to her. "Liar!"

"I am not lying. You're my friend and..."

"You are not our friend!" she spat, interrupting him. **"You tried to kill our sister, blame us for it, and when that failed, you tried to take our cubs away from us. Friends wouldn't do that!"**

Clear Seas didn't respond, but she could smell his guilt. She hissed at him again, grabbed her prey in her mouth, and backed up further.

"Marsee, they didn't understand and were afraid of your instinct and how it tried to kill Little Flower and your father before," her uncle signed as he swam out of the gloom. She trusted her uncle. He'd never hurt them, not like her father had. *My father?* She looked at the first person, trying to remember. *Is he my father? Who is he, and why can't I remember?*

Lies. I would never hurt our sister, her instinct insisted. ***He may be our father, but he tried to kill us. I don't trust him. He'll kill us if he gets close enough and take our prey for himself.***

Quiet, she told her instinct. She couldn't think over its demands and pressure to act. She shook her head and rubbed at it with her paws, trying to remember. *Had they hunted Little Flower?*

"I am so proud of you, Marsee. I love you," her father signed.

Lies! her instinct screeched. ***He left us for dead to keep his power. Remember our claws.***

"*Shut up!*" she growled at both of them but looked down at her broken claws anyway. Her prey had done that, not her father, she remembered. She realized her instinct was lying and tried to turn it off, but it refused.

No! He'll kill us if he gets any closer! If you won't do what's best for us, then I'll have to do it!

Her instinct fought her for control of her body, but she didn't like that at all and fought back with everything she had.

Her father swam closer. "You're an amazing crafter, incredible translator. Your family loves you. Remember your mother, Little Flower, Hope, GrandFather, your grandparents, and your siblings and their cubs. They all love you, and they want you back."

"I love you too, Marsee," her uncle signed, also swimming forward.

She hissed at Marcus and winced in pain as her instinct struggled to force her to act. "Please, back off!" she begged them.

Her uncle stopped, but her father didn't, and her control slipped enough that she swiped at her father, even though he was still out of reach.

"No," she growled, clenching her paw, and backed up out of range, but he kept slowly moving forward.

He's going to kill us! her instinct screeched!

"Stormy would be devastated to lose you, as would your mentor, Ellie, as would I," Clear Seas signed. "I know you have no reason to trust me, but trust Stormy. He loves you. He's your biggest fan, remember?"

Her instinct tried to force her to attack again as her father moved within range. "NO!" she cried out. "No, stop!"

She wasn't sure who she was yelling at, her father or her instinct. She grabbed her head with her claws, trying to stop the monster inside her, trying to use the pain to control her instinct and snap her out of it. "No, don't hurt him!" she yelled.

Her father was now only an arm's length away.

She didn't know if she could maintain control. Her arms were shaking, and she could smell her own blood where her claws dug in. "You're too close. I can't control it," she warned him as she fought and struggled to keep from lashing out at him now that he was within claw's reach.

"Marsee, you can do this. I believe in you. Fight it with everything you've got. I'm not going to hurt you, and I trust you not to hurt me. Please, come back to me. Fight it!" her father begged.

It took everything she had to keep from clawing and biting him as he gently pulled her claws away from her head. She knew he might kill her, was probably going to kill her, but she didn't fight him, just stared into his eyes, seeing nothing but love there as she fought hard against her instinct's desire to kill him.

He slowly wrapped her in a hug, pinning her arms down to her side. "I've got your body. You don't need to worry about it or me. Come back to me." He shifted her around and grabbed her gently by the back of the scruff with his teeth.

Her instinct roared at the indignity of being treated like a cub and the fear that he would kill her, but her body reacted anyway. She relaxed her fight over her body with relief. Trusting her father could control it, she closed her eyes and turned her full attention to her instinct.

The world around her shifted, and it was like she was no longer in the canyon but out in the Wilds like she'd been with her father. But instead of her father, the ephemeral glowing shape of her instinct growled and circled, preparing to attack.

I've had enough of this. I'm tired of you ruining my life! she growled at it.

I saved your life. I am your life, it hissed back as it continued to circle her. ***You'd be dead in that cave if it weren't for me. You'd be dead now, too, and if we don't act, he'll kill us.***

No, he won't. If he was going to, he would have already. You're trying to hurt the people I love. So either you go back where you belong, or I kill you too.

You can't. You can't exist without me, but I can exist without you, her instinct growled.

Try me, she roared back.

Her instinct leapt at her, and she batted it aside, just like her father had done to her.

Is that all you've got? she hissed at it.

It leapt again, this time grabbing ahold of her, and she screamed. She felt her father's arms hugging her tighter, holding her together as the beast inside her tried to tear her mind apart.

NO! Not today. I beat one monster, and I can and will beat you too!

She clawed at it with her back feet, trying to rip it off her.

You didn't defeat him. I did. You're nothing without me.

Perhaps, but I'd rather die than hurt the people I care about, she replied and dug her claws in deeply.

Pain radiated through her, but she ignored it. With another frantic kick, she sent it flying. Before it could recover, she pounced on it, pinning it to the ground, and bit its neck. Pain exploded inside of her, more intense than anything she'd ever experienced before. Her body spasmed, and she screamed, but she didn't let go, nor did her father. She shook the beast inside her until it hung limp and dead in her mouth. When she dropped it, it disappeared instantly with a poof. With a huge sigh of relief, she relaxed back into *her* body and slumped against her father as she tried to breathe through the excruciating pain she was now feeling.

Her father let go of the grip on her neck but continued to hold onto her tightly. "Marsee?" There was such fear in that one word that it nearly broke her.

"It's okay, Papa. I won," she mumbled. "I'm me again. I've killed it, and it's never coming back."

"Thank the moons," he whispered, but he still didn't let go of her, and she didn't try to move. She couldn't. She hurt too much.

Instead of settling, the pain grew, and she started shaking uncontrollably.

"What's wrong? Is it your instinct again?"

"I hurt," she whimpered. "Ancient Gods, why do I hurt so much?"

"Where do you hurt?"

"Everywhere...my paw...my head," she said, trying and failing to breathe through the pain, her voice now coming out in ragged gasps.

"Marcus, something's wrong with her," her father called out.

Her uncle swam over and picked up her paw, examining it. Pain flared, and she yelped, but it was nothing compared to the pain in her head.

"I think the adrenalin from her fight must be wearing off, and she's going into shock without her instinct to protect her. We should get her to the Trauma Center," Marcus said. "Marsee, do you think you can use your drone?"

She just whimpered. It felt like she was still being shocked by Rip, only worse. Every inch of her body felt like it was on fire, and it was all she could do to keep breathing. The edges of her vision were darkening again. *Had it been telling the truth? Will I die without it,* she wondered and then shrugged. *So be it,* she decided. It was worth it if those she cared about were safe. She just prayed it would be quick. She wasn't sure how much longer she could endure the agony.

Her father scooped her up as Clear Seas swam over with their drones, and moments later, they flew towards the platform as fast as the drone would go. They met up with Temperate and several others as they were swimming back with tools, and she watched, vaguely aware, as several trauma ships dove down to land at the platform.

By the time her father made it to the nearest ship, the pain was so overwhelming she couldn't make sense of anything around her. She heard the sounds of whimpering, but it took her a long time to realize they were coming from her. Pain was her entire world now. There was no beginning or end to it as a crushing weight settled on her chest. She struggled, gasping to breathe, but her lungs wouldn't work. There was no air, and she felt her body spasm with the need to breathe.

Healers started triaging her, but she couldn't understand what they were saying. Suddenly, one of the healers yanked her out of her father's arms and bolted onto the ship. They placed her in a tube, and she watched as it closed over her and sighed with relief as her pain vanished and the blissful peace of stasis pulled her under.

CHAPTER 4

Jer: Honor Guard

Jer knew the moment the healer yanked Marsee out of his hands and bolted for the ship that she was in serious trouble, far more than her broken hand would account for. He followed them to the ship, but another healer prevented him from boarding.

"Sir, we'll need the space for the others."

He grabbed the fur on the back of his neck as he stared at the sight of Marsee's still body in the stasis unit, trying to figure out what to do next. In the light of the ship and free of the bloody carnage, he could see the angry red welts of new burns that fanned out in a jagged pattern from her wrist and side and wrapped around her neck. *How did I not see them before?*

He felt a touch on his shoulder and looked up to see Clear Seas.

"They'll take good care of her," Clear Seas said, but even he couldn't keep the hint of worry off his skin.

Jer nodded. "How are the others?"

"Stormy woke on the way back. He has first and second-degree burns on his arm but should be fine," Clear Seas replied. "Avery and the Master Builder were still unconscious. They left on the first ship. I ordered Tamarin to go with them. I didn't want to leave Stormy unprotected. I hope you don't mind me borrowing your guard."

He shook his head. "Of course not. Did Stormy say what happened before we arrived?"

"Yes. He said that Marsee ordered Avery to find a light and rope so they could drop it down the mine shaft. They had just found the cave when Rip snuck up on them. Rip must have caught Avery as he left the canyon."

Jer growled and lashed his tail, furious with the guard who should have been protecting his daughter and not caring that anyone saw him angry. "Avery should have known better."

"Yes, he should have, but your children are very persuasive. Even the Senior Council doesn't argue with them anymore."

Jer snorted bitterly, knowing just how true that was, and tried to bring his emotions back under control but failed miserably. They watched as two more trauma ships landed until Clear Seas shifted his attention to peer over Jer's shoulder. He spun to see the captives being helped out. The healers on the newly arrived ships swarmed to meet them, and he gasped as he recognized one of the victims, Petra. Temperate was helping her swim out, holding onto her harness with his uninjured arm. She looked awful. Her wings were shredded, and he was pretty sure both were broken based on the sharp and unnatural angle they hung at. He scanned the others but didn't see any other Flyers in the group or anyone else he knew.

He swam over to her. "What happened? And where's Willow?"

She looked up at him weakly. "Dead. Leaf too. They tricked me out here, saying we were going to the Jeweled Caverns, but stopped on the way and stunned me. When I woke, Rip killed them in front of me. He forced me to say I killed Ellie on my mother's orders, but I swear I didn't do it, nor did she."

A healer interrupted and started scanning Petra.

"Is she really dead?" Petra asked, wincing as the healer took her from Temperate.

Jer frowned but didn't answer. It was obvious that Petra had been tortured, but they had her messages to incriminate her and no solid proof it wasn't her, outside of Marsee's comments, and there were far too many people around to tell her the truth.

Petra took his lack of an answer as a yes and slumped with grief as the healer carried her off.

"Councilor, this was left behind. It belongs to your daughter." Temperate pulled a flowing silver and purple object out of the sling his arm was strapped in and handed it to him.

"I've never seen this before. What is it?" he asked, holding it up.

"It's a symbol of great respect given by our people for someone who has risked their life to save another," Clear Seas said, taking the cloak reverently from him and swimming onto the ship with it. The healers and the other Sprites all paused briefly as he swam by, flashing purple and silver as he gently laid the cloak over the stasis tube. "Thank you for saving my son," Clear Seas signed, his skin lit in the same purple and sliver pattern as the others but tinged with hints of grief, shame, and worry around the edges. He bowed deeply and held it for several moments before swimming off the ship.

Moments later, the ship took off. As much as Jer wanted to fly off after Marsee, he followed the others back to the cave, using the drilled entrance, which he could easily fit through. To his surprise and relief, he found Snapper Fish's daughter there. She was emaciated and arguing with a healer.

"No. I'm fine. Help them first!" she flashed.

Jer swam over. "What's your name, child?"

"Carrie," she flashed.

"Are you Snapper Fish's daughter?"

"Yes, sir. Please, I know he's done horrible things, but that was only to protect me. Rip Current forced him, just like he forced Petra. Rip killed dozens of people, including the two green Flyers who dragged Petra in here, and he forced Petra to confess to killing the Senior Guild Master to stop him from killing me. He took their tablets and sent messages to Senior Councilor Wind Rider. I don't think he knew I could understand Flyer."

"She's telling the truth, sir," a voice said behind him, and he turned to see an injured Sprite swim up. Burns nearly as bad as the ones on Marsee covered both arms and part of his chest. "Honor Guard Red Fin, sir. He tried to kill me first, but when Petra refused to give in, he switched to shocking Carrie. Carrie's been keeping everyone alive by catching fish and trying to help me break free of my restraints."

"Red Fin? Are you Tanner's son?" Marcus asked.

"Yes, sir. I was assigned to watch the Translator and the Senior Guild Master but was knocked out. I never saw who it was and woke up here."

"Thank you," Jer replied. "We'll take your full statement after you've been treated by the healers."

Red Fin nodded and swam over to help another person out.

Jer started to unclip his tablet to record the scene when Carrie pulled on his fur to get his attention again. "What is it, child?"

She motioned for him to follow her. He did, and she swam over to a table on the other side of the open cage door and ducked underneath. Suddenly, what he thought was just a thick table popped open to reveal more documents and a tablet inside.

"Thank you very much, Carrie," he replied and began sifting through a pile of letters and other papers.

Marcus swam over to join him and frowned at the letter Jer handed him. He was sure it was about Marsee, but the author was unnamed, and the text, worryingly, was written in Saber.

Marcus let out a heavy sigh. "Gather it up. We'll sort it out later."

Jer nodded and grabbed everything while Marcus recorded footage for evidence.

Once all of Rip's victims were rescued and evacuated, they took possession of the bag containing the shredded remains of Rip Current's body and flew to the Trench above where they'd found Marsee. Jer dumped the bag over the edge with immense pleasure and watched as it drifted down until it vanished from sight.

In the distance, he heard the screech of a Leviathan.

"I hope he doesn't give the poor thing a stomach ache," he said dryly.

"It's a distinct possibility," Marcus replied.

"It's a risk I'm willing to take," Clear Seas said. "So, where to next?"

They made a quick detour and managed to locate Willow's tablet but found no sign of the pilot and decided that his body had been eaten. With everyone now located or presumed dead, they finally returned to the Trauma Center. When they arrived, Clear Seas and Temperate were brought in to see Stormy, but he and Marcus were asked to wait.

Jer paced in the waiting room. An hour later, they still hadn't been called back, but he spun as the door opened. It was Clear Seas and his family. Stormy was being released. Bandage putty wrapped around his arm, but he otherwise looked okay. Jewel, however, looked angry enough to kill, and apparently, a Sprite just about to enter the ward with the triage healer thought the same as they bolted out of her way and quickly left, leaving them in the room alone.

Stormy swam over and flashed his worry. "How's Marsee?"

"I don't know how she is. I haven't had an update yet. How are you?"

"I'm fine," Stormy replied dismissively, but his skin shifted from worry to a flash of regret and apology. "I'm sorry. It's all my fault she's hurt. I was so excited about finding the others that I didn't realize she wasn't following until she started screaming. I tried to stop him, but I wasn't big enough."

Jer raised a paw to stop the child. "It's not your fault. We saw what you did, and she'd probably be dead if you hadn't tried. Once again, I owe you for saving my daughter. Is there anything I can do to repay you?"

Stormy blinked at him, and flickers of surprise flashed around the edges of his apology. "No, I don't want anything. She saved my life, too. We're even. When you see her, give her my thanks."

Jer nodded. "Of course."

Jewel glared at Clear Seas before herding Stormy and his older brother out of the trauma ward. They watched them swim out in silence.

"I have a feeling I'm going to be sleeping in my office tonight," Clear Seas said when they were finally gone.

He snorted. "I doubt an entire contingent of guards will be enough to protect me once Myra finds out I let Marsee swim off and get hurt again."

"You're not wrong there," his brother said. "I'm personally thinking about hiding in Marsee's cave. I'm just not sure that'll be far enough away."

"I doubt it," Jer replied. "If she can track down Damon, there isn't a place on all five planets that's safe."

"Well, it's been nice knowing the both of you," Clear Seas said with a brief bubble of humor, but then he sobered. "How is she, really?"

"I honestly don't know. No one has been back to tell me anything yet." He sighed with a mix of frustration and fear. "For all I know, she's still in stasis while they treat the others."

Clear Seas flashed his sympathy. "If you need me, call. I'll be in my office filling out the paperwork for Rip's verdict and execution. I'll take care of it all. Stay and focus on your daughter."

"Thank you," Jer replied with a nod.

Clear Seas nodded back and swam off.

Marcus left periodically to begin taking statements from those rescued once the healers cleared them enough to talk, but was back waiting with him hours later when the Senior Healer finally appeared and led them back to her office.

She shut the door behind them and sat at her desk. Her skin was dark and professional, but she let out a heavy sigh before beginning. "She's alive, but I'll be honest, her long-term prognosis is not good. The damage she incurred this time is far worse. We're seeing more of the effects we expected to see last time. In addition to second and third-degree burns from electrocution, she experienced extensive compression injuries as her mask failed. We've done what we can, for now, but several of her organs have started to fail, including her heart, liver, and kidneys. They were just too badly damaged. In addition, her lungs partially collapsed. We've placed her back in stasis until the new organs can be printed, but we don't know if she'll survive the surgeries or if other organs might begin to fail. It's risky enough to replace one organ, but multiple could cause her body to reject them all. Her hand will require surgery to finish repairing, but we can't do that until she's stable. The scans show signs of nerve damage, so even after being repaired, she might not have full control or feeling in that paw. We'll do what we can, but without being able to repair it now, there is a good chance she could lose that hand altogether, as she's already showing signs of an infection that's difficult to treat in the best of cases."

Jer swallowed hard as she continued to list off various injuries. "How long until the organs are ready?"

"The liver and kidneys will be ready tomorrow morning, but it will take another day for her heart to be ready, and we won't be able to put her back in stasis once we start operating. New organs can't survive stasis for at least a standard month, and we have no idea if she will even survive long enough for her second surgery. While we have her open, we'll flood her internal system with a nano wash to treat the rest of her burns and hopefully prevent further failure. Assuming she survives all three surgeries we'll need to perform, and we don't have any further complications, she'll need to spend at least a month here recovering before she'll be strong enough to jump home, quite likely more."

She paused, and Jer nodded his understanding.

"Why not wait and perform all three surgeries at the same time?" Marcus asked.

"For several reasons, the time each operation will take, the number of healers needed, and the severity of her injuries. There's also a chance her heart will recover enough that we won't need to replace it, which I would prefer, as that surgery will be the hardest and require breaking her ribs to do so. It will take nearly as long to replace as the other three combined. Plus, we'll need time to rest. There aren't many on our planet rated to treat the kinds of injuries your daughter has, and with the severity, I don't feel comfortable leaving it to anyone but myself and my best healers, and we'll need time to prepare. But that's not the most concerning problem she's facing, and frankly, it's one we haven't seen before. I've sent scans to your Healer's Guild for advice."

Hyacinth turned on the monitor and displayed a scan of Marsee's brain.

He'd seen enough brain scans over the past six months to know something was very wrong, but these looked nothing like Little Flower's scans, and not just because they were nowhere near the quality he was used to seeing. It was almost as if... "Are parts of her brain...missing?"

"I'm honestly not sure. I've never seen scans like this. Regardless, there's no activity there. We're still waiting for confirmation from the experts, but the primary areas affected are all related to low-level instinct. In our species, there's a lot of overlap with autonomous functions, such as controlling breathing or keeping the heart beating. It's less so with yours, but I don't know what this means for her long-term prognosis, as these areas appear to have been far more developed than we typically see in your species. The scans showed she was already suffering from major damage in these areas when she was placed in stasis, and as we were trying to stabilize her and treat her other injuries, we watched as her immune system attacked these specific areas and then stopped. Nothing we did slowed it, and we have no idea why it stopped any more than we do what caused it in the first place. Nor do we know if it will start again once we take her out of stasis. Hopefully not."

Jer turned to look at Marcus in horror. "I thought she was speaking figuratively, but this..."

"I have no idea, Jer. I'm still amazed we managed to bring her back at all. I've seen psychosis hundreds of times, and I've never seen anyone that far gone ever come close to recovering, and she's done it three times now, arguably four."

"Explain," the Senior Healer demanded.

Jer glanced questioningly back at Marcus, who nodded, so he told the healer everything he knew about their hunting instinct and psychosis.

The Healer floated there, her mask on, as he explained. "I'm not sure I believe what you're telling me, but Avery told me much the same the other day. If you weren't both Senior Councilors, I'd think you were yanking on my tentacles, but I suppose that's possible. I've seen stranger things before. I'll be honest. I have no idea what this means for Marsee's prognosis or what kind of disabilities she'll have after. With everything else she's facing, it might be kinder not to wake her up again. For that matter, I don't even know if she'll wake up."

Jer swallowed hard and spun away, unable to face the Senior Healer as he tried to figure out what to do. "Can I see her?" he asked, unable to decide.

"Of course," the Healer said, "Follow me."

She led them to the same room Marsee had been in only the day before. Only now, she lay still and unmoving, as the stasis chamber kept her in the same state she was in the moment she entered. The cloak Clear Seas had honored her with now fluttered in the current on a stand near the window. A light had been angled to shine on it, making the material shine and glitter.

The Healer left them, and Jer swam over to peer down at his daughter. She'd been through far too much in her short life, and the tube did nothing to hide the horrible blistering burns that now scarred her body. They hadn't been nearly as bad the first time.

Marcus swam up and wrapped his tail around him, but even his brother winced at what he saw. "I'm sorry. I didn't realize she was so badly injured. She said she was okay."

He said nothing for a while. He knew he'd never forget the sounds of her screams or the sight of her writhing in Rip's grasp when he was too far away to do anything to save her. "She once made me promise that if anything like this happened to her, I'd let her go." He snorted. "I even said I'd fight her mother over it, but now, I don't think I can. I just got her back. I can't lose her now, but what kind of life will she have if she does wake?"

Marcus pulled him in for a hug, and he cried out his agony at the decision he had to make. Myra had always made the medical decisions for the family, and he wished she were here growling at the healers to make them come up with some new and innovative technique to save their daughter, but she was back home trying to keep Little Flower alive.

Will I lose both of them? he wondered. He couldn't bear the thought.

Marcus eventually left to help Clear Seas with the mess they'd found. He knew he should have gone with him to help, but he had nothing left to give, and surprisingly, his brother hadn't grabbed him by the scruff and dragged him out as he'd expected.

After watching his brother swim out, he sent Myra a message, dreading her reply, and flopped in one of the weird nets they used for chairs to wait for her reply. With a heavy sigh, he leaned his head up against the side of the net, watching his daughter's unmoving body float as his exhausted brain spiraled into depression and guilt.

He looked up when he felt a light touch on his shoulder. "Ellie! You're awake! How are you?"

"I'll manage. I'm going in for surgery in a few, but I insisted on seeing Marsee first." She swam slowly over to Marsee's side, stiff and awkward from her own injuries.

Jer watched as she clenched and unclenched her still clawless paws, ears pinned to the side of her head, as she stared down at her protege. He wondered if she was struggling with her instinct, but he didn't move to test her. If she lost control, there was nothing he could do to stop her anyway.

"I wish there was a way we could bring Rip back to life so I could kill him again for doing this to her," she growled.

"I know exactly how you feel, but there's still Snapper Fish."

Ellie frowned and turned to face him. "Snapper Fish? As in, ex Journeyman Tech Snapper Fish?"

Jer nodded.

"Huh, I thought he died something like thirty years ago."

"Apparently not. Seems he faked his death and hacked his way into the systems, making a new account to get away from the legacy of being kicked out of the Guild and then joined the Sea Patrol. According to him, Rip found out and threatened to expose him and took his daughter as a hostage to control him. Thankfully, she's one of the ones we found, emaciated but alive."

"How under the three moons did he manage that? Every account is linked to a genetic code. They can't be duplicated, and any tampering flags the system. I would have been notified."

"He told us he was born with two genetic signatures. The Senior Healer told Marcus that this happens with their species if more than one egg is released. Rather than growing into twins, they merge since their system can't support giving birth to more than one at a time."

"Huh. Well, that's a little loophole I'll need to have fixed. That doesn't explain how he managed to get into secure systems to make that change, much less change the archives."

"You'll have to talk to Lowell about that. It went way over my head, but it's apparently based on the same code he used to hack into the Guild System, which is how Lowell found it. Marsee found your reprimand while she was at the Guild and sent it to me, which I forwarded on to Lowell, who had already identified Snapper Fish's account as being behind the altered footage. Looks to me like you weren't very nice when you kicked him out."

"No, I probably wasn't, but he did hack into my account. It's why I had the techs start adding a secondary biometric authentication to all tablets and secure systems."

"And that's probably why you and Marsee lost your claws, aside from Rip being a psychopath. He used your account to try to frame Nardal for kidnapping the others and used your claw to access the suite later."

Ellie looked stunned by the explanation. "I had no idea Snapper Fish hated me so much. After all these years? It's bad enough to pull off a claw or two, but they beat me within an inch of my life."

"Rip beat you. Snapper never entered your room, but there are others involved, the least of which are the guards that helped Rip escape. If you haven't heard, Rip killed Leaf and Willow after they brought Petra to him, and he tried to frame both Wind Rider and Petra, going so far as to force Petra to confess to killing you. Rip also threatened to kill Petra and attack the hatcheries if Wind Rider didn't confess to orchestrating it all. Lowell found those deleted messages about half an hour ago. Apakna and Sammianna's extended family were threatened, too, but as far as we know, no one else was harmed, although we still can't get ahold of Apakna. Her ship should arrive in a few days. We have no idea if anyone else is involved, but we found a secret room and filing cabinets full of blackmail. It's a mess."

Ellie snorted. "You've been hanging out with your brother too long. Mess doesn't even begin to describe the situation." She turned away from him, body tight with the suppressed pain of betrayal and grief.

He understood. "Oh, just out of curiosity. Did you put Marsee down as your preference for Acting Senior?"

She spun back around. "Marsee?! Moons' no. Nardal's my Acting Senior."

Jer grunted. "Well, you might have a mess to clean up there. She did meet with Agate this morning, although I'm not sure how much damage she could do in a day. Rip, on the other hand... Lowell's looking to see what else he might have done on both of your accounts. It might be safer to make you a new one."

"Marsee actually went along with it?" Ellie asked, looking stunned.

Jer shrugged. "She thought you'd done it because you were suspicious about the altered footage and the possibility of being attacked. Rip told her there were people in the Guild involved, and she was trying to figure out who. I tried to get her to stop, but she insisted on going out not half an hour after being released from the Trauma Center. She's shown real courage and leadership. She even managed to convince Avery to leave her unguarded in order to rescue the others."

"Huh." Ellie turned back to look at Marsee again and sighed. "Well, that doesn't surprise me. She is my protege, after all. You should have seen her the other day. I have never been more proud of her. She'll make an excellent senior someday, but then I always knew she would."

Jer snorted at Ellie's ego, but it was tinged with grief, as he wondered if Marsee would ever get the chance to become a senior.

The Senior Healer appeared at the door. "Excuse me, Senior Guild Master. The surgery is ready for you now."

"I'll be with you in just a moment," she told Hyacinth. "Jer, Hyacinth told me about Marsee's injuries. Give her a chance. Do the surgeries and see if she makes it. If her heart stops or she doesn't wake up, then let her go, but if she does wake up, let her decide if that's something she wants to live with or not. No one has any idea what this will mean for her. With everything she's fought with over the last year, maybe things will be better for her."

He sighed and nodded his approval to Hyacinth even though Myra hadn't responded yet.

Ellie took one last loving look at Marsee and, with another heavy sigh, she turned and swam out the door.

Jer went back to watching and waiting. He'd almost fallen asleep when there was another light touch on his shoulder. He startled awake and turned to see Wind Rider looking back at him with an expression of sorrow as she floated in the doorway.

"May I come in?" she asked. He nodded. "Jer, I thought I'd tell you first. I'm stepping down from the Council."

He snorted. "No, you're not. Not unless your people vote you out. No more than I am, as much as I want to. Don't tell him I said this, but Marcus had it right. If we step down, Rip wins, and our children will have suffered for no reason. I'm sorry I doubted you and your daughter."

Wind Rider shook her head. "I don't deserve your apology. I voted to kill Little Flower at the Trial and blame Marsee for it."

"I know," he replied. "So did she *before* she saw the messages."

"She knew?" Wind Rider asked, flicking her wings back in surprise. "How could she possibly trust me after what I almost did to her?"

He shrugged. "I don't know. Perhaps because of her friendship with Petra. Or perhaps because she's capable of seeing and understanding the nuances that come from the responsibilities of our position. I've never been able to understand her. She's always been leaps and bounds ahead of me. I'm pretty sure she's even smarter than Marcus. She found a dozen things we'd missed, and we're trained for this." He let out a heavy sigh, looking at her motionless body.

"I owe her everything, Jer. Whatever she needs, if I can give it, I will."

He nodded, and she left. He sat there watching Marsee for some time and then decided to head back to the ship to sleep. Nothing would change here until she was brought out of stasis, and he knew there would be many sleepless nights to come. When he left the room, he was surprised to see not one but two of his guards floating outside of Marsee's room. With only six guards, they were spread thin, especially with Avery still being treated for his injuries, then he realized that both guards had been assigned to guard Clear Seas' family. "I didn't order a guard. Did Clear Seas order you to stay?"

"No, sir," Honor Guard Aris replied. "Jewel declined our protection for her family."

He nodded his understanding. They didn't exactly have the best record at protecting her family. Stormy had snuck out under Aris's watch, and Avery had failed to protect Stormy.

"You should leave and get some sleep. With Rip dead..."

"No, sir," Aris replied. "We're not leaving."

Jer tilted his head and raised a brow, waiting for an explanation.

"Sir, this is an Honor Guard," she explained.

He gasped as he comprehended what she was saying and had to look away, unable to bear the sympathy he saw in the guards' eyes. He struggled to contain his emotions behind the mask he was expected to wear, and failing, he grabbed the back of his scruff to try and help.

While the Honor Guard served multiple purposes, such as guarding the Council, dealing with predators, rescue, psychosis, and the occasional crime, they also served another role. An Honor Guard was typically reserved for the vigil and funeral of someone who had sacrificed their life for someone else, and they could never be ordered or even requested. It was equivalent to the cloak Clear Seas had placed on Marsee. The Honor Guard would choose who they deemed worthy and just show up. There was no greater honor among his people.

"We will guard her until she's safely home," Aris promised. What wasn't said was the fact that they didn't believe she would survive and that it would be her body they would be escorting.

It was too much. With a heartbroken sob, he turned and swam away.

CHAPTER 5

Jer: Vigil

Jer bolted out of the ward, struggling hard to shove his feelings of grief and fear behind the mask he was expected to wear as a Senior Councilor, but it didn't help that there was a pair of Honor Guards at every intersection he passed on the way out of the Trauma Center.

Thankfully, the waiting room was empty as he swam through. He stopped and floated in the entryway where he'd left his drone on a hook and took several moments to calm his emotions before daring to venture outside. Finally, when he felt his mask was back in place, he swam through the outer doors but stopped short the moment he swam through and stared, jaw dropped, at the sight before him.

Surrounding the building were hundreds, if not thousands, of Sprites, all making their way to where a memorial had been erected in the park. People were attaching notes and laying flowers and other small gifts as they flashed the same purple and silver pattern Clear Seas had used when he'd laid the cloak on Marsee's stasis unit.

His presence was noted, and as he watched, a wave of purple and silver traveled through the crowd.

"Thank you. I'll be sure to let her know of the love and respect you've shown her here today." He signed the words, unable to speak through his grief, and swam off, too overwhelmed to deal with the crowd or risk being asked to answer questions he didn't have the answers to. Thankfully, they seemed to understand, as no one stopped him.

He entered the platform and trudged his way up to Ellie's ship, where he found Marcus waiting up for him.

"You're back sooner than I expected," Marcus said as he walked in. "Wind Rider's here. She said she wanted to talk to you."

"I know. I spoke to her a few minutes ago." He slumped into the seat across from his mentor. The weight of gravity after so long in the water made his legs feel weak, but it was nothing compared to the weight on his heart. "Have you been down by the Trauma Center recently?"

"No. Aside from greeting Wind Rider when she arrived, I've been here, trying to get caught up on everything. Why?"

He took a deep, shuddering breath before answering. "The locals have erected a memorial and are holding vigil for Marsee and...and she has an Honor Guard."

Marcus's whiskers and ears drooped in sorrow.

"Her door, and every door I passed on the way out, had guards stationed, both Saber and Water Sprite. I wouldn't be surprised if every exit out of the Trauma Center had one posted, too." He closed his eyes and swallowed hard as his grief threatened to overwhelm him again. Failing, he buried his face in his paws, leaning on the table in front of him as he struggled to contain his tears.

"Have you decided what you're going to do?"

He took another shuddering breath but didn't lift his head, knowing that if he looked at his brother, he'd lose it completely. "I know what Marsee wants, but I can't do it. I've got to give her a chance, but I won't drag it out like Myra did with Little Flower. I told the Senior Healer to go forward with the surgeries, but...if it doesn't work and her heart fails, I'm going to let her go."

"I think that's a fair compromise and one Marsee would agree with and understand. Besides, she's on a watch. That's out of your hands anyway."

He nearly whimpered at the reminder. "I don't know if that makes it any better or not. She wouldn't be on that watch if it weren't for me."

"What Rip did was not your fault. She would have been perfectly fine, if not for him."

"But she might not have struggled if I hadn't..." He couldn't even say it. "Gods. Did you read what she wrote? You might as well execute me now. When the rest of the Council reads it..."

His brother didn't say anything, just let out a heavy sigh. "They won't. I'm not sure how, but that folder disappeared."

He stared at his brother in absolute shock.

"Don't look at me like that. I had *nothing* to do with it."

"Hiding evidence is a capital offense, Marcus."

"I'm glad to see you were paying attention to my lessons." At his snort of disbelief, Marcus rolled his eyes. "Jer, if the Full Council or, worse, the Press got ahold of that information, Marsee's reputation would be ruined along with all of Saber's. There wasn't anything in there that wasn't readily available to the Guard or Council before, and everyone knows that her tablet was stolen and her claws taken, which means everything in her account is compromised. It won't stop someone from digging, but I see no reason to call out information that will hurt her even more than she's already been hurt or give our enemies ammunition against the people of Saber. Now, have you eaten?"

Jer snorted, surprised by the sudden change in conversation, and flicked an ear back dismissively. Food was the least of his concerns. By all rights, he should report Marcus, but he knew he wouldn't.

"That's what I thought." Marcus walked over to the kitchenette and grabbed a couple of stasis containers, two glasses, and a thermos of something to drink, not even bothering to see what they were. Setting them down on the table, Marcus shoved a container towards him. "Eat. That's an order from your mentor."

Jer snorted again and rolled his eyes at his brother but shifted to lean his head on one paw, opened the container with the other, and eyed the unfamiliar contents dubiously. "What is this?"

"Not a moons' forsaken clue. Eat it or grab something else, but you're eating, and then you're going to bed."

Jer grabbed a piece, sniffed at it, shrugged, and popped it in his mouth. "Not bad. Nothing like those fire sticks, but I suppose it'll do."

Marcus took a piece of his, shrugged in agreement, poured them both a drink, and returned to his tablet, but a few moments later, he gasped. "What in the thrice-forsaken dark moons' horror of a beverage is this?!"

Jer looked up from picking at his meal and started chuckling, but it soon turned into nearly hysterical laughter, to the point where he was laughing so hard he could barely breathe, and his tail hurt from being curled so tightly.

Every single hair on Marcus's body was sticking straight out. "If you think it's so funny, you try some," Marcus growled.

Jer picked up his own glass and sniffed at it. The scent and bubbles made his nose twitch, but he cautiously took a sip. "It's got a bit of a kick, but it's not bad," he said as his own fur started crinkling with static electricity. "But it does make my fur tickle."

"Not bad?! Jeran, it's like swallowing a lightning bolt!"

"No, it's not even close," he replied, and grabbed another bite to eat, following it up with another sip of the strange bubbling blue beverage.

"How do you know what a lightning bolt feels like?" Marcus asked, eyes glaring at him with suspicion as he tried unsuccessfully to make his fur lay back down.

"I had Clear Seas zap me so I could better understand what Marsee went through. Moons, was that only yesterday? It feels like a lifetime ago."

His brother's ears pinned flat with disbelief. "You had him do what?!"

"Zap me, with the Senior Healer present, for just a second. I'm pretty sure I whimpered in pain for about five minutes before I could uncurl and talk again. Marsee said what she went through lasted for hours. I honestly don't know how she endured it. It was by far the most painful thing I've ever experienced. I'm astounded Marsee managed to fight through it or recover so quickly. I couldn't make my muscles move at all."

Marcus grunted in acknowledgment. "Speaking of Clear Seas, I had a long talk with him this evening about psychosis and what was going on with Marsee in the canyon this afternoon. He was obviously concerned about what he witnessed, but apparently, Marsee spoke to him about it earlier and told him about the test you gave her. He wanted to know if he needed to press charges against you on her behalf. I think I managed to talk him out of it without giving too much away."

Jer frowned as he considered the implications. "I'm surprised he hasn't. If anyone did what we do during a test without knowing why, it would be considered abuse. I pray we never have to test anyone again, but I'm sure that's wishful thinking. I suppose for Marsee's sake, we can be glad he's the only one who witnessed her episode."

"Agreed," Marcus replied. "I still can't believe she came back today."

"I can't believe any of what I saw today. You know, I'd half convinced myself that what she did to me that day was a fluke, but after watching her today, I'm pretty sure I got off easy."

Marcus snorted. "That's an understatement. You know, I would trade access to my archives to have seen her beat the snot out of you. I have a feeling it would be even better than watching you get trounced by Kendra. Do you think Marsee would be willing to give me a repeat performance when she's feeling better?"

"Ha. Ha." Jer glared at his mentor with mock outrage, although he'd honestly be more than willing if it meant she was actually better. He shook his head with a hint of amusement. "You two are far too alike. We had the same conversation the day I picked her up from Ellie's. I'm sure she'd be more than willing."

His brother chuckled. "Excellent. I'll be sure to ask the next time I have a chance to talk with her."

"If you get that chance." He let out a heavy sigh as his thoughts returned to Marsee's injuries.

"If she's capable of beating both a Senior Councilor and a madman more than twice her size who could kill her with a touch, then she'll be fine. What's a few damaged organs?"

If only that's all it was, he thought bitterly and picked at the remains of his half-eaten meal, but after a few moments, he shoved it aside. His stomach was far too upset to eat. "I'll be in my room. I doubt I'll sleep, but I'll try. Surgery is scheduled for first thing in the morning. Will you wake me if I'm not up?"

Marcus said he would, so Jer dumped the remainder of his meal into the recycler and made his way down to his room. He paused as he entered. Marsee's scent was thick in the air. He settled down on the bed, which was still covered in tufts of her fur, and sniffed deeply of her beautiful scent, wishing he'd held on tighter that morning and wondering if he'd ever have the opportunity to snuggle with her again. Setting the alarm on his tablet, he curled up into a tiny ball and cried himself to sleep.

CHAPTER 6

Quinn: Night Watch

After several hours of tossing and turning, exhausted but unable to sleep, Honor Guard Quinn Bluestone gave up and stepped out onto his balcony. The night was beautiful, crisp, and clear, with just the slightest hint of a breeze. All three moons were up, but only faint slivers against a dark velvet sky, surrounded by a universe of twinkling stars that were brighter than Quinn had ever seen. He would have taken the time to observe their beauty if every hair on his neck wasn't sticking straight up. He swept his gaze over the inner compound, trying to figure out what had him so on edge.

Kendra had left him in charge of New Hope's security. After finding what little remained of Paul and Danny, he and the other half of Avery's squad had snuck in under the cover of darkness on a Trauma Ship the night before. Posing as healers, they'd been given rooms in the Trauma Center, but he hadn't slept. With only seven guards to protect the community, he'd remained awake while the others had rested. Two guards had been sent to guard Damon, followed by the rest of their squad later in the day when approval had finally come in from Jeran. He'd placed the new squad on duty guarding the community and shifted Avery's squad to focus entirely on watching Myra, Little Flower, and Nazari. Only then had he returned to his room. Three days without sleep should have meant he crashed the moment he lay down, but he was wide awake and twitchy.

Something was going to happen. He just knew it.

There were a few people out, mostly Hue-man, and he could hear the faint sounds of someone playing an instrument in the garden. He had no idea what it was, and the unfamiliar and high-pitched sounds added to his nerves. Nothing seemed out of place, though. No one was yelling or running or acting suspiciously, but his fur didn't settle. He decided, since he couldn't sleep anyway that he would take a walk around. He went back into his room, flung his carry harness on, and stepped out into the common room, where Lark was sitting over by the door.

She frowned, seeing him in uniform. "What's wrong?"

"I don't know," he replied. "I'm going to take a walk around the compound."

"Do you want company?" she asked.

"No, stay here and watch."

Lark had been assigned to the team watching Nazari, whose room was just down the hall from them. Both Myra and Nazari had been placed on a watch after using their instincts to track down Damon and the others. Nazari had taken far too long to turn hers off when Kendra had tested her in the canyon. He was honestly surprised that Kendra didn't pull her in immediately, but then there was a lot of visibility on her right now, just like all of Chenzira's family. He hadn't personally tested Myra, but Councilor Paxton and Ammond both had. And while she was as jagged as she'd been at the Trial, she'd brought Damon in unharmed. He hoped, like before, that she would settle now that her children were safe.

He was just about to hit the switch to the outer door when he heard the sounds of another door opening. Lark frowned and stood, confirming his suspicions. He waited and listened, expecting Nazari to head to the lift or the stairs at the end of the hall, but instead, she walked halfway and stopped.

"It's not right," he heard Nazari mumble and, moments later, start walking again.

He raised a brow and waited until he heard the sounds of footsteps descending the stairs and the swish of the door opening and closing at the bottom before exiting the room with Lark. They followed her trail down the stairs and outside, past the waiting trauma ships, and partway around the compound, where they found Nazari pacing under one of the shade trees that had recently been planted. The thick scent of compost was nearly overpowering, but he dismissed it as he melted into the shadows. At the same time, Lark leapt nimbly and silently onto the stone wall that surrounded the inner compound and quickly made her way ahead of Nazari.

Nazari didn't notice either of them. She muttered, but he couldn't make sense of what she was saying, random words and phrases, and he began to wonder if she was sleepwalking. It was too dark out to get a good read on her. Her steps were stilted and uncoordinated, and she seemed unaware of her surroundings, but her emotions were angry and conflicted.

"He's our cub," she muttered and took off again.

He followed at a distance, keeping to the shadows, and frowned as she passed under a light that allowed him to get a read on her briefly. Her soul boundary was twanging hard. He swore under his breath and was about to call in his squad when she suddenly stumbled and stopped.

"What the?!" she muttered and scratched the back of her neck as she turned and looked around as if trying to figure out where she was. "That's what I get for taking stimulants this morning," she muttered to herself and took off back towards the trauma center.

When she passed under the light again, her soul boundary was calm, and he could only sniff embarrassment, confusion, and a hint of worry from her.

He waited until she was long gone before stepping out of the shadows.

Lark dropped down by his side moments later. "I don't like it," she said quietly.

"It's only been a day, and she recovered before she hurt anyone," he replied. "Hopefully, she was just sleepwalking."

She snorted at him. "After all these years, I'd think you'd be more jaded about her chances."

"We don't lose them all, and she has far more training than most as an animal healer," he replied. "Go on. I'm going to take a walk around the compound."

"Yes, sir," she replied and melted into the shadows again.

He watched Lark leave, and his lips pursed into a frown at her comment before he turned and continued on his patrol. He should be far more jaded, but his heart always hoped for the best, needed and wanted to see the best in people, even though it was his job to watch for the worst in them. Several hours later, after finding nothing, he made it back to the Trauma Center and ducked into the maintenance hall to make his way down to the guard watching Little Flower.

"I didn't expect to see you here this late at night," Keeta said quietly.

"Couldn't sleep. Any issues?"

"Myra's a mess, but that's not surprising. She's sleeping in Little Flower's room right now."

Quinn frowned, honestly surprised that Myra hadn't lost control when she captured Damon, what with everything that had happened to her and her family over the past year, but his thoughts were interrupted when Myra's tablet dinged.

"Ancient Gods!" Myra prayed.

He frowned, wondering what had happened. Nothing had come in from Kendra or Avery. He checked his tablet anyway, wondering if he'd missed something. "Nothing," he said quietly.

"Hey, what's..." a voice said.

"I need you down here immediately! Your office!" Myra said.

"I'll be right there."

He frowned again as Myra bolted out of the room far more jagged than he'd seen her earlier in the day. He shifted down the hall to the port directly across from Ammond's office. He couldn't see what she put on the monitor, but her tail was fully poofed.

A minute later, Ammond appeared at a full run and breathing hard. His feet slipped on the floor, and he nearly missed the turn to his office.

"What happened?" he asked.

"Marsee..." Myra said and pointed to the screen.

"Dark moons! What happened to her?" Ammond exclaimed as he saw what was on the monitor and started flipping through scans.

Myra didn't answer.

Ammond turned to face her. "Myra?" he signed.

Quinn tensed at the jaggedness he saw, and so did Keeta beside him. She reached for the door, but he held a hand, stopping her as he counted. *One...two...come on, recover...four...*

"Myra, answer me! What happened to Marsee?"

Myra blinked, took a deep breath, and pulled herself together as she handed Ammond her tablet. "Jer said Rip escaped and tried to kill Marsee and Clear Sea's youngest son, Stormy. Marsee caught and killed Rip, but not before he nearly killed her. What are we going to do, Ammond? I don't know how to fix this. I don't even know if there's anything to fix! This makes what happened to Little Flower look like a scraped knee. Jer wants to know if we think there's any chance she'll wake if they go through with the other surgeries."

"I'm surprised they're even bothering to try," Ammond said, echoing Quinn's own thoughts, although he was relieved to hear Myra speak. *Panic or psychosis?* he wondered. Her recovery time was borderline.

Myra growled at the comment, but he could tell it was only frustration as waves of worry radiated off of her.

Ammond continued to read and looked up, ears pinned in surprise. "She killed her instinct?!"

"That's what Jer said she told him. It certainly looks like it. There's nothing left."

"We don't know for sure," Ammond said. "These scans are horrible. I haven't seen ones this bad in decades."

Quinn glanced at Keeta in surprise.

"On her own?" Keeta asked.

He shrugged. "Maybe Avery..." His tablet buzzed before he could answer that thought. He unclipped it again and raised a brow at the message that came in from Tamarin.

"Now what?" Keeta whispered.

He handed her the tablet so she could read for herself.

"I bet Avery's glad he's on another planet right now," Keeta said.

He grunted. "Avery's as good as dead. If not by Kendra, then by the Seniors for leaving Marsee and Stormy alone." His brain spun, trying to figure out if Avery was involved in this plot or had just made a stupid mistake brought on by fatigue. Stimulants and decades of training helped, but Avery was far too well-trained to leave Marsee and Stormy alone, even if she wasn't on a watch.

Keeta sighed, once again echoing his own thoughts.

His thoughts shifted to Marsee, and he wondered if she'd defeated the threat they faced or if this was only the start of it. The legend that had been passed down through the millennia claimed she would die in order to save everyone from war, but that same legend had stated they would be fighting Ice Giants, not Water Sprites. Certainly, they'd been involved, but they didn't appear to be the main player.

Unless Rip Current was a pawn in an even bigger plot.

Kendra had been ordered not to bring Marsee into the Guard by The General herself. He could barely believe it, and he'd seen those ancient orders himself. His breath hitched when he realized that if Marsee had been brought in when they normally did, she'd have never uncovered Rip's plot, or killed him, or even learned about sign language.

Had that been the General's plan? He shuddered at the thought of how bad things would be if Rip had succeeded.

Keeta caught his shifting emotions and looked up at him. "What is it?"

"Nothing," he replied. "Just an exhausted and over-active imagination."

She squinted at him. "You're a horrible liar, Quinn, but I'm sure you're not thinking anything the rest of the Guard isn't thinking right now. The question is, is this the start of the prophecy or the end?"

Quinn snorted. "Remind me never to play Rando-Tat with you. As for the prophecy, I suppose we'll know soon enough."

"Is it wrong of me to hope Marsee doesn't wake up?"

"No. I'd choose one life over a war any day, too."

He shifted back down to the other entrance, popped out of the maintenance hall, and entered an empty patient room. After flicking on the privacy screen, he placed a call to Kendra. Kendra looked livid as she answered.

"I take it you've read Tamarin's report?" he asked.

She snorted. "Please tell me you don't have more bad news."

He sighed. "I wish I could," he replied and gave her a quick status update.

She was silent for far longer than he expected. "Have you been able to confirm if Marsee transitioned?" she finally asked.

"No. I couldn't see the monitor, but I would think you'd..."

"I've been locked out of her account," she replied dryly.

He frowned, wondering if that meant Kendra was going to be arrested and killed for Avery's mistake, too, and tried pulling up Marsee's medical record. "I've been locked out, too. They're protecting her."

She nodded. "See what you can find out, but don't say anything until we know if she's going to survive her other injuries."

"And what about Myra and Nazari? Do you want me to bring them in?"

"No. Not unless they get worse. You might suggest they come in on their own if the opportunity arises, but they're both too visible right now to bring in."

He nodded, and she disconnected.

Taking a deep breath, he plastered on his calmest expression and made his way down to Ammond's office.

Both healers jumped in surprise when he appeared.

"Sorry. I didn't mean to startle you," he said.

"Has something happened?" Myra asked. Worry and fear leaked from behind her mask and filled the room.

"No. I'm here because of what happened to Marsee. What's this about her killing off her instinct?"

"How do you know about..." Myra glanced at the open door and then let out a heavy sigh. "You heard me?"

He nodded. "Marsee's on a watch. If you want to save her, tell me what you know."

She handed him her tablet, and he read Jer's message with interest, then spent the next hour with them as they examined all the scans and made sure he thoroughly understood them. He was rated the equivalent of a Journeyman Healer through his guard training, but the finer details of the brain went well above his knowledge. He shook his head slightly in disbelief. "I honestly can't believe she's still alive with these injuries. Treat her, or not, as you deem fit, but keep me informed. We'll reevaluate her condition if and when she wakes up."

Ammond nodded, but Myra flicked her ears back in surprise. "You're not going to enforce the DNR?"

"Not at this time. She saved the lives of thirty-eight people, including the children of two members of the Senior Council. I think that earns her a chance. Besides, what you learn could help others in the future, even if she doesn't wake."

"Thank you," Myra said.

He tilted his head slightly to acknowledge her thanks and left, returning to his room.

Lark remained on guard and reported there were no further incidents, so he retreated to his bedroom. As tired as he was, he didn't go to sleep. Instead, he sat out on the balcony, pulled out his tablet, and called Kendra back.

"I'm fairly certain she's transitioned, but I don't think she's going to survive her other injuries." He gave her a report, and she winced. "Do you want me to tell them about the transition?"

"No. We'll wait and see if she survives her other injuries first. Hopefully, your leniency around the DNR will come across as an apology and save that fur-brained nephew of mine."

He snorted. "You're not going to kill him yourself?"

"I haven't decided yet and probably won't until I can sniff him out in person, assuming they don't kill me first."

He frowned at that reminder. "Do you think they will?"

She actually rolled his eyes at him. "He's my protege, and I gave the Seniors a life oath that he could be trusted. I'm as good as dead. I'm honestly surprised you haven't been called in to arrest me yet."

It was his turn to wince, and he swallowed hard to control his grief.

"None of that. That was my own stupidity, and I fully accept the consequences. You do what you're ordered."

"Yes, ma'am."

Kendra disconnected, and he stared out at the night sky for several minutes, lost in worry and grief for the friends he knew he couldn't save, but then opened his tablet again and started digging. There was still a chance he could save Myra and Nazari, and the more he knew about them, the better chance he had of saving them both. And, although he wouldn't allow himself to hope, knowing it was a long shot, part of him prayed that if he could save them, it would be enough to win favor with the Seniors and help him find a way to save his mentor.

The sky was just starting to lighten with the coming dawn when the fur on his neck finally settled. Setting his tablet aside, he stood and stretched, observing the community coming to life around him. Then, with a yawn big enough to make his jaw hurt, his unexpected night watch finally over, he returned to his room and slept.

CHAPTER 7

GrandFather: The Friends and Family Discount

James woke feeling like he'd been trampled by an elephant. A sharp line of pain ran across his stomach, and his ribs ached with the effort to take a deep breath, but the worst was the throbbing pain in his head and face. His nose felt three times bigger than normal. It even hurt to blink, but it was far better than he'd felt the last time he'd woken, as it was at least manageable now, and he didn't feel like throwing up every time he moved his head. He gingerly felt his face, wincing at the pain, and wished he had a mirror to see how bad it looked.

"You look like you've been kicked by a horse, but the docs said you'll be back to your normal handsome self within a day or two. You need me to track down one of the cats?"

He turned his head to find Henry sprawled out in one of the massive chairs the Sabers used, feet propped up on one of the armrests and leaning against the other with his wide-brimmed hat tilted low over his eyes, arms crossed, and looking like he'd been there for a while. His insides squirmed, but it had nothing to do with his injuries. He'd never seen a more appealing sight. *He could be on the cover of a romance novel,* he thought and briefly wondered if the rest of him matched.

He took a deep breath to calm his racing thoughts and reacting body. "You think I'm handsome?" He gave Henry a sly grin, hoping to cover his embarrassment and shyness with humor and perhaps find out if Henry had any interest in him or if he'd only been teasing, but then winced in pain from the motion. *Who knew how much smiling could hurt?*

"Well, you were a fair sight prettier before you busted your face all up, but I've seen worse," Henry teased and sat up. "Now the real question is how much you want for that horse of yours? I ain't never seen a horse as willing or downright as smart as Buster. Saved my neck at least three times on bad foot'n and followed your trail like he knew what we were doing. They're saying we traveled close to forty miles if I've done the math right. That distance would cripple most horses, but he looks perfectly ready and willing to go again today."

"Buster's not for sale, but I think you've earned the friends and family discount on riding lessons. I'll only charge you double what I charge everyone else," James replied, trying hard not to chuckle as that hurt his stomach and sides far too much.

That didn't stop Henry, though, as he cackled with laughter.

"Seriously though, thank you," James said. "I'll probably never be able to thank you enough for what you did for my family, but for starters, I'm sponsoring you for adulthood if you're willing to put up with me as your guardian. I think you've more than earned it."

Henry tilted his head as if pausing to consider it. "Well, I've had far worse offers, but I'm not stupid enough to turn down one as good as yours. It's not necessary, but thanks. Besides, I figure you'd have done the same for me."

"Good lord, no. I'd never have made it half that distance before cramping up so bad I fell off of Buster, and with my luck, I would have been picked off by one of those four-winged buzzards while I lay there whimpering in pain. I don't think I ever went out for more than an hour or two before, and I'd be sore for days after. How are you feeling?"

"Oh, I'm fine. That used to be normal for me, back when I was young *and* stupid. Now I'm just stupid. Besides, the docs gave me enough of that miracle cream of theirs that I was almost able to take a bath in it."

James scowled. "Ah, so that's why my face is still all bruised up. You ran off with it all."

"Nah, I saved you some. There's a small jar on the table." Henry tilted his head in that direction and indicated a very small container with his fingers.

James used the controls on the bed to lift himself into a sitting position, pleased to find he wasn't dizzy but winced from the pain in his stomach and side. Once somewhat comfortably situated, he reached over to grab the rather large jar of nano cream, but he couldn't quite reach it.

Henry jumped down from his chair, walked over, unscrewed the lid, and handed it to him.

"Thanks," James said and started applying the cream to his bruised ribs. He sighed with relief as it kicked in. "If you ask me, this is the best thing the cats ever invented." He continued applying the cream to the angry red scar along his midsection.

"Ain't that the truth? Damon nearly gutted you, by the way. Doc said a fraction of an inch more, and they'd have been scraping you up off the floor."

He winced as he shifted to reach behind him to apply the cream to the bruises that ran around to his back.

"Here, lean forward." Henry took the cream back from him and gently applied a large glob to the bruises.

James sighed with relief, but that quickly changed to desire and soon spread to other parts of his body at Henry's touch. He tried hard to control his breathing and reaction, not wanting to make things awkward between the two of them. When his bruises were covered, he went to take the jar back, but Henry smiled and kept it from him.

"Lean back," Henry said, taking another gob of the cream and applying it to his forehead.

He closed his eyes and sighed as coolness seeped into his brow, and the pain vanished, but heat quickly rose elsewhere.

Henry grabbed another gob, this time applying it to his swollen lips.

James barely controlled a gasp as his desire bloomed at the touch. He opened his eyes to find Henry looking down at him with a half smile, and then, to his utter surprise and delight, Henry leaned in and kissed him. He forgot all about his pain for a long time. When they finally broke apart from their kiss, he chuckled. "Well, they've certainly improved the bedside care in the trauma ward since the last time I was here. I might have to injure myself more often."

"Sorry. First one's free. After that, we charge double. Friends and family discount, and all that."

James chuckled and ran his gaze seductively down Henry's muscular body. "Worth every credit and then some."

Henry smiled and continued to apply the cream to James's swollen and bruised face, following up each tender application with another kiss. Henry had just finished treating the last of the bruises and was closing up the jar when Myra walked in.

"Oh good, you're awake. I thought you might be. How are you feeling?"

"Much better, thanks to that miracle cream of yours," James said, trying to keep a straight face and feeling like a naughty schoolboy, but frowned at the rough edges of Myra's healer's mask, wondering if there was something wrong with Little Flower.

"Excellent. Any dizziness, lightheadedness?"

"No," James lied. Then again, he wasn't lightheaded from the injuries. He risked a glance in Henry's direction and saw that Henry was having a hard time keeping a straight face, too.

"Wonderful!" Myra replied. She pulled a light off her harness and shined it into his eyes, then made him run through the battery of tests common with head injuries before flipping through the scans on the monitor above him. "Looks like you'll be making a full recovery. I'd still like to keep you here overnight for monitoring. We've never used the bone knitter on your skulls before, and I want to make sure there aren't any complications, but if everything looks good, you should be released tomorrow morning."

"How are Little Flower and Marsee?" he asked, and he frowned with concern when she hesitated to reply.

"Little Flower's improving. No further complications, but we've decided to keep her sedated for now. She's been so depressed that I don't want her waking up in any pain when she does. As for Marsee..." Myra took a deep breath. "Rip Current escaped and attacked her again. She's not doing well, and several of her organs are failing. They have her in stasis right now while they print new ones, but they don't know if she'll be strong enough to survive the operations she'll need over the next several days."

"Oh no. Have they caught Rip?"

"They did, and he's dead. Marsee killed him, saving Clear Seas' youngest son in the process. They've also caught his accomplice, or one of them anyway, and found several dozen missing people, including Senior Councilor Wind Rider's daughter."

"Marsee killed him? Good for her. Rip clearly underestimated just how fierce she is. He's twice her size, and if she could beat him, I have no doubt she'll pull through."

Myra half-smiled at his comment, but he could tell there was something else bothering her about Marsee's condition, and from the glance in Henry's direction, she didn't want to talk about it with Henry there. He would ask later.

"Two of your people are also dead, killed by a flock of harbingers: Paul and Danny. We believe they were involved but haven't found proof yet. There was a ship with Ice Giants waiting to kill you and Little Flower, not far from where Paul and Danny were found, but Damon messed up and went in the wrong direction. The Ice Giants are dead, too. They blew up their ship rather than be captured."

"So what's going to happen with Damon?" Henry asked.

"With his crimes, I imagine he'll be executed," James answered before Myra could.

"I've not heard yet," Myra added. "Jer and Marcus need to work out joint reparations since more than one species was harmed. Plus, he destroyed Marsee's room. Executing Damon wouldn't compensate her for the damage, assuming she survives. It will also depend on what you and Little Flower want. At the very least, he won't be sentenced until Little Flower wakes and gives her statement."

"Well, I, for one, don't want his kind of hate in our community," he said.

Myra pursed her lips in a frown.

"What?" he asked, not expecting that reaction.

"I think you should watch his testimony before you make any final decisions," she replied and left.

Henry turned to him and raised his brows. "I can't even begin to imagine what Damon could have said that would've changed her mind. I thought for sure Damon was dead when I saw her leap out of the shadows and attack him. She looked like she wanted to rip his head off and eat him for breakfast."

"I have no idea." James looked around the room for his tablet. "I'm guessing my tablet's still in Little Flower's room since I'm not seeing it here."

"I can pick it up for you if you want?"

"That'd be great. Thanks," he replied.

"Of course. It's getting close to dinner. Are you hungry?"

"Ravenous, but I doubt what I want would be on the doctor's approved list, at least not for a day or two," James replied with a wink.

"Ha! Well, I'll see what I can do to find something that is." Henry kissed him again and left.

He laid back in his hospital bed to wait, smiling at this unexpected and welcome turn of events.

Twenty minutes later, Henry returned with his tablet tucked under one arm and a heaping tray of food.

"Good Lord, Henry. That's enough to feed half the compound!"

"Talk to Jordan. I tried to stop her three times, and she threatened to beat me with her rolling pin if I didn't shut up and take it. I learned a long time ago to never mess with a cook." Henry set the tray down and handed James his tablet.

"I can bump you up to an adult, but you'll have to wait until Jer's around to swear you in as a Councilor. I can't do that as Acting Senior unless I get his permission first, and with everything going on, you might have to wait until we head to the Water World for the council meeting."

Henry nodded, so James gave him the oath of adulthood, fired off a message to Jer, and grabbed his drink in a toast. "Happy Name Day, Henry."

After taking a sip, he grabbed a bowl of fruit and dug through the evidence of the past few days as he ate, realizing he had a lot of catching up to do. When he finally found Damon's testimony, he flung it up on the monitor so they could both watch.

Henry started snickering during the thirty minutes where Paxton stood there waiting out Damon as if he had all the time in the world.

"What's so funny?" James asked.

"Not five minutes before this, I gave Councilor Parner a lesson in how we train horses to ride. He's using the same principles on Damon. I guarantee once Paxton gets an answer from him, he'll have to wait for far less time for the next answer."

"It's been almost fifteen minutes so far. I wonder how long Paxton had to wait?"

Henry flashed a wicked grin. "Wanna bet? Loser has to rub more pain cream on the winner's bruises."

"I'm pretty sure I can't lose that bet either way," James replied. Grateful that he had dark skin because he was sure he was blushing, he considered the bet. "Thirty-two minutes."

"Hmm...I think he'll break sooner. He's already getting twitchy. Twenty-five minutes." They shook on it and waited while they ate. Henry was closer by a whopping ten seconds. There was some good-natured teasing, but then they both quieted as the interrogation continued, their banter replaced with seriousness.

When the recording ended, they were both silent, each lost in thought for several long moments. Henry was the first to speak. "I don't believe him for a second. He's just trying to get out of being executed."

"And if he's not?" James asked. "He's right. I did taunt him. I was trying to keep him distracted to give my granddaughter enough time to lock the shuttle door and get away. My death would have been a small price to pay if it had been successful. If I hadn't, maybe he wouldn't have snapped. For that matter, if I'd waited another few minutes, we'd have both been rescued with far fewer injuries."

"Don't you dare let him play head games with you. He tried to kill your entire family and almost succeeded. If I'd been five minutes later, he would have. And if Tabor had shown up before we controlled the situation, he'd have probably killed you both and himself rather than allowing himself to be caught. If he'd changed, he could have informed any of us what Rip Current was trying to do. Instead, he decided to trade your freedom and life for his."

James nodded and disconnected the display. Setting his tablet down on the table next to him, he swung his feet off the bed and lowered it down until his feet touched.

"Where do you think you're going?" Henry asked.

"Bathroom, and then I want to see Little Flower." The world spun hard on him as he stood, and he groaned with pain as he tried to catch himself before he fell.

Henry bolted out of his seat and caught him. "Woah, easy there!"

"I'm okay. Just stood up too fast," he said.

"Come on. I'll help you over to the bathroom. Can't have you cracking that skull they spent all that time and effort putting back together again."

He didn't complain. The world hadn't stopped spinning, and he needed the help. It was all he could do to keep from throwing up. The rooms here didn't have private bathrooms, so they made their way out to the one across the hall, where they found Ammond running towards them on all fours.

"The alarms went off at the desk. Are you feeling okay?" Ammond asked after sliding to a stop.

"Woozy, but I need to use the bathroom. I'll be okay once I lay back down," James replied.

Ammond didn't look convinced and followed them to the bathroom designed for human patients.

James was able to shoo everyone away once they arrived and collapsed onto the toilet with another groan. He stayed there long after he was done his business, leaning up against the wall until his queasiness passed before trying to stand up again. When he reached for the door handle, he had just enough time to think, '*Oh, that's not good,*' before he blacked out and fell hard against the door.

When he came to, he was back in his bed with Ammond and Myra on either side of him, and it appeared they were having a fairly animated conversation with each other as they looked at the monitor above him, their deep, rumbling voices barely audible to him. Henry was nowhere to be seen.

Ammond was the first to notice he was awake, and he nudged Myra with his paw before switching to sign language and glaring down at him with an annoyed scowl. "The next time you decide to pass out, would you mind trying not to dent our door with your head? It's really bad for my record and requires far too much paperwork to deal with afterwards."

"I'll try to remember that. Did I break something again?" He didn't feel bad, or rather no worse than he had before, and the dizziness had passed.

"Thankfully, it would appear your head is harder than the door. Except for another colorful bruise on your already bruised head, you appear uninjured," Ammond replied.

"Sampson says they have something they use for the pilots to protect their heads when testing new ships. I'm thinking we should have the Senior Council put a new law into place requiring all Hue-mans to wear them at all times," Myra muttered.

"We'd never wear them. We're too stubborn and thick-headed," James replied with a grin.

"Stubborn perhaps, but not nearly thick-headed enough." Myra scowled without the slightest hint of humor. "At least not for the amount of trouble your species seems to get themselves into on a daily basis, and I'm getting very tired of looking at brain scans. From now on, no walking or standing up without someone here to support you. You're still healing, and I expect you'll be dizzy for at least another day, if not more."

"Yes, ma'am. I promise to be a good boy and call for assistance," he signed.

Myra snorted with disbelief, turned, and left, tail lashing behind her.

Both he and Ammond frowned as they watched her leave, and when Ammond looked back at him with a sigh, he looked up into the old Saber's eyes and saw concern and a touch of grief behind the mask the healer wore.

"Marsee's really bad, isn't she?" he asked with concern and understanding.

Ammond sighed again and nodded. "Even if she survives long enough to make it through the operations, she's likely to be far worse off than Little Flower when she wakes. If she wakes." Ammond unhooked his tablet and fiddled with it for a moment before handing it to him.

"For the love of all that's holy in the universe. How is that even possible?" James asked after he finished reading the report and looking at the scans. "Am I even reading these right?"

"You are, and we have no idea. Every brain specialist in the Guild is looking at these scans right now, trying to figure out what, if anything, we can do." Ammond spent the next several minutes teaching him about the finer details of the Saber's brain and was surprised when he realized that James already knew about their hunting instinct and psychosis.

"Marsee had a small episode before the trial when we were all there, and Jer explained it in detail to me a few months ago, but not the medical aspects of it. If she did manage to kill off that part of herself, that could certainly help towards identifying a cure for the illness."

"That all depends on whether there's anything left of Marsee when she wakes. The cure might be far more of a problem than the disease. Now, I need to get back to helping Myra with this. Henry's waiting for you out in the lobby. Do you want me to send him back, or would you like me to send him home?"

"You can send him back. He's welcome anytime, but I was hoping to see Little Flower."

Ammond scooped him up and carried him into the next room, where Little Flower lay sedated. Ammond set him down gently on the oversized chair next to her bed and placed the call button next to him. "Call if you feel at all lightheaded or dizzy or ready to go back to your room."

A few minutes later, Henry joined him.

James shifted over to make space on the oversized chair and leaned up against Henry as he watched his granddaughter sleep. Henry seemed to understand he wasn't in the mood for conversation and just held him. He was grateful for the support as he thought about Marsee, Damon, and everything else that had happened over the past few days. An hour or so later, he fell asleep in Henry's arms and only woke as Ammond arrived to carry him back to his room.

After Ammond left, James turned to Henry. "Go enjoy that hot tub for me. I think I'm going to sleep for a few days."

Henry gave him a lengthy kiss goodbye and told him he'd bring breakfast in the morning.

He smiled at the idea of breakfast in bed as he gingerly rolled over onto his uninjured side and lay there thinking about all of the things he'd rather be doing right now rather than lying alone in a hospital bed, but he was hooked up to the monitors in the room, and there was no way he wanted to have to explain *that* to the healer on duty. Although, he was surprised he hadn't set off the monitors already. *I might have to try harder in the morning,* he thought and fell asleep to that lovely idea.

CHAPTER 8

Jer: Shifting Perspective

Hours before his alarm was scheduled to wake him, Jer bolted upright, panting in fear from a night terror, at first relieved to realize the terror had only been a dream, but then he shuttered with a sob and curled around his pillow when he woke enough to remember the events that triggered the night terror and the horror of reality that awaited him.

After an hour of tossing and turning and failing miserably to fall back to sleep, he dragged himself out to the main room to pick at a breakfast he had absolutely no appetite for and barely even tasted. As he ate, he started digging through his messages. To his relief, there weren't any recriminations from Myra, and while she'd agreed with his decision on Marsee's care, he was heartbroken to know she didn't know how to fix Marsee any more than the Senior Healer did.

Letting out a heavy sigh, he set his tablet down, staring at his half-eaten breakfast but not really seeing it. He was terrified he was condemning Marsee to the same fate as Little Flower, or worse, and he'd promised Marsee he wouldn't do that to her. He wasn't even sure how they'd care for her if she did wake. They'd struggled to care for Little Flower and Hope these past six months, and it had nearly torn his family apart. Even if she did recover, after what had happened in the canyon, there was a very good chance he'd still have to kill her. She'd lost control while already placed on a watch in front of three members of the Senior Council, and he should have put her down the moment he'd had her in his arms, but he hadn't been able to. Instead, he'd held onto her with every last fiber of his being as she'd whimpered and writhed in his arms, fighting the demon that had possessed her. He knew her cries would haunt his memory for the rest of his life.

With a growl, he shoved his half-eaten meal aside, unable to force another bite down. But after taking several calming breaths he started watching Damon's statement, as Myra's comments had surprised him. The last thing he'd expected from her was any form of leniency. He could barely watch as guilt clawed at his stomach. Once again, he'd failed everyone. He'd failed Damon and, quite likely, Paul and Danny, although they still had no idea if they were involved in this mess or not. Even if they hadn't been, they'd packed up and run away from New Hope and been killed trying to escape.

He kept forgetting how differently the passage of time felt for the Hue-mans. A week for him was nearly a month for them, and the few months of back and forth with the guilds to try and bend the rules for the Hue-mans felt like half a year. *How long does four years feel like to them, or the six we originally expected them to wait? Even with the longer lifespans we should be able to give them with our technology, they're not going to be able to adjust in only a few months. They're having a hard enough time just dealing with the longer days.*

He wondered how he would have handled the same situation, stripped of his adulthood after having and raising a child, banned from engaging in the activities he wanted to do, and prevented from traveling without supervision because he wasn't considered an adult anymore. Even more so if the time he'd had to wait was the equivalent of a sixth of his lifetime. Could he go fifty years as a child after having the privileges of being an adult? *No, I'd be just as angry and resentful.*

On top of that, they'd judged Damon and put him on a watch over something he hadn't been able to change or rectify on his old world. They'd never actually given him a chance, and neither had any of his own species. The Council had nearly sterilized Jer's children and grandchildren for his and Myra's actions in putting Little Flower in harm's way, and he'd been horrified, yet Little Flower's people were essentially doing the same to Damon without trial or just cause.

Did they have just cause, though? They had no way of knowing if Damon had changed or was only trying to hide his bigoted and hateful beliefs. Even if he did still think that way, did it matter if he never expressed or acted on those beliefs? How much of the Hue-man's violent past was genetically based? Would that get passed on to their offspring? Hope seemed to be a happy baby and nothing like the male that had raped and beaten Little Flower, yet there were times she was just as angry and violent.

He leaned back in his chair, considered everything Damon had ever said or done in his presence, and sighed. Damon had come to him on more than one occasion asking to leave, even offering to give up his future council position. He shook his head. *I should have given him his adulthood and let him go.*

Checking the time, he sighed again. He should leave for the Trauma Center soon, but he wasn't sure he was ready for that. The moment Marsee left stasis, the clock started ticking again. He heard the sounds of Marcus moving around, followed shortly after by a gentle knock on Jer's door. "I'm out here, Marcus."

His brother appeared a moment later. "Did you sleep at all?"

"Some. I've been trying to catch up on everything and figure out what to do with Damon."

"Damon? What's there to decide? He tried to kill multiple members of our family and put others at risk. He should be executed." Marcus started digging through the kitchen to pick something for his breakfast. "Ellie has the strangest preferences in food. I can see why Marsee insisted on going down to the market. Do you have any idea what gaftari reed is?"

"Never heard of it. As for Damon, you should read what Myra sent me." Jer pulled up the message while Marcus sat down across from him and began eating. He slid the tablet over and snagged a piece of the bright orange and red reed off Marcus's plate when his brother didn't immediately spit it out. "Not bad. Tart, but it has a satisfying crunch."

Marcus grunted in acknowledgment as he read and, when done, handed the tablet back with a sigh. "I suppose that does complicate matters. Not just in Damon's case but Snapper Fish's as well. I'll talk to Clear Seas and Wind Rider about it later today. We might want to bring this before the Full Council."

"That's what I was thinking, too."

"Well, don't worry about this for now. You should focus on Marsee. They can wait a few days for judgment."

"Speaking of Marsee, did you read the message Myra sent this morning?"

Marcus popped another piece of food in his mouth and crunched loudly before answering. "No. I haven't looked at my messages yet."

"The guards have found out about Marsee's episode. Quinn overheard Myra and Ammond discussing it."

His brother's ears drooped. "I suppose it was wishful thinking that they wouldn't find out what happened."

"Indeed. What is surprising is that they're not going to enforce the DNR."

Marcus flicked his ears back in surprise. "They're not?"

"At least not until we know more." He sighed and checked the time again. "I suppose I should head over. I'll let you know when she's out of surgery."

"Before you go, I finished scanning in the evidence we found in the cave. You should read through it while you're waiting. We have a bit of a security issue."

"And we didn't before?" Jer asked, rolling his eyes again.

"The information on the rest of those letters we found could have only come from someone high up in the Guard."

Jer frowned as he considered the one he'd read in the cave. "Leaf and Willow could have easily provided the information on that letter, too."

"Some of it, yes, but not the rest. That number referenced the ticket in the guard's system about the flag on Marsee's medical record.

That's probably where Rip got ahold of Marsee's journal. Do you trust Kendra?"

Jer pursed his lips, considering. "I want to say yes. She took quite the risk by admitting what she did the other day. She saved both of my daughters' lives from the rest of the Senior Council. That rates her pretty high in my book, but we should consider everyone a suspect until we know more. Even if she's not directly involved, someone under her could be. Even Avery's a suspect after leaving Marsee alone."

His brother shook his head. "Avery? No. I don't think so. His statement matches what Stormy told his father. Marsee ordered him out."

"Marsee doesn't have the rank or authority to order a guard around," Jer growled. "Especially not when she's on a watch."

"No, she doesn't, but her reasons and intuition were right. Avery left for that light for the same reason we went to Rip's home first, and for the same reason we both let her walk out that door yesterday morning. Finding the other missing people and figuring out who else was involved was far more important than Marsee's personal safety, no matter how much we care for her."

He stared at his brother for several long moments, trying to control his anger at Avery and Clear Seas for leaving his daughter unprotected, not wanting to admit that it was really anger towards himself that he was feeling, then stood and started pacing.

"Jer, why do you think she has that honor guard? It's not because she protected Stormy in the heat of the moment, worthy enough as it was, and it's not to make up for the guards' failure to protect her. It's because she didn't stay here hiding in fear after what Rip had already done to her. She walked out that door without hesitation and took control of the situation, risking her very life to find her friend and the thirty-seven other complete strangers who are alive today because of it. It's because she had the audacity to order an honor guard to leave his post and to order three members of the senior council around."

He tilted his head at Marcus, acknowledging his words, and left the ship unable to solidify his own thoughts enough to reply.

CHAPTER 9

GrandFather: Bias

James woke as Myra arrived to check on him, feeling a million times better than he had before. She helped him to the bathroom, and outside of a little unsteadiness, he had no problems this time. He was climbing back into bed when Henry showed up with another heaping tray of food.

"Did you leave anything for anyone else?" Myra asked him.

Henry laughed and shrugged as he set the tray down. "You'll have to ask Jordon about that, but I'm not complaining. Did the patient behave himself?"

"Slept right through the night, and since he was a good cub for once, I'm releasing him, with restrictions. GrandFather, I've spoken with Nazari. You've been taken off your work shifts and lessons at the barn for the next half week, no riding, no running, or heavy lifting. Rest as much as possible. I want to know immediately if you have a headache or experience any dizziness, and for the love of the full moons, please avoid hitting your head. If you even so much as bump it, I want you back here for a scan. Understood?"

"Yes, ma'am," he replied with a grin, unable to keep his amusement off his face at being called a cub. "How are Little Flower and Marsee doing, and who's watching Hope?"

"Hope is currently being chased around the ward by her Uncle Ammy," Myra replied.

The expression on Myra's face caused him to snicker and wonder just how that translated into her language.

"Although half the ward has been taking turns," she continued. "As for Little Flower, she's much better this morning, and we're planning to wake her this afternoon, assuming she continues to improve. As for Marsee..." Myra let out a heavy sigh, her ears drooping with concern. "I don't know. I'm still waiting for an update."

James nodded his understanding. "I'll come back over this afternoon. I'd like to be here when you wake her."

Myra nodded, and he watched as she left, tail dragging on the ground.

Sighing, he turned his attention to the tray of food. As much as Henry had brought, they decimated it. When they were done, all that remained were the few items he'd purposely set aside for Buster.

Henry groaned as he leaned back in his seat and ate the last piece of food on his plate. "If Jordon keeps feeding us like this, neither of us are going to be able to fit in that saddle for very long."

He chuckled and winked. "Well, I'm sure we could find a way to work it off."

"You're on restrictions," Henry replied. "I'm pretty sure I heard Myra say no riding."

He rolled his eyes and cautiously climbed out of the bed. When he didn't get dizzy, he made his way over to the small closet in the room, looking for something to wear besides the hospital gown he was in. While it was far better than the gowns he'd ever had the misfortune of wearing on Earth, he still had no desire to head out in public in one either.

Empty, he thought. Checking the few drawers and cabinets in the room, he found them all filled with supplies or equally as empty. "I wonder what they did with my clothes," he said when all he found were his boots.

"Knowing the Sabers, they probably threw them in the recycler. You were a bloody mess. I need to bring the tray back to the cafeteria. Do you want me to pick something up from your room on my way back? I need to head over for my shift soon, so I'll be heading back in this direction anyway."

"That would be great, thanks. I'll walk over to the barn with you, though. I want to thank Buster for putting up with you."

Henry grinned as he pulled a handful of dried star fruit out of his pocket. "He knows a good deal when he sees one."

"Oh, I see how it is, bribing my horse for friendship with treats," James teased but then glared. "Did Jordan really fill up those trays of food, or did you?"

Henry chuckled, stood up, gave James a kiss that made him forget all about his horse or the meal, and after, walked out with the empty tray in hand. Twenty minutes later, he returned with an armful of clothing and a few other items that made James frown at the necessity.

When he was fully clothed, they made their way out, stopping briefly to check on Little Flower. He smiled with relief to see Myra hadn't been lying as he examined the monitors for himself. She was doing better.

As they passed Ammond's office. Hope squealed with delight when she saw him and ran out of the room on her stubby little toddler legs.

"Gampa!!!" she squealed.

James scooped her up in a big hug, only wincing slightly. "How's my favorite little girl?" he asked, tickling her.

She giggled.

Ammond made his way out after her. "You're looking much better this morning."

"Feeling better, too. Myra let me go for good behavior," he half-signed and then set Hope down when she started wiggling. He wasn't recovered enough for that.

"What did you go and do that for?" Ammond growled as Hope ran off into the ward.

Hope squealed with laughter as her Uncle Ammy pretended to chase after her, scooped her up, and returned, carrying her upside down.

"I'm assuming Myra gave you the lecture?" Ammond asked after throwing Hope up on his shoulder.

James chuckled. "She did, but sadly, it looks like I'm going to have to postpone my plans for skydiving lessons for a few days."

"Skydiving?!" Ammond asked. "Please tell me that's not what it sounds like."

"Oh, it's nothing all that dangerous. We just jump out of perfectly good shuttles for fun," he replied, trying hard to keep a straight face.

Ammond shook his head at the ceiling in full-blown exasperation. "Ancient Gods, Myra was right. We're never going to be able to keep their species alive long enough to repopulate. Jumping out of a shuttle! What will they think of next?" With that, he turned and walked away, tail shivering with barely controlled emotion.

Laughing, they made their way to the barn. By the time they arrived, he was exhausted, and his side was throbbing.

"Are you feeling okay? You're looking a little peaked," Henry asked as they walked through the barn door.

"I may have overestimated how recovered I am," he admitted and sat down on the bench near the front door with a groan.

"You want me to find Nazari or one of the other healers?"

"No, I just need a moment. My ribs are still sore, and it hurts to take a deep breath."

Henry didn't look convinced.

"I'm fine. Go on, or you'll be late for your shift. I'll rest here until I'm sure I'm recovered. Trust me. I have no desire to face Myra's wrath today. Her bedside treatment is nowhere near as good as yours."

Henry chuckled and left.

James sat and enjoyed the sounds of the animals moving around in their stalls and munching on their breakfast. He heard Buster's distinctive nicker and figured Henry must be over at his stall. He turned his head in that direction to look down the long outer aisle of the barn and was surprised to see former Councilor Tabor coming from the far back row with a tray in her hand.

He frowned as his thoughts returned to Myra's comment. He knew what she was referring to when she made them. Little Flower and Damon had been raised with two very different sets of morals. His granddaughter had been taught love and inclusion, while Damon had obviously been taught white supremacy and hate, and yet when both felt trapped and isolated, they'd reacted the same way. Only Damon had been able to act on it, whereas his granddaughter had not.

He'd seen the rage and hate in his granddaughter's eyes that had been directed towards Brice at the Agency, and they'd been no different than the ones Damon had directed towards him. Where his granddaughter had been supported and loved, Damon had been shunned by the community and would likely be executed. He himself had avoided Damon rather than getting to know him. Henry was right in that if Damon had changed, he could have come forward with that information, but if he'd been in Damon's position, would he have risked coming forward at the risk of losing his one chance at freedom? In many ways, that would be like expecting his own grandfather to turn in someone on the underground railroad in the hopes that it would earn his freedom rather than taking the chance that had been offered to escape.

Nurture versus nature? he wondered.

"You look like you have the weight of the world on your shoulders," Tabor said as she approached, setting down the tray and sitting so she could talk easier with him.

"I do. I'm trying to figure out what to do with Damon," he replied.

"I would think it would be an easy decision after what he did to you and your family," Tabor said.

"It should be, but it's not. Our people had a long and sordid past that we were barely starting to break free from before. My grandparents were born into slavery and were owned by people who could very well have been Damon's grandparents, and, if his testimony is to be believed, raised by people who continued to feel that way. As a child, you don't know any better. You believe what your parents teach you, and it takes a lot of effort and strength to both challenge and change those beliefs. Damon stated he had changed, was trying to prove it to us, and even removed his tattoos to try and remove the visible reminder of that past, but we all judged him before we ever got to know him and pushed him away. How much of what happened was our own fault? We're the ones that isolated him rather than befriending him and helping him to learn a better way. We should have known better, too. Our history is rife with people doing terrible things because they felt isolated and ostracized. What Little Flower did in the Agency was no different. The only difference is that Damon had a chance to take action on it. Little Flower was given a chance to change and prove herself, but Damon was not. Should he be punished? Yes. But should it be a death sentence? I'm honestly not so sure anymore."

Tabor stared at him in ears back astonishment. "I don't think I could ever forgive someone if they did what he did to me or my family. Frankly, I'm astounded every day that Little Flower forgave me for what I did to her. Your species' ability to find nuance in a situation is one that I'm only just beginning to understand. For us, the consequences of our actions are far more cut and dry. None of us would think twice about executing Damon for what he did, and Little Flower would have been well within her rights to demand retribution from all of us for what we did to her, and we would have all gone to our deaths feeling that the punishment was both fair and just. Instead, Little Flower advocated for us, for her parents, and managed to flip a Senior Council verdict, something I don't think has happened in millennia, if ever. I've watched that portion of her trial so many times I've lost count. I still can't believe it, and I was on the receiving end of it. The way she thinks, the way you all seem to, is so completely different from us. After utterly destroying me in front of all five planets, she turned around a month later and not only cut short my self-imposed punishment, but she forgave me and welcomed me as a friend. And yet, she still sentenced the man who raped her to death, knowing that his kind of hatred and evil can't be allowed to continue and flourish."

James gave a half smile and a snort at her comments. "Let me ask you this. If a child had been abused by their parents and killed them in an attempt to escape that situation, how would you punish the child?"

Tabor flicked her ears back again in surprise at his question but considered for a moment before answering. "Assuming we had proof of that, the child would not be to blame. It would be considered self-defense. We would find the child a new guardian and make sure they received proper medical care to deal with their trauma. Although depending on the situation and age of the child, they might also be put on a watch list."

"As it would have in ours, or should have if our legal system had been as…honorable as yours. Damon is still only considered a child by the laws of this society, even though we all recognize that he was an adult in mine, and if what he said in his testimony is true, then from his perspective, the *adults* of this community were all abusing him, holding him prisoner, isolating him, keeping him from learning the crafts and skills he wanted to learn, and he was trying to find a way to escape, and took the first opportunity given to him."

Tabor stared at him in wide-eyed, ears back shock for several long moments. "I…I don't even know what to say to that," she stammered. "I…he…" Tabor dropped her paws, unable to complete her thought, grabbed the tray she'd been carrying and stood up, looked at him, and then down towards the end of the barn where Damon was, shook her head, and left.

James chuckled at her reaction. They had a way of breaking the Saber's brains.

A few minutes later, he decided he was feeling recovered enough to make his way over to Buster. When he arrived, Buster was happily munching on his breakfast, a large clump of hay sticking out of his mouth. The horse looked up and let out a soft knicker at his arrival.

"It's good to see you too, old boy," he replied and slid the stall door open.

Buster squinted at him and flicked his ears back but kept chewing.

"No worries, you're off the hook for today. Enjoy your breakfast. I just came over to say thank you for coming after me."

He scratched one of Buster's favorite places, and the horse groaned with pleasure as he leaned into it, a small clump of hair coming loose with each scratch.

"Starting to shed, are you? Bet that itches. Well, maybe this will help take your mind off it." James pulled out the wrapped container of fresh star fruit he'd saved, knowing it was Buster's favorite, unwrapped it, and poured it into his hand.

Buster's ears flicked forward, and he nickered and bobbed his head, dropping the mouthful of hay, far more interested in the yummy snack James held.

"Want this, do you? Well, you've earned it." James held it out, and Buster slobbered all over his hand in his enthusiasm for the fruit. "Was that really necessary?"

Buster bobbed his head again as if saying yes and then sniffed at his pockets to see if there was more.

James laughed as Buster found the other stash and started pulling on his pocket with his upper lip.

"Alright, greedy horse. Just a minute," he said as he pushed Buster's head out of the way, dug out the other dish of fruit, and handed that over, too.

Buster nickered his thanks, and James gave him another pat as the horse went back to eating his breakfast, leaving him with a slobbered hand. He flicked some of it off, washed off the rest in the nearby sink, and then sighed before making his way down to Damon's cell. There were two adult female Sabers guarding the stall that he didn't recognize.

"Name and rank, please," one of the guards demanded as she stopped him from approaching.

"GrandFather," he replied, giving his registered name sign. "James O'Neil, Acting Senior Councilor in Councilor Chenzira's absence. I'd like to speak with Damon."

The guard nodded and opened the door so he could enter.

He raised a brow, surprised. "You're not going to verify who I am? You don't know me. I could say I'm anyone."

Both guards flicked their ears back in surprise. "No one would claim to be Senior or Acting Senior if they weren't. To do so would be grounds for arrest and a possible death sentence if we had verified who you were and found out you were impersonating someone else or lying about your rank. Plus, the cell is being recorded, watched, and your access verified by Command, and it's unlikely you'd be able to do anything against the two of us."

James raised his brows and snorted at the two guards before letting them have it. "You're vastly underestimating the violence my people are capable of. We used to have weapons that could kill you in an instant from over a league away. My granddaughter wasn't lying about that at the Trial. In fact, she's quite skilled with those weapons. Don't assume that just because our people are small compared to you, that we're not dangerous to you or Damon. I could have walked into that cell and killed him before you could have stopped me. I could have disabled communications with Command before coming here, as happened at the Hallowed Eve Festival, or I could have altered the footage so that Command had no idea I was even here. Rip Current managed to kidnap Marsee while she was being guarded, alter evidence in the archives, use the account of a dead person, and then escape while under guard and watch of their Command. If he can do all that, what's to stop someone else from creating and granting themselves whatever rank they want or killing you and Damon and changing the footage afterwards? Personally verify everyone who requests access to Damon's cell, even if you think you know who they are and what their rank is. Make sure someone locally, that you *personally* trust, is aware before granting them access to the cell, and verify they're not hiding a weapon. If you don't know what something is on a person, don't let them enter the cell with it, and find out what it is. The rules of engagement have changed for your people. This wasn't just an isolated incident. This was an attempted coup, and if you think this is over, you're sadly mistaken. You need to adapt, and quickly, before someone else gets hurt."

There was a flash of movement off to his side, and he turned to see another guard standing by the corner. "You're right," he signed. "The rules have changed. Do as he says."

"Yes, sir," the other two replied.

"Who are you?" James asked.

"Honor Guard Quinn Bluestone, District Senior for Council City and Second in Command of Saber's Guard. I'm currently in charge of the guard presence here," he replied. "When you're done speaking with Damon, we should talk."

James nodded and turned back to the other two, who verified his account and began checking him over. He did chuckle when they looked at him with confusion when they found the two empty bowls he carried in his pants. When they were done, they stepped aside and motioned that he could enter.

Damon looked up from where he was sitting as the door slid open.

He took a deep breath and entered. One of the guards started to follow in, but he stopped them and motioned for them to shut the door. The guard nodded but remained watching, ready to enter at a moment's notice if Damon tried something.

James turned back and stared at Damon for several moments before sitting down across from him, both tired from his walk down the barn and wanting to put Damon at ease.

Damon tilted his head in confusion.

"Tell me about your daughter. What was her name? What was she like?" he asked.

Damon stared at him for several moments and then, to his surprise, started crying. "No one has asked me about my family since before," he said, wiping the tears away. "Her name was Sarah. She had light blond curly hair and blue eyes, just like your great-granddaughter. She was about to turn two when it happened. We had birthday presents all picked out and had a small party planned for her, unicorn-themed. She was obsessed with them. Her mother found a local farm and had managed to scrounge up the money to have them bring over one of their miniature ponies dressed up as one. She was the happiest baby I've ever seen. We never had much to spare, but I was always able to provide for them, and there was always food on the table. She never cared that I couldn't provide the latest in toys and had just as much fun pulling out all the pots and pans and banging on them on the floor or dancing with her Papa. She was super smart, talking all the time, and mostly potty trained. Between working two jobs, we'd find time to go for long walks and collect leaves and pine cones or play at the community park.

She especially loved the swings. I can still hear her squeals of laughter at times."

Damon had to pause to wipe more tears away and regain his composure. Then, he lifted his shirt to reveal a tattoo of a woman holding a newborn.

"What was her mother like?" James asked.

"Amanda was the most amazing, kind, forgiving person I've ever met. I met her at a halfway house where she was volunteering. I'd been in and out of jail for years for various crimes and battled drug addiction since I was a teenager, but she never once judged me and was probably the first person to treat me with any sort of kindness. I think I fell in love with her the moment I saw her smile, and I vowed then and there to be the kind of person worthy enough for her love."

Damon sighed and hung his head. "She'd be so disappointed in me now." Shaking his head at some internal thought, he continued. "She helped me find the first real job I'd ever had. No one hires ex-cons, and certainly, not one covered in tats like I was. It was hard work, but I managed. She even helped me study for my G.E.D. Eventually, I saved up enough for a tiny one-bedroom apartment and moved out, but I returned to help volunteer just so that I could spend time with her. It took several months, but I finally managed to gather the courage to ask her out, and to my amazement, she said yes. A year later, I asked her to marry me. We were married for three years, and well, the rest is history. Best years of my life."

Damon smiled wistfully, his gaze distant and lost in memories.

"Tell me about the other tattoos," James asked when Damon refocused on him.

Damon frowned and slumped with a heavy sigh. "I grew up in a single-parent household. My dad raised me after my mom died in a car accident when I was six. He was an abusive drunk and only got worse after. He'd been driving the car. As you probably guessed, he was a white supremacist. It's what I knew. His buddies gave me my first tattoo when I was only ten. Papa was so proud of me when I said I wanted one like his. I think it was the only time I ever made him happy after Mama died. I ran away from home when I turned sixteen and ended up on the streets. I was a scrawny kid and used the tats for protection. People left me alone, although I learned pretty quickly the first time I ended up in jail that they didn't always protect me. Ironically, it was my cellmate who changed my mind about your people. He was the nicest dude I've ever met, and I fully believe he was wrongly convicted, but I'm pretty sure he was still locked up when the asteroid hit. Anyway, I tried getting those tattoos removed, but I couldn't afford it. The cheapest I could find was a hundred dollars an inch, and it still wasn't guaranteed. I did my best to hide them and kept them covered with clothing and makeup as much as possible. Myra did it in an hour, but not before tossing me naked in a cell with Vera. I know that's why almost everyone has avoided me, and I know you won't believe me, but I feel awful for what I did. I never understood how my father could beat me. I always blamed the alcohol for his actions. I never understood how grief could so overwhelm you that you'd do anything to get away from it."

"I saw your interrogation with Paxton. I'll be honest, I don't know if I believe you or not, but I have to make a decision about what to do with you. What do you think I should do?"

Damon snorted. "Do you have any choice? The law here is pretty clear. I'm honestly surprised they haven't executed me already. I deserve it for what I did. There isn't a day that goes by that I don't wish Sarah and Amanda had made it instead of me. They'd have fit in here. They'd have been able to make something of themselves."

"You said you wanted to be a pilot. Was that to get away from here, or has that always been a dream of yours?"

"A little of both, I guess. I'd never been on a plane before. Could never afford to travel anywhere, but I used to watch the planes take off from my apartment and wonder what it was like. When they flew us here, there was something magical about seeing the world from above. Like all the cares of the world were left behind, and you could just be. I wanted to see everything, visit all of the worlds, and maybe find a home where people wouldn't know my past and give me a clean start."

"If you could make reparations, what would they be?" he insisted.

Damon snorted. "I have no idea, and frankly, I don't think you should bother. I'm sick to death of the isolation, and I'd rather you execute me than have to go back to living with that kind of loneliness. I doubt anyone in the universe will give me a chance now, and the only two friends I had here are dead. I want to be with Sarah and Amanda. God, I miss them so much." Damon lowered his head to his knees, trying to hide the sobs and tears that were streaming down his face.

He watched for a moment, debating, trying to decide if Damon's cries were real or if he was trying to gaslight his way out of an execution. His gut told him that regardless of his intentions, his grief was real. Even if he was lying about his wife and child, everyone had lost someone they'd cared about. He stood and walked over, slowly sat down beside Damon, wrapped an arm around his shoulders, and sat with him until he stopped crying.

"I miss my family, too," he said when Damon pulled away.

Damon nodded. "Thanks. For this. For asking about my family. I know I don't deserve any kindness from you, but I appreciate it more than you know. Do what you need to do. As the cats say, it'll be fair and just for what I did to you."

James nodded and stood up again, dusting the dirt off his clothing.

As he walked towards the door, the guard slid it open. James started to walk through, but he stopped and turned around. "Damon, I don't know if I believe you or if I could ever trust you again after what you did to my family, but I have no doubt that every single one of us would have tried to do the same if given the opportunity to escape our cells at the Agency, and from the reports I've seen, just about all of us reacted in violence at least once while we were in there, even me."

He exited the cell, the door closing behind him, and turned back to the two guards who had searched him. "In case you're wondering, you missed all three weapons I had hidden on me."

The look of absolute astonishment on all three cats made him chuckle to himself, knowing he'd once again broken their brains, but he glared with disapproval in Quinn's direction over the failure of his guards and, without another word, stormed off.

CHAPTER 10

Jer: Montipora

It was still early, so Jer wasn't surprised when he didn't see anyone as he left the platform, not even the normal gate attendant by the terminal entrance, but he was completely unprepared for the sight awaiting him when he swam around the platform, and the Trauma Center came into view. The crowd had swelled overnight, filling the park in every direction.

They hadn't spotted him yet, so he took a moment to record the scene, praying he would have a chance to show Marsee. Thousands of Water Sprites now floated outside the Trauma Center, holding vigil. Children darted everywhere in rippling swarms of color while others waited in line to leave their offerings at the memorial. He'd expected them to go home after paying their respects the night before, but it appeared like they were preparing to remain for days. He saw temporary waste facilities being set up, as well as people setting up booths or unloading shuttles and passing out food and supplies to the crowd, and from multiple directions, he saw long lines of shuttles approaching and being directed by the Sea Patrol for parking.

A group of musicians played quietly near the memorial, easy to hear even with so many there, while someone led a prayer in sign language to the gods of the deep. He blinked when he realized that no one, outside of the children, was speaking in Water Sprite. Everyone else was using sign language. The only thing that showed on their skin was the deep blues and blacks of mourning or the purple and silver as they placed their offering with the mountain of gifts left by the others.

Was everyone coming? he wondered. *Why? Was this all because she risked her life to save Stormy's? This all seemed so much bigger than saving the life of the Senior Councilor's son or finding the others, as important as that was.*

He watched the prayer with curiosity and respect, as while he'd been to the Water World on many occasions, he had never witnessed any of their religious ceremonies. It both fascinated and overwhelmed him as the speaker begged and pleaded with their gods to restore the Translator and the others to health, to accept their unworthy offerings in exchange for their lives, and to take back the darkness it had released from the depths and infected the people with, but the ceremony stopped as people slowly realized he was there and began flashing the silver and purple in his direction.

Overwhelmed with emotion, he swam through the growing crowd, and it parted before him, leading to the memorial and the Trauma Center beyond. He nodded to the speaker as he passed, who bowed low and flashed the silver and purple, but then he stopped to look at the memorial in the daylight and read a few of the messages that had been left behind.

Notes of love, prayers for her health, and drawings by children of the characters from her books were mixed in with physical gifts. As he examined them, he realized that people had left their best work, exquisite artwork, carvings, books bound in gilded covers, bouquets of flowers woven in ornate patterns, furniture, and everything she could possibly need to refurbish her damaged room back home and half of New Hope if she wanted to. Someone had even left replacement clothing for Little Flower.

He turned, overwhelmed with the offering, and found himself facing a mother and two young children. He nodded to them and was about to swim off but stopped and looked again as he registered the expressions on their faces, or more specifically, the color of the young male Sprite who hid behind his mother. The edges of his skin were tinged in white and grey, signifying both fear and guilt, although he was trying hard to hide it.

"What's your name, child?" he asked the boy, motioning him forward.

The child swallowed hard and flashed pure white with terror as he bolted between his mother's tentacles to hide.

"I'm not going to hurt you child. Why are you so afraid of me?"

His mother sighed with tinges of regret and exasperation. "I beg you to forgive my son for his rudeness. His name is Rock Face. He's been like this for days but won't tell me what's bothering him and has even refused to go to school."

"It's nice to meet you, Rock Face," Jer replied. "Will you tell me what's going on? Is someone hurting you at school?"

Rock Face peered out from between his mother's tentacles at him and at the crowd watching them, shook his head, and hid again, but his mother shoved him out.

The small female Sprite huffed and rolled her eyes at her older brother. "My name's Coral. My stupid brother thinks you're going to kill him."

Jer flicked his ears back in surprise. "Why would I do that?"

"Because he insulted the Translator the other day," Coral replied. "The Councilors with her were very angry at what he'd said."

"I didn't say it. You did!" Rock Face flashed. "You're the one that went up and told her, and you got it all wrong!"

"You said you didn't think it was her," Coral flashed back. "As for the rest, I didn't know the right signs. I didn't mean to insult her, but you *are* an idiot. Everyone knew it was the Translator."

"I knew she was the Translator," he flashed back in anger. "That wasn't what I said!"

The mother took a deep, exasperated breath, one he'd taken many times with his own cubs, and he struggled hard to keep his amusement off his own face, although his tail was curling.

"Marsee didn't mention being insulted. Perhaps you should tell me your side of the story," he encouraged the boy.

Rock Face glared at his sister before answering. "Coral asked me if Marsee was the Translator when we saw her in the market the other day. I responded that I thought she would have had more important things to do than swim through the market, especially if she was with the Senior Councilor, but *she...*" He scowled in his sister's direction again. "told them all that I said she wasn't the Translator and that I thought they'd never bring her to such a simple market. I never said simple. When she went missing, everyone at school said the guards were going to arrest and kill me, too. After the guards searched our home twice and brought us in for questioning, well Mama anyway, we had to wait outside, it got worse."

Jer looked up at the mother. "Too?!"

She sighed and nodded. "Coral ran off before I could stop her and approached the Translator, rudely interrupting their tour. When the Translator didn't get angry, I thought we were lucky. I've never seen the Senior Councilor so angry before. I honestly expected him to have the guards drag her off then and there, but where are *my* manners? My name is Montipora. My partner Alabaster was... He was... executed by Clear Seas for killing one of the workers at the new shipyard, but I swear he didn't do it. He wouldn't have, not unless someone attacked him first. I don't know why he didn't request an advocate or why he wouldn't tell Clear Seas what happened. After what we've learned, after what Rip did to your daughter and the others, I'm assuming Rip tortured or threatened him. Perhaps he remained silent to protect us. I may never know, but I owe your daughter everything for stopping Rip Current from hurting anyone else and for showing such kindness to my family the other day."

He nodded his understanding. "We're still investigating that incident, and while I don't know everything that happened to your partner, what I do know, from the statements given by the others we rescued, is that the protesters found out about the others being held in the cave. That's what they were trying to stop, not rescue an endangered species that never lived in that canyon. The two off-world builders who were killed were working with Rip. We're still looking for the third, but we're assuming he's dead. I'm sorry for your loss, and while I know that does nothing to lessen the pain of your grief, and I can't undo what has been done, I promise to ensure that justice is served."

Montipora took a deep, shuddering breath, and while her skin remained clear of emotion, her body language told a very different story. It didn't take much to imagine what her life must have been like after that incident if children felt comfortable bullying Rock Face for his father's crimes.

"Now, as for you two..." He glared down at both of them with the full weight of his authority.

Both flashed their fear and ducked under their mother.

He waited until they peered out. "As Marsee saw no offense, I see no reason for there to be any punishment. Coral, try to be a little more precise with your language in the future. If you're going to tell someone what someone else said, don't embellish or change their words."

"Yes, sir," she flashed, still terrified but with colors of relief creeping across her skin.

"As for you, Rock Face, did anyone hurt you at school?"

Rock Face refused to look up at him, which told him someone had. "I don't want to get anyone in trouble," he said when Jer refused to back off.

Jer nodded his understanding. "It's honorable to want to protect your friends, but in my experience, those capable of hurting others have often been hurt themselves. Will you tell me who hurt you and what happened?"

Rock Face looked around at the crowd, now watching with interest. "Do I have to?"

Jer shook his head. "No. It's your right to work out reparations on your own if you'd like, but if it continues to happen, please talk to someone."

"Yes, sir," he replied.

Jer nodded to the family and swam off, not wanting to talk to anyone else or answer questions about Marsee.

Once inside, he hung up his drone and swam back to Marsee's room, where she still remained, frozen in suspended animation inside the stasis tube. He swam up to her and placed his paw on the tube, struggling to contain his emotions.

"I don't know if you can hear me wherever you are right now, but I'm sorry, Marsee." His control slipped, and tears streamed down his face to mix with the seawater as it passed through his mask. "I hope someday you can forgive me for everything I've done to you, for the decisions I've made that have caused you so much harm and pain, and for whatever pain you still face because I can't honor my promise to you. I can't let you go without a fight, but I promise I will always love you and care for you no matter what happens, and I am so very proud of you and the amazing person you've become. Please keep fighting to live. The universe needs people like you. Hope and Little Flower need you. I need you. Please?"

He took a deep shuddering breath and tried to wipe at the tears in his eyes through the mask but failed.

"We're ready for her now," a quiet, melodic voice said behind him, and he turned to see the Senior Healer floating in the doorway, her eyes soft with sympathy, although her skin and emotions were hidden behind her mask. "You're welcome to wait here, or I can take you to one of the dry rooms if you'd be more comfortable there."

"Here's fine," he signed, not trusting his voice, which had cracked with emotion only moments before. He watched as she disconnected the stasis tube from the wall and floated Marsee out of the room, then followed out the door and continued to watch as she was transported away and down the hall. The honor guards that had been stationed at her door followed silently behind.

He prayed to the Ancient Gods to protect his daughter and returned to the room once they were out of sight. The room felt bleak and empty now, and he swam over to look at the growing crowd again and wondered what offering he could make that the gods of this world would find worthy. His gift, his skill, was as a councilor. It's what he knew and all he knew, although he doubted the gods would find it worthy after the mess he'd made of everything.

As he floated there, he caught sight of Montipora and her children again as they floated away from the memorial, but a few moments later, someone swam up and stopped in front of them. Montipora froze, rigid with tension, and he wondered if there was going to be a confrontation, and apparently, so too did the guards out front of the Trauma Center as they started approaching.

"Mother," Montipora signed with barely repressed fury.

"I'm sorry. I should have believed you. Will you forgive me?" her mother replied.

In response, Montipora crushed her mother in a fierce hug, which only ended when the children demanded their grandmother's attention and their own hugs.

That's what she would want, he decided. *For the damage done by Rip to be repaired, for families to be reunited and compensated, and for their honor to be restored.* And so he prayed to the gods of the deep, the gods of the people of this world, who loved his daughter more than he could understand. He laid his century of service before them, vowing to make right what Rip had torn asunder for Marsee, Little Flower, GrandFather, Hope, Petra, Stormy, for Montipora and her family, and everyone else who had been harmed by that monster, no matter what it took, or what price he ultimately had to pay to make that happen.

A sense of calm and purpose settled over him, the first moment of calm he'd felt since the whole mess started. So, with that vow, he turned and climbed into one of the hanging nets to wait and read through the letters Marcus had scanned in, but his calm didn't last long, and he was soon growling in frustration and barely repressed anger.

He'd hoped that they'd found everyone involved. There were still missing people among the Sea Patrol and Honor Guard, but none of them had been high enough in rank to have the kinds of information provided. Neither did the guards they'd arrested the day before. The information crossed all of the species, which, as Marcus had determined already, meant it could only be from someone who was the Senior Honor Guard for a district, if not higher. They were already investigating Senior Honor Guard Stinger for possible involvement, along with all of the top officials from Rip Current's district, but they had nothing to help them figure out who this person was.

He fired off a brief message to Marcus with his thoughts and then pulled up the ticket referenced in the first message he'd found and read through what Kendra had written. After a moment of debating with himself, he pulled up and read Marsee's journal, a journal he realized he'd encouraged Marsee to write in the first place, as it started with Little Flower's arrival. When he'd finished reading what was copied in the ticket, he logged into his daughter's account, pulled up the latest version, and continued reading. His heart was torn and bleeding by the time he finished, both for everything Marsee had silently battled on her own and feared to tell them and the harm he'd both knowingly and unknowingly caused her over the past twenty years, but when he reached the end, it shattered.

Of her time in captivity, there were only two words.

"He waited."

CHAPTER 11

Jer: Honor's Loss

The hours crept by in an agony of slowness, yet with every second that passed, Jer felt like he was running out of time. Unable to sit still with his grief and worry, he stood and paced. Eventually, he stopped his pacing to examine the strange material of the cloak.

"That's Leviathan hide," Ellie said, and he spun around to face her, not having heard her swim in. "Or so I've been told. Where did she get it? I asked Marcus when he came by to visit yesterday, but he didn't know."

"I honestly don't know. She had it with her when we rescued her yesterday, but she didn't have it when she left in the morning. As far as I know, she came here to have her paw checked and then went to the Guild for a meeting with Agate before heading straight to Clear Seas in the afternoon to visit the Habitat and platforms."

"Ah. This must be Trench's cloak. I thought it might be. It's quite the honor he bestowed on her. From the history lesson I had from him several decades ago, this tradition goes back thousands of years, and it's reserved for those who risk their lives to defend their villages from the Leviathan. Back before they joined the Consortium, they didn't have the technology or resources to fight them off behind the safety of a shuttle, and it would take dozens of people just to drive them off, much less kill one, and people routinely died. This cloak was given to his family when his older brother was killed over two hundred and fifty years ago. Trench probably wasn't much older than Stormy when that happened. From what I understand, it's one of the last ones ever bestowed. They try not to kill them anymore now that they can just drive them off with the Sea Patrol."

"But Marsee didn't drive off a Leviathan," Jer replied, confused.

"Jer, what do you think Rip was? He was the biggest Leviathan this world has ever faced, at least in recent history, and he was threatening to destroy their entire world, not just a single village. She not only drove him off with nothing more than the assistance of a tiny six-year-old fry, she killed him, which I doubt any of us could do. And in doing so, she may have sacrificed her own life, not just to save Stormy and the other missing people, but to save us all. These people love Marsee in a way you and I will never truly understand. She changed their very world. She gave them a voice, and Rip Current tried to use their love for her to discredit Clear Seas and take control of their world and the Consortium. What do you think would have happened if Stormy hadn't found Marsee first? Rip would have shown up a few days later with her mangled body and claimed to have found her and likely been designated a state hero. Clear Seas would have been discredited with his failure to protect Marsee or stripped of power and executed by you if you hadn't found out who was really behind editing the archives. I'm guessing you didn't even know that there were logs and backups to check."

He shook his head, and she continued.

"Rip would have been voted in as Senior Councilor with the unanimous blessing of the entire planet behind him. You'd have stepped down to save Marsee, and Wind Rider would have been executed based on Petra's confession and hers. But he wasn't just trying to take over the Senior Council, he was after the Guild, too. I have as much power as you do, if not more since I have authority over close to half of the people on all five planets at this point, and he was trying to get rid of the top three people and destroy all the work I've done in bringing the various worlds and disciplines together. He almost killed me, my designated heir and the person most likely to take my place if both of us were out of commission, even though Nardal told me he had absolutely no desire to be Senior Guild Master long before Marsee was even born. I don't know why he bumped Marsee up to Acting Senior unless it was to prove to others that your family had too much power and try to implicate you or Marcus somehow. Regardless, he wasn't just trying to take control of this world. He was trying to take control of all of them."

He considered Ellie's words. He'd been struggling to find a motive behind many of Rip's actions, including Marsee's promotion, and why he'd implicated Nardal in the others' kidnapping, aside from trying to cover his tracks. If they hadn't already known that Ellie's account was compromised and any communication from her suspect, Nardal would have been arrested, but the moment Paxton had arrived, Nardal had shown him the message from Ellie asking that a shuttle be sent over to New Hope. It was a common request, and he hadn't even questioned it. What Rip hadn't known was that Nardal was meticulous over all requests and had forwarded her request to his tracking system. So, even though the original message had been deleted, Nardal still had a copy of it, and it was easy to confirm that the request had come from Ellie's tablet after the tablets were taken. Nardal had been cleared of involvement within fifteen minutes of Paxton's arrival.

Ellie swam over to the window to watch the growing crowd. "All of Council Platform must be out there."

"And then some. From what I could tell, shuttles are coming in from all over. How long do you think they'll stay?"

"Until it's over, one way or another," she said. "Like the Honor Guard, they'll see her home."

"It's happening all over the planet, too," Clear Seas said, and they both turned to face him as he swam into the room. "In just about every city and village. We've run out of places to park the incoming shuttles and have had to start ferrying people in from outside the city. I wouldn't be surprised if the entire district will be here by the end of the day. I had to put out a statement asking people to attend vigils in their home cities, as we're running out of room to put everyone. We're going to have to start turning people away before long. I've never seen anything like it."

"Neither have I," Jer replied. "What are you doing here, though? I thought you were off with Marcus this morning."

"I was. We just finished unloading the evidence from Rip's home. Marcus is trying to organize it now, and Wind Rider and I came over to take a few more statements, including Petra's. She was still sedated when I came over last night."

"How is she?" Ellie asked. "I haven't made it over to her room yet."

"As well as could be expected," Clear Seas replied. "It'll be months before she'll be able to fly again for any length of time, but Hyacinth said she should make a full recovery. In case you're wondering, her statement matches what the others have said."

Ellie frowned, and for a brief moment, she had the same haunted expression Marsee had on her face when she'd given her own statement.

"Are you okay, Ellie?" he asked.

"Not really," she replied. "I still find it hard to believe Willow and Leaf were involved. They've been my pilots for decades. I thought they were happy with the position."

Clear Seas let out the Water Sprite's equivalent of a frustrated sigh as a ripple of orange flashed across his skin. "According to Petra, they were jealous of the attention you gave her and the rank and status she had as a future nest mother, along with the same beliefs Marsee mentioned in her statement about Rip, that you gave Jer's family too much power when you made Marsee your protege."

Clear Seas unclipped his tablet to let Ellie see Petra's testimony.

Ellie was growling by the time she was done. "They did this because I didn't take them to dinner? *Dinner?!*"

Neither he or Clear Seas said anything, as there was little they could say to make it right. He found it equally as baffling and horrifying, but his tenure as a Councilor had shown him how often jealousy could cause resentment, which could lead to anger and violence. He understood the belief that he and Marcus had significant sway in the Council, as they did, but to kidnap someone because they weren't brought to a function or felt like that person didn't earn the rank they had was taking it to a whole new level. And it wasn't like they didn't know what

Rip was doing, either. Perhaps not the full extent of it, but according to Petra, they didn't seem the least bit surprised about the others held in captivity there.

Ellie turned away to face the window and stared out at the crowd again, but Jer had a feeling she wasn't seeing any of it. "You know, half the reason I haven't promoted anyone outside of appointing guild masters for the last half century or more was because I saw how jealous people got when I did. No one ever did anything like this, but on more than one occasion, I've had to move people around. I honestly thought things had changed. So much of the grumbling and infighting between the various disciplines that we had when I combined them stopped decades ago, and Marsee was so well-loved and popular for all of her hard work and the difference she's made for both New Hope and here. I had hundreds, if not thousands, of masters and guild masters reach out to me, asking to be her mentor. I never meant for anything like this to happen to her, but I should have known better."

Ellie sighed into the silence that followed.

"Well, to be fair, it wasn't your Guild that did this," Jer replied.

Ellie snorted. "Half the Ship's Guild is my guild, between shipping and building the ships themselves. There are others involved. I'm sure of it. The real question is, who did Rip intend to replace me with? Although I suppose he could have been trying to get rid of the Guild entirely."

"I'll let you know if we find anything to that matter," Clear Seas replied. "But, there's another issue we should discuss. I sort of played a little subterfuge to protect you." Clear Seas scratched at his ear fins, trying to figure out how to explain.

"Marcus already told me," Ellie replied. "Thank you. I hate the pain and grief that it caused everyone, but I understand why you did it."

"Thank you for understanding," Clear Seas said. "I'm curious, though. How do you want to go about coming back to life? It's going to take us time to dig through all of Rip's documents to try and figure out who else was involved and targeted, so I don't know if you're still at risk or not."

She snorted. "I'm sure I am, but it doesn't matter much to me either way. I've informed those people I most care about that I'm still alive and there are benefits to being dead. It's kind of nice not having to answer a million messages every day. What's easier for you and your investigation? Let everyone know I'm alive, or wait and surprise them at the trial? If we wait too long, though, I might be voted out of a job. Although, I'm honestly not sure I want it anymore."

"I know that feeling," Jer mumbled. "However, at a minimum, we know no one else besides Rip and Snapper was in the suite, and whether anyone else involved knew what Rip was planning is anyone's guess at this point. From what Marsee said, there was no love lost between Rip and the Guild. So, my guess is that this was a destabilizing event rather than trying to put someone else in power. I don't see any bene-fit to keeping you dead any longer, and I think we could all use some good news."

Ellie flicked an ear back dismissively. "I had a quick rundown from Agate. She's collecting everything she can find on Rip and Snapper now. Rip was profitable for the Guild in any event. Most of the crafters here charged him double the hours just for his attitude. I've also ordered an investigation into the guild hall in his district. However, I know for a fact that Wallah Fish couldn't stand Rip. I had several complaints from him over the years."

Clear Seas sighed. "I had no idea Rip was giving the Guild trouble until Marcus shared Marsee's comments with me. It's inexcusable be-havior, and I apologize on behalf of the Council. If anyone else is giving you grief, let me know. Please."

"Wallah Fish?" Jer asked. "Any relation to Snapper?"

"Not that I know of. But it is a fairly common name," Ellie replied and then turned to Clear Seas. "Well, shall we give the crowd something to talk about while they wait?"

Clear Seas flashed his humor, and they swam out at Ellie's much slower pace.

Jer swam up to the window to watch the crowd's reaction. He wasn't disappointed. A rainbow of confusion, shock, and joy spread through the crowd as they appeared, and people realized who was with Clear Seas. Most of Ellie's fur had been shaved off to treat her injuries, so it wasn't surprising that it took them a moment to recognize her without her distinctive black fur and white heart-shaped spot on her chest. Shaved, her skin was a light gray, and large, ugly bruises still covered her white spot.

Ellie returned to the room after stopping to visit briefly with Petra and remained with him to wait for word on Marsee's status, but Clear Seas left to deal with the crowds and the fallout from the past several days. Marcus stopped in periodically throughout the day, as did Wind Rider. One of the healers arrived with the noon meal, which they barely touched. Marsee had been right. The food here was atrocious, but to his immense relief, Marcus hunted down Opal's contact information and ordered food for everyone, although he still found it hard to eat with his stomach twisted in knots of anger, guilt, and worry.

When he couldn't stand the empty room any longer, he paced in the hall and eventually gave up and swam down to the surgery bay.

Avery and Tamarin now floated outside the room. They said nothing to him as he approached.

He knew he wasn't able to keep his emotions entirely hidden behind his mask, and both guards clearly sensed his displeasure by their rapid snap to attention when he appeared around the corner. He was still furious with Avery for leaving his daughter unprotected, even though Marcus was right. He hadn't stopped Marsee from leaving that morning either.

Part of him wondered if Avery was their mystery guard. While he wasn't a district senior, he was Kendra's protege and had been given a rank unique in the universe. He'd been chosen by all five senior honor guards and ratified by the Senior Council as the Senior Honor Guard for the Earth Delegation. While not quite the rank of General, it had given him the authority to declare war if the Hue-mans had proven to be dangerous and, in doing so, had temporarily put him above all five Senior Honor Guards. That authority and access had been limited in duration and stripped once he'd returned home with the survivors, but from his observation, Avery was still granted the same level of respect by the other guards.

Avery's squad had remained at the Agency to help care for the Hue-mans and had been prepared to defend the Hue-mans against the actions of the Council at the Trial. While that could have been seen as treason, Jer understood and approved. The Hue-mans had needed their protection, and it wasn't surprising that Avery would feel protective towards them. He'd given a year of his life on that mission and had lost a member of his squad in the rescue attempt. Avery had also put his name in for consideration for Senior Honor Guard when the Hue-mans decided to have their own guard, and his squad had already volunteered to transfer species if that happened.

He wondered what the guard was thinking and what his real intentions were: regaining power or protecting the Hue-mans. Avery was young for that kind of rank and authority but no younger than Kendra had been when she'd been promoted to Senior, but Avery had left Marsee and Stormy unprotected. Even if Rip hadn't escaped, they could have been attacked by some other kind of predator. Kendra had placed her life on Avery's honor before they'd left, and if Avery was involved in this mess, then Jer had every right to execute Kendra for Avery's crimes as well, both by her oath and as his mentor and senior.

He shifted his attention from Avery and stared through the window at the teams of healers surrounding the operating tube. He reassured himself that her damaged heart was still beating but was unable to see more than a brief glimpse of his daughter, the flash of her mask-covered face, tubes and wires everywhere, and the scrawny tip of her furless and limp tail. While the filtration systems in the tube kept blood from clouding the water, he could still smell it, a sweet mix of copper and rust against the salt water and the burnt harshness of a suture wand.

With a heavy sigh, he turned away from the window and found himself facing Avery again.

Avery's gaze was straight ahead, at full attention, or as full as possible while floating in water. Even his ears were up and forward.

Jer said nothing as he stared at the guard, wondering if Avery would break under his glare, but after several long moments, Jer turned and swam away. As angry as he was at Avery, he was far angrier at himself for the harm he'd caused his daughter, and he knew if he let any of that anger out, he might not be able to control it.

He paused after rounding the corner in the hall, curious if the guards would say anything. They didn't for a while, perhaps making sure he was gone, but then Tamarin spoke, quietly enough that he had to strain to hear.

"I can't believe he hasn't said anything to you yet."

Avery snorted. "I can't believe I haven't been demoted, executed, or dragged through the streets by the locals either." He let out a heavy sigh. "I just hope he only punishes me for my stupid mistake and not Kendra."

That made Jer's brows raise.

Tamarin snorted again. "Well, I suppose he could be leaving your punishment up to Kendra to deal with."

Avery groaned. "I might as well turn myself over to the locals. It would be quicker and far less painful."

"You might be right there. Have you heard anything from her yet?"

"Nope."

It was all Jer could do to keep from laughing at the tone in Avery's voice, and he wondered if he should just let Kendra deal with it.

"Well, it was nice knowing you," Tamarin replied.

Avery grunted in response but said nothing else.

Tail curled at the exchange, he waited another minute or two to see if they had anything else to say before swimming back to the room to continue pacing. He had no real proof, but his gut said Avery wasn't their mystery guard, just young and inexperienced, and had just made a stupid mistake. No one was perfect, and Jer knew his entire life was full of one stupid mistake after another. If you were lucky enough to survive them, it was how you learned.

It wasn't until close to sunset before Marsee was floated back in, and around-the-clock monitoring began as they struggled to keep her alive until her replacement heart was ready. There was at least one healer in the room at all times with them, if not more, trying to control the swelling and infection that was now ravaging her broken hand and manage her other vitals that continued to weaken.

Additional sleeping nets were hung for them, but no one slept. They just watched and prayed as they kept out of the way. Time slowed to a standstill. Every ragged pause in Marsee's fading heart caused his own to seize, and the rasping wheezes of her damaged lungs over the hiss of the life support systems that kept her breathing made him pin his ears back. He'd never hated a sound so much before, but the absence was even worse. He timed his breathing to hers as if it had any chance of helping and willed her heart to keep beating with every fiber of his being.

Fight. Live. Come back to me, he prayed over and over again. *Ancient Gods, please. I'll do anything. Just let her live!*

CHAPTER 12

Marcus: Rotten Fish

Marcus stared at the mountain of evidence in front of him. Clear Seas and Wind Rider sat beside him, doing the same. No one said anything as they continued to stare at the pile. Nor did anyone move.

"We're not going to make any progress if we just sit here and stare at it," Clear Seas said eventually.

"No, but I have a feeling we're not going to like what we're going to find either," Marcus replied.

"You always were such a master of understatement," Wind Rider said. "I'd rather eat a mountain of three-day-old rotten fish than dig through that pile."

Marcus snorted and turned to grin at Wind Rider wickedly. "That could easily be arranged. I'll give Opal a call right now if you want."

Wind Rider rolled her eyes at him and then paused as if considering.

Chuckling at her expression, he untangled himself from the net the Sprites used for a chair and swam over, grabbing a box at random off the top of the stack. Rip had kept everything organized by name, not guild affiliation or planet, which would make digging through it all that much harder. They needed to figure out who else was involved, and they had very little time to do it in, even if he, too, would rather eat three-day-old rotten fish.

Setting the box down on the table, he opened it and pulled out a stack of files, handing them off. He tangled himself back up in his net and opened his first file, which turned out to be on one of the Water Sprite councilors. The first dozen pages or so all appeared to be information easily gathered from their public page, voting records, family members, hobbies, and such, but then it changed. Several votes had been highlighted. It didn't say what the votes were for, just the reference numbers and how they'd voted.

He pulled up that information on his tablet and read through the first case with a frown, and the next, and the next, trying to figure out what Rip was interested in. More often than not, the case ended up being dropped or stated that the parties had agreed to reparations, but that wasn't unusual in many of these cases. Often, people would choose to settle the issue rather than face a criminal record and, quite likely, far more severe consequences. In several cases, if someone had been found guilty, they could have faced the death penalty. It wasn't until he got further into the information Rip had collected that he realized what was going on. The councilor was being paid off. It didn't take him long to confirm the information Rip had gathered either. One instance of it would have been enough to have that councilor removed from office, but there were dozens of examples in the file.

Several hours later, he finished recording everything, shut the file, and sighed. The others looked up from their own investigations. "Fraud. Councilor Beryl. Multiple instances of taking bribes."

Clear Seas flashed his surprise and then sighed with colors of frustration before returning to his own file.

Marcus set the file aside and grabbed another. This one was significantly smaller and contained nothing particularly incriminating. It had similar basic information on the Guild Master in question, but it also included multiple pictures of her family in what should have been a private setting. *Did he threaten them with harm?*

"How do we want to organize these once we're done with a first pass?" Marcus asked.

"We're never going to get through all of this before the council meeting," Wind Rider stated. "I say we start by separating them into crime and not crime but focus on those in the Council and Guard first for a more in-depth investigation. Speaking of which, Councilor Breydhik, murder, and treason by the looks of it. Several letters indicate he was working with Rip on his little coup and helped to make some of Rip's other... 'problems' disappear down a crevasse or two. I'm fairly sure he was behind the trap that was set for your niece on Saber. I've confirmed that he has two sons by the names of Brack and Eenowk. That can't be a coincidence."

Marcus groaned and rubbed at his forehead. He was already starting to get a headache. "Do we arrest now or wait?"

"Wait," Clear Seas replied. "Breydhik should already be on his way here. At this point, all anyone knows is that Rip was killed and that we have Damon and Snapper Fish in custody. They might very well be hoping we didn't find anything else and thinking that he was acting alone. If it weren't for Snapper, we would have never found that room."

Marcus nodded, placed Wind Rider's file on top of Beryl's, and handed her another one before grabbing one for himself. "I don't know about you, Wind Rider, but that three-day-old rotten fish is starting to sound a lot more appealing."

Wind Rider snorted and tilted her head, considering, but, with a heavy sigh of her own, returned to her investigation.

CHAPTER 13

Little Flower: Baby Steps

Little Flower's eyes were glued shut, and her stomach roiled, but she recognized the usual effects that sedation always had on her. It was honestly a vast improvement from the last time she'd been awake, as she was no longer in pain. The last memory she had was of Henry Curtis coming to rescue them and of her mother leaping over her. Knowing she was safe, she'd stopped fighting to stay awake and had succumbed to her injuries.

She lay there listening to the murmur of voices around her as she waited for the queasiness to pass and then gasped as she realized she was actually listening to the murmur of voices.

Carefully and slowly turning her head in the direction of the sounds, knowing any movement could cause the room to start spinning, she managed to peel her eyes open enough to see her grandfather in the middle of an animated conversation with Henry. They hadn't noticed she was awake, and she smiled. They were sitting side by side in one of the Saber's giant chairs, ever so slightly closer than was strictly necessary, laughing about something.

There is something between them! she thought with a grin. Henry was one of the few people she'd allowed to visit her, knowing he and her grandfather were becoming good friends. She wanted him to be happy and had seen how lonely and grief-stricken he'd been after Ben had died in the Cataclysm.

"What's so funny?" she asked, and they both turned to look at her.

"Hey, you're awake!" her grandfather signed. "We weren't expecting that for another hour at least. How are you feeling?"

"Queasy from the sedative, but hungry. I feel like I haven't eaten for days," she replied.

"You haven't. It's been about three days since you last had anything," her grandfather said.

"I'll let her mother know she's awake and see about finding something for her to eat," Henry said and slid down out of the chair, making slightly more contact with her grandfather than was strictly necessary, too.

She grinned with excitement at both their growing relationship and the sound of Henry's deep voice. It was the first time in over three years that she'd been able to hear anyone speak, and his voice was beautiful. "Tell her I want some star fruit juice and a cookie," she hollered after him and winced as her voice sounded far louder to her than she was used to.

It was her GrandFather's turn to gasp. "Did you hear him?"

She turned her head back to look at him. "I did! You too!" she said with a massive grin and then blanched as the room spun. She'd moved her head too quickly. "Oooh, I shouldn't have done that." She closed her eyes and breathed hard to try and calm her stomach. "I *hate* that sedative."

"Jessica, your mother's here," her grandfather said a minute or two later, and she sighed with happiness. It had been years since she'd heard her birth name. Opening her eyes, she looked into her mother's enormous face, her eyes glowing with concern and a touch of hope.

"GrandFather said you heard him?" her mother signed.

"I did! Henry too! I didn't hear you enter the room, though," she signed back.

Her mother's face broke into a huge grin, and she called something out that she could almost hear. A moment later, Ammond walked into the room, and there was that almost heard sound, like thunder, far off in the distance as she spoke to him. His face split into a huge grin, too, and his tail curled with happiness. She didn't often see the old healer with anything but a scowl on his face unless he was in the hot tub, and it completely transformed him into the loving uncle she knew him to be.

"That's wonderful news!" he signed. "How are you feeling?"

"Queasy from the sedative and hungry," she repeated.

Her mother picked up the thermos she must have brought in with her, poured her a cup, and carefully helped her to drink. She felt her stomach calm almost immediately.

"Better?" her mother asked afterwards.

"Much, thanks," she replied. "I really hate that sedative."

"It does tend to have that effect on your species. I wish we could figure out why," her mother replied.

"I'm sure we will eventually," Ammond said. "Now, let's see how well everything else is progressing, and then we'll test your hearing."

They spent the next half hour performing a physical examination on her, and overall, she hadn't lost anything from the swelling on her brain, but she did get woozy again when they had her sit up. She was so furious that she let out a litany of swears, which made her grandfather chuckle.

"It's okay, Little Flower," her mother said after she collapsed back on the bed with a groan. "Nothing's wrong. You just haven't had anything to eat in days. Here." Her mother handed her a bowl of fruit, and she smiled to see her favorites. Her mother was right. Once she had something in her, she felt significantly better, and the last of the dizziness finally went away.

As she ate, they caught her up on everything that had happened over the past few days, and her heart shattered when she heard about Marsee's ordeal. She was relieved to know that they now believed everyone directly involved had been caught, but she still seethed at what Damon had done, and her loathing of him only increased when she found out about the damage to Marsee's room.

"Why hasn't he been punished yet?"

"We still need your testimony, and the execution can't occur without both the authority and witness of the victim's Senior Council," her mother explained. "Your father will be on the Water World for some time caring for Marsee and figuring out the mess Rip Current left behind. Plus, Marsee has claims against Damon, too, and those wouldn't be satisfied with his execution. Just about everything the two of you owned has been destroyed, and the months and years of work put into both of your crafts lost. More than likely, he'll be required to pay that back in some way before he'll be executed for his other crimes."

She nodded. "I guess that makes sense, although I don't know how he'll ever restore what was broken or destroyed. He doesn't own much of anything himself, and as far as I know, he doesn't have the skills to repair any of it either."

"I don't know," her mother said and then changed the subject. "Do you feel well enough to try standing up now?"

"I think so. The room has stopped spinning, at least." She handed her mother the bowl and swung her legs off the bed. She sat there for a moment, making sure she didn't get dizzy again, and grinned at how much easier it was.

Her mother lowered the bed down as far as it would go and then sat down in front of her, holding out her tail for her to use for support.

Keeping her fingers crossed, Little Flower slid down off the bed and pulled herself up into a standing position. She wobbled unsteadily for a moment until she found her balance.

Her mother grinned at her. "That's your best time yet! Try letting go. You're not using much to balance yourself right now. If you wobble or start to fall, I'll catch you." Her mother put her paws on either side of her, close but not touching.

She nodded and cautiously let go, keeping her hands close to her mother's tail just in case. She wobbled and quickly grabbed for support. Once she'd recovered, she tried again and managed nearly ten seconds before wobbling and grabbing for her mother.

Her grandfather and Henry both whooped with delight, and she let out a huge grin. That was the longest she'd been able to stand unassisted on her own since Hope had been born.

"Oh, well done!" Ammond signed. "Do you want to try taking a few steps?"

She took a deep, nervous breath and nodded. Holding tightly to her mother's strong tail, she moved her right leg forward, and, for the first time in the past two months, it actually went where she wanted it to, and she didn't have to readjust or try again. Gaining courage and hope, she tried with the other leg, and while she wobbled, she didn't fall. They weren't big steps, but they felt huge.

Two more steps later, she made it to her mother and collapsed against her. Her mother wrapped her arms around her and scooped her up in a fierce hug that made her squeak. GrandFather must have signed something because her mother eased off a bit and gently set her back down.

Once she was stable again, her mother shuffled back a little and had her try again. This time, however, she tried letting go as she took a step and almost managed to make it without having to grab for support. Encouraged, she tried again and this time succeeded! Everyone cheered except for her mother, who was staying completely focused on her, although the very tip of her tail curled up in happiness. Little Flower took another wobbling step and then another. She nearly lost her balance then, but her mother caught her and steadied her before slowly removing her paws.

She was standing there with a huge grin when the sound of tiny running feet and squeals of childish laughter caught her attention. She turned her head to see Hope running by with Brice 'chasing' her. Hope looked over as she ran by and veered suddenly towards them, causing Brice to have to scramble and sidestep to avoid running into her.

"Mama!" Hope squealed.

Her knees buckled at the sound before her mother, who had also turned her head to see where she was looking, could catch her, and she landed hard on her butt, but she didn't even notice. She held out her arms to Hope, who ran straight to her and practically knocked her over with enthusiasm.

She crushed her daughter in a hug, tears streaming unchecked down her face until Hope squirmed to get away. She relaxed her grip and smiled into her child's face, then tickled her sides.

Hope squealed with laughter.

It was the most beautiful sound she'd ever heard. She tickled her again and again and again until Hope signed 'stop' and pushed away.

Hope climbed off her lap. "Chase me!" she signed and ran out the door. Brice followed behind, and squeals of laughter echoed down the hall behind them.

She looked over and saw tears running down her grandfather's face and a look of pure joy on her mother's. Looking over to Ammond, she wiped the tears off her own face. "Thank you. Thank you both for giving me that moment."

Ammond nodded. His face lit up in a grin bigger than she'd ever seen from him before, and his tail spiraled with joy, almost as much as her mother's. "Nothing has ever made me happier!" he signed. "Now, shall we see just how good of a job I've done with your hearing?"

She nodded, and somehow, he managed to smile wider, although his eyes now squinted with mischief.

"Good. I'll see you in my office in a few minutes. I expect you to walk the entire way there."

She glared back at him. "Ammond, I take back all the nice things I've ever said about you. You're as bad as my mother!"

His tail corkscrewed with amusement. "No, child. I'm far, far worse." With that, he turned and walked out, tail still corkscrewed tightly behind him, followed by the glorious sounds of everyone's laughter.

CHAPTER 14

Little Flower: Trauma Response

It took Little Flower half an hour to shuffle her slow way down to Ammond's office, and she was sweating and breathing hard from the effort. Her legs were shaking, and her mother had to catch her more than once, but she made it. Her mother lifted her up onto the examination chair, grinning at her success, and she collapsed back with relief, eyes closed and gasping as she tried to catch her breath.

When she opened her eyes again, Ammond grinned at her. "Well done, child. I knew you could do it."

Ammond turned to grab his equipment but stopped when Brice knocked on the door. "I figured you might not have seen the message from Council Platform. They've taken Marsee in for her second surgery."

"Thank you for letting me know," her mother signed back and pulled out her tablet to read the latest report.

Brice nodded and left.

"How bad is she, really?" Little Flower asked when her mother looked up. "I could tell there's something you weren't telling me before."

Her mother frowned and then shut Ammond's door and hit a switch on Ammond's desk before answering.

She wondered what that was for but didn't ask as she was far more worried about Marsee.

Her mother's tail and ears drooped as she dropped her mask. "There is. It appears she may have somehow killed off her hunting instinct. She had a major episode of psychosis after killing Rip Current. She tore him to shreds and then almost fought your father for the body before she was able to beat it back. We don't know how or why, but her immune system attacked various areas of her brain. So far, whatever it was appears to have stopped, but we have absolutely no idea what kind of issues she'll have when she wakes. If she even wakes. Your brain was damaged, but there was something for us to repair. We don't have that with Marsee. As far as we can tell from the scans they've been able to take, those areas are just gone. We won't know for sure until we can take Ammond's equipment to the Water World. Their equipment isn't anywhere near as good as his."

Little Flower looked at her mother in horror. She wouldn't wish what she'd been through these past few months on anyone. To know that her sister would likely be far worse, and possibly permanently, devastated her.

"Mama, if she ends up like I did or worse, and there's nothing you can do to fix her, please don't let her suffer. It was horrible and degrading, and I hated every second of the past two months. You said you could fix me, and Hope needed me for food, and that was the only thing that kept me going most days. Marsee held me while I cried myself to sleep almost every night. She won't have that hope, and she deserves better than that."

Her mother looked crushed. "Was it really that bad?"

She frowned and then took a deep breath. She needed to get the words out now that she could, now that her hands worked well enough to sign again. "Worse. I can't even begin to describe how bad those first few weeks were. I couldn't sign, couldn't tell you how sick I felt, how hopeless. I couldn't feed myself, go to the bathroom, or even roll over in bed to a more comfortable position. The trauma of having someone have to clean me brought back memories of that awful day every single time, and you know what I did when GrandFather tried to care for me. I was an adult trapped in a newborn body with all the memories of what I had once been able to do. I had no way to protect myself. I had no value to anyone but Hope as a source of food, and I felt like a burden to everyone else. I saw how exhausted and worn down you all were. Every minute of every hour of every day, I wanted to die, and yet you'd push me to work harder, even when I'd be so sick I'd throw up all over you. I couldn't do anything to protect GrandFather or Hope from Damon, and I had to lay there and watch as my family was kidnapped and my grandfather nearly hung from a tree. All because I couldn't manage to sit up and walk the three steps to lock the crawler's door or walk across the room to lock the door behind GrandFather when he went for breakfast that morning. I never want to feel that helpless or hopeless again, and I beg of you, if it ever happens to me again, please don't wake me up. Let me die with a shred of my dignity left."

It was the most she'd signed in months, and her arms shook from a combination of effort, emotion, and the overwhelming need to say what she'd only ever been able to whisper to Marsee in the middle of the night.

Her mother looked heartbroken, but she couldn't quite read Ammond's expression. If anything, it almost looked as if he'd felt validated by her words.

"I had no idea it was that bad for you," her mother signed. "I was so pleased with the progress you were making in such a short amount of time, and I thought you were too."

"It was all an act, Mama. The thing you all seem to keep forgetting is how differently time feels for us. For you, it may have only been two months out of your exceptionally long lifespan, but for me, it's been half a year of non-stop exhaustion, pain, trauma, and depression. Every year on this world is worth three of mine, and each day is nearly twice the length of the days on Earth. And that doesn't even account for the fact that your species will live three or four times as long as we will, and that's assuming you're able to extend our life spans. Ammond, may I ask how old you are?"

"I'm two hundred and seventy-three," he replied without hesitation.

"That would make you...eight hundred and nineteen years old to me. We didn't even have electricity until you were about two hundred years old. You aren't just old, you're ancient."

Ammond looked astonished. "I felt old before, but now I really feel old."

"Well, I've always said you don't look a day over eight hundred," Myra teased, to which Ammond scowled back.

"I am beginning to understand how you Hue-mans must feel," Ammond said. "I don't have many years left, and I'm already beginning to feel the effects of my advanced age that our technology can't fix. The nanos don't work all that well on me anymore. A hundred years ago, I felt like I had forever to do everything I wanted to do, and now I wake up feeling like I'm running out of time and worrying that I'll become a burden to my family and lose my dignity as my body wears out. Without the technology to extend your life, we would grow old and die around the same time. Yet I will have lived many of your lifetimes to your one. It's no wonder why your species feels the need to do everything and know everything now. For you, there is no tomorrow, is there?"

Her mother looked at Ammond with worry and grief etched on her face. "Are you in a lot of pain? I see you moving slower, but you've never complained about it."

"Some days, yes, but it hasn't been so bad since I've come to live here. The heat does wonders for my old bones, and the hot tub is the most amazing invention the Hue-mans have brought with them. But what helps the most is having a purpose again. Ask Theresa. She'll tell you I was a downright grump for months. I'd lost my sense of identity after I retired. I didn't know who I was without being the Ear Healer, but I found it again after coming here, thanks to this wonderful little Hue-man and her damaged ear *and* her skull that isn't nearly thick enough. Speaking of which, Myra, did I tell you GrandFather said their people jump out of shuttles for fun."

"You're pulling my tail," her mother scoffed.

"He's not," Little Flower said. "I've done it once. It's exhilarating. My friend Susie took me with her a few months before the Cataclysm. You strap on a...a harness with a bag containing a giant piece of fabric attached to a rope, and you jump out of a shuttle and free fall for a while until you deploy the fabric, and it slows your descent. Someone even managed to jump from the edge of space once and survived unhurt."

"Three moons! Why would you do that?" Myra exclaimed.

"Because it's fun. Do you remember before the trial when your family was here and we danced together? It's the same feeling. For a few moments, nothing in the world matters as you fly through the air but the experience and that moment. The thinking, worrying part of your brain shuts off, and you just are. For a moment, you're free, only so much more. I don't even know if I can explain it. Nothing else matters but that moment because nothing else can matter. If you lose focus for even a second, you could die or get seriously hurt. Your senses change and become heightened. Your reflexes quicken. Your body becomes faster, stronger, less sensitive to pain..."

Her mother's expression changed, and Little Flower struggled to place where she'd seen it before, somehow becoming more primal. She must have made a face because Ammond turned to look at her mother and the next thing she knew, she was being yanked off the chair and practically flung behind Ammond, and placed on a shelf behind him, as far away from her mother as Ammond could put her.

"Shut it off now, Myra!" he signed, bolting between them, looking ready to attack.

Her mother blinked and shook her head as if clearing her thoughts. "I'm okay," she signed back, but Ammond didn't relax. "Seriously, Ammond, I'm fine."

"No, you're not. Shut it off," he signed back.

"What are you talking about? It is off," she replied.

"No, it's not. Your eyes are still dilated, your nose is flared, and your claws are out. Shut it off now!"

Her mother looked down at her claws, flicking her ears back in surprise. "I never turned it on. I was just remembering what it had been like to hunt Damon. It felt exactly like what Little Flower was describing."

Ammond's ears laid flat to his skull, and his tail poofed out. She had never seen Ammond react like that, or any of the healers for that matter, save for her mother at the Trial. He grabbed his scanner off his desk and pointed it towards her mother.

"All of the same centers on Marsee's brain that have been damaged are lit up on the scanner right now. It's on. Shut it off," he demanded.

"And I'm telling you, it's not on," Myra growled back.

Faster than Little Flower could even watch, Ammond swung at her mother, and somehow, her mother blocked it, growled at him, and then scrambled back.

"Dark moons! It is on! How? It doesn't feel like it's on. Why can't I shut it off? Am I losing control?" Her mother grabbed her tail, her fur now spiking out in pure fear.

"I don't understand. What's going on?" Little Flower asked.

"My hunting instinct," her mother signed with an absolutely terrified and frantic expression.

Then Little Flower remembered where she'd seen that look before. It was the same one Marsee had looked at her with that night in the garden, not the one when she'd been out of control, but when she'd managed to bring her instinct back under control. She awkwardly slid down off the shelf and started making her way over to her mother, holding on to the examination chair for support.

"What are you doing? Stay back!" her mother signed and tried to press herself further into the corner.

Ammond tried to block her from approaching.

"Let me through. She's not going to hurt me. I'm part of her pride or pack, or whatever you call a collection of Sabers," she signed.

"What are you talking about?" Myra replied. "You don't know that! I could attack at any moment!"

Little Flower snorted and shoved at Ammond, almost falling over with the effort.

He moved, letting her by, but she could tell he didn't want to, and he stayed close, ready to grab her in an instant if her mother did attack.

She ignored him and wobbled up to her mother, shifting her grasp from the chair to Ammond's desk.

Her mother tried to scamper away, but there wasn't anywhere else for her to go in the room.

"Mama, stop. You don't need to be afraid. Sniff me. Let your instinct really know me. What does it tell you? You're not going to hurt me any more than Marsee would or could. I'm your cub, and I trust you not to hurt me."

Her mother blinked but then did as requested, and then her ears flicked forward, surprised. "You're right. You smell good, but there's no urge to hunt you. It trusts you too and wants to protect you and...hunt *with* you?" She seemed almost confused by that. "So why does it not feel like it's on, and why can't I shut it off?"

"Because it's part of you, just like it was for Marsee in the garden. But we don't need to go hunting. We have plenty of food here, and the bad people have all been caught. Lay down."

Her mother shrugged and did as asked, which brought them face to face.

She carefully let go of the desk, took the three tiny steps to her mother, and ran her hand across the side of her mother's enormous face, just like she'd done with Marsee.

Her mother started purring loudly and closed her eyes.

It surprised her how loud it was, as she'd never heard it before, only felt it. She walked closer, past her mother's head, and hugged her, wrapping her arms as best she could around her mother's neck. Her mother continued to purr, and her tail came around and wrapped around her waist, returning the hug.

When Little Flower backed off, and her mother opened her eyes and looked at her again, they were back to normal.

"How did you do that?" her mother asked.

"You just needed to be reminded that you were safe and loved, just like me that day with GrandFather," she replied and then wobbled as she nearly lost her balance.

Her mother picked her up before she could fall and set her back on the chair.

"Your species spends your whole life hiding from and trying to control your instinct," Little Flower signed once she was situated. "I think we must spend ours trying to find it. We can't turn it on or off like you can, so we have to try other ways to experience it, by doing things like jumping out of perfectly good shuttles or climbing to the top of the bandala tree, and it can take time to come back down from the adrenaline and excitement. It can get out of control for us, too, but usually, it's because we're stuck remembering a bad experience, like me with GrandFather. I had no idea who he was. I thought he was trying to hurt me, and I ended up hurting him instead, but Marsee is a member of my pride. She was my protection, and I felt safe in her arms pretty much from the first day I met her. She was able to snap me out of it, just like I was able to snap her out of it in the garden. I've started to learn how to control them by thinking of myself wrapped safely in her comforting arms when it happens. We call them panic attacks or flash-backs, and when they become chronic, post-traumatic stress disorder. My Papa was a…guard is probably the closest sign I have, when he was younger, and he was in many fights. I learned at a very young age never to touch him when he was sleeping because he would react before he was fully awake. His instinct was in control long before he woke up. It was necessary for his survival."

"Your people have a hunter's instinct, too?" Ammond asked. "I understand trauma responses, but I never thought they were related to hunter's instinct."

"Instinct is instinct, is it not? It certainly sounds like they're the same thing. Mama reacted as if she were back in the same situation with Damon. I imagine for a moment she was stuck in that memory."

Her mother nodded. "I was. Until Ammond spoke to me, I was re-living the moments before I attacked and how there was nothing but that moment and finding the exact second to pounce. Too soon, and you and your grandfather would have been hurt, and too late, Henry."

"From your mind's perspective, I imagine it was no different than if you were in that situation, so it released all of the same chemicals you would need to survive. I can't remember if it was Papa or Marcus who said that psychosis often occurs in people who have had to hunt for survival. That would sound to me like a very traumatic experience. So would the trauma of being ostracized because you don't fit into an established mold or being an only cub in a society where that's exceptionally rare."

Both Ammond and Myra seemed shocked by that possibility.

"So, how did your people treat psychosis," Ammond asked.

"Not well, honestly. After the attack that occurred at my school, they tried making us talk to healers who specialized in trauma, but they just made things worse. What helped me the most was talking about it with Susie. Knowing we were having the same experiences helped."

"Why did your classmate attack the other students?" Ammond asked.

"Jake was always a bit of a troublemaker, often acting out in school, and he had few friends, if any. After it happened, we found out he'd been abused at home, and he'd been beaten the night before for failing a test. He killed his teacher along with two of my classmates and injured dozens more before he shot himself. It was only one room away from my classroom, and I can still hear the sounds of those shots and the screams. I'll never forget the hours we hid, bunched into a corner away from the door, until the guards arrived and cleared the school."

Ammond nodded sadly but then pursed his lips as a thought occurred to him. "If your species has such a hard time with it, why would you purposely trigger your psychosis?"

She thought for a moment before answering. "I've never really thought about it before, but fear and excitement are much the same, only the context is different. When you're in control of it, and you know you're safe, it can be fun to experience those heightened senses. When you're in a real life-or-death situation, those instincts can save your life. Training them to be able to use them when you need them makes sense, even if you never have to. It's only when your body reacts when you don't want it to that it becomes a problem. If you have a fear of heights, the best way to get rid of it is to spend so much time up high that your body gets used to it, but that fear makes sense from a survival perspective because it makes you cautious."

"I know this would be asking a lot, but would you be willing to allow me to scan your brain during one of these panic attacks?" Ammond asked. "It might help the others by giving us a better way to treat this disease in both our species."

Little Flower nodded, "Sure, but I want a cookie afterwards."

Both her mother and Ammond chuckled.

"You and your cookies," her mother teased, shaking her head.

She rolled her eyes at her mother, as it was a constant battle between the two of them. Her mother wasn't all that impressed with the cookies or their lack of nutritional value, and it was usually Marsee who raided the kitchen after dark for her.

She turned back to Ammond. "It would be easy enough to trigger. I have a harder time not triggering them. Right before bedtime is the worst because I get stuck going over and over what I should have done differently. As for the cookies, it's good for my mental health. They make me feel better, even if it's just for a few minutes. Plus, they remind me of my mother. She used to make them for a living." She swallowed hard as a wave of grief for her lost family hit her.

Both her mother's and Ammond's expressions changed to one of sympathy.

"Do you want to do that now or later?" Ammond asked.

"Might as well get it over with," she replied.

Ammond nodded and put the stretchy hat on her again, and she decided to think about what had just happened to her. It was far fresher in her memory. She thought about how she felt watching her grandfather beaten, her fear of watching Damon take Hope and hold a knife to her throat. Of watching her grandfather knocked out and the hours spent traveling deep into the Wilds, and for who knew what purpose, and finally, the horror of watching Damon drag her grandfather towards the tree. She started shaking, and her rage and fear nearly overwhelmed her. Then suddenly, her mother was there, holding her and purring, and she calmed, remembering where she was and that she was safe.

"Thank you," Ammond said. "I'll examine these later. Now for that hearing test..."

Fifteen minutes later, the test was complete, and after a quick review, Ammond threw the results up on the wall.

"This was from when I tested you back in Myra's office," Ammond said, throwing the chart she remembered up on the screen. And this...," Ammond said with a flourish as a second line of colored dots was displayed, "is from today."

Instead of the four blue dots and the handful of green ones, there was a beautiful, if jagged, blue line.

"It would appear that you've regained about half of your hearing. More towards the middle and lower ranges than the higher. And I can probably boost this a little more with hearing aids if you want."

She whooped in joy. That was more than good enough, and the lower ranges were far more advantageous here anyway.

"But wait! There's more."

Both she and her mother looked at him as he brought up the scans of her brain.

"This is the before, and this is the after. It looks like the cochlear nerve on your other ear has grown some. I don't know if it will continue to improve or not. It's not very much, but it's a very interesting and unexpected result of the nanos we injected. We'll re-evaluate in a month or two and see if there's any additional progress, but this could have far-reaching impact for people with nerve injuries."

"Like Marsee with her hand?" Little Flower asked.

"Exactly," Ammond replied. "And the other areas we injected are also looking much better. Now there's only one other test left that we can do without GrandFather here." Ammond pulled out the paper she'd written on before and handed her a pencil.

She took several deep breaths and took it. Last time, Ammond had needed to put bandage putty on her hand to hold it in place. This time, she was able to grasp it in her hand, which was encouraging, and she began to write the words on the page. Her hand still shook, and it was nowhere near as clear as it used to be, but it was far better than it had been before.

She sighed, not sure whether to be encouraged or disappointed.

"That's actually far better than I expected. I wasn't sure if you'd have the grip strength to hold the pencil even though your dexterity and ability to sign is significantly improved." Ammond took the paper from her and put it back in her file. "Now, let's discuss goals for the next month. I want your input on what we focus on, as well as what *you* think is reasonably achievable in that time. From now on, we'll go at your pace." He glared pointedly at her mother. "If you need a day off to do nothing but float in the hot tub, then that's what you do."

He glared at her mother again, and her mother glared back but eventually nodded. It was all Little Flower could do to keep from chuckling at the expressions that passed between the two. Her mother might be significantly larger than Ammond, but Ammond had more than enough attitude to make up for it.

"Now, here's what *I* think you should be able to accomplish over the next month. First off, it'll be a stretch, but considering how well you did today walking to my office, I think you should be able to walk around the inner loop unassisted by the end of the month and, with assistance, manage a ramp or set of stairs. I'd also like to focus on your finger strength and dexterity with the goal of making your writing far more legible. I have examples of your original handwriting from your pictionary, so I'd like to try and get about halfway back to where you were before. I would like to see you drawing again, but I understand that it's a bit of a touchy subject. So, rather than even attempting to draw, I had an idea. I picked something up at the Guild this morning for Hope, and I thought it might work for you, too, as a starting point to work back up to where you were with your drawing."

He reached into his desk drawer and pulled out, of all things, a coloring book, two of them actually. "I thought it might be fun for the two of you to color together. As you can see, Hope had a great deal of fun this morning." He flipped open one of them to reveal wild scribbles that were nowhere near filling in any of the lines. "There are fifty pages in this book. I want to see you color one page every day. I think you'll see significant improvement by the end of the month, but the only way you'll get your ability to draw back is if you practice. What do you think?"

She thought about it for a while. So much of her frustration had been because Hope had been able to do far more than she could that she'd felt infantilized, but she knew she could do better than Hope at coloring, even if she couldn't stay within the lines, and she really did want to draw again. It was practically a primal need at this point. Walking sounded boring, though. "I'll give the coloring book a try, but I'll need pencils. It sounds like mine were all destroyed."

Ammond grinned, reached into his drawer, pulled out a large box of colored pencils, and slapped them on the desk.

"And some blank paper would be nice, too," she said.

His grin widened, and he reached into his drawer, pulled out a brand new sketchbook, and set that down, too.

"Anything else?" he asked with a smile.

"Yes. I have absolutely no desire to spend every day walking around the loop. I want to go riding. It'll work on balance, coordination, leg strength, and even finger dexterity."

Ammond considered it, frowning. "I'm not comfortable with you doing anything that could result in another injury to your brain, but I'll agree to it on two conditions. First, you have some form of protection for your head. I understand that was something you were looking into before everything happened, and I'd feel a lot better if there was a way to protect you from injuring yourself in some other fashion if you fell. That new rib bone of yours will take a few weeks before it's fully integrated and as strong as the rest. And two, you need to be able to walk from your room to the barn, with assistance, *before* you get on that horse. I don't care how well he's trained. I've seen how quickly they can move, and you don't have the strength to hold on or balance if they were to move unexpectedly."

She held her hand out. "Deal."

Ammond looked at it, confused.

"Hue-man's shake paws when they make a deal," she explained.

He raised an eyebrow but gently took her hand in his massive paw, and they shook.

"Good, now get out of here. I have research to do," he said, returning to his normally gruff exterior.

Laughing, her mother helped her out of the chair and carried the drawing supplies but made her walk back to her room. She made it about halfway before her legs quite literally gave out from exhaustion. Although she tried to stand back up after a short rest, her mother had to carry her the rest of the way back, and she was asleep before her mother laid her back on her bed.

CHAPTER 15

Nazari: Lost Chance

Nazari's heart stopped when she saw her cub running through the garden chasing one of the seed pods that flitted through the air. "Sari," she whispered and then shook her head. *His name is Brent now,* she reminded herself. She hated the name and its ugly, harsh sound. It didn't fit him at all. It was impossible to say, and he didn't respond to it, but then he didn't respond to anything. He wasn't signing or speaking yet, and she wondered if he would. He'd been isolated during the formative part of his childhood when language first developed for his species.

His mother was calling his name, but he didn't react to it at all. Instead, he continued to dance to some unknown beat under the bandala tree as the wind knocked more of the seed pods free. He stopped and grabbed one that landed on the ground and threw it back up in the air, where it spiraled, and he laughed as he spiraled to match it. She could hear his laughter now, thanks to Ammond's new hearing aids. It was such a beautiful sound, so free and uninhibited by the stresses of the world, like nothing mattered but that moment. She wished she could be as carefree as him.

"Come on, Brent. It's time for your nap," Councilor Harding said. She could understand the basics of Hue-man now, too, as that had been one of the Council's major complaints, but she couldn't speak it all that well. So many of the sounds were impossible to reproduce.

He didn't respond, as if he hadn't even heard. His mother picked him up, but he started screaming and struggling to get away.

Go after him! He doesn't want to go with her. Protect him! Don't abandon him too!

Shut up! She growled at the constant thoughts that had been running through her brain since that horrible council meeting when she'd lost her bid to become his mother. They'd grown stronger and far more insistent since she'd used her instinct to track Buster's scent. She knew what that meant, even if she didn't want to believe it. Her nightmares were full of Sari being the child she'd tracked down and rescued, not Hope, and she'd been halfway to the apartments before she realized where she was.

Her control was slipping, but she didn't know what to do. She knew she should report it, but that was a death sentence. She'd been tested by Kendra herself after Damon was secured, and it had taken her far too long to turn her instinct off. She'd been absolutely terrified when it hadn't turned off right away, and that had made it even harder. Surprisingly, Kendra hadn't killed her then and there. The only reason she could think of was because Henry had been there. Kendra had put her on a watch, and the stares of the guards roaming New Hope were unnerving. It was like they could see into her very soul. She had avoided public spaces as much as possible because of it, but she was starting to feel trapped and had come to the garden in the hopes that it might calm her down. It had until Sari had appeared.

Brent, she growled to herself. *His name is Brent.*

Council Harding spotted her, frowned, and turned to leave the garden with him, even as he struggled to get out of her grasp.

He's not our cub anymore, she reminded herself, digging her claws into the ground to keep from running after him like she wanted to.

They had no right to take him from us.

How many times had she thought that since that awful day? *They had every right,* she told herself, even though her heart fumed at the injustice. She turned and bolted in the other direction, away from the desire and pressure to act.

She didn't get far before a guard suddenly appeared in front of her. She gasped and skidded to a stop, startled and unnerved. He'd appeared out of the shadows, out of nowhere, and it took everything she had not to run in the other direction. The guard gave a single tilted nod of his head to follow. She sighed, terrified, but followed anyway, wondering where he was taking her.

Away from here to put her down without witnesses?

Her instinct growled and pressured her to run. She squashed it with everything she had, but she still felt it pacing and on guard for an attack. They left the inner compound and walked until they were on the far side of the massive greenhouses when he suddenly stopped and sat down.

"You looked like you could use someone to talk to," he said, motioning to the spot beside him. "My name's Quinn. You're Nazari?"

She snorted. "You know perfectly well who I am. I've seen you following me, and I know why."

He tilted his head in acknowledgment but didn't reply. She sighed and sat down beside him, waiting. He said nothing, and they sat there for several minutes before she spoke, deciding it was better she came clean about what was going on with her. She knew the guards could sometimes help. Everything she'd been trying had failed, and she knew she needed help before it was too late.

"I'm worried. It's been...harder to control my desire to go after him these past few days. I know he's not mine and that in another week or so, I might lose him entirely. I may have already lost him by going after Hope and the others, but I would do it again in a heartbeat. GrandFather and Henry are my apprentices, and I've grown to love both of them, too. And Myra's family. I know she would do the same for me."

He said nothing for several long moments, long enough to make her uncomfortable.

"So are you going to kill me now, or wait until the six months are up and do it then?" she asked.

"I'd rather not kill you at all," he replied. "You're still in control, and it takes time for our instincts to settle after a traumatic event. It's not surprising to me that it's pushing you right now. There's no bond stronger than the one between a mother and her child." He turned his attention away slightly and nodded. "But you're right. You may have lost him by going out after the others. That you're on the watch, even though it's not a criminal watch, will play heavily on the decision for many in the Council, especially our own. You may want to withdraw your appeal until after your watch is up."

She sighed at the delay and felt an emotion she wasn't expecting, one that wasn't hers: confusion. It was almost as if her instinct didn't understand why saving another cub would mean they'd lose their own. But that was ridiculous. Her instinct was her. It didn't have its own thoughts, and she fully understood why they might lose their case.

She refocused her attention outward and found Quinn staring at her, his gaze focused and intent and his body tense. She didn't dare look away, knowing that could be taken badly. She checked, making sure her instinct was off anyway. It was.

He finally relaxed some, although his gaze was no less intent. "You were struggling just now."

She raised a brow, wondering how he'd known, and shrugged, even though it hadn't been a question. "I don't know if struggling is the right word. It... This probably sounds strange, but I don't think my instinct understands why we would lose our cub for saving another."

"Hmm..." he said, tilting his head again as he considered. "Our laws are supposed to be fair, equal, and just, but far too often, they're not. They hurt those they're supposed to protect, or as Little Flower said, often have unforeseen consequences. You should be honored by the Council for the risk you took in saving the others, but I doubt you will, and perhaps to you, it seems like you're being punished for it, but you're not."

She frowned at him.

"Kendra gave you a chance. I've rarely seen her do that, not with someone who struggled as hard as you did to turn off your instinct. You're managing far better than I expected, but you're struggling badly. You were halfway to the apartments before you regained control last night."

She sighed. "You know about that?"

"Of course. You are being watched, after all. You were very lucky. I was ready to call in my guards when you regained control. That you did is the only reason you're alive right now."

She swallowed hard. "How do you know I was out of control last night? I thought I was sleepwalking."

One corner of his mouth turned up in a half smile, but he didn't answer. "I'd like to help you if I can. Normally, I'd recommend coming into the Guard for training. We could use healers with your skills, but the timing of everything will make that difficult since you're scheduled to leave for the Water World in a few days."

She sighed. "I'm honestly terrified of what will happen if I don't win the appeal," she admitted. "It was almost impossible handing him over and walking out of the council chamber that first time. I don't know if I can do that again, but I'm more afraid of what will happen if I don't try."

"I know. I'm worried for you too. That's why we need to work on your control now."

She nodded. "I've been doing everything I was taught in the Healer's Guild, but it's not working very well."

"That's not surprising. It's one thing to remain calm and in control around prey species or blood as you've been trained to do, and another when you and your instinct are in agreement to act and protect those you care about. It wants what you want, only more so, especially when they're in line with our primal needs. For now, I recommend avoiding anywhere the child might go. Stick to the barn or your rooms between now and the meeting. Travel on a different ship, and do anything and everything that you find enjoyable or calming, whether that's reading a book, listening to music, or going for a run. Your instinct will continue to push you to act. For some, it's easier to control if you give in a little rather than fighting. For example, if your instinct is insisting on hunting, get something to eat in the cafeteria, or if it's pressuring you to go after your cub, spend time with other cubs, or go for a run. Redirect its demands and give yourself a safer outlet."

"That makes sense." She considered what might help. Her claws felt twitchy with the need to act. "I think a run would be good."

He smiled. "A run it is, then. I could do with stretching my legs a little. I'm impressed at how far you traveled to rescue the others. Your endurance is fantastic, but I wonder how fast you are?"

She sized him up. He was several feet shorter than her but large and muscular for a male and beautiful to look at. She knew her mating instinct would have picked him in a heartbeat with her two past litters. He was the epitome of male virility, and part of her wished she could drag him to a mating clinic for another litter. *That would be quite the distraction,* she thought with a grin but sighed. She'd already been through two heats, not that she couldn't make that happen herself if she really wanted to, but her second heat... She pushed that thought away hard. Thinking of her daughter just made things worse.

She shook her drifting thoughts aside and refocused on Quinn and his question. The guards trained hard, but her profession meant she was fairly active, and she'd had no problems the other day outside of a little stiffness that was easily treated. She had a much longer stride than he did, and she decided she could take him and flicked an ear back dismissively. "Fast enough to keep up with you."

He laughed. "I seriously doubt that, but if you're that confident, what do you say we make it a little interesting?"

She squinted at him. Everyone knew how much the guards enjoyed a good bet. "Fine. The first person to that scrub tree," she pointed off in the distance, "has to muck out the horse stalls."

He grinned wickedly. "Deal."

She stood, stretched, as did he, and then took off without warning. She let herself relax into the run, letting her anger and stress out with every stride. She heard the sounds of his feet behind her and risked a glance back to see him, ears pinned and focused on catching up, and he was. She pinned her own ears and dug deeper. To her surprise, he caught up and started to pass her.

Letting off a growl of frustration, which he responded to with a chuckle, she dug even deeper and managed to catch up with him again. They matched their strides beat for beat as they traveled over the rough ground, her claws digging deep for added traction. Sometimes he was ahead, other times she was, but when they arrived at the tree, it was a tie. She didn't stop, and neither did he. They ran together, side by side, until she came gasping to a stumbling stop and flopped down.

"Stand up. Keep walking," he ordered. "If you don't, you'll regret it tomorrow."

She pinned her ears at him, which just made him chuckle, but heaved herself back to her feet and kept walking, not sure if that was an order she could refuse. He finally stopped and sat down. She collapsed next to him, still panting but better than before.

"I'm impressed," he said. "It's been a long time since anyone has been able to keep up with me."

She chuckled. "My profession means chasing after my wards on a regular basis, and usually in knee-deep mud. If you want a real challenge, try collecting an egg from one of the geese. Even wearing a shield, I still get bit." She shifted some of the fur aside on her leg to show him the bruise that was there from that morning's adventure.

He raised a brow. "I might just take you up on that challenge."

"You're welcome anytime. No one else even dares," she replied, laughing. "Ten credits, you'll lose."

He grinned at her. "There, that's better."

She looked at him in confusion. She'd expected him to take her up on the bet.

"You've settled some. You're not so jagged anymore," he replied.

"Jagged?" she asked.

He just smiled. "Join the guard, and I'll tell you more, but I can't until you do. For what it's worth, I think you'd make an excellent guard."

She snorted. "I seriously doubt that. Why do you think I ended up as an animal healer out in the middle of nowhere? My mouth would get me in trouble within five minutes of joining."

That made him chuckle. "You wouldn't be the first, but like I said, we could always use healers like you in the Guard. Think about it."

She raised a brow but didn't comment.

He stood and stretched. "Come on, that's enough of a rest. I believe you have stalls to muck out."

"And you would be wrong," she said as she stood and stretched. "It was a tie. Besides, Henry's the one who mucks out the horse stalls, one of the benefits of rank and all that. I would have won that bet either way."

Quinn burst out laughing. "I should have known better. You were far too confident."

She shrugged. "I wasn't born yesterday. I never make a bet I'm not absolutely sure I'll win."

He chuckled again. "I'll keep that in mind." They were silent for a few minutes before he spoke again. "We should go out running every day, once in the morning and again in the evening, or any time you feel the need to run. Call any time, day or night, or even just speak it aloud. Someone will hear you."

She nodded, knowing it wasn't a suggestion, but she honestly felt better than she had in days. "Thank you."

He tilted his head, acknowledging her, but they walked the rest of the way back in silence.

"I'll meet you at the barn tomorrow morning at seven," he said when they made it back to the compound. "Apparently, I have a sparring match with a goose, whatever that is."

"I'll be sure to bring the bone knitter and nano cream," she replied, her tail curling in amusement.

He glared at her. "That won't be necessary."

"Alright, but don't come crawling to me for treatment if it is," she replied, and laughed as he rolled his eyes at her and disappeared into the crowd.

CHAPTER 16

Little Flower: Toddler

Little Flower opened her eyes to a dark room, lit up only by the dim light streaming in through the hall, and glanced over at the strange clock the Sabers used to confirm it was in the middle of the night. She'd slept for hours, and she was both starving and had to pee. From her bed, she could see the bathroom just across the hall.

I can make it, she thought. *It's what, thirty or forty steps, maybe?*

She hadn't gone to the bathroom by herself in months, and looking around the room, she realized no one was there to help her. She could use the call button but decided to give it a try. Worse case, she fell, and she had to yell for help.

Sitting up and swinging her legs over the side of the bed, she marveled at how much easier it was than it had been a week before. The floor was a long way down, so she looked around for the bed controls, but they were sitting on the table, just past her reach. Rolling over on her stomach, she grabbed ahold of the sheet and slid down. She almost fell but managed to catch herself in time. *Okay, the scary part is done,* she thought, breathing hard. *The rest should be a piece of cake, right? Oh, cake. I wonder if Jordan has reinvented that yet?*

Holding on to the bed, she made her way down to the end and stopped. There on the floor, curled up in a ball and sound asleep, was her mother.

Smiling, she looked back up. *It's only a few steps to the door. You can do this,* she told herself. She wobbled a bit as she let go of the bed but didn't fall. Several very slow, cautious steps later, she made it to the door.

"Yes!" she cheered and then cringed to look back at her mother, hoping she hadn't woken her up. *Still sleeping, phew! Okay, now for the hallway. One step at a time.*

She was about halfway across when she wobbled and fell over backwards with an 'oof,' landing hard on her butt. "Stinky moon cheese," she muttered. That was one of the Saber's swears that she'd badly mistranslated when first learning them, but she loved the ridiculousness of it and used it regularly.

Sitting there, she looked at the far side of the hallway. *Why do their hallways have to be so moons' forsaken wide?*

She didn't want to crawl that far, so she considered how to stand back up. Rolling over onto her stomach, she pushed herself to a kneeling position and tried to bring one foot forward but fell over. Swearing, she tried again and managed to get her foot forward, but when she tried to stand, she wobbled and fell again.

After the fourth attempt, she lay on the floor, panting and trying to figure out what to do. *I guess I could just lay here and wait for someone to find me, but I'll pee all over the floor before that happens.* Sighing, she looked back at her room, wondering if she could yell loud enough for her mother to hear and wake her, but her mother was already sitting there watching her.

"You're doing a wonderful job. You can do this. Try again. See if you can get yourself into a squatting position and push straight up. That might be easier," her mother suggested.

She considered and rolled over again into a sitting position this time, tucked her feet in under her, and rocked forward, trying to get up into a squat. She rocked too far forward but caught herself and readjusted.

Ok, on the count of three. One, two, two and a half, two and three quarters... Oh, quit stalling. You can do this. Three! With a loud groan, she pushed against her knees and almost made it before falling over.

It had worked better than before, so she tried again. It took her three more tries, but she finally managed to stand up on her own, and a few minutes later, she'd made it to the far side. Grabbing onto the doorsill with relief, she looked back and found her mother sitting in the doorway of her room with a huge smile on her face and her tail curled and wrapped by her feet.

"I knew you could do it!" she signed. "I'm very proud of you!"

Smiling, Little Flower turned and wobbled into the bathroom, carefully shutting the door behind her. She'd never been more excited to use the bathroom before. It was the first time in months she'd been able to do it on her own. On the return trip, she almost lost her balance opening the door and twice more crossing the hallway, but she managed without falling.

Her mother recorded the return trip and then moved out of the way so she could make it back to her bed.

She made it over to the table, but she couldn't quite reach the controls, so her mother slid them closer and then watched as she crawled back into her bed. It wasn't graceful, but she managed. Panting from the effort, she rolled over and lay face up on the bed with a huge smile on her face. She'd done it! She was pretty sure she had a bruise on her backside and at least one scraped elbow, but she'd done it!

"Can I have some nano cream and something to eat? I'm starving," she asked her mother.

"Of course. I'll be right back," her mother replied and left. A few minutes later, she returned with a tray heaping with food and a jar of nano cream. "Where do you hurt?" her mother asked after setting it all down.

Little Flower lifted her arm to show the scrape.

"You Hue-mans damage far too easily," her mother signed with a frown but unscrewed the jar, scooped out some of the miracle cream, and applied it to her scraped elbow.

She sighed with relief as the cream took effect and numbed the pain. When her other bruises were treated, her mother slid the tray of food over so she could reach it. "Yes! A cookie!" Little Flower signed and reached for it first.

Her mother glared at her for going for the sweets first, but she didn't care.

"This is a celebration! It's taken months, but I'm finally potty trained!" She broke off half and handed it to her mother. "Cheers!"

Her mother laughed and took the proffered piece, eating it in one bite.

"Oh, this is so good!" she groaned. "Tell Jordan she's amazing!" It wasn't just the cookie, though. Everything she ate tasted wonderful. "Mama, was my sense of smell and taste affected too? This food tastes so much better than before."

"Quite likely, but then things always do seem to taste better when you're happy," her mother replied, stealing some of her food and popping it in her mouth.

"Where's Hope?" she asked next.

"She's staying with GrandFather in his suite for the night. He'll bring her by in the morning for the other healers to fight over who gets to watch her. I wouldn't be surprised if half of the staff decide they want another litter of cubs before you're out of here."

Little Flower chuckled, remembering Hope running down the halls with the healers chasing after her, and then sobered. "How's Marsee doing?"

"She's still in surgery," her mother replied.

"Still? Why don't you go to her? I'm fine, and so is GrandFather. She needs you."

"I want to, but right now, I'm far more useful to her here. I'd be unable to communicate with the healers while we jump, and I don't like the idea of not knowing what's going on. Here, it's only a couple of hours delay, and I can work with the specialists who have agreed to help. On that note, I did get some encouraging news while you slept. Rowena has agreed to take Marsee's case."

"Who's Rowena?"

"Only the Universe's most brilliant brain specialist and leading expert on psychosis. Just don't tell Ammond I said that. She and Ammond had the same mentor, and they've been competing against each other since the day they met. Rowena retired decades ago and only takes those cases she's the most interested in now. She rarely travels from her home on Digger as it's just too hard for her, but if anyone can find a way to fix Marsee, it's her."

"She's a Digger?" Little Flower asked, surprised.

"Yes," her mother nodded.

"Why would a Digger be an expert on psychosis? I thought you didn't talk about this illness with the other species."

"We typically don't, but Rowena grew up in the guard. Her father was here as part of an exchange program. She and Ammond were classmates for the year she was here, but they kept in touch after they returned home. Her father eventually became the Senior Honor Guard for Digger, and she joined and was in the guard for a while herself. Several of her pups and grand-pups are still there. It takes a different kind of Digger to be in the Guard, and you'll recognize it immediately if you ever get a chance to meet her, but my understanding is that she lost a close friend to psychosis and made it her mission in life to figure out a cure. That's why she went to Master Bresdone, Ammond's mentor, as he was our leading brain expert at the time and essentially demanded that he mentor her. She's the one who invented nanotech, and she helped find treatments for many of the injured at the Agency and helped us with your case, too."

"Ammond was a brain specialist before? I thought he was an ear doctor."

"He's both and one of the best. He didn't switch to specializing in hearing loss until Sina was born."

"So, how did you end up with Ammond as your mentor?"

Her mother grinned. "*That* is entirely Ellie's fault, that and her rocking chair. I wasn't even an apprentice yet. I'd just arrived that day and made the mistake of trying to treat her on my own. Out here, where healers are few and far between, everyone knows basic first aid, and we pick up whatever skills we can, wherever we can. It can mean the difference between life and death. I knew at a very young age that I wanted to be a healer, so I read everything I could and was illegally treating patients long before I was old enough to join the Healer's Guild. It's something the Council and Guard overlook because there just aren't enough healers in this part of the world. It seemed like a very simple dislocation, even if Ellie was screaming loud enough to wake the dead, and she agreed to let me try treating her. I was...*not* as good as I thought. Anyway, we ended up going to the trauma center, and Ammond happened to be on his very first rotation as a newly promoted Master and had been assigned to the night shift, which was apparently his very last choice, and he was in a foul mood because of it, or so he claims. Ellie didn't say anything, knowing I'd get in trouble, but Ammond took one look at her tail and figured it out. He made the mistake of trying to lecture me instead of treating Ellie first, and I let him have it. Bresdone heard the whole thing and ordered Ammond to walk me through fixing the mess I'd made of Ellie's tail. Ammond grumbled but did as ordered and then tried to start lecturing me again for treating an injury I wasn't rated for. I refused to let him get away with it. Bresdone, to his credit, listened and then, after running me through my paces, decided we were both right and ordered Ammond to mentor me."

"He ordered? I thought mentorship had to be offered."

"Well, it was a very strongly worded suggestion, and you're right. It's supposed to be. There are all sorts of legal ramifications associated with mentorship, and it's even worse in the Healer's Guild. You legally can't teach anyone, much less take a protege until you're a Master, and it takes twice as long as any other profession to earn that rank because there's so much to learn. If I messed up and killed someone, Ammond could be held liable. Ammond rightly refused and even put a mark against my application, stating I had been practicing without a license. I was furious, but I had broken the law, even if Ellie didn't press charges. No one would take me on, and I no longer qualified for the training courses offered by the Healer's Guild. I took a maintenance job at the trauma center, hoping someone would eventually give me a chance.

They didn't. What I didn't realize was that Bresdone was apparently just as annoyed with Ammond and dragged both Ammond and Rowena out to a small clinic in the South District to teach him a lesson. A year later, they returned, and after watching me clean up a bloody mess without complaint or issue, Ammond apologized and mentored me on the spot."

"Why did Bresdone drag Rowena out there?"

"It was beneficial for her research. Percentage-wise, psychosis happens more often out here than it does in the cities. Likely because there's more need to use our instincts and because more children unfortunately end up as single cubs. Plus, you go wherever your mentor goes or says you go. Legally, Ammond has the right to demote me or kick me out of the guild entirely and punish me in any way he deems fit if I don't do what he says. That's part of the contract. I could end the contract or fight the orders, but then I'd lose all the benefits that come with having a mentor, such as having his help on any case I need."

"*Any* way?" she asked with a frown.

Her mother nodded. "It's the one aspect of our society where violence is accepted. My poor performance risks his life, so it's in his best interest to ensure I'm properly trained, and if I get in trouble, so does he. Plus, there's far more likelihood that I would lose control as a healer than any other profession besides the Guard and Council, and he has the legal right to kill me if he even suspects I'm losing control. I'm honestly surprised he didn't yesterday, and since I haven't been dragged off by the guard, I'm guessing he hasn't reported it either."

She frowned. "Do you think he will?"

Her mother stared off into the distance for a while before answering. "If I have another episode, yes, but if that happens, perhaps it will help him find a cure for Marsee. Outside of what happened yesterday, I feel like I'm in control, so hopefully, it was nothing more than a trauma response, as you suggested."

"So what benefit does the mentor get from the relationship?" she asked.

"Mostly, a higher compensation rate based on the number and rank of their proteges, but there are unofficial privileges, such as having someone do the work you don't want or have the time to do. Just like I could ask for his help, he could pull me in to help on any of his projects or cases."

"Seems like it could be easily abused."

Her mother shook her head. "I suppose it could, but that doesn't happen. If I felt what he was doing was abuse, I could have him arrested or end my contract on those grounds, and he would, at a minimum, get kicked out of the guild, or worse, if I pressed charges."

She nodded the point. "Wait. You said Rowena knew Ammond when they were children. I thought Diggers only lived to about two hundred."

Her mother smiled at her. "I'm pretty sure she's staying alive just so she can outlive Ammond and say she's older than him for once. He's been pulling rank for years on that excuse. She's the oldest living Digger in recorded history by about fifty years, thanks to the tech she's invented, and probably the only person I've ever met who can intimidate both Ellie and Marcus, Ammond too, but he refuses to admit it. Rumor has it she once made Kendra run off with her tail between her legs, but she won't tell me if that's true or not. Don't worry about her age, though. Diggers are unique in the universe. They don't forget anything, ever, and they only get smarter as they age. Their bodies break down long before their brains do. You'll like her. She has your attitude."

"I like her already, then," she said and grabbed another piece of fruit. "So why can't you communicate during jump?"

Her mother rubbed the back of her head and made a face, trying to figure out how to explain. Then, she carefully tore out a piece of paper from the drawing pad, grabbed a pencil, and drew two circles on either side of the paper. "Let's say this is our world, and this one is the Water World. You'd think the shortest distance between these two points would be a straight line, right?"

She nodded.

"That's true if you're only in two dimensions, but if we make it three…" Myra took the paper and folded it into an m shape with the two dots on the top. "Now, the shortest distance is from here to here. Jump basically takes our three-dimensional space and turns it into four, and we travel from this point to this one, but while we're between places, we're really not in the same three-dimensional reality. We do the same thing with data packets, but they can go much faster because they don't need to account for the limitations of our frail bodies. Your father took an experimental ship to the Water World. It got him there in half a day instead of almost four, but he said they were all sick the entire time. The ships that rescued you had our best relay technology and are able to communicate while in jump, but most of the other ships don't, at least not yet anyway. Your father's ship is scheduled to get that enhancement, but not until next month, and even then, it will be delayed and limited to essential communication."

"That makes sense," Little Flower replied. That sounds a lot like what some of our scientists were working on to circumvent the speed of light, or at least one of the videos I saw trying to explain it."

Her mother flipped her ears back in astonishment. "You were already working on how to jump? It took us hundreds of our years to even figure out the concept, much less make something work."

"I didn't say we had anything working, just that it was one idea we had on how to get around the laws of physics as we knew them. Plus, we really wanted to know what was out there."

Her mother nodded. "Anyway, depending on how Marsee's doing, I'm planning to go with the others as a healer on the council ship. I've traded spots with Brice."

"I'm going too," Little Flower said. "I know we talked before about not attending, but that was before my surgery."

Her mother frowned. "I don't know."

"Why not? I feel so much better than I did a week ago. I want to see Marsee. I miss her. Besides, I don't want to be left alone here if everyone is going to be there."

Most of the time since Marsee had left, she'd been unconscious or kidnapped, so she hadn't had a lot of time to miss her, but when Marsee had first been kidnapped, it had felt like part of her had been stolen, and now with her in such critical condition, she hated not being there with her. Her sister would need someone who knew what she was going through when she woke.

"Ship travel can be hard and is not easy on a person, especially if they're already injured. I'll consider it, but that will all depend on how well you're doing when it's time to jump," her mother finally said. "Printed organs don't do well with jump, which is why Marsee will be stuck on the Water World for at least a month before she can come home. Bones aren't usually as delicate, but there can be problems."

"I guess that's fair," Little Flower replied, although she wasn't happy about it.

When they were done eating, her mother brought the tray back and returned to the room. She tried to get her mother to go back home where she'd be more comfortable, but her mother flat-out refused and curled up on the floor again.

Little Flower wasn't in the least bit tired, though, so she decided to try coloring. Flipping through the book, she found a page that interested her and seemed easy enough to manage, even with her unsteady hands. She stared at the page for a long time before picking up a pencil and starting. Within seconds, she went outside the lines. She erased it and tried again, and again, and again, and then her pencil snapped. With a growl, she swore and threw it across the room.

Her mother's head snapped up. "Did you need something from me?"

"Hands that didn't shake would be nice," she muttered under her breath. "No, I was just frustrated," she signed instead. "I kept messing up, and then the pencil snapped."

Her mother peered over at the book on her lap. "Well, considering that you couldn't hold a pencil last week, what you've done so far looks fantastic. Keep trying. I'll pick you up a sharpener from the Guild in the morning, but just remember, whatever pencils you throw, you'll have to pick up." Her mother had a wicked glint in her eyes and laid back down before she could reply.

She glared at her mother for several moments before sighing, picking out another pencil, and trying again. Fifteen minutes later, she had to stop. Her hand was cramping, and she'd barely made any progress.

"At this rate, it will take me all week to finish one page," she muttered and grabbed her tablet to read instead. Marsee had been helping her through one of her favorite books before she'd left. It was slow going, as she still had to look up words all the time, but it was entertaining and something to do.

Hours later, when just before dawn, she heard several low tones. Her mother's head snapped up, and she pulled out her tablet, rubbing at her eyes. "It's from your father. Marsee just finished her second surgery. She survived, but the infection in her hand is worse, and several of her other systems are starting to fail because of it. They're contemplating amputating her paw to stop the infection."

Little Flower cried and opened her arms up for a hug.

Her mother came around the bed and scooped her up. They sat there comforting each other until another message arrived, this time from the Senior Healer with more detailed medical information, and her mother left to review it.

GrandFather appeared moments later with her breakfast and Hope, and she held her daughter for a minute, but Hope wasn't in the mood to sit still.

"Want down!" Hope signed, and the moment her little feet hit the floor, she was off and running with GrandFather chasing right behind.

While they were gone, she decided to make another trip to the hole of muck, this time managing not to fall on her butt, although she came close a few times. She was halfway back when Hope came running around the corner.

"Mama!" Hope yelled.

She looked over to see her grandfather's shocked expression at seeing her walking unassisted, but before she could say anything, Hope barreled into her and knocked her over.

"Jessica!" her grandfather yelled and ran over. "Are you hurt?" he asked, squatting down and pulling Hope off her.

Hope giggled. "Mama faw down!"

"Yes, your mama fell down, you little imp," her grandfather said. "You have to be careful around your mother."

Her mother, having heard her grandfather yell, came bolting out of her office.

Hope saw her, growled, and struggled to get down. GrandFather set her down, and she ran right over to Myra, who scooped her up and growled back.

Was Hope speaking in Saber? Little Flower wondered. *She was communicating in a mix of English and Sign, but was she learning Saber, too? Marsee said she was. Could she really hear them? She could barely hear her mother.* "Did Hope say something to you, Mama?"

"Yes. Well, kind of. She was trying to say one of our words for grandmother, but it's missing many of the syllables. It's very cute, though," her mother said after Hope wiggled to be put down again and took off running.

GrandFather sighed and started chasing after her. "I'm getting too old for this!" he yelled back.

Laughing, she looked up at her mother. "Are you going to help me up?"

"Not a chance," her mother replied. "If you can do it once, you can do it again."

"That's what I thought," she grumbled back and rolled herself over. It only took her two tries to stand back up this time. Once she was up, though. Her mother held out her tail so she could use it to stabilize herself.

"Now that you're up, let's see how far you can get. If you make it around the loop in the ward, I'll bring you another cookie for lunch. I'll be nice, though, and let you hold onto my tail."

Little Flower thought about it for a moment. The loop was really far, but two, maybe three times around would be about how far it would be from here to the Barn, and that cookie had been really good. "Deal."

It took her over an hour to make it around. Even holding on to her mother's tail, she fell several times, but she did it. She had a cheering squad when she came around the triage desk. Hope must have passed her at least a dozen times, with a different person chasing her each time. By the time she made it back to her room, her legs were shaking with fatigue, and the moment she made it to her bed, she collapsed face down on it, too tired to even try to bring her legs up.

Her mother took pity on her and lifted her in. "Well done! I honestly didn't think you'd make it halfway around," her mother signed after she rolled over.

"Then I want two cookies," she signed back with an annoyed glare.

Her mother laughed but agreed and left to continue her research. She rolled over on her side, yawning but grinning from her victory, and watched as her child ran past, chased by yet another healer.

She might not have won any races, but she'd completed one, and for the first time in months, she didn't feel like an infant anymore. *I've leveled up to toddler*, she thought and then chuckled.

I hope Mama's prepared for me to go through the terrible twos tomorrow.

CHAPTER 17

Quinn: George and Matilda

Quinn woke early and made his way to the cafeteria for breakfast. The place was packed, but he found an out-of-the-way corner to read his latest reports and observe the crowd over his tablet.

A few noticed his presence, but most were oblivious, as he'd intended, and the rest soon ignored him. Nearly half were talking about recent events, and a large monitor on one wall had the morning press report, which was currently discussing the unexpected announcement that the Senior Guild Master wasn't dead after all.

While he was greatly relieved himself, his focus was on the crowd. He watched the room carefully, checking for anyone who seemed angry or upset about the announcement, but didn't sniff anything, although several who walked in and saw it for the first time stood and stared at the news report, radiating waves of relief, especially the visiting masters from the Guild.

With his meal done, he returned the tray and took the long way around to the barn. Overall, the general mood was significantly better, especially among the Hue-mans, who were going about their morning as if nothing had happened, while the other species still seemed anxious and jittery. The Hue-mans' reaction completely baffled him. They didn't seem at all concerned for their safety, and he wondered if it was because they'd expected it or because they were used to violence. He even saw one person sign that she was relieved that it had finally happened and to have proof that the other species weren't as perfect as they pretended to be.

His conversation with GrandFather the day before had been enlightening, to say the least. After his comments to the other guards about not finding several weapons, he'd asked and been allowed to examine GrandFather for himself. Even he hadn't found all three knives that had been hidden on GrandFather or even considered the ten other things that GrandFather followed up with that he identified on himself as potential weapons. That had led to a long conversation, and he realized that the Hue-mans considered everything a weapon, even themselves, as frail as they were. None of the other species bothered with weapons outside of the stunners because all the other species had sharp teeth and claws or other similar defenses, and long-range lethal weapons had been banned for so long that they only existed in the history books, at least as far as he knew.

Their conversation had transitioned into some of GrandFather's experiences with war and coups on Earth. It had left him feeling anxious long after GrandFather had left, claiming fatigue from his injuries. That much had been true, but Quinn had a feeling GrandFather had barely begun to scratch at the surface of what the Hue-mans used to do on Earth. He was still learning to read the Hue-mans, but there had been a look a time or two that Quinn recognized. He'd seen it often enough. It was the same look Marsee had given during her testimony, haunted and distant, and he wondered if it was from his recent trauma or something that had happened on Earth.

GrandFather had shared with him part of a history book that he was working on, thankfully already translated by Marsee. What he'd read so far was horrifying and far more than Little Flower had alluded to at the Trial, even during the private session with the Senior Council that he'd be privy to.

As he walked, he considered the Hue-mans that he passed with that new information. They seemed so harmless compared to the other species, but their history showed they were perhaps the most dangerous. He wondered if that would change with time. Everyone here seemed friendly and mostly happy, a far cry from the last time he'd been here. The transformation over the past few months was rather astounding. Councilor Chenzira had done good work with them for the most part, Damon notwithstanding, but then they'd always expected at least a few incidents as the Hue-mans learned to adjust to their new society and laws.

He eventually made his way to the barn, where Nazari was already waiting for him, watching the animals graze in their paddocks with a small box at her side.

Two guards were now stationed over by the door to the barn, and he knew the day guard watching Nazari was around somewhere, although she was doing an admirable job at staying hidden.

Great, witnesses, he thought and then shrugged. It just added to the challenge. Plus, with a prisoner held inside, the newly added feeds in and around the Barn were being watched around the clock by Command.

"Are you ready to meet George and Matilda, or do you need to warm up first?" Nazari asked with a grin.

He snorted at her. None of the animals he saw here seemed all that dangerous. They were downright puny compared to most of the creatures on his world. "So, which ones are they?"

She pointed to the pen in front of her, and he burst out laughing at the small flock of tiny wobbling creatures inside and the warning written in all six languages on the fence in front.

"Them?!" he asked. "You're pulling my tail."

"No, but they will be," she replied. "You see that small structure over there. That's one of the places they like to nest. You'll need to find whatever eggs they've laid, put them in this box, and get out before they attack." She opened the box, which turned out to be a padded stasis chamber with something egg-shaped in it already. "These are decoy eggs. Replace any you find with these. We'll put the real eggs in an incubator until they hatch and then swap them out. As the Hue-mans say, good luck. Oh, and don't touch the inner fence. It's electrified."

"Electrified?" he asked, surprised.

"We tried a static shield, but they destroyed it in the first week," Nazari replied. "It won't harm you, but it will hurt. The fence, that is. I can't say the same for the geese."

With that, Nazari closed up the box, handed it to him, and pointed to the gate with a wicked grin.

He glared at her but cautiously entered, honestly expecting this to be nothing more than a prank as amused as she was. He worked his way around the outside. None of the creatures paid him any attention. Chuckling to himself about the prank that had obviously been played on him, he walked over to the small structure and peered inside.

One of the geese lay on a small nest that appeared to be made up of dried grass and feathers. The goose peered back at him, hissed a warning, and fluttered its wings.

Alright, not completely a prank, he thought, and took one slow step towards it.

The goose exploded forward, hissing and honking and flapping her wings at him.

He backed away quickly, hoping to draw the goose out, and she followed. The other geese let up a matching clamor, and he glanced back to see what they were doing.

Matilda took advantage and struck. He barely managed to step out of the way and circled, dodging into the small hut and slamming the door behind him.

Outside, the geese continued to honk and clamor, but it mostly died down once they could no longer see him.

He walked over to the nest to find a single tiny egg and carefully swapped it out for one of the decoys. Once secured, he checked the other nests, found nothing, and returned to the door and peeked out.

Most of the geese had gone back to whatever they were doing before, but Matilda was still hissing and honking right outside.

He tapped a claw as he considered his options. She'd been faster than he'd expected after seeing their gangly walk. Deciding there was nothing else to do, he opened the door and bolted out.

The geese exploded in a clamor again, most running away from him, but Matilda charged.

He dodged out of the way, keeping his focus on Matilda.

Suddenly, sharp pain radiated up from the tip of his tail, and he spun to find another goose biting the end of it. He yanked his tail away and spun again as Matilda took advantage of his distraction and charged.

He bolted, tail tucked, for the gate where Nazari waited, her tail spiraling with humor, but to his annoyance, she didn't open the gate.

He growled at her as he fumbled for the latch and felt another sharp bite on his leg. Finally, the gate opened, and he bolted out, barely shutting it behind him. When he was sure it was latched, he turned and handed the case to Nazari. "You could have opened the gate," he growled at her.

"No one ever opens it for me," she replied and walked away with her tail curled tightly behind her.

He snorted but followed, curious what she would do with the egg now, and glared at the two guards by the entrance to the barn, whose tails were just as tightly curled.

They wisely said nothing until he was through, but he did hear one of them say, 'pay up' a few moments later.

He had a feeling that the footage from the cameras monitored by Command had been pulled and shared with half the guards in the Consortium already. He chuckled. It wasn't often that anything got the best of him, and it was a good reminder that just because something looked small and innocent didn't mean it was.

CHAPTER 18

Little Flower: First Words

When Little Flower's mother woke her for lunch, she brought with her two cookies as promised. Like before, Little Flower shared, and they waited together for an update. And waited.

"Mama, how do you say your name?"

Her mother growled something that she couldn't quite hear.

She frowned. "Can you say it in a higher pitch?"

Her mother did, and she could hear that a lot better. Still, it took her several tries to be able to say it correctly.

"Are you able to hear my voice easily, or do I need to lower it?" she asked.

"I can hear you. It's very high-pitched, though. Ammond tested my hearing when I first heard Hope. Apparently, my hearing is better than normal, too. Although not nearly as good as Marsee's."

Little Flower tried again, lowering it, which made her throat tickle.

"Yes, I can hear that much better," her mother said. "That's my first name. Myra," which she spelled out. "Chenzira sounds like this."

It took her even longer to pronounce that. She practically had to swallow her tongue, and she struggled to hear the differences in the sounds they made. Everything just sounded like growls, meows, and hisses to her. They spent the next hour going through the names of the various family members and their variations until she could say them reasonably well. It was a good distraction, if nothing else.

"Now that you can hear, how do you want to be called?" her mother asked.

"Honestly, it doesn't matter much to me. Little Flower is my legal name now, but GrandFather still calls me Jessica."

Her mother tried saying her name and had an equally difficult time saying it. It came out sounding more like yesss-eega.

"Most of my friends from before would call me Jess. You can, too, if that's easier." It took some practice, but her mother was eventually able to get it to sound more like chess than yes. It was good enough, especially since she was sure she'd mangled her mother's name just as badly.

By the middle of the afternoon, her mother was pacing in the hallway, too nervous to even focus on trying to solve the other issues Marsee was facing, and it was getting on Little Flower's nerves. It was time to distract her mother again.

"Mama!" she called out. That was one of the other words she'd learned, and her mother stopped her pacing and looked in. "I'm all rested up. Shall we take another walk around the loop?"

Her mother's ears flipped back in wide-eyed astonishment, and Little Flower had to chuckle at the expression. To be fair, it was the first time she'd initiated any kind of physical therapy. Usually, she was trying to get out of it.

"Gladly!" her mother said, blinking out of her surprise. They were about halfway around when her mother's tablet went off. Her mother froze, took several deep breaths, and pulled her tablet off her harness. "They're bringing her in for surgery to operate on her hand," her mother told her after reading.

"Are they amputating it?" Little Flower asked, terrified of the answer.

"No. They're going to try to repair it first and see if they can clean out the infection at the same time."

"When will we know how it went?" she asked.

"A few hours, either way," her mother answered. "However, her other vitals have improved some, and there's been no sign of rejection."

"Thank the moons!" she replied, causing her mother to chuckle. "What?" she asked, not expecting that reaction.

"It just seems so funny coming from your species. It's like when a cub swears for the first time."

She rolled her eyes and followed it up with several far more colorful swears in sign language that made her mother burst out laughing.

"Where did you learn those?" her mother asked.

"From Marsee and Sina, the night after we watched the video where I accidentally swore at Healer Brice on purpose."

Her mother chuckled again, put her tablet away, and they continued on their walk as they taught each other how to swear in each other's spoken languages. They were laughing so hard at one point that she fell and appropriately swore in Saber. One of the other healers walking by at the time stopped, looked back at her, flicked their whiskers back, snorted, and kept walking.

She improved on her time by several minutes, mostly because she only fell the one time. She spent some time coloring with Hope and sent Marsee a message before GrandFather came and took her for the evening, then took a nap. She woke a few hours later and made her way to the hole of muck and back, but her legs were achy and stiff. Once back, she grabbed the nano cream and was rubbing it on her legs when her mother appeared.

"Are you hurting?" her mother asked.

"My legs are sore," she replied and slathered a large glob on her aching muscles. "So, how long do I have to stay here, anyway?"

"Medically, you're cleared, but we haven't cleaned the tower, and it's easier for me to work on trying to find a way to help Marsee here. Frankly, I'm not comfortable letting you stay by yourself, even if you are walking. We have no idea if we've caught everyone involved."

"I can understand that, and if staying here makes it easier for you to help Marsee, then I'm all for it, but do you need to work now?"

"I'm not on shift, and I am taking a break from staring at your sister's scans. Why? Did you want to do something?"

"Yes, I'd like to go to the pool if you have the time to help me there. I'd like to sit in the hot tub and see how well I can swim. If we're going to the Water World, I want to make sure I can get around."

Her mother frowned.

"Is there a problem with going in the pool?" she asked, wondering if she needed more time for her incisions to heal or something like that.

"No. It's just that your swimming clothes were destroyed, and the replacements I ordered haven't arrived yet."

"Were all of my clothes destroyed?"

"No, just the ones that were in your sister's room."

"Oh, good. Then my pink t-shirt and blue shorts will work just as well."

"Well, come on then. Let's get you changed." Her mother scooped her up and carried her out, stopping briefly to let Brice know where they were heading.

As they climbed the tower, Little Flower enjoyed the view. While the sun had set, it was still more than bright enough for her to see. So much had changed since she'd been in her coma that she hardly recognized the place.

"Mama, what's that building over there?" she asked, pointing to a new structure. It glittered in the moonlight, but only a few rooms were lit.

"That's the Water Sprite habitat. It's connected by tunnels to the Council Chamber, Guild Wing, and Trauma Center so far." Her mother pointed out each of the various new buildings as they slowly made their way around the tower but stopped short as she flicked on the light in the room. The damaged playpen and old food had been cleared out, so while the room appeared emptier, there was no sign of what had happened when they arrived.

"GrandFather must have cleaned everything up," Little Flower signed.

Her mother nodded and brought her over to the cabinet Marsee had made to hold her clothing.

"I still don't feel comfortable having you stay here alone," her mother signed.

"I can't. I can barely handle the door to the waste room, much less the outer door, on my own right now."

"I've already spoken to your father about that. They're going to put in a new security system and powered doors so you can lock or unlock them remotely if you need to."

She smiled with relief to hear that and quickly changed into clothes for the pool. Then, she set aside clothing she wanted brought to her hospital room for later. She was tired of walking around in one of the gowns.

"Mama, can I see Marsee's room before we go?"

Her mother hesitated but nodded and carried her up the ramp. "Are you sure?" her mother asked.

She nodded. She needed to see it in person. Her mother opened the door, and she gasped at the devastation.

The pictures hadn't even come close to showing her the extent of the damage, even though it looked like someone had started cleaning up. Her mother carried her through the room, unwilling to let her down. Granted, there was still far too much debris for her to manage safely anyway.

How did he do so much damage without us knowing? she wondered.

When she saw the mangled remains of her painting, she cried and buried her head in her mother's fur. She'd spent so many hours on that painting, and if her earlier attempts at coloring were any indication, there was a good chance she'd never be able to do anything anywhere near as good again.

Without another word, her mother turned and left.

CHAPTER 19

Little Flower: Child's Play

When they made it to the pool, the place was packed with members of several species, which was normal for late afternoon.

"Pool or hot tub?" her mother asked, pointing to each.

"Hot tub," Little Flower replied, so her mother carried her over to one of the empty ones and stuck the tip of her tail in.

"I don't know. It seems far too hot to me," her mother awkwardly signed.

"Let me see," she replied, so her mother sat her down next to it. She shifted forward and stuck her feet in. "Oh, no. This is perfect!"

"Are you sure? Your feet are already turning red. Are you sure you're not burning yourself?" Her mother started to unclip her scanner to check.

"I'm sure," she signed, stopping her mother, and slowly lowered herself in. The hot tub itself was massive, designed to fit both their species, with a much deeper end on the other side.

Her mother walked around to face her, laid down on the edge, stuck her front paw in, and winced from the heat. "How are you managing this? Are you sure you're okay?" her mother asked with concern.

"I'm fine. I used to take showers hotter than this," she replied, and then closed her eyes and leaned back, enjoying the heat and listening to the sounds around her: children screaming with laughter, water splashing, bubbles from one of the other tubs, and the murmur of dozens of people all talking and laughing together. They were such wonderful sounds!

She heard the low growl of Saber speech close by and opened her eyes to see Ammond talking with her mother.

She frowned at the two, wondering if Ammond had heard something about Marsee, but her mother shook her head. "No update yet."

Interestingly, she found it easier to hear Ammond than her mother and wondered if the males had higher voices due to their smaller sizes or if Ammond was purposely raising his voice so she could hear it better.

"Good afternoon, Little Flower. How are you feeling?"

"Much better now that I'm here. My legs were killing me from my race around the trauma ward with Hope today."

He laughed. "She's very fast for one so small and seems to know only two speeds: run and sleep. Do you want the jets on?"

"Please!" she replied.

He walked over to a switch on a pole near the tub, and the jets started. She shifted to make better use of them and groaned. The water splashed as Ammond entered, and he let out a sigh of equal contentment.

"Join us, Myra," he signed.

"It's hot!" she signed back.

"That's the whole point! It'll do you good, and it won't burn you, I promise. But stay too long, and I will throw you in the pool," he teased, although that was unlikely as her mother was several feet taller and far more massive than he was.

She wouldn't put it past him to try, though, and smiled at the memory, glad that particular drawing was in her parent's room.

Laughing, her mother stuck her paw in again and left it there for a bit before pulling it out and checking it for burns. When she determined her paw was still unharmed, she sat upright again and removed her harness. Looking around, she found a nearby hook, hung it up, and carefully stepped down into the tub. She hissed as she did, but after a few moments, relaxed as she acclimated to the temperature.

They sat there in companionable silence for a while, and Jessica took the opportunity to look around and see who else was in the pool. She didn't recognize half the people there. Then again, she'd barely started to get to know the others before Hope's birth, and the compound had exploded in size over the past six months, so it wasn't surprising.

She looked over at the shallow end of the pool and smiled. Grand-Father, Henry, and Hope were there, playing with some of the other kids her age. There were even a few younger Saber cubs and a baby Flyer with them, too. The adorable little weyrling looked just like a miniature dragon. Then again, their parent looked like a full-sized dragon, and she wished she'd gone with that for their species name and not the more direct translation of their own name. *Oh well,* she thought.

When GrandFather looked in their direction, she waved.

He waved back. "Do you want us to come over there?" he signed.

"No. Hope is having fun. Let her play," she replied.

The others looked to see who she was talking to and then turned back around.

"So, Mama, what do you think of the hot tub?"

"It's surprisingly relaxing once you get used to the temperature," her mother replied. Water splashed everywhere as she signed.

"Hey, watch it!" Ammond muttered and splashed her back.

Her mother laughed and splashed him back on purpose.

"Alright, you two. Don't make me come over there and turn this hot tub around," Little Flower signed.

They both looked at her with matching expressions of utter con-fusion, which made her giggle. After explaining, she closed her eyes, leaned back against the jets, listened to the rumble of their conversation, and grinned with contentment. She didn't open them again until she felt the water shift and looked up to see former Senior Councilor Tabor joining them.

"You're looking better than the last time I saw you," Tabor signed.

Little Flower frowned in confusion. She hadn't seen Tabor since before Hope was born.

"Tabor flew the Trauma Ship that picked you up the other day," her mother explained.

"Ahh. Thank you!"

"Actually, it's you I have to thank. I'm finding being a trauma pilot far more rewarding than being on the Council ever was. The people I have to deal with don't argue nearly as much," Tabor replied with a wink.

"Never pee on a Hue-man when knives are in a line," Little Flower signed, which made everyone's heads tilt in confusion.

After realizing that the quote had been badly mangled in translation and a lot of laughter on her part when she realized what they'd thought she'd said, she gave them a brief synopsis of The Princess Bride, which made them all laugh.

She sighed. "You know, I think, out of everything we lost, that pains me the most. I must have watched that movie a hundred times or more."

"Then you should work with Marsee to recreate it," Tabor said.

"Agreed," her mother replied. "Marsee would love it!"

"I just hope I get the chance," she said, and as she did, the jets shut off.

"Alright, you. Out," Ammond signed. "That's as much as you Hue-mans should be in here before cooling off. Go jump in the other pool."

"Five more minutes?" she asked. "Pleeeeese?"

He laughed. "No. Go on."

Her mother started to swim over to help her out of the hot tub, but Ammond stopped her. "She can do this on her own."

Little Flower glared at him. "GrrRrrRrr!"

Tabor looked shocked, and her mother amused, but Ammond just flicked an ear back as if getting sworn at was a normal occurrence.

"If you're going to learn to swear in our language, get it right," he said. "It's Grr Rrrrr RrrRrrRrr." Or at least that's what it sounded like to her, and everyone burst out laughing.

She dutifully tried repeating it, and he nodded. "Much better. Now go on."

Laughing, she shifted herself over to the railing, pulled herself up to a standing position, and wobbled hard. Once she steadied herself, she lifted her leg, which was fairly easy to do in the deeper water, and pushed herself up a step. The next step was much harder since she didn't have the water to help her, but she managed. The railing helped a great deal.

She struggled with the last step, however. The railing didn't go quite far enough. She tried several times but couldn't quite get the nerve to pull herself up. She felt the water shift, and the next thing she knew, her mother's dripping wet paw was on her other side. With the second handhold, she was able to make the final step.

"Thanks. The railing isn't long enough."

"I'll put in a work order to have them extended," her mother replied. "Do you want a tail over to the other pool?"

"No. I think I can do it. Relax and enjoy yourself," she told her mother, and then slowly started making her way over to her grandfather. It was a long way, and the footing wasn't as even as the loop around the hospital ward. The cement, or whatever it was they used, had irregular grooves and was angled slightly so that the water would drain back into the pool, and her legs were all rubbery from being in the hot tub and tired from her workout earlier.

She finally made it, and to her relief, without falling, but sat down next to her grandfather harder than she'd intended to and winced, sure she had another bruise. The water in this part of the pool was very shallow, only an inch or two deep, with some gentle jets that shot up into the air at random intervals, making the kids squeal with laughter as they tried to stomp on them before they went out. Along one edge was a sandy beach where several other children were making sand castles and moats. About fifteen feet out, the pool started to deepen, where a group of older children were having a water fight.

She remembered the water fights she had with Marsee, and her heart panged with worry. She prayed to whatever gods might be protecting Marsee. *Please let her be okay.*

"Is everything alright?" one of the Flyers asked her.

"I'm worried about my sister. She's very sick, and the cubs playing over there reminded me of when we used to do that. I haven't been away from her this long before, and I really miss her. Far more than I thought I would."

He nodded in understanding. "We don't often realize what we have until it's taken from us. I, too, worry for your sister. She's an amazing person, and what was done to her was just horrible. I'm glad the person who did it is now dead and can never hurt anyone again. Do you know when the others will be sentenced?"

She shook her head, but GrandFather replied. "At the Full Council meeting. They found evidence that Rip was targeting all six members of the Senior Council, and with members of four species actually harmed or killed, figuring out the reparations is proving to be a challenge. Plus, they're all waiting to see if Marsee and the rest of the victims survive. Councilor Surellis sent me a message about an hour ago, letting me know."

Gasps of shock ran through the others. "I had no idea it was that big of a conspiracy. I thought he was just going after Clear Seas. Well, I, for one, am glad he wasn't successful."

Murmurs of agreement followed.

Hope looked up from playing with a rubber ducky at one of the water fountains and saw her. "Mama!" she squealed and ran over.

Little Flower grabbed her with a big hug before her little imp could knock her over again.

Hope pushed away, and when she set her back down, Hope grabbed her hand. "Mama pway!" Hope said and started pulling.

"Okay, Hope, I'm coming," she replied, grinning at how cute Hope sounded, not being able to say l's appropriately.

GrandFather helped her up and over as the footing was slippery. Hope didn't stop pulling on her until she was by the jets. She sat back down, more carefully this time, and grabbed the rubber ducky, pushed it down on the fountain, and let go. The duck shot up into the air.

Hope squealed with delight and chased after it. They did that for a while before Hope suddenly tired of the game and ran off to play in the sand.

GrandFather followed after Hope, so she decided to push herself further out into the water since she was already close to the area where it started to drop off, rather than going back to talk with the others. She didn't want to gossip about everything that had happened. Talking about Marsee just made her miss her that much more.

It didn't take her long to shift her way over into the deeper water. When she was about chest deep while sitting, she flipped over and walked herself, using her hands, over to the pool's edge so she'd have something to hold onto to stand up. The angle of the pool was steep, so she wasn't sure if she'd have the balance to stand up on her own or not, especially with the waves from the kids playing. Once there, she grabbed the side and pulled herself up far easier than she'd expected.

She looked over and saw her mother still chatting with the others. Two others that she didn't know had joined them. Her mother looked far more relaxed than she'd seen her in a very long time. The hot tub was doing her good.

Smiling, she started walking along the edge out into the deeper water.

She was about chest deep when her foot slipped, and she went down and, to her immense surprise, sank. She'd never had a problem floating before. Swimming hard, she tried to bring herself up to the surface and pull her feet under her to stand again, but the waves had pushed her out over her head.

She managed to break free and grab a breath, but she couldn't stay above the water and went back under. She turned over and tried to swim towards the wall, and the shallows, but a jet circulating the water gave just enough pressure to counteract what she could manage in her weakened state. She wasn't moving anywhere and kept sinking.

I can't swim! she realized, starting to panic. *Wait until you hit bottom and kick up,* she thought, franticly trying to figure out what to do.

Letting herself sink, wincing from the pressure and pain in her ears, she waited until her feet touched and then pushed up with everything she had, trying hard to make her way to the surface. She didn't even come close. Her vision started clouding around the edges, and her lungs were convulsing with the need to breathe until she couldn't control it anymore, and she gasped in a lung full of water.

The water hurt, and her body spasmed. Darkness had nearly taken her when she saw the splash of something large entering the water above her. Moments later, she felt herself being scooped out of the water and deposited on the side of the pool.

Her vision gone, and barely aware of her surroundings, she tried to gasp for breath, but her lungs were full of water. She felt someone pinch her nose and began breathing into her mouth. Two breaths in, she started coughing up the water, gasping, and her vision cleared enough to see her grandfather looking down with an expression of terror and relief, with her mother and Ammond beside him. Someone she didn't know, a guard based on the badge on her harness, still stood in the pool, wet fur dripping and plastered to her body.

Her grandfather rolled her over and held her while coughing wracked her body. When she could finally breathe somewhat normally, she slumped to the floor, exhausted and wheezing, staring at her grandfather's scraped and bloody knees where he'd slid onto the cement, coming to her rescue.

"You really need to stop doing that," her grandfather said. "You've already used up, what, at least five of your nine lives this past year?"

That made her chuckle, which triggered another round of coughing.

Before she could answer, her mother scooped her up and carried her back to the Trauma Center, followed by Ammond and, to her surprise, the guard, although somewhere between when they entered the Trauma Center and when she was placed on a trauma bed, the guard disappeared. Half an hour later, she'd been treated for the remaining water in her lungs, dried off, and dumped unceremoniously back in her room.

Her mother was muttering something fierce, and her tail was lashing as she examined the monitor above the bed.

"I'm sorry. I shouldn't have gone out so far."

Her mother's ears went straight back. "You're sorry?! I'm the one that should be apologizing. I shouldn't have let you go in the pool by yourself until we knew if you could swim or not. You almost drowned! If it weren't for the guard... I didn't even realize you were in trouble." Her mother shuddered in barely controlled horror.

"Mama, it's not your fault. I've been swimming since I was Hope's age. I don't even remember not being able to swim. Swimming wasn't really the problem. I couldn't float. I sank like a rock."

Her mother's tail still lashed, and she kept muttering.

GrandFather showed up then with Hope and her mother's harness, which her mother had left behind in her haste to treat her.

"Mama, I'm fine. No harm done, and now I know I need to be far more careful in the pool."

Her mother growled her thanks to GrandFather for the harness and stormed out, still muttering.

"Now you've gone and done it," her grandfather chuckled.

"Who knew I couldn't float?"

"Duh, you're nothing but skin and bones. What did you expect?" her grandfather replied, handing her a still-damp and sleepy child.

Hope snuggled in and was soon fast asleep in her arms.

GrandFather shook his head and climbed up into the oversized chair. Once situated, he grabbed her jar of nano cream and started slathering it on his skinned knees.

"Thanks for banging up your knees to save me."

"Do me a favor and go a few days without trying to kill yourself. I've barely healed up from the last time," he muttered but softened it with a wink.

"I'll see what I can do, but I can't promise anything," she chuckled as she gently stroked her daughter's soft blond hair. *It's so much like Mitch's. I wonder if she'll be like him, too?* She blanched at the very idea and shoved the thought away hard, hating herself for even thinking it.

"Do you want to talk about it?" GrandFather asked.

"No. Not really."

He sighed but surprisingly didn't press the issue. They chatted quietly about unimportant things while Hope slept for about an hour, and then he left, taking Hope with him.

She hated to see her daughter go, but she wasn't ready to take care of her on her own. She rolled over and curled around a pillow, lost in thought about everything that had happened over the past year and a half. She was still curled around her pillow when her mother arrived with their dinner, which included another cookie. She shoved her racing thoughts aside and sat up to eat. Her mother's emotions were neatly tucked behind her mask again, but her tail thwapped rhythmically with impatience, and she checked her tablet regularly.

They were about halfway through their meal when her mother's tablet dinged with the same low tones as before, and she took a deep breath before opening it.

Little Flower sighed with relief when the tension left her mother's body.

"It's from your father. They were able to save her paw and clear out much of the infection, and several of her other vitals are starting to improve," her mother signed a moment later and went back to reading. "They're unsure about one of the bones in her paw. It was an awkward break, so it might need further surgery later if it doesn't heal right."

They celebrated the good news by sharing the cookie.

After dinner, her mother left to review the latest information sent by Marsee's healers, so she pulled out the coloring book again. She'd only been drawing for five or ten minutes when Ammond stopped in and brought her a tracing book used to help teach cubs how to write in Saber for her to practice with and checked out what she'd done so far.

"I haven't finished the page yet. It's taking a lot longer than I thought it would."

He smiled at her. "I'm very impressed at what you've accomplished so far."

She squinted at him, unsure if he was being serious or not.

"I'm serious. If you keep putting this much effort into everything as you did today, you'll be back to your old self far sooner than you think," he replied.

"Do you really think so, or are you just trying to keep my hopes up?"

"If you want it bad enough, you'll be even better," he replied. "Take your drawing, for example. Say the shake doesn't quite go away. It's clear to me you haven't lost the concepts behind good artwork from what you've done so far, so change up what you use to draw. I know you prefer to use pencils, but paint or even graphic arts might be more forgiving and allow you to work around those limitations. You might find you're an even better artist in ways you might not have even tried before. Don't be afraid to explore. Just because you struggle in one area doesn't mean you'll be horrible in another."

She raised her brows to consider and looked back down at her coloring. Could she figure out a way to make the shakiness work with her drawing? She looked back up at him. "Thanks, I'll consider it."

Shortly after he left, her mother arrived with a small box, looking decidedly annoyed.

Little Flower opened it and found what looked like nothing more than a metallic ring. "What is it?"

"It's a mask that will allow you to breathe underwater," her mother replied. "The guard who rescued you dropped it off a few minutes ago." With that, her mother turned and stormed out.

Chuckling at her mother's annoyed expression, she set the mask aside and pulled out her coloring book. She colored until her hand cramped again. Setting everything aside, she adjusted the bed so it was flat and curled up on her side, wrapping herself around a pillow and tried to fall asleep, but her back was cold, and she really wanted to snuggle into her sister's warm fur, like she used to, but her sister wasn't there, and even if she was, she'd lost all of her fur thanks to that awful scum-sucker. She grabbed the blanket at the foot of the bed and tried rolling it up behind her, but it didn't help. She flipped over and over again, but no matter what she tried, she couldn't get comfortable.

For months, she'd either been so exhausted that the moment she laid down, she fell right to sleep or had been cradled by Marsee as she cried out the day's frustrations, but now she couldn't sleep, and every time she closed her eyes, she was seeing Damon drag her grandfather off, or envisioning what Marsee had gone through.

She needed to talk to someone, but right now, she was all alone. Her mother had gone who knows where, probably back to her office to work on Marsee's treatment, or for all she knew, out for a run to work off some of her own frustration, and really, Marsee was the one she needed to talk to. Marsee was the only one she'd been able to open up to and the only one who was ever able to chase away her demons. She hated being here, a universe away, and not being able to do the same for her sister. Her mother at least could help with the medical aspect of Marsee's issues. All she could do was lay there and worry, and the beeps and noises of the ward, after living in silence for so long, were irritating.

With a frustrated growl, she slid off her bed and slowly made her way down to her mother's office. As expected, her mother was there, leaning over her tablet, head propped up by one arm.

"Mama," she called out, knocking on the door.

Her mother looked up, surprised to see her there. "Hey, what's up? Are you feeling okay?"

"I can't sleep," she said. "I miss Marsee. I'm so worried about her, and I'm scared. Every time I close my eyes, I see Damon drag off GrandFather, and Marsee isn't here to protect my back and scare away the nightmares like she used to. And, well, I can't believe I'm saying this, but it's too loud in here. Could you come lay down with me until I fall asleep, or maybe give me something?"

Her mother looked at her sadly but nodded. She picked her up and carried her first to the supply closet, grabbed the sedative, and then brought her back to her room and set the hypo down on the table next to the bed. But rather than sedating her, her mother climbed onto the bed, curled up, and helped her find a comfortable spot. Once she settled, her mother started purring, and when, after an hour, she still hadn't fallen asleep, finally gave her the sedative.

CHAPTER 20

Little Flower: Horse Play

When Little Flower woke the next morning, she was still wrapped in her mother's embrace. Her mother was sound asleep and snoring. She lay there feeling warm and protected, but it wasn't quite the same as waking up in Marsee's arms. Her mother was too big, and she didn't fit quite right.

Why do I miss Marsee so much? she wondered. *Is it just because I'm so worried about her?*

She was lying there trying to make sense of her rambling thoughts when Ammond appeared at the door and smiled softly at them. She could see the love he had for her mother in his old eyes.

"Let her sleep. She needs it, but I wanted to let you know that Marsee improved significantly overnight. The infection in her hand is finally receding. They've cautiously changed her condition from critical to serious, and they think she's going to make it. They're planning to see if they can wake her soon."

Tears started streaming down her face. "Thank you," she signed and carefully wiped the tears from her eyes, trying not to wake her mother.

He nodded and left.

It was probably an hour later before she had to wake her mother. She really had to pee. As she rolled over, her mother woke. When she told her the good news, her mother nearly crushed her with a hug.

She had to push her away. "Mama, if you keep squeezing like that, I'm going to pee all over you!"

Her mother laughed and then surprised her by climbing off the bed and carrying her over to the hole of muck rather than making her walk. She didn't care. She really had to go. While she was in the bathroom, her mother ran to her office and returned carrying her tablet. Her whiskers were buried in the report, reading up on the latest information, but there was a grin a mile wide on her mother's face.

"She's improved even more in the last hour, and they've changed her condition again from serious to stable!"

"That's wonderful! Shall we go for a walk before breakfast, then? Work up an appetite?" Little Flower asked.

Her mother grinned and then squinted at her. "Is this newfound enthusiasm for doing laps because you want to go to the Water World or because you want to go riding?"

"Both," she replied, "and I want to go back to the pool today and try out that mask."

Her mother's tail twitched slightly with consideration. "If you can make it around the loop without falling, I'll get you another cookie with your breakfast."

"Two cookies," she glared. "I'm hungry."

"One per lap," her mother countered, eyes now glinting with mischief.

"One per lap and an extra if I don't fall during that lap."

Her mother flicked an ear back slightly as she considered the offer, then held out her tail. "Deal."

She grinned and shook the offered tail once before taking off. She knew she was being bribed with treats, but the cookies were more than worth it and far better motivation than a claw to the back of the leg.

She not only managed not to fall, but she managed almost two laps in the same amount of time before her legs gave out. She was only two rooms away, but her mother was pleased enough with her effort that she decided to count it anyway.

Later that morning, she was busy coloring, for lack of anything better to do, when her mother and grandfather walked in with mischievous smiles on their faces. They were each carrying a box.

"A package arrived for you," her grandfather said as her mother handed her a square box.

Little Flower set her coloring book and pencils aside and opened the box, revealing a very funny-looking helmet. She put it on and was trying to figure out how to adjust it when she suddenly felt it shift and form around her head until it fit perfectly.

"Now, if we can just get you to wear that all the time," her mother signed with a scowl.

Little Flower rolled her eyes but looked back into the box as there was something else in there. She picked it up to reveal what looked like nothing more than a belt loop with a small canister on the back. There was also a piece of paper inside. She pulled that out and read the Saber script. There were several words she didn't know, so she handed it off to her mother.

"It says to put this on around your waist, and if it detects a fall, it will wrap you in an airbag. There's a button on the end to turn it on. Push the same button to turn it off or deactivate it after a fall."

GrandFather set his box down and took the belt from her. "Let's try it out," he said, putting it on around his waist and walking out into the hallway where there was more room. He pushed the button and then tried jumping. Nothing happened. Apparently, not enough motion. "Myra, pick me up and drop me," he signed and motioned to the height he wanted.

She flicked her ears back. "You must be joking," her mother replied.

"No, I'm not. We need to know what height and speed will trigger it. If I'm going to trust my granddaughter's life with this thing, I want to make sure it'll work, and if something does go wrong, I'm right here to be treated. It might hurt, but I've fallen from that height without injury before. If it can't protect me from a straight drop, I'm not even going to attempt anything at speed, and this is about the equivalent of Buster's height."

Her mother frowned but walked over, carefully picked him up, held her arms out, and let go. The instant she did, a bright orange bag exploded around him, and GrandFather bounced and rolled down the hall. Myra stopped him, and the bag deflated to reveal GrandFather lying on the ground, laughing. She immediately started scanning him for injuries, but he waved her away.

"I'm unhurt. We'll need to get Buster used to this, but it was effective, at least from a straight drop. We'll still need to try this out at a higher velocity, such as having you throw me, which would simulate Little Flower getting bucked off."

"I am not throwing you. Don't even ask. You're not recovered enough for that," her mother replied with some force and kept scanning.

GrandFather ignored her, climbed back to his feet, and took the belt off as he walked back into the room. "No worries. I'll figure something else out. Now for my surprise," he said, tossing the belt on the bed and handing her the other box.

She opened it to find a new set of riding clothes, a pair of brand-new riding boots, and a padded vest. "So, does this mean I can go riding now?"

"Well, do you think you're up to making it to the barn?" her mother asked, "And, do you promise not to hurt yourself today, or at least *try* not to?"

"I think I can. It's not that far from here. It's worth a try. If I fall on the way over or take a break, does that still count?"

Her mother considered it. "You're lucky. I'm in a good mood right now, so yes, but I'd feel a lot better if you *didn't* fall."

"I'd feel a lot better if *I* didn't fall, too," Little Flower signed. "My butt is still bruised from yesterday. I have absolutely no padding there anymore. I'm not sure about walking over there in these boots, though." She lifted up the boot to look at the heel. It wasn't a very tall heel, just enough to protect her foot from slipping through the stirrups, but she was barely stable on flat feet, and there was very little tread. "My shoes were still in Marsee's room."

"I'll check to see if they were damaged or not while you change," her grandfather said and disappeared. A trip to the bathroom and a quick change, and she was ready. GrandFather took longer than expected to return, however. So, while she waited, she tried walking in the boots. As expected, she was wobbly, and she needed her mother's help to keep her balance, but they were the most comfortable pair of riding boots she'd ever owned.

"We're going to use these boots for your laps later, I think. Make things a little more challenging for you."

She rolled her eyes. "Mama, these boots are not made for walking." This only confused her mother. "Sorry, Hue-man reference. It's an old song." She signed what she could remember of it.

Her mother laughed, and an almost feral glint appeared in her expression. "Sounds to me like you should wear them to the trial."

"Does that mean I can go?" she asked, hopeful.

"No, it does not. But if you keep improving and working hard like you have these past two days *and* avoid trying to break your neck or drown yourself, maybe."

Little Flower laughed and promised she would try.

A few minutes later, GrandFather returned. "Sorry. It took me a while to find them, and then the laces were cut. I had to run over to the Guild for a new set. Hope you like purple!" He lifted the shoes up to show her.

"Love it!" she said, swapping out the boots for the shoes. "Everything else fits perfectly. Thank you!"

It took her over an hour to make it to the barn with GrandFather, but she did it. She only fell twice on the hill but had to stop several times to rest as it was a lot farther than she thought. Her mother had work to do but wanted to watch her ride. Since they knew it would take her a long time to make her way over, they decided to send a message when she was about ready to try riding. On the way, they stopped and talked about the various Earth creatures they were passing. She was still amazed to see a giraffe and just how friendly it was, too. Her grandfather thought it must have been someone's pet or possibly part of a rescue or small zoo, which New Hope was becoming.

As evidence of that, there was a small cubs' tour from the school in Sand Dune present, about twenty wiggly cubs, along with their teachers and chaperones. Nazari was directing the tour, and they stopped to watch part of it. Most of the cubs were no bigger than she was, which meant they were young, and they acted just like a group of kindergarteners.

"Here we have two geese by the names of George and Matilda and their offspring. Don't let their small size and fluffy appearance fool you. Out of all the creatures rescued from Earth, these are the most dangerous."

"Are they poisonous?" one of the cubs signed.

"No. Poisonous means that they would make us sick if we bite them. Venomous means that we would get sick if they bite us. They are neither, but they're faster than they look, and their beaks are very painful. I've been informed that civilizations on Earth used geese as guards throughout their history as well as a food source."

"Nuh-uh," another cub signed. "Those tiny things are guards?"

"So I've been told. They're very loud when there's a threat, and even though I've been bitten by them several times, I didn't believe it entirely until yesterday morning when I witnessed none other than the Senior Honor Guard's Second running for his life from them, tail tucked between his legs."

Nazari tucked her tail between her legs and made an expression of panic that made all the cubs laugh.

"What was he doing in the pen?" GrandFather asked.

"I bet him ten credits he couldn't get one of Matilda's eggs away from her without being bitten," Nazari replied.

"Did you win?" one of the teachers asked, tail curled.

Nazari grinned. "I never make a bet I won't win. If you see him, be sure to ask how his tail is feeling."

After the laughter died down, Nazari continued telling the cubs about the geese.

GrandFather leaned over to her. "I'm pretty sure those two geese were from our farm, too. Our neighbors down the road moved to Florida about a month before and left them behind. We called them Thanksgiving and Christmas dinner. Unfortunately, their offspring seemed to have inherited their attitude."

"Well, they'll need it here," Little Flower replied.

"True. I just wish Ben had survived and not them."

She gave him a hug and followed after Nazari as the tour moved down to the next pen.

The cubs asked a million questions, which Nazari could barely keep up with, and it was all the teachers could do to keep them from running off.

"Who knew herding cats could be so difficult," she said to her grandfather as they kept walking.

He laughed. "I thought keeping up with Hope was hard enough. I don't know how they manage with litters of five or more."

"With a lot of help and usually several partners, according to Marsee. When you've got half a dozen litter-mates to help out with the care, it's a lot easier."

He looked at her quizzically, and she explained what Marsee had told her about how partnership normally worked for the Sabers. "Ahh, that makes so much more sense. I've wondered why some of the females were being called Papa by their cubs."

"So what's going on with you and Henry?" she asked, and he immediately blushed like a schoolboy with his first crush. She gave him a hug. "I'm really happy for you. I like Henry, and I think Grampa Ben would approve. So have you, you know?"

If anything, her grandfather blushed even more.

"You have!" she crowed. "So, how was it?"

"A gentleman never kisses and tells," he said, but he was smiling so hard, she knew.

"So that explains why you're moving so slowly this morning," she teased.

"Jessica!" he yelped in embarrassment.

She laughed but then immediately sobered as a thought occurred to her.

"What's the matter, pumpkin?" he asked.

"I just realized I'll probably never get to experience that. I've met all the men, and I'm not even remotely attracted to any of them, and well, frankly, the idea of 'mating' with them terrifies me. I'm not sure I could without seeing *him* every time."

"What about the women? Are you attracted to any of them?"

"Not that I've noticed. There's no one my age, and most of the others still see me as a child anyway."

"Well, you don't exactly have a lot of people to choose from. None of us do, but it could just be that you're demisexual. You'll need to form a close attachment to someone before you could ever feel comfortable having a more intimate relationship with them, but even if you're asexual, that's okay, too. You won't need to have sex if you want to have another child someday, and you don't need another person to feel that way if that's what you want to experience. As far as having a partner, why not do what the Sabers do and find someone you want to raise Hope with? Maybe one of the other single women or even your sister. You're practically litter-mates, and that would fit with their customs. For that matter, if you wanted to have a more intimate relationship someday with her, you wouldn't have to worry about any genetic issues with cubs or STDs. Plus, she's changed more of Hope's poopy diapers than any of us."

She looked at her grandfather in surprise and then considered what he had to say. Marsee was her adopted sister, but only recently, and they were two entirely different species with two very different cultures and customs. The Sabers didn't even have any restrictions on mating with their siblings or littermates because the Healers were needed to manage conception since the species had lost true males millennia before, and any genetic issues could easily be avoided. Every single Saber was a test tube baby. The only restrictions they had, as far as she could tell, were between parent and child. That being said, the females only went into heat twice in their lives. Marsee would have to mate with one of her own kind, but they already had far more of a physical relationship than she ever had with anyone, family or friend, back on Earth, even though there was nothing remotely sexual about it. She needed physical contact to counteract the trauma of her isolation at the agency, and Marsee seemed to want and need just as much.

"You're seriously okay with that?" she asked.

"Why wouldn't I be? As long as it's consensual. For most of my life, I could have been arrested for partnering with Ben for both his sex and race. Plus, as far as I can tell, there are no racial restrictions among the other species, and within our own species, they somehow managed to rescue a rather wide variety of cultures and beliefs. From the conversations I've had and overheard, I wouldn't be surprised if there weren't more than a few cross-species relationships by the end of the year." He blushed and then grinned. "You know, Ben had quite the...uh...collection of alien romance novels."

She nearly fell over in surprise. "You're joking?"

He shook his head. "He claimed they belonged to your grandmother, but more than a few were added to the collection every year. He once told me he bought them in memory of her. It certainly made for some interesting evenings, that's for sure. If you're interested, there are already a few that have been written, although none of them have made it into the library or over to Marsee to translate. I'll send you a copy, although I'll warn you. You'll never look at the Water Sprites the same way again."

She snorted and could just imagine.

They walked in silence the rest of the way, each completely lost in their own thoughts, thoughts that shifted as they walked past the two guards now stationed outside and reminded her of the horror of the past few days. She expected to be challenged, but they only nodded to them as they approached. Once they were inside, she sat on the bench by the door to change into her boots and rest for a bit. Her legs were screaming from the effort of the walk, and she rubbed at them to try and stop the myriad of tiny muscle twitches that started the moment she sat down.

GrandFather must have seen her wince as he pursed his lips. "I'll saddle and groom him this time, but next time you're helping. You know the rules," he said before disappearing down the aisle.

That made her both laugh and sigh with the reminder of Grampa Ben and the rules of the barn back home. Just about every time she'd arrived at the barn, there had been a muck rake waiting for her outside Buster's stall. She wasn't sure she could manage to maintain her balance enough to muck the stall, but she had no doubt her grandfather would require it eventually, even if that meant she fell face-first into a pile of horse manure. Once her boots were on, she shifted to lean against the back of the bench to wait. The sounds of the barn made her smile again, and she felt herself relax as she looked around at the airy and well-maintained space. *Grampa Ben would have loved it here.*

While she waited, she watched as the tour entered the barn, and Nazari began telling them about the various habitats for the creatures. A few minutes later, they disappeared down another aisle, followed a minute or two later by a pair of guards who entered and took off in different directions on patrol. She frowned at the need for the guards, had hoped that they'd never need them, and recognized that what happened to her likely wouldn't have happened if she'd allowed the guards in the first place.

"Every decision you make, Councilor..." she muttered under her breath and then wondered if she'd ever feel safe here again and if her father now intended a permanent guard, regardless of what the rest of the Council decided, or if they were only here until the trial and Damon was dealt with.

It wasn't long before she heard the familiar clip-clop of Buster's large hoofs coming towards her. She grinned with happiness at the sound, so much a part of her childhood and filled with nothing but good memories that they shoved the constant fear she now had into the background.

She turned her head and watched as they appeared around the corner. Out of all the creatures rescued, she was beyond grateful that

Buster had been one of them. They'd be dead now if it weren't for this horse, but he had been part of her life since before she could remember.

"I sent your mother a message, and I'll meet you in the arena," he said as they approached.

"What? No ride over?" she asked.

"Nope. Buster needs to work off a little energy before you get on him," he replied, coming to a stop next to her.

Buster was half asleep, head bobbing and lower lip drooping.

She slid carefully off the bench and stood, reaching out to give him a scratch. His head drooped lower, and his eyes started to close with the attention. "If you work any more energy off him, he's going to fall asleep while I'm riding."

Her grandfather laughed. "He may be now, but I want that safety belt of yours. The last thing we need is for it to go off and for Buster to decide you're a sand spinner."

She handed him the belt, and he left her behind to make her own way, with Buster slowly clopping along beside him, still half asleep. Twenty minutes or so later, she made her way over to the arena, thankful for the wall to hold onto. GrandFather was still free-lunging Buster in the arena, and the horse was cantering around the far side. She watched for a moment, catching her breath, as his powerful muscles dug into the sand. She loved watching horses run. There was something so primal and free about them.

"Gate!" she called out, letting him know she was there.

Her grandfather brought Buster down to a walk and called him over as she made her way awkwardly in through the large swinging gate and latched it behind her. She wobbled hard in the soft-packed dirt and held tightly to the wall as she made her way over to the mounting block. She smiled when she saw it. It was tall enough for her to be able to swing her leg over Buster's back and sit down rather than trying to climb up, and there was even a railing for her to hold onto.

She made it there about the same time GrandFather did with Buster. "I'm really glad there's a railing," she said.

"Thank Henry. He added it this morning when he saw how hard you struggled with the steps in the hot tub last night."

"I will," she replied and stared at the four large steps she still needed to climb. "I think I'm going to need help with these stairs, though. Will you walk behind me so I don't fall over backwards with these boots?"

"Of course, but have a seat for now. We have some spook training to do first," he replied and then turned towards the gate. "Hey, Henry! We're ready for you!"

Henry showed up a minute later and walked in. "Mornin' Little Flower," Henry said as he walked over and picked up the belt that was lying on the top of the mounting block and peered dubiously at it. "So, how does this thing work anyway?"

"Push the button on the end of that canister to turn it on or off," GrandFather said.

Henry found the button, pushed it, shrugged, and put it on before hopping up the stairs of the mounting block. "Ready?" he asked GrandFather.

GrandFather nodded, so Henry jumped off. An instant before he hit, the bag exploded around him, and he rolled off towards Buster.

Buster snorted loudly at it and lifted his head, but other than that, he didn't even so much as take a step back.

A few moments later, the bag deactivated, and Henry reappeared, chuckling. "That was an experience. How'd he do?"

"Snorted, but that's all," GrandFather replied.

"Best dang horse I've ever seen. You sure you won't sell him to me?"

"Nope, still not for sale."

Little Flower laughed. "I guess you'll just have to marry my grandfather." She had no idea a man with such dark skin could visibly blush, but blush, he did.

GrandFather crossed his arms and scowled at Henry. "So *that's* why you've been so friendly lately. You just want me for my horse!"

"What can I say? I missed riding," Henry retorted.

It was GrandFather's turn to blush and stammer, and she nearly fell off the step she was sitting on, howling with laughter.

"Keep it up, missy, and I'll bring Buster back to his stall," Grand-Father growled at her.

"That's what he said!" she replied and then did fall off the step, laughing.

GrandFather glared at her, but he was having a hard time keeping a straight face, as was Henry.

Buster looked positively bored.

"Alright, time to see how well that belt really works," Henry said after helping her back onto the step. He walked over, swung himself up into the saddle, and took off across the arena, testing out various gates to make sure the belt wouldn't go off accidentally. Then, when he was in the middle of the arena, he purposely rolled off the saddle. The airbag deployed, and Henry rolled nearly a quarter of the way across the arena before he stopped.

Buster shifted away slightly and came to a stop after Henry fell off, snorted, walked over to the ball, and sniffed at it. He snorted again when Henry deactivated the belt and then nudged him with his big nose as if to say, 'What are you doing down there?'

It took Henry a few tries to stand up and walk straight, but he was laughing and unhurt. "That was rather fun, all things considered. Wish I had one of these when I was in the rodeo."

"Alright, Jess, your turn," her grandfather said and helped her stand up.

Henry handed her the belt, which she put on and adjusted, and then GrandFather used that to help support her on the way up. It was a good thing he was there, as she almost pitched over backwards on the third step. They were even taller than she'd thought, and it took every bit of strength to step up, even with her grandfather's help. Henry brought Buster over and side-stepped him neatly into position. GrandFather helped her on, and then he and Henry both adjusted the stirrups so they fit her.

"Do you want us to walk with you first, or do you want to try it on your own?" GrandFather asked.

After the fiasco of the day before, she was not taking any chances. "I'd rather you walked first so I can see how well I can balance and not have to worry about steering."

He walked down the mounting block and flipped the reins back over so he could hold them. "Ready?"

She grabbed a fistful of Buster's long, wavy-blonde mane, took a deep breath to control her nerves, and nodded.

GrandFather clucked Buster forward.

Two steps in, she almost fell, but Henry caught her and steadied her.

They made their slow way around the arena, and by the time they were back to the mounting block, she felt like her balance was good enough to try it on her own. GrandFather flipped the reins back over, and they did another lap, with her in control, but the two continued walking on either side for protection. A second lap completed, she told them she felt good and started off on her own and tried a very gentle figure eight.

Buster plodded along, head drooped and half asleep, bored with how easy of a task he was being given but willing and responsive anyway.

She almost lost it with the first turn but managed to catch herself and readjust, and when she turned to walk back to the mounting block, she looked up and saw that there was a crowd of kindergarten Sabers all clamoring to see over the gate. The teachers were standing behind them, with their jaws all dropped in absolute astonishment. She waved and then changed her directions to walk over to the gate.

Buster lifted his head at the crowd, ears forward, but she didn't sense any nervousness from him. If anything, he picked his pace. She knew he liked children and briefly wondered if he realized these were children, too.

When she stopped, close enough for the cubs to pat Buster, she dropped the reigns so she could sign. "This is Buster. He belonged to my grandfather Ben before."

"This is *the* Buster? The one that ran fifty leagues to save Little Flower?" one of the cubs signed.

"He is. I'm Little Flower," she replied, and everyone's eyes lit up, and their ears flicked forward.

"I told you it was her!" one of the other cubs signed.

"It's okay. I probably look very different without my hair and wearing this helmet. That taller man over there is Henry Curtis. He's the one who rode Buster to save us, and the other man is James O'Neil, my grandfather."

"But he's no bigger than we are! How could he have gone fifty leagues without getting eaten!" another cub signed.

"The predators all took one look at him and said, 'Nope, he might try to ride us too. We leave that one alone,'" she signed back, and they all laughed.

Buster shifted forward and leaned his big head over the side of the arena door, and one of the cubs closest reached up and carefully pat him. Buster closed his eyes in contentment and let out a little groan, not even the least bit concerned about the wall of furry predators in front of him.

"Can we ride Buster?" another cub asked, and there was a flurry of 'pleases' and 'can wes?' from the rest of the group.

She looked back at GrandFather to see what he thought, and he walked over.

"I am not sure how he would tolerate a Saber on his back. He seems to have no issue here, but he is still a prey animal," GrandFather replied. The look of disappointment on the group clearly broke him. "But, we can try."

Buster snorted as the cubs all cheered.

"Sucker," she teased her grandfather.

He grinned and looked up at her with a shrug. "Now, while Henry helps Little Flower down, there are some ground rules..."

She took that as her cue to dismount and backed Buster away from the door and over to Henry. Rather than helping her step off onto the mounting block, Henry caught her and spun her around to sit on the edge. She shifted out of the way as GrandFather led the cub who had first asked in.

"I doubt your helmet will fit, but can we have the belt?" her grandfather asked. "I really don't want an angry Saber after me if Buster spooks and their cub gets hurt."

She unhooked it, and he put it on the cub.

"This will protect you if you fall," he told the cub.

"I can land safely from twice that height," the cub said. "I'm really good at jumping."

"I'm sure you can. This is added protection for me. I don't want your Mama mad at me if you get hurt."

"Oh. Yeah, that's probably a good idea. My mama's pretty scary when she's mad," the cub replied.

I'm sure she is, Little Flower thought with a chuckle. She knew she'd never forget the ferocity of her mother leaping over her to capture Damon or the time she'd pounced on Marcus to protect Marsee.

"Okay, let's see how he does with you up here. Go ahead and give him a pat on his side so he knows you're there. Remember, no claws."

The cub did, and Buster didn't so much as twitch.

"Alright, he seems to like you. Go ahead and grab the saddle and swing a leg over, nice and slowly."

Buster looked up at the weight on his back, but other than that, he didn't seem to care.

GrandFather quickly ran down. The Saber's much wider feet didn't fit in the stirrups, so the cub just put a few claws in for balance, and GrandFather started leading Buster around.

Fifteen or twenty trips later, everyone had their turn, and the first cub spoke up again. "Thank you very much, GrandFather! That was a lot of fun! I was wondering. Could we see what Buster can really do?"

"Henry, do you want to take this one?" GrandFather asked. "I'm not cleared for riding yet."

Well, horseback riding anyway, Little Flower thought with an audible snort. They both glared at her, but she just grinned wickedly back.

Blushing slightly, Henry nodded and then surprised everyone by taking both the saddle and reins off. Grabbing a fistful of mane, he swung himself up and on and took off at a full gallop around the arena.

Halfway around, he turned Buster into the center, changed leads, and took off again in the other direction. He came to a sliding stop and then had him back up, spin around, and take off in the other direction. He stopped again and had Buster sidestep several paces before turning and walking back to the middle of the arena. He jumped off and then had Buster take a bow before walking back over to the group.

Buster followed without Henry even having a halter or lead on him. Even GrandFather seemed impressed.

Everyone cheered, and she saw one of the cubs sign, 'How did he do that?' and another, 'I want to be able to do that. I wonder if Mama would get me a horse.'

Oh, that poor mother. Horse crazy at first sight, she thought.

"When did you teach him all that?" GrandFather asked in English.

Henry chuckled but didn't answer.

GrandFather glared at Henry. "You *are* trying to steal my horse, aren't you?"

Henry just chuckled again.

"Alright, cubs. We have more to see. Tell everyone thank you," one of the teachers signed.

A chorus of disappointed 'Awwws' followed by signs of 'thank yous' came, and the teachers herded their charges back out the door.

As she watched them leave, she chuckled over the fact that the Saber's groan of disappointment was apparently the same between their species. *I wonder if that's a universal constant, too?*

When she turned back to look at her grandfather, he was still sending daggers in Henry's direction, and Henry was having a hard time keeping a straight face.

"Oh, get a room, you too," she teased.

"Jessica!" Her grandfather's scowl redirected towards her as his face darkened with another blush.

Howling with laughter, she nearly fell off the mounting block again.

CHAPTER 21

Jer: Hey Papa

Outside the vigil grew until Clear Seas was forced to close the city. Jer often found himself staring out the window at the crowd, praying along with the religious speakers, knowing he should be working, but he couldn't make himself leave the room. If she didn't make it, he wanted to be there with her. There were several close calls as Marsee's heart faltered before her new one was ready, but she survived. The infection and swelling in her paw made Jer sick to look at, and he could smell it, even through the static shield. He wished he could hold her good paw, but the healers wouldn't allow it.

Clear Seas asked permission to give updates on Marsee's status, and he agreed, with restrictions. He watched from the window the first time, not willing to leave Marsee's room, and the flash of blue at Clear Seas' words that she'd survived her first surgery nearly blinded him. The wave of sadness and grief as Clear Seas spoke of her other injuries and their uncertainty of her survival nearly crushed him, and he'd had to turn away.

He hadn't watched after that, but even still, he'd been able to see the flash of blue each time Clear Seas informed the crowd that she was still alive. Occasionally, there was an unexpected flash of blue, and he checked those out to see that someone had been released. He smiled at the love the crowd gave them, but those were few and far between. Most had injuries as severe as Marsee, if not worse: burns, broken bones, malnutrition, and infection, and they'd be recovering for some time.

Finally, several local days later, the Senior Healer deemed Marsee recovered enough to wake her for a short time so they could assess the damage to her brain and start figuring out what they needed to do next. She fully expected that Marsee would be in significant pain, but a pain block would prevent them from finding out how systemic her injuries were. They all held their breath as the Healer applied the anti-sedative and waited for it to clear Marsee's system.

"Marsee, sweetheart, can you hear me?" Jer asked, carefully taking her good paw in his, allowed for the first time.

Marsee's eyes fluttered open, "Hey, Papa," she whispered.

It was all he could do to keep from crying out in joy. They were the two most beautiful words he'd ever heard. He watched her eyes closely, but he saw no sign of an internal struggle, and her claws had remained sheathed. "How are you feeling?" he asked.

"I'm okay. Really tired. Is Stormy okay? And the others?"

"They're fine. We found Petra in the cave, too," Jer replied. "She was injured, but she'll recover."

Marsee closed her eyes and sighed with relief. "Oh good."

Her voice trailed off, and for a moment, he thought she'd fallen back to sleep.

The Senior Healer swam up and lightly touched Marsee's arm.

Marsee opened her eyes again and shifted her gaze to look at the healer.

"Marsee, I need to examine you to see how badly you've been injured. If the pain gets too bad, let me know."

Marsee nodded slightly.

His hope soared as she responded to the tests. She was moving, responding, and following instructions, if slowly. She was weak, but it was far better than where Little Flower had been when she'd woken from her coma, at least from his perspective.

When the Healer was done, she motioned that they could continue visiting and swam back to confer with the other healers in the room.

Ellie swam up, "Hey there. Who said you could take a vacation?"

The slightest of grins crossed Marsee's face, and her tail curled at her mentor's teasing. "I did. I outrank you now. If I remember correctly, I'm pretty sure I demoted you."

Ellie burst out laughing. "That you did, and I've heard you did a fine job in my place, too."

"I suppose I should fix that. Poof, you're a...whatever you want again." Marsee yawned and gave a small, tired wave of her injured paw.

"You're so kind," Ellie said with a smile. "I quite liked being an apprentice again. Maybe I'll stick with that."

"You demoted Ellie?" Jer asked.

Marsee shifted her eyes towards him again. "Yeah, she was being really annoying." This made the whole room laugh. She chuckled slightly with them but then frowned.

"Is the pain getting to be too much for you?" he asked.

"No. I don't hurt like before. That was awful. Maybe a little achy. Mostly, I just feel weird, hollow, and really weak."

"Well, you haven't eaten for about four days," Jer replied.

"Four?! Tell Opal I'm going to need more than a few fire sticks then." She let out another yawn. "I think I'm going to go back to sleep now." She was asleep almost before she'd finished saying it.

Jer turned to the Senior Healer with a huge smile on his face, but the Healer wasn't smiling. "What's wrong?" he asked.

"Marsee appears to have lost her reflexes. She didn't blink when I flicked my hand near her face or even twitch when I touched her eyelid. Nor did she react normally to the small electric jolt I gave her. She said she felt my hand, but she didn't jerk her hand away as most people would. She should be in severe pain, and I honestly expected her to start screaming or writhing the moment we woke her, but she didn't even make a face like she was trying to hide being in pain, and she just told you she only ached a little."

"She said she was in a lot of pain before. Maybe it just doesn't seem as bad compared to what Rip did."

"Hold out your hand, Councilor."

He did, afraid he was going to be zapped like Clear Seas had the other day, but when she touched him, he just yelped and pulled his hand away, shaking it to clear the tingles in his fingers.

"Even if it wasn't painful, she should have at least had a small flinch."

"So what does this mean for her?" he asked.

"Well, without being able to feel pain or react instinctively, something could easily get in her eye and blind her because she won't react to it or even know if there's something in her eye to be removed. She might not remove her hand if she placed it on something hot and could get far more serious burns, or she might not recognize a severe injury like a broken bone. She's certainly not reacting to her bad paw and even moved it without the slightest show of pain. We don't know what else she might be missing and might not for a while. I'll have a team research if anyone else has had issues like hers before and see what we can do for her. I know I've never seen anything like it among my own species. On the positive side, though, she can still feel and move her fingers on her injured hand and has strength in all of her limbs, so I expect she'll be able to move normally once her strength returns. She's speaking well, and her memories appear to be intact, which is a good sign that there aren't any major cognitive impairments. Overall, her vitals are improving, so I believe she's going to pull through. I'll have someone bring something back for her to eat when she wakes up next, but no fire sticks. Her system isn't ready for it, and she'll be on a strict diet for several weeks at least. Absolutely no exceptions."

Jer sighed with relief. He would take it. He'd been afraid she'd be so much worse. "Thank you. She's awake and talking, and that's enough for right now. We'll figure out the rest when she's stronger. I suppose I should probably let the crowd know." After taking another long look at Marsee, he swam out.

Avery and Tamarin were grinning from ear to ear, and he smiled at them before swimming on. He stopped at each honor guard station to thank them and let them know she was awake and that the Senior Healer believed she was going to pull through. He was not going to get tired of saying that any time soon.

As he swam out, the crowd stilled and turned to face him. It was the first time he'd left the Trauma Center since she'd gone in for surgery, and he saw flashes of concern and worry from many of them. "SHE'S AWAKE!" he both yelled and signed.

The crowd roared for several minutes and flashed bright blue with their joy. Then, a wave of silver and purple began to flood the crowd, and their attention shifted as people pointed up at one of the windows.

He turned to look and found Marcus cradling Marsee and holding her up to the window. *She must have been woken by their cheering,* he thought.

In one motion, the crowd bowed deeply with respect. When they rose, she weakly signed 'thank you' before leaning back against Marcus, and he turned and carried her away from the window.

When Jer had their attention again, he called out. "The Senior Healer says she has a long road to recovery ahead of her, but they believe she'll pull through. Thank you so much for your show of support and your prayers. I can't even begin to tell you how much it has meant to all of us. Now, please, go home and get some sleep. I know I intend to."

A combination of happiness and humor flashed through the crowd as his words were carried back. He turned and made his way back inside the Trauma Center and up to her room. Marsee was asleep before he made it back.

"She insisted, and who am I to argue with someone capable of demoting Ellie?" Marcus said when Jer swam in and saw Marsee's sleeping form.

He hoped that moving her hadn't done her any harm, but the healer on duty watching her right now didn't seem concerned. He chuckled and swam over to one of the sleeping nets. He sent Myra a message that Marsee had woken and had even joked with them, knowing that the Senior Healer would send all of the detailed medical information along. That done, Jer closed his eyes and fell instantly into the first real sleep he'd had in nearly a week.

CHAPTER 22

Little Flower: Saber Growth Hormone

"For all those cubs are nearly as tall as us, they still do act an awful lot like children," Henry chuckled after the last of the group had left the arena.

"That's because they *are* children," GrandFather said and turned back to face her. "Jessica, do you want to ride again?"

She going to say yes but frowned with worry as a thought occurred to her. Her mother still hadn't shown up. *Has something happened to Marsee? Mama would tell me if something happened, wouldn't she?* Her breath hitched at the very idea.

GrandFather noticed and pulled her in for a hug. "What's the matter, pumpkin?"

"Mama didn't show up. Something must be wrong with Marsee. Can we go back now?"

He squeezed her tighter before letting go. "Of course, pumpkin. You can ride Buster back."

"Really?" she asked, surprised out of her impending panic.

"Yup," he replied and handed her the belt, which she quickly put on. Then, to her surprise, he only put Buster's halter and lead rope back on and had Henry throw her up on Buster bareback since he still couldn't lift anything heavy. "You just hold on. I'll steer. It'll work your legs as much as the walk back would, if not more."

Henry picked up the saddle and bridle and carried them off to be put away and then followed them all the way to the Trauma Center, where he helped her down. Henry brought Buster back to the barn while GrandFather helped her inside. He'd been right. Her legs were wobbling so much she could barely stand, but the boots didn't help either. Healer Samin was manning the triage booth, staring at them as they entered with the same open-mouthed shock that the school teachers had earlier.

"It's so easy to break the Saber's brains," GrandFather said to her.

She chuckled and turned to Samin. "Do you know where my mother is?"

Samin blinked and shook herself out of her surprise. "Last I knew, she was in her office."

She thanked the healer and kept walking. She could hear the deep rolling rumbles of a fairly animated conversation long before she arrived, but she paused in an instant panic the moment she could peer into her mother's office. Her mother was sitting at her desk, her head held between both paws, grabbing the back of her scruff and staring at her tablet, while both Ammond and Brice were looking at the monitors and frowning.

Something has happened to Marsee, she realized. "Mama?" she squeaked and then lowered her voice. "Mama?"

Her mother looked up, and for a brief moment, there was anguish on her face before it disappeared behind her mask.

"Hey, Little Flower. Come on in. How was your ride?" her mother asked, but Little Flower didn't answer.

"What's wrong with Marsee? Is she..." She couldn't finish.

Her mother took a deep breath. "Marsee's alive. They just woke her up, and she was able to speak and joke with the others before falling back to sleep."

"But..." Little Flower signed, confused. That was wonderful news. *Why are they so upset?*

"But she doesn't have any reflexes," her mother replied.

"What does that mean? Is she paralyzed like I was?"

"No, she appears to have the ability to feel and move her limbs with reasonable strength, considering her other injuries. What it means is that she isn't flinching when something comes near her eyes, and she's not reacting to pain. She should have been screaming with pain from her surgeries and burns, but she was laughing and joking with everyone."

"I don't understand. Wouldn't it be a good thing that she's not in pain?" she asked. "Maybe because she went through so much, her other injuries just don't seem painful."

"No. The healer gave her a slight shock when she didn't react to her other tests, and she didn't even flinch or notice it happened. Not being able to feel pain is very dangerous. You wouldn't know if you cut yourself or broke a bone or even if you were on fire. She'd be more likely to choke on something or have something get in her eyes, too, and we don't know what else might be affected. We might not know until she hurts herself."

"Can you fix it? Like you did with me? Inject her with those nanos?"

"As far as we can tell, there's nothing there for us to fix," her mother said sadly. "That part of her brain is gone."

"So we have to be extra careful. We'll figure it out," Little Flower said dismissively, not really understanding why they were so upset. Marsee could talk and move, which was far more than she'd been able to do for the past two months.

"Little Flower, how much has Marsee told you about our growth spurt?" Ammond asked.

"Just that it's really painful and that you spend a year in a special ward to help manage the pain."

Ammond nodded. "That's what I figured. We don't normally talk about what happens during that year with our cubs because it would be too frightening. Before the Great Awakening, we were much smaller than we are now, honestly, probably not much bigger than Marsee is now, or so our legends say, and our lives were only about as long as yours. One of the scientists of that time was trying to figure out how to treat psychosis, which was a major issue then, especially with the males of our species. We still don't know what causes it, but in the process, that scientist thought they'd figured out a vaccine for it and either messed up or created a breakthrough, depending on which camp you're in. In addition to killing off the males of our species, he ended up extending our lives nearly tenfold, but it caused us to grow much larger than our bodies are designed to support. Our bones end up growing far faster than the rest of us, and we end up needing dozens of surgeries to correct it."

"Yeah, Marsee told me something happened to the males. That's why you get to choose what sex you are and why mating requires a healer to accomplish it. So Marsee won't be in pain through that?"

"No, and that's the problem," her mother replied. "We've found a few instances of people born without the sense of pain, and none of them have ever made it through their growth spurt. Every scar we have is a potential failure point, and she's covered in them. They literally tore themselves apart without knowing about it, and that's assuming they lived long enough even to make it to their growth spurt. In her case, what's really dangerous are her new organs. Printed organs don't grow the way others do, and they'll be the first to fail."

"So you mean…"

Her mother nodded. "Marsee has maybe twenty years left to live, max."

Overcome with emotion, her mother stood and started pacing.

"So why don't you stop the growth spurt, like you do for the males of your species?" her grandfather asked.

Her mother stopped and stared at him and then looked back at Ammond. "Has anyone ever tried that?"

"Not that I'm aware of," he replied. "Aside from this instance, I can't even think of a reason to do that. Not at her age, anyway. I don't know what would happen if we put in an implant before her growth spurt started. I'm assuming it would work the same."

"Jer triggered his early," her mother commented. "He was only thirty, but he wanted to be ready when I came into heat."

Ammond nodded. "Triggering it early is normal, but we don't usually recommend doing so any earlier than that because it means spending more time in the clinic to reach adult sizes."

"We would do that sometimes if a child started puberty too early to stunt the growth of severely disabled children. It made it easier for their parents to care for them when they were older, although many people were adamantly against it, for good reasons, as it also made it easier for the child to be abused by their caregivers," GrandFather said.

"Marsee would never be able to have her own cubs," her mother replied. "She'd be male but far too small for any female to choose during their heat, and she's told me in the past that she doesn't want to be male."

"Can you stop her growth but keep her female?" Little Flower asked.

Myra shook her head, but it was Ammond who spoke first. "Technically, it's possible." Her mother looked at Ammond with surprise. "There's really not much difference between the male and female implant aside from the changes that make the males smell male and react to a female in heat. We could easily give her a female implant and stop her heat, but she'd be far too small to have cubs. We have a hard enough time as it is when fully grown. If she were to have any chance of having genetic offspring, she'd have to have a male implant and find a partner willing to have her cubs."

"She'd be alive, though," Little Flower replied, although her heart broke for Marsee. She knew how much her sister wanted cubs of her own someday.

Her mother continued to stare at Ammond. "I thought it wasn't possible to delay our first heat. Are you telling me I could have waited to have my first litter?"

Ammond nodded. "You could have, but the risks of something happening during that first heat are significantly greater if you wait, on par with a second or third heat. It's far safer to go into heat naturally the first time."

"Why didn't you ever tell me that before?" she asked.

He flicked an ear back. "I figured you already knew from the decade you spent specializing at the mating clinic. I didn't realize it myself until I was researching Sina's birth defect. I'll send you the study I found on it."

Her mother nodded, and they began a mad flurry of conversation and research that was well outside of her ability to understand, so she excused herself and made her way back to her room. She absolutely reeked of horse, and her new riding pants were covered in dirt and horse hair. She threw her clothes into the cleaning unit and showered, reveling in the fact that she was able to do so herself. Then, cleaned and dressed again, she returned to her room, climbed into bed, and grabbed her coloring book to try and process her emotions from the news about Marsee.

Her grandfather had been teasing her about losing several of her nine lives the night before, but in reality, Marsee only had one of her nine lives left. Marsee had been absolutely horrified when she first found out about the human lifespan, and now there was a very real chance that she would likely outlive Marsee by several human lifetimes.

For Marsee, it must feel like she only has a few years left to live, yet to me, she's got sixty or more, which feels like forever. She must be absolutely terrified, or maybe they haven't told her yet. Probably not. I bet they're waiting for her to recover some first. If Mama had told me I only had a year or two to live when I first woke up, I'd have given up a long time ago. I've barely made it through the last two months, and that was only because I had to stay alive to feed Hope. Marsee's not going to have that. She's never going to have that. She's never going to have a partner or mate or have cubs and grand cubs.

GrandFather brought her lunch and left again, but she felt sick to her stomach with worry for Marsee and couldn't eat. Curling around her pillow, she tried to nap, but as tired and sore as she was, she couldn't fall asleep. She looked up at a touch to her shoulder to find her mother sitting beside her bed, looking haggard and barely holding it together.

"Oh gods..." Little Flower signed. "What happened?"

CHAPTER 23

Marsee: All Three Moons

Marsee drifted between awake and asleep for an unknown length of time. Sometimes, she heard people talking. Other times, she dreamt she was back in the cave or fighting Rip Current in the canyon again, and she'd wake with a start, only to fall back to sleep almost immediately.

Eventually, she managed to claw herself awake but didn't open her eyes. Instead, she lay there thinking how surreal it was to be sleeping underwater. There were no pressure points, and at first, she had a hard time telling up from down or even feeling her own body against the warm, soothing water, which was so different from the cooler water they'd used to treat her hypothermia before. The only thing she could really feel was a gentle current traveling from her head to her feet and a slight pressure keeping her in place.

She didn't feel any pain, but her hand felt stiff and numb. She tried to move it but then remembered that there was a cast on it. She felt incredibly weak, and the very idea of doing anything, even opening her eyes, seemed exhausting. She still felt hollow, as if something important was missing, but she couldn't quite pinpoint it, and after a while gave up trying, as her thoughts were slow and sluggish.

She tried not to think about her encounter with Rip or what had happened after. It was too raw, and she was terrified that if she even thought about it, she'd slip back into the void she'd almost lost herself to. Instead, she tried to focus on the feeling of the current and the warm, soothing water around her, but her thoughts kept drifting back to her fights.

The fight with her instinct had felt so real, even though it had just been in her head. She was relieved that Rip was dead and couldn't hurt her or those she cared about ever again, but both wished she'd made him suffer longer and was absolutely horrified by how she'd tortured him before she'd killed him. It had been her right, although others deserved a piece of him, too. She'd managed to rescue Petra and the others in the process, so it had been worth it to get the information, but she didn't like who she'd become in that moment when it had been her desire to see Rip suffer and had reveled in the sounds of his screams and drooled at the taste of his fear. She'd given herself over completely to that part of herself and had nearly succumbed to it. Was she any better than him? Was that her desire or her instincts? Was there any difference? Had she truly beaten it like it had seemed, or would it come back and hurt someone she cared about later? She honestly didn't know, and that terrified her.

Warm and comfortable, it was tempting to fall back to sleep again, but she forced herself to open her eyes and look around the room instead. Her father and Ellie both hung in their separate sleeping nets, sound asleep. Through the open door, she could see Avery floating outside. His body was still, but his ears swiveled to catch the slightest of sounds. She turned her head and found the cloak she'd been given hanging up by the window and a healer she didn't know floating in one of the chair nets, quietly tapping away on a tablet.

"Hey," she whispered.

The healer looked up and smiled at her. "Good morning," the healer signed. "How are you feeling?"

She tried to sign back, but the tube got in her way.

The healer swam over and did something. The outer tube vanished, and the static shield shifted out, only noticeable by the faint glimmer and shift in the water around her it caused. "There, you should be able to sign easier now. I can speak your language if that would be easier for you."

"I don't want to wake them," she signed back.

The healer nodded her understanding and asked her again how she was feeling.

"Tired and weak, but okay," she replied.

"Are you in any pain?"

"No, but my hand feels stiff and kind of numb."

"Well, try not to move around too much even if it doesn't hurt, and go slow when you do. We had to replace four of your internal organs due to how badly damaged they were from electrical burns. I expect it will be another several days before it will be safe for you to leave the tube. While we had you open, we flushed your internal system with nanos to treat the other burns and injuries you sustained. They appear to be working, but it will take time. The numbness in your hand is likely due to nerve damage you had from the re-broken bones. You'll probably need another surgery when you're stronger, depending on how one of the bones heals. It was shattered into several pieces. We have a new bone printing just in case it doesn't take."

She nodded her understanding. She was honestly surprised her paw was working as well as it was after what Rip did to it.

"Are you hungry?"

"No, I don't think so," she replied.

The healer frowned at that. "Are you feeling sick to your stomach?"

"No, I feel fine."

The healer frowned again.

"What?" she asked.

"You're sure you're not hungry? You haven't eaten in days. You should be starving."

"I don't *feel* hungry, just...hollow, but I guess I could try to eat something," she replied.

The healer nodded. "I'll be right back," she signed and floated away.

She closed her eyes and had nearly fallen back to sleep when she felt the healer's touch on her shoulder. She jumped in surprise, not having heard her swim back in.

"Sorry. I didn't mean to scare you. Would you like to sit up a little?"

Marsee nodded, so the healer adjusted the shield. She felt her upper body being lifted. It was weird not being able to see the bed she was on, although she could feel the gentle pressure still holding her in place from the static shield above her.

The healer handed her an odd container, and Marsee frowned at it, trying to figure out how it worked.

"You're on a liquid diet for at least the first week until we're sure everything is working correctly. Obviously, cups and glasses wouldn't work here. Put your mouth on the end piece here and suck."

Marsee did and was surprised to find a very unique but thick and flavorful drink. *At least if I'm stuck drinking this for a week, it tastes good,* she thought, but then frowned. She couldn't remember how to swallow. *It shouldn't be that hard. Why can't I do this?*

"What's wrong?" The healer asked. "Does it not taste good? My understanding is that this flavor is the most popular for your species, but I could get you something else."

She didn't really want to admit what was wrong. It seemed so strange, but she had to do something. Her mouth was full of whatever this liquid concoction was. "I...It'll probably sound really strange, but...I...I don't remember how to swallow," she signed.

The healer was a professional, at least, and didn't show the least amount of surprise. "Are you having difficulty moving the muscle in your throat or your tongue? Or is the angle perhaps too shallow? Sometimes, that can make it difficult."

"I'm not sure. I could try sitting up more," she signed back. The healer adjusted the shield until she was about three-quarters of the way upright, and she tried again. She tried tilting her head back, but that didn't help. *She said tongue and throat muscles. Push the liquid back. Got that, but how do I activate my throat muscles? I've never even thought about how to swallow before.* She shook her head no after trying for a bit.

The healer stuck her hand through the shield and started massaging her neck in a downward motion. Suddenly, she swallowed.

"Why was that so hard?" she asked.

The healer examined her scans for a moment before looking back at her. "You had third-degree burns around your neck from the shock you took, and your brain uses electricity to control your muscles. Both could account for it, although it could be nothing more than a lack of use. Everything else appears to be healing well, but I'll have the Senior Healer confirm. We've honestly been far more focused on the more life-threatening injuries you sustained. Why don't you try again."

Marsee looked closely at the Healer, as she had the impression that there was something that they weren't telling her, but she tried again anyway. Again, she had difficulty, but by repeating what the healer had done to her throat, she was able to swallow. She paid attention to how the muscles felt as she swallowed, and on the third attempt, was able to drink without having to do the weird neck massage.

When she managed that, the healer smiled.

Marsee drank a few more sips, but it was hard work. She had to focus on every sip. After a little bit, she handed the strange thermos back to the healer.

"You've hardly had anything," the healer flashed, frowning at the level indicator on the side. Are you feeling full or in any discomfort?"

"No and no," she replied.

"But you're not hungry either?"

Marsee shook her head.

The healer frowned and then shrugged. "I'll leave this here. If you feel hungry, drink. Even if you don't feel hungry, try to drink as much as you can. Take a sip every ten or fifteen minutes."

"Okay," she replied. "Do you know where my tablet is?"

In response, the healer swam over to a drawer, pulled out her tablet, and swam back, handing it to her.

"Thank you," she signed.

The healer nodded, swam back over to her net, and resumed tapping away on her own tablet.

Marsee opened hers and gasped. There were literally hundreds of millions of unread messages waiting for her from people she'd never even heard of, and a message at the top that read 'Storage Full: 483,324,237 messages remaining on the server.' Her message box was full? She didn't even know that was possible. She picked a few at random.

My Dearest Translator,

I am absolutely horrified by what happened to you after all you've done for our people. I know it's not nearly enough to make up for what was done to you, but I'm donating an hour of my time to your account for every hour you were held by that miserable slime-sucking trench-dweller. I hope that will make up for some of the time lost while you recover. We are not all like him. I wish you a quick and full recovery.

With all my love, Wave Dancer

Dear Translator,

Thank you so much for saving my friend, Stormy. You're the absolute best, and I love the Adventures of Super Stormy! I hope you write another one, maybe about how you both saved the others?

Your second biggest fan, Bramble Weed

To Translator Chenzira,

Thank you for slaying the Leviathan that threatened to destroy our world. I've heard that you will have a long

> *recovery. If you are ever in my district and would like a tour of the Jeweled Caverns, please let me know. It would be an honor to show you around. I'm sending you one of the crystals I hand-picked from the cavern. I hope that its light and beauty will make up for a little of what was done to you. Wishing you a full recovery.*
>
> *Senior Scientist of the Jeweled Caverns, Granite*

After reading a dozen similar messages, she flipped over to her Guild account and blinked hard. She had to be reading her balance wrong. No, it didn't change. Correction, it did change. It kept going up, even as she watched.

"Three moons! I'll never have to work another day in my life!" she exclaimed, far louder than she intended. It was enough to wake the others.

"Hey there, Kit...sweetheart." her father said. "You're awake. How are you feeling?"

"Absolutely gobsmacked. Ellie, have you seen my guild balance?"

"No, why?" Ellie asked.

"Because I'm pretty sure I can afford to buy a small moon now. Maybe even a large one," she replied, holding out her tablet.

Ellie awkwardly untangled herself from her sleeping net and swam over. Taking the tablet from her, Ellie glanced down and whistled. "I'm pretty sure you can afford to buy all three with this balance." Ellie's ears drooped, and she let out a heartbroken sigh. "I'm never going to see another book from you again, am I? You could sit on a beach for the rest of your life doing nothing if you wanted to. What are you going to do with all of this?"

"I have absolutely no idea. There's no way I could even begin to use all of this, and it's not like I need anything. Maybe donate it somewhere else, although I suppose I could buy my own ship with this. It'll take me months just to thank everyone. I could easily afford to hire a few dozen staffers to do that for me, although that seems a little disingenuous..." She trailed off, thinking about all that she could do now.

"About that..." her father began and then paused as if reconsidering having said anything.

"What?" she asked.

"I hesitate to tell you, but before kidnapping your sister, Damon broke into your room and destroyed almost everything in it. It will all need to be replaced.

"He did what?!" she yelled. "Why that no good..." she muttered off a string of curses that made the healer flash her amusement, and then Marsee gasped. "Little Flower's painting?! Oh, please tell me he didn't destroy that, too!"

Her father looked miserable and nodded.

"Let me see," she growled.

Her father frowned but flipped open his tablet, pulled up the footage Paxton had taken, and handed it to her.

She was fuming by the time she'd finished and threw the tablet hard in her fury. It didn't go far in the water, but alarms started blaring on the monitor above her head a moment later.

The healer swam over and started flipping through the scans, frowning.

"What's wrong?" she asked as she started feeling lightheaded and queasy. "I don't feel so good."

"I should think not."

It was the last thing she heard as the world went dark around her.

CHAPTER 24

Jer: Heartbreaking Mistake

Jer's heart nearly stopped as Marsee slumped, and additional alarms started blaring. The healer slammed a switch on the bed. Within seconds, Marsee was horizontal, and the tube reactivated and closed in around her. Before he could ask what was going on, healers swarmed into the room from every direction.

"How in the bottomless depths did she manage to do that?!" the Senior Healer exclaimed, then started flashing commands faster than he could follow. Several healers bolted to cabinets around the room, grabbing supplies, while another shoved him back out of the way. To his shock, they didn't float her out but began operating on her right there in the room.

Blood instantly filled the tube she was in until he couldn't see her, and even the filtration system struggled to keep up so that the healers could see what they were doing. He felt his control slipping from the combination of his fear and the thick, coppery scent of the blood. His instinct demanded he protect his daughter, reacting as if the healers were the ones harming her, not trying to save her life, but he knew there was nothing he could do to help her. He knew he should leave the room, but he couldn't move. He tried to tell the others that he needed help, but he couldn't talk. He couldn't even sign. All he could do was stare as his daughter bled out in front of him and watch as the healers frantically tried to save her life.

He pushed hard against his instinct, but it wouldn't turn off and continued to pressure him to act, to save her. When that failed, he tried a different tactic. He and Marcus had trained for this eventuality.

I need Marcus, he thought. *He'll know how to save her.*

His instinct relaxed ever so slightly, and he managed to make his arm move enough to hit the emergency beacon he kept attached to his harness. It would place an urgent call to his brother and notify the guards if it wasn't shut off in time.

He was honestly surprised that they hadn't noticed yet, but everyone was focused entirely on Marsee. He couldn't see anything in the tube she was in. It was now dark red with her blood, so he watched the monitors and the weak and fluttering beat of her heart.

beep beep ... beep beep ... beep ...

...

...

No! He didn't want to believe it. Healers scrambled to save her, but he didn't understand why. He hadn't removed the DNR on her account. He knew he should stop them, but he couldn't form the words, wouldn't form the words. It wasn't his instinct stopping him now. It was him. Even though he'd promised Marsee not to and knew what her life would be like, he couldn't do it, and surprisingly, neither did the guards.

...

...

Marsee! Please come back! he prayed over and over, watching the monitor for the slightest flicker of a beep.

...

...

Suddenly, he felt himself being pulled out of the room hard by his scruff. He didn't resist even though he felt his control return before he'd even made it through the door. His instinct recognized Marcus by his scent and rolled over, belly up and throat exposed.

Marcus spun him and stared into his eyes with concern.

"Marsee," he whimpered. *Her heart stopped.* He couldn't say it. Couldn't admit what it meant."Oh gods, no!"

His brother crushed him in a hug and held him tightly by the back of his scruff as he cried out his grief, and he felt his brother shaking with his own grief and silent tears.

beep...beep

He gasped, not daring to believe what he'd heard. He pushed away from Marcus and spun to look back into the room. Marcus let him spin but kept hold of him. The healers were still operating, but Marsee's heart was beating again. Weak and unsteady, but it was there.

beep......beep

...

beep......beep

...

"Stay with me," he whispered. "Fight."

beep...beep

"What happened?" Marcus asked.

He couldn't answer. To do so would admit that his own actions had nearly killed his daughter. Again.

"Jer!" Marcus snapped. "Look at me."

He turned his head and blinked but still didn't answer. He swallowed hard, trying to find the words, but they weren't there.

His brother's face was blank at first but then softened with under-standing. "Come on, Little Brother. Let's get some fresh air and give them room to work."

He blinked at his brother again, barely processing what Marcus was saying.

beep...beep

He turned and looked back into the room at Marsee, not wanting to leave, afraid if he did, it would be the last time he ever saw her, but Marcus grabbed him by the scruff and dragged him off down the hall. He didn't resist, even though leaving Marsee behind was the hardest thing he'd ever done. Halfway down the hall, Marcus practically shoved him into an empty room. He stumbled as they passed through a shield into a dry room and heard his brother shut and lock the door, followed by the faint whine of the privacy screen as it activated.

"Jer, talk to me," Marcus both said and signed. "What happened."

"I made another stupid mistake," he muttered and turned to walk over to the window. In the park below, a work crew was packing the gifts left for Marsee and the others. He wondered if she would ever see them.

"Jer..."

He sighed and gave a slight nod to the window.

Marcus walked up beside him and looked out.

"People are donating credit, too. Her guild balance is in the millions. When Ellie asked what she was going to do with it all, she responded that she didn't know because she didn't need anything. I made the mistake of telling her about her room, and when she saw what Damon did, she threw her tablet. Moments later, alarms started going off, and they didn't even bother floating her out. They just started operating right there in front of me."

"Is that why you alerted? Because of the blood?"

He nodded. "My instinct wanted to act, to protect her. I froze. I knew I should leave, but I couldn't. I couldn't ask for help either, talk or sign, but I managed the alert. That's twice in less than a week. I know what that means. Tell my family I love them, and I'm sorry."

Marcus said nothing but slammed his mask in place, grabbed him by the scruff, and turned him around before placing his other paw under his jaw.

He stared at his brother, honestly surprised that his instinct wasn't reacting to the threat yet. But then they had trained for this, too, and the reaction he now felt was entirely different from the fear of a few moments before. He closed his eyes and sighed with pleasure, allowing himself that brief moment of bliss, honestly glad it would end this way. When death didn't come immediately, he opened his eyes again.

Marcus stared back at him for several long moments and then swallowed hard. "Turn it on." The command came out barely above a whisper.

He did, fully expecting the beast inside him to react, but nothing happened outside of the world sharpening and his brother's earthy brown scent appearing around him. He breathed deeply and smiled. *Marsee was right. He does smell like old books.*

"Why are you smiling?" Marcus asked him, frowning with confusion.

"Because your training is still working, and your scent is a mix of green and brown and smells like old books."

Marcus flicked his ears back in surprise at the comment.

"It reminded me of a conversation I had with Marsee about what she could see. That was the day I first saw any beauty in our instincts. Marsee's scent is a beautiful blue like the joy of a Water Sprite, only so much more. It glows. Myra's is the gold of early morning sunlight reflected off a gentle stream. Little Flower's is indigo mixed with hints of the chocolate chip cookies Marsee sneaks out for her every night, but lately, it's been tinged with black and harsh with her depression. Hope's was indigo, too, but it's turning pink." He allowed himself to think of every member of his family, wanting them to be his last thoughts.

Deep inside, he felt his instinct finally start to react to his coming death. "Now, big brother." His voice shook with the effort, and soon, his limbs started to, too, as he fought for control. He didn't want to hurt his brother, didn't want to hurt any of his family anymore. He knew they would be better off without him. With his death, they would no longer be a target.

His instinct seemed to accept his decision, settle, and then turned off. He was pretty sure it wasn't his doing, as his instinct now cowered in a corner of his brain, waiting for the end and wondering if it would hurt. It was such an unusual and odd feeling.

Marsee had once told him that hers had shoved her forward, recognizing that if it didn't, they would die. Was his instinct doing the same, a last-ditch effort to save their lives? He was essentially committing suicide by not resisting, which he didn't think was even possible.

Marcus frowned at him with confusion.

He smiled back with love at his brother. "It's alright. I love you, and I forgive you. Make it quick for both of us."

"I love you too, little brother," Marcus said and, to Jer's shock, pulled him in for a hug instead. "But I'm not killing you today. I think you're fine and experienced a normal stress reaction, but you did the right thing in contacting me. It's also not surprising you couldn't ask for help. If you had said something, Avery probably would have killed you."

Jer snorted and turned away to look out the window again. "I don't understand you sometimes, brother. Why didn't you kill me?"

"Jer, this week has been impossible. I would expect no less from anyone else in your position, but I don't think you're a risk."

He snorted. "I would put me down. I've lost control twice, and I've admitted to going non-verbal. I couldn't even sign."

"In a situation where speaking would have gotten you killed."

He shrugged. "Semantics."

"Semantics that make all the difference. Besides, not many would have been able to stand there, knowing they were about to die and turn their instinct off as you just did."

"I didn't," he replied.

Marcus frowned at him through the reflection in the window. "What do you mean? It looks off."

"It is, but that was my instincts doing. I'm honestly not sure what just happened. Marsee told me after being rescued from the cave that it felt like her instinct shoved her forward, knowing that if it didn't, Avery would kill her. I think mine might have just done the same. I wanted you to kill me. I'm so tired of hurting my family just by being alive."

"And you don't think your death would hurt them? It would devastate me."

He sighed. "I don't know how to protect them from me, much less everyone else who wants to hurt them because of me."

"By fighting people like Rip and ensuring they never take power."

He said nothing.

Marcus reached over and wrapped an arm around him, pulling him in for another hug. They stood there, staring out the window in silence for a long time, and didn't move until there was a knock on the door.

They turned as the door slid open to find Avery floating out in the hallway. "Councilors, the Senior Healer would like to see you in Marsee's room."

Jer took a deep breath, slammed his emotions down hard, and nodded. As they made their way to Marsee's room, the last of the healers, save for Hyacinth, swam out, leaving only them and Ellie behind.

Ears drooped with worry, Ellie floated beside Marsee, holding her uninjured paw through a portal in the tube.

Marsee lay still, but her chest rose and fell. There was still a faint hint of blood in the room, but he couldn't see it anymore, and to his relief, his instinct didn't react to it. His eyes drifted from his daughter to the monitor and the steady beep of her heart.

beep beep...beep beep...beep beep

It was such a beautiful sound.

Hyacinth turned as they entered. "She's alive and stable. She was very lucky there was a healer in the room with her. She tore out several of the sutures on her new organs and nearly bled to death before we could repair them. How she managed that, I have no idea."

"She got angry and threw her tablet," Jer replied, swimming over to Marsee's side. Ellie moved out of the way, and he took Marsee's paw in his. Without her fur, it looked so tiny and strange. He rubbed his thumb over the webbing between her fingers.

"She shouldn't even be strong enough to do that," the Healer said, scratching an ear fin. "Regardless, I'm going to place her in a body cast until she heals enough that it's no longer a risk if she moves too quickly. Lily's printing it now. We'll need to tell her what's going on so she's more careful in the future, but before we do that, there's something you should know."

He closed his eyes, bracing for more bad news.

When she didn't continue right away, he opened his eyes and swallowed hard when he saw her look of regret and compassion.

"I've heard back from your Healer's Guild about her other injuries. I'm sorry to have to tell you this..."

He shook with barely controlled grief. "How long?"

"I don't know. After what just happened..." The Healer sighed. "If she's very careful, a few years, perhaps. But, no one born with her condition has ever survived their growth spurt. Most never even make it that far and die in childhood. She'll likely spend the rest of her short life in one trauma center after another. I would normally recommend sedating her until she's healed more, but long-term use of the sedative is just as dangerous with new organs as stasis, and we had to use far more than normal to keep her sedated during this last operation. If she's developing a resistance to it, we'll need to be very cautious about when and how long we use it to save it for emergencies in the future."

He shook his head, not wanting to believe it. "Myra will find a way to fix her," he said. "We'll just have to be careful until then."

"Councilor, I commend your optimism and faith in your partner's skills, but I don't believe there's anything left for her to fix."

"We can't tell Marsee that," Jer said, "She needs to believe she's going to get better. I've seen what that lack of hope did to her sister. She doesn't want that kind of life, and without her instinct, there's nothing to stop her from trying to end it."

"We have to tell her, or she'll hurt herself again," Hyacinth countered.

Lily swam in carrying the printed cast for Marsee. He moved out of the way so they could secure it in place.

His already shattered heart broke further as he watched the healers work. *How many casts would she wear until it ultimately killed her?* He turned away and grabbed his scruff, trying to decide what the right thing to do was when his last words to her had nearly killed her.

"Papa?"

CHAPTER 25

Marsee: Lost Instinct

It felt like only a moment later, but when Marsee opened her eyes, the light in the room had shifted, and her father was pacing, grabbing the back of his scruff. Her uncle and Ellie were there, too, and all three looked frazzled and upset.

"Papa?"

He spun around and swam over to her. "You're awake!"

"What happened?" she asked and realized there was something tight and constricting around her midsection, making it hard to take a deep breath. She lifted a paw to feel it. "What's this?"

"You ripped out half the sutures on your new organs, and you just spent several hours in surgery to repair them," he replied.

She blinked, thoroughly surprised. "I did?"

"You did. That's why they've put you in a body cast, so you won't do it again," he explained.

"Are you in any pain, Marsee?"

She turned her head to see the Senior Healer floating on the other side of her. "No," she replied. "But it's really hard to take a deep breath in this. Does it have to be so tight?"

Senior Healer pursed her lips but nodded. "Yes. Marsee, you should be writhing in pain right now, but you're not, and you clearly didn't notice that you'd hurt yourself by throwing that tablet." The Senior

Healer picked up her uninjured hand and frowned again. "I want you to look away from me and wiggle each finger as I touch it."

Marsee shrugged but did as asked.

"Is your hand in any pain?"

She frowned at the scars on her arm and paw from where she'd been burned, but they looked mostly healed. "No. Should it be?"

"Councilor, your hand, please."

Her father hesitated but held his hand across to her. The moment their hands touched, her father yelped and swore, shaking it hard.

"Marsee, I just did the same thing to you, and you didn't even notice. It would appear that you've lost your sense of pain. Lily said you had trouble swallowing earlier and didn't feel hungry. Is that true? Do you feel hungry now?"

"Yes, Yes, and...I don't think so. I feel hollow but not hungry, like something's missing, but I can't tell what it is. What's going on, and what does this mean?" She was starting to worry, not liking the expressions she saw on the other's faces or seeing her uncle upset and without his mask. That rarely happened.

The Senior Healer looked over at her father and uncle.

Her uncle nodded, took a deep breath, slammed his mask down, and swam over to her. Somehow, the sudden sight of his mask scared her even more. This wasn't her uncle. This was her Senior Councilor. "Marsee, I need you to turn on your instinct for me."

She frowned and shook her head, panicking. She was terrified of what would happen if she tried. It had felt like she'd beaten it, but she wasn't sure what would happen if she tried using it again. "No. No, I don't want to. Never again. Please don't make me!"

Her uncle closed his eyes and took a deep breath, and beside him, her father actually gasped. When she looked over at him, his face was slammed tightly behind his mask, too, but his feelings were obvious as his fists were tightly curled. He was scared. Motion caught her attention, and she watched as Avery swam inside the room. His face was blank, too.

Above her, the quiet beep of the monitor changed as her heart rate spiked. "What's going on?"

"Marsee, this isn't a request. It's an order. Turn your instinct on now," her uncle commanded, not answering her question.

She frowned, absolutely terrified by the harsh tone of his voice, but nodded, braced herself, fearing it would attack again, and tried to flick it on.

Nothing happened.

She focused and tried remembering how she felt when she gave up control, but there was nothing but that same sense of hollowness. She tried channeling her anger at Rip and Damon and imagined tearing them to shreds, but still nothing. She tentatively tried speaking to her instinct, but there was no reply, just a wave of hollowness that grew so intense that it nearly swallowed her whole.

"I...I can't," she whispered, nearly crying from the feeling and the fear of what would happen if she didn't obey his order.

Her father stiffened, and Avery swam a little closer.

"Please try," her uncle said again. Misunderstanding her.

"No, I mean, I can't turn it on. I tried, and nothing happened. It's like it's gone. I think that might be what's missing. When I try, I just feel even hollower. Oh, gods. What an awful feeling. I can't even begin to describe it." She shuddered hard and tried to take a deep breath to control the feeling, but the cast constricted her breathing, and the feeling just continued to grow. Finally, she thought to try turning her instinct off. The feeling receded some, but it didn't go away entirely.

Marcus gave her father a look, and her panic flared again as her father gave a slight, worried shake of his head.

"I promise! I really tried! Please! You have to believe me!"

Her uncle turned back to her, and his face softened with compassion and regret. "I do believe you, but..." He let out a heavy sigh and then glanced over as Avery swam up to her tube. Both her father and uncle stiffened at the sight of the guard but said nothing.

She was nearly in a full-blown panic at this point, and knew if she had any fur left on her tail, it would be sticking straight out.

Avery hit a button, and part of the tube slid down. She shook with fear as he reached in and grabbed her chin. Not hard, but there was a hint of his claws in warning not to pull away. "Try again," Avery ordered.

She tried with everything she had, but nothing happened outside of another wave of hollowness that caused her to whimper.

"What did you experience in the canyon right before you regained control?" he asked.

She fought through her fear and the wave of hollowness to explain, honestly doubting he'd believe her. "My instinct thought my father was going to kill us and tried to take control to stop me from letting him get any closer. I don't even know how to explain it, but for a time, it felt like I was back on Saber out in the Wilds and fighting my instinct just like I fought with my father, only it was ephemeral, translucent, and glowing like it was in the cave. Every strike it landed, and every strike I landed hurt, but I eventually killed it or imagined killing it. It disappeared with a poof, and it felt like I fell back into my body."

"Do you still have it on?"

"I...I don't know. I did what I always did, but the only thing that's changed is the feeling of hollowness. It keeps getting worse."

"Try turning it off," Avery said.

She did and sighed as the feeling receded again.

Avery glanced up at the monitors as her heart rate came down, nodded, and backed away. "I believe she's telling the truth. For now, we'll continue to watch."

Her father sighed with evident relief and swam forward, took her good hand in one of his, and caressed the side of her face with the other. "Marsee, you told me that you killed it and that it's never coming back. We think you really did."

The Senior Healer continued. "Your immune system attacked and destroyed several parts of your brain that are used to control the things we're born instinctively knowing how to do, and in your case apparently controlled your ability to know when you need to swallow, your sense of pain, and even knowing if you're hungry or not, and perhaps others we might not know of yet."

"So what does that mean for me?" Marsee asked with a mix of confusion, worry, and relief when she realized they weren't going to kill her.

"Well, without your sense of pain, you're not going to know when you've seriously hurt yourself like you just did, so you're going to have to be beyond careful," the Senior Healer explained. "You'll have to set alarms to ensure you eat and drink enough, and you'll probably want to start wearing eye protection, if not a static mask, to prevent something from getting in your eyes or impacting you without you knowing it. You could literally break your leg or catch on fire and not know it, and I'm sorry, but it will eventually be fatal, and likely sooner rather than later. We've found a few records of people born without the ability to feel pain in your species, and none of them survived the transition into your adult stage."

Her ears flicked back, and she looked at the Senior Healer in horror. "No..."

"I'm sorry, Marsee," the Healer said.

"NO!" Marsee screamed at the Healer. "No. You're wrong! You have to be wrong!" She pulled her hand away from her father and tried sticking a claw into her palm but felt nothing and watched as blood started to drift away, carried off by the current. "No... No, this can't be!"

"Marsee, you need to remain calm. You could seriously hurt yourself again," the Healer said as she tried to grab her paw to treat it.

Marsee yanked her paw back and hissed. "NO! Don't you dare tell me what I need to do! You just told me I'm going to die before I can ever have children, that I'll have to spend the rest of my pitifully short life wrapped in padding, unable to do anything because I might hurt or blind myself and not know it. I'll be angry and upset if I want to. Leave me alone!"

"Kitten, I know this is..."

She snapped her head to face her father and yelped as a wave of pain and fear washed over her. Everything Rip had said to her about her father came rushing back. She growled as the simmering anger she had towards him exploded into a boil, unlike anything she'd ever experienced before. She'd hated Rip, but this was something entirely different. This hate had the pain of betrayal behind it and nothing to temper it. It was so encompassing that it was almost as if she'd never experienced an emotion before.

She didn't know how she could both feel pain and not feel it, but she wrapped the pain of his betrayal around her like her cloak, pinned her ears flat to her skull, and hissed at him. "This is all *your* fault!"

He flinched back as if she'd slapped him and then swallowed hard with guilt, telling her she was right.

"You said you were only trying to test me, but that's not true. If you hadn't attacked me, I might have been able to trust you enough to regain control without damaging myself, but *you...* You *wanted* me to lose control, didn't you? You weren't trying to save me. You were trying to push me over the edge so you could have an excuse to kill me."

"That's not true at all," he replied.

She ignored him. "Of course it is. It's why you didn't step down before Rip tore my claws out and why you let me kill him instead of doing it yourself, isn't it? You wanted to get rid of your diseased and disappointing daughter, just like he said. It's why you didn't back off when I wasn't done tearing him to shreds. All you had to do was back off and give me time to recover, but you didn't!"

"I'm so sorry..."

"I can't believe I fought my instinct to save you. It was right about you all along, and so was Rip. What I don't understand is why you even bothered to treat me. You had your chance to get rid of me. You even promised me you wouldn't let me end up like my sister. Unless you're going to kill me anyway later or let the Guard do it. How long do I have? A few weeks after returning home, where you can hide my death?"

"No, of course not! If you're telling the truth..."

"If *I'm* telling the truth? You've broken your word to me twice now. How am I ever supposed to trust you again?"

He swallowed hard but then straightened. "I am sorry that I couldn't honor either of those promises. I gave my oath to protect the people, even at the expense of my family. I should have put you down on more than one occasion, but I broke that oath to give you a chance. You…"

"Some chance," she spat. "Get out of my room."

"Marsee, please. We'll figure something out. Your Mama can fix anything. I know it!"

She pinned her ears flat again, lashed her tail, and growled. "GET OUT! I hate you and never want to see your lying face ever again. GUARDS!"

Avery and the other guard bolted forward, and each grabbed one of her father's arms.

"Marsee, please…" he said as the guards dragged him out of the room. "I'm sorry!"

She wanted to claw her father's throat out for everything he'd done to her, but she couldn't move in the body cast, although she tried. Suddenly, she felt the static shield pressing her flat and restricting her motions.

She hissed at the healer. "What are you doing? Let go of me!"

"Marsee, you need to calm down, or you're going to hurt yourself," the Senior Healer replied, pulling out a hypo.

She spat at the healer, letting off a litany of swears, and ordered her to stop, then ordered the guards to stop her.

But the healer didn't, and neither did the guards or anyone else.

CHAPTER 26

Clear Seas: Oh the Irony

Clear Seas sat in his office, staring at his tablet and the massive backlog he needed to attend to. The fact that he had a coup to investigate didn't stop the normal affairs of state, and he was woefully behind, even more so than usual. It was days like this he really wished he had the small army of junior councilors, like the other species did, and it didn't help that he'd already identified that his Senior Staffer had been involved. Everything she'd ever worked on would have to be reviewed. He was seriously considering stepping down and letting someone else deal with the mess. Only there wasn't anyone he could trust on his council to pick up the pieces.

I need to talk to Temperate. I really need a Junior Councilor.

Oh, who are you kidding? You know he doesn't want the position, and it'll be years yet before Stormy's an adult. You're just going to have to make due.

Sighing, he checked the time and frowned. Marcus's tablet had blared with an alert, and he'd bolted out of their meeting without an explanation. He figured something must have happened with Marsee, but it had been hours without an update. Wind Rider had left shortly after to be with her daughter, who was going in for another surgery herself, and he'd retreated to his office and the relative safety of the work that needed to be done there.

I should check on them, he decided, after realizing he'd read the same paragraph twice. It was getting close to dinner time anyway, and he always tried to eat meals with his family whenever he could. Yawning, he closed the ticket he was working on and was just about to fold up his tablet when an urgent call came in from Stinger.

Swearing to himself, wondering what new catastrophe awaited him, he answered. "What is it this time?" he asked, not entirely sure he was able to keep the exhaustion off his face or skin.

Stinger was in Command and didn't look particularly happy to be calling him either and hesitated slightly before answering. "The Translator...just had her father forcibly removed from her room and accused him of attacking her," Stinger replied. "Marcus was there, and for some reason, Avery let him go instead of bringing him in. At her accusation, I examined her record. She's been placed on a watch in the last few days, which I was not informed of, and there's also a flag on her medical record, but for some reason, I can't access it or the tickets associated with either of them. Do you want me to arrest him?"

He sighed. "No. I'll handle it. Send me whatever footage you have, and keep this incident quiet for now. If this is the same situation, Marsee already informed me about it, and it's not an issue. The watch is probably from killing Rip. That's required as part of their Charter."

"That was my first thought, too, but the watch was added before she killed him."

He frowned. He knew about the watch but had hoped to keep it quiet. "I'll handle it," he repeated.

"Yes, sir," Stinger said and hung up.

Great, this is all we needed.

A moment later, the ticket arrived from Stinger. When the video ended, he stared at the blank screen as he considered what he'd seen. He was saddened to learn of Marsee's long-term prognosis, but it wasn't really any different than they'd been expecting. He'd seen people react far worse to bad news, but the whole scene set his scales on edge. He didn't like it at all.

What's really going on? he wondered. He couldn't remember the last time he'd seen Marcus break his mask, but he'd flinched, and Jer had actually gasped at Marsee's refusal, and they had medical proof she had a brain injury. Not only that, but it was almost as if they'd expected Avery to kill her, and they weren't stopping him either. Avery had no legal right to do so unless she was actively hurting someone, and she'd been perfectly in control until she'd been told of her diagnosis. Even then, she was far too injured to actually hurt anyone and restrained behind a shield.

The scene after she'd been told of her injuries was concerning, too. The way her behavior towards her father had changed had been sudden and drastic. He replayed the recording and watched that section again. *She reacted as if he hit her.* He was fully fluent in their language but still checked to ensure he had the meaning of the words right. *Why would the word kitten make her react that way?*

He pulled up the medical flag Stinger had mentioned, frowned at the listed injuries, and opened the linked ticket. Kendra's assessment was sparse, simply stating that it had been investigated and wasn't an issue. He opened the attached document and realized it was Marsee's personal journal. It didn't take him long to find her comments on the incident. He read through it with hints of orange and red escaping his control, not liking what he read at all as it was far more than either Marsee or Marcus had indicated. He then switched to Marsee's account, pulled up the latest version, and jumped to the end to see if she'd written anything about her captivity, wondering what exactly Rip had said.

What she wrote took his breath away. He'd never seen two words hit with more of an impact in his life.

"He waited."

It was much of an accusation as Little Flower's drawings had been and one he'd been wondering himself. He would have gladly given up his position to save his children and had wondered several times why Jer hadn't done the same for Marsee before he'd left Saber. He saved the latest copy to his account, intending to read the entire thing later.

Sighing, he closed his tablet and swam out, locking his office door behind him. As he swam out of the Council Building, he saw Jer leaving the Trauma Center and taking off at full speed on his drone. So did others, and he saw them flashing their concern and wondering if the Translator had died.

That's going to be a problem, he thought.

He now had guards stationed outside the Council Building at all times, not that he particularly trusted any of them, but there were a few he still trusted. One of those, Red Fin, was currently floating out front. "Follow Councilor Chenzira. Keep out of sight if you can. He's had some bad news and probably isn't paying attention to his surroundings."

"Yes, sir," Red Fin flashed and took off in a direction that should meet up with Jer if he didn't change directions.

"Sir is the Translator...Is she dead?" the other guard asked, flashing his concern.

"She's alive, or she was as of a few minutes ago," Clear Seas replied and swam across to the Trauma Center.

He had to answer the same question at least a dozen times as he crossed the park and even had the head of the Press Guild call him with an urgent call, but he finally made it inside.

"Sir, the Senior Healer is waiting for you in her office," the Triage Healer said the moment he swam through the main door.

He nodded, sure there was probably a report from her in his inbox by now, and swam down the hall.

Her door was open, and she looked up as he entered and flashed her surprise. "That was quick. I just sent off my report."

"I haven't read it," he said, shutting her door. "Stinger called me."

"Ah," she replied. "Well, to make a long story short, there's a flag on her medical record that would corroborate her claims that he attacked her."

"I'm aware of it and spoke to her the other day about it. She didn't want to press charges then."

"Are you also aware that there's a recently added council-ordered DNR on her medical record, too?"

"No," he replied with a frown. Who authorized it?"

"That's the strange part. It's the system account. I've never seen that." She pulled up Marsee's record to show him. "When I first discussed Marsee's injuries with Jeran, I honestly didn't expect she'd survive, much less wake, and recommended it. A few hours later, Jeran agreed if her heart stopped during her surgeries. I went to add a temporary DNR and realized there was already one there. When I saw who added it or *what* rather, I put in a ticket asking about it. I'll be honest. With both a flag on her record and the oddity of that DNR, I felt uncomfortable and ignored it today. Her heart stopped briefly when she ripped out her sutures before we could repair them. I fully accept whatever punishment the Council deems fit."

"There won't be any," he replied. "My backlog would fill the trench right now. I must have missed it. You were right to question it, and regardless of her statement today about not wanting to end up like her sister, I order you to ignore it if something else should happen. I've seen her behavior before when people are given bad news, and after everything that's happened to her, I want her to have time to process her injuries and trauma before making that decision. If you need an excuse, I'm willing to use her brain injury as a reason to question her competence, even if she appears to be lucid."

Hyacinth sighed with relief. "I was hoping you'd say that. It's going to be hard enough to keep her alive as it is. As upset as she is right now, I wouldn't put it past her to attempt suicide. She's going to be spending the rest of her life in trauma centers, and I wouldn't wish that on anyone."

"Nor would I," he replied. "Do you have any idea why she reacted so drastically when her father spoke, specifically her reaction to the word kitten?"

"I'm pretty sure Rip did that. She reacted just as badly to it, if not more so, when we first rescued her. I tried using that term to reassure her she was safe, and she reacted as if I was attacking her. Avery told me not to use it going forward, and I told Jeran. He frowned and did it anyway. At the time, I thought he was trying to see it for himself. Marsee flinched badly and asked him not to use it but didn't say why, at least not while I was present."

"Do you think he used it intentionally today?"

She was still for several moments and then shook her head. "He only found out about her long-term prognosis moments before Marsee unexpectedly woke up and was rather distraught over the news. I don't think he would want to cause her more harm, but something made her mad enough to throw her tablet."

"Unexpectedly?"

"I gave her enough sedative to sedate an adult of her species for hours. She's developing a resistance to it. We have others, but they're not as safe and require intubation. I've ordered my healers not to use it if we can. I'd rather save it for emergencies."

"Didn't you just give her some?"

"No. I gave her a narcotic that causes drowsiness and has a calming effect. With her injuries, knocking her out doesn't take much, but it may cause hallucinations when she wakes, depending on how long she sleeps."

He nodded his understanding and spent the next several minutes reviewing Marsee's current medical status and Hyacinth's assessment of the injuries in the flag before swimming down to Marsee's room. The guards were outside, floating at attention, and the door shut. When he hit the switch, he was startled by the volume in the room, and he noticed both guards turned to look.

"I can't believe it!" Ellie yelled. "You knew, and you did nothing?!" Her back was to him, ears pinned flat, and tail lashing. He'd seen her angry on many occasions but never this angry.

Wind Rider was there too, and both she and Marcus looked over as he swam in and activated the privacy screen again. Ellie glanced back at him but then refocused her anger on Marcus, who floated there perfectly calmly as if this was a normal conversation.

"Of course I knew, Ellie. The Guard and Council are notified anytime a flag is entered on someone's medical record, and Marsee was still on a watch at the time. Kendra was notified immediately and investigated. Jer thought she was losing control and chased her away from New Hope before anyone could get hurt. Do you honestly think I'd let my brother abuse my own niece?"

"Yes, I do. You knew and did nothing. Dark Moons, he broke her shoulder, and you seem to think that's acceptable behavior!" Ellie yelled. "That's not chasing her away. He attacked her both physically and verbally. He..."

Marcus glared at Ellie. "If you knew what happened, why didn't *you* report it? That makes you an accessory."

"Because *she* made me promise not to. I was honoring her wishes at the time and trying to gain her trust enough to tell me what was really going on. Why do you think I moved my office to New Hope? I was keeping an eye on him to ensure he didn't hurt her again since no one else seemed to care."

"Of course, I care. Gods, Ellie. I've given her more chances than anyone. She was spraying trees and purposely using her instinct. For that matter, Jer's lucky he's alive. She had him pinned by the throat and drew blood. I've never known anyone with psychosis to do that and walk away."

"Did it never once occur to you that maybe she doesn't *have* psychosis? Her behavior as a child could just as easily be explained by a trauma response to child abuse. If he's capable of hurting her once, what's to say he hasn't hurt her before?"

Marcus sighed and rubbed at the back of his scruff, then turned to look back at Marsee's sleeping body. "She's gone non-verbal, she's hunted, and she's sprayed. Those are all signs of psychosis, and there's nothing in her medical record that would indicate abuse has happened before. Kendra herself investigated and signed off on it."

"Bruises could easily be hidden under her fur, and Myra could have treated everything else."

"Do you honestly think Myra would let Jer get away with abuse?"

"Jer's a Senior Councilor, Marcus. He could easily be abusing Myra, too."

"That's a serious accusation without any proof to back it," Marcus replied. "And I seriously doubt Myra would let him get away with abuse. She'd maul him if he so much as raised a paw to her."

"She can't, you pedantic, fur-brained, walking encyclopedia."

"Ellie," Clear Seas warned, although he was honestly amused by the rather apt description.

Ellie took a deep breath. "Myra's been on a watch, too, and I imagine she's back on one now after going after Damon. She can't raise a paw to defend herself any more than Marsee can without risking her own execution, and no one on the Council would believe her if she tried to press charges."

"Of course, I would," Marcus replied.

Ellie snorted. "No, you wouldn't. All Jer would have to say is, 'She's on a watch. I thought she was losing control, and I was testing her.' Tell me you and the rest of the Council wouldn't take his side because that's exactly what you did to Marsee."

"Marsee never came to me or said anything about the incident."

"Would *you* risk the population finding out you had psychosis to stop abuse or just take the beating? Gods, Marcus. You were ready to kill her today, and you have medical proof she has a severe brain injury."

"I am well aware of her injuries and had no intentions of killing her."

"Don't you dare lie to me. I saw that look when she said she didn't want to turn it on, and you didn't do anything to stop Avery from approaching. I know you well enough to know you thought he was going to kill her. So did she."

"Refusing or even hesitating to turn on your instinct is seen as grounds for an immediate execution because it means you know you're not in control. Avery has the right to execute anyone he deems is a threat."

"Only if they're actively hurting someone, which she wasn't, and you have the responsibility to ensure that right isn't abused!" Ellie snarled. "Which you didn't. Neither of you did. I'm honestly disgusted by the both of you right now. You didn't even give her a chance!"

"I have given her more chances than anyone, ever. No one ever stops on their first hunt. The fact that she didn't kill Little Flower is astounding unless she's hunted before and lied about it. Then, that night in the garden, she was fully gone the moment she turned it on. By her own admission, she didn't understand anything her father was saying or know who she was, but she came back. No one ever does, or they didn't until her. Then we found out she was practicing on her own and hiding it from both her father and me. I fully expected Kendra to order her execution, but she allowed it to continue as long as Marsee didn't start hunting or struggling. We never expected to get her back once we realized she was being tortured, and what I saw the other day... I honestly can't believe she managed to come back from that, either. If it weren't for her brain scans, I would have had no choice but to put her down today the moment she refused to turn it on. She's lied before, and she could be lying now. It's my responsibility to protect the people from harm, as is Avery's. How many chances do I give her before she hurts someone?"

"As many as she needs," Ellie spat back. "What crime has she committed? She has an illness that no one understands, has been tortured and beaten for days, and is now apparently disabled and will be dealing with the challenges of those injuries for the rest of her short life. She hasn't hurt anyone, under circumstances that would push any of us over the edge, as Jer nearly did with this *test* of his, yet you're treating her like she's the criminal. You weren't the one having to pick up the pieces. I did. She was a mess for weeks, and you didn't even stop by to make sure she was okay."

"I was well aware of how she was doing. I had daily reports from Kendra and watched from a distance on several occasions. Kendra advised me to stay away unless she reached out to me first for fear my sudden appearance might trigger her. Ellie, you know there wasn't a cure, much less a treatment before. You've seen it on several occasions. Can you blame us for being cautious?"

Ellie glared at Marcus, and Clear Seas was very glad that glare wasn't directed at him. He was honestly surprised it hadn't come to blows yet, as angry as she was, even if her paws were still in casts.

"There's a very fine line between being cautious and abuse. Jer crossed it, and you know it. Why are you protecting him?"

Marcus sighed with barely controlled frustration. "Because if I'd been in his situation, I would have killed her, but I'll talk to her when she wakes and see if she wants to press charges or if there have been any other instances of abuse, and I'll check with Myra, too."

"You will do no such thing," Wind Rider hissed. "You're too close to the situation. Clear Seas and I will take over the investigation."

"Do you honestly think she's going to open up to the two of you after what *you* almost did to her?" Marcus retorted.

Ellie frowned at them in confusion.

"She told me about what happened before," Clear Seas said. "I'll talk to her."

"She's my citizen," Marcus replied. "You have no jurisdiction here."

Both he and Wind Rider snorted.

"Marcus, I'm beginning to wonder if someone hasn't hit you over the head," Clear Seas said. "A member of the Senior Council has been accused of a crime. That person is both your brother and protege. You should recuse yourself. You've already had the opportunity to investigate and did nothing. As far as I'm concerned, by her actions today, Marsee has now appealed that decision and brought it forth to the rest of the Senior Council. I was notified by my Senior Guard and Senior Healer, not just of the flag on her medical record and what happened today, but the fact that my senior guard can't access the related ticket and the fact that there's a council-ordered DNR on her medical record. Do you want to explain that?"

"That?" Marcus snorted. "I protected the ticket to protect Marsee. As for the DNR, the guard has her on a watch for psychosis. It's standard procedure, not that..."

"Standard procedure?!" they all exclaimed.

"Are you telling me you DNR everyone with this illness?" Clear Seas asked, flashing his shock.

"Of course. What point would there be to bring someone back to life if they're just going to turn into a wild animal and hurt someone?" Marcus retorted, seemingly honestly surprised by their reaction.

"Your niece would be dead right now if my Senior Healer had honored that DNR. I've ordered her to ignore it, and if you try to change it, I will have you arrested."

Marcus closed his eyes and took several deep breaths. When he opened his eyes again, his face was calm. "You don't understand this illness. We lost our last planet because of it, and dozens of people are injured and killed every year, including trained guards. I am not recusing myself. Jer did what he was trained to do, what *all* of Saber's councilors have been trained to do for the past ten thousand years."

"I'm beginning to think you don't understand this illness either," Clear Seas replied. "This DNR is a violation of her rights."

"It is not. It's no different than a DNR placed on a council or guard-ordered execution."

"Of course it is," he replied. "Ellie's right. She hasn't committed any crimes or hurt anyone."

"She's hunted," Marcus countered. "That's a crime for our species, one that is punishable by death unless it's necessary for survival, and..."

"That's a load of Leviathan poop, and you know it," Clear Seas spat. "For one, the definition of hunting, *per your charter*, indicates that she would have had to track *and* kill some prey animal. She has not, and for another..." He paused, remembering that Ellie was in the room and that she didn't know about the Council's tests. "I'm not allowing you to execute or treat someone as a criminal for something I've done on more than one occasion."

"You have no jurisdiction over what another species considers a crime. Marsee nearly killed Little Flower..."

"I'm not. I'm basing this off of your own laws. Marsee stopped. That's an important distinction that *you* seem to be forgetting. I took Tabor's word that she was dangerous and would lose control at the slightest sign of violence. I was wrong, and so was Tabor, and so are you."

"You saw what happened in the canyon. Do you honestly think she's safe?"

"Yes," he replied. "I don't know what I saw in the canyon, but I do know she was badly injured, and according to my Senior Healer, those injuries would or could account for any sort of odd behavior, even violence. She obviously didn't trust her father, yet she stayed in control, gave him multiple chances to back off, *which he didn't*, and still didn't hurt him, even though she believed he was going to kill her. If she can do that, if she can survive what Rip did to her and not hurt my son, then she's safe, and you need to stop treating her like a criminal."

"Are you really willing to risk your people's lives on that?"

"I'm willing to risk *my* life on it. She saved my son's life, and I will do *everything* in my power to save her and others like her. And I mean *everything*."

"As will I," Wind Rider added.

"And I," Ellie said, crossing her arms with a glare.

Marcus glared at him, upset enough that his tail was actually twitching. "I'll allow your right to override the DNR in this case, but I'm not going to allow you to change the policy around psychosis, at least not yet. When we have more proof that sign language works as a treatment, I'll consider changing the policy, but not until I'm sure my people are safe. To do so would be irresponsible, and I am not recusing myself from this case either, not because of Jer, but to protect my people."

They all glared at each other for several long moments, but Marcus didn't back down.

"Fine," Clear Seas finally spat. "I'll allow you to question her first, but I reserve the right to question her myself and take over the investigation if she chooses to press charges or if I sense you're pressuring her or Myra in any way."

Marcus sighed but gave a single nod of agreement.

"What I want to know," Ellie said. "Is how Rip found out about her illness."

Marcus took a deep breath before answering. "Likely, it's from her personal journal. He had a copy of it. I don't know if he found it from the flag on her record or pulled it off of her account when he stole her tablet."

Ellie sighed, but Clear Seas was furious, and so was Wind Rider.

"Why isn't that in the evidence?" Clear Seas demanded. "I've read everything linked to Marsee's ticket in our investigation. Twice."

Marcus sighed again. "Because her folder is still in my office, and I haven't scanned it in yet. Before you get upset, I did it to protect Marsee, not Jer. I didn't want the entire council to get their hands on it. Every last item is linked in some way to her psychosis. It's all readily available from her record or account, but I don't see any need to call it out. Trust me, if my council read what was in there, they'd call for her immediate execution, not his. The fact is, many already are."

He glared at Marcus. "Have you hidden anything else?"

"No, just that. On my oath."

"I honestly don't know if I believe you, but let me be perfectly clear. She may be your citizen, but as long as she's here, she's under *my* protection. Harm her in *any* way, and I will personally make sure you suffer as much as she has before I have you executed, whether there's a majority vote or not."

Marcus's eyes widened in surprise at the threat.

"Seconded," Wind Rider stated with a glare.

Ellie said nothing, but he noticed her claws flash in warning, and so too did Marcus. His eyes widened further as Ellie's expression changed from anger to a wicked promise of violence.

Once again, he was very glad her glare was not directed towards him. The economic damage alone she could do to Saber was threat enough. He turned and swam out, not waiting for a reply, but stopped and turned to face Avery, leaving the door open behind him. "I'm granting Marsee residency for as long as she needs or chooses to stay here. Whatever your policy is around her illness back on Saber, you will ignore it. Restrain if necessary, but no matter what happens, do not execute or allow anyone else to execute her without my direct authority. If you, or those on her door, can't obey those orders, you can leave."

"I have no problems obeying those orders, sir," Avery replied. "I don't believe Marsee is a risk to anyone but herself at this point. If there were going to be issues, it would have happened when I tested her."

It surprised him that Avery would have such a different reaction than Marcus. He would think that if psychosis was as dangerous as Marcus seemed to believe, their guard would feel as strongly. "Come find me when your shift is over. I should be in my office or the conference room this evening."

"Yes, sir."

With one last glance at Marsee's sleeping body and a pointed glare directed at Marcus, he left to find Jer, fully aware of the irony of their swapped situations, and he absently wondered if there would be anyone left on the Council by the end of the week.

CHAPTER 27

Marcus: What a Mess

Marcus was at a complete loss as to how to salvage the entire moons' forsaken situation. If Marsee chose to press charges, it could ruin Saber's entire reputation, and there would be nothing he could do to save Jer without completely destroying Marsee in the process or putting his people at risk. Both Clear Seas and Wind Rider had essentially declared they would go to war to protect Marsee, and he shuddered to think what they could do with Ellie's backing.

"Papa, no," Marsee muttered.

He turned to look at his niece. Her paws, ears, and tail twitched furiously with a night terror.

"Please stop! Why are you doing this?"

"She's been kidnapped and tortured for days, yet her night terrors are of her father," Ellie said quietly beside him. "If that isn't proof that he's been abusing her, I don't know what is."

He closed his eyes and took a deep breath to contain the grief he felt, knowing that even if Marsee didn't press charges, he would still likely have to kill his little brother. Jer's episode scared him, even if he'd decided it was a natural reaction and not a sign of impending psychosis, but he knew he was only fooling himself. When he opened his eyes, his mask was firmly in place, and he gave a single nod. Both Ellie and Wind Rider relaxed.

"Call me when she wakes," he told Ellie and swam out. He returned to his office and slumped in his seat with a groan as he rubbed at his forehead. When the pain didn't recede, he pulled out the emergency stash of pain pills he kept in all of his offices and took two before unclipping his tablet and firing off messages to Myra. Then, on the off chance, he sent one to Myra's other children as well.

With a heart-weary sigh, he began digging for further evidence of abuse. He'd already read Marsee's journal twice. Once when Kendra had originally posted it to the ticket and again after realizing Rip had found it. Still, he opened it again, scrolled to the relevant part, and read it a third time to confirm what he remembered.

There, he thought and took several images for evidence.

He says it was just a test, that he didn't mean what he said, and that he only did it to make me angry enough to be sure I was safe and in control, but why does it still hurt so much? How could he say and do those things to me? He's my Papa. He's supposed to care for my injuries, not make them. I could never do that to Hope. All I've ever wanted was for him to be proud of me, but no matter what I do, I'm a disappointment. I left Little Flower alone, and now she's dying. I'm so far behind in my studies that I doubt anyone will mentor me now, not that it matters.

All that matters is learning enough about the Hue-mans so that they'll let me keep Hope when Little Flower dies. Papa will never let me keep her, not with my psychosis, but I'll be damned to the dark side of the moons if I let him keep her. He's too busy with his duties as Senior Councilor to take care of a cub, and if he can hurt me like he just did, what's to stop him from hurting Hope? His honor? Pah! He promised he wouldn't pounce on me again, and an hour later, he tried to kill me. He's never broken his oath before.

Why this time? Because I was upset? Will I ever be allowed to be angry or upset without him worrying that I'm losing control, or is it only a matter of time before he decides I'm too dangerous to keep around and finally kills me like I thought he was going to do today?

He highlighted several points, which he could use as evidence that there hadn't been other attacks, but still dug into the rest of Marsee's account, reading back for the past year her conversations with her father and opening random files to see if there were further hidden documents. When his investigation of Marsee's account uncovered nothing, he switched into Jer's account, knowing Jer would receive a notification of it, but he found nothing there either, not that he expected to find anything. As a member of the Council, Jer knew his account was recorded. If he had anything written down, it would likely be in a hand-written journal like Rip did and like most in the Council did, including himself. Myra's account was also clean.

Tapping a claw on his desk, he fired off a message to Lowell to look for any messages or files that might have been deleted from any of their accounts and leaned back in his chair with a sigh. Everything pointed to Jer testing Marsee, not abuse, but their laws were clear. If Marsee felt it was abuse, then it was abuse, and based on her written journal and her injuries, she had every right to execute him for it, too.

They'd found enough evidence so far with the rest of their investigation that multiple members of the Council would be executed for far less than what Jer did to Marsee. How could he order their deaths and not Jer's? He knew he was going to have a hard enough time executing his peers and friends. He didn't think he could kill his brother, too. He hadn't been able to earlier, even though he knew his brother was losing control and had admitted to being non-verbal. It hadn't even been his instinct stopping him. He'd just loved him too much to do it. *How can I kill Jer for doing what he was trained to do, for what I trained him to do?* He buried his face in his paws. *Gods. What a mess.*

CHAPTER 28

Quinn: Cub's Tour

Quinn guarded the cub's tour disguised as a chaperone and groaned inwardly as Nazari told everyone about his failure to retrieve the egg unscathed, knowing he would be teased mercilessly by the rest of his squad for it later. The two currently guarding the entrance to the barn were highly amused. To be fair, he had completely underestimated the seemingly docile creatures, and he'd chosen not to treat his bruises as a reminder not to underestimate the creatures of Earth in the future. *Who knew such a tiny creature could have such an attitude or such a painful bite?*

His attention shifted to Little Flower and GrandFather slowly making their way to the barn, and he snorted. *If she could take on the Senior Council, I should have known better. I wonder if that's a common trait for Earth creatures? They are small, so they would have to be fierce to defend themselves from predators. Henry Curtis traveled close to fifty leagues and confronted Damon with nothing more than a flimsy knife to defend himself.*

He made a note to add knife defense to that evening's training regimen. It had been some time since he'd worked on disarming techniques, and they should familiarize themselves with the tiny weapon the Huemans seemed to prefer. *They have nothing in the way of natural defenses. It's not surprising they'd make claws of their own. The question is, have they made more than that?* He'd spent several hours reviewing the logs of everything printed in the Guild and hadn't identified anything, but nearly half of the items were completely unknown to him, and nothing would prevent someone from sending the plans for a weapon to someone else to manufacture, or for someone to purchase a printer of their own.

He refocused his thoughts on his primary duties at the moment and shifted his attention briefly to the guards trailing Little Flower and GrandFather, and then scanned the surrounding area. Having the cubs here was a risk, but while people were still jagged and on edge, they'd found little evidence of anyone else in the community being involved in the events of the past few days, and with Rip dead and Damon in custody, the Hue-man Council had decided to go ahead with it.

The trip had been planned for some time, and someone had to be the first group to visit, but they were taking precautions. An additional squad had flown in, vetted by Kendra, and he was spending his morning herding kittens, which was proving to be far more challenging and interesting than he'd expected.

They were a rambunctious group and full of non-stop questions, even though they were still learning how to sign. Nazari was a riot and a natural with children, and he found his tail curled more often than not at the stories she told of the various creatures and the challenges they'd had in learning to care for them, and he found himself learning just as much as the cubs.

In his last visit to New Hope, he'd not spent any time in the barn as he'd been focused on Marsee, and while he'd toured the facility after they decided to guard Damon there, he'd not paid much attention to the creatures themselves, as he'd been far more focused on identifying potential security issues.

He relaxed slightly as they started to enter the relative safety of the barn.

"Are you the Honor Guard that was chased by the geese?" one of the cubs asked one of the guards at the door as they entered.

"No child. I wouldn't have been stupid enough to take that bet. The creatures of Earth may be small, but they're fierce, especially when protecting their young," the guard replied.

Quinn glared at the guard, but that just made her even more amused, especially knowing he couldn't say anything to defend himself to the cubs while in disguise.

Once the last of the cubs were inside, he gave the guard another glare. "And I wouldn't be stupid enough to call my senior stupid in public, even if he was. I'll see you here first thing tomorrow morning to see if you can do any better."

The other guard snorted with amusement as he ducked inside, and Quinn heard the sounds of a bet being placed as the door shut behind him.

He followed Nazari, his attention only half on the tour, but it wasn't long before his ears picked up the sounds of hoofbeats coming from the direction of the arena.

The cubs eventually noticed, too, so Nazari changed directions, and they made their way over to find out what was going on since the cubs had no interest in anything else at that point.

Quinn was just as impressed to see Little Flower riding the horse, even knowing what Henry had done. She could barely walk or maintain her balance and struggled to hold the strange leash the creature was wearing, yet the horse followed her commands without the slightest hint of hesitation.

What surprised him even more were the emotions coming off the horse. This creature not only trusted Little Flower but cared for her and was happy to do what she asked. If anything, Buster seemed bored with how easy of a task he'd been given. Quinn was even more surprised when the horse not only didn't seem scared by the wall of excited and clamoring cubs but welcomed their attention. But that was nothing compared to his astonishment when Buster allowed the cubs to ride on him without even the slightest issue.

Both Little Flower and Nazari had stated that horses were a prey species, and for it to allow a predator to willingly sit on its back in the most vulnerable of positions was unheard of. It wasn't just that it was well trained, but it trusted the Hue-mans around him not to put him in a dangerous position.

Nor did any of the cubs have any sort of issue with their own hunter's instinct, which he had been worried about. If anything, the cubs were completely enamored with the strange-looking Earth creature, and as far as he could tell, the horse knew it.

He hit the button on the camera attached to his carry harness to flag the recording for further review later, knowing it would automatically show up on the main monitors in Command. He chuckled, wondering what they were thinking right now, and half expected someone to contact him for confirmation that his feed hadn't been tampered with. To be fair, he was beginning to wonder if his own senses had been tampered with. There was intelligence and curiosity in those dark brown eyes, and as he watched Henry Curtis ride, he began to wonder if the horse was sentient and decided to come back later for further observation.

After they left the Arena, they moved on to the second level, where many of the smaller creatures were housed, and he found himself laughing hard as Nazari told tale after tale about the various creatures and even brought several out for them to interact with. One creature they were told was called a skunk and was born with a defensive mechanism that sprayed a very noxious odor, but they'd since learned how to remove the scent gland and found out that the creature was actually very friendly. She was one of the ones that they'd managed to figure out how to clone so far, and her tiny kittens were adorable.

The feline exhibits were the most interesting from his own perspective, tiny miniature versions of themselves. The biggest of the feline species could have easily been mistaken for one of their own cubs. While he'd frequented the mating centers often in his youth, none of the females he'd mated with had ever offered a partnership after. That didn't bother him, though. It had been enjoyable, but there hadn't been any sense of attachment. His proteges were his children, and he helped care for the children of the other guards, but these felines were so adorable that they made him smile wistfully.

"Can they talk?" one of the cubs asked.

"I suppose that depends on what you consider talking," Nazari replied. "They make many of the same sounds we do and for the same reasons. They growl and hiss and purr, and their body language is very similar. It's not difficult to understand how they're feeling. The cubs are far more vocal and social than their parents, but they've never said anything more than any of our young cubs do before they learn how to speak. Perhaps with time, they'll learn our language or we theirs. They are genetically very different from us, even though they look very similar. This is a prime example of convergent evolution, where creatures who take up the same ecological niche develop similar characteristics. I'm told that the Hue-mans had even larger felines, some bigger than you."

"Like the saber tooth tiger?" another cub asked.

"Exactly. However, that creature went extinct around three thousand standard years ago on Earth, after the end of their last ice age. They were unable to adapt to the changing temperatures and the loss of many of their primary food sources, like the mammoth, another example of convergent evolution. However, unlike our chenzies, the mammoth was designed for cold weather habitation."

Quinn frowned when Nazari brought one of the tiny kittens out for them to see as he sniffed grief and longing from her and she twanged hard before leaving their pen. Thankfully, she recovered quickly, and no one else appeared to notice.

The rest of the tour was uneventful, if informative. The last stop was a small booth where the cubs were able to choose a souvenir. Many chose a copy of Little Flower's book on Earth creatures or the latest of Marsee's translations, while others picked out small stuffies in the shapes of the various creatures. They did have to break up a small squabble when they ran out of the stuffed horses. It was no surprise that everyone wanted a Buster stuffy.

Nazari walked up to him. "I see I'm going to have to order more of those. I have a feeling Buster is going to be very popular."

Quinn chuckled. "If the Senior Guild Master is smart, she's already got people working on it."

Once the cubs were safely on their shuttles back to Sand Dune, he turned to Nazari. "Shall we go for that run now?"

Nazari nodded, and they took off. The pace wasn't nearly as punishing as the day before, and Nazari stopped once they were out of sight of New Hope.

"What's bothering you?" Quinn asked, although he already had a pretty good idea. "I saw you struggle to leave the feline pens."

Nazari sat with a sigh, and he sensed waves of sadness rolling off her. "They were my wards at the Agency, too, and the mother reminds me of one of my daughters. She only lived for a few days."

"Did she have a name?" Quinn asked.

Nazari shook her head. "She didn't live to her name day, and nothing ever fit. I knew that she wasn't going to survive. She was born too early and had too many complications. I think a part of me knew it would be even harder if she had a name. I had the trauma center deal with her body. I couldn't bring myself to look at her, to admit that she was gone. I don't even know what they did with her. Did you know that's how I met Myra? She was in the trauma center with Marsee at the same time. She'd lost one of her cubs and both her parents the week before and Marsee was barely holding on. Even after her own losses, she checked on me. I don't think I would have survived without her support and friendship. I've always been a bit of an outsider, never really fitting in, and had few close friends at the time. I had a real attitude when I was younger."

"And you don't now?" Quinn teased.

Nazari snorted and rolled her eyes. "Like I said, I never did well with authority. The only one who ever really put up with me was my mentor. How she managed was beyond me. Thankfully, my patients don't seem to care about my attitude. If anything, it's an advantage. I've found that the Hue-mans are just as snarky, and I fit here better than I have anywhere else in my life, even if many still don't trust me. They have no respect for authority either. GrandFather and Henry challenge everything I teach them, but I've learned a lot from them too. I suppose if you do end up killing me, I couldn't think of two better people to give my life up for. Do me a favor, though…"

Quinn tilted his head for her to continue.

"If you do have to put me down, come up with some other reason for it. Blame it on a sand spinner or something. I don't want them to know it was because I went after them. They already have enough trauma to deal with."

Quinn nodded. That wasn't a problem. They often hid the cause of death when it was from psychosis.

Nazari twanged hard and visibly flinched.

"Are you alright, Nazari?" he signed.

"Not really," she replied, thankfully still speaking. "I think another run would be good."

So run they did. She pushed the pace hard this time, to the point he was starting to tire before she finally stumbled to a walk and turned back in the direction of New Hope.

"Better?" he asked.

"I think so," she replied. "Or at least no worse."

"Is your instinct speaking to you?"

She looked over at him and shrugged. "Maybe? Sometimes I think it might be. I'm not sure how to describe it. Before, there was just this constant pressure to go after him, but since the other day, there have been times when it almost seems like it is. I'm probably going mad, but…at times, it seems wholly separate from me, and struggling to understand our culture and customs, as if it's waking up and looking around for the first time. I've found myself trying to explain as if it were a small cub, and that sometimes helps. Take just now, it… It can't decide if you're a friend or a threat and doesn't understand why you see it as a threat as it's never hurt anyone and only wants to protect our cubs."

Quinn raised a brow. This was very different from his own experiences and the vast majority of those brought into the Guard. He'd only ever heard his own instinct once, right before he transitioned, and it had wanted to kill Kendra. But so, too, were her circumstances. He'd been sparing at the time. Curious to see what would happen, he decided to respond as if it were its own entity. "I'm both, but I'd much rather be a friend. I find that works better in the long run, even if I am down by ten credits and probably won't hear the end of it for the next decade."

She snorted in amusement. "I warned you."

"So you did. However, I'm not one to pass up a challenge," he replied. "Is it pressuring you to hunt at all?"

"No, just go after him. That's all it wants, and it's prepared to fight for him, but it doesn't really care how we get him back, just that we do."

"Hmm. I'll admit, your reaction and its demands are unusual. Although I suppose protecting our children is about as instinctive as it gets."

"Like I said yesterday, it doesn't understand why we would be punished for saving another cub or why you would kill me for using it to do so in the first place, or at least that's the sense I get. Intellectually, I understand why, but I suppose my heart doesn't."

"There's nothing inherently wrong with using your instinct. Its whole purpose is to protect us when we need it. It's when it pressures you into doing something that you don't want to do that it's bad, like it did the other night when it made you go to the apartments. As long as you remain in control and don't hurt anyone, there's no problem."

Nazari twanged hard again, and she tilted her head as if listening. Suddenly, her eyes went unfocused, dilating, and he tensed.

"Nazari? Are you alright?" he signed again.

"Why was our cub taken from us?"

Nazari's voice was flat and stilted, and he frowned, surprised by the question. He was worried Nazari was losing control, but she wasn't acting violently, and she was talking, so he decided to see where this would go. He'd only ever heard of Marsee using plural pronouns, but then everything about Marsee's case was unique.

"Because the Hue-mans did not trust you to care for the cub properly. We made mistakes in their care that hurt them, that hurt your cub, too. He is not your cub, even though you love him. He was born to a mother of another species, and the leaders of his species decided he was better off with one of their own."

"We raised him, cared for him, protected him. They had no right to take him from us."

"Yes, you did protect him, and I believe he should have gone to you, but that was their right to decide, just as it is our right to decide with our own species, but at this point, he's likely to have developed an attachment to his new mother, and to take him from his mother now would only hurt him more. You don't want to hurt him, do you?"

"We would never hurt our cub, but we want him back. How do we get him back?"

"By proving you can be trusted. Give Nazari back control and never take it from her again unless she gives you permission. Listen to her. She understands what needs to be done. It might not work, but it's the only chance you have. If you try to take him by force or do not give back control, I will kill you. Give back control, and I will do everything within my power to help you get your cub back."

She was silent and perfectly still for several long moments, although her soul boundary twanged hard. "You promise? This is not a trick?"

"I give you my word," Quinn replied, thinking this was the strangest conversation he'd ever had.

Suddenly, Nazari collapsed and started panting hard. "Ancient Gods!" she swore.

"Are you all right?" he asked, helping her sit up.

"I honestly have no idea. That was the strangest experience of my life." She rubbed a paw against the back of her head. "It said it wanted to ask questions, but I didn't expect that!"

"That makes two of us," he replied. "How do you feel now? Has it backed off?"

"Yes and no. It's waiting to see what you do," she replied after a moment and rubbed at her head again. "Gah, that's such a weird feeling."

"I gave you my word, and I *never* break my word. I'll reach out to the Senior Council on your behalf and see what we can do."

"Are you going to tell them what happened here?" she asked with a worried frown.

He paused to consider and shook his head. "No, I don't think they'll understand. I'll discuss your concerns about being on the watch and how that would unfairly affect your case."

She nodded and sighed with relief as her instinct settled.

"Better?" he asked.

"Much. I can still sense it, but it's backed off considerably," she replied.

"Well, I suppose that's an improvement."

She nodded her agreement and rubbed at her head again, harder this time.

He watched her closely. "I need to see that you're still in control. Turn it on for me."

She did and turned it off again without issue. "Is this normal?" she asked. "I learned about psychosis, but I've never seen or treated anyone with it, and none of this was in my training."

"Yes and no," he replied. "It's very concerning. Historically, hearing it speak or speaking in plural, as you just did, is a very bad sign. I've only known one other who regained control after that happened, but I'd much rather be able to negotiate a truce than the alternative, if that's even a possibility. I should bring you in, but I'm not going to, not as long as you remain in control. You've shown no signs of violence, and you remained verbal. I want to see where this goes. As far as I'm concerned, anything we can do to improve a person's chances of survival is worth the risk."

Nazari frowned. "I'm really that bad?"

He nodded sadly. "You are, but if Marsee can recover, so can you."

"Marsee? Myra didn't..." She wilted, her ears drooping with grief. "Oh... Her injuries are a cover, aren't they? That's why she has an honor guard already?"

Quinn shook his head. "I figured Myra or GrandFather would have told you. She's the first to recover from an advanced case. Thankfully, sign language cuts through. Her injuries are not a front, at least not yet anyway. Who knows what they'll find when she wakes up? She's surprised us before, and I have a feeling she will again, too. As for her honor guard, no, that has nothing to do with her past history of psychosis. She's more than earned it, perhaps more than anyone in centuries."

"What Marsee went through was horrific, but I don't understand why I'm having trouble. I've been through far more traumatic experiences in my life than hunting down Damon. Why would this be a problem now?"

"For two reasons. One, because you used your instinct for a significant length of time and because you haven't dealt with the underlying trauma yet, which has been compounded by your current custody battle and by going after the others. It may have happened twenty years ago, but that doesn't lessen your grief or the fact that you abandoned your daughter."

She flinched as if slapped and then took a long shuddering breath, but even though she tried hard not to, tears began streaming down her face.

"Perhaps it's time you gave her a name and found out where they buried her," he said softly.

"I don't know if I can," she replied, wiping the tears away.

"Would you like me to find out for you?" he asked. He already knew, but he wasn't going to tell her that.

Nazari sighed but didn't respond. Instead, she started walking for New Hope again. It wasn't until they were in sight of the compound that she stopped, sat down, and broke the silence. "Do you really think it would help?"

"Holding onto grief and guilt never helps."

She nodded. "Find out, but I'm not sure I'm ready to know just yet." She stood and walked off.

He watched her leave, knowing she was done talking. He sighed when she was out of sight, both worried and intrigued by what had happened earlier, and was just about to open his tablet to send messages to the Senior Council and Kendra when his comms went off, blaring with an alert.

CHAPTER 29

Little Flower:
Healer Samin

"Marsee woke, found out about her room, and threw her tablet in anger. She ripped out half the sutures in her new organs. Thankfully, there was a healer with her when it happened because Marsee didn't feel a thing."

"Dark moons..." Little Flower signed.

Her mother just stood there looking lost and forlorn. Little Flower set aside her coloring book and pencils and tapped the side of her bed. Her mother nodded and climbed in carefully next to her, and they cuddled, each trying to comfort the other. Her mother was too scared to purr. She was still wrapped in her mother's arms when Ammond appeared.

"She's still sedated, but they intend to tell her what's going on when she wakes up," Ammond said. He handed Myra her tablet, which she'd left in her office so that she could review the medical reports herself.

"She doesn't know yet?" Little Flower asked.

"No, we wanted to protect her until we knew more about what she was facing, but we don't really have much of a choice now," Ammond replied. "She'll have to learn to be very cautious about everything she does."

"If she reacted that badly to her room, she's going to be inconsolable about this. I hope they'll be ready to sedate her," Little Flower said.

Ammond nodded sadly and left.

Her mother continued to snuggle with her as they waited for an update on how Marsee took the news, and about an hour later, her mother's tablet dinged. She frowned, then stiffened.

"I take it. It didn't go well?" she asked after waving to get her mother's attention.

Her mother looked up from the screen and shook her head. "It's from Marcus. He says he had her turn her instinct on, but she refused at first and then said she couldn't. He's choosing to believe her for now." Her mother swallowed hard.

"What aren't you telling me?"

"He could have killed her for refusing and still might. I'm not aware of anyone who can't use their instinct. There was no mention of that in the other cases we found, and it certainly never came up in any of my training. More often than not, it's the other way around, where a traumatic brain injury causes people to lose control."

Her mother went back to reading, but moments later, her ears flicked back.

"Now what?"

"Marsee blamed her father for her injuries and had the guards drag him out of the room."

"Why is she blaming Papa? That doesn't make any sense."

Her mother kept reading. "Apparently, for letting her kill Rip Current as if he hadn't, she might not be in this situation."

"Ahh, I guess I can see her point, but isn't that her right since he tried to kill her?" Little Flower asked.

"It is, and frankly, if she was as out of control as her father said at that point, he'd have never been able to get her 'prey' away from her without a fight." Her mother went back to reading and then started growling, or at least that's what she thought the sound was, as she could barely hear it, and bolted out of the room, tail lashing behind her.

What's going on now? she wondered and carefully made her way out of the room after her. Her mother rarely got that angry.

Down at the end of the hall, by the triage desk, she saw her mother, ears pinned and tail lashing as she hissed and growled at Journeyman Healer Samin.

The poor healer's tail was tucked between her legs and fully poofed in fright, but she was giving it back to her mother just as loudly.

GrandFather must have just entered the ward as he was standing about halfway down the hall, holding a large tray of food for their supper and watching the commotion.

Ammond came barreling past her on all fours, grabbed her mother by the scruff, and pulled her way from the other healer. He growled something at her, pointed in the direction of his office, and shoved hard.

Her mother stormed past her with Ammond right behind, both of their tails lashing. He slammed the door shut, but it did nothing to block the growls and yells coming from his office.

"What the heck is going on?" GrandFather asked when he walked up beside her.

"I don't know, but I'm glad I'm not Healer Samin right now."

They stood there and watched for a few minutes before the door opened, and Ammond walked out. He turned back to face his office, arms crossed, tail thwapping hard, and glaring at her mother as he waited. He was normally gruff, but she'd never seen him angry before, and he was downright livid.

A minute later, her mother left the room, healer's mask firmly in place, and walked past them again.

Ammond followed closely behind.

She said something to Healer Samin, who nodded, and then her mother turned and stormed out of the Trauma Center.

"What was that all about? Is something wrong with Marsee?" she asked Ammond when he returned, but he just shook his head and walked back into his office, slamming the door behind him.

CHAPTER 30

Quinn: Alert

Quinn frowned as he listened to the coded alert coming in from the guard watching Myra, then hit his comms. "I'm about two leagues out. ETA six minutes," he replied and took off at full speed.

A few minutes later, the guard called back. "Be advised. Target just left. Do you want me to follow or stay here?"

"Stay. I'll handle it."

He hadn't made it back when Myra came barreling out of the compound over by the Tower and took off at a full run. He winced when he saw just how jagged she was.

"Target spotted, heading west out into the Wilds. All available guards, Alert level four, pursue but do not approach. Command, notify Kendra, and request backup. Trauma Ship One on standby."

He took off after Myra, staying back far enough that she wasn't aware of him. He wanted her as far away from New Hope as possible if she did lose control. Even with the added guards flown in for the cub's tour, they would be hard-pressed to contain the situation without someone getting hurt if she lost control. It wasn't long before the other guards caught up with him.

They ran for leagues before she finally came to a stop in a small, protected grove of ghost trees. With a ferocious snarl, she swiped hard at one and let off a litany of swears before stopping to pick out the thorns embedded in her paw.

He breathed a sigh of relief that she was still talking but frowned when she switched to using her teeth to try and work them out and then followed it up by licking at her paw after spitting a thorn out.

Instinctive grooming or trained medical response? he wondered.

He motioned for his guards to circle and stay out of sight. They split off and disappeared. He took a deep breath and another before slowly approaching. When he was close but still out of her range, he sat down, waiting for her to notice him and trying to appear as nonthreatening as possible. If he could calm her, there was still a chance he could save her.

She paused her licking to dig at another thorn, muttered under her breath, and spit that one out, too. When she apparently had all the thorns out, she stood and started pacing again but jumped when she saw him, startled by his presence, and pinned her ears back with a low growl. "What are *you* doing here?" she hissed at him.

"Following you, obviously," Quinn replied, flicking his ears back at her attitude towards him, which was incredibly rare. People usually reacted in fear to the guards, but Myra was furious. "What happened?"

"What *happened* is that my soon-to-be *former* partner attacked my child several months ago, and now she's dying in a trauma center because of it." Ears still pinned to her skull and tail lashing, she turned and swiped at the tree again with a growl of rage, sending large clumps of wood flying. If she'd picked up more thorns, she didn't react to it.

"No," he said quietly. "He did not attack her. He was testing her control."

"How do *you* know what happened?" she spat, turning her glare back to him, and started pacing again.

"Because I'm the one that investigated the flag, along with Kendra, and watched her the entire time she was in Council City. I also guarded her on her return trip to New Hope and was here for several weeks after he returned to make sure nothing else happened, even though Kendra dropped the watch."

She stopped her pacing and looked at him with surprise. "Why didn't you tell me what he did so I could protect her?"

"Because Marsee didn't want you to know," he replied calmly.

"But I'm her mother!"

"And she's an adult and old enough to make her own decisions. She didn't want you to worry about her with everything else going on."

She glared at him, but he could tell she wasn't mad at him. He was just there. "What possible reason could he have had that would justify breaking her shoulder and clawing her?! That kind of attack would put anyone over the edge."

"He wanted her away from New Hope because he thought she *was* losing control," he replied. "Just like you're dangerously close to losing control right now."

She pinned her ears and huffed at him. "I'm perfectly in control of my instinct. I'm *talking* to you, aren't I? *I'm* the one that wants to claw him for what he did to my daughter, not my instinct."

"Is that a threat?" he asked.

She snorted. "How? The last I checked, he was on the Water World. I'm livid, but that doesn't mean I'm going to act on it. Why do you think I'm out here clawing trees instead? Be honest. You'd feel the same if it was your own children."

He nodded the point. "I don't have children, but I understand your anger. Councilor Chenzira was doing what he was trained to do, and... that's one of the hardest parts of being in the Council or the Guard. From everything I learned, he had just cause, too. He would not have been able to control her on his own if she had been losing control, and he nearly died to protect New Hope. Marsee pinned him *after* she broke her shoulder."

"Like I believe that," Myra huffed.

"Your daughter just killed a fully grown adult Water Sprite, capable of killing her with a touch, and she did it with a badly broken paw. I know what those shocks feel like. I train with the Sprites often. I've never once been able to fight through even a fraction of the pain she experienced, but she did. Taking on Councilor Chenzira would have been cub's play in comparison. She won that fight with her father, had him pinned with his neck in her mouth, and walked away. It's the only reason she's alive today. Not only should she have been put down that day for the behavior he witnessed, but what she learned in that fight likely saved her life when fighting Rip. For what it's worth, the broken shoulder was an accident. He deflected one of her attacks, and she landed badly."

Myra huffed again and sat down, facing away from him. She was still angry, but she was also pleased that Marsee had won, and some of her jaggedness went away. Only then did she look at her paw and start digging another thorn out.

"Stupid tree," he heard her mutter, "and stupid thorns."

He sighed with relief and walked over to face her.

She looked up at him, paw in her mouth and with a crooked expression as she continued to dig at the thorn. She eventually got ahold of it and spit it out. "What kind of behavior?"

"She was clawing trees, just like you, and then she sprayed them."

Myra winced and looked away. "Are you sure that's what happened?"

He nodded. "The trail she left behind was quite clear."

She sighed and then looked back at him. "Why didn't you bring her in?"

"Everything about your daughter is unique. You're right. What he did should have put her over the edge, but it didn't. We chose to watch and learn instead. Now, I need you to turn on your instinct for me."

She huffed at him again and rolled her eyes, thoroughly annoyed, but did as requested without hesitation.

He waited for several minutes, watching her closely, frowning at the jagged twangs he saw. She was dangerously close to losing control, and he debated whether he should bring her into the guard or kill her now before it was too late.

"So how did you find out?" he asked, wondering if she could still speak.

"Marcus messaged me to find out if Jer had hurt me, too. As if I'd let him get away with raising a claw to me. Apparently, when Marsee found out about the full extent of her injuries, she blamed Jer for her loss of control and had the guards throw him out of the room."

He snorted and flicked his ears back in astonishment. "You're serious? She had him dragged out, a member of the Senior Council?"

Myra preened with pride for her daughter. "Serves him right. He should know better than to mess with my children."

"When it comes to *your* children, the gods themselves should know better. You can turn it off now."

She did without hesitation, which surprised him. People that jagged usually struggled. *Perhaps she is just angry. She has every reason to be after everything that has been done to her family.* He signaled for the rest of his guards to stand down.

Only then did she notice them, and she gasped when she realized what was really going on. "I swear I'm in control of my instinct! I'm just angry."

"It was a precaution. Myra, I'll be honest with you. You are *not* as in control as you think you are. What's been done to your family would put anyone over the edge. You've gone from one trauma to the next for the past year or more. You need to take some time off and do something you find enjoyable before it becomes too late."

"I don't have time for that. Marsee's..."

"Marsee will recover."

"You don't know that!" she hissed.

"I do. If she's awake and talking, she'll recover."

"No, she won't! Not in the long run." Myra's anger vanished, replaced with a sob of heartbroken grief. "She has no instinct anymore. She can't turn it on, or so she says, and she has no sense of pain or even any reflexes anymore. Without them, she'll never survive her growth spurt, assuming you all don't put her down first."

He shook his head. "No. We won't do that. Not unless she starts acting violently. There are protocols when someone has a brain injury."

Myra frowned. "I'm not aware of anyone not being able to use their instinct, and I've been studying psychosis for the last decade."

"It's probably because it's not listed as psychosis, and more often than not, the person has other, far more limiting disabilities that make it moot anyway. Regardless, I wouldn't worry about Marsee. She has the heart of an Honor Guard and will face this challenge head-on, just like she has all the rest. How well she recovers depends on you. You'll be able to help her better if *you* take some time to rest and recover. No one thinks clearly when they're exhausted. You need to heal yourself before you can heal anyone else. Your ability to control your emotions is severely lacking right now. That's understandable with everything you've been through, but it's also a symptom of not treating your own trauma or giving yourself time to recover. Your instinct will take advantage of that sooner rather than later if you don't do something about it. If your protege did what you did today, what would you do?"

She sighed. "I'd probably tell them the same or relieve them of duty." Growling with frustration, she stood and started pacing again.

"What's really bothering you?"

"That isn't enough?" she snapped.

He said nothing, just waited.

Myra growled and huffed before stopping, her back to him again and her claws digging into the ground. Guilt radiated off her in waves.

"I think the person you're really angry with is yourself," Quinn said softly.

She growled again, which told him he was right.

"Why?" he pressed.

"Because I'm their mother, and I'm supposed to be their protector!" she growled out.

"And you failed to protect them."

It wasn't a question, but she nodded. "I failed them both. I knew something had happened to Marsee when she left unexpectedly with Ellie, but I believed Jer when he said she was struggling with dealing with her sister's illness and the changes to New Hope. I should have talked to her about it, but I was too busy focusing on Little Flower, and I failed Little Flower, too. I should have stayed in the room with them like Jer told me to. I didn't even pay enough attention to keep her from nearly drowning yesterday."

"Why didn't you stay in the room?" he asked.

"Because I was stupid," she muttered.

"And?"

"And exhausted," she finally admitted and slumped back down. "I'd been up for four days straight taking care of Little Flower after her surgery, and I didn't think that anyone would go after them. I thought they were targeting Jer. I should have known better."

"How could you? You were exhausted, just as you are now. Sleep deprivation is just as disabling as being under the influence of a narcotic, and you know it."

She sighed but didn't turn around to face him. "I'm honestly afraid to go to sleep now. I'm afraid if I do, they'll be gone when I wake up, and when I do finally sleep, my dreams are full of night terrors. Yesterday, I took a few minutes for myself, and look what happened? My daughter nearly died because of it."

"There are multiple guards watching your children now. They'll protect them, just like they did yesterday," Quinn replied.

"The guards were protecting Marsee, and that didn't stop Rip from kidnapping her or letting Rip escape and attack her a second time," Myra turned and spat at him.

He sighed. "You're right. We failed to protect your children, too. I failed to get here in time. I failed to recognize the full extent of the threat that Damon posed when I was here before. The guards on the Water World were betrayed by the very people they should have been able to trust, and Avery left your daughter alone. However, Marsee ordered Avery away, GrandFather ordered you away, and Little Flower is an adult and chose to go in the pool on her own. You can choose to blame yourself, blame the guards, blame your family for sending their protection away, or put the blame where it really belongs, on those who tried to kill them. We can only ever do our best, and far too often, that's not good enough. Just like you can't save everyone under your care, we can't anticipate every threat, even though we try. That being said, your children are probably the most guarded people on all five planets right now, and I can personally vouch for every single guard stationed here."

"How do you know they weren't working with Rip, too?" she asked.

"Because every single one of them was willing to commit treason to protect your daughter and her people from the Senior Council, as was I, and I have worked with these guards for decades, and I know their character and trust them with my life. They would willingly give their lives to protect your family and to protect the Consortium from the likes of people like Rip Current. Our oath is not to the Council. It's to the people, to ensure that their rights and freedoms are protected. We guard the Council's honor because we know that power breeds corruption, and we guard ourselves against that as well, viciously."

She turned away from him again. "I don't know how I will trust anyone again, guard, council, or otherwise. Every time I turn around, that trust is being broken. I don't even trust myself anymore."

"I know," he replied. "None of us are perfect. If we were, we'd be gods, and even then, I wonder. But you can trust me. I will do everything I can to protect your family. I'd rather not have to protect your family from you, but I will if I have to. Get some rest. That's an order."

With that, he stood and walked away, knowing she needed time to gather her thoughts, but once out of her sight, he circled back around to keep watch from a distance and saw his own guards hadn't gone far either. He nodded with approval before disappearing from sight.

As he waited and watched, his thoughts drifted to Marsee, and rather than feeling relief to hear that she'd survived her injuries and woken, he was terrified of what was to come, and he felt horrible for wishing she'd died.

CHAPTER 31

Jer: Guilty as Charged

Jer punched the drone as fast as it would go, but it wasn't nearly fast enough to outrun the guilt and self-loathing he felt. Every time he turned around, he made the wrong decisions, said the wrong things, and hurt those he loved. He was crushed by Marsee's words, but he knew he deserved every one of them. People jumped out of the way and flashed his concern as he barreled through the market, but he paid them absolutely no attention. He didn't stop until suddenly, there was nothing but the open sea in front of him.

Blinking in surprise, he finally looked around and realized where he was. He'd come all the way out to the Trench. He didn't even remember the path he'd taken to get there. He looked down over the edge at the darkness that Marsee had been trapped in and shuddered. He was terrified of the dark, and Marsee had spent more than two days down there because of him, because he hadn't immediately given in to Rip's demands. He'd waited. Not that he ever expected Rip to honor his end of the ransom and return Marsee alive. So much had been done to her in that time, but she'd been stronger than him and survived. She'd beaten Rip Current with nothing more than her teeth and claws and had gone back out, not even fully recovered to try and save the others, but now she was dying, and it was all because of him.

Rip had wanted to destroy him, had used Marsee to do so, and it had worked. He had nothing left to give. Nothing he could do or give her would ever make it right. She hated him for what he'd done to her, but it was no less than how much he hated himself. Rip hadn't taken her future from her. He had. She'd killed a part of herself to avoid killing him, had sacrificed hundreds of years of her life for him, and he didn't deserve it. He should have been the one to protect her, not the other way around. He should be the one lying in the Trauma Center, not her. A big part of him wanted to throw himself over the ledge, his life for the years he'd stolen from her, but unlike before with Marcus, his instinct now held him fast.

Remember your oath, the voice that wasn't his said again. *You promised the gods of the deep to make things right for everyone else if she woke. The gods gave you your wish. Now you know their price.*

He sighed, unsure if he could bear the weight of that price and everything that was to come, if what the others were already finding was any indication, but he had given his oath. Marsee had woken, and he would do everything in his power to make things right for her, somehow. Granted, he might not get a chance if she decided to press charges against him. He was honestly surprised Avery had let him go.

If she wants my life for hers, so be it, he thought with a sigh so heavy it was almost a sob. It was really the only thing he had to give her.

"I wouldn't jump if I were you. It's a long way down, and you'll get bored long before you hit bottom."

He spun to find Clear Seas floating a few feet behind him. "What are you doing here?" he growled. The last thing he wanted to do right now was talk to anyone.

"Trying to decide whether I need to arrest you or not," Clear Seas replied. "It's not every day a member of the Senior Council gets thrown out of a room by the guards. Plus, half the people in Council Platform saw you leave the Trauma Center and take off like a Leviathan was chasing you. Rumor was spreading that Marsee was dead. I've heard from Stinger and Hyacinth about the incident, and even the head of the Press Guild called to find out if Marsee had died."

"You might as well kill me now. I won't fight the charges. She's as good as dead, and it's all my fault," he said, turning around, unable to look at Clear Seas' flash of sympathy. What he deserved was anger or revulsion.

"What really happened between you and Marsee?" The sympathy that had been there a moment before vanished, and Clear Sea's voice now had a hardness he had never heard before.

Jer spun back to look at Clear Seas in confusion. "You already know what happened."

"Do I? Or is she right? *Were* you trying to get rid of her?"

"Of course not!" He sighed, all fight going out of him, as he admitted to himself that it wasn't entirely true. "The last thing I want to do is kill my daughter, but I took an oath to protect the people before myself and my family. I was sure she was losing control. She was showing all the signs of slipping, and I didn't want anyone to get hurt or for anyone to see it if I had to put her down. We might not be able to save people, but we do everything we can to protect their reputations."

"Have you hurt her otherwise?"

Jer snorted. "Every decision I've made throughout her entire life has hurt her in one way or another, although that was never my intention."

Clear Seas frowned. "Is that an admission of guilt?"

He shrugged. "I never considered it abuse before, but I suppose it was. I've only hit her one other time. That, too, was a test. I hated to do even that. It happened just after the trial. I saw her bolt onto my ship and found her with her instinct on. She didn't even know it was on. She was in control but was overwhelmed with the construction, crowds, and anger at you and the rest of the Senior Council for what you nearly did to her."

"She had every reason to be angry," Clear Seas replied. "But what else did you mean?"

"You know how much time the Council takes away from our families. Between Myra's career and my own and the remote location of our home, she spent much of her childhood alone and in that tower of hers or with Myra at the clinic. The months Myra was at the Agency were the worst. I didn't even realize for over a month when she stopped attending her guild classes in person. She never seemed to mind being alone. If anything, she preferred it. She was happiest when I brought her to Marcus's so she could lose herself in his library. She's always valued her independence and privacy and hated going anywhere where there was a crowd. We didn't know until Little Flower arrived that her hearing was bothering her. Well, we did, but we always thought it was an excuse to get out of doing something she didn't want to do."

He turned to stare out at the empty sea again. "I never believed her, not when it mattered. It's no wonder she doesn't trust me. Every time she needed me, I wasn't there, or I did the wrong thing, just like I did in the canyon. I was trying to save her life, but I didn't listen to her. I didn't listen to what she needed, and instead of helping her, all I've done is take her children and hundreds of years of her life from her."

Clear Seas swam up beside him and placed a hand on his shoulder. "Jer, we could all get into a shuttle accident tomorrow. None of our lives are guaranteed. Just because we *can* live for hundreds of years doesn't mean we do."

He looked over at Clear Seas, shaking his head. "But if I hadn't let her kill him, she might still have had a full and happy life."

"It was her right to kill him, and if she hadn't killed him right then and there, he might have gotten away. We didn't have a shock collar to contain his charge, and I'm not sure I would have been able to kill him before he killed all three of us."

"Perhaps, but if you'd seen her today..."

"I saw the recording, and I'll be honest, I haven't made up my mind about that test, but I've seen that kind of anger before. Heck, I've been on the receiving end of it on more than one occasion. I'm sure you have, too. She was angry at the situation, not you. If you're telling the truth, she'll get over it once she's had time to process everything, and I have a feeling she'll forgive you eventually."

"I doubt it," he muttered. "I wouldn't."

Clear Seas briefly bubbled his amusement. "Well, we've already determined she's far better than you at just about everything. I imagine this will be no different."

"Thanks. You're so kind." He turned away to look out at the dark, empty sea in front of him.

"Any time," Clear Seas replied. "Now, what's really bothering you?"

He snorted. "You mean besides being a complete failure to the people I'm supposed to represent and my utter lack of ability to protect my family and people or make a decision that doesn't hurt the people I care about?"

Clear Seas chuckled. "Welcome to the club, Senior Councilor."

He rolled his eyes but didn't reply.

"Jer, being a Senior Councilor is the hardest thing I've ever done, and I was quite literally raised with the expectation that I would be the next Senior Councilor when my father died. Little Flower understood that when she gave you this role. She knew how difficult it would be, and she knew that you would be capable of managing it because she saw you make those difficult decisions and choose to protect her and her people before yourself. What was it she said to Jennette? 'Every decision you make, Councilor, has the potential for unforeseen consequences.' I've been a Senior Councilor for over a hundred years now, and yet for the past twenty, there's been a Leviathan in my midst killing my people, and I welcomed him with open arms. Rip was one of my trusted advisors. His father was one of my best friends, and I transferred that loyalty and friendship to his son without question, gave him committee positions he didn't even qualify for, and he repaid me by trying to kill both of my sons and the two most beloved people this world has ever known, and *then* he tried to frame me for it. Your daughter risked her very soul to save my son when I was too far away to protect him. I was supposed to be the one protecting her, but I was stuck on my ship, waiting for authorization. I should have made her wait. Although if we did, Petra and the others would probably be dead now. So if you're going to blame anyone for what happened, blame me. Or better yet, put the blame where it really belongs, on the now horribly shredded and permanently dead Rip Current. Little Flower was right. The darkness was here all along, and you and I, we're the last defense for our people. It's going to take a long time for our worlds to overcome the shock of what happened and learn to trust us again, assuming I don't have to kill you, and a lot of hard work and difficult and painful decisions to ensure it doesn't happen again."

"You make us sound like the superheroes from the Hue-man stories," Jer said.

"We're the closest thing this world has, but we have to make sure we don't turn into the villains in the process."

He snorted. "I'm pretty sure that's already too late for me."

There was a loud screech off in the distance that made both of them jump.

"No doubt. Now, come on. Let's get out of here. I have no desire to fight off a Leviathan today. I've had more than enough of that for one week, and I think it's long past time we had that little talk."

Jer snorted again but followed Clear Seas away from the Trench as the Leviathan once again screeched, this time sounding closer. The sound made his instinct stir, reacting to the danger, and it pushed him to leave. As much as he wished the pain in his heart would go away, along with the unbearable guilt he felt, deep down inside, he had no real desire to fight off a Leviathan or become its next meal either.

CHAPTER 32

Stormy: Super Spy

Stormy leaned back in his net and stretched as he examined the gift he was making for the Translator. It was both a thank you and an apology. He was struggling hard with his guilt. He'd swum off after promising his father to do as he was told, and Marsee had been hurt because of it. He should have stayed and protected her after the guard had left. At the very least, he should have ensured she'd followed him. Maybe then, she wouldn't be fighting for her life in the Trauma Center. But he hadn't. He'd wanted to live up to her belief that he was brave, to be the superhero she thought he was, but all he'd been was stupid.

He winced as he stretched. His entire body still felt stiff and ached, but he wasn't going to complain about it. He was lucky. The others had endured far more. He looked down at his arm, where a thin, jagged scar remained from his ordeal. The Senior Healer said it would fade with time, but he honestly hoped it didn't. He wanted the reminder that his ego and stupidity had gotten Marsee hurt. When he'd heard Marsee scream for help, he'd swum back immediately but had then frozen in fear and indecision as Rip had attacked her. He'd been pretty sure Marsee had been trying to lead Rip away from the cave to protect him, but he hadn't been able to make himself leave the cave to swim for help or to help her. It wasn't until he realized what Rip was really doing that he'd been able to act. He still hadn't been able to bring himself to talk to his father about that.

He traced the line with his other hand, as he'd been doing often these past few days. The burns were healed, but he could still feel that awful pain. It was so much more than he'd ever experienced in shock practice, or in his entire life for that matter, and he wondered how Marsee had endured it or even fought back. He hadn't been able to. Yet she'd not only fought back, she'd caught and killed Rip. *She's the real superhero. I'm nothing but a sidekick.*

He knew he'd never forget the expression on her face as she launched her attack to rescue him. It was the last thing he'd seen before he'd passed out. He was trying hard to capture that ferocity in his drawing, but he wasn't nearly skilled enough, and none of the pictures of her or any other Saber truly showed it. He sighed as he peered at his drawing and shifted the light before picking up his tablet and examining the picture again. It was hard, as his memory of her that day was without her fur and snarling, yet every picture he could find was of her furred and either smiling or serious. Only one picture even came close, and that was the moment Tabor had been about to deny Little Flower's chosen reparations at the Trial. She wasn't snarling, but there was the same look in her eyes, a simmering rage.

He examined his drawing. *The eyes are right, but something's still missing.* The light caught his scar, and he grinned as he realized what it was. He was drawing her with her fur, but that hid her scars. They'd changed her expression, made her fiercer.

A superhero should have a sigil, he decided. Grabbing a white pen, he added a few bolts along the side of her face and wrists and one larger, jagged scar along her chest, using his own scar as a reference. When he was done, he leaned back and smiled. *Perfect! Now, she really does look like a superhero.*

Satisfied, he dug through his desk for the sealer to protect it. The ink he'd used was designed for use underwater, but the sealer would ensure it would last longer and give the whole thing a glossy finish that made the grain of the wood it was drawn on pop.

He was nearly done when he heard the sound of the front door open and close.

"Councilor Chenzira, welcome," he heard his mother say. "How's Marsee?"

He swam over to his door and propped it open to hear better.

"She's still alive and talking," he replied. "but..."

Stormy's heart dropped at the pause.

"Clear told me there were injuries you didn't release to the press?"

"There are. She's lost her sense of pain, and the few people the healers have found with similar conditions didn't survive their growth spurts because of it."

Stormy flashed a mix of dark blue and grey with his grief and guilt and struggled hard to keep from crying out. *No! I've killed her!*

"How horrible. Still, that's some time off, is it not?"

"It is. I just hope Myra can find another miracle and fix her like she did with Littler Flower."

"Oh? Marsee told us Little Flower wasn't doing well. Has she improved?"

"Thankfully, yes. Just before all this happened, Ammond and Myra performed another surgery, which appears to have had a great deal of success. She's walking on her own again and even regained some of her hearing. She still has a long way to go, but I'll take any improvement."

"That's wonderful news, and I'm sure if Myra can figure out how to fix Little Flower, when we know so little about her species, she'll find a way to fix Marsee, too. Please let them both know I'm praying for them."

"I will. Thank you."

"Of course. Now, I must apologize for my rudeness, but I wasn't aware you were coming for dinner, and I was just about to head back out. There's a problem at the museum I need to attend to."

"There's nothing to apologize for. My visit was unplanned, and it's work-related anyway."

"How long do you expect to be?" his father asked. "We have a meeting this evening?"

"I'm not sure. A few hours, probably. I was going to take Stormy with me as Temperate left to visit with Melody, but if you're going to be here for a while…"

"I'll watch him," his father replied. "If you're not back before we leave, I'll bring him with me to my office. You can pick him up when you're done."

"Thank you. He's been holed up in his room all afternoon, working on a gift for Marsee. There's food in the kitchen if you're hungry. Councilor, I hope you'll join us for dinner some evening soon?"

"I'd like that, thank you," Jer replied.

Stormy quickly slid his door most of the way shut but peaked through and watched as his father and the councilor swam past. He frowned at the haggard look on Councilor Chenzira's face and the tight mask on his father's. *Is Marsee worse than he told Mama, or is something else going on? Why would they come here to discuss Council business and not talk in their offices? Because it's not recorded?* He couldn't think of any other reasons why the two would come here to talk.

Making an instant decision, knowing that he would get in a trench full of trouble if his father found out, he shut and locked his door and then swam over to the hidden door and hit the latch to open it. Lighting up his skin just enough so he could see, he ducked in and shut it behind him, but rather than taking the tunnel that would lead out, he swam in the other direction, heading towards his father's office. This section of the tunnel was narrow, twisty, and far too small for anyone else in the family to swim through, and he wondered if his father even knew about it.

There were other exits scattered throughout the cave system that made up their home and easier tunnels to access them that the whole family could use, but he knew there were sensors in those areas that would notify his father if he swam through. He'd looked hard one night when he couldn't sleep and hadn't found anything in this direction, but he was getting too big to fit. He had to twist and turn just right to make it through and nearly got stuck. *I'll need to make this spot wider,* he thought as he wiggled his way through a tight section. *I wonder if I can borrow Papa's tools without him noticing.*

A small beam of light poked through the hole in the wall, lighting up the tunnel and showing where his father's office was. He went dark, swam up as quietly as he could, and peered through.

"Fuzzle Knocker?" his father asked.

"Please," Jer replied.

His father pulled a bottle of something out of a cabinet, reached for a cup, then changed his mind and handed Jer the entire bottle. Jer took a large drink of it and sighed. Then, both Jer and his father stared at each other for several minutes without talking. The only interruption came as Jer took another sip of whatever a Fuzzle Knocker was.

"Well, this is an exciting conversation," his father said. "Shall I go first or you?"

"I can't exactly claim the moral high ground anymore," Jer replied. "So you might as well go first."

Stormy blinked in surprise and honestly wondered if he was translating the Senior Councilor's words correctly. He might not be able to speak the language yet, but he'd been learning to understand and read all the languages for as long as he could remember.

"Alright. Tell me exactly what happened that day. Don't leave anything out."

"Does it really matter? If she wants to press charges, I'm not going to fight it."

"Yes, it does. Marsee's feelings aside, you're right. We have both taken an oath to protect our people. If Marsee was out of control, it was your responsibility to stop her, just as it was my responsibility to decide if the Hue-mans were safe enough to continue existing. Tell me what happened."

Jer sighed, nodded, and took another sip before he began his story.

It was all Stormy could do to contain his emotions and stay dark as he listened. His father dug into everything Jer said, tearing at him with laser-sharp focus, questioning the smallest details, and when Jer was done, they sat in silence for another several minutes before his father spoke again.

"I'll admit, I don't fully understand your instinct or her illness, but I believe you're both right. You believed you were doing what you needed to do to protect the people of New Hope, but it would have felt like abuse to Marsee because she didn't know what was happening. I'm still not convinced this test is appropriate. It honestly seems like it would do more harm than good."

Jer took another large sip of his drink. "I won't argue with you there. It certainly didn't help her, but in every test I've ever had to witness, the person never made it past the first swipe. Half never survive turning it on. I'm told one in a thousand make it as far as Marsee did, but they all lose it at the taste of blood, and they never come back, no matter how much time we give them. Or they didn't until sign language. We don't bring people in to be tested until they're close to losing control anyway. Usually, after they've gone non-verbal, hunted, or hurt someone."

His father eventually gave a single nod. "Well, until we have Marsee's statement, I'm not arresting you. She told me before she wasn't pressing charges. If she's changed her mind, I'll need to understand why and make sure what happened today wasn't just the result of hearing bad news."

Jer snorted derisively. "Bad news? Clear, I've killed her. Her injuries are a direct result of her not trusting me and having to kill off her instinct. How she managed that, I still have no idea." He took another long drink.

"It's far more likely her injuries were caused by repeated electrocution and her failing mask, regardless of what she thinks, and that's not your fault. I should have realized how badly she was hurt, even though she recovered so quickly, but I didn't. All I saw was Stormy's lifeless body, and I panicked."

"I don't blame you for that," Jer said. "I didn't even see her burns until she was on the trauma ship." He shook the bottle. "Got any more?"

"The water was murky, and there wasn't a lot of natural light in that canyon," his father said as he swam over to the cabinet again and held up another bottle. "Are you sure? I've never seen you drink more than a glass before."

Jer nodded. "I want to be thoroughly drunk before you kill me."

"Trust me. It won't help," his father replied, but he tossed the bottle over anyway and swam to the window to look out.

Jer took a sip and was silent for several minutes. "You had every right to decide if the Hue-mans deserved to live, but why did you decide to blame Little Flower's murder on my daughter or decide to kill her at all? You could have just killed Little Flower."

Stormy flashed his surprise before he managed to control it, but his father's back was still turned, and Jeran didn't seem to notice.

His father let out a ripple of regret that reflected in the window. "Tabor was convinced that you and Marcus were lying about Marsee's recovery and using her status as Little Flower's translator to protect her. I had no experience with this illness, only your daughter's written testimony and Tabor's insistence that she was a dangerous threat. We couldn't think of any way to separate the two without raising suspicions, and Tabor was adamant that Marsee would attack at the first hint of violence or something amiss. We didn't want to publicly order the execution because we knew it would cause a riot and more people might have been hurt. Little Flower was popular, and the public sentiment was that she was exaggerating to make her species appear more dangerous. Tabor insisted her people at least wouldn't question it if Marsee had lost control, especially with Marsee's statement to back it. It wouldn't have mattered what we planned anyway. We never got a chance. Kendra took proactive measures long before we made our decision. Quinn refused to leave Little Flower's side on the grounds that Tabor had been accused of a crime and then warned Little Flower about my ability to shock. None of us would have been able to get within striking distance of her or Marsee. Marsee remained calm through the whole thing, outside of a poofed tail, and continued to translate, making me mistrust Tabor about your daughter's illness and wonder if she was trying to get rid of the evidence of her crimes, as Quinn implied. When Little Flower agreed to share everything with us, we did everything we could to trip her up, questioning her until she was practically asleep on her feet to see if her answers would change. It was Little Flower's trust in Marsee the next day that ultimately changed my mind about both Marsee and the Hue-mans. If she could trust Marsee after everything that was done to her, how could we do any less for her? It's not lost on me that my own son would be dead now if I'd gone through with our plans."

Stormy couldn't believe what he was hearing and felt sick to his stomach. His own father had planned both genocide and to kill Marsee and Little Flower. It was nearly as bad as what Rip did, even if he hadn't followed through.

"But tell me this?" his father continued. "Is what I planned to do any different than what you did to Marsee? It was for the same reason: to protect our people. I knew there was a good chance I would have been executed regardless of the authority granted to the Senior Council, but I considered that a small price for ensuring that a violent species didn't continue to exist, only it would appear mine is far worse."

"It's not just your species that was involved," Jer muttered. "But I suppose you're right. It was much the same, and there are no right answers sometimes."

His father snorted. "Jer, you'll soon come to learn that there are no right answers. No matter what we do, someone always gets hurt. Take Rip, for example. I imagine his mother is grieving right now. As far as I know, she's always lived an honorable life, but my people will likely ostracize her, and assuming we don't find anything on her, I expect she'll be dead within a year, if not sooner. Rip's named heir is already dead. Whether by suicide or murder, I don't know and probably never will. On the plus side, that's one less member of my family I'll have to execute."

Stormy frowned at that statement. He hadn't realized that Rip was family, and he wondered who else was involved.

"I don't know how you're going to do it. I couldn't with Marsee."

His father said nothing but looked far more emotional than he'd ever seen him and then changed the subject again. "So, outside of this fiasco, how are you managing as the Hue-man's Senior?"

"Honestly, I'm completely overwhelmed. For all Little Flower and GrandFather insisted their people craved power, I can barely get them to do more than show up for the weekly meetings. Paul, Danny, and Damon were the most vocal about having to wait for their adulthood. Perhaps this craving for power only affected a few individuals, or we got lucky with who we rescued, but Damon even offered to give up his council position once to leave New Hope as an adult. I should have let him go."

Jer took another drink. "Most of the time, I don't understand them. I don't think there's been a vote or meeting that has gone the way I expected it to. The way they think... Their ability to innovate is astounding. It's on par with the Digger's math skills, the cubs even more so. If you give them a problem, they'll find a hundred different ways to solve it and ten times faster than I ever could, but I'm worried about them, too. It wouldn't surprise me if Ben graduates from primary school by the end of the year. By our best estimates, he's only four standard, but he runs off all the time. The last time, we found him sound asleep halfway up the bandala tree. He won't talk about his past, and none of the other cubs are much better. Brent still can't talk, and for as smart as they are, GrandFather says they're still behind in their development. No one else has come forward to adopt them either, at least not among the Hue-mans. Several of the healers have expressed their interest, but no one dares try after what happened with Nazari. I can believe it, though. Most of the adults are in more than one guild or discipline. That might be nothing more than exploring what's available, but they jump from one interest to another practically daily. Marsee's a lot like them. She's always been leagues ahead of me and went wherever her interests took her. I'm pretty sure she's even smarter than Marcus. Did you know she learned your visual language in less than a month? She's better now than I am after a hundred years."

"You're serious? I thought you'd been teaching her all along."

"No, she didn't know more than the basics taught in primary school in any of the languages until a month or so after the Cataclysm. That's when she switched to the Writer's Guild. She learned all the languages in less than a year, although she was pretty rusty at speaking it, more from a lack of opportunity than anything. She's fully fluent in the Hue-man's primary spoken and written languages. She even knows some of the others and is helping to record those languages for posterity. I've never seen anything like it. It took me decades to become half as fluent as she is, but it's like she never forgets a word once she learns it."

"Well, that's why she's the Translator. I'm just glad I don't have to try to speak in Flyer anymore. That language is impossible."

"If you want impossible, try learning Hue-man. I swear they change the meaning of words on a daily basis. That or it's an elaborate prank that they're all in on. Don't even bother trying to put it through the translator. The last time I tried translating a message left at my office, I got 'The purple fish flies at midnight.' When I asked Little Flower, she didn't stop snickering for an hour. Everyone I've asked has given me a different meaning, and that phrase is now on the menu in the cafeteria. I still don't know what it means."

His father snorted. "Are you sure Wind Rider didn't put them up to it? It sounds like something she would do."

Jer shook his head. "Oh no. This is all their doing. They're even worse than the Flyers when it comes to pranks. They have a holiday entirely devoted to it. And before you ask, yes, she knows about it. Last I heard, Wind Rider was proposing they adopt it as a holiday, too."

"Gods. And here I was, worried about bombs. I clearly failed to see the real threat."

Jer chuckled, rubbed at his eyes, and yawned before taking another sip of his drink. "Well, if you're not going to arrest me, I think I'm going to call it quits for tonight. I'm exhausted and won't be good for anything now anyway." He stared at the bottle and gave it a little shake before taking another sip and setting it down on his father's desk.

"With the amount you've drunk, I should probably call the guards to escort you back, but if they're not still following you, I'll need to have words with Stinger. Go on. I'll probably execute you in the morning, but until then, have a good night and try to get some rest."

Jeran snorted and swam out, bouncing off the open doorway on his way through.

His father stared at the door for a moment, seemingly lost in thought, and then his gaze turned to focus in Stormy's direction. He knew there was no way his father could see him, but it felt like his father was staring right into his soul. He quickly checked to make sure his skin was still dark before looking back up.

His father's expression changed slightly, seemingly amused at some thought before he floated up out of his chair and swam out.

Breathing a sigh of relief, Stormy flipped and wiggled to turn around in the tight space and quickly swam back to his room, worried his father was heading out and would stop at his room to collect him.

In his haste and the low light, he misjudged the narrow section and found himself thoroughly stuck, tightly enough that he was having difficulty breathing. Frantic, he wiggled his tentacles until he found purchase on a rock and pushed with everything he had. He came free with a painful scrape. When he made it to a roomier section of the tunnel, he looked back and saw that he was bleeding.

Great. How am I going to explain that? he wondered and took off again. When he made it back to his room, he flipped open the spy hole and peered in. His door was still shut, and the room appeared empty. Flashing his relief, he flipped the hidden latch and swam in but froze as he turned to shut the door behind him.

His father was sitting in his sleeping net, arms crossed and glaring at him.

CHAPTER 33

Clear Seas: A Shocking Development

History sure has a way of repeating itself, Clear Seas thought with some amusement as he intentionally glared at his son with the full weight his authority. He wasn't angry, far from it. He'd known Stormy was there the entire time. A hundred years of practice was the only thing that kept him from laughing at the predicament his son now found himself in, one he himself had been in when he was only a few years older than Stormy. Granted, he'd been in far more trouble at the time. It had been a defining moment for him, and he absently wondered what his son would think of this moment a hundred years from now or if he'd even remember it.

It bothered him how much his son had been forced to grow up this past week, but he was proud of him nonetheless. Stormy had shown his honor on several occasions, risking his life to find and save Marsee, and had even been honest about his disobedience. His son was growing up and starting to act like an adult. On several occasions, he'd returned home to find his son watching the news broadcasts rather than playing with his toys or watching one of his favorite entertainment programs, and their conversations over the evening meals had changed ever since Marsee's first visit. While she'd been amused by Stormy's enthusiasm to meet her, she'd treated him like an adult, and Stormy had responded.

He, too, had been impressed with his son's observations and questions, even if they still had the innocence of youth behind them.

Is it time to pick an heir? he wondered. *Can I really put it off any longer, or will I just be dooming my children to another assassination attempt if I do?*

He knew what happened against him was because of the hereditary nature of his position and the anger passed down by the faction that had lost their last war. His grandfather had fought in it, and he'd grown up hearing the stories his father passed on of how bad it used to be, but he hadn't expected anyone to go after his children or the children of the other Seniors. He thought they'd moved past that sordid part of their history, even if he'd been well aware of the minor and not-so-minor infractions still occurring in many of the districts.

Cultures took time to change, and he'd been strategic in what he'd enforced over the century, wanting the culture to change organically and not be forced, knowing that would breed resentment, just as his father and grandfather had done before him. He'd never once put in his name for the vote, but his people had voted for him anyway, and he'd always expected to lose the Senior Council position long before his district voted him out. Nearly a third of the Council had voted against him at the last election, and he'd honestly been disappointed to be reelected.

What kind of Council would we have if they'd won? His heart was already breaking from what they'd uncovered so far. People he'd trusted had done unspeakable things because of the power they had. *Was it any different from what Jer and I did?* he wondered. *Intent? We have no idea why many of those actions occurred. If Jer was telling the truth, then he was protecting his people, but from Marsee's perspective, it was abuse. How can I allow Jer to walk free and kill others for similar crimes? Heck, even Marcus has admitted to hiding evidence, which is a capital offense, even if he was doing so to protect his people's reputation. Is that any different from what my grandfather did in removing evidence of the war from the archives?* He sighed at the coming decisions he knew he had to make, knowing he could no longer let things slide.

As his thoughts drifted, Stormy gently shut the door, took a deep breath, and squared his shoulders. From experience, he knew how much his silence and the blankness of his mask unnerved people, and he was curious just how long his son would last before breaking. His own father had been able to make him squirm with nothing more than a glance.

He had to give his son credit as he was managing to keep his emotions off his skin. No small feat for someone Stormy's age, regardless of the situation. Learning to control his skin and body expressions had been one of the hardest parts of learning to become a councilor, and he'd worked hard with all of his children to develop that skill as it was useful even if they never took up that mantle. However, a flash of unhappiness slipped through his own control when he realized his son was bleeding.

"Come over here," he ordered, breaking the silence.

Stormy swallowed hard, and a hint of white appeared around the edges, but he swam over. He turned his son so he could better look at the scrape. "This is deep. I think it might need suturing. Come on."

He led his son to where the first aid kit was stored and placed a temporary bandage over the wound to stop the bleeding, saying nothing the entire time, then led his son up to the trauma center to have it properly cared for. His discussion with his son could wait until after it was treated. Stormy remained dark beside him the entire way.

"How can I help you, sir?" the Triage Healer asked.

"My son managed to get himself into a bit of a scrape, and I think it might need suturing." He shifted his son so that the bandage was visible.

The young healer took out her scanner and gave Stormy's wound a quick once-over. "Yes, it looks like it needs cleaning, too. I'm sorry, but there might be a bit of a wait. Please have a seat. A healer will be with you as soon as they can."

He nodded his understanding. That much was obvious. The waiting room was packed with people, many already waiting without a seat. Several people shifted to give up theirs, but he waived them back down.

Stormy's injury wasn't serious. They were healthy, and they didn't need the convenience of a seat. He tried very hard not to abuse the privileges that people insisted on giving him as their Senior and tried to instill the same in his children, but as he expected, it wasn't long before Hyacinth swam through the doors to find them.

"Councilor, what seems to be the problem?"

"A minor scrape that can wait. The others were here first."

She nodded, checked the board to see who was next in line, and pulled them back. Half an hour later, they were still waiting. More people had arrived with far more serious issues than his son's, and he insisted that they were treated first, too.

Stormy said nothing the entire time as he floated next to him, although he did pull out his tablet to distract himself.

He glanced over at one point to see what his son was doing and resisted reacting to what he read. His son was researching Marsee's illness. He said nothing and doubted his son even knew he'd looked.

He's taking it seriously, at least, and not relying on what Jer said, although I doubt he'll find much if Hyacinth couldn't find more than the basics on the illness, and that had all been significantly out of date.

That fact bothered him. While some medical information was only taught to people once they'd earned a specific rank, almost everything was publicly available so that people could research and advocate for themselves. Only a few items were deemed dangerous enough to be restricted, but there shouldn't be any restrictions between Senior Healers, which meant either Nerissa was hiding something or they weren't even bothering to look for a cure. The most recent article was well over a hundred years old. He made a mental note to look into that further.

Eventually, it was their turn, and Hyacinth led them back to a room. "I'm sorry about the wait."

"No worries," he replied. "I could see you were busy tonight."

"Busy is an understatement. I've had to call in extra help. Stormy, hop up on the bed."

He frowned as Stormy swam up and turned around to face the Senior Healer. "Extra help? Is there a problem?"

She flashed a shrug. "I haven't had a chance to look at the numbers, but in addition to caring for Rip's victims, people are coming in for treatment since they were already here for the vigil, and we're seeing an early uptick in the seasonal flu, likely caused by the vigil."

"Why aren't people getting care in their home communities?"

The look she gave him nearly made him squirm. "You know very well that not every community has a clinic or master level healers staffing them."

He tilted his head, nodding the point. Several new clinics had been postponed for nearly a year because of the needs of the Hue-mans. He knew that had made people angry. *I need to discuss that with the others,* he thought and put that on his bottomless list.

She went dark as she examined his son on the large monitor above the bed. Suddenly, she turned and ripped the bandage off Stormy's side, causing his son to wince. "I see someone's in a hurry to grow up."

"What makes you say that?" Clear Seas asked, surprised out of his thoughts by the unexpected comment.

"Well, from his wounds, I'd say he got himself thoroughly stuck. In addition to the scrape, there's a solid ring of bruising around his midsection."

Stormy nodded, flashing his surprise. "I've never had any problems in that section of our home before, but I wasn't paying attention and got myself wedged in so tight I could barely breathe."

"I imagine not, and that's because you've grown an entire inch since the last time I saw you."

Clear Seas' century of training couldn't stop him from flashing his surprise. "He's started his growth spurt?"

They didn't grow nearly as much or as quickly as the other species did, but they still had a growth spurt and would grow several feet in length before reaching physical maturity. When that happened, Stormy would be about the same size as the adult Hue-mans but would continue to grow at a slower rate for the rest of his life. An inch in only a few days was exceptionally fast.

Hyacinth nodded as she continued to treat Stormy. "So it would appear."

"Already? But, I was more than twice his age before I started mine, and I don't think I've given the oath of adulthood to anyone under the age of ten before."

"Twelve is about when it normally starts, give or take a year or two, but I've seen it start as young as five. Stormy's was likely triggered and accelerated by his fight with Rip."

That worried him greatly. He knew there could be all sorts of unexpected complications from electrocution. "This is an injury from being shocked? Is anything else wrong?"

"No, not as far as I can see. What he's experiencing is quite normal, although less common these days, especially as people move to the safety of the cities. Our pituitary gland controls both our growth and our ability to shock. Using his full shock against Rip triggered his gland to produce a higher concentration of growth hormones. It's a defensive mechanism. The more dangerous our environment, the quicker we grow. Haven't you ever wondered why you're the same size as someone nearly twice your age?"

"Honestly, I've never once thought about it," he replied. "Everyone's a different size. I wish I had known. I might have realized something was up with Rip sooner. He was nearly as big as I was, and he was half my age."

"There are medical conditions that can trigger it, too. Some people naturally grow faster or hunt more for their survival, so don't assume that just because someone is longer for their age they've been up to something nefarious."

"I can really get bigger just by using my shock?" Stormy asked.

"Yes, but it will leave you unprotected for a day or two while you recharge. It's a dangerous trade-off. I expect it may continue until you reach physical maturity, likely by the end of the year if it stays at the same rate. I can give you something to stop it if you're not ready for that. I usually recommend it for anyone under the age of eight, but in your case, I think it would be...safer if you didn't."

"Are there any health risks to maturing so young?" Clear Seas asked.

"Physically, no, outside of discomfort and stiffness, which can be treated, but maturing young can be emotionally difficult if the person isn't ready for adult responsibilities. Stormy, please turn around." Stormy shifted so his back was to the healer. A faint line of bruises now showed across his back. "He'd be quite young for an adult of our species but about the same as the Hue-mans. I'm told their females mature even younger, with the average being somewhere between three and four standard years of age. Little Flower was only five when she became pregnant."

He felt his entire worldview around the Hue-mans shift with that single statement. He'd known Little Flower was young, a cub by every species reconning at that point, but he'd forgotten just how young as she'd proven how capable she was at the trial. Stormy was older than her by a few months, if he remembered correctly, yet until this past week, he'd seen his son as a child.

How much of adulthood is societal expectations versus physical maturity? he wondered. *Would his son be ready in a year, or is he ready now?*

While the actual age varied for each species, the one thing they all agreed on was that regardless of the age set by individual charter, once a female reached physical maturity, they were considered a legal adult. The males were different in that they didn't have to deal with the legal and physical consequences of a pregnancy, so their age of adulthood was usually determined by age.

In practice, however, most parents presented their male children for adulthood once they were physically mature, too. The Hue-mans hadn't, but he understood why they were being cautious with the males who had been rescued after what had happened to Little Flower. Damon had proven they couldn't be trusted, but then Rip had done far worse.

I would have been cautious with their history, too, but that's Damon's whole argument. He'd been an adult before but had lost those rights. He's only what, ten standard? That's barely an adult for any of the other species. I certainly wasn't making adult decisions at that age.

No, but Little Flower had made decisions for her entire people at half that and had acted with far more grace and maturity than people ten times her age, he countered himself.

He'd been twelve when he'd become an adult but hadn't acted like one. His father had made him his heir the same day he'd reached adulthood, and he'd spent the next several years trying to prove his father wrong and getting into all sorts of trouble to get out of it. He hadn't wanted the position. *I still don't want the position,* he thought with a snort. *Stormy's acting like more of an adult than I did for years.*

As he thought, he watched his son's bruises vanish under the Senior Healer's treatment.

"You can turn back around," she said, eventually. She put her equipment away and then turned back to face him. "Do you want me to stop the growth spurt?"

"Stormy is old enough to decide for himself," he replied. "It's not my life to live."

Stormy shook his head hard. "No. I don't want you to stop it. I wasn't big enough to kill Rip. I don't ever want to be in that position again. Can I speed it up even more, or would it just continue at the same rate?"

"It's basically an on/off switch," she replied. "Assuming you have triggered your growth spurt, it will continue at the same rate until you're physically mature. The rest of the time, the effect usually lasts for about three months before tapering off.

He agreed to his son's decision, and the Healer gave a single nod back.

"I'll mark it on your chart and send you information on what to expect over the next year. If you have any questions, feel free to ask. Come back tomorrow to remove the bandage on that cut. If you notice any skin discoloration outside the bandage or a fever, come back immediately. You should also plan on a wellness check in two or three months to make sure everything is progressing normally."

He nodded his understanding, thanked the healer, and ushered his son out, wondering what other unexpected news this day would bring.

CHAPTER 34

Clear Seas: Future Heir

Lost in thought, Clear Seas absently motioned Stormy inside his office and shut the door behind them, which automatically activated his privacy screen. He swam over to his window and looked out at the children playing in the park below. It was one of his favorite views as it reminded him why he ultimately accepted his hereditary fate. The children were about the same age as Stormy and playing a rambunctious game of shock tag. Flashes of their laughter made him smile wistfully at the memory of how much fun he'd had at their age with his friends. But his smile vanished with the adulthood realization that the skills they were learning as a part of a simple children's game could mean the difference between life and death.

His son had risked his life twice now to save Marsee, had gone out after Rip alone, knowing the guards would never believe a child, had faced down a Leviathan, rescued Deep Current from that same Leviathan, and would have killed Rip if he'd been big enough. That thought decided him. His son was already making life-or-death decisions. Most children would swim away, but Stormy hadn't. He'd swum to help.

Plastering his mask back on, he turned to face his son. Stormy floated just inside the door, looking nervous and unsure. It was rare that he brought his son with him to his office. In the past, he usually brought him to the nursery unless he was picking something up, but current situation aside, he was not leaving his son with guards he wasn't sure he could trust anymore. He swam over to his desk and sat down, but Stormy remained floating by the door.

"Have a seat," he ordered his son, pointing to the net across from him.

Stormy reluctantly swam over and climbed in. He was far too small for the large net. It practically swallowed him whole. He could hardly believe that his son would be physically mature in less than a year. He'd thought he had years before that would happen, but the Senior Healer was right. It was a blessing in a way. His son would need that added protection.

He glared at his son, although Stormy continued to hide his emotions reasonably well. "Do you have anything to say for yourself?" he finally asked, breaking the silence.

"I'm sorry. I know I shouldn't have listened, but... Is she really going to die?"

He sighed, heartbroken for Marsee and for his son, who practically worshiped her. He'd never hidden anything from his son if he asked, and he had no intentions of starting now. "Probably. How long she survives is anyone's guess at this point. This morning, she tore out the sutures in her new organs and nearly died. She never felt a thing. Their growth spurt is far more aggressive than ours. Without her sense of pain, she'll quite literally tear herself apart, but that's not for another twenty years."

"Can they stop her growth spurt, like the healer suggested with mine?"

"I don't know. Hyacinth says they're looking into it, but regardless, it will still be very easy for her to seriously hurt herself without knowing, just like she did today. If she's careful, she might live a long life. Her mother is a very talented healer, and Myra's mentor is one of the best brain specialists in the Consortium. If they can fix Little Flower, I'm sure they'll figure something out with Marsee."

Stormy nodded and looked away as he tried to control his emotions. After a few deep breaths, Stormy shifted his gaze to look back at him and squared his shoulders. "So, how much trouble am I in?"

"You've completed your first year of charter studies. You tell me."

Stormy flashed his surprise, then went dark for several minutes as he considered. "None?" he finally replied, with a hint of surprise and confusion on his skin.

"Explain your reasoning."

"There are no laws against what someone might see or hear, only laws restricting what you can do with that information and how it can be obtained. You can't blackmail someone to keep them from telling, and if you find out something but don't report a crime, then you might be held as an accessory in that crime. There are laws against recording people in the privacy of their own homes without their knowledge, but I didn't record the conversation. There are laws against breaking and entering, but it was in my own home, and I was already there, which you knew. You've never said I couldn't go in the tunnels. In fact, you've encouraged me to practice running them in the dark, and if you wanted to ensure I didn't overhear you, you could have activated your privacy screen. I could have just as easily listened from outside your door, which you left open." Stormy flashed surprise as he realized that. "Also, I was confused as to why you'd be discussing council business at home when you both have your own offices and conference room. Both your expressions said something was seriously wrong, and the only reason I could think of was that your office at home isn't recorded like it is here."

"So you thought we might be doing something illegal?"

"No. I thought there was something going on that you didn't want anyone else to know about, like that one of the other Seniors was involved with Rip or that Marsee was far worse off than Councilor Chenzira told Mama."

"So why didn't you wait and ask me?"

"Because people never tell children anything, or if they do, they leave a lot out, thinking we won't understand."

"I have never hidden anything from you."

"You didn't tell me what you planned to do at the Trial," his son countered.

He nodded the point. "Correction, I've never hidden anything from you that you've asked about, but you're right. I have simplified my responses based on what I believed you would understand. I won't any longer. If you don't understand something, I expect you to ask. Do you have any questions about what you heard?"

"Lots," Stormy replied. "What are you going to do about Councilor Chenzira?"

"I don't know. That all depends on whether or not Marsee decides to press charges. Even if she doesn't, I'm considering a vote of no confidence. What do you think I should do?"

His son considered the question. "I don't know either. It feels like abuse, but I don't know enough about her illness or culture to say one way or another, and I've only heard his side of the story. When you test me on my shock or skin control, I know what you're doing, so I don't take anything you say or do personally. The few times I've asked you to stop, you've stopped. It sounds like he didn't, and you've never done more than a light shock to surprise me. She needed medical care."

He nodded and let a brief flash of pride slip through, which made his son light up blue before regaining control.

"You're right on all accounts, and that's as good of a place to start as any."

"Start what?"

"Your training, of course." It was all he could do not to chuckle at his son's reaction as he ran through multiple emotions before going dark again.

"Training? I'm not in trouble?"

"Of course not. You argued your case quite convincingly. Besides, I knew you were there the entire time. If I hadn't wanted you to listen in, you wouldn't have, and you're right. I left the door open, knowing you were home."

His son frowned. "How did you know I was there? I've checked multiple times for sensors, and I never found anything."

"That's because there aren't any. The rock behind the opening is reflective. That spot on my wall goes dark when you're in front of it, although I recommend you take the other tunnel in the future. There's no point in injuring yourself when I fully expect you to be listening in on future conversations."

Stormy blinked at him as if not believing what he'd just heard. "You *want* me to spy on your conversations?"

"Of course. How better for you to learn? You're quite right that people rarely tell children anything, and from my experience, they won't open up either if they know you're there, and much to both our surprises, you're going to be an adult soon, which means it's time to start your formal training, assuming you have any interest in being on the Council."

His son stared at him in open-mouthed shock. However, he managed to keep most of it off his skin this time. Only a slight tinge of white crept around the edges. "I thought Temperate was your heir," his son finally replied.

"No, and neither are you, yet. I haven't officially picked one. This job is impossible, and I won't force it on any of my children. Your sister has already stated she doesn't want the position but would do her duty if the people voted for her. Your brother hasn't said either way, but all he's ever wanted was to be a pilot in the Sea Patrol. If my life is blessed, it'll be a long time before that day happens. However, I could really use a Junior Councilor I can trust."

His son blinked. "You want to be your Junior Councilor?" This time, he wasn't able to keep the surprise off his skin.

"No, well, yes, I suppose, eventually. I'm asking if you have any interest in *someday* becoming a Junior Councilor and if you would like to start your training as a Staffer."

Stormy blinked again. "What about my schooling?"

"You'll still need to finish your schooling and graduate from primary school at the very least, and I won't stop you if you want to go to secondary school or learn a trade. My time to work with you will be limited until after the meeting, but I should be able to squeeze in an hour each day to work with you and more after. There'll be a lot of study at first anyway, and I'll have you research specific cases and give your verdict. Before you say either way, I want you to be aware of the risks. Joining will make you even more of a target than you already are. There are far more people involved than just Rip, including other members of our extended family. I'm still trying to figure out everyone involved, and I hope we can resolve this before anyone else gets hurt. You can't trust anyone right now, and you can't tell anyone anything you learn as part of your training, including what you heard tonight."

"I promise. Are any of them people I know?"

He nodded sadly. "I can't tell you who, either. Not because I don't trust you, but to protect you, and you're right. This room is recorded. If they had any inclination you knew, they'd come after you, either to find out what you knew or to use you against me."

Stormy looked down at his arm, ran his thumb along the thin scar from the electrical burns he'd received, and was silent for a long time.

He waited, fairly sure his son would rise to the challenge.

His young son took a deep breath, squared his tiny shoulders, and looked him in the eye. "If the darkness has already spread to our family, then there's no choice but to learn everything I can to fight it, even if I never become a councilor. To do otherwise would make me complicit. People like Rip can't ever be allowed to take power. I accept."

He smiled and flashed his skin bright with pride for his son. "Do you, Stormy Seas, promise to study hard and devote your life to the betterment of the people, to learn the Charter and live by its laws, and to keep in confidence anything you learn as part of your training?"

"I do," Stormy replied.

"Then it is my pleasure to be the first to welcome you to the Council, Apprentice Staffer Stormy Seas."

"Does this mean I'm an adult now?"

He grinned but managed to keep the bubbles of humor off his skin, just barely. "Of course. You can't be a Staffer without being a legal adult, but I figured we'd better wait for your mother before giving you the oath of adulthood. She'd never forgive me if I didn't."

Stormy frowned. "What if she says no?"

"She won't. I, however, will likely be sleeping in the living room tonight for not talking to her about it first. Now, I have no expectations that you'll move out, although as a legal adult, you now have that right. You are still very young. And until things settle, I don't think it's safe for you to go anywhere by yourself and I would prefer if you stayed with us, where your mother, brother, and I can protect you."

"Yes, sir. Do I still have a bedtime?"

That did make him chuckle. "Yes. Even superheroes need their sleep."

Stormy glared at him.

He raised a hand to ward off his son's righteous anger, amused that his son's first thought as an adult was about his bedtime. "I'm not trying to restrict your newfound rights. You can stay up as late as you want, but you'll find you'll need far more sleep as you go through your growth spurt, and it's going to be significantly harder to wake up in the morning for school if you don't go to bed on time. As a councilor, you should sleep whenever you can because you never know when a call is going to come in."

Stormy stopped glaring and nodded.

He stared at his son for a moment before floating out of his chair and swam into the waste room. "Come over here. I want to check on that bandage."

Stormy frowned at him but followed his orders.

Once Stormy was inside, he shut the door and then swam up to the ceiling and pressed a spot on the mural. A door popped in and slid to the side. "There are access tunnels that run throughout the Council Chamber and most public buildings that the guards use. However, this part of the building was built by your great-grandfather after the war but before First Contact, and no one alive should know about them except myself and now you. I haven't even told your siblings."

He swam down the narrow tunnel and showed where the spy hole was for his office. "Even with the shield on, you'll be able to see and hear inside. There's an exit in every waste room and a spy hole over every Senior Councilor's office and the Senior's conference room."

"I'm not sure how I feel about spying on the other Seniors in their offices, especially if they believe their conversations are private."

Clear Seas nodded. "I felt the same when my father showed me, but remember, knowledge is power. What we do with that knowledge determines the kind of people we are. Rip used his access to gain blackmail over people rather than bringing them forth to be tried. I have rarely felt the need to spy on the other Seniors, but then, before this week, I've trusted most of them. Now, I don't know who I can trust, and the safety and lives of not just our people but everyone in the Consortium may depend on what we learn."

Stormy frowned but nodded his understanding.

He pointed out each exit and spy hold, then showed Stormy where the tunnel exited into the maintenance tunnels. "Always check first. If, for some reason, you need to escape out this way, follow the blue line to the nearest exit or the red line to Command. There are sensors in every access port that will trigger in Command, except for this one, so don't use it unless you absolutely have to, and there are sensors in the hidden section that will notify me, or should anyway."

"Do you think Rip found out about the tunnels?"

"I never had an alert, but I suppose it's possible he found out and disabled the sensors. I'll set up new ones tomorrow. Regardless, everything in these offices is recorded, and with everything else he did, he could have easily hacked those feeds, too. You should always assume that everything you say or write could become public knowledge and guard your words carefully."

After showing Stormy how to open the access port from the other side, they returned to his office and spent the next hour discussing everything Stormy had overheard until Jewel arrived. To say she was surprised was an understatement, but after a rather lengthy conversation, he gave his son the oath of adulthood, and Jewel escorted his newest Council Staffer home.

CHAPTER 35

Little Flower: In-betweener

When nothing else happened, Little Flower shrugged and returned to her room to attack the meal GrandFather had brought with him. As they ate, they tried to figure out what had her mother so upset, which shifted into talking about how badly Marsee had taken the news and everything she would be facing.

When she asked her grandfather what had actually been done to Marsee, he pulled out his tablet and brought up her statement. The Sprite doing the translation looked a little sick around the gills several times, and she didn't feel much better. It was so much worse than she'd been through with Damon, and she knew from experience that the healers wouldn't know how to treat that kind of trauma.

"Can we go back to the barn?" she asked after it was done.

"I don't know. It's getting late. Why?" he asked with a look of confusion at her sudden change of topic.

"I want to show Marsee what I can do now. Maybe it will give her a little hope if she can see what Mama and Ammond accomplished. The healers won't know how to treat her mental state any more than they know how to treat her physical injuries. They tried with me before Hope was born, but they just didn't have any frame of reference to understand what I was going through."

"That's a really good idea. Are you up for another walk back?"

"I won't know until I try," she said. So, he handed her her riding clothes and stepped out of the room while she changed.

"And just where do the two of you think you're going?" Ammond asked with a grin and curl of his tail as they neared the entrance to the ward, where they found him talking with Samin.

She grinned back, as the comment made her feel like she was a naughty teenager sneaking out behind her parents' backs and up to no good, a far cry from being treated like an infant for the past two months. "Back to the barn. I want to show Marsee what I can do. Maybe it will help."

"That, child, is an excellent idea, and I want to see this, too." To her immense surprise, he picked her up and carried her out rather than making her walk.

GrandFather grabbed Buster out of his paddock on the way over and brought him inside, but once Buster was hooked up in the crossties, GrandFather had Ammond set her down and handed her a brush.

She chuckled but didn't complain. At least he wasn't making her clean the stall first, and he didn't even ask her to pick out Buster's feet, which he did in a bit of a rush, and then she grinned as she realized what was going on.

"What's got you in such a hurry tonight? Got a date with your *boyfriend*?" she teased.

"As a matter of fact, I do, but don't worry. I'll be back in plenty of time to pick up Hope for the night."

"Well, why didn't you say so? We could have done this in the morning."

"Honestly, I'm just glad you're even asking to leave your room, and you're right. Marsee isn't going to have the help she needs. If this helps even a little, then it's worth the delay. Besides, if Henry doesn't understand, then he's not the right person for me. I let him know I would be late and why," he said as he finished the last hoof.

That done, he put the grooming supplies away and quickly tacked up Buster. "Thanks to Ammond, I'll have time to go back to my room and clean up before meeting him, and I won't have to worry about smelling like a horse. Even if I am beginning to think he likes my horse better than me," he said with a wink that made her laugh.

She kept her mouth shut, though. There were far, far too many jokes she could have followed up with, none of which she wanted to risk someone else overhearing, but it was *so* tempting.

In the arena, it took her three tries to get the words she wanted to say out without messing up, and then she climbed on Buster with GrandFather's help.

Ammond's expression as he watched her little demonstration was priceless. Even knowing what the horse could do, and had done, didn't change his amazement, and she hoped Marsee's expression would match.

When she was done, GrandFather helped her down, and she wobbled over to check out the recording. Satisfied, she sent it off, hoping it would help her sister until she could make it there and hug her in person. There was so much more she wanted to say, but it wasn't the kind of thing she could say in front of the others. She would do that later, in private.

Ammond left to return to his research while GrandFather put Buster away, and she started making her slow way back. Ammond had offered to carry her back, but she'd insisted on walking on her own and told GrandFather to go on ahead without her when he eventually caught up to her. She wanted, needed, to be there for her sister, and she was bound and determined to make it on that ship in a few days, but more than anything, she wanted to be by herself for a while. It had been a very long time since she'd been left to manage on her own, and she felt safe with the guards stationed outside the barn.

She made it about halfway back when her legs started to wobble from exhaustion, so she shifted off the path to sit down on the grass where she could watch the animals still out in their paddocks during the cooler evening air, lit up by a glorious sunset on the horizon. She took a few pictures in the hopes that she would one day be recovered enough to draw the scene. She was still sitting there when her mother came padding around the massive greenhouse that contained all of the plants from Earth and saw her.

"What are you doing out here by yourself?" her mother asked, shifting from all fours to two feet as she approached so she could better talk.

She frowned at the phrasing her mother used. Unlike Ammond, her mother's phrasing made her feel like a child, and she was sick and tired of being treated that way by her mother, but she explained anyway. "Ammond, GrandFather, and I went to the barn to take a video to send to Marsee, hoping to cheer her up. They offered to help me back, but I wanted to walk and told them to go back to what they were doing. I wanted some time to think, and GrandFather has a date tonight. I didn't want him to be late."

"Date?" she asked, clearly confused. "What does the date have to do with anything?"

"No," she chuckled. "He and Henry are interested in each other. It's a...Hue-man mating ritual," she signed, trying to explain it.

"Ah. I thought they might be. GrandFather smells differently when Henry's around. I hope it works out. Henry would make a good addition to the family. Mind if I join you, or do you want to be alone?"

"You can stay. I wasn't making any progress with my thoughts anyway, and it'll be a bit before I'm recovered enough to move again."

Her mother sat down near her but angled so they could talk. "So what's bothering you?" her mother asked after a while.

"Everything," she signed with a heavy sigh.

"It has been a rather eventful week," her mother replied. "Anything in particular?"

Little Flower snorted at the understatement and then sighed again. "I watched Marsee's statement tonight."

Her mother matched her sigh and nodded her understanding.

"I'm worried about her. The healers aren't going to know how to care for her."

"She has the best healers on that planet working on her case, plus the best brain specialists in our Healer's Guild," her mother replied.

"Physically, sure, but mentally, no. You've all tried, but you don't have the frame of reference. This is so much more than the trauma that comes from an accident or the death of a loved one. You never get over it. The nightmares, the second-guessing, looking over your shoulder to see who's behind you. It's not feeling safe in your own home or having words, sights, and smells all trigger you and drag you back into that horror. And thanks to her injuries, Marsee's never going to have another day in her life where she's not reminded of what happened to her, just like I can't look at Hope without being reminded of *him,* or worse."

"I didn't understand before, but I do now, and you're right. We don't know how to treat that. I'm afraid to go to sleep now for fear you'll be missing when I wake up again," her mother replied and then tilted her head at her. "What did you mean by worse?"

She sighed, trying to form the words, and gave up and stared out into the distance for some time. "There have been times where I've looked at her and hated her."

"Who, Hope?" her mother asked.

She nodded and looked away again, not able to meet her mother's eyes. "I love her and would do anything for her, but she has his hair and eyes and sometimes looks just like him, and this rage builds up inside of me. There are days I hate myself for making the decision to keep her, hate her for needing me to keep her alive when all I wanted to do was crawl off the balcony. Every time I saw her do something I couldn't do anymore, I wanted to scream at the injustice of it all. What kind of mother am I going to be if I have those kinds of thoughts towards her? I can't care for her on my own. I don't even know how to take care of her. I've never even changed one of her diapers. Marsee did all of that. I can't pick her up or keep her from running off. I can't protect her from predators. I couldn't even walk three moons' forsaken steps to protect her. That's all I had to do, just walk three steps."

Tears started streaming down her face, and her arms began to shake with the guilt of her failure and inability to protect her child. She wiped her eyes and dropped her arms, unable to continue.

"What you have been through, no one should ever have to go through. Being a parent is the hardest thing you'll ever do, even without all of the trauma you've endured. If it's too much, I'll care for her, and so will Marsee if you'd prefer. I don't know if she told you or not, but Marsee was her primary guardian for the last month or so of your coma and intended to adopt Hope if you didn't wake. We all thought you were dying. If you had, I would have been brought before your council for sentencing again, and your people were still very angry at your father and me. I fully expected they would call for my execution, and I had no intentions of fighting it, but I was worried about what would happen to Hope. I was honestly relieved when Marsee asked for custody because I knew Hope would be cared for and loved. I will always feel guilty for the harm my actions caused you, and every time I see your injuries, I'm reminded of them. Perhaps that's why I pushed you so hard. I needed to make things right for you. As for being a parent, you're doing a wonderful job, far better than I am. I should have stayed in the room with you and protected you. I should have gone with you over to the pool and not lounged about neglecting my duty to you, and I should have done a better job of protecting you at the Agency. I am so sorry you keep getting hurt because of my negligence."

She didn't reply. She couldn't make the words form that she knew her mother wanted to hear: that it was okay. Because it wasn't, even if she had forgiven her mother a long time ago for what had occurred at the Agency, even if she knew her mother hadn't been the one to hurt her and had done everything she could to make up for that harm, not just for her but for all of her people. It didn't change how she felt about her own ability to protect her daughter or any of the hundred other conflicting emotions and thoughts scrambled up in her brain right now.

They sat there in silence for a long time. The suns had nearly set before she gave up trying to make sense of it all and turned to her mother, deciding to change the subject. "Mama, why were you so mad at Healer Samin earlier?"

Her mother frowned and let out a low growl before answering. "I don't have all the details yet, but back when you were in your coma, your father thought Marsee was losing control and chased her out into the Wilds to test her. Apparently, rather than just having her turn her instinct on and off again, he attacked her, and she was injured. He broke her shoulder, and she needed several cuts to be sutured, but she never told me. She even insisted that the record of her treatment be hidden from me." Her mother sighed. "Which is her right as an adult. Samin flagged it, though. It upset Marsee enough when it happened originally that she left and spent several weeks living with Ellie. I knew there was something going on between her and her father, but I had no idea what had happened. I thought she was just struggling with all of the changes and the grief of you being so sick. Marcus is waiting for her to wake up to get her side of the story and see if he needs to arrest your father for abuse. I was mad at Samin for hiding it from me, but she did the right thing. She had no way of knowing if I'd been the one to hurt Marsee or not, and it was Marsee's right to hide it from me."

"Why would Papa attack Marsee?" she asked. "Wouldn't that put her over the edge?"

"Marcus says that's exactly what he was trying to do, to see if she could control her instinct when angry and stressed. It's when she'd be most likely to have an issue. She had no problems then. Only it ultimately made it harder for her to regain control when she really needed to because she no longer fully trusted your father."

"Oh. Papa must be devastated."

Her mother frowned at her and then looked back out at the sunset. "I don't understand you sometimes. I'm not so forgiving. I will be ending my partnership with your father."

"What?! Why?" Little Flower cried.

Her mother's ears flicked back in astonishment. "He purposely attacked and injured your sister. I can't live with someone who could do that to my children. I would charge him myself if I still had the legal right to do so."

"But wasn't he just trying to protect us and help Marsee? I've been on the receiving end of her psychosis multiple times. She's absolutely terrifying when she's out of control. He wouldn't have done it, not unless he had a reason to suspect she was going to hurt someone."

"It doesn't matter," her mother said with a sigh. "He still hurt her."

Little Flower fumed. "So intent doesn't matter to you, just the actions? Or is it that it's okay when *you* claw your children, just not when someone else does?"

Her mother's ears flicked back in astonishment. "I would *never* attack my children!"

"Oh really? And just how many claws did *you* stick in the back of my legs over the past two months? Even when I asked you to stop, you never did. How is *that* any different?"

Little Flower glared at her mother, who just sat there and blinked in astonishment at her. Throwing her arms up in frustration, she wobbled to her feet and stormed away as fast as her shaky legs could take her. The fact that she couldn't effectively run off made her even angrier. She almost lost her balance as she yanked the door open and then slammed it behind her. She fumed the entire way back to her room, slammed the door, and just stood there looking at the stark, nearly empty room, and then flopped face down on her bed and screamed into a pillow.

She didn't want to be in this stupid room anymore, but she didn't have anywhere else to go. Marsee's room was destroyed. Her room in the tower felt like just as much of a hospital room as this one did. It certainly wasn't her room. She had no say in who came or went there, and frankly, after everything that had happened, she had no desire to ever sleep in that room again. She wouldn't even be able to manage the door on her own yet, much less climb the ramp to her room.

Her parents were splitting up. Her grandfather was off spending time with Henry, probably doing what she'd never be able to do with another person. Her sister was stuck, injured, and traumatized on another planet, half a universe away, and she'd barely even seen her own child today. She'd spent the last two months held to the whims of her mother with little say in her own life, and then literally the day she started being able to do a little more, she was kidnapped and held at the whims of a madman, and forced to watch as her family was nearly killed in front of her.

She screamed into her pillow again and again, but her screams turned to wracking sobs as she fell apart without her sister's strong arms around her, the only thing in the universe capable of holding her together.

She didn't look up until she felt the light touch of a paw on her shoulder and frowned to see someone she didn't recognize at first, not until she saw the badge on his harness. It was the guard who had protected her at the trial. She scrambled to sit up and wiped the tears off her face. "You?! What are you doing here? Has something happened? Marsee? Is she okay? Did she arrest Papa?"

"Please do not worry. Nothing has happened. I am in charge of the guards stationed here," he signed. His signs were hesitant, and he paused a few times to think of the right motions. It was obvious he was still learning, but the meaning came across clearly. "I saw your talk with your mother and…"

She swallowed hard, thinking about everything she'd said in front of the guards who were stationed outside of the barn. She'd forgotten all about them.

"From the sounds of your cries and your tears. I thought you might need a hug or someone to talk to."

She blinked in surprise as that was not what she was expecting at all. She raised her hands to answer, but like earlier, the words just weren't there, and she dropped them with a sigh.

He seemed to understand as his face softened. "I am sorry," he replied.

She blinked at him again. "For what?"

"I not…I did not get here in time to protect you."

"My grandfather told me what happened. It's not your fault the crawler broke. It's my fault for not letting the guards be here in the first place. Thank you for trying anyway. He said you were hurt. Are you okay?"

He nodded. "A piece of the ship hit me," he signed and then touched the back of his head. "I am unhurt. I have a hard head."

She chuckled, and he frowned at her. "Sorry. I'm not laughing at your injury, but that you said you have a hard head. That's not a good thing in our language. Usually, it's an insult, meaning that someone's skull is so thick that new information can't get inside, stubborn, unwilling to change."

He frowned again at that answer, and she wasn't sure if he was trying to understand or if he'd taken it as an insult, but then he smiled. "Ah, fur-brained?" It was one of the insults Sina had taught her and apparently far stronger than her interpretation of it.

"Exactly," she replied with a grin. "Not that I think that of you."

He snorted, "Well, my mentor has called me that a time or two. How do you say this in your language?"

The next ten minutes were spent trading insults, which was not what she'd expected, but it did a lot to calm her raging emotions, only that calm didn't last long, as his face changed to be the more serious expression she was used to seeing with the guards.

"I take it you aren't just here to cheer me up?"

He sighed and shook his head. "Your feelings towards your child. Have you hurt her?"

She snorted. "How? Until a week ago, I could barely stand, even with assistance. For that matter, I haven't even been left alone for more than a few minutes since I woke up. If anyone has to worry about being abused, it's me. She knocked me over yesterday, trying to give me a hug. She's far stronger than I am and faster and I would never hurt her. The very idea makes me sick, but it doesn't stop me from seeing him when I look at her or worrying that she'll be like him or that I'll slip up and say something in anger because of what he did to me."

He nodded and seemed to take her at her word. "What of your mother? Do you wish to press charges against her for abuse?"

"Moons, no!" she replied. "That wasn't my point at all. I was trying to get her to see that what Papa did wasn't abuse. At least, I don't think it was, or at least I don't think that was his intent. He wouldn't have hurt her if he didn't have a very good reason to do so."

"Kendra and I investigated it. We found no signs of abuse and very clear signs of issues to warrant a test and drive her away from New Hope. He would not have been able to stop her on his own and nearly died. I have watched since to make sure she was safe."

She frowned. "Safe from Papa or safe from psychosis?"

"Both," he replied.

"Mama said she can't use her instinct anymore."

"I know. She will still be on a watch."

She frowned at that. "Why?"

"She has killed. It's the law, and to be sure that she's telling the truth."

"Are you ever going to believe her?"

He nodded. "She would be dead if Avery didn't believe her now. There are protocols when there is a brain injury."

"Avery's the guard who left her alone?"

He sighed but nodded, and a hint of worry crossed his face before it was hidden behind his mask.

"You're worried about him, aren't you?"

He nodded again. "And Kendra. She is our mentor, and she promised Avery could be trusted, on her life, before your father left. Your father could execute them both for Avery's mistake."

She frowned. "I thought Marsee ordered him away."

"She does not have the authority to do so, even if it was for a good reason. Now, back to your mother. You said she clawed you."

"No, not really. She never broke the skin. She used pressure to make me move when I didn't want to." She did her best to explain, and he insisted on having her show exactly how much pressure her mother had used."

When she had answered all of his questions, he sat and thought for a moment. "This is how you teach horses your language?"

She hadn't even considered that, and it annoyed her. "Great, I'm back to being an animal," she muttered.

"I do not understand," he signed.

"It doesn't matter."

"It does. You're annoyed. Why?"

"Because it makes me feel like an animal again and uncomfortable about my treatment towards Buster."

"Ah. You see Buster as a person?"

She shrugged. "He's very much his own individual, and I care a great deal for him, but if you're asking if he's sentient? That I don't know. He's smart and willing to do anything I've ever asked of him, but he's certainly not going to be arguing with the Council anytime soon."

That made Quinn chuckle.

"But for the past two months, he's been able to communicate as well, if not better than I have. My mother wouldn't take me off of medical leave or let me go to the council meetings even though I could understand everything. I just couldn't move or sign, and my spoken words got mixed up, but Marsee understood me."

"I'm surprised you let her."

"What choice did I have? I couldn't even go to the bathroom on my own until two days ago, and if I had taken myself off medical leave, then I would have made things even harder for everyone else."

"How very honorable of you."

She squinted at him, pretty sure he didn't mean it as a compliment. "What do you mean by that?"

"If you truly cared about how tired your family was, why then did you resist your physical therapy? I would think you'd want to push yourself to get better as quickly as possible."

Her squint turned into a glare, and she saw a twinkle of amusement in his eyes that he'd hit a nerve.

"I think you didn't want to get better. It's easy to fight for others but hard to fight for ourselves. You're a champion of your people and those you care about. You bent the very laws of the universe to save them, yet you gave up on yourself. If you want to be treated like a Councilor, perhaps it's time you started acting like one."

Without another word, he stood and left.

She waited until she was pretty sure he was out of earshot and then grabbed a pillow and threw it as hard as she could at the wall with a frustrated scream. "Moon's forsaken fur-brained guards. They're nearly as bad as healers." That wasn't nearly good enough to calm her frustration, so she grabbed the nearly empty jar of nano cream and threw that, too. To her surprise, the jar shattered.

Sighing at the mess it made, she crawled off the bed and retrieved her pillow. She tossed it back on the bed, nearly falling over with the effort, and walked out to find something to clean up the rest. She stopped short, though, to find Quinn actually leaning up against the opposite wall, arms crossed and tail neatly curled by his feet. Leaning against the wall next to him was a human-sized broom and dustpan.

She glared at him and his amused expression. "What? Never seen someone throw a temper tantrum before?"

He snorted, and his tail curled further. "On a daily basis. I guard the Council, remember?"

She rolled her eyes and wobbled her way across the hall, grabbed the broom and dustpan, and returned to her room. It took her over an hour to clean the mess up, but she managed without falling or cutting herself. When she exited, Quinn was still there.

He said nothing as she glared at him, wondering why he was hanging around, but he said nothing. Instead, he hit a switch on the wall next to him, and a door swung open to reveal a utility closet. She waddled her way back over and put the broom and dustpan away.

"Any idea where my mother is?"

"I ordered her to get some rest, so she *should* be in her room, sleeping, but I can find out."

She shook her head. "No. She needs the rest. *That* particular conversation can wait until morning. My daughter?"

"The last time I saw her, she was being cared for by Ammond in his office."

She nodded her thanks and started making her way down the hall. As she turned to cross the hall to Ammond's office, she glanced back in Quinn's direction, but he was nowhere to be found. "Overgrown fur-ball," she muttered, but Quinn was right. She had been giving up on herself. She squared her shoulders, determined to take her life back, starting first with her daughter.

CHAPTER 36

Marsee: Rainbow Paws

Marsee struggled to fight the effects of whatever it was the healer had given her. She felt strange and disconnected from her body. She could hear people arguing but couldn't focus enough to tell what they were saying, and moments later, those growls shifted into night terrors as the medication won, and she found herself trapped back in the cave.

"You're a feisty one, Little Kitten. I'll give you that much. It's a shame your father chose his power over you, but then you always knew he would. What will it be? Shall I send him your oh-so-distinctive tail to remind him I mean business, or how about these beautiful ears? Do you think that will change his mind? Do you think he'll give up all the power in the universe for you, one diseased and disappointing little kitten? One that reminds him of his own failings, of how he lost control and killed your grandparents?"

The nightmare shifted, and it was her father, not Rip, who swam forward out of the darkness through water now thick with blood. He snarled and swiped at her.

"Papa, no!"

He didn't stop, and she turned to run, but he was right there chasing her and swiped at her again.

She whimpered in pain and fear. "Papa, stop! Why are you doing this?"

"Can you blame me? You always were such a disappointment. It's been fun, but I think it's time for you to die now."

She growled and prepared to attack but suddenly felt something holding her down. She couldn't breathe as it constricted her chest. She fought and struggled but couldn't move. She was trapped and helpless, and all she could do was watch and growl as he stalked her with a wicked snarl on his face.

"Say hello to your grandparents," he sneered and struck.

"Papa, NO!"

"Marsee, wake up!" Ellie yelled.

Her eyes snapped open at the yell, but she couldn't make sense of anything. It was too bright, and the face in front of her seemed to stretch and melt and morph from Ellie's face back into her father's. She growled and swiped at him.

"You're safe. It was just a night terror. He's gone."

She frowned as the words didn't make sense. Her thoughts were slow, and she couldn't tell if she was awake or still dreaming. "Getawayfromme!" Her words felt thick and sluggish in her mouth as if her tongue was three sizes too big. She swiped again, but this time, watched as her paw left rainbow streaks in the water. *I must still be asleep,* she thought and completely forgot about her Not-Father as she wiggled her paw and giggled at the rainbow streaks.

"Maybe she's still asleep," another voice said, and she turned her head to peer at a giant white blob with a face that kept changing, too.

"Wazwrongwithyourface?" she asked. "Izzallmelty."

"No, I think she's awake," the white melty blob said. "I'll go find the Healer."

"Kay. Feel better," Marsee said and went back to wiggling her paw and giggled again as she started drawing shapes in the water with it. Her sister had mentioned lucid dreaming before, but she had never experienced it. *This is fun,* she thought. *Can I control it? Purple,* she thought. Nothing happened. Frowning, she wiggled her paw a little harder. "Purple purple purple."

She looked closer at her paw, trying to see if it was any more purple than before. *Maybe?*

The Not Father sighed, reminding Marsee that he was there. She hissed again, more on principle than anything, and frowned as the face melted again into someone she almost recognized. "Ellie?"

"Yes."

"You look funny."

"I'm sure I do. You're drunk."

"No, I'm not. I haven't had anything to drink in days. Papa said so." She frowned as her sluggish thoughts returned to her father, and she looked around the room with worry.

"He's gone. You're safe."

"You sure?"

"I'm sure. If he comes anywhere near you again, I'll claw him myself."

"Kay," she replied and went back to watching her rainbow paw, confident that Ellie could handle her father if this wasn't a dream, even if she looked funny.

She was still waving her paw when the door slid open, and Rip swam in. Instantly terrified, she growled and hissed and backed away but found herself back up against the wall of the cave. "Look out! It's Rip! He's back!"

Ellie spun and sighed. "Marsee, it's just the Senior Healer. You're safe."

"I promise you. I am not that vile monster," Rip signed.

She frowned. It certainly looked like Rip. *It must be a trick*, she decided, and hissed again.

"I think the narcotics are confusing her," Ellie said. "She's been laughing at her paw for the past several minutes."

"Obviously," the healer replied in a voice that was very melodic, not the harsh sounds she remembered.

Marsee looked down at her paw and wiggled it, then looked back up at the Water Sprite. "You're not Rip?"

"How could I be? You tore him to shreds."

"Oh yeah, I did. Didn't I." She wiggled her paw again. "My paw's made of rainbows."

"Definitely the narcotic," Ellie said.

Marsee yawned, suddenly very tired, but that confused her. *How could you be tired in a dream?*

"Why don't you try going back to sleep? You'll feel better when you wake up," the Not-Rip Sprite said.

She peered at the Sprite, trying to decide if this was another trick. "You sure you're not Rip?"

"I wouldn't let Rip anywhere near you," Ellie said. "You're safe. Go back to sleep."

"Kay." She flopped down on her side and watched her rainbow paw until her eyelids grew too heavy to keep open.

CHAPTER 37

Ellie: Signs of Abuse

Ellie shook her head as Marsee started snoring and turned to the Senior Healer. "Rainbow paws? I don't know whether to be worried or disappointed I didn't get any of what you gave her."

Hyacinth chuckled as she swam up to examine the monitors. "When I was an apprentice, my mentor had me try one of the narcotics so I could understand what my patients experienced on them. I completely forgot what windows were and was convinced I could see through the walls."

Ellie chuckled, but her laughter died off as the healer continued to stare at the monitors. "Is there a problem?"

"Far too many," she replied with a sigh and looked down at Marsee's sleeping body. "The worst part about being a healer is when you don't know what to do. I can fix her immediate problems. The rest...?" Hyacinth shook her head. "After everything she's survived, she deserves far better."

"Myra will figure out how to fix her," Ellie said. Hyacinth turned to face her, and it looked like she was going to disagree. Ellie raised a paw to stop her. "The only thing I agree with Jer on right now is that Marsee needs to believe that her mother will find a way to fix her, whether that's true or not."

Hyacinth tilted her head slightly. "I have found that false hope does more harm in the long run than the truth, but you know your protege better than I do. She should sleep for a few hours. When she wakes, try to get her to drink something."

Ellie nodded. "Thank you for disobeying the DNR. I hope you didn't get in trouble for that."

Humor bubbled across Hyacinth's skin. "That's one nest of cave vipers I am more than willing to stick my tentacles into, even if I didn't have Clear Sea's backing. Besides, the worst that would happen is that I'd be demoted, and frankly, I could use a vacation."

Ellie grinned. "I'll have to admit, it was nice being dead for a few days."

"I might have to try that next time. Sadly, I doubt my Second would believe me if I called in dead."

"The trick is to have someone else call it in," Ellie replied. "It's far more effective that way. If you do it yourself, they'll never believe you."

Hyacinth chuckled but looked up as an alarm dinged. She nodded to Ellie and swam out.

Ellie turned her attention back to Marsee and carefully caressed the side of her face.

Marsee's paw twitched, and she growled, but her eyes didn't open.

"Shhh. You're safe. I won't let anyone hurt you."

"M'kay," Marsee mumbled.

Ellie laid her head carefully across Marsee's casted side and purred. Marsee gave a short, happy purr back before it trailed off, and her paws began twitching again with another dream. She could still hear the wheeze in Marsee's breathing, but she was alive and healing, and that was all that mattered for now.

The door slid open again, and Wind Rider poked her head in. "How is she?"

"She has a serious case of rainbow paw," Ellie said quietly. "But I think she'll survive."

Wind Rider chuckled. "I wanted to let you know Petra's out of surgery. They said everything went well."

Ellie sighed with relief and sat up. "I am so sorry she was hurt because of me. You trusted me to protect her, and I didn't even know she was missing."

Wind Rider stepped in and shut the door behind her. "It's not your fault, any more than what happened to Marsee is. It's Rip's fault. Don't ever forget that. Just because we have power doesn't mean we're not allowed to love or have a family. What Rip did and got others to do was unconscionable." Wind Rider glanced towards Marsee. "She's a very special person, and you're very lucky to have her as a protege for however long she has left. She would have made an excellent Senior. I'll admit it took me a long time to realize it, and I've not always treated her fairly. Yet she didn't let her feelings towards me cloud her judgment, and my daughter and I are alive because of it. I don't know what's really going on between her and her father, and it would seem I don't understand this illness she has either, but I have known her uncle and her grandfather for most of my life and have never known them to be anything but honorable. Don't you dare tell Marcus, but I have always looked up to him, even if it is my life's mission to ruffle his fur."

One corner of Ellie's mouth curled up in a slight grin, as she felt much the same when it came to Marcus, but the phrasing made her worried. *Is she taking Jer's side?*

"Marcus tends to have that effect on people," she replied.

"That he does. And, while I find it hard to believe that Jer abused Marsee or that Marcus would cover for him, I promise you I will make sure that it doesn't happen again. What do you know of this test?"

Ellie sighed with relief and told everything she knew.

"Have you seen any signs of abuse since?"

She shrugged. "Nothing I could bring before the Council as evidence. I expected her to return after Jer did, but she didn't, stating that Little Flower was worse and that she wanted to remain for however long she had left. It was certainly a valid enough reason, but then one of her instructors contacted me, concerned because she'd missed several classes, so I unofficially moved my office to New Hope. When I arrived, she looked as bad as the day she left with me. She was exhausted, and both she and Myra had lost weight. When I asked, she said everything was fine, but there were signs it wasn't. Any time Jer entered the room, she would stop whatever she was doing, pick up Hope, and move her away from him, and sometimes, when she didn't think anyone was watching, she'd have this look on her face that I don't even have the words for. That's a big part of why I scheduled this trip. I wanted her to have some time away from him. I don't know if anything else has happened or if she was still struggling to get over what had happened before, but it doesn't make any sense to me why he would have done what he did. I've lost count of the number of children in the Guild who've died because of psychosis brought on by child abuse."

"I thought this was a brain defect?"

"We don't really know what makes someone more vulnerable than someone else. It's far more common in single cubs and can be triggered by traumatic events, overuse of our instincts, or something as simple as a single taste of meat. I've been on a watch at least a half a dozen times in my life, have had to put down four people before the guards could arrive, and have reported hundreds of others. As far as I know, none of them ever survived."

"That many?" Wind Rider asked, appalled.

"It's the worst part of my job."

"What made you think Marsee doesn't have psychosis?"

"Well, for one, she didn't hurt Little Flower, and that was before they found out about sign language. Marcus was right about that. People don't stop on their first hunt, but she did. For another, I'm not convinced she actually knew how to use her instinct before that day in the garden, intentionally anyway."

"Is that something you're taught?"

"I was. It's one of the few memories I have of my mother. I was an only cub, too." Ellie looked away from Wind Rider, lost in ancient memories.

"There's something else, isn't there?"

Ellie sighed and nodded. "I recognize a lot of myself in Marsee."

"You said you've been watched. Did you have issues?"

"Not the way Marsee did, but…I did lose control. Once." She took a deep breath and swallowed hard at the memory. "I have never told anyone this, and I don't want anyone else to know, *especially* not Marcus and Jer."

"Why? Because you fear they'll hurt you too?"

She snorted. "I'd like to see them try. No, because I don't want to see someone else hurt."

Wind Rider tilted her head at her, both acknowledging the request and expressing her curiosity.

She took another deep breath. "I was abused as a child."

Wind Rider flipped her wings back in surprise. "You were? By whom?"

Ellie nodded. "My aunt. I was only three when my parents and my cousin Reighly died in a house fire. The fire brigade deemed it an accident, but it was my fault. My mother watched Ry while his mother worked. My father worked nights at the local healer's clinic, and we were all supposed to be sleeping during the afternoon rest period, but we weren't the least bit tired and snuck outside. The shed attached to the house was off-limits, but what did I know of limits at that age?"

"You still don't," Wind Rider teased.

"Fair point, well made. Anyway, I was trying to get something down off of one of the shelves to play with, and somehow, I knocked over the shelf with our emergency oil lanterns. The oil got all over Ry, and something sparked it. I don't remember what happened next. My instinct took over, and I ran. The fire spread to the house, and everyone died. Everyone thought I had died in the fire, too, but when they didn't find my body, the guard was called in. They eventually found me, but it was almost a week before I could speak. I was terrified they were going to kill me. I'm honestly surprised they didn't, but I was still a cub and not completely feral. I was taken in briefly by one of the guards until I calmed enough to say what happened."

"There weren't any alarms or fire suppression systems?"

She shrugged. "I honestly don't know. If there were, they clearly didn't work. After they deemed I was safe, my aunt took me in. We were all the family each other had left. Things were fine until Ry's name day, about a month later. I was sound asleep when she dragged me out of my room by the scruff into his room and proceeded to beat me, stating it was her right to punish me however she deemed fit. She did the same on my parents' name days. I never said anything because I blamed myself, too, and at the time, it seemed fair and just, and I had no reason to believe she was lying. She told me on many occasions that the fact I didn't lose control during those beatings meant I knew I deserved it. It was years before I realized I was being abused and not punished, but it wasn't until my litter was stillborn that I truly understood her pain. She's still alive, I think. I get a letter from her every year on their name days, blaming me for their deaths, telling me about everything they would have done over the past year if they were still alive."

"That's horrible!"

"You know, I used to think so, too, but now I look forward to them."

Wind Rider flicked her wings back in surprise.

She shrugged. "I've learned more about my parents through those letters than I ever knew as a child, and the life she's made for Ry is full of heroics and adventure. I've considered turning them into a novel. Anyway, even now, even after all she did to me, I just want her to say she forgives me and that she's proud of me. The way Marsee looks at her father is the same way I looked at my aunt. If he's in the room, her attention is entirely focused on him. Every action is geared towards protecting Hope or making herself appear unthreatening. She flinches at the slightest sign of his displeasure, and she's terrified of making a mistake, of not being good enough. The slightest praise from him is enough to make her tail spiral with joy, yet she never seems to believe it either. She had absolutely no self-esteem when I first met her, and she still doesn't, even though she's absolutely brilliant in just about everything but math. She couldn't even believe anything she'd done was good enough for me to mentor her, even though I'd been mentoring her for months, and she still doesn't believe me when I compliment her on something. She about passed out the first time I gave her a compliment."

"Well, you do tend to have that effect on people," Wind Rider teased.

Ellie chuckled. "Another fair point, well made."

"If violence can cause your people to lose control, why do you think you didn't?"

Ellie shrugged. "I've asked myself that question so many times I've lost count. I think, at first, it was because I felt guilty and felt the beatings were justified. Outside of the name-day beatings, she hit me regularly, but it was only when I messed up, and I never feared for my life, even during the worst of the beatings. She never used her claws or hit hard enough for me to need medical care. I loved my aunt, and I think she loved me, too, even if there were days she hated my very existence. As much as she hurt me, she also taught me my craft. Her insistence on perfection got me where I am today, but living with her was impossible at times. Once I earned my adulthood, I left home and never went back."

"The cookies are getting away," Marsee mumbled in her sleep.

Both she and Wind Rider snorted. "I might have to find out what they gave her," Wind Rider said.

"I wish I had thought to record her earlier," Ellie said, waiving her paw slowly through the air. "My paw is made of rainbows."

Wind Rider chuckled and then squinted at her. "You aren't suggesting blackmail, are you?"

"Of course not," Ellie replied and put on her most innocent-looking face. "Bring it up when she's promoted to Senior Guild Master, absolutely."

Wind Rider snorted. "I always knew you had a bit of Flyer in you."

It was Ellie's turn to snort. "After all the pranks that have been pulled on me over the years, I'm surprised you haven't made me an honorary member of your species."

Wind Rider pulled her head back with an appraising look and then fluttered her wings in a dismissive shrug. "Perhaps someday, but you've got a long way to go before earning *that* honor. Your unexpected resurrection was rather impressive, but that was really Clear Sea's doing. If you're looking for a mentor in that regard, I might be willing to offer up my services, but I'll need to see some effort on your part first."

Ellie's tail spiraled with humor. "Challenge accepted."

Wind Rider grinned. "I look forward to it. Now, I need to get back to my daughter. The sedative should be wearing off soon. Call me if you need anything."

Ellie turned to Marsee after Wind Rider left. "You'd better get better quickly because I fully intend to have you help."

"Purple," Marsee replied.

"My thoughts exactly," Ellie replied with a chuckle and laid her head back down on Marsee's side.

Marsee settled into a deeper sleep, and Ellie floated there, listening to the wheeze of Marsee's breathing for several hours, lost in thought about her childhood, about her life's work, and how it had harmed those she cared about.

The problem with rank and authority is that everyone needed you for something and only ever saw that rank. They never saw the real person behind that rank. You could never truly know who your friends were. Even though she'd been angry with Myra for years, Myra had welcomed her back with open arms and a well-deserved thwack upside the head. Myra was the closest thing she had to a sister, and she loved Marsee as if she were her own child, yet she had nearly lost her again twice today. She'd blamed Marcus and Jer for not acting to save Marsee when Avery had approached, but she hadn't either. She'd frozen, knowing that if she moved, Avery could have killed her, too.

I am a coward, she thought, *just like my aunt said I was. Marsee's not, though. She fought back, injured and broken, to defend Stormy. She would have made an incredible Senior. Maybe I should just retire now and let her have it. She practically owns the Guild at this point anyway.*

She sighed and lifted her head to look down at her protege. Marsee started twitching again, so she reached out and stroked her head. "Shh, you're okay. I'm sorry you were hurt because of me. That will never happen again."

Marsee didn't respond this time, fast asleep, but then coughed. She frowned as she listened to Marsee's breathing. Marsee coughed again and again, and the slight wheezing she'd heard before changed to gasping breaths, but she didn't wake up. Before she could reach for the call button, alarms started going off, and moments later, a pair of healers she didn't know swarmed into the room.

She moved out of the way while they worked and prayed to the Ancient Gods to save Marsee for the third time that day. *Come on, Marsee! Keep fighting!*

One healer slapped a different mask over Marsee's face while the other healer swam back out.

"What's wrong?" Ellie asked.

"Her lung fall," the healer said in rough Saber as she applied something to Marsee's side.

Ellie frowned with guilt. "It collapsed? That's my fault, isn't it? I was resting my head on her side. I thought the cast would…"

"Not you fault," the healer said, grabbing another tool. "Her has new mona."

"New mona? Do you mean pneumonia?"

The healer turned to face her and switched to Water Sprite. "Do you understand Water Sprite? My sign is even worse than Saber."

"Well enough, if you don't go too fast," Ellie replied in both Saber and sign, hoping the meaning would come across.

The healer nodded. "Pneumonia is the closest word I know in your language. She has an infection in her lungs. It looks to be the same one she has in her paw, so I'm guessing it spread when they operated earlier."

"The Senior Healer was just in here, not an hour ago, and didn't say anything about an infection," Ellie replied.

"This particular infection is nasty in your species and can spread rapidly, especially in someone as weak as she is."

The healer who had left returned carrying several items, which the first grabbed from them. "No worry. I fix it," she said in Saber as she turned away and went to work.

Please let her be telling the truth!

CHAPTER 38

Clear Seas: Abdication

Clear Seas watched Stormy and Jewel swim across the park in the direction of the Market until they were out of sight. Praying he'd made the right decision and that no harm would come to Stormy, he turned and swam over to the small kitchenette in his office and peered at the food inside but then shut the door. He had no idea if any of it was tampered with. *Maybe I should head down to the market?*

Before he could, there was a knock on his door. He swam over, peered out to see who it was, and opened it. "I didn't expect you until later," he said, waiving Avery in.

"The additional guards Kendra sent after us just arrived. I need your authority to let them disembark."

He raised a brow. It didn't surprise him that Kendra had sent additional guards, but he was surprised at Avery's request. "Why the formality now? We've never bothered with it before?"

"We haven't had a coup attempt before either," Avery replied. "And there's a full contingent, not just the normal two squads."

He snorted and shook his head slightly, which made Avery frown. "I'm not denying the request, far from it. I'm just surprised. An entire contingent just to arrest me?"

"We didn't know what we were flying into."

Clear Seas nodded. "I suppose that makes sense. I was honestly surprised that Jer and Marcus arrived with so few guards. Permission granted. Pair them up with my guards and have them start sweeping the Council Building and city for the meeting."

"Yes, sir," Avery replied.

He motioned over to the seat that Stormy had so recently vacated. Avery climbed in but said nothing as Clear Seas took his own seat. He considered his words carefully. "I am decidedly uncomfortable about what I saw today in Marsee's room," he started and paused. "Did you intend to kill her?"

"Yes," Avery replied.

Clear Seas found himself taken aback by both the honesty and complete nonchalance and threat of Avery's reply. There was no regret in the answer, simply fact. With that one word, Clear Seas knew to the very tips of his tentacles that Avery had killed before and often. Nor would he hesitate to do so in the future.

"Why?" he demanded. "She wasn't hurting anyone and had a medically documented injury that clearly showed her low-level instinct was damaged."

"She refused when her uncle told her to turn it on. That's grounds for immediate execution."

"Why, though?"

Avery seemed surprised by the question. "She's on a watch," he replied as if that answered everything. At his glare, Avery continued. "More often than not, severe brain injuries like hers result in psychosis, not the other way around. When I tested her before, she was nervous but didn't hesitate. She didn't just hesitate today. She was terrified. That's more than enough proof to tell me she knew she wasn't fully in control anymore. I wouldn't expect either Jeran or Marcus to be able to kill a member of their family, and I needed to be sure she wasn't lying."

"What made you decide she was telling the truth?"

"She was absolutely terrified I was going to kill her, but there wasn't even the slightest change in her pupil dilation. If she had been lying, you would have known. Her instinct would have taken control to save her life or at least tried to, and she remained verbal the entire time, but what sealed it for me was her rage towards her father. As angry as she was, she didn't lose control, and she's admitted to struggling with her control towards him."

"What do you know of what happened between them?"

"He thought she was losing control and drove her away from New Hope before testing her. She passed that test, which is surprising in itself, but struggled hard after. Marsee's emotions after being rescued were understandably conflicted, but she didn't act negatively towards her father until she found out about the ransom demands. They had an argument and appeared to have worked it out. Certainly, her reaction towards him when she first woke up was not anger, and I think she would have been perfectly fine with him if he hadn't slipped and used what is obviously a term of endearment."

"You don't think that was done on purpose?"

"Not at all. Watch the recording. He winced as soon as he said it, and I've heard him nearly slip up a few times and correct himself immediately."

"Why did you let him go?"

"Because no crime had been committed. The flag on her record had already been investigated by both Kendra and Quinn, and by her own words, she knew it was a test. What happened in the room today was a result of the torture and psychological manipulation she experienced during her captivity, not because of what her father did."

"You've heard her admit this?"

"She told you as much the other day at your house."

That surprised him. "You heard that conversation? I didn't realize your species could hear that well."

Avery nodded. "Sound travels differently in water. But if you need written proof, it's also in her journal, which is linked to the ticket on her flag."

He nodded the point. "How do you feel about this test?"

"Honestly, I hate it. Every member of the Guard does. We'd much rather bring people in and try to work with them, but we don't always get that chance."

"Why do you hate it?"

"Would you want to see children attacked, turned into wild animals, and then have to put them down?"

"No, I suppose I wouldn't," he replied and then squinted. "Are you implying that this test turns children into wild animals?"

Avery was silent for longer than he expected, but he waited the guard out.

"No," Avery finally replied. "They were already turning. It merely exposes the issues that were already there." Avery looked away and sighed. "I have witnessed far too many tests in my career and dealt with far too many already gone. If there's an issue on patrol, we normally do a single-strike test to see how quickly people can recover, but more often than not, we know long before that strike happens that there's a problem, usually a well-documented trail of problems. Just like there was with Marsee?"

"So why didn't you bring Marsee in?"

He sighed again. "The last recorded issue happened more than a year prior to Marcus putting her on a watch, but he took her off only hours later. We believed that both Jeran and Marcus were more than capable of determining if she was safe, and bringing her in would have tampered with the Trial by removing Little Flower's chosen translator. There were no signs of any issues at the Trial, which is the main reason why Kendra didn't bring her in or put her on a formal watch. It was also a unique situation since New Hope started out as her home, and the Hue-mans refused a guard. However, she's had a full watch on her from the moment the flag appeared on her medical record, and she failed to fill out the appropriate paperwork before leaving for Council City with Ellie."

That shocked him. While technically on the same planet, legally New Hope and Council City were different worlds. "Why would she do that? She'd be risking an immediate execution."

"We're not entirely sure, but both Jeran and Marcus were in jump at the time. My understanding from what Kendra told me was that she let it slide because getting away from her father before he returned home was the right decision on Marsee's part. There's nowhere else for her to go in New Hope. And because she was technically under guard at the time, even if she never knew it. Quinn overheard the conversation about her leaving with Ellie and flew back with them in case there was a problem."

"Ellie knew what was going on?"

Avery shook his head. "No. She didn't find out until the end of Marsee's stay. Ellie wasn't even sure she was on a watch until Quinn showed up. After Jeran returned, Kendra ordered Jeran to stay away from Marsee, and when he unexpectedly showed up at Ellie's house a few weeks later, Kendra called out several squads, expecting something to occur. Nothing did. Quinn remained in New Hope right up until Marsee left for her trip here but ended his watch and returned home to Council City after finding no further signs of abuse, just exhaustion from caring for Little Flower and Hope."

He frowned at that knowledge. "Do you think Rip knew that Quinn had left New Hope unguarded?"

Avery shrugged. "I have no idea. Jeran didn't even know Quinn was there, but it was public record that the Hue-mans had decided not to form their own guard. I think it's more likely that what happened in New Hope was timed to coincide with his plans here."

He nodded at that, as it fit with the information they'd uncovered so far. "So, in your opinion, Marsee is safe, and her father has not abused her?"

Avery was silent for a bit before answering again. "I believe that Marsee is safe for now and that she was unable to turn her instinct on earlier today, but I am concerned about any treatment they may try to fix this issue. It may end up causing more problems than it solves. As for Jeran, what he did was necessary, but whether it was abuse is entirely up to Marsee. We've found no other evidence of abuse, but that doesn't mean it hasn't happened. I also believe that there may be grounds to find her incompetent to stand trial based on her current injuries."

"Thank you," he said and dismissed the guard.

He stared at the closed door, mulling over what Avery had told him, sighed, and left to attend his meeting. It was close to midnight before he finally left to return home, exhausted and heartbroken about his continued investigation into the coup. As he approached his home, he was surprised to see a light on and found Temperate waiting for him in the family room.

"You're up late," he said.

"I wanted to talk to you. Mother says you made Stormy a Staffer today?"

"I did. I haven't officially posted it yet. Your mother asked that we wait until after the meeting to protect him, and we both agreed. I did give him the equivalent access rights, but that isn't publicly posted."

"He want's it?"

Clear Seas shrugged. "I can't say if he wants it, but he accepted, knowing the risks, and for the right reasons."

Temperate sighed with relief. "He's grown up a lot this past week."

"He's been forced to. I take it from your reaction that you don't want to be my heir?"

Temperate nodded. "I hope you're not upset."

"Of course not. I've known for years you didn't want the position, although if something happens to me, you might still get voted in anyway. Even if he is legally an adult, people aren't going to vote for him, no matter how popular he is right now."

"I know, and I'll do what I have to until he's ready if that happens, but I have a pretty good idea of what's coming, and I don't think I can do that. I don't think I can kill or even order someone's death. That's not who I am. I've also decided to leave the active patrol and put in a request for consideration for the next available command position."

"Command?! I thought you loved being a pilot?"

"I do, but..."

"You're having a hard time flying since your accident?" he guessed.

"That's part of it..." His son rubbed the back of his ear fins and then smiled sheepishly. "Papa, Melody's pregnant. We're having a girl."

Clear Seas floated there so completely flabbergasted that his skin didn't even react, but then it quickly changed to the bright blue of joy, and he crushed his son in a hug. "A girl! Oh, Temperate. I'm so happy for you. Have you told your mother?"

Temperate nodded and beamed his own joy, but then it dimmed. "When Melody told me, I offered to partner with her, but she said no. She's worried about becoming a target, and she's right. Being your son puts them both at risk and the very thought of someone doing to them what Rip did to Marsee and Petra... I just can't, Papa."

His heart broke, crushed by the pain he saw in his son's face. "I know. That thought terrifies me, too. I would step down if there was anyone I could trust right now or if doing so wouldn't put every other member of the Council and their families at risk. What I care about is that you're happy. Whether you're officially partnered or not, she's welcome in our family, and we'll love them both. Hopefully, this will all be over soon, but if not, we'll figure something out."

"Thank you, Papa." Temperate hugged him again and then left to spend the rest of the night with Melody.

He watched his son swim out, struggling hard to contain his emotions until his son had left, then turned to find Jewel watching him from the hallway, concern etched on her face and skin. He said nothing as he followed her back to their room and shut the door behind him. Only here did he ever allow his mask to slip. Jewel had seen the best and worst of him and hugged him as he started crying, horrified by the pain and risk he caused his family simply by being a part of it. Like Jer, he had no idea how to protect them.

As always, Jewel shared in his pain and then began harmonizing with a voice he still found mesmerizing even after more than half a century. It wasn't long before she reminded him of one of the many joys of being part of this family that made his life worth living, and to his utter surprise, he didn't end up spending the night in the family room, although he didn't get much sleep either.

CHAPTER 39

Jer: Fuzzle Knocked

Thoroughly drunk and not caring in the slightest, Jer left Clear Sea's home, but rather than returning to the ship to sleep, he stumbled his way back to his office and pulled out the bottle he kept stored there. He rarely drank, and then never more than a single glass, for fear that his instinct would take advantage, but there were days as part of his profession when he needed to forget everything, and today was one of them. If he was lucky, he would drink himself into oblivion before Marsee called for his execution. He was honestly surprised Clear Seas hadn't arrested him, and the irony that he was now the one facing a death sentence wasn't lost on him, not that he cared if Marsee called for his death.

"Fair and just," he muttered and took a long sip directly from the bottle, reveling in the burn on the way down.

Hours later, he sat sprawled in his chair by the window, bottle empty and tossed aside, yet sadly still conscious. The light in his office had long since turned off, and he stared out his window at the park below, not seeing any of it. Numb with grief and guilt and sluggish from the effects of the alcohol, he was at a loss for how to make things right. Not only was he losing Marsee, but he was losing the rest of his family, too. Myra had informed him that she was filing papers for separation and had then blocked him. He could override the block, but he wouldn't. Her last words to him had cut deeply, but he had no intentions of even trying to change her mind, knowing it was safer for them this way.

There was a knock at the door, but he didn't bother answering. The door opened anyway, and the lights flickered on. Squinting, he watched through the reflection in the window as his brother peered in, saw that he was there, and stepped in through the static shield. Jer sighed but didn't turn around.

"We need to talk," Marcus said as he deactivated his mask and sat down in a nearby chair.

Jer snorted. "Just talk? I figured you were here to arrest me."

"Not yet. I went by earlier, but Marsee's still sleeping. I'll try again in the morning."

He grunted. Now or in a few hours, it didn't matter. The result would be the same, but he was worried about his daughter. "Still? Is she alright?"

His brother grinned slightly. "Ellie said she woke briefly and stated her paw was made of rainbows before passing out again and then mumbled something about chasing cookies." His expression turned more serious. "But she had another setback. Her lung collapsed again, and she has pneumonia on top of everything else. It's the same infection as in her paw, and they think it spread when they opened her up. It's serious, but she's responding to treatment."

"Gods," he whispered. "How much more can she take before my stupidity kills her?"

Marcus frowned and let out a disappointed sigh. "What really happened that day?"

"I've already told you everything. I'm too drunk to talk about it anyway. Not drunk enough, though. Any chance you've got another bottle of fuzzles in your office or whatever they gave Marsee?" He lifted his paw. "Rainbow paws, huh?"

"So Ellie said, and you know I don't drink."

There was a touch of humor in his brother's voice, but his face, reflected in the window, was blank, hidden behind his mask, and he knew why. If Marsee demanded his death, Marcus would be the one who would have to kill him, assuming Marsee didn't. *Then again, she might have Clear Seas zap me.*

"There isn't anything she could ask for that would hurt more than the pain I'm in already. If she wants my death, so be it. It would be fair and just. I've already lost everything that matters. She wants nothing to do with me. I can't even get an update on her status anymore. I tried texting Ellie, and I got a 'you'll find out if she's dead or not when everyone else does' response from her, and Myra's ending our partnership. I expect you'll be getting the request from her shortly if you haven't already. I can't blame her. I would do the same in her place. I'm assuming you're the one that let her know?"

"I had no choice. I needed to know if there had been any other instances of abuse against her or Marsee, and I'm sorry, but Hyacinth and Stinger both informed Clear Seas, and Wind Rider heard it all from Petra's room. It was all I could do to keep them from taking over the investigation without starting a war. I should recuse myself, but I'm not. You did what I taught you to do, and I would have likely done the same."

"No. You would have killed her. That's what you taught me to do. I couldn't do that, or so I thought. I've killed her anyway."

"Jer, I would never expect you to be able to kill your own daughter, even if she had been fully gone."

He shrugged. "Looks like Rip is going to get his way after all. At least this way, I won't be able to hurt her anymore."

Marcus frowned at him. "Jeran Frederick, *have* you hurt her any other time besides that test?"

He spun in his chair, ears back in surprise that his brother would even ask, and nearly fell out of it as his head spun. "Of course not! I hated what I had to do that day, but she was...I...I really thought she was losing control again."

"Then why didn't you call in the guard?"

"Because then I would have had to kill her, and you know it."

"What really happened, Jer?" Marcus pressed again.

"I've already told you everything."

"Tell me anyway. That's an order."

He snorted and rubbed at his face. "I've never seen anything like it. She wasn't like the others. She was showing every sign of losing control, yet she was still verbal if talking in plural like she did the other day. I didn't know what to do. I wasn't sure if she was out of control or completely in control, so I kept pushing her to see what she'd do. Her first few attacks were clumsy, like a cub's, but then they changed. She managed to swipe me several times and then did this move that I can't even begin to describe. She flipped through the air and pinned me. She had me caught in her jaws just like she had with Rip before I could even react, and I thought for sure I was dead, but after I stopped struggling, she just yelled at me for several minutes and stormed away, and that was after she broke her shoulder."

We could do the same if you let us.

Jer froze and clamped down hard on his instinct, but it was already off.

Marcus saw his look of panic and spun around to make sure no one had entered but then turned back with worry and confusion on his face. "What's wrong, Jer?"

He shook his head, regretted it immediately, grabbed it to stop the world from spinning, and turned away from his brother, unable to explain. *Ancient gods! A third time?*

"Jer, talk to me," Marcus demanded.

He rubbed the back of his head and grabbed at his fur. *Am I losing my mind, too?*

Of course not, the voice inside his head snorted. *How can you lose what's always been there?*

Jer shook his head again and then looked down at his claws. He had to blink several times to focus on them. *Still sheathed,* he thought.

Marcus stood and walked over in front of him. He tried to turn away, but his brother stopped him, forced his head back around, and stared into his eyes, frowning. "What's going on with you, Jer," Marcus demanded. When he didn't respond, Marcus switched to sign. "Talk to me, please."

He sighed as he peered into his brother's eyes and shrugged, far too drunk to really be scared. He was dead either way, whether by his brother's paws now or Marsee's later. "I s'pose my fuzzer's knockled. Knocker's fuzzled?" He shook his head to clear it but regretted it immediately. He closed his eyes, swallowed hard, and took several deep breaths to keep from throwing up. When he opened them again, Marcus was still staring at him, frowning with concern. "D'you remember when Avery was questioning Marsee about her instinct the other day? How he asked if her instinct still spoke to her?"

Marcus frowned but nodded. "I wasn't sure what he meant by that, but for Marsee's sake, I was too afraid to ask. Why?"

"Well, either I'm drunker than I thought, or mine is too."

Marcus's ears flicked back, nearly pinned, and he examined him again. "It doesn't look like your instinct is on now, and I saw no signs of it a moment ago. Just how much have you had to drink?"

He shrugged. "Not nearly enough. Two, three bottles?" He tried to remember and looked down at his paws to count. "There was one here and one, two, two bottles at Clear Seas, but the first wasn't full, and I had something at the market. No idea what that was or if it was even alcoholic."

Marcus raised a brow. "Three bottles? How are you still conscious?"

He shrugged. "Pretty sure the gods hate me, too."

His brother snorted. "No doubt. Flick it on," he commanded.

Jer did, almost afraid of what would happen, but it was no different than normal, although he winced at how bright the room was and then blanched as the stronger smells hit his stomach. "Before you hit me, I need to throw up." He bolted towards the waste room, bouncing off the corner of his desk, and struggled to find the switch to the waste hole, gave up, and threw up in the sink. When he was done heaving, he leaned back against the wall and slowly slid down until he was sitting on the floor, landing with an oof.

Marcus handed him a towel and a glass of water and sat down across from him. "You're going to feel miserable in the morning."

"Too late. I'm already miserable."

"What just happened?'"

"It's too bright, and everything stinks," he said, squinting and rubbing at his nose.

Out of nowhere, Marcus swung hard at him. He tried to block but missed completely. Marcus connected hard with the side of his head, knocking him to the floor. He lay there looking up at his brother and started laughing as he'd completely forgotten that his instinct was still on, and apparently, when drunk, it did him no good. "If you're going to hit me, at least do me the favor of knocking me out."

"I'll remember that for next time. Now turn it off," Marcus demanded.

He turned it off without issue and sighed with relief as the room darkened back down to more manageable levels, although now his head hurt.

Marcus stared at him before sighing and leaning back against the cabinet under the sink. "Are you alright?"

"No." He rolled over and looked up at the ceiling, which had been painted to look like the sea. He almost forgot his brother was there as he got lost in the mural, which seemed almost alive as his vision swam in and out of focus.

"Sorry about that."

"Huh? 'Bout what?" he asked, trying to remember what they'd been discussing.

"Hitting so hard. I had a feeling you wouldn't be able to block, but I wasn't sure. We know next to nothing about our instinct except for when it goes wrong, and we have so little reason to use it that we have no real understanding of what's possible. Certainly, everything about Marsee's condition is new, and you used it quite a bit the other day."

"Not jus' the other day," Jer replied. "Used it lots of times. I wonder what kind of fish that is. It's rather silly looking."

Marcus frowned. "Explain." The command came out at nearly a growl.

"It's all poofy," he replied, poofing his own cheeks out in demonstration and crossing his eyes.

"Not the fish," his brother growled in exasperation, "about using your instinct."

"Oh, that? Kendra said Marsee should do whatever helped to keep her calm. I've gone running with her a few times and sat with her in the garden while she drew, partly to try to rebuild our relationship, but I also wanted to understand what she was experiencing. I know it was a risk, and I would have said something if I felt any sense of being out of control. It was stronger every time I used it, but there was no urge to hunt, and Marsee was right. The world is beautiful with it on unless you're drunk, then it really stinks. I honestly don't think I would have been able to figure everything out in the suite if I hadn't had that practice."

His brother was silent for a while, hidden behind his mask, and Jer absently wondered if he was going to kill him then and there, but he was far too drunk to care and soon lost himself in the mural again. "You know, I never even noticed the mural before. So much effort for a waste room that only a few people would ever see. I wonder who painted it. It looks so real."

Marcus looked up and grunted but was quiet again, lost in thought. "I'm thinking once this is all over, we should take another trip out into the Wilds," his brother finally said.

"More work on my control?" His instinct actually purred at that idea.

"Perhaps. I was thinking more like training, assuming Marsee doesn't demand your immediate death, or perhaps even if she does. If I'm going to have to kill you anyway, we might as well try to learn something from this catastrophe. Marsee might have been perfectly fine if she'd never been traumatized by Rip, and I certainly don't blame you for wanting to understand what Marsee was going through or for wanting to kill him. I wanted to tear him to shreds, too, and what happened this morning in her room would terrify any parent. Have you used it intentionally since the suite?"

Jer pursed his lips, trying to remember. "It's come on several times for legitimate reasons when I was startled and worried about being attacked, and I purposely turned it on in the canyon when Marsee started screaming. I thought we were going to have a real fight on our paws, and I had no idea how I was going to beat him without it, even with Clear Seas' help."

Marcus nodded. "As did I. Well, if Marsee was in full control of her instinct the whole time she fought with you, then likely that's how she was able to beat an adult Water Sprite nearly twice her size. She had at least a little practice at fighting. She may hate you for it, but I have a feeling she and Stormy would both be dead now if it weren't for that experience, and you and I both know no one has ever come back from as far gone as she was. Perhaps that has something to do with it, too."

"I shouldn't have let her kill him," Jer said with a half sob.

"You had no choice there. It was her right, and frankly, you'd never have been able to take him away from her. She was losing control long before she killed him. I offered while you were finding help, and she growled at me for even suggesting I take over. No, I think where you messed up was not backing off when she asked. I can certainly see how that would have scared her and made it harder for her to turn her instinct off. Either way, it's done now, and we can't change it, and until I speak to Marsee, you're still on the Senior Council. I don't believe what you did was abuse. It's fairly well documented in her journal, and you were doing what you were trained to do, but we don't have any precedent here. No one has ever survived to press charges before. I'm personally hoping that she'll be calmer once she's had some time to process her injuries. Thankfully, Tabor set precedence for what happens when a Senior is charged with a crime, so if she does press charges, I'll agree with your decision to take whatever Marsee asks for in reparations as fair and just. It's probably best if you don't fight it, for her sake and Saber's. Now, since you didn't come back to the ship, I'm assuming you've been here drinking all night. You need to rest. We have a mess to clean up."

Jer snorted. "Mess doesn't even begin to describe it."

With Marcus's help, he climbed to his feet with a groan, but they hadn't made it halfway to the door before both their tablets dinged.

They both wore matching frowns as they started reading. Jer sighed as he squinted his way through Quinn's report, and it took everything he had to keep from throwing his tablet across the room.

"Myra was in full control when Quinn tested her," Marcus said softly. "She's strong. She can manage this."

Jer grabbed his scruff tightly to keep from crying. "She's slipping, and you know it."

"She's been through a lot this past year. Nothing she's done is unreasonable in these circumstances. She brought Damon in unharmed. If she can do that, she'll be fine. I'm honestly more worried about Nazari. Quinn's assessment of the situation is spot on. Hearing her case while she's on a watch will expose everything and kill any chance she has of winning. Yet if we vote against her, she's liable to lose control right in the middle of the meeting."

Jer snorted, "Her and half your council. What's going to happen when we announce their convictions?" He sighed and rubbed at his eyes. "Let's discuss it with the others. I can't stink rate...stink straight? No that's not right...think..."

"Think straight. I'm surprised you can even stand straight." Marcus surprised him by pulling him in for a hug. "It'll work out, little brother. Just give it time. But if not...I promise she won't suffer...or you."

His breath hitched, and tears started streaming down his face as he was nearly swallowed whole by the guilt he felt at the harm he'd caused his family. His knees buckled, unable to bear the weight.

Marcus gently set him down but continued to hold him as he cried out his grief and guilt. Then, when the tears finally stopped, too emotionally spent to even think about finding the energy to return to the ship, he curled himself into a tiny ball and buried his face under the thick fur of his tail. He sobbed again as, moments later, Marcus curled around him, purring to protect him from the loneliness of his broken heart, and held the broken pieces together for him until he finally cried himself to sleep.

CHAPTER 40

Marsee: Midnight Promises

Marsee bolted awake from a night terror to an unfamiliar room cloaked in darkness. Confused and still groggy from the narcotic, her dream merged with her surroundings as a shape moved in the deep shadows of the corner.

Dark Moons! He's back! But I thought we killed him!

She tried to flick on her instinct, but nothing happened, and only then did she remember that she'd killed it. Frantic, she tried to swim away, but a tentacle wrapped around her arm and grabbed at her face, pulling her back. She clawed at it, but it wouldn't let go. Terrified, she screamed.

Light pierced the room as the door slid open, and a pair of guards swarmed inside.

"Help!" she yelled and clawed at the tentacle as they hit the light switch.

"It's alright, Marsee," one of the guards said and signed. "It's just an oxygen mask."

"You're safe," the other guard flashed. "I promise."

She spun to look behind her, and sure enough, a long white tube floated behind her, attached to the wall. Glancing over in the corner, she realized her attacker was none other than Ellie, who was struggling to untangle herself from her sleeping net, her tail lashing with frustration.

All four feet had slipped through the net, and it had somehow twisted into a knot.

"Gods, Ellie. You about gave me a heart attack."

She turned to the guards. "I'm sorry. When I woke, the room was dark, and I thought Ellie was Rip."

"It's alright, ma'am. You've been through enough to give any of us night terrors," the Saber guard said as the second one, a Sprite, swam over to help Ellie out of her tangled mess.

"I can certainly see how you'd make that mistake in the dark," the Sprite said and peered at the net, trying to figure out how to untangle Ellie. "How in the depths did you manage to do this?"

"Moons if I know," Ellie growled. "These nets are impossible. I've been coming here for a century, and I still don't know how you manage to sleep in them."

The Sprite flashed her humor. "I'm sure I would have as much difficulty in one of your beds. I don't know how you avoid rolling off them."

"We don't," Ellie said and then yipped in surprise as the guard did something and Ellie spun and suddenly somersaulted out of her net. The guard caught her before she could hit anything, flipped her back around, and made sure she was stable before letting go.

Ellie glared at the guard. "You did that on purpose."

Humor flashed again. "Of course I did. It was the easiest way to get you out."

"Thanks. I think," Ellie replied with another glare and gingerly sat back in her untangled net.

"You're very welcome," the Sprite said and swam back out.

She didn't know either of them, although the Saber looked familiar. It took her a bit to remember that the guard had been stationed outside of Clear Seas home, and she frowned as her memories of everything that had happened that day came back.

"Try not to worry," the Saber Guard said. "You're safe here. There are guards at every entrance to the ward, on both ends of the hall, and there are two guards on your door at all times. No one is even allowed down this hall if we don't know them."

She wasn't sure if that helped or not, and the guard seemed to understand.

"The guard is here to protect you from anyone who might want to harm you, and that includes your father and uncle. Clear Seas has granted you residency for as long as you want to stay and has placed you under his protection."

She blinked in surprise. "He has?"

"Wind Rider, too," Ellie said. "I know your grandparents and some of your cousins live on Flyer. If you want to move here or there, once you're better, I'll move with you."

She stared at Ellie. She wasn't sure what surprised her more, that Clear Seas and Wind Rider were now fighting against her uncle on her behalf after voting to kill her less than a year before *because* of her illness or that Ellie would move to be with her.

"You'd really move?"

Ellie nodded. "If you're not safe back on Saber or Little Earth with me, then I certainly wouldn't expect you to stay there. I'll go wherever you want to. You're my protege, and I knew the risks around your illness and what you were facing when I offered to be your mentor. Granted, I didn't expect any of this, but we'll figure it out. I know your mother. She won't stop until she finds a way to fix you, and no matter what happens, I'll take care of you."

She sighed as she realized that leaving would mean leaving her home and, more importantly, Little Flower and Hope. She wouldn't ask her sister to leave her people. Did it really matter, though? She'd be spending the rest of her pitifully short life in one trauma center after another. Even if no one attacked her again, she was still going to die.

"Thanks," she said, but her heart wasn't in it. She turned back to the guard. "What's your name?" she asked, her eyes flicking briefly to the Sprite outside her door. She was far enough away from the guard that she couldn't quite read her badge.

"I'm Aris Zatara, and that's Tanner. I came with your father. If you're worried because Tanner's a Sprite, don't be. I've known her since I was a cub. She's one of the best guards on all five planets."

Tanner heard this and ducked back into the room. "On my life, Translator. I promise no one will harm you on my watch. My son was one of the missing guards who had been assigned to protect you. They found him, injured but alive, chained with the others in the cave. I owe you everything for saving his life and will gladly give mine to save yours in the hopes that it will restore even a little of his lost honor in failing to protect you." Tanner flashed the silver and purple, bowed low, and swam back out before she could respond.

She didn't even know what to say to that. She wasn't sure if Clear Seas protection meant she was also safe from the guards putting her down, as Aris implied, but it was better than nothing, and it helped to know that at least one guard was on her side.

She nodded to Aris, who turned and swam back out to join the other guard, shutting the door behind her.

Her immediate panic over, she flopped back over on her side and gave a slight tug on the mask. "What's up with this?"

"You managed to get yourself a nasty case of pneumonia and started having trouble breathing," Ellie replied.

She let out a defeated sigh. "I don't know why you're even bothering. I'm just going to die anyway."

"Your mother will find a way to fix you," Ellie repeated.

"If I don't kill myself with a sneeze first," she replied bitterly.

"Well, that would be an inventive way to die, I suppose. Better than being strangled by your sleeping net. Gods. I just remembered the guards have cameras on their harnesses. I bet the recording of me caught in my net is halfway across the universe by now."

Marsee chuckled, "You're officially doomed, but I imagine it'll be a close second to me fighting my oxygen mask."

"You're just lucky they weren't in here earlier. You had a nasty case of rainbow paw from the narcotic they gave you. Ellie waved her paw and made a silly face.

She groaned. "That wasn't a dream?"

"Nope," Ellie replied and gave her a wicked grin.

"Please tell me you didn't record that?"

"Sadly, I didn't think of it until after you passed out again."

She breathed a sigh of relief.

"However, Wind Rider was here."

She groaned and buried her face in her paws. "That's who the white melty blob was?"

"None other," Ellie replied with a grin.

"I'm never going to be able to show my face in public again. Maybe I should just have the guards come back in here and kill me."

"Nah. You and I have work to do," Ellie replied.

She peered out from under her paws to frown at Ellie. "Work? I'm on medical leave, and I have enough credit that I never have to work another day in my life."

"That won't stop you from helping me come up with a Flyer-worthy prank. I haven't quite decided who I want to prank, though. Your father is at the top of my list, but Marcus is a close second."

She frowned in confusion. She wanted to claw her father, not prank him.

Ellie saw her confusion and explained. "Wind Rider said she'd consider mentoring me in the art of pranking others, but I needed to show some initiative first. I certainly can't let an insult like that go unanswered. Can you imagine? *Me* not showing initiative?"

Marsee snorted, not expecting that at all. "Why would that have even come up in conversation?"

Ellie grinned wickedly. "You'll just have to make it to Senior Guild Master to find out."

All humor vanished instantly, and she sagged with a sigh that turned into tears as all of the stress and fear of the past week caught up with her, and she buried her face in her paws again.

"It'll be alright. Your mother *will* fix this."

"No, she won't!" she wailed. "The healer said no one ever survived."

Ellie bolted out of her net and swam over to her, but she didn't notice, too caught up in her grief and jerked back, startled when Ellie went to caress the side of her face.

"Sorry, I didn't mean to startle you. Hug?"

She nodded, and Ellie pulled her in for a hug and purred for several minutes while she cried her grief out. "It'll work out. We're alive. We survived, and that's a start. Your mother and Ammond will figure out something. They saved your sister. They'll find a way to save you, too."

"I don't want to end up like Little Flower, crippled and broken and dependent on someone else to care for me for the rest of my pitifully short life."

"You won't. You're already so much better than she is. You're going to have a long, happy, healthy life. I promise."

"Don't make promises you can't keep."

Ellie sighed but continued to hold her until she finally stopped crying. "Now, why did you flinch from me? I don't want to do anything that triggers you. Has your father been hitting you?"

"No. Outside of the test, he's only ever swung at me one other time. That was a test, too, he said. It was that first day of construction, and I was overwhelmed. Papa caught me with my instinct on, and I didn't even know it. He didn't hurt me, just startled me."

Ellie nodded. "I've been through that test a few times in my life. It's unnerving for sure, but I've never had anyone attack me like he did to you."

She leaned back in her bed with a sigh.

"So why the flinch?" Ellie asked again after a few moments of silence.

She reached up and touched her face where Ellie had. "I don't know. You surprised me, and it was where you touched. Rip would wake me by hitting me in the face with slimy fish and..."

She swallowed hard, trying to find the words, and Ellie started purring again.

"Every time he touched me, he shocked me. I know you can't and that I can't even feel it anymore, but..." She dropped her paw, unable to explain.

Ellie's purr turned to a low growl. "That monster. I wish you'd left something of him for me to claw, but I'm glad he's dead. He can't ever hurt you again, and I won't either, not a tail or slap upside the head ever again. I don't want to hurt you, even by accident, and if I do or say anything that bothers you, you tell me immediately, and I'll stop."

Marsee snorted, once again surprised. Ellie never hurt when she hit, and most of the time, Marsee was actively trying to rile up her mentor, specifically to get a reaction. It was play, teasing, and frankly, it meant a lot to her that she could tease Ellie and mostly get away with it. "Like I said, don't make promises you can't keep, Senior Guild Master. I know you too well. I give you a week, maybe two, depending on how your paw feels before my snark gets the best of me and you run out of patience."

Ellie chuckled. "Well, I promise to try."

She shook her head. "Don't. I don't want you to change, and I don't want to feel broken and brittle, even if I am broken and brittle. "

Ellie nodded. "If you're sure."

"I'm sure." Closing her eyes, she yawned, suddenly very tired. "I think I'm going back to sleep now."

"Do you think you can drink something first?" Ellie asked.

The only response was a light snore.

Ellie rolled her eyes and gave a very light tap on Marsee's nose. "Impudent Apprentice. Poof."

The very tip of Marsee's tail curled in response.

Ellie grinned at the tell, but before returning with her drink, Marsee was sound asleep and twitching with another dream. She set the drink in the net beside Marsee's bed. "Fine. I'll let you get away with it this time, but don't make a habit of it." She shook her head. "Good Apprentices are so hard to find these days."

Marsee: Alone

Marsee woke with a start early the next morning as the Senior Healer touched her shoulder.

"You're looking better this morning," the healer said.

Marsee glared up at the Healer, angry about being woken and furious about what she'd done the day before. "Don't ever restrain me again or give me something against my wishes. Do it again, and I'll have you arrested."

"Marsee, that was uncalled for," Ellie said.

She swore at Ellie in Hue-man, knowing that neither of them would understand.

"It's alright. I promise it won't happen again as long as you remain calm until your sutures heal."

She hissed at the healer. "Don't you dare tell me what to do or how to feel. I'm sick of having to act perfectly happy and calm around others, even when I'm not. I have every right to be angry."

"Yes, you do. What was done to you was unthinkable. I am not trying to deny your feelings or take your rights from you. I only want to keep you from hurting yourself again. I would normally sedate you until you healed, just like we did with Ellie, but you're not responding well to the normal medication we use, so we'll have to do it the hard way. That means you need to stay still and in the tube for a few days.

Feel free to swear and yell at me all you want. Although, if you do swear at me in Hue-man, I would appreciate a translation. We keep a log of new and inventive swears and give a prize to whoever collects the most at the end of each year. Sadly, I'm woefully behind."

She snorted, surprised out of her anger.

Hyacinth looked up at the monitor. "Your infection appears to be going away. I think it's cleared up enough to take this mask off so you can eat. I'll come back in an hour or so and give you another treatment." After taking the mask off, she swam out.

"Here, drink," Ellie said, holding up one of the odd cups.

Marsee laid her head back down and sighed. "I'm not hungry."

"Marsee, it's been days. If you don't eat something soon, you're going to die."

"So what? I'm going to die anyway," Marsee muttered. She knew she was being childish, especially after just ranting that everyone was trying to kill her, but she didn't care as her emotions swung rapidly from anger to despair and self-pity.

"Not for another twenty years or more. Your mother *will* find a way to fix this. Drink. If you need to, consider this an order from your mentor."

"I quit," she muttered. "Go away."

Ellie swam around to the other side of the bed to face her. "Nope, you're not allowed to quit. Drink."

Marsee grabbed the drink and threw it, although far more cautiously this time.

Ellie sighed, swam over, and brought it back. "I will do this all day if I have to."

"I. Don't. Care. *I'm not hungry.*" She hissed at Ellie for added emphasis and rolled over again.

"Obviously. Now drink." Ellie held the drink in front of front of her face and bopped her on the nose with it.

She pinned her ears and growled before taking the drink and throwing it again. "Give me one good reason why I shouldn't just claw my throat out and save everyone the effort."

"Because I love you, and I want to spend every last minute you have left with you, and I'd rather that be twenty years than a few days, and I'll be damned if my protege gives up the moment things get a little tough. At least give us time to figure this out."

"Gets tough?! Dark Moons! Ellie, if this past week hasn't qualified as tough, then I want nothing to do with being in the Guild. Look what being your protege has gotten me. In the last week, I've been kidnapped, tortured, rescued, attacked, *and* tortured again. I've killed someone, had multiple organs replaced, had who knows how many surgeries, lost all my fur, which I may never get back, had my claws ripped out, and my hand broken twice, and now I apparently can't swallow, know when I'm hungry, or even know if I've torn my insides out. I can't do any of my crafts now because I could get a splitter in my eye and lose my vision. I'll never grow up, never have a partner or mate, and I'll never have cubs or grand cubs..."

"I can't have children either," Ellie said quietly, interrupting her rant.

The grief in Ellie's voice stopped Marsee cold.

"Something went wrong with my first heat, and I nearly died. The healers spent years trying to figure out what went wrong before daring to let me try again. I managed to get pregnant the second time, but my cubs were all stillborn. The healers refused to try a third time, even though I begged them for years. I tried compensating by taking a protege. She... She died, too. Everyone assumed that I didn't take another protege because I was elected Senior Guild Master shortly after, but I just couldn't handle losing any more children. I stopped visiting with your mother because I couldn't stand to see her so happy having so many cubs and grand cubs. Even after nearly a hundred years, it was too much. You were the most adorable cub I'd ever seen, and I think I fell in love with you the day I first met you. I would have taken you on as my protege years ago if I hadn't been afraid of losing you to your instinct, but I did what I could by ensuring you had the best instructors in whatever you were interested in, and I'll be condemned to the dark side of the moons before I lose you too. *NOW DRINK.*"

Marsee stared at her mentor for several moments, absolutely stunned. "You love me?"

Ellie rolled her eyes. "Of course I do. Do you honestly think I'd take a protege after a hundred years if I didn't?"

She didn't even know what to say and just stared at Ellie, jaw dropped. Rip had tried to make her believe that Ellie had only picked her because she was close to the Hue-mans, but Ellie loved her? Had loved her since she was a cub?

"Moons to Marsee," Ellie said and bopped her on the nose with the drink again.

She glared at Ellie as she rubbed at her nose. It hadn't hurt, but it felt weird.

"Drink."

She took the bottle from her and forced a few sips down.

"All of it."

It took her nearly an hour to complete it, with Ellie glaring at her, arms crossed, the entire time.

"Now, can I go back to my misery?" she asked when she was done.

"No. You're going to start responding to everyone and thanking them for their kind words and gifts, and you're going to apologize to the Senior Healer for your atrocious behavior."

Marsee growled at Ellie. "No."

"Growl at me all you want, but no protege of mine treats anyone like you treated her. Your father, I can understand. He deserves to be clawed, but Hyacinth has spent days trying to save your life. The least you can do is listen to her and be polite."

"She restrained me and injected me with something against my will. She deserves my anger, and I already told you I quit the Guild."

"She was trying to save your life, and I already told you you can't."

"Why not?"

"Because I said so."

Marsee snorted and rolled her eyes at that response, but before she could formulate an adequately snarky reply, the monitor's alarms started blaring. "Oh great. Now, what's wrong with me?" Marsee muttered under her breath as she tried to figure out what was wrong. Nothing hurt, and outside of that awful hollow feeling, she felt reasonably okay, if still exhausted, short of breath, and incredibly weak.

The Senior Healer, along with several others, swarmed through the door and started triaging her, but after a few moments, the Senior Healer snorted and briefly flashed her humor before shooing the others out and turning back to face her. "*You...*need to pee."

"Are you... Are you telling me I can't even tell when I need to go to the moon's forsaken waste room now? For all that's cursed under the thrice dark moons, just kill me now. What else could go wrong?"

"You need to poop too," the Senior Healer replied, with barely controlled humor.

She groaned and covered her face with her paws. When she peered through her claws, the Healer was still there and staring at her.

"What else is wrong with me?" she growled.

"Nothing. Yet. I'm waiting for you to go to make sure you can and that we don't need to insert a catheter or colostomy."

"Gah. No wonder my sister wanted to die after she came out of her coma. This is downright degrading. Can you at least turn around?"

They thankfully humored her, and apparently, the moons blessed her, and she was able to go without assistance.

Marsee muttered and swore for a full twenty minutes after the Senior Healer reapplied the other mask with her next treatment and left. She only stopped when she couldn't think of anything new to say and started repeating herself in different languages.

"Feel better?" Ellie asked when she paused to catch her breath.

"No, and if you keep asking stupid questions, I'm going to demote you again."

Ellie chuckled as she swam over to the small desk in the room and pulled out Marsee's tablet. "You can't. You just said you quit. Now, here, I figure if you start now, you might just finish replying to everyone before you die. I had the techs organize your messages for you. You started receiving so many that you broke the server. They've been categorized by people in your contacts and then by age, figuring you'd want to start replying to the children first. I also figured you'd prefer to have most of the physical gifts donated to New Hope so they're being shipped there. Agate is organizing the gifts and messages that were left at the various vigils. Flowers and plants have been sent to decorate the local Trauma Centers and clinics in your name along with any toys gifted, with instructions that they're to be handed out to children being treated or stored for later, which apparently has done wonders for morale. I've also sent my best crafters to see what they can do to restore your room and see if it's possible to salvage Little Flower's paintings."

"Thanks," Marsee muttered as she took the tablet. She was rather overwhelmed with everything Ellie had done while she'd been asleep, but she was far too grumpy to admit it.

"You're very welcome," Ellie said, beaming as if Marsee had waxed poetic for an hour in thanks instead of pouting like a cub and then swam over to her net.

She rolled over on her side but didn't open her tablet. Instead, she stared at the light bouncing off the wall as she tried to make sense of everything that happened. Ellie was fixing her room, but did it even matter? She couldn't go home. The last few months had been impossible, and she knew it would be even worse going forward. Her people would be afraid of her now, not just her father. Even without the risk of losing control, she didn't think she could stay in the same community with her father anymore, much less two rooms away, but she didn't know if she'd be any safer anywhere else. *Who did Rip tell about my illness,* she wondered.

Intellectually, she'd understood why her father had attacked her, but the doubts Rip had infected her with continued to swirl in her brain. She'd chosen her father over Rip, had fought and killed her instinct to keep from killing her father, and had even felt her death was worth it to protect him. *So why am I so mad at him now? Am I really mad, or is this all Rip's doing? I wasn't mad at him until he said that word.*

Her thoughts swirled, along with her emotions, until she was broken out of it when her tablet dinged with her urgent message tone. She rarely got those. Flipping it open, she saw it was from her mother but had been sent the day before. The urgent messages were designed to go off every hour if not answered.

"You didn't answer it?" Marsee asked.

"I may have access to your account as your mentor, but I am not going to invade your privacy unless it's to save your life. You have my word on it, and I never break my promises."

She nodded and played the recording. Her mother was sitting outside the compound somewhere. The edges of her healer's mask were ragged and torn, and fury was seeping out.

What else has happened? she wondered.

"Hey, Sweetheart, I just heard from Marcus about what your father did to you. I wish you'd told me, but I understand why you didn't. I'm livid at what he did, and I don't care what his reasons were. It obviously didn't help you and only made things worse. Anyway, I figured you should hear this from me before you hear it from anyone else. I'm ending my partnership with your father. I can't live with someone who would harm my children, and I want you to know that you'll be safe from him when you come home. I wish I was there to protect and care for you, but I'll be there as soon as I can. The Council ships will be leaving in a few days, and I swapped places with Brice. Stay strong. Do what the healers say. We're working on a solution. Ammond is bringing his equipment so we can get a better scan of your brain, and GrandFather gave us an idea, which half the Healers Guild is working on right now. I promise I won't give up on you. We'll get through this. Give Ellie a hug from me. I love you, and I'll see you soon."

She tossed her tablet aside and let out a heavy sigh that came out a half sob.

"Do you want to talk about it?" Ellie asked softly.

"No."

Surprisingly, Ellie didn't push. Her mother had gotten rid of one of her problems. She should be happy that she could go home, but she wasn't. Instead, it felt like her world was falling apart, and a piece of that hollow, broken shell, all that remained of her brittle and broken life, had crumbled and fallen away.

CHAPTER 42

Marsee: Statement

Marsee floated on her bed, flopped over on her side, absently watching sunlight reflect and dance on the wall. She was far too exhausted and emotionally spent to do anything else. Thankfully, Ellie didn't press her.

The Senior Healer stopped in again, briefly checked on her treatment, and swam out, leaving the mask on. Marsee just floated on her bed like the furless lump she was and ignored her. Ellie's sigh of disapproval was the only thing to break the silence. She ignored that, too.

Sometime later, she heard the door open and shut but didn't bother rolling over to check who it was.

"How is she?" she heard her uncle ask quietly.

"Grumpy. She hasn't said more than three words in the past hour," Ellie replied, "and based on the look she gave me, I'm pretty sure two of the three were swears. I need to learn more Hue-man."

He chuckled. "They do have a rather extensive lexicon of profanity. Is she awake?"

"I don't know. She's been staring at that wall for an hour, but I haven't heard any snoring."

"I don't snore, and there's not exactly anything else to look at in here," she muttered, not bothering to roll over. "They could have at least put the bed by the window."

Her uncle swam around the bed. "Hey there. How are you feeling?"

She rolled her eyes.

"That good, eh? Do you feel up to talking for a few minutes, or should I come back later?"

"I suppose that depends on what you want to talk about."

"I'm sure you have a pretty good idea of why I'm here," he replied. "I came to talk to you about your father."

"My father? I thought he wasn't anymore. Mama said…"

"I haven't signed off on the paperwork yet. So technically, he's still your father."

"Why not?"

"I wanted to talk to you and your mother first," he replied. "I need to know what really happened between you and your father and whether you intend to press charges against him."

She snorted, honestly surprised. "For what? Doing what he's legally allowed to do?"

"You had the guards remove him from your room, claiming he attacked you. We haven't officially arrested him yet, as we only have his side of the story. We need your statement first."

"Why now? You took his word for it before."

"I had no reason to believe anything else had happened," he replied.

"How would you know? You never even asked me what happened. The guards never came and asked me either, but then I don't have any rights on Saber, do I? I'm just a diseased monster and one angry outburst away from being put down. I'm honestly surprised you haven't killed me already."

"You are not a monster, and you have the same rights as every other citizen."

"No, I don't, and you don't even see it, do you? I think that's one of the things Rip was right about. I lost my rights long before I hunted Little Flower."

There was the faintest change to his expression. If she didn't know him so well, she would have missed it. She'd surprised him, and that didn't happen very often.

He was silent for several moments before speaking. "What makes you believe you don't have any rights?"

"Well, for one, I was the one kidnapped and tortured, yet I'm the one placed on a watch. I'm assuming you didn't remove it."

"The guard has the right to watch anyone they deem a risk, and regardless of your current medical status, it's the law for anyone who has had to kill."

"*You* are the law. You could change it if you wanted to, but you don't trust me, do you?"

His face hardened briefly. He honestly seemed angry, but she wasn't sure. It wasn't one she'd ever seen on him before, and all she could smell was the faint chemicals of her breathing treatment.

He took a deep breath. "Marsee, if I didn't trust you, I'd have killed you the moment you indicated you didn't want to turn your instinct back on. Any refusal or hesitation to do so is seen as proof that you know you're losing control and grounds for immediate execution. I'm honestly surprised Avery didn't. I've not once seen a guard do otherwise."

She stared at him in shock and horror. She'd always known that refusing an order by the Senior Council or Guard had serious consequences, but this was an order she couldn't follow. "What if someone asks me to turn it on in the future? I swear I can't. I've tried several times. All that happens is that hollow feeling gets worse."

He sighed. "That, I don't know. I'm still trying to figure it out. There's no precedent, and that's partly why you're being watched. We need to know if this is a permanent injury or not."

"So if Mama figures out how to fix me, you may end up killing me anyway?"

"I seriously hope that's not the case, but your condition is unique. As far as I'm concerned, there's enough medical evidence to prove you're telling the truth. If you want to challenge your watch, you can bring it before the Full Council. That is your right, but I wouldn't recommend it as it would expose your illness to the population, and I don't think people would understand or trust you if they knew, even with medical evidence. The safest path for you is to wait out the six months, as people expect. Then, if there's no change in your medical status, I can record your disability as permanent. That may not stop someone from asking you to try, but it will give you some protection."

"Some?" she replied with a snort. "Like I said, no rights. If I can't even fight a watch with medical proof that I'm no longer a risk, how can I bring charges against Papa for what he did? The Council will take one look at my watch and side with him, or worse, demand my execution."

"Your father has stated he won't fight it if you choose to press charges and will accept whatever you want for reparations, so it won't need to go to trial."

Surprised, she flicked her ears back and then pinned them as she squinted at him with suspicion. "You're going to believe me about that, but not about my control? Somehow, I find that hard to believe."

"I do believe you about your control. If I didn't, you'd be dead, but I fully understand why you don't trust me. You're right. I should have come to speak to you about what happened and not taken your father's word for it. I wasn't aware you weren't spoken to by the guard about it. You should have been, and I promise I'll look into it. If you would prefer, I can recuse myself and ask one of the other seniors to swim over. Frankly, they would be happier if I did, but I thought you'd be more comfortable and open talking with me. Regardless, you will need to give your statement to one of us. It doesn't need to be detailed, but it needs to be the truth. Simply state whether or not he was abusing you and what you want for reparations, and if you don't want the rest of the Council to know, I can restrict access to the Seniors."

She blinked at him. "You're serious? If I tell you he was abusing me and call for his death, you're going to kill him without even trying to save his life?"

Her uncle sighed but gave a single nod. "To go to trial to try and save him would put all of Saber at risk, and our laws are clear. If you feel what he did to you was abuse, then it's abuse, and if your father isn't going to fight it, then I have no grounds to represent him."

She rolled over and looked up at the ceiling as she tried to decide if she would feel more comfortable talking with him or one of the others. They had all lost her trust in one way or another, except for her uncle. He was the only one who would really understand what was going on. The problem was she didn't know if that would help her case or not. She shrugged. "I suppose it doesn't matter."

"I'll take that as consent to continue." He unclipped his tablet, fiddled with it for a second, and then clipped it back to his harness. A tiny blue light indicated the camera was on. "This conversation is now being recorded. At any time you wish to stop the recording, say so. Please state your full name for the record."

She sighed and rolled over to look at him again. "Marsee Bet Chenzira."

"Marsee, has your father, Senior Council Jeran Frederick Chenzira, been abusing you?"

She didn't answer. She honestly didn't know what to say. It felt like abuse, but Rip had twisted her thoughts and feelings about the incident so much that even though she knew what her father said he'd been doing and why, she wasn't so sure anymore. She wasn't even sure about her own actions that day anymore. On top of that, her emotions were all over the place: simmering rage one minute, depression the next. She hated him and loved him. Wanted to claw his throat out and felt horrible about what she'd said, and was both relieved and devastated to hear her mother was separating from him. Regardless of the rage she currently felt, she wasn't sure she wanted to press charges. To do so would mean that Rip would win. Yet, leaving someone capable of abuse in charge seemed equally bad. But was it abuse or a test? That she didn't know.

"You need to answer the question," her uncle said after a minute or two of silence.

She still didn't answer. She didn't know how.

"Or did you attack someone? Is he covering for you?"

She frowned at her uncle, and it took everything she had not to pin her ears back in anger, feeling trapped and betrayed by his questioning. He said he trusted her, but with those words, he proved he really didn't.

"I didn't hurt anyone. I have *never* hurt anyone who wasn't hurting me or someone else first. I was upset and went out for a run," she replied, then rolled back over to stare up at the ceiling again. She couldn't bring herself to look at her uncle or the blankness of his now fully hardened and masked face. She was starting to loathe that mask.

"What were you upset about?" he prompted after further silence.

"Everything. Mostly my sister. I felt guilty for not being there when she went into labor, and the noise of construction and people everywhere was grating on my nerves. There wasn't anywhere in New Hope I could go where it was quiet. My ears hurt from wearing the hearing aids all the time, and I needed a few minutes of peace and quiet to get away from it all, only I practically ran into Papa on my way out of the tower."

"Is that how you got hurt?"

She pursed her lips, fighting to control the snark that wanted to come out. He wasn't exactly making it easy to avoid talking about her illness. "No. Papa tried to stop me. I didn't want to talk to anyone, certainly not out where everyone could hear, so I kept running. I didn't realize it was a command from a Senior Councilor and not a request from my father. He chased after me and pinned me to the ground, biting my scruff hard enough to draw blood. I didn't realize it was him at first and struggled to get away. I thought some predator had attacked."

"How long before you realized it was him?"

"A few seconds, maybe. When I yelled at him to stop, he backed off."

Her uncle frowned slightly. "That wouldn't account for all of your injuries. How did you break your shoulder?"

She glared at him. "I thought I didn't have to go into details."

"What I've heard so far is not abuse, nor does it match with the injuries on your medical record. I need to understand why and what upset you so much that you would have the guards drag your father off yesterday."

She sighed as she considered her words. "We argued. I told him to leave me alone and then ran off again. About an hour later, he caught up with me, and we spoke for a bit, but I really wanted to be alone and wasn't ready to talk, so I took off again. This time, he chased after me, but instead of stopping me, he forced me to keep running. He clawed me several times in the process. After repeatedly asking him to stop, I had enough and fought back. Eventually, I managed to pin him, gave him a piece of my mind, as the Hue-mans say, and limped off. I was absolutely terrified he would attack again if I let him up, but I knew you'd never believe me if I killed him. As for my shoulder, I broke it when he deflected one of my attacks, and I landed hard on a rock. He *claims* he didn't mean any of what he said and was just testing my control."

"What makes you think he wasn't?"

"Because it felt like abuse at the time, and there was a moment I thought he was going to kill me. It took me a long time to get over what he said to me, and what Rip did to me has me so...so messed up inside that I honestly don't know what's real anymore."

"Has your father ever attacked you before?"

"No."

"What did Rip do to make you mistrust your father?"

She winced at the memory and flexed her unbroken paw but answered anyway, knowing he would keep pressing if she didn't. "He said it was Papa's fault he was hurting me because Papa chose his power over me and hadn't stepped down, that Papa wanted his diseased daughter to die. He used Papa's term of endearment every time he shocked me. Even though I can't feel pain anymore, I can feel Rip shocking me every time I hear that phrase and feel just as terrified as I was in the cave." She paused, trying to collect her thoughts.

"Is that why you reacted so strongly yesterday?"

"That's part of it," she replied. "I don't even know what emotions are mine anymore. I feel like I'm feeling everything and nothing at the same time, but when he said it, I felt this rage build up in me like I've never felt before, and everything Rip did and claimed came rushing back."

"Like what?" he pressed.

She shook her head. "I don't want it on record. I don't even want to think about it."

Surprisingly, he stopped the recording. "I understand how difficult it must be to talk about what happened to you, but if there is more and you can tell us, it will help our investigation, even if everything he said was a lie."

"I haven't told you a fraction of what happened. I can't."

"Why not? Is someone else threatening you to keep you quiet?"

"No. It's just...I don't even have words for some of it." She lifted her broken paw and rubbed at it with her good one. "I can't explain how I don't feel pain, yet I can still feel what he did to me, every excruciating moment." She put the paw down and stared at the ceiling instead. "Most of the time, he would shock me until I stopped screaming and then talk while I recovered. Sometimes, it was about me, about what he was going to do to me next. Sometimes, it was about others, like you and Ellie, but mostly he focused on Papa. He knew everything about my past, took what I thought were normal or innocent experiences, and twisted them to make them seem like neglect and abuse. I don't even know what's true and what isn't anymore, and I'm not going to put on record something that might not be true and probably isn't, especially when I have no way of proving any of it. I've already told you what I'm sure of and what I've had a chance to look into."

"What kinds of things did he say?" he asked again.

She shook her head.

"Marsee, wouldn't it be better to find out the truth than always wonder?"

She shook her head again. "I honestly don't know if it would do more harm than good. Rip wanted me to mistrust all of you. I don't want to give his words any more weight than they already have, and I need time to process and do my own research. If I find something, I'll let you know."

He nodded. "That's fair. Now, while we're off the record, why don't you tell me what really happened with your father? In as much detail as you can remember."

She rolled her eyes but told him everything, or most of it anyway. There were parts she wasn't sure of anymore and parts she didn't want him to know about, but then she should have realized he already knew.

"Your father says you marked a tree," he said after she was done.

She sighed and nodded. She'd purposely left that part out. "My instinct felt trapped in the tower with everyone around us. I suppose I did, too. I figured giving up a little control was safer than losing it completely. That's part of the reason I took off again. It was furious that Papa was in territory it had just marked, and I left because I was afraid I would hurt him."

"So you were losing control?"

"I didn't think so at the time. It wasn't like before with Little Flower. I was fully in control of my body and how much control I gave up to it, but I was also overwhelmed with everything else going on, and I didn't want to risk it."

"And you believe this test made it harder for you to control your instinct in the canyon?"

"Not just in the canyon. From that very moment. Every time Papa was around, my instinct growled at him. I didn't trust him, and I was afraid to show any emotion around him after that, but I was just as worried about what would happen if I said nothing. The day he came to pick me up from Ellie's, it was all I could do to keep from clawing him. But that was as much me as my instinct, and I nearly lost control the day he took custody of Hope back. My instinct saw Hope as our cub and wanted me to take her back. I promised I would tell him if I had any issues, and I did. We went out for a run, and that helped a lot. We even sat and watched a small herd of doba, but we didn't have any problems. Kendra followed us if you need proof. We've been working through it. He's been spending time with me while I practice. That helped a lot, too. I think we would have been fine if it weren't for Rip, but he targeted every doubt I still had and twisted them into a tangled mess. In the canyon, I didn't remember who Papa was at first, but my instinct did, and all it remembered was the threat he posed and how he'd hurt us before. Clear Seas, too. I honestly don't know why it didn't see you as a threat. Out of everyone, it's you I have to worry about, isn't it?"

He didn't answer.

They sat there in silence, staring at each other until Ellie's tablet dinged. She'd forgotten her mentor was in the room. She'd told Ellie some of what had happened that day but not everything, not the specifics. She glanced over at Ellie. Her mentor looked positively livid, although she was doing her best to remain calm.

"Why would he do that?" Ellie growled. "What possible reason could he have to justify that kind of abuse? A swipe or two, maybe, but this?"

Her uncle sighed. "Ellie, we've been over this. Jer did what he was trained and authorized to do as part of being a Councilor. He believed that Marsee was losing control again. He not only chased her away from New Hope so that she wouldn't hurt anyone, but was also administering the test the Council uses to determine if someone is in control of their instinct, or part of it anyway."

"Part of it!" Ellie spat, ears pinned back and tail instantly lashing with fury. "Are you telling me you do this to everyone?"

Marcus nodded. "If necessary. Most people don't survive the first swipe if they're having issues, and I've never known anyone with psychosis to catch someone as Marsee did to her father and not lose control, not once in the hundred and forty-five years I've been a councilor."

"That's no excuse!" Ellie growled. "And you should know better!" Her tail was lashing hard enough now to cause visible waves in the water, which made everything ripple as the light refracted through it.

Marcus flicked his ears back in surprise at Ellie's venom. "Ellie, it's our responsibility to ensure the safety of the population."

"By trapping people into defending themselves and then killing them when they do?" Ellie spat back.

He sighed. "It's not like that at all. Most everyone we test is on the verge of losing control the moment they're brought in. Half the time, just having them turn it on is enough, just like it was for Marsee that day in the garden. A normal person would recover once they realized the threat was over. People with psychosis don't come back. You've seen it enough to know that."

"If anyone else did what Jer did, you'd execute them for abuse and attempted murder. Not only did he continue to threaten her after repeated demands for him to stop, he pushed her to the point she feared for her own life, even after she was injured and broke her shoulder. If she had killed him, it would have been self-defense, but you'd have executed her because of her medical history, no matter what she said in her defense. You probably wouldn't have even given her a chance to explain herself. To think how many children I reported. No wonder they all died."

With that, Ellie growled at Marcus, swam out, slamming the door switch open, and, to her surprise, growled at the guards floating outside. "You're as bad as the Council if you allow this...this *abomination* of a test to occur!" she hissed at them and swam off down the hall.

From where she lay, she could only see Avery in the doorway. He watched Ellie for a moment and then turned to look back at her and Marcus. She had no doubt he'd heard Ellie's rant. It had certainly been loud enough. His expression was a mask, though, and he simply reached up and hit the door switch, giving them privacy again.

"Papa told me you tested him as badly, if not worse, for months," she said, eventually breaking the awkward silence.

Her uncle sighed and turned to look back at her. "He's not wrong. I'm sure I said just as many equally harsh things to him at that time, but there's a big difference. He knew what I was trying to do when I was doing it and consented to it. *You* did not. Regardless of his intentions, he broke his word and your trust, and he hurt you in the process. Ellie's right. If this had been done by anyone else for any other reason, it would be considered abuse, and I believe you have grounds to charge him for it and more than enough evidence to prove it. Do you want to press charges?"

She sighed and looked up at the ceiling again, trying to decide what she wanted.

He waited this time.

"No."

"Are you sure?" he asked. "You are well within your rights to have him executed. Although, if you do want that, your father and I have already discussed exploring what our instincts can do. If I have to kill him, I'd like to get some value out of it, at least."

She flicked her ears back, surprised that he would even question her answer. "Are you trying to get him killed?"

"Of course not," he replied. "My feelings towards him are immaterial in this situation. You seemed hesitant in your answer. I don't want you to hesitate to press charges if you're fearing that he might attack you again in retribution."

She thought about it for a moment. *Was there even anything he could give me to make up for what happened? His death won't give me my life or the ability to have cubs back, and Mama already took his cubs from him.* She couldn't think of anything she wanted from him. "Yeah. I'm sure. As horrible as it was at the time, I understand what he was trying to do." She let out a heavy sigh. "I'm scared and angry, but I don't want him to die or step down. If he did, Rip would win. Besides, I did this to myself to keep from killing him in the first place. What point would there be to kill him now? He was here, and it was easier to blame him for what happened to me rather than accept that I'd done it to myself, and, if I'm being truly honest with myself, I don't think my instinct would have let Papa be the one to execute Rip anyway. We both wanted it way too much, although now... "

She rolled over away from him, unable and unwilling to discuss it any further, but her uncle wasn't done questioning her.

"Before I have you record that officially, and as we're alone, I do have another question for you. The other day, when Avery questioned you in the ship, he asked you if your instinct still spoke to you. Was it actually speaking to you in words?"

"Yeah. Yours doesn't?" she replied, lifting her head and looking back, surprised.

He raised an eyebrow at that and considered. "No. The only time I really used it, it never spoke to me. I just knew how to do what I needed to do. Have you always been able to speak with your instinct?"

She flopped back down but didn't roll back over to face him. "No. Just since that first day with Little Flower. Before that, it was just the 'pounce on everything' reflex. That day, it changed and gained a voice and...a body. Perhaps it was just my imagination. We could talk even when it wasn't on, and I bounced ideas off it all the time. It's how I knew Deep Current was telling the truth and why I knew both Clear Seas and Petra were innocent. I know it must sound kind of crazy, but that's just how it was for me. In the cave, it grew even stronger. I swear I could see it walk beside me. I even felt it curl around me in an attempt to keep me warm at one point. We had long conversations as it tried to teach me what it could, to be able to fight back the next time Rip showed up. It encouraged me to keep walking, talked me out of drowning myself half a dozen times, and protected me while I slept. After that day in the garden, it stopped pressuring me like it had before and questioned my motives, but it never tried to take control, even when I was in danger, not until Papa got close enough to kill me."

She shook her head. "No. That's not entirely true. It recognized the threat when Rip grabbed my mask and killed him before I even realized what was going on. But I wanted Rip dead just as much as my instinct did, and I didn't try to stop it. It didn't feel like I lost control but more like it was protecting me, and I was in control again immediately after, or at least I felt I was, right up until the end. It felt that I wasn't taking the threat Papa posed seriously, and it argued hard to make me stop him. It said something like, 'If you won't do what's necessary, I'll have to do it for us.' That's when I started to fight back, even though I was sure Papa was going to kill us, too. Now I just feel hollow and empty and...I don't know. I'm really lonely too. I keep forgetting and try to ask it a question, and the silence makes me grieve all over again."

She rubbed at the back of her head and the hollowness she felt there. "Is it wrong to miss something that tried to harm you?"

"No, I don't think so. You've lost a significant part of yourself, and anyone would grieve over that. The way you describe it, it sounds almost like it was a friend or perhaps even a mentor to you in a way, helping you when no one else could, and having to destroy the fragile trust you'd built over these past few months couldn't have been easy."

"You don't think I'm crazy?" she asked, lifting her head to look back at him.

"No. Not at all. You did what you had to. You've been through more life-threatening situations than anyone should ever have to go through. Besides, you're the first person to survive an advanced case of psychosis. Who would I be to say if how you handled it was sane or not? It clearly worked."

"Ha!" she muttered darkly. "Some success..."

"You have another twenty years to live. That's more than you had the other day. If you hadn't regained control, you would not have left that canyon alive. Only the fact that you were still trying to fight it and hadn't gone non-verbal stopped me from having to kill you. When you said you were losing control... I have never hated my job as much as I did in that moment." He reached out to caress the side of her face, but she flinched away, and he dropped his paw with a look of sorrow in his eyes, although nothing else about his expression changed. "As far as I'm concerned, it was a miracle we got any of you back at all. And besides, it's not all bad."

"Oh? What makes you say that?" She squinted at him with suspicion.

"Well, for one, I now know I can trust you not to lose control, which means I can trust you in my ancient archives room."

"What? Really?! *That's* why you haven't let me in there all these years?" She glared at him, trying to determine whether he was joking or not.

"Well, that and I wanted to ensure you were trained on how to handle them properly. Now, before you start daydreaming about all the books in there, let's get this statement out of the way."

She sighed, and he turned on the recording again.

"Marsee, do you feel what what your father did to you was abuse?"

"Yes and no, she replied. It felt like abuse at the time, but I understand why he did it, and if I had been losing control, he would have been right to do everything in his power to get me away from New Hope."

"Do you want to press charges?"

"No. He promised never to do it again, and he hasn't. He put himself at risk to protect the people of New Hope, and I won that fight, so I consider us even. Rip Current tried hard to make me question my father's intentions, but Rip is the one I really blame for this, not my father. I'm pretty sure that if we hadn't fought that day, I wouldn't have survived what Rip did to me. I needed to know I was strong enough to survive and win."

Her uncle turned off the recording, and she rolled over away from him. She heard him sigh and then the sounds of the door as it swished open and closed again.

Ellie returned a few minutes later in a far calmer mood than she'd been when she'd left, although the tip of her tail was still twitching. She came over, gave her a hug, and then returned to her net.

Marsee tried going back to sleep again, but moments later, her tablet started to ding. She muttered and flipped over to see what was going off.

Reminder: Time to pee

Marsee groaned. "You set up a reminder to tell me when I need to pee?"

Ellie chuckled. "If you think I'm going to tell you every few hours, you're sadly mistaken, and I know how you crafters are. I'm guessing you probably forgot before, on more than one occasion, completely focused on whatever project you were working on at the time."

Marsee muttered. "Fair." Sure enough, she needed to go. "Gah, peeing in water is just weird."

Ellie chuckled.

She growled at her mentor but was grateful for the current that pulled it away. *How did the Water Sprites pee?* She hadn't seen one of their bathrooms in the tour of Clear Seas home and then shuddered, realizing she was probably swimming in their pee and the pee of all of the other creatures that made up this world. *Ewww.... No, don't think about that.* Still, she shuddered again.

"Are you okay?" Ellie asked, frowning with concern.

"Did you ever think about the fact that we're swimming in fish poop?" Marsee asked.

"Trust me. It's better if you don't," Ellie said with a matching shudder of her own.

Chuckling slightly at her mentor's horrified and disgusted expression, she closed her eyes and was instantly asleep.

CHAPTER 43

Marcus: No Wonder They All Died

Marcus swam away from his niece's room, deep in thought. He was relieved that she had decided not to press charges, but the entire situation weighed heavily on him. Her lack of trust in him had hurt, but he supposed he deserved it. He was a risk to her, although one he considered minor, as he was fairly certain she was telling the truth, but what bothered him more was her accusation that he and the Guard had not done their due diligence, and in that, she was right. He had taken both his brother's and Kendra's words for what happened. Even though he trusted his brother implicitly, he should have spoken to Marsee about it. More so, Kendra should have.

Why didn't she? he wondered. *Is it because she found her journal? It is fairly well documented in there. Or is something else going on? What better way to assassinate someone than by turning their own child against them? No one would have thought twice if Jer had been killed by someone with psychosis, especially by his own daughter. I'm pretty sure that's what Rip was trying to do, but was Kendra working with him? Is she our mystery guard? Why though? What motive would she have? I've done my best to address every issue she's brought forward.*

No wonder they all died.

He shook his head as Ellie's words clobbered him hard and cut deeply into his soul. The worst part of being a Councillor had been administering the test, yet he'd never once questioned its need, not until it was his own niece facing it. As a Councilor, he needed to be there whenever any of the citizens of his district were tested, but it was the Senior's responsibility to sign off on it and be prepared to perform the execution. Most of the time, Kendra and her guards did that horrible deed simply due to numbers. He rarely had to get involved, although every test was a risk. He'd been hurt far more often administering the Junior Advocate's test. He'd seen so many people brought in lose control before the test even started. He'd never even once suspected that they might be the cause of it, not the other way around. Yet, from what Marsee said, that test made everything harder for her to control and the reason why she'd ultimately lost control. He'd seen more than a few children lost to abuse over the years, but he'd never once considered that the Council's test for psychosis was abusive.

Harsh and violent, yes, if they made it past the first swipe, but abusive?

Then again, no one ever survived to challenge it. Seen from Marsee's perspective, Jer had been attacking her without cause, and she would have been well within her rights to kill him, but she and Ellie were both right, too. I probably would have ordered her execution, and if Jer had killed her, I wouldn't have even questioned it. Was the test a trap, as Ellie believed?

He thought back to each of the tests he'd observed in his long career. No one survived the test once they'd gone non-verbal or hunted. At that point, it was mostly a formality, but it was the one chance they had to prove themselves. He shook his head, deciding it wasn't a trap. Almost all lost control just turning it on or with the first swipe, and if the Council could recover, so should they if they weren't a risk. Even still, for Marsee to draw blood and walk away when she feared for her life and when her instinct wanted to kill was unheard of. Yet she'd done it on more than one occasion. He wondered if he would have walked away in a similar situation.

Be honest with yourself. You would have killed him at the first strike, but you have that right.

He stopped and blinked. *Is that what Marsee really meant about not having the same rights?* As a senior councilor, he could kill anyone he deemed a threat, and any citizen could kill in self-defense, but Marsee couldn't. Any sign of violence on her part while on a watch could be cause for execution.

No wonder they all died!

But that was the case for anyone who acted with violence towards another, and she said she'd lost her rights long before she'd ever hunted. Is that true?

He shook his head, unable to find any instance where her rights had been violated or restricted prior to her hunt. When she was on the watch, they'd done everything they could to ensure her life was as normal as possible. Even when she'd bitten her classmate's tail as a cub, it had been justified, and there'd been no repercussions outside of a watch. The Guard had found proof that she and her friend were being bullied, not just by her peers but by her teacher, as well.

He frowned, remembering that Kendra had investigated that incident. She'd found evidence of further crimes after Marsee's teacher went non-verbal during her investigation, which included the physical abuse of her own children and dozens of complaints that had been filed by other parents and ignored by the School Master. Marsee's teacher had been brought in to be tested and had failed after going non-verbal in front of Kendra, and the School Master demoted, although he was pretty sure Marsee didn't know that. They hadn't wanted to upset her or her classmates.

Did Rip find out about that incident from Kendra, or did he just pull it off her record?

The only other incident that he could remember was when she'd been caught using her instinct by her friend's mother. As a minor, he'd tried to protect her by scaring her out of using it, which had seemed to help at the time, or so he'd thought, but they hadn't been able to save her friend. She'd been completely non-verbal before he had returned with Tabor and hadn't made it past the first swipe. They hadn't told Marsee about that either and had blamed it on a sand spinner, both to protect Marsee and her friend's reputation. Marsee had been distraught enough about the loss of her friend as it was.

If Rip found out... I wonder if that's what she won't tell us? He made a mental note to see if Rip had a file on Marsee's friend.

The only thing he could think of was the DNR. Wind Rider and Clear Seas certainly believed it was a violation of her rights, and he wouldn't be surprised if they tried to force the issue by bringing it before the Full Council, but he didn't think Marsee knew about it. Ellie had agreed not to tell her for fear she might try to kill herself. Granted, with a terminal illness, it didn't really matter. That was her right.

I need more information about how sign language is working.

He sent out a message to Kendra asking for the latest reports on psychosis, their trials, and her recommendations going forward on when and how they should test someone. He hadn't been called in to test anyone yet, which seemed to be more than a coincidence at this point. His council was not particularly comfortable with his current recommendations but were willing to try for the sake of science and the hope that they could save even a few more children each year.

He then sent out a message to his Senior Healer, ordering her to assign a team to study psychosis and see if anything they were learning with Marsee could be used to help the others, although he was sure she was already looking into it. They hadn't had a breakthrough like this in thousands of years, and he'd rather give someone twenty years than kill them outright if they could find a way to reproduce it safely and painlessly.

It was the best he could do for now. He couldn't change the past, and he still needed to protect his people, but he could try to help others in the future and, if nothing else, give them the same chances he was giving his niece and brother.

NO WONDER THEY ALL DIED!

He snorted as Ellie's words hit him again. *Knowing Ellie, she'll probably have those words carved on my tombstone.*

CHAPTER 44

Marcus: Instinctive Measures

When Marcus arrived back at the Seniors' Conference room, the others were all there, including Sammianna and Apakna, who had arrived earlier that morning. Sammie had her nose buried in her tablet, squinting at something, but Apakna was glaring at Clear Seas, who was glaring right back with flickers of orange and red. Sparkles of ice crystals floated up around Apakna in the chilled current used to keep her cool enough. He always liked the effect, a snowstorm in reverse. It made her look magical. Today, with her scowl and crossed arms, it made her look dangerous.

What's going on here? he wondered.

That morning, they'd had a rather heated conversation as they brought the two up to speed on the latest developments, but Jer had been the one to take the brunt of it as the other Seniors had interrogated him. His brother stared off into the distance, one arm propped against the side of his net as he absently rubbed at his scruff, seemingly lost in thought and waiting to find out his verdict.

He was terrified for his brother. Jer had been practically non-verbal with his own grief and guilt that morning, barely answering the rapid-fire questions the others had directed at him. It had been all he could do to advocate for his brother, and he hoped the others would drop the issue with Marsee's decision. Even if she wasn't pressing charges, they could still vote Jer out, and he was pretty sure his brother wanted them to.

They all stopped what they were doing and watched as he swam in, but no one spoke.

Clear Seas finally asked the question they were all wondering. "So, did she press charges?"

"Surprisingly, no," Marcus replied, taking his seat. "As I expected, she's in a far calmer mood this morning and even told me that she believes she wouldn't have survived what Rip did to her if she hadn't fought with Jer before."

They all looked at him in surprise, even Sammianna, but no one was more surprised than his brother.

"You're serious?" Jer asked. "She really dropped the charges?"

"I am." He threw her statement up on the monitor, knowing they would want to see it. He watched the others as they watched the statement. Their faces were all the blank masks he expected to see, outside of Jer's, who flinched on several occasions.

Apakna was the first to speak. "I still find it hard to believe that she beat Jer in a fight. Jer, did you let her win?"

His brother shook his head, but Clear Seas burst out laughing and spoke before Jer could. "With all due respect, *Senior* Councilor. Marsee may be small, but I personally witnessed her catch and kill one of my own species after he nearly killed her and my son. If she can do that, she's more than capable of beating her father."

"So you say," Apakna replied, glaring at Clear Seas, not the least bit amused by his laughter or the slight barb.

Granted, he was just as surprised by the barb. That wasn't like Clear Seas at all. *Just what happened while I was gone?*

"You don't believe me?" Clear Seas asked, now flashing astonishment.

"No, I don't," she hissed back. "I don't believe any of you at the moment. I've been stuck on a ship for the past eight standard days with a faulty communication system while all of this happened. The last I knew, you were the one being arrested, not Jer. So excuse me if I hold judgment until I've had a chance to review all the evidence, *Senior* Councilor."

Clear Seas's astonishment changed to anger, and the room lit up an orange-red with it.

"It has been quite the week," Marcus said, trying to defuse the situation, "but Clear's right. Marsee is more than capable of it. We typically have an entire contingent of guards on hand during a test to contain the situation, and dozens of guards are killed or permanently injured every year. In all my years, I've never once witnessed anyone with psychosis not lose control with the first taste of blood and not seriously injure or kill the other person. Jer's lucky he survived, both that day and in the canyon. She was fighting hard to maintain her control the entire time."

Clear Seas turned his glare on Marcus, and his skin shifted to a solid red. "Stop trying to make Marsee appear to be more of a threat than she is. There's more than enough medical proof that she's unable to use her instinct anymore. She was verbal the entire time in the canyon and didn't show the slightest bit of violence towards anyone but Rip until Jer refused to back off, and frankly, she had every right to be angry and mistrust him after what he did to her."

"Stop trying to downplay the threat of psychosis," Marcus countered. "You haven't had to deal with this illness. I have, for half a century longer than you've been a councilor. She was terrified to turn her instinct on yesterday, and she struggled hard to turn it off in the canyon. Don't try to deny it."

"I'm denying your interpretation of that loss of control," Clear Seas said. "I don't believe it was psychosis."

Marcus snorted. "What else could it be? She herself said she was losing control."

"Confusion from the lack of oxygen because of her failing mask compounded by the severity of her injuries," Clear Seas replied with a scowl. "You *yourself* told me your instincts help to block pain. She should have been writhing in pain the entire time from what Rip did to her, but she didn't even cry out until she tried to turn it off. Personally, I think it was cruel to make her turn it off before her pain had been managed by a healer. I don't think you realize just how painful it is to be electrocuted, and I don't think you'd be able to turn yours off if you were half as injured as she was, but I'd be more than willing to test out that hypothesis."

Marcus scowled at both Clear Seas' claim and the threat. "If she hadn't turned it off, she would have killed her father or started eating Rip's body."

"If he'd done what she'd asked and backed off, she wouldn't have seen him as a threat," Clear Seas countered. "As for Rip, that would have been her right, too, although I seriously doubt she would have. She didn't seem to have any interest in that, only shredding him into tiny pieces, like he deserved."

They glared at each other for several tense moments before Sammi-anna spoke. "Clear Seas brings up a good point. We don't know how painful the Sprite's shock is." She held her hand over to Clear Seas. "Show me."

Clear Seas flashed his surprise briefly, but before he could respond, Apakna snorted.

"You're seriously going to let him shock you?" Apakna asked. "He could kill you."

"He could reach over and kill me at any moment," Sammie replied, not lowering her hand. "We either need to trust him and the evidence or vote him out. The evidence says he's innocent, and we should fully understand what was done to the victims." She looked back at Clear Seas and raised a brow.

"Close your mouth tightly and make a fist with your hands," Clear Seas said.

Sammie did, and Clear Seas reached out and lightly made contact. She yelped and instantly curled up in her shell.

"Are you alright?" Clear Seas asked.

The only response was a whimper, and it took her nearly a minute to uncurl. "Well, that was informative," she replied as she rubbed at her hand, "and an experience I never want to repeat."

"For the record, that's only a tiny fraction of what I'm capable of generating," Clear Seas said, "and far less than Marsee experienced based on the severity of her burns."

After Sammie's bravery, he had no excuse not to follow her lead. He glared at Clear Seas's evident amusement when he held out his hand but endured the pain, managing not to yelp, even though it was far more painful than he expected. He wasn't one to pass up a challenge, though. "Show me what she really endured," he said after.

"No. If I did what was done to her, I could easily kill you." Clear Seas said, shaking his head. "I don't even know how she survived."

"I'll take that risk," he said.

"No." Clear Seas replied with some force. "My threat notwithstanding. I'm not doing that to you or anyone."

"Yes. You will. You were right. I don't know if I could turn off my instinct if I had the same injuries. That was far more painful than anything I've ever experienced."

Clear Seas frowned at him. "Not without a healer present, and we'll try it first at the same level. If you can't do it there, there's no point in trying anything more."

"Fair," he replied, so they called in Hyacinth.

While they waited, Wind Rider and Apakna both did the same, although it took Apakna some time to decide if she trusted Clear Seas enough to allow it.

Hyacinth arrived a few minutes later and frowned when he explained what he wanted to try. "For the record, I think you're absolutely fur-brained, but I understand your reasoning."

They all snorted, and Clear Seas bubbled bright blue with laughter.

"I won't disagree," Marcus replied and held his clenched paw across the table to Clear Seas, turned his instinct on, and nodded.

Rather than a light touch, Clear Seas grabbed his wrist. Pain exploded throughout his body, and it seized. He couldn't think, couldn't breathe. Even with his instinct on, he couldn't block the pain or fight back to try and escape Clear Seas' grasp. He tried to turn his instinct off, but he couldn't. It wasn't that it was fighting him, but he couldn't focus enough through the pain to turn it off or even tell Clear Seas to stop, and eventually, he passed out from the lack of oxygen. When he woke, every part of his body throbbed, and he rubbed at his wrist where Clear Seas had grabbed him. "Ancient Gods," he swore. "How did she fight through that?"

"I honestly don't know," Clear Seas said, his skin now shifting to dark blue. "So, were you able to turn your instinct off?"

Marcus snorted, "Not even close. I will concede your point that her injuries alone could have prevented her from turning off her instinct, regardless of her statement that she felt like she was losing control. I will inform my council and guard to take that into consideration in the future and ensure that pain is managed before asking someone to turn it off, assuming they're in control and not hurting anyone. Thank you, Hyacinth."

She nodded and swam out.

"Now, what about Jer?" Marcus asked. "As Marsee's not pressing charges, are we good there?"

"No," Apakna growled. "Not even close. Marsee had the guards drag him out of her room, and what she wrote in her journal shows it clearly traumatized her. She may not be pressing charges, but she was hurt both physically and mentally enough to leave home for weeks. It may be standard practice to test people, but according to both of you, he didn't even follow the standard procedure by not calling in the guards. I vote no confidence. He should step down, and I think you should, too. I'm not comfortable at all about having Senior Councilors who believe attacking children is acceptable in any context."

"Would you rather we just killed them?" he countered.

"If they were truly gone or hurting someone, yes. It would be far kinder. Otherwise no. Frankly, I think it's highly suspicious that after ten thousand years you haven't found a cure. My decision stands. What Jer did was abuse, and as you're his mentor, you're equally responsible. I am putting forth a vote of no confidence against both of you. Please leave so we can discuss."

Jer sighed and started to swim out but stopped as Marcus let out a huff of frustration. Jer turned to look back at him, surprised.

Marcus pursed his lips at the Ice Planet's Senior Councilor and stood. "I understand your concern. If you should decide to vote us out, I ask that you do not publicize the reason, not to protect us, but to protect my people. I will gladly step down or take whatever punishment you deem fit as long as my people remain safe."

He pointed to the wall of boxes they'd yet to dig through. "But also consider who among those remaining do you trust enough to take our place?" He turned his attention back to Apakna, pulling every ounce of authority he still had as a Senior Councilor, and directed it entirely towards her. She matched him just as fiercely, frost flakes glittering as she breathed out. "Or whether we should be the ones putting forth a vote of no confidence against you. None of us in this room are free of scandal, not even you, Senior Councilor Apakna. Don't think I don't know that every single one of you planned to kill my niece and let her take the blame for Little Flower's death and commit genocide against a people you imprisoned and isolated for almost a year."

Clear Seas and Wind Rider looked away. Sammianna showed no emotion but nodded the point. Apakna continued to glare at him, not budging an inch.

"Are you seriously blackmailing us for honoring a decision your council made?" Apakna asked. "On top of everything else?"

"No. I am reminding you of a decision you made to protect your people, one that no one outside of this room would truly understand. I took an oath to protect my people before myself and my family, but that doesn't mean I stop loving my family. I should have killed Marsee on several occasions, but I couldn't, and neither could Jer. I gave her a chance, just like you ultimately gave the Hue-mans a chance. Tell me truthfully that it's any different."

Apakna continued to stare at him.

He snorted, full of derision at her. "We'll be in my office. Let us know when you decide what kind of Council you want to be."

CHAPTER 45

Nazari: Confronting the Past

With her nightly rounds complete, Nazari returned to the feline pens and lay down in their enclosure. The latest batch of kittens swarmed her almost immediately, and she purred, content to let them chase her tail. It wasn't exactly what her instinct wanted, but it helped. It didn't hurt that they were absolutely adorable miniature balls of fluff.

The mother, who looked so much like her daughter, tolerated her now but was nowhere near as affectionate as her cubs and lay sprawled along one of the branches, observing. Her tail swayed gently as it hung from the branch, but she didn't seem upset. If anything, she seemed pleased to have her cubs distracted.

"They are quite rambunctious," she said.

Nala, the name the Hue-mans had given her, yawned without lifting her head, and a paw slipped to hang drooped from the branch.

"I bet they do tire you out. I would be, too, with a litter this big." She lay there, head on her paws and absently twitching her tail for the cubs and letting them climb on her for some time. Her thoughts drifted to her daughter, wondering if Quinn was right about needing to put closure on her death. She'd thought she'd accepted that loss a long time ago, but the grief she felt told her she hadn't. She'd only hidden it.

"You seem quite content at the moment."

She looked up and found Quinn in the doorway. "Oh, I'm sorry. I must have lost track of time."

"No worries. I've been watching you for a while. This is clearly helping." He stepped carefully inside and plunked down beside her to take a closer look at one of the cubs, who waddled over to check him out. Quinn wiggled his tail, and the cub pounced. "They really aren't much different than our cubs, are they?"

"Genetically, they're very different, but behavioral-wise, they are much the same. The cubs are far more social than their mother. GrandFather says it only takes ten or twelve generations of selective breeding to domesticate a wild animal. All it takes is breeding based on behavior."

"That's all?" he asked, surprised.

"So he says. I can believe it. The difference in only two generations is astounding. Nala tolerates me now, but I still can't touch her without sedating her first." She sat up slowly, peeling kittens off her back in the process, and looked at the feline that reminded her so much of her daughter and then over at Quinn. "Did you find out?"

He nodded. "Mostly. You'll need to ask Myra where she's buried."

"*Myra* took her?!"

He nodded again.

"Oh. I have a feeling I know where she is then." She stood and walked out, deciding she'd better get it over with before she lost her nerve.

Quinn walked out with her in silence, and she was surprised to find the sun had already set. She'd been in the pen for hours, far longer than she'd thought. It was still bright out and easy to see, with the first of the moons making an appearance over the distant mountains. The garden was beautiful as always and glowing with life. Myra had done an exceptional job in creating her desert oasis, and the Hue-mans had expanded it out into the courtyard. She made her way back to the small, protected glade where she knew Myra's parents were buried. She hadn't seen a marker in the glade when she'd first found it, but if her daughter was buried anywhere, it would be with them.

To her surprise, Myra was there pruning flowers on a large bush. Myra looked up and smiled at her. "Nazari! How are you? I've been meaning to come over and thank you for coming with me the other day."

"No thanks are necessary. They're family." Surprised that Myra didn't mention or react to Quinn's presence, she looked back and realized he'd vanished, giving her privacy, although she was sure he was still around. She looked back at Myra and scratched at her scruff. "I've...I've been talking with Quinn."

Myra's eyes darkened, and she frowned.

"I'll be honest, Myra. I'm struggling badly."

Myra's ears drooped as she realized what she was saying. "Oh gods, Nazari. I never meant for..."

She raised a paw, stopping Myra. "I know, and I would have gone out after them on my own even if you hadn't been there. GrandFather and Henry are my proteges, and I would do it again. However, my instinct is...pressuring me to go after Brent now. Quinn believes it would help if I put closure on..." She paused, struggling to find the words. "He says that you...that you took her?"

There was a brief look of confusion and then understanding and compassion. "They brought her body down to the morgue when I was there to collect Hope and my parents. They said you weren't taking her, and I just couldn't see her buried alone, so I figured she could keep my daughter company. I know we'd only just met, but I don't think I would have survived those awful weeks if it weren't for you. I hope you don't mind."

Tears started streaming down her face. "So she is here?"

Myra nodded and crushed her in a hug until she regained her composure and then led her over to a small but beautifully carved marker. She pushed a large flowering bush aside. Under her parents' names, hidden by the flowers, were the words 'Hope Chenzira and Sari Jabri. Lived, but a moment. Loved forever.'

She collapsed to her knees with a gasp. "Sari..." she whispered and reached out and touched her paw to the name. "You named her?"

"I know that was presumptuous. I'm sorry. You mentioned that name in one of our conversations. If you have a different name, I'll have it changed."

"I did?" She honestly had no memory of that.

"Well, not exactly. I had mentioned how difficult it had been coming up with names for my first litter, but how Marsee's name had just fit. You said you'd been thinking about naming yours after your grandfather to follow in the same pattern you'd picked for your first litter. I did a little research, and since he was the only grandparent left that you hadn't picked, I guessed that's who you meant."

"I don't even remember saying that."

Myra wrapped an arm and tail around her and pulled her in for another hug. "I had her and Hope placed in my mother's arms. She's never been alone for a moment."

A large hiccuping sob broke free, and it was a long time before she could stop crying. Her daughter hadn't been abandoned. She'd been loved and protected all these years. "Why didn't you say anything?" she finally asked.

"I figured you would ask when you were ready."

She sighed. "I couldn't even bring myself to look at her after Nadine told me she died. Somehow, it felt too final, as if by not acknowledging it, it might mean she was still alive."

"I understand. I didn't tell Marsee about Hope until this past year. I don't even know how to explain it, but part of me wonders if my granddaughter now carries a part of her soul. The moment Little Flower said what her name was... I can't even explain what it felt like. It was almost like part of me recognized her. Who knows what happens to our souls when we die? Many of the Hue-mans believe in reincarnation. Perhaps the reason you're so attached to Brent is because your soul recognizes your daughter in him. Maybe that's why you picked the same name for him?"

She looked over at Myra, wondering if that was even possible. "I suppose that's possible. Although perhaps my instinct is confusing the two. I don't know if that makes it easier to think part of her might still be out there or harder to know that I might lose her all over again. Oh, who am I kidding? I'm going to lose him. Quinn thinks it might be best if I put off my appeal until my watch is over, but I don't know if I'll make it that long. He says he was going to reach out to Jer and Marcus on my behalf, but I haven't heard anything."

Myra sighed. "I was never happy with that verdict, even if I understand where it came from, and I know Jer and Marcus weren't either. You helped save our family. As angry as I am at Jer right now, I have a feeling he'll fight for you. I'll help in any way I can. I already gave GrandFather a character reference for you, and I'm more than willing to speak for you at the trial if you think it'll help."

"Thanks. I appreciate that more than you know. Why are you mad at Jer?"

Myra snorted. "I would have thought it would have been all over the compound by now. Jer attacked Marsee a few months ago. Everyone claims he was testing her control, but...it's probably a good thing he's not on the planet right now. I was so angry I nearly got dragged off by the guards today. I was ordered to rest, but I couldn't sleep, so I came here instead."

"Gods. On top of everything else? That's the last thing you need. How is Marsee? I heard she's awake."

"Honestly, not good. She can't use her instinct anymore and has no reflexes or sense of pain, but she's able to move her limbs and talk. I don't know how to fix her."

Nazari flicked her ears back in surprise. "She can't use her instinct? I didn't know that was possible."

"Neither did I, but without her sense of pain, she won't survive her growth spurt. Right now, the only idea we have is to stop it, but she's said repeatedly that she doesn't want to be male. The idea of taking her cubs from her after everything she's been through..." Myra shook her head and sighed.

Nazari gave Myra a squeeze with her tail. "I'm sure you'll figure something out. That's one of the things I like about you. You don't give up. If she can't use her instinct, perhaps it'll be better for her. Quinn said she's survived psychosis three times now?"

"Four, if you count the day she hunted Little Flower."

"When did she hunt Little Flower?"

"The day after I brought her home. Marsee stopped on her own, and I didn't know how bad she was until it was almost too late. I thought she'd just pounced on the leash to stop Little Flower from running off. You know, the one thing I still can't understand is how she didn't have any issues that day with the chenzie."

Nazari snorted with laughter at the memory. "I wonder how long it took Marsee to get the smell out of her fur?"

"She complained about it for days," Myra replied. "I snicker every time I see that drawing. Ow ow ow ow ow!"

Nazari's tail spiraled. "Somehow, I don't think animal healing is in her future."

"Probably not, but she's stubborn enough to be one." Myra winked at her, and she chuckled.

"I'll take that as a compliment."

Laughing, Myra stood and walked over to a floating cart, where she grabbed a small pot, filled it with dirt, and walked back over. Then, carefully, she picked a flowering branch off of the bush in front of the memorial. "Here. The clipping will regrow. Keep it out of direct sunlight and drench it in water once a week or if the leaves start to wilt."

"Thank you," she said. "I apologize ahead of time if I kill it. I was never good at keeping plants alive."

"Well, we can't all be perfect, but I'd be glad to teach you. It's not that hard. They'll tell you exactly what they need *if* you know what to look for."

She snorted at Myra. She'd said the exact same thing to Myra the day she'd come to her asking to learn how to care for her neighbor's animals. She smiled at her friend. "You know, I think I'd like that."

Myra gave her another hug and then turned to her with a wicked grin. "Come on."

"Where are we going?" Nazari asked, although she had a pretty good idea if Myra was repeating history.

"I hope you're prepared to get your paws dirty. You have an appointment with the compost heap."

Laughing, she stood and gave Myra another hug. "Thank you for everything."

The next hour was probably one of the best she'd had in a long time, ridiculous, stinky, and full of hysterical laughter as Myra taught her all about the compost from the plant's perspective. It was exactly what they both needed. That night, rather than returning home, she stayed and had dinner with Myra and talked long into the night about the issues they were both facing. Then, long after midnight, they curled around each other and did their best to comfort and hold each other together.

It had been years since she'd had the physical comfort of another, outside of her time with Brent, and she decided that if she did survive and somehow managed to gain custody of Brent, it was time to start looking for a partner. *I wonder if Quinn would be interested.* And, with that yummy thought, she purred herself to sleep.

CHAPTER 46

Marsee: Rough Seas

Later that afternoon, Marsee was woken when there was a knock on her door. She forced her eyes open to see the Senior Healer peering in. "I wanted to know if you were up for visitors. The Senior Councilor and Stormy are here to see you."

She sighed but nodded. "Stormy's always welcome." She would always make time for him. He'd risked his life for her twice now, after all. It wasn't his fault her life was now doomed to be short and meaningless. She adjusted the shield and rubbed at her face and the mask she was *still* wearing. It was starting to bother her. "How long do I have to wear this? It's starting to itch."

Hyacinth swam over and checked her scans. "You're not fully recovered, and I'd rather not take any chances with this infection. It's a nasty one. This particular mask is designed with the expectation that you would have fur to buffer it. I'll see if I can find something to make it more comfortable." She swam out and returned a minute later and injected something into Marsee's arm. "I didn't find anything, but this should help with the itching."

"Thanks."

The healer nodded and swam out again. A few minutes later, Clear Seas and Stormy swam in. Stormy flashed a rainbow of emotions as he entered before bringing his skin under control. He was delighted to see her sitting up but apparently not expecting to see the angry red incisions from her various surgeries that were not in any way hidden by the cast, her complete lack of fur, or the oxygen mask.

"Hey, Stormy. How are you feeling?" she asked.

"Me?! I'm fine. You're the one that's been in here for days," he flashed as his hands were full, holding a large wrapped package. "How are you?"

"I'm much better," she lied. "It seems I have you to thank you for saving my life again."

"Nah, we're even. You saved mine, too. Anyway, I brought you something. Papa said you lost everything back home, so I wanted to get you something to replace what you lost. I hope you like it." Stormy swam over and handed her the package.

She carefully unwrapped the beautiful fabric and stared, completely unprepared and overwhelmed by the sight in front of her. On the lid of what appeared to be a wooden box was a drawing of her in her Leviathan cape with her ears pinned back, teeth and claws bared, snarling ferociously. Surrounding it were the words 'The Translator's Sharpening Kit. Guaranteed to make your claws and teeth so sharp they'll slice through the toughest of supervillains.'"

When she looked up, hints of nervousness crept around the edges of Stormy's skin.

"Papa said you can't use your instinct anymore, but I want you to know you'll always be my superhero."

She stared at him, more shocked by his words than the drawing. "You know?" She glanced at Clear Seas.

"It's not official yet, but Stormy will be my heir if he still wants to be when he finishes his training," Clear Seas said. "I've started his training with current affairs, which includes you and both your illness and current injuries."

She winced and looked away, not sure how to handle the knowledge that Stormy knew about her illness.

Suddenly, she found herself wrapped in tiny arms as Stormy hugged her. "I...trust...you," he said in halting, half-formed Saber. She was surprised, both by his words and by the fact that he could say them. She didn't think he was old enough to speak her language at all yet. She hugged him back, struggling to control her own emotions.

When she pulled back, he let go and switched to sign language. "I have known about your illness since the day you were rescued. I have never feared you any more than you've ever feared me. We're both alive because of your superpowers when mine weren't good enough. I know I'm not strong enough to protect you, but if you're looking for a sidekick, I'd like to put in my application."

She snorted with surprised laughter. "I think it should be the other way around. I've lost my superpower. Can I be your sidekick?"

He looked up as if considering. "Well, I suppose I could use someone with claws and teeth around as a supervillain shredder, but you're going to have to learn to swim faster if you're going to keep up with me."

She chuckled, and her tail curled. "I'll see what I can do."

"Do you like it?" he asked, nodding toward the box.

"Oh, Stormy, I love it," she replied. "Did you draw this?"

He nodded. "I made the box, too."

She lifted it to show Ellie and then looked closer at the box. It was fairly simple but sturdy and far better than she could have done at his age. Opening it, she found an assortment of high-quality nail clippers and other grooming supplies, far nicer than any she'd ever owned. "You're very talented. Thank you. This is exactly what I needed. My claws are looking a tad scruffy these days." She held up her good paw and wiggled her claws with a fake snarl to match the picture.

Stormy flashed a bright blue, and Clear Seas appeared to be having difficulty keeping the laughter off his own skin as she saw slight bubbles around the edges.

A moment later, a yawn slipped out, even though she tried hard not to. All she'd done was sleep, but she was still exhausted.

"We should be going soon. Marsee needs her rest," Clear Seas said to his son.

"Okay, Papa," Stormy signed, then gave her another hug. "I'm glad you're feeling better. I was so worried about you."

"I was worried about you, too."

"She was," Ellie said. "You're the first person she asked about when she woke."

Stormy flashed his happiness and started swimming for the door.

She expected Clear Seas to follow, but he turned to Ellie instead. "Ellie, would you mind swimming out to the waiting room with Stormy? I would like to talk with Marsee alone for a minute."

Ellie frowned and looked over at her.

"It's alright, Ellie."

Ellie nodded and swam out with Stormy.

Clear Seas shut the door behind them and then hit a switch next to the door.

She frowned, wondering what the switch was, as she didn't notice anything different about the room.

"I assure you, you're safe. If you're uncomfortable with the privacy screen on, I can turn it back off or ask the guards to come in," he said in response to her frown.

"It's alright," she replied. She was worried, but not about him. She'd always heard her parent's privacy screen activate before and wondered why she couldn't hear it now. *Am I losing my hearing, too?*

"You don't look alright," he replied and started to turn it off, but she raised a paw to stop him.

"I'm not worried about you. I'm worried because I can't hear it. I could always hear it buzz before."

Clear Seas gave a slight shudder. "I hate that buzz. I never understood how the other species could stand it. It's almost as bad as the lights. The ones in your uncle's office are the worst. Thankfully, we rarely meet there. I didn't notice it so much in New Hope, though."

"You can hear the lights, too? I thought I was the only one."

"Sound travels differently in water. We don't so much hear it as feel it. It makes our skin itch. That's one of the reasons why all the electronics are double insulated, and our walls are textured. It helps defuse it."

"That explains why it's so much quieter here. As for New Hope, I may or may not have purchased an order of very expensive lightbulbs when I was a cub and secretly 'misplaced' the old ones at the neighbor's house. Ellie, thankfully, took my hearing into consideration when designing New Hope and ordered the same brand for the build. I'll add the privacy screens to the list and make sure your offices and apartments are updated. They don't bother me so much because the buzz helps me to know it's working. So, what do you want to know?"

He flashed his humor and thanks, but rather than answering, he swam over, closer but still out of reach. "I know that look you gave earlier. I thought you might like to talk about it."

She scrunched her brow in confusion. "What look?"

"The look you gave when you saw the box. I thank you for the kindness you showed my son, but I could tell it bothered you, and I have a pretty good idea of why."

"It didn't bother me," she lied but turned her attention back to the box. It had bothered her more than she wanted to admit, even if she was touched by the effort he'd gone to.

"Killing someone, even when they deserve it, is never easy, especially the first time."

"No. Killing Rip was easy. It was the easiest thing I've ever done. Living with it, however..." She sighed, shook her head at a loss for the right words, and then ran her paw over the drawing. "Your son sees me as a superhero. I can't even begin to fathom it, much less how the rest of your people see me. For most of my life, I've been an outcast to my people, a monster to be ridiculed and feared, and it turns out they were right all along. I enjoyed every second of every scream I tore from him, the smell and taste of his fear and blood, and I'm mad it didn't go on longer. I nearly killed my father over his shredded carcass because I wasn't done making Rip suffer, even though I knew he was already dead and couldn't feel it."

"He deserved to suffer."

"Yes, he did. But I didn't need to enjoy it so much. That makes me no better than him."

"No, it doesn't. If you were like him, you wouldn't question it at all. You're better than I am in that regard. I wasn't much older than you the first time I had to kill someone, and I've killed so many times now I no longer even react to it. That disassociation meant innocent people died, by my hands, because I took Rip's word and his evidence at face value, never once questioning it. *That* is a feeling you never want to experience. Trust me. It's far worse. You killed for the right reasons, and your feelings were just. Don't let whatever he said make you think otherwise. He deserved to be treated exactly the way he treated everyone else, the way he treated you. That's why it was your right to kill him however you wanted to. Sadly, there are at least thirty-seven others who won't get that opportunity, but I have a feeling they sleep better knowing you made sure there was nothing left of him. I know I do."

She couldn't look up at him, too overwhelmed with her own emotions.

He swam over in front of her bed. "Marsee, look at me."

She sighed but looked up at his command.

"I don't see anything in front of me that needs to be changed, but if you don't like who you've become, find a way to be the kind of person you want to be. Maybe the Guild isn't right for you. You have the honor of a guard and the heart and justice of a councilor, the good ones, anyway. What I saw the other day is someone brave enough to go back out there and fight for those who didn't have anyone fighting for them, who was willing to risk their very soul to save my son and dozens of people she didn't even know, people *I* didn't even know were missing. That's something Rip would never have done, and that's why Trench gave you his cloak and my son this drawing. You are not a monster. You're the hero I should have been but wasn't and the hero with the superpowers we needed."

"You really believe that?" She stared into his eyes, wishing she could still sniff out if he was telling the truth.

"I do," he replied. "So do my people. So does Stormy." He paused and tilted his head as a thought occurred. "I thought your illness only started last year. What else has happened?"

She shrugged, not sure how to explain. "It changed this past year, but I've always struggled with my instinct, and the stigma and ridicule that comes with it is hard to live with. No one believed me when I said I didn't understand how to stop pouncing on things. I had no idea how to stop something that just happened, and practicing got me in a lot of trouble."

"Explain," he demanded.

She raised a brow at the slight hint of anger she saw on his skin and the harshness of his normally melodic voice. She realized this had just gone from a friendly conversation to a formal investigation by a member of the Senior Council. For him to break his mask in this way was as unusual as seeing her uncle do the same. Somehow, that tiny bit of anger soothed something in her soul. He had once taken Tabor's word for her sanity, but he now believed her and was angry for her.

"When I was ten, I started attending school in person in Sand Dune, and within a few days, my classmates found out I was still pouncing on tails. So was my classmate Halinah. We were bullied by both our classmates and our teacher, but no one believed us. I tried telling everyone, including my parents, uncle, and the School Master, but they all said that I needed to work on my control and that the teasing would go away when I stopped pouncing. It wasn't long before my classmates started getting physical about it with her. She was quite a bit smaller than I was and almost a year younger, and I decided that if we were going to get bullied for being monsters, I'd act like one. So, one afternoon, when they went after her during our play break, I pretended to be completely out of control and pounced on the main bully's tail and bit him hard enough that he needed surgery. It stopped the bullying, but I was nearly dragged off by the Guard. For some strange reason, the guards believed me, and our teacher was removed from her position. Lina and I became the best of friends after that. That was the best month of my childhood."

She looked away as she struggled to contain her emotions and the grief and guilt she still felt at the loss of her friend.

"Something happened?" Clear Seas guessed.

She nodded. "About a month later, I went to her house after school. It was the first time I had ever gone to someone else's house to play, outside of the few times we visited with family, and I was so excited I could barely sit still in school that day and had another flare-up. We discussed the difficulty we had controlling our instincts. She was just as confused as I was, so we decided to try practicing, as neither of us knew what else to do. Her mother caught us, and let's just say the lecture I got from everyone is one I'll never forget. Halinah's mother was mid-rant about calling the Guard on me when my uncle showed up instead of my father. He brought me to his house to wait for my father to get done with whatever council business had held him up, and I tried to explain, but like everyone else, he didn't believe me either. He told me that if he ever saw or heard that I'd used my instinct again on purpose, outside of a life-or-death situation, he would order my execution. I believed him, but I had no idea how to stop pouncing, and I was so terrified that I did everything I could to hide it. Lina pounced on a sand spinner the very next day and died from her wounds. It was my idea to practice, and I've always wondered if it was my fault. They wouldn't let me go to the funeral, and my classmates refused to have anything to do with me after that. I never had a real friend again, not until Little Flower came to live with us."

"What were you doing to practice that day?"

"Just wiggling our tails, trying not to pounce on each other and failing miserably. It was honestly a lot of fun. I'd never laughed so hard in my life until her mother walked in and found me with her tail in my mouth. I never tried practicing again until Little Flower suggested it. I'm honestly surprised Papa let me."

"Your father said you've been practicing with him. Was he lying about that?"

She shook her head. "No, but that didn't start until after the Trial. Two days after the Trial, my instinct came on without me knowing. I was overwhelmed with the construction, and my father saw it. I knew the risks, but it scared me, and I decided I needed to practice. I was worried about what would happen when the rest of the Hue-mans and creatures arrived. I would sneak out at night, sit in the garden observing the world, and then draw with it on. When I finally admitted it to my father, I thought…"

"You admitted it? They didn't catch you?"

"No. I told Ellie the night Papa came to get me from her house and then told Papa when he returned from Digger. I was tired of being treated like a monster. I wanted him to see the beauty in it, like I did, and I wanted him to know I was taking it seriously. I showed him my drawings, but he looked at them like I'd just admitted to eating babies or something equally atrocious. Instead of seeing the beauty I saw, he was horrified. I was so scared by the look he gave me that I ran and hid in my room, fairly sure he was going to kill me."

"Obviously, he didn't. Did he hurt you?"

"No. He talked to Kendra and Marcus about it, and Kendra told them to let me continue drawing and doing whatever I needed to do to remain in control as long as I wasn't hunting. Then she tested him, dislocating his shoulder in the process."

A flicker of surprise crossed his skin. "Why would she test him?"

She frowned. "I shouldn't have said that. I promised not to say."

His look changed ever so slightly, and she sighed, knowing she couldn't refuse to answer. "He told me he had issues following his Junior Advocate's test and said he couldn't trust me because he didn't trust himself. Kendra overheard. He shared the recording of Kendra testing him with me as reparations for hurting me. At the time, I considered it fair and just."

"But you don't now?"

"I honestly don't know what to think anymore. It changes from one minute to the next. I feel like…like I'm being tossed around in a storm."

"Trauma can do that."

She nodded. "Perhaps. I've seen it with my sister, but it feels like more. I didn't feel this way after I was first rescued, but now I go from anger one second to numb a moment later, and I can be excited and laughing about something, but then I'll burst into tears. It honestly scares me more than my instinct did before. What if I get angry and hurt myself or someone else when I don't really mean it? I wanted to claw Papa yesterday. Today, I'm horrified. In an hour, I'll probably want to claw him again. As for me... I don't know if this is something I can live with."

She fiddled absently with her claws.

"Twenty years is a long time to find a cure."

"If it was just an injury. I would take the years and live them to the fullest, but it's so much more than that. How do I go home knowing my entire species will fear me, where one wrong outburst or even remaining silent too long will get me killed, if not by my father or uncle, then by the guards who will be watching me for the next six months, if not the rest of my life?"

Anger flickered on his skin again. "You are welcome to stay here."

"And live as an outcast away from everyone I care about? I don't know if that's better or worse, but I thank you for the offer."

He was silent for several moments. "Did you happen to scan in any of your drawings?" he asked, returning to the prior conversation.

She nodded again and reached for her tablet. When she pulled up the first of the images, it took everything she had not to whimper. They were still beautiful, but not what she remembered, and the colors she'd only been able to see with her instinct were gone. "I imagine Damon destroyed the originals, and I don't know if you see color the way I did then, but..." She handed over her tablet.

It didn't take him long to react as his skin lit up bright blue. "These are stunning!" he exclaimed as he continued to swipe, and then looked up at her and must have picked up on her sadness. "You can't see them?"

She shook her head. "There are colors missing, and everything seems...dull and faded."

"I'm honestly not sure how our vision differs, but I don't think I've seen anything as...true before. Your sister has the ability to capture the emotion of a scene in only a few lines, but I think you captured its soul. I can almost smell these flowers."

She smiled her thanks, but it only made her wonder if she would ever paint anything as good again. She understood her sister now more than she ever had and knew why her sister wanted nothing to do with her drawing anymore. To have that ability and lose it was worse than never having that skill to begin with.

"I would really love a print."

"I wish I could share them. If my people saw, they'd…" She shook her head and sighed, not really sure what they'd do, but her gut said it would be bad.

He handed the tablet back but nodded his understanding. "I certainly wouldn't tell anyone where they came from if you're concerned about that. Do you think there was anything malicious about your father and uncle not letting you practice?"

She pinned her ears in surprise at the question and then frowned as she considered. Rip had implied much the same. "I honestly don't know. Papa once told me that the more we use it, the stronger it gets, and from my experience, that's true. I suppose it's like any skill. They all worked with me for years to get me to stop pouncing on things, but no one ever had me try to turn it on."

"What did they do?"

"Every time I pounced on something, we worked through it, trying to identify triggers so that I could spot them before my instinct reacted. Then there was all the dangerous crawly recognition. Granted, almost everything in our area is dangerous, but I learned to identify what was poisonous, venomous, or just painful. I learned what to do if I got hurt and how much time I had to get help before it was deadly. I had no problems avoiding pouncing on something deadly, but any form of moment could trigger it."

"You never practiced turning it on or off?"

"No. I didn't even understand what that meant until that day in the garden. I thought they just wanted me to stop pouncing."

"Your uncle said it's something your species just knows how to do."

She shrugged. "Maybe it is for everyone else, but I didn't, and neither did Halinah. Maybe that's the difference? Maybe some of us need to be taught. It took me time, even after that day, to recognize when it was on and learn that there were different levels of control I could give up."

"That is a reasonable hypothesis and one I intend to examine further," he replied. "Your father said you turned your instinct on before running off that day he tested you. Was that intentional?"

She sighed and nodded. "I wanted the extra speed to get away from him. I thought I'd turned away enough that he couldn't see it. That's why he attacked me, isn't it?"

Clear Seas nodded. "So he says. That and the fact you sprayed and were talking in plural like the other day."

She leaned her head back against the invisible bed and sighed, finally admitting that she'd brought it all on herself, her father's attack, accepting Ellie's offer of mentorship, going out in the arboretum by herself, not waiting for Clear Seas to get clearance, ordering her guard away, and choosing to kill Rip herself even though she knew it might put her over the edge. "So it is all my fault," she whispered.

"No. I don't believe so."

She snorted and rolled her eyes at him.

"Did you know that spraying was bad?"

She shrugged. "I didn't know it could get me killed if that's what you're asking. By that point, I'd figured out that if my instinct did react to something, like something smelling good enough to eat, I could stop it from getting worse by finding something else to eat. It had a major sweet tooth, and I could often distract it with chocolate chip cookies. My sister calls it chocolate therapy. If I felt overwhelmed, running or any form of motion helped to calm me. That day, my instinct felt like our territory had been invaded. I was an adult, but I couldn't leave the tower without someone asking where I was going. There were people everywhere I didn't know, and I was exhausted. I took off to find someplace where I could just be alone, someplace quiet where I could think. I didn't even really know what my instinct was doing at first, but it relieved the feeling of being trapped, at least until my father showed up. I was already mad at him, and my instinct felt like he was invading our newly claimed territory. Rather than fight for it, I decided to find someplace else before my instinct decided to take matters into its own paws."

"You were still on a watch then, correct?"

She nodded.

"Did you know you aren't allowed to leave your home without supervision while on a watch?"

She stared at him in openmouthed shock.

"I'll take it from your reaction that the answer is no."

"No one has ever said anything about what I could or couldn't do on a watch. I saw the guards when they were in New Hope and when I was in Council City and figured that's all it was."

He flashed his surprise, which surprised her. "You should have been informed at processing by the guard who put you on the watch."

"I was never processed. I didn't know for sure I was on a watch until I asked Papa. Ellie thought I might be and told Little Flower. Papa said it was an informal watch. After I was rescued, Avery said he was putting me back on the watch but didn't say anything, nor did my father or uncle."

Clear Seas was silent and dark for several moments. "Did your uncle pressure you to drop the charges against your father?"

She flicked her ears back, surprised at the question. "No, not at all. In fact, he said I had grounds to press charges. I said what I did of my own free will, and I meant it. I don't really know how I feel about my father or how much of my anger is my own, my injuries, or what Rip manipulated, but my father had just cause to believe I was losing control. What I do know for sure is that Rip wanted my father out of office in the worst way, and I won't give him that victory. I was angry and scared, and Papa said that word and I...I don't know."

"The Senior Healer said you reacted harshly to that word before. Was that because of Rip?"

She nodded. "He said..." She braced herself for the pain.

"You do not need to say it."

She sighed with relief. "He said Papa's term of endearment every time he shocked me. Now, when I hear it, my body reacts as if he's still shocking me."

He flashed his understanding, sympathy, and even a hint of anger. "Marcus said there were things you haven't told us about what happened to you in the cave. Is it because it's about him or your father?"

She nodded. "Some of it. Some I don't even know how to explain, like how he could make me question my own memories and motives or turn what I thought were innocent actions into malicious intent, and there are things I can't remember, too. I don't remember Stormy being there, and I feel like there's more. Something important, but it's like trying to remember a dream or a nightmare you don't want to face. For all I know, it could have been a dream. He'd shock me until I'd pass out and then start again when I woke, and I did what I could to hide from most of it."

He sighed and flashed his regret. "What you are experiencing is normal for the extreme trauma you've endured. It's not uncommon for people to block out the memory of their trauma or abuse, and people don't often recognize when something is abusive because it's all they've ever known, and it can vary widely between species and cultures. I'm sure much of our culture would make you uncomfortable if you knew about it. As I'm sure you're aware, the Consortium's Charter doesn't go into detail about what's considered abusive, leaving that up to the local charters to define, but there are council training materials that I could share with you. They are difficult to read, but perhaps they might give you the words you're looking for, or at least a framework to begin talking about it."

She nodded. "I'd like that. I tried looking for information to help Little Flower through her trauma, but I didn't find much."

"It's considered restricted information because we don't want people to use that information against others, as was sadly done to you. If you need someone to talk to, call me at any time. I know I'm not a healer, but I am a good listener, and, unfortunately, I've probably heard it all."

She looked at him with a frown.

"My people still have a lot of work to do. Abuse is far more common than I would like to admit, even among members of my council, it would appear. In any event, even if everything Rip told you was a flat-out lie, it would be good for us to know what he said. We don't know what he's told anyone else, and if he was spreading lies, it would be better if we were prepared to counter them. If you can't tell us in person, perhaps try writing it down. If there's something you want me to look into but don't want your father or uncle to know, I'll make sure they never know it was from you."

She nodded her understanding and looked up at the ceiling as she tried to decide if she could trust him.

He said nothing as he waited for her to decide.

"He...claimed that my grandparent's shuttle accident wasn't an accident. He claimed my father lost control, killed them, and hid it using the storm."

Clear Seas' skin remained blank for at least a minute before shaking his head. "It's possible the accident was malicious, which I will look into, but your father didn't lose control and kill them. I was there when they left the Trauma Center to borrow his shuttle to return home. In fact, he tried hard to get them to stay and wait out the storm, and I was still there when word came in about the accident about an hour later. He never left your side or mine."

She closed her eyes, sighed with relief, and then opened them to look back at him. "I didn't realize you were there."

"I was on the planet for a council meeting and stopped in for a visit. Your father and I have been friends since before either of us were in office. Neither of us wanted the position, even if it was expected by both our fathers, and we often got ourselves into a lot of trouble during council meetings and state dinners."

"You can't be talking about the same person. *My* father got in trouble? This I have to hear."

Humor flickered across Clear Sea's skin, and he turned to swim out. "Sorry. That information is classified. Senior's eyes only."

She snorted and glared at him. "You can't drop something like that in a conversation and just swim away. That's...that's got to be psychological abuse or something. I'm going to be up all night trying to figure out what you did."

That caused him to burst out laughing. "My apologies, Translator, but I do look forward to hearing whatever you come up with. I'm sure it will be...inventive."

She chuckled. "Clear, wait."

He stopped by the door and turned back.

"Thank you."

"For what?" he asked, flashing his confusion.

"For not seeing me as the monster my own people do."

A ripple of color flashed across his skin in a pattern she hadn't been taught. "I did once, but I was very wrong. A person's capacity for violence doesn't make them a monster. It's what they do with that ability. You risked your very soul to save my son and thirty-seven others from the real monster infesting these waters. You are nothing like him, and I will spend the rest of my life thanking every god in the universe that I realized that in time. If there is *anything* I can do, please let me know."

He flashed silver and purple, bowed low, and swam out.

After he left, she stared down at the box and rubbed her paw over the image again, thinking about what Clear Seas had said, feeling both conflicted and relieved to have told someone about how she felt and the secret she'd been keeping.

"Who am I?" she asked the universe. "A monster or a superhero?" Stormy thought she was a superhero. Her people, if they knew the truth, would think she was a monster. She was neither now. She'd lost her superpowers, not that anyone believed her. Her own family couldn't even decide.

If nothing else, she was glad she'd been able to save Stormy and find the others, but she wondered what would become of her life. She'd never live long enough to become the Senior Guild Master like Ellie wanted. Although, at this point, she wanted nothing to do with the Guild and the pain it had brought her. Becoming a councilor would also take far longer than she had, too. She'd be lucky even to make it to Junior Councilor, and the decade of being a Staffer didn't interest her in the slightest. She'd never once considered being in the Guard. Her injuries would likely make that impossible, and the idea of spending hours every day just floating outside of a door was worse than the thought of attending another requisition meeting.

I suppose I could translate more books. The worst I'd have to worry about there is a paper cut, not that I need to.

She had enough credit now to do anything and nothing, but the only thing she'd ever really wanted was to raise a family, and that was no longer an option. Little Flower was better and wouldn't need her help soon, and she'd never have her own cubs.

Ellie swam in then and came over to take a closer look at the box. "It's really very good. Shame he'll be a councilor someday. We could use his talent in the Guild. I should check to see if he'd let us make these kits. We'd sell out in seconds."

"Oh no," Marsee replied. This one's all mine, and I am not sharing." It was bad enough that there were toys based on her drawings. Shuddering at the thought of everyone having their own kit, she pulled out the nail clippers and cleaned up her front claws, but she couldn't reach her back ones with the cast on. Even though she couldn't see anything, she could still feel pieces of Rip on her claws.

At her growl of frustration, Ellie took the nail clippers from her and cleaned her back paws for her. It was a strange sensation having someone physically care for her, but Ellie said nothing, just cleaned and sharpened them with a tenderness that belied the fact that Ellie was one of the most powerful people in the universe and, more often than not, hid her kindness behind a very gruff exterior.

"Thanks," she said. "I just hope I get to use those brushes." Ellie's fur had already started to grow back, making her look fuzzy, even in the water, but Marsee's hadn't at all yet.

"I'm sure you will," Ellie replied. "On the plus side, it does make clipping your claws a lot easier."

She grunted, not sure what to say, and flicked up the next claw.

"There. How does that feel?" Ellie asked when she was done.

She let out a heavy sigh, and Ellie looked up at her with concern.

"What is it?" Ellie asked.

"I can still feel him, what I did to him." She rubbed at her paws, trying to get rid of the sensation.

Ellie shifted over and grabbed her paws. "Don't. You'll hurt yourself, and it won't help."

She glared at Ellie. "How would you know?"

Ellie reached up and caressed the side of her face. "I have been around for a long time and have been on more than a few watches in my day. The second worst part about my job has been dealing with those lost to psychosis before the guards could arrive. That's likely the only reason I'm not on a watch now. I've proven my ability to kill and not lose control."

"You've had to kill?"

Ellie nodded. "Four times and none of them were any older than you. They were all fully gone. The only thing that ever helped me was distraction. I could have some craft supplies sent over if you want. Do you like to knit?"

"I never did much past the basics. It was always too slow for me." She wondered if she'd be strong enough to do the same if she somehow survived long enough to be Senior Guild Master. *If they were already gone, perhaps.* She paused her wandering thoughts and looked back at Ellie. "Wait. Second worst? What could be worse than that?"

"Requisition meetings," Ellie replied with a fake shudder.

She snorted, and her tail curled in surprised humor at the joke.

"Now, get some rest," Ellie said. "That and time will help more than anything." As Ellie put the clippers back in the box and stored the kit in one of the drawers, Marsee rolled over to stare at her cloak as she continued to think about her conversation with Clear Seas.

Let's see how you do without your cloak. You don't deserve it anyway!

Rip's words haunted her. She wanted to believe everything he'd said was a lie, but she knew, in this, he was right. She wasn't the hero everyone thought she was. She was a monster who drooled at the taste of her prey's fear. With a sigh, she rolled over away from the cloak and silently cried herself to sleep.

CHAPTER 47

Stormy: Staffer 101

Stormy followed his father into his father's office in the council building, both nervous and excited. While his father had answered many of his questions the night before, this was his first official training session as a Staffer, and he was worried he'd already messed up. He wasn't supposed to let anyone know what he learned, but he'd slipped trying to comfort Marsee.

His father motioned him over to the small table in his office where they could work together, side by side.

"I'm sorry, Papa."

"For what?" his father asked, briefly flashing his surprise.

"For slipping up that I knew about Marsee's illness. I know I promised to keep anything I learned secret and that you didn't want anyone to know I was training to be a councilor."

His father shrugged. "I am not worried about Marsee or Ellie betraying your confidence, and it's good that they know. I'm actually very proud of your actions today."

Stormy frowned in confusion. "You are? Why?"

"Because you gave Marsee exactly what she needed. You are perhaps the first person to know about her illness and not only trust her but see her psychosis as a blessing instead of a curse. She will need a friend like you to help her through her recovery and the challenges she'll face in the future."

His father leaned back in his net, eyes unfocused as he thought about something. "I think now is perhaps the right time to share the first lesson I ever had from my father after he named me his heir. Never apologize, at least not in public. Seniors don't make mistakes. People need to see you as confident and infallible. That's where your power and authority come from. You can, however, change your decision or make reparations if new information is brought forth."

Stormy stared at his father. "*Never* apologize?"

"Never. The fact is, there is no right decision, only a weighing of the pros and cons. Every decision you make will both hurt and harm someone. Your job will be to find the path in which the least amount of people will be hurt, and where the most good can be done. You will need to stand behind every decision you make and accept and deal with the consequences."

Stormy thought about it for a moment and then nodded his understanding.

"You will need to learn to listen more and speak less. Take time before answering questions or making any decisions. Be sure of your words before you speak them. If you don't have an answer, tell people you'll look into it and will get back to them, but make sure you do. People will respect you more for taking the time to research, and I've found that, more often than not, silence will make people uncomfortable, and they'll give away far more than they intended. Now, let's talk about what I learned from Marsee and how to investigate her claims before I go have a conversation with the others about it."

On several occasions, he failed to keep the surprise off his skin as his father explained what Marsee had told him, but his father said nothing about his lack of control. As they dug into each claim, his concern grew, not just about Jeran but also about Marcus and the rest of Saber's council. And while it didn't show on his father's skin, he knew his father well enough to know he was concerned, too.

When they found and watched the recording of Kendra's testing of Jeran, on Marsee's account, he had to swim hard into the waste room to make it in time before throwing up. His father said nothing as he returned to his seat but watched him with an expression he couldn't quite decipher.

"If they had a way to stop psychosis, why didn't they do so with Marsee?" he finally asked.

"That is a very good question," his father replied, "and I think it's time to find out."

After his father left, Stormy bolted back to the waste room and into the tunnels, quickly making his way to the Senior's conference room. He still wasn't sure how he felt about spying on their conversations or what it meant that his great-grandfather had felt it necessary to make that a possibility, but he understood the need.

His father swam in moments after he arrived. The others were all there, digging through what looked like a mountain of paperwork.

"I wasn't expecting you back so soon," Marcus said. "Is everything alright?"

His father said nothing as he took his seat, but the others all stopped what they were doing and gave his father their undivided attention. He stared at Jeran for several moments before displaying the recording of Jeran's conversation with Kendra on the central monitor.

Jeran slid down into his seat and grabbed the back of his scruff the moment it started, and Marcus sighed.

"When were you going to inform us that you had issues with your control?" His father asked after it was done.

"Never," Jeran replied.

His father stared at Jeran until Jeran started to squirm, but it was Marcus who broke first.

"It's not uncommon for new Junior Advocates and Councilors to have issues. That's the whole point of our test. No one can stop on their first hunt, and quite a few don't come back. But the real test is after when newly elected Councilors have to give their first test, as at that point, our instincts have hunted and tasted meat and can get confused in the heat of the moment."

"How often does this happen?" Sammianna asked.

"Everyone has issues at some point, some worse than others," Marcus replied. "Our test is designed to scare people into never using their instinct again."

Jeran raised a brow. "I always thought I was the exception. My juniors have never had any issues, even Samantha, which I would expect after I hurt her."

Marcus shrugged. "I think that says more about you than them. You take the time to build a bond with your juniors. Not everyone does, and that can make a real difference in their success."

"This method you mentioned to Kendra, why didn't you do the same for Marsee?" Wind Rider asked. "Although, I can't see how more violence would help when what Jer did to her made it harder for her to control."

Neither councilor answered.

His father leaned forward in his seat and flashed his anger. "Answer the question," he demanded in a voice harsher than Stormy had ever heard before. "Or I will make sure neither of you leave this room again."

Jer looked away, and Marcus rubbed at the back of his scruff. None of the other Seniors moved or reacted to his father's threat, and he was surprised at how long it took before Marcus finally spoke.

"Because we didn't tell Kendra everything, and neither of us could do what I did to Jer to Marsee."

Stormy wasn't as familiar with body language for Sabers as he was his own species, but he honestly thought both councilors looked embarrassed.

"What I'm about to tell you, I don't think anyone outside of our council knows," Marcus continued. "Back before the Great Awakening, psychosis was rampant among our people. We lost our planet after fifty years of war because of it."

"I'm well aware of that fact," his father scoffed. "I learned that in primary school, although I was taught that psychosis had been cured millennia ago."

Marcus grunted. "As you can imagine, they tried everything they could to find a way to cure this illness or find a way to bring people back. Outside of the treatment that ultimately ended in our growth spurts, longer life spans, and loss of true males, they found another way to stop psychosis when it happened, but it was too controversial to implement in its entirety. What they learned was that a specific act of dominance could sometimes snap people out of an episode. It's the whole reason our society is now structured the way it is and the reason for our mentorship programs."

"You're referring to grabbing or biting the scruff?" his father asked. "I wondered why Jer did that to Marsee in the canyon. I thought he was going to kill her."

Jer nodded, but Marcus continued. "In cubs, it causes our bodies to relax. We believe this is a holdover from a time before we knew how to walk on two feet and needed a way to carry our cubs. When our bodies relax it can sometimes snap us out of an instinctive reaction. As we mature, it transfers over to our mating instinct. Our instinct is to seek out the strongest partner. As we are all technically female, I made liberal use of those instincts to establish dominance over Jer."

"You mated with him?" Apakna asked.

Marcus shrugged. "Mating is too kind of a word for what I did. By any other species standards and even ours, if Jer didn't consent to it, it would be considered rape. I would push him until his instinct reacted and then pin him by his scruff and...well, you get the idea. Once I was sure I could control him, I had him fast until his instinct took over to save his life and made sure I could stop him mid-hunt. Only then did we return to society with the understanding that if he hurt anyone, I would be liable and executed along with him."

"Is this standard practice for your council?" Wind Rider asked.

"No. Standard practice whenever someone loses control enough to hurt someone is immediate execution. Most mentors won't even attempt it due to the risk involved and the moral implications. Samantha gave Jer a chance, and I would gladly risk my life to save my brother. This method only works if there's a strong bond of trust between the two. Now, however, if he has an issue, I can snap him out of it with nothing more than a tug to his scruff."

"Are you still having issues?" Apakna asked. "You're rubbing at your scruff now."

Jer sighed and lowered his paw.

She leaned in with a scowl. "You have, haven't you? How bad?"

Jer nodded. "This week has been impossible. I nearly lost control investigating the suite and again yesterday when Marsee crashed. Thankfully, Marcus's training worked."

"I'm keeping a close watch on the situation," Marcus said. "He was in full control as of last night, even though he was three bottles into the hangover he has now. If it gets any worse, I'll deal with it."

"That's why you left in such a hurry?" his father asked.

Marcus nodded again. "Jer wears a tracker on his harness that allows him to contact me when he needs help. If I don't respond in time, it'll notify the guards."

"Moral and legal implications aside, why didn't you do this with Marsee?" Sammianna asked.

"Because without an implant, it would have triggered her heat. A heat at her age would kill her, and we didn't find out she was still having issues until right before the Trial. We didn't have the time if we were going to save the others."

"I begged my father to take her," Jer said. "But he didn't believe he had a strong enough relationship with Marsee for it to work. They've only met in person a few times. Plus, implants for our species are highly regulated, and I didn't think Tabor would give her that chance, which meant I would have had to steal one. I was still considering it when Marsee came and found me, but if I'm honest with myself, I don't think I would have. There were too many other lives at stake, and I just couldn't do that to her. When Marsee came to find me to discuss practicing, I thought for sure I was going to have to put her down then and there, but the ancient gods gave us a miracle instead."

"Thankfully, sign language works far better than any other treatment we've ever had before and without any of the moral or legal implications," Marcus added. "But this brings up a bigger issue."

"Bigger than one of our Senior Councilors turning into a wild animal and another admitting to rape?" Apakna scoffed. "Gods, can this day get any better?"

"It wasn't rape," Jer said. "I knew what he was going to do, and I agreed to it wholeheartedly. I was horrified by what I did to Sam and fully expected to die for it. I still can't believe she gave me a chance. Any fear or pain I experienced was fair and just for what I did to her. I'm alive today because of what Marcus did, and I owe him everything for risking his life to save mine. And...while much of it was...violent, it was also four of the most...indescribable months of my life. In many ways, far more enjoyable than what I had with Myra during both of her heats or since."

Marcus rubbed the back of his scruff, looking embarrassed. "Which is also part of the reason we don't tell anyone about this method. We don't want it to turn into an even bigger issue."

Wind Rider snorted, Apakna raised a brow, and Sammianna looked confused. But then, the Digger's reproductive cycle was different from any of the other species. Like the Flyers, they laid eggs, but they were fertilized after they were laid, not before. Stormy wasn't entirely sure what Marcus was implying, but he got the general idea.

His father pinched his nose and took a deep breath. "So what's this bigger problem?"

Marcus nodded in the direction of the growing pile. "When we announce their verdicts and punishments, there's likely to be mayhem, and not just from those trying to finish the coup that Rip started. I expect more than a few will lose control, and not just those arrested. If fighting breaks out, there's the potential we could lose every Saber in that room."

"You just had to go and challenge the gods, didn't you?" Clear Seas asked Apakna.

Wind Rider snorted and shook her head. "I always wondered why none of your species ever came before the Full Council to appeal an execution."

"If they're guilty, they never survive long enough to make it before the Council," Marcus replied. "Everyone knows the law and what the punishment will be for breaking it. Those who actually make it to trial are almost always innocent or believe they were justified by their actions, and the vast majority of the time, they are."

"How is it then that Myra didn't lose control or any of your council at the Trial?" Sammie asked.

"Hope," Marcus replied. "And Honor. Jer's sacrifice is what likely allowed the others to maintain control. I never doubted that you'd find Little Flower sentient, and Myra was trying to save her protege, children, and the other healers at the Agency. She expected to die and felt her death was fair and just. I think she would have remained in control until her execution, but if you had harmed Marsee, she would have lost it then and there to protect her, and Marsee probably would have, too."

"And I would have been right beside her," Jer said.

Apakna frowned. "You're the one that gave us the precedent. Tabor was convinced you did that because you knew there was a problem and couldn't bring yourself to deal with the situation."

Jer flinched as if Apakna had struck him.

"Was that your plan? Did you intend to push Marsee over the edge?" Apakna pressed.

"Gods, no," Jer replied. "I wanted you to change the precedent and go with victim's choice, just as I said in my vote. I hoped that Little Flower would figure out a way around it, and I thought you would all be just as horrified as I was when we found it, but apparently not."

The conversation devolved at that point, with far more yelling than Stormy expected. It was nearly an hour before Stormy's father regained control and pressed the rest of the issues they'd gone over and asked Jeran and Marcus to leave so they could discuss them. Stormy followed the two back to Marcus's office. Jeran flopped down on the couch and grabbed the back of his scruff tightly by both paws.

Marcus sat down in front of him and stared at his brother for several moments. "For what it's worth, I would do it all over again to save you, and I believe you made the right decision with Marsee. Papa wouldn't have had a strong enough bond with her, and she would have killed him. Even your bond wouldn't have been strong enough. If it had been, she would have responded to you in the garden. What she needed was the unconditional love and trust of her sister."

"I don't know if that helps or not," Jeran said. "to know that my love wasn't enough."

Marcus pulled Jer in for a hug, and they were silent after that. He considered returning to listen to the other senior's conversation, but his father appeared only a few minutes later.

"We have decided not to vote either of you out at this time."

Jer pinched his nose. "So much for getting the night off."

Both Marcus and his father snorted, and his father swam out.

"I believe you're the one who said that hangover was fair and just. It's not my fault you chose not to get treatment for it."

Jeran rolled his eyes at Marcus.

"Come on. It's time for supper, and I'm hungry," Marcus said, and they swam out.

Stormy made his way back to his father's office, where he found his father looking out his window. Stormy swam up beside him and watched as Jeran and Marcus swam across the park.

Eventually, his father sighed and turned to face him. "Do you have any questions about what you heard?"

Stormy nodded. "Does rape really cause the Sabers to go into heat?"

"So they believe. Their Senior Healer informed us at Little Flower's trial that they don't know for sure as they don't have true males anymore, but it was documented in the precedent. As things stand now, males of their species react almost instantly to the presence of mating pheromones and within three days release the eggs the healer's need for conception, so it seems entirely plausible."

Stormy looked away.

"What's bothering you, son?"

He sighed. "Before you arrived in the canyon, I think that's what Rip was trying to do."

"What makes you say that?" his father asked.

"Well, he had a tight grip on her scruff and was shocking her sides about where our scales would be. But it's what he said." He explained what Rip had said as best as he could remember.

His father's skin rippled with a frustrated sigh. "It's entirely likely and something we're watching for. She told me that she's blocked out much of what happened to her."

Stormy sighed. "I don't understand how someone could do that to another person. It's not like Little Flower's rapist, who may have thought he had no choice to earn his freedom."

"I don't know. I may never know why Rip hated us so much or did the things he did, but power changes people, and you need to remain vigilant about it. Never let the power of your authority get to you. While rank comes with its privileges, never use it for personal gain and never use it to hurt another unless there is just cause. You will be the law, but you won't be above the law."

"So why are you allowing Jeran and Marcus to remain in power? I followed them rather than watching your deliberation to see if they would give anything away," he explained when a brief look of confusion crossed his father's face at the question.

"Because by their laws, they have done nothing wrong, even if we all feel otherwise, but I am not comfortable with this decision, and I still want your input."

"Why are you not comfortable with your decision?" Stormy asked, surprised that his father would admit it.

"Because I'm worried that they will try to harm Marsee in the future. If not them, then whoever follows them, and I don't know if I'll be able to do anything to stop them."

CHAPTER 48

Marsee: A Backlog of Messages

"One double berry mix, a house specialty. I hear it's Translator's favorite. I had to pay a fortune to get you a bottle. I hope you like it."

Marsee growled at her mentor for waking her up, rolled her eyes at the comment, forced the drink down, and rolled over to go back to sleep. As soon as she did, though, her reminder to pee went off. She growled and threw the tablet across the room, peed, and had almost fallen asleep again when the Senior Healer entered and started checking her vitals. She growled at the Healer and rolled away.

"Marsee..." Ellie growled at her in a warning.

Marsee ignored her and the Senior Healer and tried to go back to sleep.

"Well, Marsee, you've managed to go a whole day without tearing out your sutures again. How are you feeling?"

Marsee swore under her breath.

"Wonderful! Sounds like you're ready to start your physical therapy. You can join Ellie with hers tonight."

"No thanks," Marsee muttered. "I'm tired, and I'd rather sleep."

"Suit yourself. Another day in the casts is probably for the best, anyway. Ellie, if you'll follow me."

Marsee rolled over to find herself in an empty room, swore at the Healer, and rolled back over, angry enough now that she couldn't fall back to sleep. "Moons' forsaken healers are all alike." Eventually, she sat herself up and grabbed her tablet, which had been collected and left beside her bed. For lack of anything better to do, she started scrolling through her messages. She'd been ignoring them all day, mostly out of spite but also because she didn't want to hear any more bad news.

Near the top, she found a handwritten message from Clear Seas with several documents attached.

I spoke to both Avery and your father regarding the miscommunication around your watch, and it would appear that it may have been an oversight. I'll leave that for you to decide. Your father states that he believed the informal nature of your first watch didn't warrant it, and Avery believed you were already aware of the restrictions.

While I do not believe your current watch is warranted, I have attached the appropriate documentation for your edification and acknowledgment. Much to my unexpected annoyance, it would appear that I cannot remove the watch of another species, even on my own planet, but I can offer my protection. At a minimum, I believe it would be safest if you remained here until your watch is over. I also believe that it is in your best interest to maintain your visible honor guard, at the very least, until after the meeting. If you do not trust any of those guards posted on your door, for whatever reason, please let me know, and I will see that they are reassigned.

Regarding the discussion on your training, I have had widely varying and troubling conversations. It would appear that there is no formalized or standard training around this particular issue, leaving the responsibility up to each parent. Due to the severity of risk involved, I find that highly surprising. Our children receive formal shock training as part of their education. I suggested this for your people, but the reaction I received was also surprising. Avery is very much for and your uncle against, while your mentor suggests that additional training for parents might be in order. When it comes to issues that are uniquely species-oriented, I rarely get involved, and I have rarely disagreed with your uncle in matters of state. I do now. However, both you and your uncle have stated that pressing this issue before the Full Council would do your species more harm than good, and I fully understand your concern. I will leave that decision up to you and will support you in whatever you decide.

I have also attached the documentation you requested. It is my hope that it brings you and your sister a modicum of clarity in an otherwise senseless situation. Please feel free to contact me at any time to discuss them.

Regarding the other issues we discussed, I am still investigating and will let you know as soon as I know anything.

I pray the gods bring you a full recovery, and when you're feeling better, it would be my honor if you would join my family again for another meal. Until then.

She read the message three times. She was surprised that he took the time to hand-write a message rather than typing it out, but his elegant script implied just as much as his words did. Not only did he not trust her father and uncle to protect her, he felt they had neglected her training and that she was still in danger from someone else, specifically someone in the guard.

She looked over at the door. Aris now floated outside. Could she trust the guards that had come with her father? She didn't know. Avery had let her live, which was something, but the Senior Healer had been in the room at the time, too. Aris had said they were protecting her, not protecting others from her. Was she lying? Would they just kill her if she returned home, as Clear Seas believed, or did they believe her? If they did believe her, why hadn't Avery removed the watch? Her uncle had implied that it would be more dangerous for her if he did. Were the guards doing the same, or was this a ploy to reassure everyone else that they were safe from her?

Frowning at all the unanswered questions, she pulled up the first of the documents. It was a short document, but her tail was twitching by the time she was halfway through reading, and she simmered, at a near boil, by the time she was finished. She was furious at everyone, but especially her father, for hiding this from her. It would have saved her so much frustration and could very well have saved her life.

- Travel between districts and planets is prohibited without prior authorization and a minimum of one day's notice, except in a life-threatening emergency or if accompanied by a member of the Council or Guard.

- Travel outside of your home village, town, or city is restricted without prior authorization and a minimum of twelve hours' notice, except in a life-threatening emergency or if accompanied by a member of the Council or Guard.

- Travel from your home to a place of work, schooling, trauma center, and the homes of registered friends and family members is allowed but must be reported or scheduled prior to departure, except in a life-threatening emergency or if accompanied by a member of the Council or Guard.

- All other travel is restricted to a five-league radius of your primary residence unless accompanied by a member of the Council or Guard.

- You must have your tablet with you at all times and/or inform a family member of where you are going and the expected duration unless accompanied by a member of the Council or Guard.

- Failure to follow any of these rules may result in your arrest and/or execution.

- Failure to locate within an hour, except in the case of a life-threatening medical emergency, may also result in your arrest and/or execution.

- Deliberate attempts to hide or run from the Guard or Council and/or refusal of any reasonable and legal order **will** result in your immediate execution.

The rest of the document was a link to the various forms she needed to fill out for travel notices and further qualifications on each item, including what did and did not constitute a life-threatening medical emergency. Her anger boiled over, and she copied the list and sent it to her father.

Didn't warrant it? You could have gotten me killed by not informing me. I can understand perhaps not thinking it was necessary for the first watch, but you should have informed me once Avery put me back on. I'm seriously beginning to regret my decision. Were you trying to get me killed?

Notice of his typing appeared moments later.

> *No, of course not. I was trying to make your life as normal as possible and took care of all the paperwork for you. I am sorry for the harm I have caused you, and I understand if you want to change your mind. Whatever you want, I freely give you to make up for the harm I have done.*

She stared at that message for several minutes before deciding on a reply.

> *Paperwork?! You think I'm upset about paperwork? Gods. Is there even a single brain cell in that clueless, fur-brained head of yours? "Deliberate attempts to hide or run from the Guard or Council and/or refusal of any reasonable and legal order will result in your immediate execution." You didn't think that was important enough to mention? What else have you been hiding from me?*

There wasn't an answer right away. She could see him typing and then a pause before typing again, and again.

> *I won't argue with you there. I am a clueless fur-brained idiot, and no, I'm pretty sure there isn't a brain cell left. If there was anything left, your uncle knocked it out of me last night. You know there are many things I can't tell you. However, I thought you already knew that last point. I know that's not the*

answer you want to hear, and it's not the answer I want to give, but it's the truth. All I can do is say I'm sorry for the harm I've caused you and the harm I will cause you in the future.

Is that a threat?

No. It's simply the reality of my position and the oath I've taken.

"That damn oath," she muttered.

I heard that, and I agree completely. I am beginning to loathe ever taking that oath.

So why don't you step down?

You know the Hue-mans better than I do. Do you think any of them are ready? Half my Council is pregnant or out on maternity leave. The rest have shown no interest in leadership and barely show up for the weekly meetings. They may be adults, but they still think like children and are still learning about their new world and what it has to offer. If I step down, it puts the next Senior Councilor at risk. Do you want to put GrandFather or Jordan in front of that target?

> *I'm willing to give my life to protect my people, to be that target, even at the expense of my family.*

She growled with frustration.

> *What makes our lives more valuable than theirs? There are millions of us and only a few hundred of them. Every one of their lives is far more valuable because the loss of even one of their lives could mean the extinction of an entire species.*

He would have to use my own words against me.

> *I heard that, too, and I know you understand. I don't expect your forgiveness, and I fully deserve your anger, but I hope you know that I love you. I have always loved you, and I will always love you.*

She snorted. Not sure how to respond, she closed the message and found several from her sister. Filtering her inbox, she pulled up the first message and played the recording.

It looked like Little Flower was in the barn, although she couldn't quite tell from the angle and lighting. Her sister was wearing a funny-looking hat and clothes that she'd never seen before.

"Hey, Chenzie Butt. I hope you're feeling better. Mama told me what was going on. It sounds like you used up eight of your nine lives this past week, and you're having a really hard time dealing with it. I completely understand. I've wanted to die just about every day since I woke up. It was so hard and degrading to need someone to help me use the waste room or clean myself, and you know how traumatic it was, too. I couldn't do the things I used to be able to do, and life felt purposeless. How many nights did you purr me to sleep or hold me through my grief and terror? I wish I could be there right now to do the same for you, but until then, I wanted you to know it gets better."

She was amazed at how well her sister was signing, and for that matter, that she was even bothering to sign in the first place. Her sister had improved so much in just a few days, and she was completely right about how degrading it was not to be able to do things on her own.

"You and Mama both made me promise to give it time while they figured out how to fix me, so I'm making you promise me the same, and I wanted to show you what's possible," her sister continued. The video backed up, and Marsee gasped. Her sister was standing on her own, and if that wasn't enough, she watched as her sister took several wobbly but unassisted steps forward.

"I can't believe it!" she whispered.

"This is Buster. I can't wait for you to meet him," Little Flower signed. Then, she grabbed the leash on the strange harness attached to Buster's head and made a noise.

Buster started moving forward, and she watched in amazement as her sister made the horse do a few circles and then returned to face the camera. "If Mama and Ammond can make it so I can do this in just a few months, they'll figure something out for you. They're already working on it, along with every brain specialist on the planet. So don't you dare give up on me. I'm going to be working really hard, so Mama will let me travel with the others for the Council Meeting, and I expect you to be working just as hard, if not harder, on your end. Mama's in a *really* bad mood, and trust me, you do not want her in control of your pickle torture when she's in a bad mood. Love you to the moons and back!"

She pulled up the next message.

"Hey, Chenzie Butt. Hope wanted to say she misses you and she wanted to show you the drawing she made for you. She worked really hard on it. Go on, Hope. Hold the picture up for your Auntie Marsee!"

Little Flower helped Hope hold the picture up, and Marsee chuckled at the scribbles. Little Flower tickled Hope, and she giggled and then squirmed to get down, and she heard squeals of laughter trailing away. She sighed with relief to know she could still hear Hope.

"Auntie Brice is chasing her down the hall as we speak," Little Flower continued. "I think Hope's painting has merit. It's a little abstract, but I think it more than accurately represents this past week's worth of chaos. What do you think? Anyway, she's been giving me pointers and says if I keep working hard, I'll be as good as her someday."

The image flipped around to show another drawing. One that Little Flower had obviously started but that Hope had scribbled all over. Marsee nearly cried for joy to see that her sister was drawing again.

"Seriously, though. I'd ask how you were doing, but I don't need to. I'm a complete mess, and you went through so much worse than I did. I saw your statement, and I'm sure that wasn't even half of what that monster did to you. I'm proud of you, though. You survived where everyone else would have died. You beat him, and he can never harm you again. If you want to talk about it, I'm here. If you don't, that's okay, too. Oh, it sounds like Hope is making her way back. Guess I'd better sign off for now. I'll message you later when it's quieter around here. Keep fighting to live. I don't know what I'd do without you. I love you, Marsee."

Marsee stared at the tablet. *Sounds like? She said, 'Sounds like'! She can hear? Wait? She said my name! She must be able to hear! What did Mama and Uncle Ammond do after I left? Little Flower can walk, talk, hear, and draw again? How?! Granted, she's still not back to where she was, but still! Maybe they will be able to fix me.*

She replayed the video, stopped at the scene with them holding Hope's drawing up, and just stared at the image. They were the reason she'd ultimately been able to claw her way back. It was thoughts of her cub that had cut through the haze of her instinct.

Little Flower's cub, not mine, Marsee growled. *I'm never having my own cubs, and Hope is Little Flower's, not mine.*

Swallowing the pain of grief, the only pain she really felt now, she pulled up the next message.

Little Flower was mad, and her eyes were puffy and red from crying. "Gods, I miss you. Mama just told me she's ending her partnership with Papa. I don't even know what to say. She says she can't live with someone who would do that to her child, yet she sticks her claws in me practically daily if I don't work hard enough in my pickle torture. How do you feel about it? I imagine you must have been terrified, angry, and felt betrayed at the time, but now? I heard you kicked him out of your room. That must have been quite the scene. Oh, GrandFather and Henry are dating. I'm happy for him." Her sister sighed and ended the message, looking anything but happy.

She hit reply but couldn't find the words and canceled it. Instead, she closed her tablet and rolled over.

"Rise and shine! Time for another drink!" Ellie said cheerfully as she swam into the room.

"Ugh, I just laid down!" Marsee groaned but sat back up again and took the stupid drink.

"I've been gone for hours. What were you doing?" Ellie asked.

"I couldn't fall back to sleep, so I went through some of my messages," she replied after forcing down a few sips. "I can't wait until I can eat something else," she muttered. "I swear it tastes worse with every bottle. Can you sneak something in from Opal's for me?"

Ellie shook her head. "Sorry. You're on a strict diet. So, anything exciting?"

"Yes and no. You wouldn't believe how much Little Flower has improved. She's walking and drawing again, and it sounds like she's regained some of her hearing too, and I found out that Papa's been hiding things from me again."

"Oof. I see what you mean. What did he do this time?"

Rather than answer, she just handed Ellie her tablet and let her read everything for herself.

Ellie looked up with a frown. "You didn't know?"

She shook her head.

"I'm sorry. I should have realized that when you told me you ran off."

She shrugged. "What's done is done."

"Now, what's this about Little Flower drawing again?" she asked, handing the tablet back.

Marsee opened the message and showed her the first bit.

"Hope shows promise. Little Flower's got a long way to go, but at least *she's* trying again," Ellie replied with a glare.

Marsee purposely ignored the barb and opened the message with Little Flower riding. The look on Ellie's face was comical. She didn't think she'd ever seen her mentor so surprised.

"Well, your sister's right about one thing," Ellie finally said. "You do not want to be around your mother when she's grumpy."

"That's an understatement. Have you been hanging around my uncle?"

"No, child. He's been hanging around me. Alright, you. Get some sleep already. You're a real grump when you're tired."

"Finally!" Marsee muttered and rolled over. Still, as tired as she was, she couldn't fall asleep as her thoughts began to spiral.

"Ellie?"

"Yeah?"

"Did I do the right thing?"

"About what?"

"Papa."

She heard Ellie sigh, but she didn't speak for a long time. "What specifically has you second-guessing your decision?" she asked instead. "The information about your watch."

"Yes and no. I can't get my feelings on it to settle. I've never felt like this before."

She heard the sounds of Ellie swimming over, but she didn't open her eyes. Ellie laid her head over Marsee's shoulder in a hug. She shifted to lean into it and sighed. Eventually, Ellie sat up and began stroking her head. Thankfully, there was no flinch this time.

"It's not surprising your emotions are a mess. He hurt you, but he's your father. You hate what he did, whether it was for a good reason or not, but you still love him. I have my own personal feelings about the situation and want to claw our entire Council right now, especially your father and uncle, but I'm not the one who has to live with that decision. You are. Decisions like this are never easy. There's no right or wrong answer, and you never know what will happen because of it. Perhaps what you're going through will help someone else in the future. Maybe they'll be able to find a cure someday because of your injuries. I don't know if that would justify what your father did, and I don't know if keeping him on the Council will do more harm than good. He's done wonders with the Hue-mans, and I don't think anyone else on the Council could advocate for them the way they need it, even your uncle. Everyone else would let their egos and beliefs get in the way, but your father is letting them chart their own path, for better or worse. Unfortunately, people like Rip will stop at nothing to claim that power for themselves. I don't know if the Hue-mans are really ready to take on that battle. If someone should decide to go after them directly, they'll have little defense, only a handful of borrowed guards. Your father knows that. He was prepared to fight the entire council to protect them and would have had to kill your mother if Little Flower had chosen that path. I'm furious about what he did to you, but if he's telling the truth, he was honoring his oath to protect the people before you, just like he did by not stepping down and just like he did when he took the position in the first place."

"My head knows all that, too, but my heart is screaming with rage so loudly I can't hear it."

Ellie sighed. "Do you think he'll hurt you again?"

She considered the question. "Probably. Do I think he'll attack me again? No, not unless I'm out of control. But if it's a choice between his oath and me..." She sighed. "I'll be out of claws by the end of the week. He said as much."

"And would you rather have a father that protected you but left his people vulnerable?"

She sighed. "No. I would vote for him over people like Rip any day, even if it meant my death."

"Well, there's your answer."

"So why does it hurt so much?"

"Because he's your father, and you love him, and it feels like a betrayal."

"But I didn't feel like this before. The whole time I fought with my instinct, it was to protect Papa. Even right after, when I thought I was dying, I was happy that Papa was safe. But the moment he said...that word, I was hit with an intense rage unlike anything I've ever experienced before. More even than I felt towards Rip. My emotions are all over the place. I'm worried something else is wrong and that I'll hurt someone without meaning to."

"I suppose there could be something else going on. Do you want me to get the healer?"

She nodded, and Ellie left. She heard them return a few minutes later but didn't open her eyes or roll over to look.

"Marsee," the Senior Healer said several minutes later.

She opened her eyes to find the healer in front of her. "I'm not sure if there's anything wrong. There are several minor hormonal changes that could account for mood swings, although they're still within my understanding of your species' norms. I've sent them off to your mother for consultation. In the meantime, I can give you something to calm you."

"What you gave me before?"

Hyacinth nodded.

She shook her head. "No, thank you. Ellie doesn't need any more blackmail than she already has."

Hyacinth's skin bubbled with humor. "What, you didn't like having rainbow paws?"

Marsee growled at the healer. "That and I don't want to be fuddle-headed if someone should attack."

The healer nodded her understanding. "I'll ask your mother if she has any other suggestions. Most of what I have here is not safe for your species, but she could bring something with her."

She nodded her thanks and rolled over, but it was a long time before she finally fell asleep.

CHAPTER 49

Marsee: Leviathan Poop

Marsee bolted awake from another night terror, but thankfully managed not to scream this time. The lights were off, but there was a glow from the corner where Ellie sat in her net.

"Are you okay?" Ellie asked.

"Just another night terror. Please leave a light on. It's too dark in here without them, and since I'm probably not going to be able to fall back to sleep for a while, you might as well bring me another one of those moons' forsaken drinks."

Ellie chuckled and swam off. She returned a few minutes later, and Marsee forced a sip down.

"Gah. These things *are* getting worse. I can't drink this," she said, tossing it away.

Ellie frowned, swam over to the bottle, took a sip, and flicked her ears back.

"I know, horrible, right?" Marsee half chuckled at her mentor's horrified expression.

"No, Marsee. The problem isn't with the drink."

It took her a second to realize what she meant, and with a howl of despair, she rolled over away from her mentor.

Ellie swam over and put a paw on her shoulder, but she shrugged it off, too upset to be comforted. She *was* getting worse. She'd been able to taste before. Why couldn't she now? What did that mean for the rest of her senses? Was she going to lose those too? Everything already seemed so much duller than before. *Ancient Gods, please don't let me lose my sight too. I don't think I could handle being in the dark all the time.* She grabbed her tail and held it for comfort, too scared to damage it to twist it like she wanted to. Without her fur, it just felt weird and not comforting at all, but she held it anyway and curled into as much of a ball as the stupid cast would allow.

She heard the door open and close several times but didn't bother to roll over to see who was there, too trapped in her own grief and fear to care.

After what felt like an hour later, she felt another touch on her shoulder, but she shrugged it off, too.

"Marsee, you're okay. There's nothing wrong with your sense of taste that we can't fix. You're not getting worse, I promise."

She opened her eyes to see a very tired-looking Senior Healer floating in front of her.

"Are you sure? Everything is so much duller than before, not just my sense of taste. Smells, hearing, even my sight."

"Yes, I'm sure. You still have burns to your mouth, nose, and throat that the nano wash can't get to. It's probably what's causing your difficulty swallowing, as we haven't been able to find any other cause. The shields and nano wash are likely affecting your other senses. There's no sign of any further damage to your brain, and overall, you're doing much better." She held up a bottle. "This is a nano solution. I want you to take a large sip of this and hold it in your mouth for as long as you can before swallowing it. It's going to taste absolutely revolting, but it will speed up the healing process. It may take a few days, but you will get your sense of taste back once your burns finish healing."

Marsee took the bottle from the healer and drank. It was all she could do not to throw up. Revolting was too kind of a word for how bad it was. The creature Rip had fed her had tasted better. "Ugh, what's in this?" she signed, as her face contorted, trying to keep from spewing the vile concoction all over the Senior Healer.

The Healer flashed her humor. "You're better off not knowing, but on the bright side, the drink will taste better afterwards."

"That's not exactly a ringing endorsement. I'm pretty sure Leviathan poop would taste better."

"Sadly, I don't think we have any of that on the menu, but if you'd like, I could send someone out for some," the Healer teased.

Marsee pinned her ears and growled at the Healer, which just caused her to laugh even brighter.

"Okay, you can swallow now."

Marsee forced it down. Her stomach lurched, and it nearly came right back up, but she somehow managed to keep it down.

"Wait an hour before trying your drink again to give the nanos time to work," the Healer signed and then swam out of the room.

Ellie didn't say anything, just swam over with her tablet and the drink that had floated away and crawled back into her sleeping net.

Marsee flipped open the tablet as she tried and failed to get the horrid taste out of her mouth. She read through dozens of messages when one came in from Ammond. Surprised to be getting one from him, she opened it and snorted as she read it.

"What's so funny?" Ellie asked.

"Mama made the mistake of making Little Flower mad. They apparently had an epic fight in the Trauma Center. Furious, Little Flower transferred her care to Ammond, and Mama was apparently muttering and moping so badly that Ammond had to order her home and relieve her of duty. He even took her tablet from her so she couldn't work and stated that if she didn't go home and sleep, he would sedate her and leave her behind when the council ships left."

"What did they fight about?"

"Ammond said Mama wasn't going to let Little Flower attend the Council Meeting."

"Well, she was injured. Jump can be hard on people if they haven't fully recovered."

"That was Mama's excuse, but Little Flower stated that if Grand-Father was healed enough to be cleared to go, she should be too.

GrandFather was hurt far worse than she was, and if it was safe enough for her to ride Buster, then it should be safe enough for her to jump. Then she went into a full twenty-minute rant on how she was sick of being treated like a baby and not having any say in her care and demanded to be transferred over to Ammond since he at least listened to her. She stated that she was a legal adult, member of her species Council, and victim of the crimes being tried and that if Mama wasn't going to let her go on the council ship, she'd fly herself in Papa's or take public transport if that's what it took to get there. Either way, she was going. Tabor apparently witnessed the whole thing and offered to fly Little Flower in her own ship. Mama turned on Tabor, and Tabor gave Mama what for, too, stating that if Little Flower wants something badly enough, she gets it and that she's learned to stay out of her way, and it would be best if Mama did too. Then Mama stormed off, stating that if Little Flower wanted to go, fine, but if she got sick, she could clean up her own mess. Anyway, Ammond wanted me to know that he felt that Little Flower was perfectly capable of attending if she could take on Mama and win but that I might want to warn the Seniors that she's coming."

Ellie laughed so hard she nearly fell out of her net. "Moons! I wish I could have seen that! I might have to ask your sister if she'll be my mentor. I could use some lessons from her. I've been on the receiving end of your mother's wrath before, and it's not fun."

"What did happen anyway?" Marsee asked, and Ellie finally told her the tale, which had her laughing. "So, *are* you the Senior Guild Master or not?" Marsee teased.

"I can't remember. Did you promote or demote me last?"

Marsee frowned, trying to remember, and then shrugged. "I honestly don't remember. Either way, poof. Consider yourself promoted again. I have no desire to spend the rest of my pitifully short existence stuck in requisition meetings."

"Fair. I'll just have to promote your sister instead," Ellie replied as she tried to find a comfortable position in her net. "She should be able to handle the Council and a few grumpy guild masters."

"Moons! Those poor councilors," Marsee chuckled. "Then again, if she's there, those meetings might actually be interesting. Nah. Still not worth it."

"It would serve them right. Anyway, It's been an hour or so. Try that drink again and go back to bed. We have pickle torture in the morning." Ellie flopped again, and one foot slipped through one of the holes in the net. "Moons' forsaken fish nets."

Marsee wasn't sure whether to grumble about therapy or laugh at Ellie's difficulty with the net. Humor won out as every attempt Ellie took to extricate herself from the net ended up tangling her up worse, to the point that Marsee wondered if she'd have to call the guards in to help untangle her again.

"You think it's easy? I'll trade with you," Ellie muttered at her.

"Do you want me to call the guards in to help?" Marsee asked sweetly.

Ellie just pinned her ears at her, huffed, and gave up, laying where she was, all four feet now hanging through the net, and her face smushed awkwardly into the side.

Chuckling, Marsee snapped a picture and sent it off to Little Flower, knowing she would be just as amused by it. Then she grabbed the thermos. She took a tentative sip and frowned. "I can't tell if it's any better or if it's just that the nanos were so horrible."

"Want me to ask the Healer to fetch you that Leviathan poop?" Ellie teased.

She glared at her mentor and threw the bottle at her. It didn't even make it halfway across the room.

Ellie growled and stared at it, knowing she was too tangled at the moment to retrieve it.

Marsee smirked and rolled over. Behind her, she heard Ellie grunt and mutter as she tried to extricate herself from her tangled mess and then sigh with defeat. Her tail curled with humor as she drifted back to sleep, wondering just how long Ellie would struggle before calling for help.

CHAPTER 50

Nazari: Council Decision

Nazari sat in her office on the third floor of the barn, staring at her tablet and the message that had just arrived from Senior Councilor Surellis. It took everything she had not to throw her tablet out the window or keep from crying with the first words she read, *'I'm sorry to inform you.'* She closed her eyes and took several deep breaths to calm herself before reading on.

Master Animal Healer Nazari Jabri,

I am sorry to inform you that the Senior Council has decided not to bring your case before the Full Council due to the current challenges we're facing. While Jeran and I owe you everything for saving our family, we recognize that your current status on the watch list would not bode well in your favor.

To protect your reputation and that of Saber's, we discussed pushing off the appeal for another six months. The consensus was that it would not be fair to the child, who would have developed an attachment to his new mother and, at that point, would have spent more time with her.

Nazari growled, even if part of her agreed and understood. Her instinct roared with anger, and she struggled hard to contain it. Eventually, it settled enough that she was able to keep reading.

> *However, we also agree that the circumstances around your case are less than ideal. While it is the right of any council to deny off-world adoptions regardless of the circumstances, you were the closest thing he had to a mother for a good portion of his early life, and that should have been honored. As a Healer, you knew the risks before going after my family, knowing fully well that it might hamper your own case.*
>
> *As such, we're granting you visitation rights of two hours a day until the child reaches the age of two standard years. At that point, we will allow the child to decide who he wants for his mother.*
>
> *Senior Councilor Marcus Surellis*

Nazari's heart started beating again when she realized that she still had a chance and would actually get to see and hold him again.

The rest of the message contained detailed information regarding what was and wasn't allowed during visitation and the paperwork she had to sign to acknowledge receipt and understanding of the verdict. As she had requested a Full Council trial with her appeal, she still had the right to bring it forward at the next meeting with an advocate to argue her case and present additional information if she didn't accept their verdict.

It wasn't a hard decision for her to make. Try again for full custody, knowing she would likely lose or take the chance they'd given her. She wanted to see him now, to hold him again, and to hopefully build a relationship with him, strong enough that he would choose her, or at the very least be able to prove to his mother that she wasn't the monster his mother seemed to think she was. If nothing else, there was the chance she might be able to continue visiting with him if he didn't choose her.

She acknowledged receipt of the verdict and set her tablet down on the desk as she considered how best to win his affection. Her instinct purred with happiness with the thought of seeing their cub again and pushed to have her go to him now, but she calmed it with promises that they would see him soon. She couldn't initiate contact until Councilor Harding had acknowledged receipt of the verdict, too.

She sat there in her office for over an hour, waiting for a response, when her ears picked up the sounds of tiny running feet coming down the hall, and she smiled, knowing it was him. Unable to resist the pressure from her instinct, she stood and quickly walked out into the hall.

He stopped running the moment she appeared and stared up at her.

Does he remember me, or is he afraid? She lay down, making herself as small and unthreatening as she could.

His mother walked up behind him. They stared at each other, but his mother said nothing and waited to see what he would do.

Suddenly, he let out a high-pitched squeal and started running towards her as fast as his little legs would go.

Her heart soared with joy, and unable to contain herself any longer, she ran to meet him and scooped him up, enveloping him in a fierce hug. She closed her eyes, trying to contain her tears, and purred her heart out until he wiggled in her arms. When she looked down at him, he smiled back up at her.

"Hello," she signed.

He didn't say anything back, just snuggled into her fur like he always had.

She watched him for a few moments before looking over at his mother.

Councilor Harding's lips were pursed in a frown as if angry, but then she let out a heavy sigh. "Not once," she said, shaking her head.

Nazari tilted her head in confusion, wondering if she'd heard correctly. She didn't have her hearing aids on, and Councilor Harding's voice was right on the edge of her hearing.

"Not once, in all this time, has he reacted to seeing me like he did for you just now," Councilor Harding continued in sign language. "It's like I don't even exist most days. I don't think we have to wait until he's two. He might not be able to speak, but he's made his decision. I'll let the Senior Council know." She turned and started walking away, shoulders slumped in defeat.

Nazari sat there stunned for several moments, sure she was dreaming. "Wait," she called out.

Councilor Harding turned around with surprise on her face.

Nazari wondered if she was surprised that she'd stopped her or that she'd spoken in her language.

"You love him?" she asked carefully, pitching her voice as high as she could make it.

"I do, but he obviously loves you more," the councilor replied.

"Then stay," Nazari said. "Partner with me. Let's raise him together. Your council was right. I don't know your culture, and he could use that guidance from you." Her words were halting as she struggled to form the strange high-pitched sounds, but she was pretty sure she got them right. She half-signed with her free hand as well, hoping the meaning was coming across.

Councilor Harding stood unmoving for several moments and then shook her head again. "No. If I've learned anything these past few days, it's that our culture is rotten to the core. I offered to adopt him, not because I wanted him, but because I wanted to hurt you, even though I didn't even know you. It's the same thing I did to Damon, and look how well that turned out. Yet you stayed and continued to care for us and the other children without complaint and risked your life to save members of my people. I don't know how to raise him or treat the issues he's dealing with, especially when I don't even know how to take care of my own. He's better off with you. Congratulations Mama. It's a boy." With that, she turned and walked away.

Nazari sat stunned long after Councilor Harding disappeared from view. Then she looked down at the child in her arms and smiled. He'd fallen asleep. She gently moved a tiny piece of his head fur off his face as her heart bloomed with love and joy.

"Sari...My beautiful Sari," she whispered, but moments later gasped as she felt something snap into place as her instinct finally settled, content with their victory, back to slumber where it belonged.

The silence without the constant pressure and demands to act, even after it had settled some after that strange conversation the other day, was so profound that she started crying, knowing just how close she'd come to losing control.

She closed her eyes, took several deep breaths, and wiped the tears away.

When she opened them again, it was to see Quinn standing at the end of the hall, watching her with that same intense look he'd given her that first day.

She smiled at him, unsure what to say. Would he even believe her?

His expression softened, and a matching smile lit up his face. Then, with a nod, he turned and walked away.

CHAPTER 51

Marsee: Recovery Ward

It was far too early when Marsee was woken by a very chipper Senior Healer. Ellie sat in her sleeping net as if nothing had happened the night before, tapping away on her tablet, but the very tip of her tail was curled with suppressed humor. The thermos she'd thrown was nowhere to be found.

Marsee glared at them both, highly suspicious, then turned to the healer. "When my mother acts as cheerful as you are, it either means I'm dying, or I'm going to wish I was dying in a few minutes. Which is it?"

The Healer's skin bubbled brightly with laughter. "Neither. Well, maybe the latter. It all depends on how everything goes this morning. Once I've checked you over, assuming everything looks good, you're being transferred to one of the dry recovery rooms."

"Oh, no wonder you're so happy. You won't have to put up with me anymore." While it came out as a mutter, she was pleased to know she had improved enough to leave the trauma ward. "I'll admit, I've been a bit of a grouch. Sorry about that."

The Senior Healer chuckled. "I'm always happy when one of my patients recovers enough to move to the recovery ward. As for being grouchy, you've been one of the less grouchy patients I've had in here in a while. No one ever deals well with bad news, and you've had far more than your fair share. Besides, it's been rather entertaining. I've learned several wonderful new swears, which have bumped me up significantly in the ranks. Thank you. And it's not every day we see parents or members of the Senior Council dragged off by the Guard."

Marsee rolled her eyes. "Glad I could be so entertaining."

"Do me a favor, though. Don't come back for another stay. I'd rather you stayed in one piece and out of here."

"You and me, both," Marsee agreed.

"Now, let's get you out of that nano wash and see how well you're doing." The Healer swapped out Marsee's face mask for the full-body one, then shut down the nano-wash and shield.

Marsee sighed with relief as the room visibly brightened and the sounds of the ward sharpened. She couldn't tell much difference in her sense of smell, but it shifted from the slightly acrid smell of the nano-wash to a more antiseptic and briny smell of the highly filtered and treated water. It was much closer to what she normally sensed, if not what she'd been able to do with her instinct. She knew she would always miss that beauty, but at least she wasn't any worse off than she'd been before. *I can still hear Little Flower and Hope, and that's all that really matters,* she thought.

"Better?" The Healer asked.

Marsee nodded. "Much."

"Good. Now let's take this cast off."

The Healer ran a wand along Marsee's sides, and the mesh cast split neatly in two.

Marsee didn't dare move for fear of hurting something again, but she did take a deep breath.

"You can relax. Your incisions are healed enough that as long as you don't take an impact to your stomach, you should be fine. Now, let me see that paw."

Marsee held up her injured paw, and the Healer took that cast off as well.

"Make a fist for me. Excellent, now extend each claw individually."

Marsee did as requested.

"Are you feeling any stiffness or numbness?"

"Yes, these three fingers feel numb." Marsee pointed them out.

"That's what I expected. There's a nerve that runs along here that splits out to those fingers. Can you feel this?" The healer ran her fingers along her paw and the indicated fingers.

"Kind of. It's all tingly," Marsee replied. "Like when you sleep on your arm wrong."

"We don't get that sensation, but I hear it's awful."

"It's prickly but not painful. Annoying more than anything," she replied.

The healer examined the scans for a minute. "The nerve is still inflamed, and there's still quite a bit of swelling. You can move your paw and still feel, so I expect once the swelling goes down, the numbness should go away, too. Nerves tend to heal a lot slower than other injuries, so it may take a few weeks, depending on how much you use your paw. You'll want to rub nano cream in here at least twice a day until it goes away. Now, nice and easy, I'd like you to sit up and then swim over to the door and back. If you feel dizzy at all or if anything feels even remotely odd or different, let me know."

Marsee sat up and swung her legs off the invisible bed. "I hope you realize how strange it is to have a bed you can't see."

The Healer looked at her funny. "You can't see it?"

Marsee's face dropped, and she started to hyperventilate with panic again.

"Calm down, Marsee," Ellie said, not looking up from her tablet. "I can't see it either."

The Healer shook her head. "I've been treating your species for decades, and not one of them has said they can't see the beds. I wonder..." The healer did something, and suddenly, the bed was there.

"I can see it now," Marsee said. "It's all shimmery, but I can see it."

"As can I," Ellie said.

The Healer shook her head. "You'd think someone would have mentioned it. Anyway..." The Healer tilted her head, indicating Marsee should get moving, so she did.

It took every bit of energy she had to swim over to the door and back.

"How do you feel?"

"Exhausted. My muscles feel like I just ran for leagues, and even without the cast, I still can't breathe."

The Healer nodded and indicated she should lay back down on her bed as she examined the scans for several minutes.

"The good news is you didn't damage or injure anything. The less good news is you have a lot of hard work ahead of you to recover your strength. You might not feel it, but your body is still recovering. As for your lungs, they're much better. The infection appears to be gone, but I expect you'll continue to feel short of breath for several days, perhaps as much as a week. Every time you think about it, try breathing as deeply as you can. This will help them recover faster. For everything else, you're going to have to start paying closer attention to how your body feels and moves. That you can feel the fatigue in your limbs is a good thing. Pay attention to that, or any numbness, stiffness, or any time it doesn't do what you expect, as that could indicate you've injured something. Rest for now. I'll return in an hour or so, and we'll swim over to your new room."

The Healer gave her a wicked grin and left.

"Why do I have a sinking feeling that my new room is about as far away from here as it could possibly get?" she muttered.

Ellie's tail spiraled, but she didn't look up from whatever had her attention.

She was not wrong. An hour later, the Healer returned with a bag to transport her few belongings, and they made their slow way to the new room, flanked by her guards, who were looking decidedly menacing that morning. Everyone who saw them turned and swam in a different direction. The guards she passed all saluted, bowed, or flashed the silver and purple, depending on species. It wasn't just her father's guards or the Water Sprites, but Flyer's as well. She didn't see any Diggers or Ice Giants.

Avery must have picked up on her curiosity when she spotted a pair of Flyers outside a room.

"Right now, there are only a handful of Flyer and Digger guards on the planet, those that came with Wind Rider and Sammianna. Senior Councilor Apakna is here, but she left before everything happened. There's also a full contingent of our guards that arrived the other day."

She raised a brow. "A full contingent? I thought only two squads were allowed for council meetings."

"They were sent after you were kidnapped, and Clear Seas gave his authorization for them to stay. Most are helping to secure the city in preparation for the meeting."

She nodded. "How is Petra?" Marsee asked.

"Her wings were badly damaged, but she should make a full recovery and be flying again in a few months," the Senior Healer answered.

She stopped and peered in when they passed Petra's room. Petra was asleep on a bed similar to hers, but her wings were fully extended. The shimmer of a shield surrounded her. She swallowed hard at the sight of them. They looked horrible.

"It's not as bad as it looks," the Senior Healer said. "Repairing wings is complicated but fairly common. For all their size, their wings are rather delicate and break or tear often. It's one of the most common injuries we treat for them here. Thankfully, Rip didn't cut any of the major nerves or tendons. The challenge with her is the sheer amount of damage that needs to be repaired. We're still printing her replacement skin. It's a rather painful process, as their wings are very sensitive, so we're keeping her sedated as much as possible."

She nodded and kept swimming. She had to stop and rest at least a dozen times. Her muscles were so weak that it felt almost like she was trying to swim through thick mud instead of water. By the time she made it to her room, she was panting hard, even with the Healer's help, and the moment she stepped into the room, her legs collapsed out from under her. She was so exhausted she didn't even have the strength to take her mask off. Gravity pulled her head down, and moments later, she was asleep. She didn't even wake up when the guards picked her up and moved her to the bed.

CHAPTER 52

Marsee: Truce

To her shock and surprise, they actually let her sleep, or if they came to check on her, she never knew it. It was nearly evening before she woke again, screaming from another night terror. Ellie woke with a snort. The guards checked in, saw she was unharmed, and returned to their duty.

"Another night terror?" Ellie asked.

Marsee snorted and rolled her eyes at her mentor. "No, I was dreaming I was trapped in a requisition meeting and screamed just to liven things up a bit."

Ellie's tail spiraled with humor. "I might have to try that next time. Well, since you're finally awake, I'll get you something to drink."

"Yay," Marsee replied. "Just what I always wanted, berry-flavored liquid Leviathan poop."

Ellie laughed and limped her way out of the room. She sighed at the visible reminder of her mentor's injuries. In the water, it had been easy to forget that Ellie had been hurt, too, as aside from her shorn fur, most of her visible injuries had healed.

When Ellie returned, her tail was still tightly curled. "In case you're wondering, your father is pouting out in the waiting room. Apparently, no one would come back to ask if you wanted to see him."

Marsee took the drink and frowned as it didn't taste any better than before, but she forced the sip down anyway. After making a disgusted face, which made Ellie chuckle, she sighed and looked over at the guards floating outside her room. "Hey, Avery."

He turned to look in the door. "Yes, ma'am?"

"Would you please drag my father in here?"

"Are you sure?" he asked.

She nodded. "I need someone else to growl at. Ellie and the Senior Healer are far too chipper today."

"Yes, ma'am," he replied with a grin and curl of his own tail as he took off, making her wonder if Avery would take her instructions literally.

Her father appeared at the door a few minutes later, sadly not being dragged by his scruff, but he did look like he'd been called into the School Master's office.

Before either of them could say anything, Ellie growled at her father. "Upset her, and I'll have Avery throw you in the Trench."

Her father nodded, not the least bit upset about the fact that Ellie had just threatened him.

Avery looked like he wanted to do just that as he stepped inside after her father did, apparently ready to ensure nothing happened.

"Hey, Kitten, how are..." He stopped and winced as she gasped. "I'm sorry, Sweetheart. I keep forgetting."

"No. Say it again," she demanded.

His brow furrowed with worry and concern. "I don't want to hurt you."

"Say it again. The whole phrase, like he did."

"Little kitten," he whispered.

"Again," she demanded.

He sighed. "Little kitten."

A slow smile crept across her face. "It doesn't hurt, Papa. It doesn't hurt! Little Kitten. Little Kitten. Little Kitten! Blessed Moons! It doesn't hurt!" Tears started streaming down her face, and he rushed over and scooped her in for a hug. The tears turned from happiness to anguish as the days of fear and grief welled up in her, mixed with her relief that her father's term of endearment no longer physically hurt. Still, she wondered how long it would take to forget what had happened every time she heard it.

He held her until she cried herself out. "Better?" he asked as he gently laid her back down.

"A little. Papa, I want you to keep saying it. I refuse to allow him to take that from me, too. That's yours, not his."

"Whatever you want, my beautiful, amazing, wonderful little kitten," he replied and hugged her again. "I am so very sorry for how my actions have hurt you."

"I know," she replied. "And I forgive you."

He pulled back and looked at her with wide eyes and a jaw dropped in both shock and astonishment. "You're really forgiving me?"

"I guess I am, or a truce at least. I'm still angry and hurt and having a really hard time controlling my emotions. I'll probably be mad at you again tomorrow." She let out a heavy sigh. "But I've been stupid. You had good reasons to think I was losing control. What I do know is that I could have easily killed you."

"I should have backed off when you asked."

She looked away from him and rubbed at her paw. "Perhaps. Or perhaps I wouldn't have come back in time. I think I knew I was dying. Right before I killed my instinct, it said, 'You can't live without me, but I can live without you.' I couldn't breathe, and the pain was worse than anything I'd ever experienced, but I was glad you were still alive. I felt my death was worth it if it meant saving you. I wasn't even angry at you until you said kitten. That's when everything Rip did came rushing back, all the fear and pain and the twisted lies he told me. He wanted me to mistrust you, to lose control and attack you, and I nearly did, even without my instinct."

"I deserve your mistrust," he replied. "I've broken it far too many times. I was never there for you when you needed me, and I have hurt you, both physically and emotionally, and I am sorry. I have not been a good father to you. I don't deserve your forgiveness, but I thank you. If there is anything I can do to make up for it, please let me know."

Before she could answer, her alarm went off. She groaned and reached over to shut it off. "If you'll excuse me, it's apparently time for my appointment with the waste room."

Her father looked at her in confusion, and she wondered if he knew about her latest setback. "Lucky me, in addition to everything else, I can't tell when I need to pee either," she grumbled as she struggled to sit up. Gravity was so much stronger than she remembered. When she attempted to stand, she nearly fell over as her legs buckled out from under her again, but her father caught her before she could fall.

"Easy there, Kitten," he said as he helped her sit back on the bed. "Are you hurt?"

"I don't think so, just a lot weaker than I thought. That or the Senior Healer has turned up the gravity in the room as payback for my attitude."

"I warned you," Ellie said from the other bed.

She hissed at Ellie, who muttered something about impudent apprentices.

Her father chuckled at the exchange, carefully picked her up, carried her into the other room, and then brought her back when she was done. Even the effort needed to squat over the hole was enough to make her legs shake.

She was just lying back in bed when the Senior Healer arrived and started examining the monitors from the hall, along with two other healers who could enter the room. "Your heart rate set off the alarms, but I'm not seeing anything that would cause it. Are you feeling okay?"

Marsee sighed. "I just went to the waste room. It was exhausting. Papa had to carry me because my legs gave out."

"Ahh, yes, that would do it. You shouldn't try to leave your bed without assistance for at least a few days. It's going to take you time to get used to gravity again and build your strength back up."

"So I noticed," she muttered.

"Well, since you're awake, I'll bring you your supper. Do you want it before or after the nano drink?"

"Ugh, I have to have another one of those?"

"It would be best. I'm seeing improvement, but you're not fully healed yet."

She let out a disgusted sigh. "Ellie just brought me another drink, but I'll take the nanos first. That way, I can wash the horrible taste out with the other horrible taste."

The Healer chuckled and left with the others.

"What's with the nano drink?" her father asked.

"It's to treat the burns that the nano wash couldn't treat. I started losing my sense of taste on top of everything else. The Healer says this should fix it and my difficulty swallowing, but it's revolting, and that's being kind. I'd rather eat that slimy creature Rip threw at me."

A few minutes later, a healer returned with the nano drink. It was just as revolting, if not more so than before. She wasn't sure if that meant it was working or not, and just like the first time, it made her stomach lurch when she swallowed. While she waited, they chatted, and he caught her up on everything.

"Ugh, another moon's forsaken trial?"

"Well, at least this time, you don't have to stand in front of everyone translating," Ellie teased.

"I suppose," Marsee muttered.

"So anyway, we need to know what you want for reparations from Damon regarding your damaged room," her father said.

She snorted. "Like that matters. Ellie said she has crafters working to fix it if they can. I just want it so he can never hurt our family again. I'm good with whatever Little Flower wants."

When the hour was up, she forced her meal down. It still didn't taste any better, although she did notice it was slightly easier to swallow. Her father left to continue with his investigation while she was dragged out for another round of physical therapy. She didn't even make it one slow lap around the ward before passing out.

CHAPTER 53

Marsee: Still a Monster

When Marsee woke again, she was back in her room, and it was dark out. Ellie had kept the light on, but she still woke up screaming.

Her father, apparently sleeping on the floor, was by her side in moments.

"Shhh, it's okay. You're safe. It was just a night terror," he whispered, holding her close as she shook from the adrenalin. After helping her to the waste room, he offered to curl around her, like he had in the ship. She nodded, shifting over to make room. She snuggled in close to his warm fur with a happy purr on both their parts, and she was asleep again in seconds.

Marsee walked along a stream in the Wilds, enjoying the beautiful day. Her back was warm with the afternoon sunshine, and the flowers of spring bloomed all around her. She took a deep breath, enjoying the scent, and went to flick her instinct on so she could see the colors of that scent in the gentle breeze, but nothing happened. She frowned, remembering she'd killed off her instinct.

The world darkened as a cloud covered the sun, and she heard the rumble of thunder off in the distance but then frowned again when she realized it wasn't thunder. It was a growl. Turning to look behind her, she found her father barreling down on her, fangs bared and claws out, and he swiped at her. She bolted out of the way and took off.

"How will you ever protect your cubs if you can't defend yourself from me? You're nothing but an injured kitten. You don't even have your instinct to fall back on," he snarled at her.

"Leave me alone!" she yelled at him.

"No. You need to learn to fight and run faster," he snarled and pounced, pinning her to the ground by her scruff. She fought and struggled to get away, but she couldn't move.

"Let me go, Papa! Why are you doing this to me?" she growled.

"Because you need to be stronger."

She struggled, broke free, and attacked with everything she had. She smelled blood as she made contact and roared with her success, but suddenly, she was pinned down, unable to move again.

"Marsee! Wake up!" Aris yelled.

She snapped awake, staring at the two guards who had her pinned. She collapsed back into her bed, panting and frowned, realizing she still smelled blood. It hadn't been in her dream.

"I smell blood. Who did I hurt?" she asked in a panicked whisper as Aris backed off now that she was sure she was awake.

"It's just a scratch," her father said as a pair of healers came streaming through the door, notified by the alarm on her monitor. They examined her monitors and then checked her father over before disappearing and returning a few minutes later. One went over to her father to suture the cuts she'd given him while the other healer began treating her.

"You re-broke one of the bones in your paw, but we should be able to set it without surgery. You also pulled a muscle in your shoulder, but that's minor, and some nano cream should take care of it," the healer explained as she began treating her broken paw.

She stared at her paw in surprise. She had no idea she'd even broken it.

When it was set, the healer rubbed some nano cream into both her shoulder and paw before leaving.

Marsee just continued to stare at her paw.

"Are you alright, Kitten," her father said, sitting on the edge of her bed.

She looked up at him in horror. "No. I hurt you."

"It's alright. It was just a scratch, and I'm all better now. Do you want to talk about your night terror?"

She shook her head. There was no way she was going to tell him she'd been dreaming that he was attacking her again.

You need to be stronger.

His words from her dream played over and over in her head. How was she going to defend herself or her family now that she had no instinct or if she could break a bone in her sleep and not even know it?

"Papa, I'm scared," she whispered.

"I know, Kitten," he replied, pulling her in for another hug.

When she stopped shaking, he helped her over to the waste room and back, but when he tried to curl up around her, she shook her head at the slight hint of fear she smelled. "You'd better not. I don't want to hurt you again."

"I don't care if you claw my throat out, in your sleep or awake. If it helps you heal, I'll do anything."

"I know."

He sighed but nodded and curled up at the foot of her bed again.

She rolled over, curled into a ball, as she stared at her paw. She could still smell blood under the minty smell of the nano cream, and she shook with silent tears as she realized she would never be able to sleep with her sister or Hope again for fear she'd kill them in her sleep. She'd lost that, too.

It was early morning before she finally fell asleep, and she was in the middle of another night terror when her father woke her by touching her paw to say goodbye. Still half asleep and thinking that Rip was after another claw, she growled and swiped at him, nearly falling out of bed before she woke up.

He scrambled out of the way and then back to catch her before she fell. "I'm sorry. I didn't mean to startle you."

She could smell the reek of fear on him, even after he regained his composure.

Even without my instinct, I'm still a monster. Will he ever trust me?

"I need to head out for a meeting, but I'll be back at noon."

She grunted, rolled over away from him, and curled into a tiny ball.

He sat down on the edge of the bed and placed a paw on her shoulder. "What's the matter, Kitten?"

"Everything," she replied.

"Do you want to talk about it?"

"No. Go away."

He sighed and left.

Half an hour later, she was still wallowing in her misery when there was a commotion at her door. She looked up and saw that Avery had stopped a Saber Healer she didn't know and was verifying who he was. Tamarin, the other guard at her door, had her hand on her stunner, and both were blocking the door. Eventually, Avery confirmed the Healer's identity and let him in.

She frowned as he hesitated before stepping through the door, and once through the shield, she could smell his fear.

It's going to be like this with everyone, she realized.

"Hello, Marsee, my name is..."

"Go away," Marsee said, curling up in a ball again.

"Marsee..." Ellie warned.

She lifted her head and hissed at Ellie before looking back at the healer, who had startled at her hiss. "I said go away."

He spun and left.

"Guards, I don't want him back in my room."

"Yes, ma'am," Avery replied.

"Marsee, that was uncalled for," Ellie said, her disapproval evident in her tone. "He did nothing wrong."

"He reeked of fear. I'm not having someone care for me that thinks I'm a monster, and it doesn't matter anyway. There's no point in trying to get better. I'm just going to die."

"Marsee, you're not..."

"Either shut up or leave," she hissed at Ellie and rolled over so her back was to her, then started to shake with fear and grief. The hollowness of her missing instinct grew until felt like it was going to swallow her whole, but she didn't even bother trying to turn it off. She welcomed it. She wanted it to swallow her whole.

Ellie sighed, and a moment later, she felt Ellie's paw stroking her head. "You're not a monster. Please don't give up."

She shifted away from Ellie's paw. "Leave me alone."

"Marsee…"

"Leave me alone, or I'll have the guards make you," she hissed.

Ellie sighed again but returned to her side of the room.

She curled tighter and hid under her furless tail as she slid down into a deep well of despair and hopelessness and eventually cried herself back to sleep.

CHAPTER 54

Marsee: Change of Guard

Over the next several hours, Marsee kicked out every healer they sent her and refused to leave her room when the Senior Healer came for her physical therapy. There were only so many healers on the planet that could even enter her room, and every one of them was a Saber and smelled of fear, even if their expressions were neatly tucked behind their healer's mask.

She listened as Ellie, Hyacinth, and her primary guards discussed moving her back to a wet room but hadn't bothered contributing to the conversation. She honestly didn't care what they did. She was surprised that Ellie wasn't pressing the issue about accepting one of the other healers, even if she could tell that Ellie was thoroughly annoyed with her.

"I'm not moving her to a wet room," Hyacinth stated. "She needs the gravity of a dry room. She's already spent too much time underwater."

"I could just leave and save you all the hassle," she muttered.

"By all means," Hyacinth replied. "You're welcome to leave at any time."

Marsee glared at the Senior Healer. "You're serious?"

"Without a council order, I can't make you stay. I don't think you've recovered enough to leave yet, and I won't clear you to jump for at least a month, but if you'd be more comfortable in a suite, that can be arranged." Hyacinth fiddled with something on her tablet, then shifted and motioned down the hall.

She glared at Hyacinth but grabbed her tablet and mask and carefully slid off her bed. Her legs buckled out from under her, but she didn't let that stop her. She crawled her way to the door and out. The guards followed her silently.

She never made it to the exit. When she woke, she found Tamarin sitting beside her in an otherwise empty room. She huffed at the guard and rolled over. "You could have brought me to a suite or Ellie's ship instead of back here."

"I can help you better here than in Ellie's ship," Tamarin said. "And if you can't walk across your room, you won't be able to manage a suite, even with my help."

"Your help?" she asked.

Tamarin nodded. "I'm your primary healer now, and unlike the others, you're not going to get rid of me so easily."

She lifted her head to glare at Tamarin. "You're a guard, not a healer."

"Every guard has the equivalent training as a Journeyman Healer before we're allowed out on patrol, even if we don't have the certification. Our focus is more on first aid, trauma, and physical therapy, and I've been managing my squad's care for long enough that I'd probably qualify for my Masters with a specialty in physical therapy if I'd bothered with the exams before, but if you're worried, Hyacinth has agreed to mentor me and proctor my Journeyman's exam this evening. Aris will care for you during the night shift. She already has her Journeyman's."

Marsee shrugged and flopped back down. "I suppose it's not like I have any choice since I can't disobey you while I'm on a watch."

Tamarin shifted to the other side of her bed and sat down again. "You *do* have a choice. I won't force you to accept my care. Legally, I can't, but I truly want to help you, and I understand why you kicked those other healers out. I wouldn't want someone caring for me that reeks of fear either."

"You could smell it, too?"

"Of course we could. Why do you think we gave them so much trouble before letting them in the room?"

She blinked, as that thought hadn't even crossed her mind.

"Now, why don't you tell me what's really bothering you."

"You wouldn't understand."

"No? Well, let's see. You've been kidnapped and tortured for days and can't trust anyone to talk about it. You're dealing with a terminal injury, and one the Council doesn't know what to do with, and all you want to do is go home and forget it all. Only going home means facing friends and family who will fear and mistrust you. Oh, and the food here is atrocious. Did I miss anything?"

Marsee snorted. "Let's not forget about an uncle that's liable to kill me if I sneeze wrong."

"Well, there's that, too, but if I can survive. You can, too."

"You? You had psychosis?"

Tamarin nodded. "Many of us in the guard struggled with our instincts as children. We're the lucky ones who got help early enough and survived, but our friends and family never trusted us after, either. Only my litter mate still keeps in touch. My parents turned me over to the guard when I was only five, but I found a new family there. We would gladly welcome you if you wanted to join us. You've more than proved yourself."

She was shocked by Tamarin's offer but horrified for the reason why. They wanted her because she was a killer. She hid her anguish behind humor. "And spend all day standing out in the hall? I think not. I can't even stand up right now."

Tamarin grinned. "You'll get better. I'll make sure of that. Besides, I've never been one to pass up a challenge."

Marsee rolled her eyes at Tamarin, but she didn't kick the guard out.

"Get some rest. Good job pushing yourself earlier. We'll try to get a little further next time."

Marsee growled, which only caused Tamarin to chuckle on her way out.

Once out in the hall, she heard Tamarin say, "Pay up," to Avery.

"She growled at you," Avery replied.

"The bet was swearing. Growling is not swearing. Pay up."

"How much was the bet?" Marsee called out.

"Trust me, you don't want to know, but I thank you for your politeness," Tamarin replied, "and you should be very glad Avery's not in charge of your care right now."

"I can demote you," Avery growled at Tamarin, but Marsee heard the ding of credit being transferred.

"You can, but you won't," Tamarin replied. "You're far too honorable for that."

Chuckling slightly at the exchange, she curled up, closed her eyes, and was instantly asleep. Only her sleep was riddled with nightmares, not of Rip or her father, but of everyone running from her in fear, and instead of waking screaming, she woke crying.

Ellie was back and tried to comfort her, but she shrugged Ellie's arm off and buried herself under a blanket. Tamarin came in and tried to get her to talk about it, but she swore at the guard and ordered her out. To her surprise, Tamarin left, although Avery muttered that he should have specified the end of the day as the time frame for the bet. When Tamarin brought her meal later, she ignored it. When she said it was time for therapy, Marsee once again refused, honestly more curious to see if Tamarin had been telling the truth about not forcing her. Tamarin seemed to accept her lie that she was too tired but helped her to the waste room and back and left her to sleep. Only she didn't get a chance to sleep. A few minutes later, her uncle showed up.

"If this is another interrogation, you can leave," she muttered at him.

"It's not. I had a few minutes and thought I'd come by and see how you were doing. I brought you a book I think you might like. It's one of my favorites."

She grunted but didn't take it from him.

He set it on the table beside her and sat down. "I hear you're having a bad day?"

"Yup," she replied. "And I really don't want to talk about it. Certainly not with you."

"Why not?" he asked.

She snorted at him. "Thank you for the book, but please go away, Uncle. I'm not in the mood for company."

"Marsee, why don't you want to talk to me?" He paused for a bit, waiting for an answer. "I am sorry I didn't listen to you in the past, but I'm listening now. How can I..."

"Are you?" she spat. "Or are you just looking for evidence to use against me? I'm sure you're only here because Papa told you how I clawed him in my sleep and how I turned all the healers away because they reeked of fear, just like you do now. You're not here to try and comfort me. You're here because you think the monster is still lurking inside me, waiting to pounce, and nothing I ever do or say will change your mind. Either kill me and put me out of my misery, or trust me and go. I honestly don't care either way."

To her surprise, both guards stepped inside, stunners out, and focused on her uncle.

He looked up at their entrance, and the weapons pointed at him. To her further surprise, he said nothing about their threat. Instead, he turned back to face her, gave a single tilted nod of his head, and left.

The guards followed him out of the room and stayed focused on him as he swam away.

"Thank you," she said when they resumed their guard position.

"There's no need," Avery replied. "I have given my oath to Clear Seas that I would not let your father or uncle hurt you, as has every guard in this building."

She blinked. "Isn't that treason?"

"No," Avery replied. "Clear Seas placed you under his jurisdiction when he gave you temporary residency, and my oath was given in your uncle's presence and was a stipulation for remaining on guard. As he didn't object, he agreed to those stipulations. That oath extends to every guard under my command, which, at this time, includes every Saber guard on the planet. Regardless, I would have responded the same. My oath is to the people, not the Council, and as long as you stay here, your uncle has no grounds or authority to execute you, and as long as you aren't committing any crimes or actively out of control, I will protect you from them, just as I will anyone else who tries to hurt you."

"As will I," Tamarin said. "With my life if necessary."

"Why, though? Why would you risk your life for me?"

"Because you risked your life for us," Tamarin replied. "For me."

Marsee frowned. "I don't understand. I didn't even know you before I killed Rip."

"This isn't about Rip, as honorable as that action was," Tamarin replied. "You earned our respect a long time ago. Why do you think the Guard has given you so many chances this past year? It's not because we don't know what to do with you. It's because you risked your life by giving your statement about your experiences with psychosis, not to save your life, but to help others, and I don't think you really knew what you were risking by doing so, but I think you do now."

"You think my uncle will kill me if I return home?"

Both guards were silent, and their silence said everything.

"I think Clear Seas is right," Ellie said. "Marsee shouldn't go home until the watch is up."

"Staying here would be safer," Avery replied.

"I'll start making plans," Ellie said.

"Don't bother," she told Ellie. "I don't want you to live in exile, too. And besides, I quit the Guild, remember? I release you from your obligation to me."

"I don't accept," Ellie replied, walking over to her. "I promised I would stay with you, wherever you are, and I keep my promises."

"What's the point of fighting it? I'm just going to die anyway."

"Well, for one, it'll annoy your uncle," Ellie replied. "And annoying your uncle is a major driving force in my life."

Marsee snorted and rolled over, but unlike before, she didn't shove Ellie away as Ellie laid her head over Marsee's side and purred. Ellie smelled of fear, too, but she knew Ellie was afraid for her, not because of her. "And for another?"

"Someone has to be first, and I want to make sure you won't be the last."

Little Flower: Council Ship

Little Flower paced in her room as they waited for the ships to arrive, positive she forgot to pack something. Or at least that's what she was telling herself. Her dreams had been full of nightmares, each one worse than the next, and she was exhausted, grumpy, and worried.

She was still furious with her mother for refusing to take her off medical leave, although watching Ammond drag her out of the Trauma Center had been entertaining. No one, especially not her mother, was going to prevent her from being there for her sister or see Damon hang for his crimes. She just prayed she'd get there in time. The last message she'd received from Marsee terrified her. She was spiraling rapidly into a depression, and when Marsee'd said that she'd kicked her healer out, she knew she'd been right about them not knowing how to help.

"I'm pretty sure if you've forgotten something, they'll have it there for you. My suite was fully stocked last time," her grandfather said. GrandFather and Henry were waiting with her, their bags already packed and leaning against the wall, and were helping to distract Hope, who had picked up on her mother's nerves and had been cranky all morning.

"I know. I helped design the manifest for the Council suites, remember? I'm more worried about the trip," she replied as she dug through her bags for the fourth time. She had plenty of diapers since they could easily be sanitized and reused, Hope's clothing, wetsuit, a pair of the most adorable tiny flippers she'd ever seen, a child-sized mask, her favorite stuffed animal, Sir Fuzzleton McFuzzface the Third, who was looking decidedly more frazzled than fuzzy at this point, and several other toys. Her bag contained her own underwater equipment, a small selection of clothing, her tablet, several coloring books, pencils, and a blank drawing pad.

"Toothbrush!" Wobbling over to the shelf, she grabbed her toothbrush and the Saber's equivalent of toothpaste just as Ammond arrived to inform them that the ships had arrived right on time. She dug out her tablet, sent Marsee a quick message, and shoved it back in her bag.

GrandFather helped her put Hope into her newly purchased carry sack. She'd practiced for hours, carrying a large melon the day before after trying out every variety they had in the warehouse to ensure she could safely walk while carrying Hope. Then, once Hope was situated, he grabbed one of her bags for her. Henry picked up the other one, and they made their way out.

It felt like it took her forever to make her way out to where the ships had landed, but she knew she had plenty of time. She had practiced that walk, too, even though Ammond had offered to carry her out. Far too big for the shuttle bay, the two large ships had landed in an open section of desert outside the compound. Dust and sand still billowed in the air, making it hard to get a good look at them. She'd expected one of the massive public transport ships she'd seen before when they'd visited the shipyard, but these were smaller, only capable of supporting two hundred passengers each, not the five thousand of the public transports. The only ships she'd ever traveled on were Ellie's and her father's, and while this one was nice and well-maintained, it wasn't designed for her species. The new ones hadn't been completed yet, and these had a feeling of age to them. She could have taken her father's ship, but she wanted to spend time with the others and remind everyone that she was a member of the Council.

They were one of the last to arrive, and Ammond helped her up into the ship as the steps were too high for her to climb safely while carrying Hope, but rather than setting her down, he carried her over to the last row of remaining seats, then helped her to secure and sedate Hope and then adjusted her straps, which she couldn't quite manage, while her grandfather and Henry secured their belongings in their sleeping berths.

"Remember, keep your head facing forward and against the back of the seat when we take off. If you need them, there are more anti-nausea tablets and bags in the table in front of you. You can have one tablet every hour. Let me know if it gets to be too much, and I'll sedate you.

She nodded. He'd offered to sedate her for the takeoff and jump, but she'd refused. There was no way she was going to allow herself to miss this experience or give them an opportunity to remove her from the ship before they were on their way. She trusted Ammond, but she wouldn't put it past her mother to try.

Damon was being transported on the other ship, and he would be guarded the entire time. She'd been told that the Senior Honor Guard herself was on that ship.

Twenty minutes later, the ship was loaded, and they took off. She had a window seat and spent the first few minutes looking out the window as the ship rose and moved away from New Hope.

"Head back, Jessica," her grandfather warned as the ship started to tilt.

Head in place, she waited. Suddenly, the engines roared to life, and she was forced back into her seat.

"I've been on rollercoasters more intense than this," she muttered to her grandfather, who chuckled beside her.

"I know. Just wait until jump. Trust me, it's like nothing you've ever experienced," he replied.

When the gravity systems engaged, she checked on Hope, who was still sleeping, and then looked out the window as the planet quickly fell away. She could have sat there watching the planet spin for days if given the opportunity, but far too quickly, the warning for jump sounded. The universe imploded on her, and an instant and eternity later, it exploded back out, and the blackness of space changed to one of a rainbow of colors.

Her head spun for a few seconds, but after a few deep breaths, the feeling passed, and she chuckled, "That's quite the experience for sure. I see now why you couldn't explain how it felt," she told her grandfather as she checked on Hope again.

When she looked up at her grandfather, he looked decidedly green. Henry had unbuckled his harness the moment they were out and flipped open the table to grab a bag to throw up in. From the sounds of things, other people were also sick.

"How are you not sick?" GrandFather asked, popping another anti-nausea pill.

"I've been dizzy and sick for the better part of the last two months. That was nothing in comparison, and it passed quickly," she replied.

Several of the more experienced healers, including Ammond and her Mother, were up and checking on everyone and bringing the babies out of sedation now that they were safely in jump.

Her mother did a double take when she realized that she was perfectly fine and not even the least bit sick.

Little Flower raised an eyebrow at her, unable to keep the smirk off her face at her mother's expression.

Her mother snorted and applied the anti-sedative to Hope. "You would be the one person in the entire universe not sick after their first jump," her mother signed.

Ammond saw and burst out laughing. Her mother glared at Ammond, who just laughed louder. "You really need to stop underestimating them, Myra, especially Little Flower. She is your daughter, after all," he replied and handed Henry another bag and some water.

Nearly half of the people left their seats to lie down.

She followed Henry and GrandFather back to her room but left after she dug out her tablet, the coloring books, and some toys for Hope. She'd downloaded all of the evidence for the upcoming meeting and intended to dig through it on her way to the Water World. She'd had a fairly heated argument with GrandFather the day before regarding

Damon's punishment. She wanted Damon dead, but GrandFather, surprisingly, wasn't so sure. Everyone had recovered without consequences, and even Marsee's room was being restored at no cost to her thanks to the gifts from the Water Sprites. They were even working to repair her ripped painting.

It didn't matter what her grandfather said, though. There was no way she'd ever be able to trust Damon, and she honestly couldn't believe her grandfather wanted leniency.

Marsee's case was far more complicated. Rip was dead, so it was a matter of determining what role Snapper Fish had played and whether or not he was responsible since he was being forced to perform those crimes to protect his own daughter. From what the Seniors could tell, most of the victims had been taken to cover up Rip's tracks, for blackmail, or for 'practice' as he'd told Marsee, and the more they dug into Rip's past, the more they found. Hundreds of people had been affected or harmed by his decisions over the past two and a half decades in the Council, and from what they'd been able to tell, for more than a decade prior. Rip's death didn't even begin to cover the reparations needed. Interestingly enough, while Damon and Snapper Fish were entitled to representation, both had declined it.

When she returned to her seat, she let Hope out of her jump seat and handed her the toys. Hope played quietly for a while and then slid down off her seat and ran off to play with the other toddlers. There were enough aunties and uncles keeping watch and no place where Hope could go to get in trouble, which gave her plenty of time to curl up and read or watch the translations.

When she watched all she could, she took a break to let her blood pressure come back down and switched over to review some of the other items on the agenda so she could try to make at least a partially informed decision. She was months behind and woefully unprepared to vote on many of the issues, thanks to her mother's insistence that she wasn't fit for duty.

After a while, she set her tablet aside, yawned, and wobbled to the small kitchen to see what they had to eat. Grabbing a bowl of fruit, some juice, and a cookie, she returned to her seat, set everything down, and wandered down the seats to find her errant child. Hope was curled up, sound asleep in Uncle Ammy's arms.

"She's asleep already? Bring her back when she wakes. I have food for her."

He nodded, and she returned to her seat and pulled out her coloring book to think about everything while she ate.

"Mind if I join you?" her mother asked.

She shook her head and set the book and pencils aside.

Her mother took the currently empty seat across from the table, swiveled it around to face her so they could talk, and looked at the half-finished drawing on the table between them. "You're making progress."

She shrugged. It was a little easier, but she still wasn't anywhere close to where she'd been before.

"I'm sorry," her mother signed.

"For?" she asked when her mother didn't continue.

Her mother's ears flicked back. "For hurting you, of course. That was never my intention."

She raised a brow but didn't respond.

"I should have never used my claws on you. That was wrong of me, and it will never happen again."

She shook her head. "Wrong answer."

Her mother's ears flicked back in astonishment but then frowned with confusion. "I don't understand."

"Obviously," she replied and then sighed. "Mama, *why* did you use your claws on me?"

"You'd given up before even trying. I needed you to push yourself because I knew you'd never get better if you didn't. By making you angry at me, you forgot your limitations and pushed harder. That's when you made the most progress."

"So the ends justified the means?"

Her mother nodded and then shook her head. "I was wrong to use my claws to make that happen, but you did get stronger."

"And if you hadn't been able to perform the second surgery and make things better, I would have dragged myself off the balcony the first time you left me alone. Would the ends have justified the means, then?"

Her mother looked horrified. "Would you have really done that? You were making so much progress."

"Yes, I would have because I didn't see the progress. I only saw one day after another, after another of pickle torture, stuck in a broken and useless body and treated with less autonomy than my own child. I couldn't handle the idea of being treated as an infant for the rest of my life, unable to make my own decisions or live or not live my own life to the best of my ability. The only person who saw me as wholly unbroken was Marsee."

"That's not true, Little Flower," her mother interrupted.

"Isn't it, though? I was perfectly capable of being able to understand and vote on issues, but you saw me as medically unfit to attend Council Meetings because my *body* wasn't fully functional. I was capable of understanding the goals and timeline for recovery, but you saw me as an infant who didn't know better and made all of the medical decisions for me, without consulting with me, without giving me any basis to know if I was actually improving quickly or not, and against my wishes, or even giving me a chance to say, 'I feel really sick right now, let's do this tomorrow.' Or at least not until such time as my body improved enough that I could communicate quickly enough for you not to lose patience with me trying to point to words in the book. I tried so many times to tell you no, but you never listened. You never asked why. I had to go before the Full Council to prove I was a sentient adult, and half a year later, you took that away from me, and then you have the audacity to blame Papa for trying to help Marsee through an illness that none of you understand, and without even talking to him about why he did what he did. Marsee doesn't blame him for what happened anymore. In fact, she credits him with giving her the knowledge that she was capable of beating someone bigger than her. She was just upset about her injuries, and he was a safe person to yell at. Rip Current twisted her brain into mush to make her think that Papa didn't care for her. None of you understand what it's like to go through something like what Marsee went through, and you're only making it worse by making her feel like she's to blame for you and Papa breaking up when she needs to focus on herself. She needs to find reasons to live, not feel like her world is falling apart."

Her mother sat and thought about what she'd said for a long time before responding. "I am sorry for treating you like a child. It will not happen again, and I will talk with your father, but I do *not* promise to change my mind about what he did. I can't see any reason why he would have done what he did and thought it would help her."

"Thank you," Little Flower replied. It wasn't perfect, but it was better than nothing.

"I have harmed you. Do you want reparations?" she asked.

"No, just do better so you don't make the same mistakes with Marsee or the next person," she replied. "There are a lot of very hurt and traumatized people on the Water World right now, with no coping mechanisms, and no one who understands or even knows how to treat their trauma, and likely a bunch of healers that mean well, but are doing all the wrong things."

Her mother nodded. "I promise to do better."

"Good," she said and then sighed. "I suppose I should get back to work preparing for the Council Meeting."

Her mother nodded and stood but stopped before she left. "Have you watched Damon's testimony yet?"

"No, why would I? There's nothing he could say that would change my mind. He tried to kill me and several members of my family."

"I think perhaps you should watch his testimony," her mother said and left.

If her ears could go back, they would have. Curious about what could have changed both her mother's and her grandfather's opinions, she took several deep breaths and pulled up his statement. When she was done, she stared at her tablet and swore in every language she knew.

CHAPTER 56

Stormy: Shades of Darkness

Stormy sprawled upside down in his favorite net, tentacles weaved through the holes. He absently pushed against the wall just hard enough to make the net sway in the gentle current of the family room. While it wasn't a school day, he'd woken early and spent the entire day fins-deep in his research and council training and was currently devouring a detailed guide on the cultural practices of Saber that his father had sent him, which he found utterly fascinating. There were already dozens of sections he couldn't wait to talk to his father about, or better yet, someone from Saber.

He'd discussed many of them with his brother earlier, but Temperate was currently holed up in his room talking with Melody, who had just returned home from her work shift. His brother hadn't said anything about his unexpected promotion outside of teasing him for getting stuck, but he had spent most of the day helping him with his investigation, and hadn't shown any signs of displeasure or annoyance at the dozens of questions he'd asked. If anything, his brother seemed to grow more anxious and focused as the day went on, but then what they were both learning was troubling, and his brother had a longer and closer relationship with Jeran and Marcus than he did.

The past week had changed both of them, and he wondered if his brother would finally decide to be his father's heir or step down now that he was stepping up. It didn't matter to him either way. He would happily support his brother in whatever capacity his brother wanted. What mattered was ridding the universe of people like Rip. Only what he was learning was that fighting the darkness wasn't as simple as he once thought. It wasn't just black and white. It was shaded with nuances of grey, where a single word or action could turn something that at first glance seemed legal and honorable into a crime, just like it had with the villain the Night Flyer had fought, or where dishonorable actions, like spying on the others could mean the difference between life and death for his people.

He understood now why his father was so conflicted about his decision, as he was finding it far more difficult to make his own decision with every new piece of information he learned. On top of that, much of his investigation, such as reading Marsee's private journal, felt like an invasion of her privacy, even though he knew it was a necessary part of the position.

He jumped, startled by a knock at the door. Surprised by a visitor this late when his parents weren't home, he called out to his brother before clipping his tablet to his harness and unwinding from his net to swim over to see who it was. He unclipped the brand-new stunner his father had taught him to use that morning and cautiously peered out the window. Seeing only Councilor Chenzira floating outside, he clipped his stunner back on his harness and opened the door. "Good evening, sir. My father's not home yet."

"I know. I just spoke to him. I'm actually here to see you."

"Me?!" Stormy asked, flashing his surprise.

"Yes. I came to ask you a favor. May I come in?"

"Oh, of course," he replied, swimming aside to let him in. "What can I do for you?"

"I was hoping you could help me with Marsee," Jeran replied.

"Gladly, but how?"

"It's my understanding that you're aware of her injuries and illness?" he asked rather than answering his question.

"I am. Papa told me about it and what you did. Were you trying to hurt her?"

"Yes," he replied, surprising Stormy that he'd admit it. "In order to fully test someone's control, we need to make that person scared or upset enough that they'll stop focusing on it."

He frowned as Jeran's explanation sounded like their shock or skin practice and not the more violent description he'd read in Marsee's journal or what he witnessed with Kendra's test. "How can you tell the difference between someone acting in self-defense and a loss of control?"

"That's a very good question. The biggest sign is losing the ability to understand speech or speak back."

"How do you know they're not just too upset or scared to speak?"

"It can be difficult to tell. I couldn't tell with Marsee when she first ran off, as she didn't respond to several of my commands. That's why we look at a person's entire behavior. In her case, she was spraying trees, which is a very bad sign. Marsee's the first to ever come back from an advanced case of psychosis, and none of us knew what that meant or if she would continue to have issues. You don't need to worry about her hurting you, though. We believe she can no longer use her instinct."

"I wasn't worried about her before. She won't hurt me anymore than I would hurt her."

"And that's exactly why I'm here. Marsee's not handling her injuries well and has been refusing treatment and visitors for the past several days. Our instinct's whole purpose is to keep us alive, and without it, I'm worried that she might hurt herself. I was hoping that you might have better luck than the rest of us in getting her to talk or, at the very least, participate in her physical therapy. Ellie says the only time she's really perked up was when you visited."

"I would gladly visit with her again if you think it would help," Stormy replied, then swam up so he was face to face with the Senior Council and squared his shoulders. "On one condition."

Jeran tilted his head, asking.

"That you never hurt her again," Stormy demanded.

There was no change in Jeran's expression, just a slight shift acknowledging his demand. "I see she has a very powerful protector in you," the Senior Councilor replied. "However, as much as I want to, I can't make that promise. My oath is to protect the people before myself and my family. That oath has already put a target on my family, and if necessary, I would kill my daughter to protect my people. That is an oath you will have to take if you become a Councilor someday."

"He's right, Stormy," Temperate said from behind him. He spun to look at his brother, who floated by the entrance to the hallway. "That's the whole reason I don't want to be Papa's heir. I have no problems giving my own life to protect the people. That's what I risk every day when I fly, but I don't think I can put a target on the backs of those I care about or kill them if they do something wrong. I'm not strong enough for that."

"Someone has to," Stormy replied.

His brother smiled at him and flashed pride tinged with sadness. "With those three words, little brother, you've shown me how incredible of a Senior Councilor you'll be, and it'll be my honor to vote for you when that time comes."

Stormy frowned, realizing exactly what his brother was saying, and then straightened with the weight of it before turning back to Councilor Chenzira, who was still staring at Temperate. "You believed you were protecting your people by attacking her?" he asked when the Councilor's attention focused back on him.

Jeran nodded. "And Marsee."

He flashed his confusion. "How would attacking her protect her?"

"I didn't want anyone to witness her out of control or being dragged off by the guards, assuming they didn't kill her outright. They'd already given her more chances than anyone I've ever seen. By testing her myself, I was able to protect her reputation and save her life."

He thought about what they were both saying and the fact that Jeran was being very honest with him about what he'd done but was still here trying to help his daughter. "I think I understand. My father says there are no right decisions. Sometimes, even when we're trying hard to do the right thing, people can still die or get hurt, like Little Flower told Councilor Tabor."

"Exactly. The unintended consequences can often be worse than what you tried to avoid. All you can do is your best to anticipate them and try to pick the pieces up after."

Stormy turned back to his brother. "I'm going up to the Trauma Center. Do you want to come with me?"

His brother briefly flashed amusement, which Stormy assumed was because he wasn't asking for permission. "Gladly, little brother. I need to visit Petra, too. I should have gone over a while ago."

"Good. I'll be right back."

He bolted to his room, grabbed one of the framed drawings off his wall, and quickly swam back. Neither said anything as he swam past them and out the door. They both followed after him, although he checked often to ensure that the Senior Councilor kept up with him. He wasn't making that mistake ever again.

He did his best to ignore the looks and flashes of animated conversation as the people they passed wondered what was happening and why he was in the lead. He wondered how long it would take for his people to recognize and acknowledge him as their next Senior. Like his father, he didn't think anyone would vote for someone his age, even if he was legally an adult and older than Little Flower, but people were talking about it. Word of his adulthood status had made the press before they'd even arrived home, but when asked, his father simply stated that he saw no reason to wait when his son was already acting like an adult and risking his life to save others.

He just prayed to the gods of the deep that he could actually live up to the oaths he knew he would now one day make.

CHAPTER 57

Stormy: Sounds of Silence

The Senior Healer led Stormy and and his brother to a section of the Trauma Center he'd never been to before. She stopped and grabbed a bottle from a refrigeration unit, then led them up several floors and down another hall.

When they swam up, they found Marsee curled tightly in a ball on a raised bed with her back to the door while Ellie sat in a chair working on her tablet. Honor Guards Aris and Tanner floated outside the room, but neither stopped them.

Unlike before, they couldn't enter the room as it was a dry room, and he examined it with curiosity. Outside of the Senior's rooms, this was the first dry room he'd ever seen in person, and it seemed stark and empty, not remotely fitting for their Translator. Outside of a pair of beds, the chair Ellie was sitting in, and a small table next to each bed, there wasn't much in the room. Marsee's cloak hung on a hook, and a small bouquet of flowers sat on one of the tables. He wondered why the room hadn't been decorated with all of the gifts that had been left behind, but he was glad he had brought the drawing with him because there wasn't even any artwork on the walls to look at. At least not on the walls that he could see.

The Senior Healer set the drink on the floor. "Marsee, I've brought your supper, and you have visitors."

"I said I didn't want to see anyone," Marsee mumbled back, not bothering to look to see who was there. "Go away."

The Senior Healer flashed 'good luck' at him and swam off.

"Not even your biggest fan?" Ellie asked as she stood to retrieve the drink.

Marsee sighed but lifted her head to peer over at him with little enthusiasm. "Hey, Stormy. Thank you for coming, but..."

"My brother's here, too," Stormy interrupted before she could ask him to leave again and floated over so his brother could fit in the doorway, too.

Marsee sighed again and rolled over so she could see them better, but curled back up in her ball, head resting on her paws and ignored the drink that Ellie tried to hand her. Ellie set it on the bed beside her and sat back down.

"How's your arm?" Marsee asked Temperate.

"Mostly better," his brother replied. "I'll probably be stuck in physical therapy for another week or two, but overall pretty good. You?"

"Weaker than a newborn kitten, but there's no pain. I can't decide if that's a blessing or a curse. I broke my hand again last night and didn't even notice." Marsee let out a depressed huff, and her ears drooped even further.

Stormy looked down at the scar on his arm. "I have never experienced anything as painful as what he did to me that day. I still hurt, and you were hurt far worse than I was. I think you should consider it a blessing. Plus, it is a rather cool superpower. I suppose it's a decent trade."

She flicked an ear back dismissively. "Superpower? How could this possibly be a superpower? I'm going to die before I ever grow up."

"Well, for one, if someone tried to hurt you again, you'd be able to kill them while they float there trying to figure out why you weren't screaming in pain." He did his best to act out the scene, pretending to shock the guard next to him, acting all confused when nothing happened. Then he pretended to knock himself out with a visible crackle of electricity, trying to find out if it still worked.

It was silly enough to make the others laugh, including the guards who went along with his play-acting. While Marsee didn't, when he opened his eyes again, some of the gloominess seemed to have faded from Marsee's expression. Her ears weren't quite as drooped anyway, and the very tip of her tail curled slightly. He flipped back around. "Please don't wait for us to eat. We've already had dinner."

She flicked an ear back dismissively. "Thank you, but I'm not hungry. I'll eat later."

"Obviously," Stormy said. "Papa said you can't tell when you're hungry either. If the healer says it's time for you to eat, you should eat."

Marsee glared at him. "Did they put you up to this?"

"Up to what?" he asked. "I finished another drawing for you." He grabbed the frame from where it had drifted and purposely angled it so she couldn't see the picture.

Marsee continued to glare, trying to tell if he was being serious or not, and apparently decided he was, or at least decided to be polite. "Thank you. Ellie, would you mind bringing it over?"

"Not a chance," Ellie said. "If you want to see it, you need to climb out of that bed and get it yourself."

"I'm too tired," Marsee complained.

"Well, you won't get any stronger if you won't even try," Ellie replied.

Marsee hissed at Ellie, and Ellie rolled her eyes. "My apologies for my incredibly rude *apprentice*. Poof. She's been like this all day."

Stormy flashed his happiness, which made them both frown. "My mother says that when I'm sick and get a case of the grumps, that it means I'm getting better," he quickly explained, not wanting them to think he was happy about Marsee being demoted. Although he was pretty sure Ellie was only joking.

Both Ellie and Marsee snorted.

"I don't know how accurate that is. She's been grumpy from the moment she woke," Ellie replied.

"I'm right here, you know," Marsee muttered, "and you can't demote me. I demoted you last. Poof."

"It has been very informative, at least," Ellie continued, not paying any attention to Marsee. "I had no idea the Hue-mans had so many swears. I've learned at least a dozen new ones today alone."

"They do?" Stormy asked. No adult had ever brought up swearing around him. "What's their favorite?"

Ellie made a sound, which he tried to reproduce.

Marsee rolled her eyes at Ellie. "It's an uh sound, not an ooh, and needs to be sharper at the end. Clip it off." She demonstrated, and they both tried again. "It's one of their words for mating," Marsee explained. "They use it in every grammatical context, too."

"One of their words?" Stormy asked. "They have more than one for mating?"

"Dozens. At least as many as Flyer has for 'mother,' if not more." She coughed, took a swallow of her drink, frowned, and set it back down. "Still made of Leviathan poop," she muttered.

"That bad?" he asked.

Marsee let off a litany that combined swears from all of the spoken languages, which had him blinking in surprise while the others all burst out laughing, even the guards.

"I'm not even sure that's physically possible," Honor Guard Tanner said beside him, lifting one of her tentacles to consider it.

"Might make for an interesting evening, though," Aris replied.

He frowned at the two guards, sure he had missed something in translation. They both grinned at his evident confusion and went back to guarding. Ellie snorted, and Marsee rolled her eyes at both guards, but her tail had curled some more.

"I'll explain it to you later," Temperate said.

"Why not now?" he asked.

Temperate flashed embarrassment, and the guards and Ellie howled with laughter, but they still didn't explain. However, the next half-hour turned into the most ridiculous language lesson he'd ever had, which made him laugh uncontrollably on several occasions and even had Marsee giggling a few times as she taught them new swears to describe her drink every time she took a sip.

Surprisingly, he found he could make most of the Hue-man sounds, which was an interesting discovery for all of them. It was a little harder for his brother, but only when trying to make the sounds in the higher pitches that the Hue-mans could hear. The hard part was how staccato their words were, but he was fairly confident he could figure that out with some practice.

"You know Stormy sounds a lot like them when they're singing," Marsee mused to Ellie. "Have you heard Henry sing?"

"No, I haven't," Ellie replied, "but I've heard he has a beautiful voice."

Marsee shifted and groaned her way over to her tablet. He noticed that her arms shook with the effort to shift on the bed, but a minute later, a beautiful, child-like voice filled the air, and Stormy flashed bright blue at the sound. The tone was so pure and perfect. Better than he could do, and it took everything he had not to harmonize with it.

"Oh, I need to have a conversation with Henry," Ellie said when the song was done. "That was beautiful. What did it mean?"

"The song is called 'The Sound of Silence,'" Marsee said and was quiet for a moment before she started singing in Saber. Marsee's voice was raspy, and her breath short from her injuries, but he knew he would never forget this moment. There was so much emotion in her voice and the words... Even the guards turned to listen. He glanced up and blinked in surprise. Honor Guard Aris's mask was completely dropped, and she seemed almost shaken, which made him wonder if he was translating something wrong.

When Marsee was done, they were all staring. "What?" she asked. "Did I do something wrong?"

"Of course not. Did you have that translated before?" Ellie asked.

"Not officially, but I've listened to it many times," Marsee replied. "It's one of my favorite Hue-man songs, and I sang it often to help pass the time in the cave. It seemed appropriate somehow. Why?"

"I have translators on my staff that don't even come close to translating them as well as you did, and you have a beautiful voice."

"Thanks," Marsee said, although she seemed almost upset by the compliment. He had a pretty good idea why. "It's the one musical talent I share with my siblings. I tried learning to play an instrument, but I couldn't stand the sound of my atrocious playing long enough to stick with it. I really wanted a drum set, but my parents refused. I believe they said something about waking the neighbors."

Ellie snorted. "In case you're wondering, Marsee's nearest neighbor was twenty leagues away."

"Twenty-five," Marsee said, "but who's counting."

"Why didn't you sing with your siblings?" Stormy asked.

Marsee groaned. "I tried once. I couldn't make myself walk out on the stage. I have horrible stage fright."

"Really? Me too," Stormy said. "I feel sick every time I have to give a book report in school, and the idea of giving a speech in front of the Council..." he let a shudder run across his skin. "I cover it up with humor in school, but somehow, I doubt the Council will appreciate it if I start cracking jokes in front of a meeting."

"I would," Ellie said. "Especially if it was during a requisition meeting. It's all I can do to stay awake during those."

His skin bubbled with amusement. "Do you have permission to share Henry's recording? I'd like to learn it."

"I do, but I thought your species didn't sing outside of mating," Marsee replied.

Temperate shook his head. "The other species' songs are quite popular, and we'll sing those if we can. Many believe it's inappropriate, but I have a feeling it has more to do with a lack of ability than impropriety. Flyer is especially beautiful to listen to but absolutely impossible for any of us to reproduce."

"There are quite a few Water Sprites who record in the other languages," Ellie said. "Most post under their mentor's accounts or are listed as musicians on their albums rather than vocalists to keep their identities hidden."

"I want to learn more, Hue-man, too, and this will help," Stormy said. "Will you send me a translation, too?"

Marsee nodded, and his tablet dinged a moment later. "I'll write up the translation later. Do you have the language guide? My sister recorded her spoken words there."

"I do, but I can't hear her the way I can this person or you," Stormy said.

"Ahh. We recently added a setting on the site so you can lower the frequency," Marsee said, "and Ammond has built new hearing aids so we can hear them better. I don't know if there are any designed for the other species yet."

"We're working on it," Ellie said.

He flashed his excitement and thanks and wondered how much a set would cost.

"I can send you a recording," Aris said, tapping the camera on her harness. "It won't be professional quality, but it should be good enough to help you learn the language."

"Thank you!" he replied and flashed his happiness.

Ellie grinned. "I'd like a copy too, Aris. Marsee, when you're feeling better, I want you and Henry to record that song professionally. Do you think you can translate and sing it in the other languages, too?"

"Me?!" Marsee squeaked. "My voice isn't good enough for that."

"Are you calling me a liar?" Ellie growled.

"No, but..." Marsee looked absolutely terrified, which surprised him.

Ellie threw a pillow at Marsee and hit her on the side of the head.

Marsee grabbed it, and he half expected her to throw it back, but she buried her head under the pillow instead.

Ellie chuckled and rolled her eyes at Marsee. "Keep it up, and I'll have you give a public performance, too. It'll help with that stage fright."

"I should have let him kill me," Marsee muttered from under the pillow. Moments later, Marsee's tablet dinged. She pulled her head out from under the pillow, looked at her tablet, and groaned again. "If you'll excuse me, I need to use the waste room. Aris?"

He shifted out of the way so that Aris could enter. She helped Marsee put on a strange harness and then used it to help her walk over to the waste room. He was pretty sure the guard was carrying most of her weight, but even still, Marsee's legs wobbled and nearly gave out on several occasions. He frowned, seeing just how weak his friend was, but managed to keep it off his skin.

Ellie made a face after Marsee entered the room. "She made it the whole way without stopping. That's a first," Ellie explained at is look of confusion.

When they returned, Marsee looked exhausted, but she had Aris help her over by the door so she could see the drawing. She lay on the floor, panting hard for several minutes, head resting on her paws, before recovering enough to lift her head or speak. "I'm half convinced the Senior Healer keeps turning the gravity up in this room," she muttered.

"I warned her," Ellie replied.

She pinned her ears and growled at her mentor but then turned back to him. "Let me see that drawing."

He slid it through the shield.

Marsee's tail stopped thwapping and spiraled as she examined it. "I love it!" she exclaimed, holding it up so Ellie could see.

"What is this creature?" Ellie asked after walking over to get a better look at it.

"It's a dolphin," Marsee replied. "I'm pretty sure it's sentient or pre-sentient at the very least, and I think that's why Rip wanted the Habitat gone, or one of the reasons. That's a picture of us interacting. It repeated everything I did and then started over. When I messed up, it corrected me. The sounds they make are even higher pitched than the Hue-mans."

Marsee had Ellie grab her tablet so she could show the recording she'd taken of them.

As Ellie watched, he noticed a motion down at the end of the hall and saw the Senior Healer swimming towards them again. "Ah, perfect," the Healer said when she arrived and saw Marsee right by the door. "Looks like you're ready for your therapy."

Marsee flicked her ears back in annoyance. "I have company."

"They can join you," the Healer said. "It's only one lap around the loop anyway, so it shouldn't take you that long."

"Actually, Stormy can," Temperate said. "I'd like to visit with Petra if she's accepting visitors."

The Senior Healer nodded. "We just woke her for her meal. A distraction would be good for her."

"Mind if I join you?" Ellie asked his brother. "I haven't been over to see her in a few while."

Marsee glared at them and growled at Ellie when Ellie handed her a mask, but she took it, put it on, and groaned as she crawled her way through the door with Aris's help.

Ellie and his brother left to visit with Petra while they took off in the other direction with the guards following them, but a moment later, there was a ding, and the Senior Healer excused herself and took off.

They didn't make it very far before Marsee stopped. "Did they make...this hall longer...while I slept?" she panted.

"Yup. Just for you," Aris replied.

"Come on, Marsee. You can do it!" Stormy said. "I'll race you."

"Please, you'd be able to make it forty-three times around before I could make it to the end of the hall."

"Stormy's fast," Aris said. "But I'm thinking only four or five unless he finds a shortcut I don't know of."

"No, he could easily do far more than that. Maybe fifteen?" Tanner replied.

Marsee rolled her eyes. "Gods, save me from guards and their bets. It wouldn't surprise me if you had a bet on who I clawed first."

"We did," Aris replied. "Sadly, I'm out ten credits. I thought for sure you'd claw your father days ago. Now, enough stalling."

Marsee snorted but kept swimming.

CHAPTER 58

Stormy: Beacon of Light

Stormy floated beside Marsee, keeping to her slow pace. "Marsee, may I ask you a personal question?"

She grunted. "I suppose it depends on what that question is."

"Do you trust your father not to hurt you?"

Marsee stopped and turned to face him. "Why do you ask?"

"I'm trying to understand why you didn't press charges."

"Your father told you what happened?"

He shook his head. "Not initially. Your father was at my house, and I overheard them talking about it."

She grunted again and kept swimming.

He figured she wasn't going to answer but kept pace with her and didn't press, deciding to try out his father's suggestion about remaining silent.

It wasn't long before she stopped again for another breather. "Yes and no," she wheezed and took several deep breaths. When she could breathe better, she continued. "I trust my father, but I also fully expect he will hurt me again. His loyalty is to his people before anyone and anything else, even me. I don't believe his intentions were to abuse me, even if it felt like abuse at the time. It's just not in his nature to hurt people. He has a gentle soul, and I can see how much it hurts him to know his actions have caused me harm. He won't even kill the crawlies that get into the compound. In case you're wondering. I've forgiven him. I forgave him a long time ago, but Rip did everything he could to make me attack my father, and it will take me time to untangle the web of lies Rip put in place."

"You really forgave him?"

"Yes. To do otherwise would mean Rip would win."

"I lost that bet, too," Aris said.

Marsee snorted at the guard and started swimming again.

He kept pace with her. Only now, he swam backwards so he could sign and flash encouragement. She stopped often, and he continued their prior conversation to distract her, asking her how to say more words in Hue-man. They were about three-quarters of the way around the loop when she stopped for a rest and closed her eyes. Moments later, she made a sound he'd never heard before, and the guards started chuckling.

"What's that sound?" he asked. "Is she alright?" It sounded like she was choking.

"She's snoring. She made it further this time, at least," Aris said as Tanner scooped Marsee up and carried her back to the room, where Aris took her and carried her inside, laying her gently on the bed. "She'll sleep for hours, I'm sure. Thank you very much for visiting."

"I'll come back tomorrow after school," Stormy replied and started to make his way out to find his brother but stopped and turned back around to face Aris. "Do you believe Marsee's still a risk because of her illness?"

"No," Aris replied. "She has shown far more control than anyone I have ever seen with her illness. Even if her instinct should recover, I don't believe that will change. Marsee has the heart of an Honor Guard. She would kill herself before she allowed herself to hurt anyone, or anyone that didn't deserve it anyway."

"You've had to deal with others with her illness?"

"That's the primary responsibility of my squad, but it's not just dealing with this illness, as you put it, but working with those in the early stages. It's why I joined the guard. I want to help others like the Guard helped me, and I'd much rather save people if I can."

Both he and Honor Guard Tanner flashed their surprise.

"You had psychosis?" Tanner asked. "I thought this illness was always fatal before sign language."

"It depends on how advanced the condition is and the cause. If we can get to people early enough, there's still a chance we can save them. My episode was due to a traumatic event. Once I knew I was safe, I recovered, which is common in those situations. The Guard helped me process my trauma and ensured I had full control."

"If I might ask, what happened, and did you forget who you were like Marsee did?"

Aris was quiet for a moment. "Someone hurt my litter-mate when we were cubs. My instinct took over to protect us, and I killed him before I even knew what I was doing. I was so scared that I ran and hid in a small cave near our home where no one could reach me. I never forgot who I was, but it took two days for the guards to track me down and convince me I was safe enough to crawl out of hiding."

"Have you been tested, like Marsee?"

"Like Marsee? No. Those who have issues and go to the Guard for help are never brought before the Council. We either learn control or don't survive our training. Historically, only about half of us ever did. The odds are much better now."

"Why isn't everyone with issues brought into the Guard for training?"

"They are now. Councilor Surellis changed the policy once he took office in an attempt to learn how effective sign language is."

"And before?"

She shrugged. "It was voluntary. We tried to save everyone we could, but not everyone accepted the help we offered, and the Council rarely sent anyone to us once they hunted or went non-verbal."

He frowned. "Why not?"

"Well, the first is a crime if not in a life or death situation, and as for the second, how can you work with someone if they can't understand you?"

He nodded the point. "So why would the Council attack them instead of just putting them down?"

Aris was silent for a long time before answering. "To give them a chance they wouldn't normally have. Before Marsee, no one with the advanced stages of this illness ever recovered. Thanks to her and Little Flower's bravery, people now are. Everything about Marsee's condition is unique, and while I loathe the test with every fiber of my being, it's our responsibility, and the Council's, to ensure she and others like her are safe. She could hurt a lot of people before we could stop her, just like I did, and the people of New Hope would have little defense if she was truly gone."

"Thank you for trusting me with your personal experiences and thoughts around this illness, Honor Guard. I promise to keep your confidence."

The guard nodded, and he made his way towards the entrance. Temperate met him halfway, and they returned home in silence as he thought about what Marsee and the guard had said.

Temperate picked up on his mood and asked him if he wanted to talk, but he shook his head and made his way up to his room. He sat at his desk and stared at the wall for a long time, lost in thought, and then started on another drawing for Marsee, seeing that she'd enjoyed the one he'd brought so much, as he continued to think. When he was done, he set it aside and sent a message to his father before climbing into his sleeping net to read before bed. It was late, and he was half asleep but still reading when his father returned home and knocked on his door.

"Come in," he replied.

His father swam in and shut the door. "You wanted to see me?"

"Yes. I have an answer for you regarding Councilor Chenzira," he replied.

His father's entire body language changed as he put on his mask and shifted from father to Senior Councilor. "Go on."

"I met with both Councilor Chenzira and the Translator today and spoke with the Honor Guard stationed outside her room. I have also reviewed their Charter along with everything I could find on this illness, and all of the evidence you sent me. I couldn't find anything regarding the test, and not much on the illness, but I did find a video of someone lost to it. The medical journal I read indicated that this illness has always been fatal once someone reaches the advanced stages, and once lost, the people become extremely violent. That was the same impression I got from Honor Guard Aris, who says she's had to deal with people lost to this illness before. It's not our place to determine what's moral and right for a species outside of what's in the Charter, but the Charter gives both the Senior Council and the Guard the right to execute anyone they deem a threat to the safety of the people. Both Jeran and Marcus could have executed her months ago when this illness first appeared, but they didn't, which tells me that they care about her, as letting her live meant putting their people at risk. As vulnerable as the Hue-mans are, they wouldn't have any defense against her. She's the first to survive the advanced stages, so it seems reasonable for them to be cautious, and if it was a choice between executing her outright and pushing her hard enough to confirm she had control, then doing so was the right thing to do. It allowed Jeran to ensure she was safe enough to live among a prey species and gave her a chance, just like you gave the Hue-mans. I believe Jeran was doing what he felt was right to protect his people and that he wouldn't have done so if he'd felt there was any other way, and so does Marsee. She says she's forgiven him and trusts him, and as such, I would drop the charges and allow him to maintain his position as long as his people want him in office."

"She trusts him not to hurt her?" his father asked.

He shook his head. "No. Not at all. She trusts him to honor his oath even if that means she gets hurt."

That surprised his father enough for it to slip through his mask, but he quickly recovered. "I find that hard to believe."

"Why?" Stormy asked. "If Marsee hadn't stopped Rip, and it was a choice between stopping Rip or saving me, what would you have done?"

His father sighed. "I would have broken my oath. I did break my oath. The moment I saw him shocking you, all that mattered was saving you. I went straight to you and left the others without even a second thought about their ability to control him in order to get you help."

"But you said Marsee had everything under control. If she hadn't, and Rip still posed a threat, I believe you would have reacted differently. If stopping him meant I died, I would forgive you."

His father looked away from him and didn't speak for a long time. Whatever he was thinking, he didn't say.

"What about what Marcus did to Jeran? Do you have any thoughts there?"

"I couldn't find anything about that method, but believe it's essentially the same as what Jeran did to Marsee. Plus, the Charter explicitly states that people can't be tried for actions that were not considered crimes at the time they performed them, and as Jeran consented to it before it happened, it wasn't a crime."

"Did he have any choice but to agree, though? It was that or death."

Stormy frowned and considered. "I believe intent and circumstances matter here. Jeran did hurt someone, and Marcus was trying to save his brother in the only way he knew how, not hurt him. Realistically, Samantha could have demanded those same actions as reparations, even if Jeran said she gave him a chance."

His father tilted his head, acknowledging that point but not necessarily agreeing with it. "And what of Marsee? Do you believe she's a risk?" his father finally asked.

"No. She never hurt Little Flower, and even with what Rip did to her, she didn't hurt me in the cave or hurt her father. Honor Guard Aris said that she believes Marsee has shown far more control than anyone with her illness and that even if her injuries did heal, she wouldn't be a threat because she has the heart of an honor guard. The Honor Guard also said that others are recovering thanks to sign language, so even if there is an issue in the future, there's a way to stop her from hurting anyone. We've both seen that. She responded to me in the cave when I used sign language but not Deep Current when he spoke in her language, and she was able to communicate with you in the canyon."

"Send me the information you've found."

He did. Expecting as much, he already had it queued up.

His father reviewed it and asked him dozens of questions about it, trying to poke holes in his reasoning. Eventually, he nodded. "I'm impressed at your thoroughness, and I will inform the rest of the Seniors of your verdict."

"My verdict?! Are you saying this wasn't just practice?"

"Technically, it will come from me, as I doubt the others will accept you yet, but yes, this is your verdict, as will any others I ask you about in the future. I expect you to take them all as seriously."

"But I thought you already made a decision?"

"It was not a unanimous decision, and I have not cast my vote yet. I still felt uncomfortable with many of the things Marsee discussed with me. Your reasoning is what I was looking for."

"Why did you leave such an important decision up to me?" he asked. "I'm not trained on this yet."

"Because you took it seriously. You recognized that you didn't have enough information to decide when I first asked you. You did your research and didn't let your own feelings for Marsee cloud your judgment. I personally expected you to find in Marsee's favor and against her father and uncle. Now, it's late, and you should get some sleep. You have school in the morning."

"Yes, Papa."

His father gave him a hug and then left.

He flopped in his sleeping net but didn't sleep, completely overwhelmed with the weight of the decision he'd made, his first real decision as Future Senior Councilor, and he couldn't think of a more monumental decision as it affected far more than just Marsee. If he was wrong, it would affect everyone. He went over and over his research, trying to poke holes in his own reasoning, even though he had done so for hours already. At first, he couldn't, but then he thought about the unintended consequences, and his brain spiraled as it followed different ideas, each one more horrific than the last.

Those thoughts kept him up until the early hours of the morning, shaking with the fear that he'd made the wrong decision until one thought finally broke through. Rip was a villain in the truest sense of the word, and he had targeted Jeran first.

He'd been trying to force Jeran to step down by targeting his children, but Rip hadn't stopped there. He'd done everything in his power to turn Marsee against her father and had almost been successful, but Marsee still trusted her father to lead with honor because he had. It was the whole reason Rip had targeted Jer first. The darkness hated the light, and Jeran was that light. As Marsee had said, he was a kind soul, and he hated the harm his decisions had caused his family, yet he'd still done it to protect his people.

Jeran had put the people first on many occasions. He hadn't hidden his partner's crime, even knowing she would likely die for it, in order to protect Little Flower and her people. He'd chosen to protect his council before himself by admitting to a crime he hadn't committed so that his planet wouldn't suffer from sanctions that would cripple them for decades. He'd accepted responsibility for the Hue-mans, knowing he might have to kill his partner and harm his daughter. And, when Rip had attacked, he hadn't stepped down before the ultimatum had passed. He'd protected the entire Consortium, knowing that his daughter was being tortured and likely wouldn't survive, and then he'd turned around and offered his own life to Marsee.

And she'd given it back to him. Not because she trusted him not to hurt her again, but because she trusted him to protect his people, even from her, even if that meant killing her in the future. Because she knew that if the light her father shined went out, then the darkness would win forever.

CHAPTER 59

Marsee: Unexpected Apology

Marsee collapsed in a sprawl on her bed, exhausted from her physical therapy. Tamarin had pushed her hard, and she'd finally made it around the loop without passing out, but it had taken everything she had, and the only reason she'd put any effort into it was because Stormy was visiting. He'd been showing up every afternoon, and she hadn't had the heart to turn him away. It wasn't lost on her that they were timing her physical therapy sessions for when he was there. He was flashing his happiness at her success, but it was all she could do to stay awake and not pass out on him like she had every other time.

"How on the dark side of the moons did you do that?" Tamarin mumbled.

"If you want to be a healer, your mask could use some work," Marsee muttered. "What did I tear this time?"

"Nothing. You broke a bone in your tail."

Marsee pulled her tail up to look at it. "Swimming? How is that even possible?"

"If I knew that, I wouldn't have asked?" Tamarin replied. "Regardless, it's an easy fix. The bone knitter will take care of it. I'll be right back."

"I'll be here," she replied. "I'm too tired to walk to the door."

Tamarin chuckled and left.

"I'll let you get some rest," Stormy flashed. "Until tomorrow?"

"Until tomorrow," she replied in Hue-man. Stormy repeated it and swam off.

She was asleep before Tamarin returned.

"Marsee, I'm going to fix your tail now," Tamarin said, waking her without touching her. The one thing she liked about Tamarin's care was that she always said what she was going to do first and made sure she was awake before touching her. She still reacted badly anytime anyone woke her by touching her.

Marsee grunted but didn't bother opening her eyes.

Tamarin gently shifted her tail and, a few moments later, shifted it back before walking out of the room.

She had nearly fallen asleep again when there was a commotion at her door. She opened her eyes with a groan to see Wind Rider and Petra floating outside with what looked like half a squad of their own guards. Avery and Tamarin were blocking the door, on high alert, with their paws on their stunners.

"I am not here to harm them, Honor Guards. You have my word," Wind Rider stated. "These guards are for my daughter's protection only."

"Let them in, Avery," Marsee ordered.

Avery let Wind Rider and Petra in but refused to allow the other guards inside.

Marsee shifted in her bed and adjusted the angle to help her sit up. She knew if she stayed lying down, she'd fall back to sleep, but she was too tired to sit up on her own.

Ellie climbed off her own bed and gave Petra a careful hug before returning to the seat.

Petra's wings were bound to her side, but she otherwise looked good. Far better than the last time Marsee had seen her.

Marsee nodded to the two and wondered if this was an official visit or another attempt to cheer her up.

To her surprise, Wind Rider shifted into the Flyer's equivalent of a bow, one knee bent, head down, curled away, and wings up and back. It was a very vulnerable position for their species, as she wouldn't be able to see an attack coming or react quickly to defend herself from that position. "I owe you everything, Marsee. After everything I have done to you, you somehow trusted me and my daughter, exonerated us both, and then put your very life at risk to find her when all the evidence pointed to us. I honestly don't know what to say except thank you and that I'm sorry for the harm I caused you in the past."

Marsee sighed and shifted her attention to Petra, who, to her surprise, also looked down and away, although she was too injured to perform a full bow. Marsee's own feelings were mixed. Petra was her friend, had shared her passion for flying, and had helped her earn her pilot's license. She'd been one of the few people she could talk to about the challenges of being the child of a Senior Councilor. Petra had been tortured and held for longer than she had, and she was one of the few she could potentially talk to about what had happened, but she hadn't been able to. She'd tried a few times to swim over to Petra's room but hadn't even been able to make herself leave the room.

She was relieved that Petra hadn't been involved and would make a full recovery, but right now, all Marsee felt towards her friend was intense jealousy. Petra would lay tens of thousands of eggs in her lifetime, so many that she only kept the ones she wanted while others raised the rest of her children for her. She would soon recover and be able to move on with her life, while Marsee would struggle for the rest of her pitifully short existence, unable to do the things she wanted to do for fear she would break, and she would never have a single cub of her own. She'd been prepared to die to kill Rip Current, but living with her trauma was turning out to be so much harder.

She shoved her feelings of jealousy down hard and tried to be as diplomatic, even though she didn't want to talk to either of them right now. "I didn't trust you, Wind Rider. I trusted your daughter. The messages didn't fit with the Petra I knew, the one who didn't want the life being forced upon her. The Petra I knew loved Ellie for giving her the freedom she desired, however short that was, and would never have hurt either of us, but I would not have been able to exonerate her or you if Rip hadn't messed up. I would never have even asked Petra whether she wanted to be a Nest Mother if my sister hadn't expressed her own concerns about how you might feel being forced into that life. Rip, though... He couldn't see how anyone would not desire that power and luxury, and apparently, neither can the males of your species if Leaf and Willow are examples. I think maybe it's time you came clean with your population about the low birth rate and start to figure out why, and maybe start listening to your daughter about what she really wants in life and figure out how to give her that instead of what you think she wants."

Petra lifted her head to look at her in astonishment and perhaps a touch of embarrassment at being called out.

Wind Rider sat up and glanced at her daughter with a heavy sigh. "We've had dozens of scientific teams studying the problem for centuries but haven't found anything. I even wear medical trackers now so the healers can study me and try to figure out why I'm so prolific, yet others are not. As far as we can tell, we're just not producing as many eggs during our mating flights. Assuming Petra is as prolific as I am, her loss would have been devastating for our species."

Marsee snorted at the look Petra gave her before hiding it.

"Did you ever think maybe there isn't a physical cause?" Marsee asked.

Wind Rider frowned at her. "What do you mean?"

"Councilor, is what you're doing to Petra and the other females of your species any different than what my sister believed was being done to her and hers at the Agency? If you strip away everything else, the pampering, rank, and authority, aren't you still forcing her to mate and give birth four times a year whether she wants to or not? If I were in that situation and wanted out, I'd cut my mating flights as short as possible to meet the 'requirement.' You might see it as a duty to your people, but not everyone does. Your daughter certainly doesn't."

Wind Rider whipped her head around to stare at her daughter. "Is this true?"

Petra sighed and shrugged but winced as the motion jarred her injured wings. "I've honestly never thought of it quite like Marsee's implying, but yeah, I guess so. I don't want to go home and be a Nest Mother. I don't want to be on the Council. I just said that so I could leave. I want to be a pilot and explore the universe. I love flying for Ellie, even though I barely fit on her ship anymore, because we get to go everywhere, but if I really had a choice, I'd be on one of the exploratory teams. I want to experience setting foot on a new planet for the very first time and see creatures and planets no one has ever seen before, but I knew the Council would never approve of that. And well, when I do clutch, I want to do it for me, with someone I care about, not whoever manages to catch me, and I want to raise *my* clutch like the other species get to do, not give them away to strangers."

Wind Rider was quiet for a long time, considering Petra's words before turning back to face Marsee. "You have given me a lot to think about and look into, and if you're right, then it seems I owe you even more. If there is *anything* I can give you to make up for the harm I have caused you in the past, and in gratitude for saving my daughter, and it's mine to give, I do so freely."

It was Marsee's turn to sigh. "Like I told Clear Seas. I understand why you made the decisions you did at the Trial, even if I don't agree with them. Your apology and support now is good enough for me. Besides, unless you know how to fix my injuries, there's nothing you could give me that I want."

Wind Rider tilted her head in acknowledgment. "I don't know how to fix your injuries, but perhaps I can give you something you want."

Marsee raised a brow. "I seriously doubt that, but go on."

"Your father tells me that you will never be able to have cubs of your own because of your injuries. You saved my daughter. I would gladly give you one of my clutch in return."

Marsee pinned her ears in surprise. "I thought that it wasn't allowed for off-worlders to adopt your children."

Wind Rider shook her head. "It's not so much that it's not allowed but that our eggs won't hatch for off-worlders, but I would gladly take the time necessary to hatch one for you if you wanted one."

Marsee blinked hard and considered. A huge part of her wanted to accept, but it wouldn't be *her* cub, and besides, she had no idea how to raise a weyrling. Learning how to care for Hope had been challenging enough, and Hope thankfully couldn't fly. She got into enough trouble on those little legs of hers as it was. There was no way she could teach a Flyer how to fly. She let out a heavy sigh and shook her head. "Thank you. That offer means more than you could know, but it would be unfair for the child for me to accept. According to the healers, I probably won't live long enough to raise one of your children to adulthood anyway, and I'm going to be dealing with a lot of medical complications from my injuries that would make it difficult for me to care for them properly."

Wind Rider nodded her understanding. "If you change your mind or think of something else, the offer still stands," she said and walked out.

Petra watched her mother leave and turned back to her. She opened her mouth to say something but noticed everyone else still there, sighed instead, and followed after her mother.

Marsee snorted and rolled over to face away from Ellie, afraid Ellie would want to discuss the meeting. Thankfully, Ellie seemed to understand. She was soon asleep but woke only a few hours later, screaming from yet another night terror.

The guards didn't even bother looking in this time.

CHAPTER 60

Marsee: Enough

"Well done, Marsee. That's a new record," the Senior Healer said after her morning pickle torture as she crawled through the door and sprawled onto her bed with Tamarin's assistance, too exhausted to swap out her mask for the one they were making her wear to protect her eyes.

"Some record. I used to be able to run for leagues, and now I can barely make it two laps around the ward," she muttered.

"With your injuries, I'm impressed you can even do that," the Healer replied as she examined her monitors from the hallway.

Marsee grunted. It was about all the energy she had, and she was nearly asleep when the healer spoke again.

"It looks like that bone in your hand didn't hold. It's shifted out of place, so we'll need to operate."

She picked up her paw and made a fist, not feeling any pain.

"Don't do that," Tamarin admonished, grabbing her paw to stop her. "You'll risk further damage."

Marsee grunted and lay back down with a heavy sigh. "Whatever." She was honestly too tired and depressed to care.

She opened her eyes again a moment later when she felt the bed move under her and realized Tamarin was pushing her out. *At least they aren't making me swim to the operating room,* she thought bitterly.

They met Ellie halfway down the hall. "What's going on?"

"Looks like I broke my hand again," Marsee replied, not bothering to move.

"How did you manage to do that?" Ellie asked in surprise.

Marsee rolled her eyes. "I clawed someone for asking stupid questions."

The guards behind her chuckled.

"Her injury from the other day didn't heal right," the Healer replied. "We half expected it. It'll be a quick repair, and we should be done in half an hour or so."

The healer floated her into an operating room and hit a switch. The solid table in the middle of the room shifted and adjusted until it was a chair with added support for her arm. "Do you want to be sedated?"

"It doesn't matter. If you wait five minutes, I'll be asleep anyway," Marsee replied with a yawn.

The Healer chuckled. "Well, if you can wait until you transfer over to the chair, I would appreciate it. I wouldn't want to drop you or anything."

She grunted but climbed off the bed and flopped into the chair. Even in the water with Tamarin's help, that effort was exhausting. Tamarin strapped her paw down on the support so it couldn't move. They didn't sedate her but did press something into her arm. Even though she couldn't feel pain, her arm went all tingly and then numb.

It was a quick repair, minor in the grand scheme of everything else they'd repaired. Within a few minutes, the bone was replaced with the one they'd already printed, and the incision repaired and covered in bandage putty, but it highlighted how the rest of her life was going to be, one unfelt injury after another. After the surgery, she shifted back onto her bed and curled up on her side, staring at the bandage putty on the back of her paw. She was so lost in thought that she didn't even realize she'd been transferred back to her room until Tamarin switched out her mask and left.

The days had begun to run together as her life changed to one of exhausting routine. Physically, she was improving, if slowly, but mentally she was falling apart. Even Ellie, for all she'd been through, didn't understand. Ellie had been unconscious through most of her trauma and recovery, and aside from her own therapy, mostly for her paws, had fully recovered. Even her fur was regrowing. Marsee looked closely at her still bare arm for any sign of regrowth, found none, and sighed.

Even though she couldn't feel pain, her body felt weird, almost disconnected, as if it wasn't her own body anymore. It didn't move or feel right, which was only heightened by the unusual feeling of everything touching her skin. She couldn't stand the rough feeling of the bedding and had already ordered replacements, but even with the softest fabric they had available, something about it still felt wrong.

The worst part was the hollowness left by her missing instinct. It intensified every day and added to the disconnected feeling. It had grown to the point where nothing else could touch it. It swallowed up every other emotion she had. Everyone tried to cheer her up, crack jokes, and pick on each other, but it didn't matter. It was so strong that she even began to wish she could still feel pain, just so she could feel something different. Even knowing that her sister was on her way wasn't enough anymore, and she didn't have the energy or will to fight it.

The only time she even tried was for Stormy. He came by every afternoon after school, accompanied by Temperate. While Temperate had been medically cleared to return to duty, he had taken a leave of absence until after the trial, as they still had no idea who had tampered with his shuttle. She welcomed those visits even as she fell deeper into her depression. Stormy was full of youthful abandon, and he was the only one who could make her laugh. He brought her drawings every day, each one more ridiculous than the last, most focusing on the characters in her books, and they covered her walls now. When she couldn't sleep, she stared at them. Occasionally, she thought about finishing her translation of the Night Flyer, but she couldn't bring herself to even bother.

Temperate also came by regularly on his own, usually in the mornings after dropping Stormy off at school, and she'd been able to open up a little to him. He was struggling with his own trauma and finding it harder each day to fly, but they mostly stuck to safe topics, their favorite books, and his curiosity about the Hue-mans. He never pushed, though, and would often just float outside her room, keeping her company if that was all she was up to, but it was no longer enough to keep her depression at bay. Nothing was.

Marsee continued to stare at her paw until the annoyance of her mask broke through. Wearing it non-stop was just as aggravating as everything else that touched her skin, and it was starting to feel like it was suffocating her. In a fit of rage and anguish at her ruined life, she unhooked the stupid thing and threw it across the room with a growl at the pointlessness of it all.

Ellie looked up from her tablet and sighed. "Marsee, you need to wear the mask."

"You wear it," Marsee spat at her. "I'm done."

"Marsee..." Ellie started.

"I'm done. I've had it. All of it. What's the point? I'm just going to die anyway. I'm going to be spending the rest of my pitifully short life stuck in the Trauma Center, going from one broken bone to the next until I tear myself apart. Why even bother trying to get stronger? It's not like I'll ever be able to do anything ever again anyway if I can break a bone doing nothing more strenuous than swimming."

Ellie set her tablet down and walked over to comfort her, sitting on the edge of the bed. "Marsee, that's not true. Your mother and Ammond will find a way to fix you. Look what they did with your sister. You need to give them time."

"My sister had a brain to fix. There's nothing left of mine *to* fix! It's gone, Ellie, just like my life. I'm stuck like this, and I can't take the hollowness of it anymore, and I'm done trying."

She reached up with her uninjured paw, claws out, to rip her own throat out. *At least it doesn't hurt,* Marsee thought bitterly as she dug the claws in.

"Marsee! NO!" Ellie screamed and grabbed her paw, trying to stop her. "Guards! Help!"

Marsee growled and fought back, trying not to hurt her mentor, but she couldn't get her paw free enough to finish the deed, so she took her injured hand and tried to do the same on the other side.

Avery and Tamarin came running in. Avery grabbed her arm and tried to pin her down.

She pulled her back legs in and clawed at him, catching his side and digging in deep. "No! Let me go! I don't want to live like this anymore!" She continued to claw with her back feet, hoping they'd end her for even daring to attack them.

Tamarin grabbed for her legs, but she writhed and kicked hard at the other guard.

Avery reached for his stunner. She shifted her legs from Tamarin to try to kick it out of his hand.

"No!" Tamarin yelled. "Her heart can't take the stunner."

In the same heartbeat, Avery dropped the stunner, grabbed her, and she found herself flying through the air, flipped over, and her arms yanked hard behind her.

"Go find a sedative," Avery growled, and Tamarin bolted out of the room.

"Why won't you let me die?" Marsee wailed as she tried to struggle free. Even though she couldn't feel pain, Avery had her pinned down with her arms held tightly behind her back and his weight pressing her to the bed. "I can't take this emptiness anymore."

"It won't always be like this, I promise," Avery said. "You need to give yourself time."

"What would you know?" she hissed at him. She managed to twist her hand around enough to dig her claws into Avery's paw. He hissed, ears back, and let go just enough to let her yank her hand free. She brought it back up to her neck, but Ellie grabbed it before she could get close enough. "LET ME GO!" she growled.

"No, Marsee. I'm not going to do that," Ellie said.

She continued to fight and struggle until Tamarin returned and sedated her.

CHAPTER 61

Ellie: One Last Chance

Ellie paced in Marsee's room, waiting for word from the healers. It hurt to walk, but that helped contain her worry and the itch of her regrowing fur. She spun as she heard someone step through the static shield.

"I came as soon as I got your message," Jer said. "What happened? Did she tear something again?"

"No. She tried to kill herself. She would have succeeded if I hadn't been sitting next to her, but she still managed to claw her throat before I could stop her and fought hard enough to injure both guards until Tamarin could sedate her. I haven't had an update yet."

Jer rubbed both paws through his fur on the back of his neck and grabbed his scruff, twisting hard. "She's been getting worse every day. I don't know what to do, Ellie."

"Everything we can until Little Flower and Hope get here," Ellie said. "She spiraled from the moment they jumped. We need to find some good news for her, anything."

"A million credits isn't good enough?" Jer snorted.

"She doesn't care about any of that. That's not a reason to live. Credits mean nothing if you can't even swim down the hallway without getting hurt. She had surgery on her paw again. I'm guessing that's what set it off."

It took another hour before they brought Marsee back in. The Senior Healer floated outside in the hallway as Tamarin hooked Marsee's bed back up. "She managed not to do any permanent damage, but she came very close to nicking a major artery. I've trimmed and rounded her claws down as far as possible, but that won't stop her from trying again. Someone needs to be awake and watching her at all times."

Jer nodded. "Avery, I want one of your guards stationed inside the room."

"Yes, sir," Avery replied and swam inside, taking up guard by the door. Four parallel strips of bandage putty ran down his side, and a patch covered the back of his paw, but if it bothered him, he didn't show it.

"How badly were you hurt?" Jer asked.

"Nothing that won't heal in a day or two," Avery replied.

"Thank you for not..." Jer started, but Avery raised his paw and stopped him.

"It was expected. We all knew it was only a matter of days before she tried something. Sir, regardless of our orders, you know we can't stop her again. She has a terminal illness. It's her right. She needs to talk to someone, and she needs to find a reason to live."

Jer turned back to look at Marsee's sleeping body. He sighed, plastered on his Senior Councilor's mask, and nodded to Tamarin. "Wake her."

Tamarin did as ordered.

Marsee groaned as the sedative wore off, then realized she was still alive and growled at Jer before trying to rip her throat out again.

Jer grabbed her arms, pinning them to the bed before she could hurt herself, and growled back. "Marsee Bet Chenzira, don't you even think about it. If you kill yourself, he wins, and everything you went through will be for nothing."

"I don't care! I can't live like this anymore!"

"Yes, you can, and you will. You're stronger than this."

"No, I'm not. My instinct was. Without it, I'm nothing but a hollow shell. I didn't defeat him. My instinct did." She hissed and struggled to escape his grasp, but he held her firmly in place.

"Your instinct is only as good as you are," Jer replied. "It can only access what's there to begin with. It amplifies it. It was your desire to save Stormy and the others, and without it, they would all be dead. You need to keep fighting to stay alive. Little Flower and Hope will be here in a few days, and if you go and kill yourself, it'll kill your sister. You're her rock. She's been miserable since you left, and she needs you to help her with her own trauma. If you can't stay alive for yourself, stay alive for her. Stay alive for Hope. Help your sister raise her cubs. She can't do it alone as much as she'd like to think she can. She needs you."

Marsee slumped and stopped struggling. "You don't *understand*, Papa. You don't know what it's like. I can't stand it anymore. I couldn't even swim down the hall without breaking my hand, and I never even knew it! I'm not going to be able to help them. I'm going to be spending the rest of my life in the Trauma Center until I rip myself apart. I've got more credit than anyone in the universe, and I can't do a moons' forsaken thing to fix it, but the worst part is the emptiness inside of me where my instinct used to be. I feel like a brittle hollow shell that will shatter with the slightest touch. The mask I have to wear to keep from going blind feels like it's choking me, and every Saber I see looks at me with fear. Even you. What's the point of living a life like this? Why did you even bother waking me up? You promised you wouldn't let me end up like Little Flower. You promised!"

Jer closed his eyes and took a deep breath before opening them. Then, he cautiously let go of Marsee and sat down on the bed next to her. "Yes, I did, and I'm sorry. I couldn't keep that promise. Perhaps it was selfish of me, but I had to give you a chance. You *are* getting better. In many ways, you're so much better than your sister. Your other injuries are healing. You can walk and talk. You're still you. The important parts are still there. I know it's hard. You're going through what no one has ever been through, and no, I don't understand what you're experiencing, but you're still alive, and that alone is a miracle."

He reached over and caressed the side of her face. "Kitten, I don't fear you. I fear for you. I'm just as worried about your future as you are. *Please* give us time to find a way to fix this. Look what your mother and Ammond have been able to do in just six months with your sister. They'll find a way to fix you, too, but you have to give them time. Please? Six months? At least give them the same amount of time they've had with Little Flower before you give up."

"And if they can't?" Marsee spat. "What then? Am I to live my life broken and useless, going from one trauma bed to another?"

"No. I won't do that to you," Jer said softly. "If your mother has not made any progress after six months, and you still feel this way, I, Jeran Frederick Chenzira, promise to end your suffering, but *only* if you promise to give us that six months and try to get better."

Marsee rolled over to face away from him, curling up into a tiny ball, and then snorted when she saw her rounded and stubby claws. "I'm surprised you didn't declaw me."

"I worked too hard to replace those claws just to take them out again," the Senior Healer said from the entryway.

Marsee snorted again but lay there for a long time thinking, and they all waited in silence. "I'm not wearing that stupid mask."

"Is it too tight?" Ellie asked as she scratched at another itch. " I could get you a bigger one, or would you prefer something like what the Hue-mans wear?"

"I can't stand the feeling around my neck," Marsee muttered. "The shield makes my skin crawl, and the collar makes me feel like he still has a tentacle wrapped around me."

"I'll find you something different," Ellie promised. "And I'll keep trying until we find something comfortable for you to wear."

"Do you promise?" Jer asked.

Marsee sighed but nodded. "Just don't tell Mama."

Jer snorted. "I'm stupid, but not *that* stupid. Now give me your oath."

Marsee let out another sigh but rolled over to look at him. "I, Marsee Bet Chenzira, promise not to take my life for six months but not a minute more."

He frowned at the wording but nodded. "You'd better keep that promise because if you don't, I will haunt you in the afterlife."

Marsee rolled her eyes and rolled over again. "Go away. I'm tired."

Jer sighed, reached over, hugged Marsee, even though she didn't respond, and then stood and walked out without another word.

When Ellie was sure Marsee was asleep, she followed to find something to use as an alternative to the mask but stopped when she saw the Senior Healer. "I'm not sure if my injuries are healing or if it's my fur growing back, but I'm really itchy. Can you give me anything for that?"

Hyacinth nodded and motioned for her to follow. When they were in an examination room, the Senior Healer motioned her over to the bed. "Let's see what's going on with you first."

Ellie swam over, hopped onto the bed she could barely see, and waited. "What is it?" Ellie asked when the Healer didn't respond for several minutes.

"I'm not sure your itchiness is from your injuries or your regrowing fur," the Healer said eventually.

"Then what is it?" Ellie asked. "An allergic reaction?"

The healer didn't respond right away and then turned to face her with a look of regret. "I'm sorry. I should have caught this before. Your implant is missing. You're not in heat yet, but you should have it replaced quickly."

Ellie's emotions bounced between joy and terror, settling on joy. "Rip took it?"

The Senior Healer nodded. "I'm not seeing any evidence of your implant from the scans we took when you were brought it. It must have been removed."

"Why would he do that? That doesn't make any sense. Did he...?" She swallowed hard.

"I honestly don't know, any more than I do with Marsee. Nothing triggered on the scans," Hyacinth replied. "Your records indicate this would be your third heat?"

Ellie shrugged. "I'm not really sure if my first heat counts, but Healers wouldn't let me try again, even though I wanted to. Wait, Marsee? The hormone changes you were talking about? Did he use my implant on Marsee?"

"No. I've already checked for signs of that. There's a bio-marker released if a heat is triggered using an implant. I'm honestly not sure if she is going into heat or if this is just another complication from her injuries, but she is showing sensitivity to touch. Her reaction to her mask and the bedding could be the early signs of rubbing or nothing more than discomfort from her lack of fur and other injuries."

"Could she be reacting to me somehow?"

"Unlikely. You're not releasing pheromones yet. Regardless, I don't have a replacement implant. You need to leave today. It would probably be best if you flew to Digger. They have..."

"I'm not leaving Marsee," Ellie said, shaking her head. "Not like she is now."

"You have a one-in-a-thousand chance of surviving a third heat," the healer countered. If you don't leave now, you'll die."

Ellie shook her head. "I don't care. I'll take that chance. How long do I have before I'm in heat?"

"I honestly don't know. A week at most. It varies per person. Please, go home and get your implant replaced."

"I'm not leaving Marsee, not like this," Ellie repeated, this time with force.

"Then I'll put in an emergency order to have one delivered. Hopefully, it'll arrive in time. Everything is delayed right now. We might be able to treat it with replacement hormones, but what I have isn't quite an exact match."

"No," Ellie replied, shaking her head. "I understand the risks, but I've wanted cubs since I was younger than Marsee. I'm taking this chance. Don't tell anyone, especially not Marsee. If she found out..."

The Senior Healer pursed her lips. "I don't recommend it, but it's your choice. I want you to come see me every day so we can monitor the situation."

Ellie nodded. "I'm assuming you can't do anything for the itch?"

The Healer's skin bubbled with humor. "Not if you want that cub."

Her tail spiraled at the very word. *Cub! Could something so wonderful come from this nightmare?*

She thanked the healer and swam off towards the Guild. It was the first time she'd left the Trauma Center since she'd been beaten, and she was honestly a little surprised at how scared she felt. *He's dead,* she reminded herself.

"Are you alright, Senior Guild Master?" the honor guard at the entrance asked.

"I'll manage," she replied but didn't swim off.

"Would you like help or an escort?" the guard asked.

She really did, but she squared her shoulders and shook her head. She refused to allow Rip Current, or whoever else was involved, to make her live the rest of her life in fear. "No, I'm good. Thank you," she replied and directed her drone towards the Guild. Wincing from the pain of trying to hold onto the drone, she stopped and reconfigured it before moving off again. Her paws were better, but they still weren't fully healed.

As she approached the main building, a bright flash of blue lit up the window of Agate's office. Ellie chuckled and wasn't the least bit surprised when Agate met her at the entrance and crushed her in a hug. She was honestly surprised Agate hadn't been by to visit yet, but they'd been chatting practically non-stop since she woke.

"How's Marsee?" Agate asked.

Ellie sighed and tilted her head towards the door.

Agate flashed her worry but followed Ellie back to her office.

She hit the privacy shield on her desk before slumping down in her seat, tired from that brief swim, and looked up into Agate's worried face. "Marsee's not doing well. I'm afraid we're going to lose her."

Agate flashed her grief, sadness, and anger. "That trench-dwelling mud-sucker. If he wasn't already dead, I'd kill him myself for what he did. What's going on? Were her new organs rejected?"

"No, she's recovering there, slowly, but there's a lot more going on than was released to the press. She...experienced a significant brain injury as well. She can't feel pain anymore, and because of that, it's quite likely she won't survive her growth spurt, if she even lives that long. She's spiraling into a depression and tried to take her life this morning. You can't tell anyone."

Agate slumped with her own worry. "That poor child. After everything she's been through..."

"That's why I'm here. I need something other than a static shield to protect Marsee's eyes. She says the collar is choking her. I want one of everything we've got that could remotely protect her eyes."

Agate nodded. "That's easy enough. I'll have someone bring that up right away." She quickly put in the order and turned her attention back to Ellie. "How are you doing?"

Ellie shrugged. "I suppose that depends on who you ask."

"I'm asking you," Agate replied with humor.

"Well, physically, I'm recovering. Mentally, I'm having just as many night terrors as Marsee is. My paws still ache something fierce, and I'm not going to win any races any time soon, but...I just had some unexpected news, which could either be really good or really bad."

"Oh?" Agate asked, flashing both curiosity, concern, and then confusion when she realized that Ellie wasn't upset.

"You can't tell anyone, especially Marsee. Promise me," Ellie demanded.

"Of course. What's wrong?"

"My implant is missing," Ellie replied. "I don't know why, but he took it out."

"Your implant...bottomless depths! What are you still doing here?" Agate asked, flashing her worry again. "We don't have that kind of tech here."

"Taking care of Marsee. I need to be sure she's okay before I leave. The Senior Healer is monitoring the situation. She said I should be good for a week. I'm not leaving until Little Flower and Hope arrive, at a minimum, but I'm hoping to make it through the trial portion of the Full Council meeting at least. I'll need you to take over after. I'll figure out some excuse."

"Of course," Agate replied and then frowned. "Have you had any thoughts about what we're going to do about Marsee's guild balance?"

"A few, but she's not in any sort of condition to talk about it right now. If I even tried to bring it up now, I'm pretty sure she'd buy a moon to spite me." Ellie sighed and shook her head. "Everything I've worked for over the past century, destroyed in a matter of days by one madman and a giant oversight."

Agate snorted, "Well, it's not like we've ever had anything like this happen before."

Ellie rolled her eyes and looked up as a Sprite swam up and knocked on her door. She turned off the privacy screen and motioned the Sprite in.

"I have your order for you, ma'am," the Sprite said, swimming over and setting it on Ellie's desk.

"Thank you, Iruki," Ellie replied.

"It's good to see you again. Please tell the Translator I'm thinking of her and hope she recovers quickly."

Ellie nodded, and Iruki swam out.

"I should be getting back," Ellie said but didn't climb out of her net.

Agate looked at her with compassion. "How are you doing, really?"

"I'm absolutely terrified," she admitted. "I'm thankful I don't remember any of what happened to me, but if it weren't for the guards outside of Marsee's door, I don't think I could sleep at night. The moment I close my eyes, it's like he's trying to crawl his way back into my room. I jump with every noise, and when I finally fall asleep, half the time, I'm woken up by Marsee screaming from another one of her night terrors. I don't know who to trust anymore, and it took everything I had to leave the Trauma Center a few minutes ago."

She let out another heavy sigh. "Agate, I thought I was doing something good with the Guild, bringing everyone together, stopping the infighting and bickering, but it very nearly got me and my protege killed. Two of my pilots are dead, and the third is lucky she survived. People I've known for decades wanted me dead because I didn't take them out to dinner. How is that even remotely a reason to justify what was done to us? How many more people feel the same way?" She swallowed hard, struggling to contain the rage and fear she felt.

Agate swam over and hugged her. "You can't justify the actions of a madman. They wanted power without doing any of the work to earn it and had no sense of responsibility or honor. I can't guarantee that there aren't others, but I suppose it would be easy enough to figure out who wants to harm you, at least among my people anyway. Just look at who didn't send Marsee a gift."

Ellie snorted. "I can't exactly have the guards arrest anyone who didn't donate hours."

"No, but it might tell you if there's an area you should focus on," Agate replied. "Maybe they could use a dinner or two, or maybe something is wrong that needs to be fixed."

She tilted her head, nodding the point. "I suppose. Granted, the Guild may be gone by next week anyway. Who knows what the Council will do when they find out how big her balance is now? Plus, Marsee's tried to quit at least a dozen times, and if she dies, everything goes to Hope. I can't exactly negotiate with a mewling cub." She let out a heavy sigh. "Well, I should get back to Marsee before she wakes up. Thank you, Agate."

Agate hugged her again, and after another heavy sigh, Ellie grabbed her packages and swam quickly back to the Trauma Center. She didn't relax until she was safely inside. When she arrived back at the room, Marsee was still sleeping, so Ellie took the opportunity to nap, now safely protected by three honor guards, but for the first time since she'd woken in the Trauma Center, she drifted off to thoughts of her cub, not the horror of the past week and dreamed of a little black kitten that looked just like her.

CHAPTER 62

Jer: Torn and Shredded

Jer could barely keep himself in check as he left the Trauma Center, wondering if Marsee would honor her oath when he hadn't. Would she try again the moment their backs were turned? Even if she did honor it, had he only postponed the inevitable, and would he be able to follow through or break yet another promise to her? Avery was right. With a terminal illness, it was her right to take her own life rather than suffer, yet he'd stripped her of that right because he wasn't strong enough to let her go. He'd once thought that killing her would be the worst decision he would ever have to make, but he realized now that forcing her to live, to endure something no one had ever been through, might very well be worse.

Rather than returning to his meeting, he punched his drone in the other direction and, before long, found himself outside of Rip's secondary residence. A pair of Saber guards now floated outside the home, keeping anyone from entering, but they didn't challenge him as he entered. He'd been here many times as Rip's guest over the years and had never once suspected anything. While it was still furnished with quality artwork, it was far more in keeping with a standard councilor's home: comfortable rather than ostentatious, with signs of wear, and designed for entertaining and collaborating with other delegates.

He swam into Rip's office and clenched his fist at the sight of the large painting behind Rip's desk. It commemorated the day Rip was sworn into office, with Clear Seas giving him his oath in front of the Council and a ghost-like image of Rip's father floating behind him, with one hand on Rip's shoulder.

Fury rose inside him, fueled by his instinct, and with a snarl as primal as the ones Marsee had directed at him that day in the canyon, he slashed at the painting again and again until his claws were raw and bloody from being worn down by the stone wall behind it. He didn't stop until an arm grabbed him, and he spun with a snarl, paw raised to defend himself, only to find Marcus looking at him with worry and concern.

"What happened?"

He couldn't say it and just started crying.

Marcus pulled him in for a hug and grabbed him gently by the scruff until he managed to pull himself together. "What's wrong, little brother?"

"She tried to kill herself," he whimpered.

"Marsee?" his brother asked for clarification.

"Yeah." He took a deep breath and pulled away, only then seeing the others.

Clear Seas' skin was a solid dark blue and black with mourning and grief. Wind Rider ducked her head under her wing, in her species expression of grief. Apakna sighed. Only Sammianna seemed unaffected, but that wasn't surprising.

"She's alive," he quickly clarified. Waves of relief crossed Clear Seas' skin, and Wind Rider came out from under her wing. "Or she was when I left the Trauma Center. Ellie and the guards stopped her, but not before she hurt herself badly enough to require surgery, and she injured both Avery and Tamarin in the process."

"They treated her?" Sammie asked, briefly showing her surprise.

"They better have," Clear Seas replied with some force. "I gave both the healers and the guards orders to if she tried. We've all been expecting it."

"But she has a terminal illness," Sammie said with a slight frown. "It's her right."

"And a brain injury and severe trauma that could be hampering her decision-making ability," Clear Seas replied. "She told me that her emotions were all over the place and that she was worried she'd hurt herself or others unintentionally. I took that as grounds to state she did not want to hurt herself, regardless of what else she might say or do later."

Sammie nodded her understanding.

"I suggested she talk to the healers, and she did," Clear Seas continued. "Hyacinth believes her mood swings to be a result of her injury, as there's some minor damage in the part of her brain that regulates emotions, and she's not seeing anything else but a slight hormonal imbalance to account for it. We decided not to tell Marsee for fear it would make things worse. She's having a hard enough time dealing with the issues she has now, much less the trauma she's endured. Myra's bringing something to try and help regulate it, as Marsee's refused the one medication we have that's safe for her. I don't blame her as it's a very strong narcotic, and she reacted poorly to it before."

"The narcotic, I understand. She had a horrible case of rainbow paws when I was there." Wind Rider said, waiving her paw and making a silly face that made everyone but Sammie chuckle. "But she seemed perfectly stable when I spoke to her the other day."

"Cognitively, I would agree," Clear Seas replied. "But she won't talk to a healer about what happened to her either. I suggested she try writing it down, and she has been adding it to her journal. I've been monitoring it, hoping to catch something before it happened and possibly find out what else happened to her. She's opened up a little to Temperate but still won't talk about what happened to her in the cave."

Jer growled, frustrated that he hadn't been informed, that he hadn't thought to do the same, and overwhelmed by the entire situation. "They treated her. However, she came very close to succeeding. Even though she begged me to let her go, I forced her to promise to give us six months to try and find a solution. She gave her oath, but I don't know if she'll honor it. She didn't calm down until I mentioned her sister and Hope. Personally, I'm hoping she'll improve once they arrive."

"What triggered it?" Wind Rider asked.

"Ellie said she re-broke her paw right before it happened, but Marsee told me she couldn't stand the hollowness anymore. I don't even know what that means. How do you fix or treat a symptom that has never existed before?"

He picked up a small object off the desk and flung it at the wall with everything he had.

To his surprise, Sammianna picked up a small table and did the same. "You know, that's surprisingly therapeutic."

Clear Seas's skin went from the worry he'd been flashing to bubbles of surprised laughter. "That's my favorite form of therapy. I have a cave in my home where I go to smash rocks. I fully intend to have this home demolished. I say we start now. If nothing else, there may be other hidden rooms or compartments."

The others agreed and began demolishing the office. Marcus, however, dragged him into the waste room to treat his bloody claws with a first aid kit they found there.

"What are you all doing here?" he asked his brother quietly as he worked.

"Clear Seas went back to his office to grab a file and saw you leave the Trauma Center. He came and got me, and the others insisted on coming, too."

He grunted and shifted a claw so Marcus could treat it.

"You did a number on these. You might want to get these looked at by a healer. Try to save your claws for the future. You might need them."

He grunted again.

After Marcus finished treating him and checked to ensure he was still in control of his instinct, his brother left him alone in the waste room to join in the mayhem and give him time to recover.

How do I keep her alive until the others arrive? he prayed. *I don't know how to help her.*

Then find someone who does, that other voice said.

But who? he wondered.

An idea came to him. It was a long shot, but the only one he had. He made several calls, sent out half a dozen messages to make arrangements, and prayed that they would agree to come and that they would get here in time. Arrangements made, he returned to the others and explained his plan. They agreed it was worth a try, and all sent messages to back his.

Marsee had saved the Consortium. It was their turn to try and save her.

Please let this work, he prayed.

The next several hours were spent destroying everything. The guards had apparently checked once to see what was going on, snorted, and returned to their posts before Jer had left the waste room. By the time he was too exhausted to lift a claw, almost nothing was left of the interior. The others were all equally exhausted and waiting in the destroyed remains of Rip Current's living room when he swam out.

"Well, I'm honestly glad we didn't find anything else. We have enough to dig through as it is," Clear Seas stated.

"I'll admit, I am feeling better." Wind Rider stated. "Exhausted, but better."

"Agreed," he replied. "And lucky for us, we have his other home to destroy later. I have a feeling we're going to need it."

"There has never been a more true statement ever uttered by this Council," Sammianna said.

They all turned to look at her and burst out laughing.

"What?" Sammie asked, squinting at them as she tilted her head. "What did I say that was so funny?"

"I'll explain it later," Wind Rider replied.

"Come on," Marcus said, "playtime is over. It's time we get back to our job."

"You always were such a spoilsport, Marcus," Wind Rider said, throwing a piece of broken furniture at him. It didn't even make it halfway to him.

Marcus chucked. "Gods forbid I spoil your fun, Wind Rider. I learned that lesson a long time ago."

Wind Rider grinned. "Well, that's what you get for calling me a smelly fish."

"You did what?" Apakna asked.

Marcus sighed. "It was an honest mistake. I was still learning Flyer at the time."

"Oh, it was no mistake," Wind Rider stated and gave a wicked grin.

"I swear I had no intentions of insulting you," he replied.

"Oh, I know that. You were purposely misinformed. It's the oldest prank in the book, and you fell for it."

The look on Marcus's face was priceless. "All this time? You've let me believe I messed up all this time? It's been over a hundred and fifty years."

Wind Rider laughed. "And I enjoyed every second of it."

Marcus shook his head. "Flyers."

"Well, someone has to keep pedantic, fur-brained, walking encyclopedias like you in line," she replied.

Marcus snorted, and Clear Seas flashed his humor, but everyone else looked at Wind Rider in surprise.

"I stand corrected," Sammianna said. "*That* is the truest statement ever made."

CHAPTER 63

Stormy: A Friend in Need

Stormy slumped in his seat at school and twirled his stylus, bored out of his mind as his teacher rambled on with a review for the upcoming science exam later that week. He already knew everything she was discussing and really wanted to get back to his council studies. They were far more interesting and useful for his future career, but his teacher would know if he didn't have his textbook open on his tablet. He was considering testing out of primary school entirely but didn't want to give up time with his classmates, even if he didn't feel particularly close with any of them. He knew building those relationships was just as important as anything else he learned in his training.

Yawning, he flipped the page when directed and stretched his tentacles, trying to wake up.

Suddenly, his tablet dinged loudly with an urgent message from his father.

The entire class and his teacher turned to look at him, as notifications were supposed to be turned off, but he wasn't paying any attention to them. It was all he could do to keep the horror off his skin as he read.

"Is there a problem, Stormy?" his teacher asked.

He looked up and saw flashes of worry from his classmates and realized he hadn't been able to keep the emotion off his skin as well as he thought he had. He took a deep breath and calmed his skin. "There is nothing you need to worry about, but I need to go," he replied and swam out, not waiting or asking for permission.

Temperate had been escorting him to and from school, but Stormy wasn't waiting until school was over. Not today. His friend needed him now. He wasn't worried about an escort as he knew guards were watching the school, and as expected, a pair of guards swam up behind him as he bolted out of the school and took off in the direction of the Trauma Center. Thankfully, they didn't question him because he wasn't taking the time to stop and explain.

A few minutes later, he arrived and swam in, bolting his way up to Marsee's ward.

"I'm sorry, sir, but Marsee's not accepting visitors today," one of the guards at the entrance to her ward said, stopping him from entering.

He swam up until he was eye-to-eye with the guard and glared. "I am not a visitor. I am Staffer Stormy Seas, future Senior Councilor of the Water World, here on official business, and you will let me pass."

The guard flashed his apology but still didn't move. "I am sorry, sir, but the Translator expressly stated she didn't want to see you today."

"I am well aware of what happened today. I have faced down Leviathans, Council Guards, and Councilors to save my friend. If you think I'm going to let you stop me today, you're sadly mistaken. Either move, or I'll have you removed." He knew he was pushing all sorts of boundaries and authority he probably didn't have, but he didn't care.

To his surprise, they moved.

Tamarin and a guard he hadn't met before floated outside Marsee's room. He was surprised not to see Avery there. Tamarin raised a paw to stop him as he approached, but he just glared her down and kept swimming.

"Marsee's not accepting visitors today," Tamarin signed.

"She will see me," he signed back, "whether she wants to or not."

Tamarin seemed amused but dropped her paw and let him approach.

He found Marsee curled up in a tight ball facing away from him, but he could see the bandage putty that wrapped around the side of her neck. Avery stood guard inside, and Ellie was curled up, sleeping on her own bed. Avery glanced over at him but didn't order him to leave. He wouldn't have obeyed those orders anyway.

"Marsee, you have a visitor," Avery said.

Ellie opened her eyes but didn't move.

"Go away," Marsee muttered.

"I not go," Stormy said in his best Hue-man as he couldn't speak well enough in Saber yet to say those words yet.

Marsee sighed. "Please go away, Stormy. I don't want to talk."

"Then you hear." He glanced at Ellie and signed. "Will you translate for me?"

Ellie nodded her agreement and sat up.

He took a deep breath as he scrambled to figure out what to say without giving away everything he knew from reading her journal. "Marsee, I know you probably think I'm nothing more than a child in love with your stories, but I'm not, or at least not for the reason you think. I've read everything you've ever translated because I wanted to get to know you better. I've wanted to meet you for years, long before the Hue-mans arrived or your father and uncle became Seniors. Your father has been to my house many times and spoke of you often and your interest in crafting, artwork, and books. I hoped with every Full Council meeting that, you would come with your father so I could meet you. I've thought about sending you a message dozens of times, but I thought you might think it was weird to get a message from someone you didn't know. I know you know what it's like to be the child of a Councilor and how isolating it can be. People only want to be my friend because I'll be Senior Councilor someday. It's even worse now. I don't know who I can trust anymore. Friends have backed away and won't talk to me now, and I don't know if that's because they're afraid they'll get hurt if they're associated with me or if their parents were involved with Rip. If you kill yourself, I won't have anyone but my brother left where I can just be me. I need you. I need your friendship. I need someone I can trust in my life. Please, if you can't live for yourself, live for me. Help me be the best Senior Councilor I can be so I can fight people like Rip and make a better world for people like you."

He waited to see if she would respond, and it took several minutes of patience on his part before she spoke.

"You don't understand," Marsee finally said, although she didn't roll over.

"Then help me to understand. I promise everything you tell me will remain private."

Several more minutes passed before she rolled over to face him but then saw Avery, Ellie, and the guards outside. "I really don't want to talk about it."

"Because of everyone else?" he asked.

She nodded.

"Guards, Elle, turn around so our conversation is private," he ordered.

Ellie immediately rolled over, but Avery frowned at him. Then walked over to the door. "Your stunner, please."

Stormy immediately handed it over, and once he did, Avery ordered the guards to turn away and then did the same himself, leaving them guarded but effectively private.

He waited.

"I don't want to live my life broken and useless, outcast from the people I love," she finally signed. "Everything that made my life worth living has been stripped away. All I've ever wanted is to feel like I belonged, to have my own family full of a half dozen cubs and a partner who will adore me as much as I adore them, but I'm never having children or a family of my own. None of my people will partner with someone who has psychosis. They're already turning away from me. The Saber Healers here all smelled of fear when they came to treat me, and so do my father and uncle when they visit, and I'm terrified my uncle will order my execution the moment I return home. Ellie says she'll move here with me, but I don't want her to give up her life for me, and I can't ask Little Flower to move here and take her and Hope away from her people. Maybe I could make a new life here, but if your people find out about my illness, they'll turn away from me, too. But it's more than that. I feel...I feel like I'm already gone. I'm hollow and disconnected from my own body. Everything feels, smells, sounds, and tastes wrong. The world is darker, colors are missing, and so am I. For a long time, it felt like my instinct was trying to push me out of my body, but then we found a truce where we could live together. I felt centered for the first time in my life. Now my body feels too big and empty and lonely. It's all I feel now: hollow and alone. Don't get me wrong. I value your friendship. It's filled the gaping hole some, and I look forward to your visits and have stared at your drawings for hours, but it's not enough. The hole just keeps growing. For so much of my life, I was alone. I can't go back to that. I can't go back to the stares and whispers, especially when they're right. I'm not a superhero or even a sidekick. I'm a monster that everyone's afraid will turn feral and hurt them."

"You are not a monster. You're my friend, and I don't fear you, and neither will the others when they see you're still you."

She looked down and sighed. "You don't know my people."

His heart broke for his friend and the loneliness that he understood, even if it was from a different cause. He didn't know what else to say or how to help her, but then a thought came to him. He swam down to the floor and carefully crawled through the shield. The first breath of air struck him like a knife, making him gasp, and the weight of gravity was so strong that it flattened him instantly to the floor, but he crawled towards her with everything he had.

"Stormy, No!" Marsee called out.

Everyone turned towards him, and Avery scooped him up before he could stop the guard and shoved him back through the shield.

"No!" he demanded. "Let me go to her or bring me to her! My friend needs a hug more than I need air."

"No!" Marsee yelled and started to shift to the edge of her bed. "Stay. I'll come to you. I don't want you hurting yourself for me."

"Can't you see that I'm already hurting?" he signed and let his pain ripple on his skin. "This is nothing. I have risked my life for you twice, and I will do it again and again and again until you realize that I care about you and that others care about you and would be devastated if you die. Your people might fear you, but my whole planet loves you, and that won't ever change, not if they're worth their scales. You're my best and only friend, and I'm not letting you throw your life away when I fought so hard to save it. You owe me! You owe Deep Current for giving his life to save yours. You owe us all to live. Don't give up. Please! Fight for yourself as hard as you fought for me."

"I don't know how!" she cried. "That part of me is dead. My instinct saved you, not me. There's no fight left in me. It died with my instinct. What's left is nothing but a hollow and broken shell."

"You can lie to yourself, but you can't lie to me. You made the decision to risk everything to save my life, not your instinct. You. It may be gone, but you're not."

When she looked away and appeared to be giving up, he swam through the shield, not bothering to swim down to the bottom. He yelped with surprise as he fell and cried out with the sharp pain of impact, but Avery didn't stop him this time.

When Marsee saw that, she scrambled off her bed and fell without the guards there to help her.

He pulled himself forward, gasping, fighting through the pain of each breath, and he wondered briefly how Deep Current had managed so long.

Marsee forced herself to her feet with a groan and frantically grabbed for the mask that was lying on her table but knocked the table and everything on it over, sending the mask rolling away.

He smiled to himself to see how frantic she was and pulled himself forward again and winced at both the pain he was feeling and the slurping sound his body made on the floor. *What a strange sound,* he thought.

She scrambled for the mask, not paying any attention to her injuries or the effort it took, caught it, slapped it on, and then bolted for him, scooping him up carefully and hopping awkwardly to the door on three feet before diving through.

He grinned up at her. "I knew you had some fight left in you," he signed and then wrapped his arms around her in a hug.

She hugged him back briefly but then pulled away. "Are you alright? Tamarin, check him over."

"I'm fine," he replied, stopping the guard, then looked up at his friend. "Don't for a second think that counts for the debt you owe me, but thank you. I had no idea gravity was so strong."

She snorted at him and then pulled him in for another hug. "Thank you for being my friend, even if I've been a lousy one in return."

"Always," he replied. It's also good to see that you've improved enough to be able to walk on your own again. Now, since you're out here, let's get those laps in."

She rolled her eyes at him but started swimming.

They did their laps in silence. He could tell she needed time to think, but he stayed close, not that he was going to win any races today. His entire body hurt.

When they returned to the room, she stopped outside the door and turned to face him. "I gave my father an oath that I would try for six months. I don't know if I'll be able to honor that oath, but I'll try."

He nodded. "That's good enough for me, for now. But I want you to call me at any time of the day or night if you need another hug or the shoulder of a friend to cry on."

She nodded and gave him another hug before turning and walking into the room. She was gasping by the time she made it to her bed and climbed in, but she managed on her own for the first time since he'd been visiting.

He waited with her until she fell asleep.

"Thank you," Ellie signed from her bed.

He nodded, took another long look at Marsee, sighed, praying he had done enough, and swam off to find the Senior Healer, wincing with every motion. He didn't want Marsee or anyone else to know how badly he'd been hurt. He knew he wasn't big enough to spend any time out of the water safely. The impact on the floor had hurt more than he'd expected, and his lungs still burned with every breath. He knew he should have gone for treatment immediately, but Marsee had been more important. He found the Senior Healer in her office.

She looked up and flashed her surprise to see him. "Stormy! You're here early. What can I do for you?"

He passed out before he could even answer.

When he woke, Temperate was floating in the room beside him. "The guards told me what you did. It was stupid, but I'm proud of you, little brother."

Stormy sat up, feeling significantly better than he had before. "There was nothing stupid about it. My friend needed a hug. Don't you dare tell Marsee or our parents that I got hurt."

"Yes, sir," his brother replied with a grin. "Come on. The Healer says you're fully recovered, but you might be short of breath for a few days. Thankfully, Marsee got you out of there in time, and her room was only at half gravity, or you would have been flatter than a ribbon fish."

He swam off the bed and followed his brother out. "That was only half gravity? Bottomless depths. How do they endure it?"

"I have no idea, little brother. I've had to experience it a few times as part of my training, and it's excruciating. What I can't understand is how Rip endured it so long just to hurt Ellie. Even if he turned the gravity down to its lowest setting in the suite, it would have still been uncomfortable and painful to breathe."

That thought had never occurred to him, and he swam out of the Trauma Center in silence and didn't say anything until they were halfway home. "Hatred has no limits, but thankfully, neither does love."

His brother turned to look at him. "You're pretty wise for one so young. Stupid, but wise."

"Careful big brother, or this stupid person might forget how to control their shocks..."

Temperate's skin bubbled with laughter. "I'm not worried. You're far too honorable for that."

"Honorable perhaps, but still stupid," he replied, then zapped his brother just hard enough to make him jump, and then took off like a Leviathan was chasing him, skin bubbling bright blue with laughter as his brother chased after.

CHAPTER 64

Jer: Old Enemies

Jer, along with the others, laughed the entire way back to the Council Building, both at Marcus's expense and the shocked expressions of the people they passed, but their humor evaporated as they entered the conference room and faced the pile of evidence that still remained untouched. No one reached for another folder. What they'd found already was bad enough. Eventually, his brother swam over to grab another box.

"Well, I suppose I can save everyone the trouble of going through any of my Council," Wind Rider said with a sigh. "I'm pretty sure we're all guilty of a crime, and it's quite likely why Petra and I were targeted, along with all of the hatcheries."

That stopped Marcus in his tracks, and he spun around. "What do you mean?"

Wind Rider was silent for a long time, long enough for his brother to return to the table and sit down. Wind Rider took a deep breath before continuing. "As I mentioned, I stopped in to visit Marsee the other day. I wanted to thank her for saving Petra, and as part of that conversation, Marsee made an observation. As you know, we highly compensate our Nest Mothers to the point that they're the most well-paid citizens on our planet, and the status that comes with being a Nest Mother often translates into a council position. My mother taught me it was my duty to our people, and I never even questioned it. I've always felt proud about being able to produce clutches as large as I have and very lucky to have produced the number of daughters I have over the years. My concern for the wellbeing of my clutch is why I run for office, but I've just learned not everyone feels that way, my youngest daughter included."

Marcus frowned. "I'm not sure I understand. How is that a crime?"

"I'm not sure if any of you are aware of it, but our population has been steadily decreasing. It's not enough to be noticeable from one year to the next, but Petra's loss would have had a fairly devastating impact on our people. We've found no reason to explain it, but at this point, we've reached a critical stage. We rarely have more than a few Nest Mothers per district now. A few are in the single digits."

Sammie frowned. "I had noticed a decline in your last census report but wasn't aware there was a trend. Your population has been fairly stable for centuries."

Wind Rider nodded. "According to my research, about five thousand years ago, we were hit with an illness that devastated our population before we found a cure. We came very close to losing all of our females, as it seemed to hit them the worst. At the time, there was a unanimous vote to require one clutch per year to save the species. Nest Mothers were heavily compensated based on the number of eggs they donated to the community, but with this vote, it changed from being a voluntary contribution to required, although compensation nearly doubled for that required clutch. It worked, and over the next few hundred years, our population stabilized, but the requirement never went away. About a thousand years ago or so, we realized that the average number of eggs we were producing in a clutch was decreasing, but none of our scientists could figure out why, so the number of required clutches went up to the current expectation of four a year. Every vote was unanimous as it was seen as the only way to save the species. However, to Marsee's point, this has likely had the reverse effect, with people choosing to cut their mating flights short to get out of the requirement as quickly as possible."

"That seems like an entirely reasonable hypothesis," Sammianna said.

"Agreed. Additionally, due to the exceptionally low numbers, our females, except for those on the Council, are rarely allowed off the planet due to the risk and are placed in the district where they're most needed. We do our best to honor their preferences, but we can't always do so. I thought my youngest daughter shared my sense of duty, which in a way she does, as she would have willingly done her duty to save our species, but Petra has absolutely no desire to be a Nest Mother, share her clutch, or mate with whoever is able to catch her during a mating flight. She had to go before our council to get permission to leave Flyer as Ellie's pilot, and the only reason it was allowed was because she'd stated a desire to be on the Council, and it was seen as a good learning opportunity for her. As Marsee stated, if we take away all of the rank and privileges that come with being a Nest Mother, we're essentially forcing our females to mate. The males of our species are also apparently unhappy that they rarely manage to earn a place on the Council. That was what Leaf and Willow told Petra as one of the reasons why they kidnapped her. They just saw the public image Petra put forward in order to get away, not believing her when she said she had absolutely no desire to live that life."

The room was silent for several moments as they all considered the implications.

"When was the last time this policy was voted on?" Sammie asked.

"About four hundred years ago," Wind Rider replied.

"And no one has brought this up since?" Sammie continued.

"Not that I'm aware of. Certainly not since I've been on the Council. I wasn't even aware that was what my daughter felt until the other day," Wind Rider replied.

"Well then, I don't see much of a problem as long as you fix the issue now that you're aware of it," Sammie said. "None of your council voted on it, and if no one has expressed concern, then how were you to know that your efforts to save your species were doing the opposite of what you'd intended."

"I agree," Marcus replied. "These should be fairly easy changes to make. Switch your compensation model back to the number of eggs donated to the community. Honor the nest mother's choice in where they're located. Just because a community needs a set number of eggs doesn't mean she needs to live there, and as far as your mating flights go, that has to be a personal choice. If someone wants an open flight, just like we do with our mating practice, then that should be their choice. If they don't, then that should be honored too. What's the reasoning for not having it that way?"

"The belief is that only the fittest would be successful, but in reality, it's usually the female that allows our choice of male to catch us. They would rarely catch up otherwise. We can fly much higher, faster, and further than most males. Only once have I been outflown, and that was a glorious flight and one of my best clutches. There is prestige for the males in succeeding, and in reality, that can often translate into a Council position, too. I've personally made an effort not to choose the same person twice, as there's also the concern about not having enough genetic diversity. As for location, most want to live near their offspring, even if they aren't raising them."

"Well, that's easy enough to resolve then. Pay them more if it's an open flight," Marcus replied. "and give the female the ability to vet whoever's is in the flight to begin with. As for not allowing them off-planet or preventing them from participating in their chosen craft, that needs to stop immediately. Unless they're on a watch, the Council should have no say in that."

"And if no one chooses to clutch?" Wind Rider asked.

"Then you raise the compensation until they do," Marcus replied. "If nothing else, try it for a year or two and re-evaluate."

Wind Rider nodded and reopened the folder she'd been working on, and they all followed her lead.

Sighing, Jer grabbed a new folder as he'd finished his last one just before Ellie had messaged him about Marsee, but it wasn't long before he was growling again.

"What did you find this time?" his brother asked wearily.

Rather than answering, he held up a picture of Myra's parents.

"Whose folder is that?" Marcus asked with ears-back surprise.

"Former Councilor Brian Casey of the South District," Jer replied.

"The councilor before you?" Clear Seas asked.

Jer nodded.

"Casey died several years ago," Marcus said. "And he retired long before Rip took office. I wonder why Rip even bothered keeping a record on him?"

"He was one of my Junior Advocates for about a year after he stepped down and then moved out to Hidden Springs, where he semi-retired until he died," Jer said. "I considered him a mentor and relied heavily on him that first year. We spoke regularly after. I never had a sense that he had anything against me or noticed anything odd about him. The district office was well organized when I took over."

"Maybe Rip was just looking into anyone associated with you?" Apakna suggested.

"Yeah, but why would Myra's parents be in this folder?" he asked.

"What else is in there?" Wind Rider asked.

"Not much, actually. Pictures of his family, like everyone else." He continued to flip through, stopped with a frown, then flipped to the next page and started shaking when he realized what he was seeing.

"What did you find?" Marcus asked.

He swallowed hard.

"Jer! Are you alright?"

He shook his head. "No," he whispered. "Gods no."

Marcus bolted to his side and spun his seat. "What's going on?"

"It'll be too much. This'll put Myra over the edge, for sure."

"What will?"

"It wasn't an accident."

Marcus grabbed the folder from him and flipped through it. "The accident report shows a faulty repair in the guidance system."

"The same as Temperate's?" Clear Seas asked, flashing his worry.

"Looks that way, but I'm not a tech," Marcus said as he continued flipping through the pages.

"His nephew was the tech who worked on it," Jer said.

"So, they were murdered?" Apakna asked.

"There's nothing here to say it was," Marcus said. "It was probably an accident. Brian's nephew was only a Journeyman, based on this report. Although, it looks like Brian may have covered it up to protect his nephew. Brandon's mentor took responsibility and a demotion, but there's a fairly substantial payoff by Brian. I can't see why they'd have gone after her parents. They were both farmers and well-liked."

"If it was intentional, they weren't going after them," Jer said. "They were going after me. It was my shuttle. I left it for servicing while I was in the hospital with Myra and Marsee. Her parents refused to stay and wanted to return home before the storm hit. Their shuttle was old and didn't have an autopilot. I told them to borrow mine. If they'd taken their own, they might still be alive."

"And you, Myra, and Marsee might be dead," Marcus stated.

"You didn't know about this before?" Wind Rider asked.

"No. I never even looked for a report. The storm was one of the worst we had in over a millennia, nearly as bad as the one we had this past year. Brian must have picked up the ticket when it came in."

"Clear, I know that look," Apakna said. "What's going through that slippery head of yours."

Clear Seas scowled at Apakna for the insult but then scratched at an ear fin. They all turned to look at him, and he sighed. "I managed to get Marsee to tell me a little of what Rip told her in the cave, but I also promised I wouldn't say where I heard it from. That was before Marsee forgave Jer."

"You know something about this?" Jer asked.

"I haven't had a chance to look into it, and I figured Rip was just messing with Marsee. He tried to convince her that you lost control, killed Myra's parents, and used the storm to cover it up."

"And you didn't think that was important enough to look into?" Apakna snapped. "What in the bottomless crevasses is going on with this group? It's one scandal after another. Sammie, do you have a scandal you'd like to share with us, too?"

Sammie frowned and shook her head. "I don't think so. I did fail a math test when I was a pup, but that's public record."

Apakna pinched her nose and shook her head. "Sarcasm, Sammie. That was Sarcasm."

"You failed a math test?" Wind Rider asked, flicking her wings back in surprise. "You? I find that hard to believe."

"I didn't fail it on purpose. I was very sick. My teacher was so worried she called for a trauma ship. It was a good thing she did. I had a bad case of the Dorrian Flu. It was one of the scariest moments of my childhood. I completely forgot how to math."

"You have an illness that makes you forget how to do math? Was it cancer?" Marcus asked. "A brain tumor?"

"Did someone named Dorrian hit you over the head?" Wind Rider added.

Jer snorted, and Clear Seas' skin bubbled with laughter. Apakna just rolled her eyes.

"Thankfully, no, on all accounts. Flu is a bit of a misnomer. It's actually a parasitic infection that, if left untreated, can cause serious problems, including our ability to process numbers. The infection was caught early and fairly easily treated, but I can't even begin to explain how terrifying it was to think I might end up so horribly disabled. I completely understand how difficult it must be for Marsee right now, but we're getting off-topic. Clear, why didn't you prioritize this?"

"Because I was with Jer that day," Clear Seas replied. "I arrived on Saber a few days early to spend time with him before the Full Council meeting. I was there when they left. Jer never left my side until the healers came to inform him of the accident. You can't fake that kind of grief. Plus, it was twenty years ago and fairly well publicized, so it wasn't surprising that Rip would have known about it. He was already on the Council by then, and if I remember correctly, Tabor mentioned something about it at the start of the meeting."

"She did," Marcus said.

"I hated to even attend that meeting, but my people were suffering from a three-year drought before the storm hit. We didn't have the resources to clean up from the storm on top of it. I missed Marsee's name day, and I wasn't there when Myra brought our other daughter and her parents home and buried them, either." He sighed and shook his head at how much he'd hurt his family over the years. He'd been hurting Marsee since her birth.

"Well, that's one less person we'll have to execute, I suppose," Marcus replied. "What's his nephew doing now?"

Jer shrugged and pulled up the information, and his ears pinned flat. He turned to look at Clear Seas and slid his tablet over.

Clear Seas took it, although it was obvious he wanted nothing to do with it. Within moments, he was bright red with anger.

"I think we just found proof of who tampered with Temperate's shuttle," Jer told the others. "Casey's nephew is one of the techs who last worked on it."

Marcus frowned. "I thought we cleared all the techs. They all had spotless records."

"We did," Clear Seas growled and held up the tablet to show an image of Casey's nephew. "He's changed his name and modified his record, but that spot pattern is very distinctive. Sammie, what are the odds of two people with the same skill set and associated with the same tampering having the same facial spot pattern?"

"Well, if you take into account the number of people that..." Sammie began.

"Sarcasm," they all said.

"Oh," Sammie replied and sighed, looking honestly disappointed. "Are you sure you don't want me to calculate it? It would be good evidence."

The others all snorted, and Apakna pinched her nose again, muttering something he couldn't quite hear, but apparently Sammie did.

"I swear I'm fully recovered," Sammie replied with a frown. "You see? This is why it would be a scandal. I should have never told you. I'm going to have to double-check my math from now on, aren't I?"

"She's just teasing," Jer said. "Trust me. Your math skills are far better than all of ours combined. I'm guessing they probably still were even when you were sick."

"Oh no. For three whole days, I couldn't even count to ten. It was awful."

"I can't imagine any disease or illness that would be more horrifying for a Digger," Wind Rider said.

Sammie squinted at Wind Rider. "Sarcasm?"

"No. Not at all," Wind Rider replied, although the tips of her wings were curled up in humor.

Sammie nodded, taking Wind Rider for her word. "You have no idea. I barely came out of my shell the entire time."

Clear Seas handed Jer his tablet back and then grabbed his own, placing a call. "Stinger, I want Master Tech Brandon Hollow brought in for questioning immediately. Inform me when he's been secured."

There was a flash of light, which Jer assumed was a 'yes, sir,' and then Clear Seas hung up.

Jer quickly read through the rest of the file on Casey and then started digging through the other boxes to see if Brandon had a file. "We really should organize these better," Jer muttered, but a few minutes later, he found a file under Brandon's original name and flipped through it. "There's not much in here, just pictures of his family and the same report that was in Brian's file."

"Blackmail then?" Apakna asked.

"It's possible," Jer replied and swam back over with the folder to show the others and then began digging into Brandon's record. "His record appears clean, high ratings from both the Guild and Ship's Guild, but if Brian or Rip was hiding other issues, they wouldn't show up."

"What about extended family?" Apakna asked.

Twenty minutes later, Jer was still digging through Brandon's family when they had a call from Stinger stating that Brandon was in custody. While it wasn't necessary, they all made their way down to the holding cell. There were guards both inside and outside the cell, and Brandon sat slumped on the half net available for seating.

"Brandon Hollow, we have evidence that you were responsible for a shuttle accident that caused the death of the Translator's grandparents. You were also the tech that last worked on my son's shuttle before his accident, where the same malfunction occurred. Do you have anything to say in your defense?" Clear Seas asked.

Brandon sighed. "I wondered when you'd come for me. The Chenzira's shuttle was an accident. I was young and impatient and made a mistake. My uncle managed to get me out of trouble, but Rip found out about it shortly after. He threatened to expose me and have my family killed if I didn't help him."

"Why didn't you come to me for help?" Jer asked.

"For one, I didn't think you'd believe me, and for another, he sent me pictures of my children, so I knew he had someone else helping him. I separated from my family and changed my name to try and keep them safe, but he found me anyway," Brandon replied.

"What did he have you do?" Marcus asked.

Brandon sighed. "Exactly what you think. Over the years, he had me modify at least a dozen shuttles, including his father's."

"I want to know who else and when," Clear Seas demanded.

Brandon nodded. "I promise to tell you everything I know but protect my family first. I don't know who else is involved, and if they know I'm being questioned, they might harm them."

"Where do they live now?" Jer asked.

Brandon gave them the information.

"That's in my district," Marcus replied. "I'll take care of it."

When the message had been sent off to have them moved to a secure location, Clear Seas turned back to Brandon. "Now tell us everything."

"When I know they're safe," Brandon replied.

Clear Seas briefly flashed his frustration but quickly brought it under control and nodded. "That's a fair request, and I'll honor it."

As it would take several hours for the guards to reply, they left and swam back to the conference room. The moment the door was shut, Clear Seas radiated a multitude of colors, which Jer completely understood.

"Ready to destroy Rip's other home now?" Jer asked.

Clear Seas snorted but calmed himself. "If he's telling the truth, what are we going to do about it? It's not much different than what Snapper Fish did to save his daughter."

"He admitted to killing Rip Current's father," Marcus replied. "That should be a death sentence."

"Is that his fault or Rip's for blackmailing him to do it?" Wind Rider replied.

"I'm not sure we can afford to show leniency," Apakna responded. "We need to stop this hard. The Pile is already far greater than I ever expected. People need to know we're going to come down hard on anyone who ever tries this again. If we don't, the people will never trust us."

"I doubt they ever will as it is," Jer muttered. "I'm honestly not sure how I'm going to swim into that Council chamber knowing so many people in that room wanted me dead."

"At least it's not your family," Clear Seas replied. "Our next family get-together is going to be very awkward. It's so nice to see you again, Jelly. I haven't seen you since the execution of your partner. How are your children doing? They hate my guts, and you want me dead, too, just wonderful! It was so nice catching up with you. Will I see you again next year?"

Marcus snorted, and Clear Seas began laughing.

"Bottomless depths," Clear Seas muttered, rubbing at his face. "What a mess."

"You do realize he was lying, don't you?" Sammianna stated, and they all turned to face her.

"What do you mean?" Apakna asked.

She actually rolled her eyes with exasperation. He'd never seen a Digger do that before. "You're picking on me about my math skills, but you can't even do basic subtraction, not that you needed it after everything we discussed earlier. Rip took office after his father died. He's been on the council for twenty-five years. He couldn't have found out about the shuttle accident and bribed Brandon to kill his father. Marsee's only twenty. Either he's lying about killing Rip's father, or Myra's parent's accident wasn't an accident."

Jer nodded. "I told you your math skills were better than ours."

"That's becoming more obvious by the minute," Sammie replied. "How you manage to balance a budget is beyond me."

"Digger Staffers," they all said in unison.

Sammie squinted at all of them.

"Not sarcasm," Apkana stated. "Brandon could be lying to protect his family if someone else is blackmailing him."

"True," Jer said and returned to his investigation, as did the others. Half an hour later, he threw his tablet across the room with a snarl.

"I take it you found something," Sammie asked. "Or do you need my help with another math problem?"

Jer snorted and then buried his face in his paws with a groan. "No. I figured this one out all on my own. Once again, it's all my fault."

"Your fault?" Wind Rider asked. "How?"

"Brandon's oldest daughter had psychosis. Hers was the first test I ever had to witness. It was about a year after I took office. I didn't realize Brian was related, but that would explain why he retired from the Council so suddenly. He probably knew about her issues and didn't want to be the one to put her down."

"Do you think he orchestrated the shuttle accident?" Marcus asked.

"Brian? No," Jer replied. "He was waiting in the district office with two bottles of Fuzzle Knockers after the execution and actually comforted me. I was a mess, but it explains why he got as drunk as I did. I don't know why Rip would have been targeting me then. I didn't even know him, and I was from a tiny district in the middle of nowhere. I suppose Brandon might have snapped when working on my shuttle."

"Rip could have been trying to get rid of you because you were my friend," Clear Seas said. "Or because you were Marcus's brother, and he was already one of the longest-running councilors and nominated several times for Senior."

"We may never know," Jer said. "But either way, I killed Brandon's daughter. If it wasn't accidental, he was trying to kill me in retaliation, and it was my insistence that made Myra's parents use my shuttle. They died because of me."

CHAPTER 65

Marsee: Rowena

That evening, Marsee lay curled up on her bed, thoroughly depressed but doing her best to appear to be honoring her oath, even though she fully intended to end it the moment they left her alone. She went through the motions of her pickle torture, drank whatever was handed to her, and obediently used the waste room when her alarm went off. Ellie never left her side, not even for her own pickle torture, and Marsee did her best to ignore Avery, who never took his eyes off her. He didn't say anything about the injuries she gave him, and she didn't apologize. She was honestly surprised that they'd even bothered to try and save her life. She considered asking them why but wasn't sure she wanted the answer.

Tired but not ready to sleep and face another night terror, she was absently scrolling through the ships she could requisition, for lack of anything better to do, when there was a commotion at her door. All three guards turned and greeted the newest arrival with deference and what appeared to be love. As she watched, Tamarin hugged one of the oldest Diggers she'd ever seen. Her shell was dull, scratched deeply, and even appeared to be missing in places, showing a mottled grey skin underneath. Her face was so wrinkled Marsee could barely see her eyes, but there was a wide grin splitting it. She couldn't remember ever seeing a Digger smile that much.

"Tamarin! My, how you've grown," the old digger said with a voice that was just as rough as her shell. "You were just a tiny kitten the last time I saw you. How's your tail?"

Tamarin chuckled. "Still attached, thankfully. I've missed you."

"Pah, I doubt you've even thought of me, but I appreciate the sentiment."

"That's not true at all. You're a legend in the Guard. I've made sure of it. I tell the story at least once a year to the new recruits."

The Digger chuckled. "That must really annoy Kendra. I fully approve."

Avery carefully helped her through the shield, and to Marsee's further surprise, she glared at Ellie. Ellie said nothing and honestly looked a bit intimidated. This seemed to both amuse and delight the old Digger, who turned to Marsee with another brilliant smile before slowly shuffling over to the side of the bed.

Who is this person? Marsee wondered, but she didn't have to wait long to find out.

"Good morning, Marsee. My name is Rowena, and I'm in charge of your care now. How are you feeling?"

She sniffed deeply but couldn't detect any sense of fear from the old healer, which was surprising as Diggers were known to curl up in their shells at the slightest hint of danger. If anything, she seemed excited. "You're not afraid of me?"

Rowena cackled with laughter. "Me afraid of you?! You're just a kitten. I was a healer for your Guard for decades, long before Kendra was even born. They're a grumpy bunch on a good day and impossible the rest of the time. There's nothing you could do or say that would surprise me. I've heard and seen it all. I'm actually very excited to be assigned to your case. Your injuries present a unique opportunity, and I'll be honest. I've been downright bored for most of the last decade."

Marsee flicked her ears back. Everyone knew a bored Digger was a dangerous thing. If this one had latched onto her, there might actually be a chance they could find a way to fix her, assuming the ancient healer didn't die first, which was entirely possible if she was as old as she implied.

Rowena squinted and shuffled closer before tapping at the monitors. "Ah, that's better," she muttered. "The monitors here are downright atrocious. I've already put in a complaint to the Council, but thankfully, your uncle informs me he's bringing his latest tech, and I can't wait to get my old fingers on that new brain scanner of his. I've been drooling over the specs for months. What he's done with the Hue-mans is incredible."

"Ammond? You know my uncle?"

She nodded. "Of course I do. I've known him since I was a pup. Ammond was a grump even then, but he's softened over the years. Twice now, he's actually said the word please when asking for my help. I didn't even know he knew the word."

She snickered. "Twice? Really?"

"The first time was with your sister. Your mother had already asked me. I worked with her remotely while she was caring for the Hue-mans at the agency, and had I already told her I would help with your sister, as long she picked on Ammond and made him beg me for it. I had quite a bit of fun making him squirm before agreeing, but don't you dare tell him that."

"You're *that* Rowena?" She'd heard her mother mention the name several times while trying to find a cure for her sister.

Rowena grinned. "I'm not just *that* Rowena. I'm *the* Rowena. The universe's most revered brain specialist."

"She's pretty good at fixing tails, too," Tamarin called out from the doorway.

Rowena chuckled and then glared at her. *"That* Rowena? What has that old coot said about me?"

Ellie snorted from the other bed, and Rowena glared at her again.

"That had better not be a comment on my age, cub. He's two months older than I am, as he regularly likes to inform me every time he tries to pull rank."

"Of course not. I've been calling him an old coot for years. He hates it."

Rowena grunted and glared at Ellie for another moment before turning her attention back to Marsee, waiting.

She was shocked to see anyone give grief to Ellie and rubbed at her scruff. "Honestly, he's never said anything to me, but my mother has mentioned you on several occasions, and she was thrilled the day you agreed to help with Little Flower."

Rowena grinned. "Well, your mother is quite brilliant in her own right, even if it was my nanotech she was modifying. Now, stop wiggling so I can get a better look at your lovely brain."

Marsee stilled and waited, feeling a bit of hope for the first time since she'd woken up.

"I figured as much," Rowena muttered after a bit, sounding absolutely disgusted.

"You can't fix me?" Marsee asked, drooping with disappointment.

"Oh, no. I'm not saying that at all. I'm muttering over this scanner. It's nowhere near good enough for what I need. Ellie, I would have thought you'd have fixed this by now?"

"Trust me, I'm trying. Nothing Ammond sent me is designed to work underwater. I have techs working on it."

"Then get me something that doesn't," Rowena snapped. "There's no water in this room, and none of Ammond's equipment is designed to work underwater, either. There was better equipment on that ancient transport ship I took to get here than what's in this room." Rowena stopped and frowned as she considered and then brightened. "I could be wrong. These old eyes aren't as sharp as they used to be, but I think I saw one of the Earth delegation ships parked on the platform when I landed. It was designed with some of the best medical tech we had at the time. It won't be as good as what Ammond's bringing, but it would be far better than this ancient piece of junk."

Ellie scrambled for her tablet and placed a call. "Wind Rider, is the ship you took still here?"

"Yes," she replied. "Petra and I are staying there until the security systems on the suites can be updated. Why?"

"Thank the moons! I'm temporarily commandeering it for Marsee. The med bay has better tech than what's available here."

"You're more than welcome to it and welcome to move her there if it helps," Wind Rider replied. "There's plenty of room."

Rowena grinned and turned back to the door. "Guards, can you hunt down Hyacinth for me?"

"Yes, ma'am," Avery said, giving a nod to Tamarin, who took off swimming.

A few minutes later, they both returned.

"Is there a problem?" The Senior Healer asked from the hallway.

"No, a possible solution. There's an Earth delegation ship parked on the platform."

Hyacinth understood immediately, and a lengthy conversation occurred about whether to move her there permanently or just for the scans. Ultimately, they decided to start with the scans and go from there, so Wind Rider had the pilots move the ship to the roof of the Trauma Center after determining that it would fit, just barely, while the three trauma ships that were normally parked there were moved to the platform.

Fifteen minutes later, Marsee was helped off the bed and started her slow trudge to the ship, grumbling the entire way out the door, annoyed that they were making her swim instead of floating her there on her bed.

"Oh, quit your belly aching," Rowena growled at her. "You're moving better than I am."

Marsee shut up after that and focused on trying not to pass out as she struggled to keep up with the pace the old healer set, but she did glare at Ellie, who chuckled, thoroughly amused by Rowena.

"I think I've changed my mind," Ellie said as she followed out and swam ahead to catch up with the healers. "Rowena, will you be my mentor? This is the first time Marsee has stopped growling in days."

"Now, why would I want a belligerent pain in my shell like you for a protege?" Rowena retorted.

"I can get you all the best equipment?" Ellie offered sweetly.

"Ha!" Rowena snorted and glared at Ellie with derision. "You've failed miserably so far. I'm not the slightest bit impressed with that offer."

"I seem to remember a nano-particle accelerator that would suggest otherwise," Ellie countered.

"*What* nano-particle accelerator? I never even saw it. Two days before it was scheduled to arrive, you rerouted it to the Agency. I'm *still* waiting for mine."

Ellie was silent, at a complete loss for words.

"I'm pretty sure my brain is more damaged than I thought," Marsee said into the silence.

"What makes you think that?" The Senior Healer asked.

"I've never seen Ellie at a loss for words. I must be hallucinating."

The others all burst out laughing, Rowena loudest of all, but Ellie glared at her, tail lashing. "Poof. Apprentice."

Marsee shrugged and kept swimming, but her tail curled.

Eventually, she dragged her exhausted body onto the ship and stopped for a breather just inside the door while Rowena went ahead to examine what was available in the med bay. Ellie and the guards kept her company while Hyacinth swam off to find a cart she could use inside.

Once her breathing calmed, she tried to make her way back, but her legs buckled out from under her after only a few steps. The guards caught her before she could fall, and Tamarin carefully picked her up and carried her back. She didn't see Petra, but guards stood outside the hallway leading towards the front of the ship. A minute later, they arrived in the med bay, stationed near the back.

The Flyers didn't use beds or even seats, so it didn't surprise her that she didn't see any, but Avery walked over, hit a button on the wall, and a bed slid out. Tamarin set her gently on it, and the monitors sprang to life around her.

"This will do for now," Rowena said, and then said nothing for a long time.

A few minutes later, the Senior Healer appeared in a cart that seemed far too small for her, but she didn't seem to mind being all scrunched up.

They poked and prodded at her, had her move every which way, speak, read, sniff at things, listen to music, and even injected her with something that made her squirm with itchiness until they gave her something else, and it stopped. Lastly, they had her try turning on her instinct. It was all she could do to keep from curling up in a ball and whimpering with the wave of hollowness that accompanied it. Even still, Avery and Tamarin watched her closely until Rowena told her to turn it off.

"Very interesting," Rowena said and turned to discuss her findings with the Senior Healer.

She barely understood one word in three, and she couldn't tell if what they were saying was good or not, as they both had their healer's mask on tightly. She couldn't even sniff anything out.

Ellie must have been just as confused as she leaned over after a good ten minutes of this had passed. "Do you think you could build a translation program for that?"

"No, I'm pretty sure they're making up words at this point," she replied. "I don't think a Level Four Master could decipher that gibberish, and besides, I'm only an apprentice. That's *way* above my pay grade."

Rowena cackled with laughter, and the Senior Healer bubbled her amusement, but they didn't stop to tell her what any of it meant.

Twenty minutes later, her father and uncle arrived.

Finally, when Marsee was about ready to start pulling her father's fur out, for lack of any of her own, Rowena turned around. "Do you want the good news or the bad news first?"

She wasn't expecting to hear any good news, so she chose that.

Rowena put the scans up on a monitor so that Marsee could see. "The good news is the damage doesn't appear to be as extensive as we first thought. This is a recording of what they witnessed when you were brought in." Marsee had thought the old healer had been exaggerating, but the quality of the scan was abysmal compared to what she was used to seeing on her mother's monitor. Still, she watched as her brain went dark, section by section, until it suddenly stopped.

"This scan is essentially useless. I haven't seen one this bad in close to fifty years. Hyacinth, how you manage to keep anyone alive around here with that ancient tech is beyond me."

"We've already approved an emergency expenditure to pay for anything Marsee and the rest of the victims need," her uncle replied before Hyacinth could.

"That's all well and good if it actually exists," Hyacinth said. "Everything I need won't work underwater. That's the whole problem."

"I'm working on it," Ellie replied with a frustrated growl.

Rowena grunted. "Anyway. This is what we can see now."

A far more detailed image was displayed, although still not to the quality she was used to seeing, but even still, she could see the difference. "It's not all gone?"

"No, it's not, and from what I can tell, it appears healthy, just inactive. I'll know for sure when your uncle gets here. Only this small section is gone entirely, but *that's* the bad news. From what I understand of your brains, this was essentially the control hub, a mini-brain for your instinct, so to speak. It was larger than I've ever seen and connected to just about every area of your brain, including several places I haven't seen before."

"So, can you fix it or not?" she asked.

"Maybe. We have something to work with, which is more than we had before. I don't want to give you any false sense of hope, but I do have a few ideas to research. The biggest problem to solve is your lack of any sense of pain. When Hyacinth shocked you during our tests, your brain did react, even if you didn't feel it. I can work with that. We might not be able to restore your sense of pain, but we should be able to monitor for it, which gives you a much better chance of survival."

"Would I be able to have children?"

The healer looked at her sadly and shook her head.

Marsee wilted as that tiny bit of hope faded away. Even though they didn't exist yet, it felt like her children had just died, again.

"Marsee, you're mother has already told me how much you want children. I don't think you would survive pregnancy and childbirth, even if you did make it to your female stage. Making it to your male stage is going to be hard enough. It would be safest if we gave you your implant now, but..."

She drooped further, fully understanding what that meant. She would be the smallest male on the planet. The odds of anyone picking her in an open mating were next to none, and she knew no one would ever choose to willingly partner with someone who had psychosis for fear they would give it to their cubs."

"I know what your goals are. There's still time, and I've never failed a patient. Not once. I don't intend to ruin my reputation now."

Marsee nodded. "What about when I tried turning on my instinct?" she asked. "You saw something there."

"Yes, I did, and that was *very* interesting." She pulled up a different scan. "My research has led me to believe that this tiny part of your brain is essentially the switch for turning on your instinct. That was surprisingly undamaged. When you tried, it lit up, but there was nowhere for the signal to go, and then several other areas of your brain activated that I wasn't expecting, like your immune system and the part of your brain that controls pain."

Marsee frowned in confusion. "But I can't feel pain."

"Exactly. *That's* why it was so interesting. What exactly do you feel when you turn it on?"

"The only way I can describe it is hollow. I always feel that way now, but it's so much worse when I turn it on. It's not painful the way I've always experienced pain, but it's awful. It makes me feel like I'm going shatter into a million pieces, and it washes over me in waves."

"Interesting. Does it change at all when you have it off?"

"It feels worse every day, harder to ignore, especially after my pickle torture or when I'm trying to sleep."

To her surprise, Rowena grinned.

"Now that is very, *very* interesting. Marsee, I want you to close your eyes, ignore everything else, and tell me if that feeling changes at all."

Marsee shrugged and did as requested. She felt a slight touch on her arm and nothing else for a while. Then the sense of hollowness grew, and she couldn't help but wince. "It's a lot stronger now."

"Fantastic!" Rowena exclaimed. "Marsee, you can open your eyes."

She peered up, and everyone in the room was smiling. "What's going on?"

"I believe you *can* feel your pain," Rowena replied. "It's significantly muted, but it's still there."

"I had to up the charge quite a bit before you reacted," Hyacinth replied. "It wasn't enough to harm you, but if I did that to anyone else, they'd be screaming."

"But you did feel it," Rowena added. "That's something we can work with."

"So why does it get worse when I try to turn on my instinct?"

"Phantom pain, probably. People who lose a limb often claim their missing limbs still hurt or itch. I imagine this is no different. Your brain knows something is very wrong and is responding to it. You should still be in significant pain from your other injuries, which would explain why the feeling is stronger after your pickle torture. By the way, I love that term. And also why it's worse when you're trying to sleep. Pain is always worse when we're exhausted or upset."

Rowena dug through the cabinets and drawers until she found what she was looking for and injected something into Marsee's arm.

The feeling of hollowness slowly receded. It didn't go away entirely, but it was manageable again. She almost started crying from relief. "Oh, that's better. It's still there, but I feel like I can breathe again."

Her father reached over and squeezed her good hand. She looked up into his face and saw that he *was* crying.

"I'm sorry, Marsee," The Senior Healer said. "I didn't even consider it might be pain."

"There's nothing to apologize for. I didn't think it was either," she replied and turned back to Rowena. "What about my mood swings?"

Rowena squinted at the monitor again and gave a slight shrug. "I'm honestly not seeing anything that would account for that. Those areas of your brain were not damaged, although they appeared to be in the original scans. It's possible there was something there that has since healed. There are hormonal changes, but not anything I would be concerned about. They're still within normal ranges for your species. Electrical shocks can do all sorts of strange things to our bodies. Have they been leveling out at all?"

"Not really. They're just as strong, but they've mostly been stuck on thoroughly depressed for the last several days," Marsee replied.

"Hmm," Rowena grunted. "Well, I have a feeling what you're experiencing is a normal trauma response, intensified by the pain you weren't being treated for, and it will improve as you heal and your body stabilizes. As far as depression, that's entirely expected with what you're going through. I suggest you try to do something enjoyable, like listen to music or read a favorite book. I've been informed that you're better when young Stormy visits?"

She shrugged. "I guess. I try to make an effort when he's around."

"It's pretty much the only time I hear her laugh," Ellie added.

"Well, if being around children brings you joy, I suggest visiting with those in the children's ward. As popular as you are here, they would certainly value your visit. Perhaps you can read them one of your stories."

She smiled at the idea and nodded. "I'll give it a try. Assuming you don't run me into the ground with my pickle torture first."

Rowena chuckled. "The children's ward is on the other side of the trauma center. We'll do both."

Marsee snorted and rolled her eyes. "Why does *that* not surprise me?" she muttered to the laughter of the others.

"So does this mean you have proof that Marsee can't turn on her instinct?" her uncle asked.

"That depends on what you mean by turning it on. She can flip the switch, but the switch isn't hooked up anymore. The parts of her brain that would normally turn on are not, but she is reacting to it, both with pain and a measurable increase in her immune response. It might actually be beneficial for her to turn it on as much as possible. It might help speed up her healing."

She stared at Rowena in shock. "You're serious? You want me to keep my instinct on?"

"I am. Our brains routinely build new neurological pathways all the time as we learn new skills. Your brain recognizes that something is wrong and appears to be trying to fix it. It would be worth trying at the very least."

"I don't know if I can. That feeling is awful."

"I imagine so. The way your brain is lighting up, if you could feel it, it would be excruciating. However, we should be able to manage that."

"Do you think she'll ever be able to use her instinct again?" her father asked.

"No. I don't think so, at least not in the same way."

"So, the risk of another episode of psychosis?" her father asked.

"Non-existent from everything I know about the illness. I still don't know for sure what causes it. I really wish I had a detailed scan of Marsee's brain before, but my current hypothesis is that the switch gets stuck. How, I haven't been able to figure out, much less figure out a way to medically treat it, but there's nothing for it to turn on, so even if it did get stuck on, she wouldn't have issues, or at least not the same issues."

"How does sign language help stop psychosis?" her father asked.

"I haven't figured that out yet. The main benefit appears to be that it gives the afflicted a way to communicate and remember who they are, at which point they're able to reactivate the thinking parts of their brains. The reason that those with psychosis go non-verbal is that there are no pathways from your instinct to the part of your brain that controls speech. Well, usually. Marsee's unique there, too, as she had a fairly well-developed pathway to that area."

"Is that why I could hear my instinct talk?"

"You could?" Rowena asked. Her tiny eyes twinkled with excitement.

Marsee nodded. "Ever since the day I first hunted Little Flower. I don't know how to explain it, but it felt like a separate person, complete with its own thoughts, fighting for control of my body at times. That day in the garden, it felt like we merged. Sometimes, it was a separate entity. Sometimes, we were one. We talked all the time, even when it was off. I could give as little or as much control as I wanted but still be in control. Occasionally, it would activate on its own. For example, moving me out of harm's way, but most of the time, it would ask for more control or clarification. I was able to hold off on killing Rip because I wanted to find the others, but then it refused to give up control later because it felt my father would kill us if he got too close and that I wasn't taking the risk seriously. It even said, 'I can live without you, but you can't live without me.' before I was able to kill it off."

"How extraordinary!" Rowena exclaimed. "I always thought it was just an on-off switch. Is it the same for the rest of you?"

"It's just an on or off state for me, and I've never heard anything," Ellie said.

"Same," her uncle added.

"It's just on or off for me," her father said. "I've never even thought about trying to control the level, but it has gotten stronger as I've used it." He glanced at the guards and then down at her. "And I've heard a voice a time or two."

Both Avery and Tamarin stiffened, hands reaching for their stunners.

"How often and recently has this happened?" Avery demanded. His voice was sharp enough that both her father and uncle jumped.

"Why? Is this bad?" her uncle asked.

"As bad as going non-verbal. If not more so," Avery replied. "*Answer my question.*"

"Only once, that I'm sure of. The first time it happened was the day I examined the suite. That was the only time I heard it when my instinct was on. Then there were two, maybe three times when it wasn't on. It sounds different than my normal thoughts."

"Have you had any issues with your control?" Avery pressed.

Her father looked away from Avery and gave a slight nod.

Avery sighed. "How often and when?"

"Three, maybe four times this past week," her father replied softly. "And I was non-verbal once."

She swallowed hard, realizing what that meant, and noticed that his claws flashed briefly as he said it.

So did Avery and Tamarin. Avery stepped closer to her father, and to her surprise, her uncle jumped in between the two, raising a paw to stop Avery.

"He was in full control when I tested him this morning, and I believe those situations were warranted, even the non..."

Avery ignored her uncle and motioned for him to move aside. Her uncle didn't move, and Avery glared at him. "He just stated he's been non-verbal. You know as well as I do what that means."

"It's alright, Marcus," her father said and stepped around her uncle. "Avery's right and I have no desire to lose control and hurt someone. If I am slipping, then it would be better for everyone if you're not the one to have to handle it."

"Papa?" Marsee squeaked.

"It's alright, Kitten. Whatever happens, this is not your fault, and I love you."

Avery never took his eyes off her father, but his body was tense. "Turn it on."

"Hold up," Rowena said, stopping them both.

Avery turned to look at Rowena with astonishment.

"Don't get your tail in a bunch, Honor Guard. If you're going to test him, let me scan him while you do. It might help Marsee or others if he's starting to have issues. You know as well as I do how rare it is to have someone have their instinct talk and still be in any sort of control. If nothing else, it'll give us something to compare later."

Avery nodded his acceptance and hit another switch on the wall, causing another bed to pop out. Her father climbed up and sat on it. When Rowena indicated she was ready, her father turned his instinct on.

"Can you still understand me?" Avery asked.

"Perfectly," her father replied.

Marsee watched the scans with interest as her father's brain lit up on the monitors, or what she could see of it, as most of it was blocked by the two healers.

"Yes, he does have a small pathway to the speech center, but nowhere near as developed as Marsee's. The rest appears to be fairly normal. Slightly larger in the olfactory section. Can you try changing the amount of control you give up?"

"I don't even know how," her father replied.

"I didn't either for a while," Marsee said. "But then I tried just turning off my heightened sense of smell, and it worked. After that, I played around to see what I could do."

Her father frowned as he focused. The monitor flickered several times, and then he wobbled and grabbed the bed.

Both guards tensed again.

"I'm still in control," her father said. "But I can't turn it down without turning it off. I tried a few times. The rapid on/off made me dizzy."

"Can you give up more control?" Rowena asked.

Avery and Tamarin both tensed yet again, but her father just sat there and shook his head after a moment. "I'm not experiencing anything more than what I was experiencing before. The best I was able to do was focus in on specific scents, but I don't *feel* any different."

Suddenly, Avery swung hard at her father.

Her father blocked and grunted with the effort but otherwise didn't react.

"Turn it off," Avery ordered.

Her father must have because Avery gave a single nod.

They all waited in tense silence as Avery considered and then glanced at Tamarin, who scratched at the back of her scruff and eventually shrugged. "If he hadn't admitted to having issues, I wouldn't have known there was an issue," Tamarin said and turned to Marcus. "What makes you believe these issues were warranted?"

"Jer wanted to kill Rip after determining he was one of the people in the suite but was still verbal and managed to stop himself before leaving.

The second incident I'm aware of was when Marsee crashed in her room, and they started operating. He didn't hurt anyone and managed to contact me for help."

"That's what was going on?" Avery asked and seemed honestly surprised.

"That's when I was non-verbal," her father added. "My instinct wanted to protect Marsee, but I didn't know how, and I couldn't make myself leave or ask for help."

"That's why I think the non-verbal episode was warranted," Marcus added. "Speaking up would have meant his death, and I personally think it was a normal stress reaction. Any parent would panic if their child crashed and healers suddenly started operating in front of them, especially with the amount of blood that was in the room at the time. The third time was later that evening. I was there when he believed his instinct spoke to him. He was drunk enough to be sick but was still in full control of his instinct."

Avery nodded. "The recent circumstances have been extreme, but I agree, you do appear to be in full control, Councilor. I want to know immediately if you hear it again or have any further issues, warranted or otherwise."

"If he has *any* issues, I'll take care of it," her uncle replied, his face a cold, hard mask that scared her.

Avery shook his head. "I applaud your commitment to your oath, Councilor, but please come to us first if you can. If given the option, I'd rather try and save him, and regardless, I imagine Rowena would like another scan."

"That, Rowena would," Rowena replied.

Her uncle nodded at Avery and turned back to Rowena. "Healer, if you have the time, I'd like a more detailed explanation of what you've found and a recorded statement on Marsee's status and inability to use her instinct."

Rowena nodded. "Of course, Councilor." She turned back to face Marsee. "Marsee, you can head back to your room now."

"We can have some of this moved to the Trauma Center if that would be easier," her father said.

Rowena nodded. "It most certainly would. At a minimum, that monitor for my office and this bed for Marsee's room, if you can, without destroying the ship."

"I'll get someone working on it right away," Ellie said.

Tamarin once again picked her up and started carrying her out.

"I expect her to swim from the ship back," Rowena called out as they left the med bay.

"Yes, ma'am," Tamarin replied.

Marsee groaned. "You're as bad as Ammond!"

"Oh no, child. I'm far worse!" Rowena replied. "Tamarin, take the long way back!"

"Yes, ma'am," Tamarin replied with a wicked grin.

Marsee glared at the guard.

"Trust me," Tamarin said. "Kendra doesn't even mess with her. I don't recommend you start."

She wasn't sure what surprised her more, that Kendra was afraid of the ancient healer or the peels of cackling laughter from Rowena that followed them down the hall.

"Are you going to tell me why Kendra is afraid of Rowena?"

"Maybe someday," Tamarin replied with a chuckle as she stepped through the ship's door. "But today is not that day. Now get swimming."

Marsee glared at the guards, who all looked thoroughly amused. "So what's with your tail? Did Ellie roll over it with one of her rocking chairs?"

Laughter followed her question, but Tamarin just grinned. "Nice try. Get moving. That's an order."

She rolled her eyes but started swimming. "Watch the attitude, Guard. I'm the Translator, remember? If I can demote Ellie, I can demote you, too."

Avery chuckled. "She's got a point, Tam. Five credits says she demotes you by the end of the week."

Tamarin snorted. "Please. I'll be lucky to make it back to the room. The real question is who she likes better. You or me."

"Avery, obviously," Marsee replied. "You're the one making me swim."

"Fair point, well made, *Translator*," Tamarin replied. "Turn left."

Marsee groaned as it was in the opposite direction she'd come from. To their utter amusement, it took everything she had not to demote Tamarin on the spot, but it wasn't long before her injuries caught up, and she passed out. She didn't wake until Tamarin was laying her back on her bed. She waited until the guard took up her post outside again.

"Hey, Tamarin?"

"Yes, *Translator*?"

"Poof!"

Both guards chuckled, but she heard the ding of credits being transferred a moment later. With a slight chuckle of her own, she closed her eyes again, laying there trying to decide if the events of the day were a win or not. She was worried about her father even if he had passed the guards' test. While he'd said it wasn't her fault, she knew it was, although part of her, the part that was still angry at him, felt it was fair and just that he was struggling now, too. Only, that thought made her as sick to her stomach as knowing how much she'd enjoyed killing Rip had.

She was glad to know that the hollow feeling could be managed and relieved to know what it was, but she was also grieving the loss of any chance of future cubs. She knew Rowena was trying to keep her hopes up. She might live longer, not tearing herself apart during her growth spurt, but at what cost and how much longer would that get her before some other injury did her in?

On the slight chance that using her instinct would help, she turned it on and gritted her teeth as the hollow feeling washed over her. It wasn't quite as bad as before due to whatever they'd given her, but she could only endure it for a few minutes. The moment she turned it off, she sighed with relief, yawned, and fell asleep.

CHAPTER 66

Jer: Heat

Jer watched the guards carry his daughter out, honestly surprised to still be alive, and listened until he heard the door shut behind her before letting out a heavy sigh.

"You stupid fool!" Marcus hissed at him and, without warning, hit him in the back of the head hard enough to knock him off the bed. "What were you thinking? Telling the guards that you've gone non-verbal? Were you trying to get yourself killed?"

"I love you too, brother," Jer said, rubbing at his head as he picked himself up off the floor. "But if you keep hitting me like that, Rowena won't even be able to fix me."

"I do love a challenge," Rowena teased.

"Personally, I don't think you hit him hard enough," Ellie said. "I'd be glad to volunteer my services."

"Love you too, Ellie," Jer replied with a smirk.

"That's Senior Guild Master to you, *Councilor*. Marsee might have forgiven you, but *I* haven't."

Jer nodded. "That's fair, and I deserve it."

Marcus growled with frustration but then pulled him in for a hug. "I almost lost you," he whispered. "Don't do it again."

Jer hugged him back but said nothing. He knew he was on borrowed time.

Eventually, Marcus pulled away. "Seriously, Jer. What were you thinking?"

"I was trying to help Marsee, and we needed the information. Now we know hearing our instincts is bad, and if I do lose control, perhaps some good will come of it. And I meant what I said earlier. I don't want you to be the one to do it. Let the guards handle it."

Marcus grunted at him. "You're going to drive me to start drinking, and you know how much I loathe the stuff."

"It grows on you," he replied. "Although I'm not sure I ever want to touch it again. I have never been so sick in my life."

"Serves you right," Marcus muttered.

Jer hit a switch on the wall. The bed transformed into a seat, and he flopped in it with a heavy sigh. "Gods, I hope that was enough. Thank you for coming so quickly, Rowena."

"And miss an opportunity to get my hands on her lovely brain before Ammond does? Not a chance. I appreciate the use of the ship, though. This old shell isn't up to the rigors of public transport anymore, and I have never had a more comfortable trip, even if emergency jump was a bit unsettling."

"You're responsible for this?" Ellie asked him. "How? Last I knew, your ship was still on Saber, and it doesn't have emergency jump capabilities."

Jer grinned. "No, but a certain commander in the Ships Guild informed me that yours does, along with long-range communications. I am curious how the Senior Guild Master managed to get experimental tech added to her ship before official testing's complete or before the Senior Council, for that matter."

Ellie shrugged and looked at a claw innocently. "You can get anything if you're willing to pay for it *and* take the risks. I travel between planets far more than just about anyone, including the Senior Council, and have been testing out improvements for years. If you think I'm going to authorize tech that puts others' lives at risk without testing it myself, you're sadly mistaken."

She looked up from her claws and glared at him. "But if you tell *anyone* that I have advanced communications, I *will* claw you, Senior Councilor or not. Jump is the only vacation I get. Consider this your only warning."

He snorted. He could have her arrested for that threat, and she knew it, and she knew he wouldn't.

"And before you even think about arresting me for threatening you, I will remind you that you stole my ship."

"Commandeered, which is my right in an emergency. We took over your ship the day Marsee was released from the trauma center. It was the one place we knew we could secure. I sent Sampson to beg for me in case my message wasn't good enough. He promises me he returned it in better shape than when it left and with a few new toys, courtesy of the Council. Marcus slept in his office last night, and I figured you wouldn't even notice."

She glared at him but then conceded the point. "I didn't, but you could have asked. I would have said yes in a heartbeat."

"I know, but I didn't want to take that time. I was afraid we didn't have it."

She rolled her eyes at him. "So why didn't you hire a ship on Digger?"

"He did," Rowena replied. "But your ship was better equipped for what I needed, both in monitors and cargo space, and you don't need to dismantle this ship. Everything I need for now is in your cargo bay."

"So this was a ruse, too?" Ellie asked, waving her hand at the ship.

Rowena grinned. "Well, it will take time to set everything up, and I don't have time to waste. My clock is ticking even faster than Marsee's these days. Besides, you saw how hard she worked on the way up here. It was good for her."

"You haven't changed at all. Have you?" Ellie asked, shaking her head. "You sure you won't be my mentor?"

"Ha! Not a chance. On both accounts. I don't have time to mess with protocol or unruly proteges, but enough of that, we have far more serious things to discuss."

Jer swallowed hard at the sudden change in tone. "Something else is wrong with Marsee, isn't there?"

"Very much so, Councilor," Rowena replied. "I believe your daughter is in heat."

If he hadn't already been sitting, he would have fallen down. He stared at Rowena, then started laughing when he realized it was impossible. Marcus and Ellie turned and looked at him like he'd gone mad.

"Master Bresdone would have been proud," Jer said, trying and failing to uncurl his tail. "You had me there for a second. Good one!" Her expression didn't change, and he felt the blood slowly drain out of his face as his tail went limp, hitting the floor with a soft thud. He shook his head. "Please tell me you're joking."

"I'm not joking, Councilor. My mentor's formidable legacy aside, I wouldn't joke about something this serious."

He shook his head again. "But that's not possible. I would have noticed. So would Marcus and Avery."

"She's not releasing pheromones yet, but she's already rubbing at her paw, which is how we think she re-broke it."

"The paw isn't from a heat," Ellie said. "She's trying to rub out the feeling of killing Rip. I know from experience that feeling never goes away."

Rowena tilted her head briefly. "I'll take your word for that, but she's still showing elevated hormone levels consistent with someone going into their first heat."

"How would that even be possible?" Ellie asked. "She's far too young, and Hyacinth said..."

"That we don't know," Rowena interrupted. "A medically induced heat should leave a bio-marker that we can pick up for at least a month on the scanners, and there's no sign that she was raped, but that doesn't mean it didn't happen."

"Raped?!" Ellie exclaimed. "How would that trigger a heat?"

"It just does," Marcus replied.

Jer buried his face in his paws and shook as he realized what must have happened. "Gods. It's my fault."

Marcus sighed as he realized what he meant. "I suppose that's possible."

"Jeran Frederick Chenzira!" Ellie growled. "What have you done to her?"

"I was trying to save her life," he replied. "In the canyon, I..."

"By raping her?!" Ellie hissed.

Before he could answer, Ellie growled and lunged at him.

Marcus bolted between them and deflected Ellie's attack, knocking her hard into the bed.

"Ellie, stop!" Marcus growled as he grabbed her hard by the scruff and pinned her down. "Jer did not rape her."

Ellie hissed at Marcus as she struggled to get away. Even though she was so much bigger than him, her injuries meant he had no problem controlling her.

"If you don't stop struggling, I'll have no choice but to kill you," Marcus growled as he grabbed at her paw to further restrain her.

She yelped in pain and tried to pull away, but Marcus held on tightly.

"It's bad enough you let him get away with abusing her," she hissed. "You're going to let him get away with raping her, too?"

Jer sighed with relief to see that Ellie was still able to talk.

"I'm not condoning anything," Marcus replied. "I was there and saw what happened. He did not rape her."

She glared at him and huffed but stopped struggling. Marcus cautiously let her go and backed off. She pushed herself up off the table and winced as she flexed her injured paw, but then crossed her arms. "Explain."

"Jer bit Marsee on the scruff to try and snap her out of her psychosis," Marcus replied. "Just like it causes cubs to relax, it can sometimes knock people out of an episode of psychosis. It's possible Marsee's old enough that her instinct mistook that for rape. It's far more likely Rip..."

"You swear that's all that happened?" Ellie asked, interrupting Marcus.

"On my oath," Marcus replied.

"And mine," Jer added.

She sighed. "I'm sorry for assuming the worst and attacking you."

"I forgive you," Jer replied. "I'm honestly glad Marsee has such a fierce protector in you. I'm impressed you've held off this long as it is."

She snorted. "Trust me. It hasn't been easy. I've wanted to claw you for months."

"And I would have fully deserved it if you had," he replied. "Would it make you feel better to have a swipe at me now?"

Marcus snorted and rolled his eyes. "I don't know why I even bothered."

Ellie's claws tapped briefly, and she gave him a wicked grin but then winced again and stopped tapping. "It would, but you're in luck. For some reason, my paw hurts."

He grinned. "I'll admit, I was counting on that. However, I'll let you have a rain check."

"A what?" Everyone asked.

"It's a Hue-man expression. Basically, it means you can take me up on that offer at a later date when you're feeling better. Free of charge."

Ellie raised a brow but said nothing.

There was a brief pause in their conversation while Rowena treated Ellie's paw, which Marcus had managed to break.

"So what are we going to do about Marsee?" Jer asked.

"The best option all around would be to give her an implant," Hyacinth said. "She's too injured to survive a heat, much less pregnancy, and we're not equipped to perform an implantation here. She'd never survive the jump necessary to return to Saber. However, with her current mental status, if she were to find out, I think it would be too much."

"You want to give her the implant without telling her?" Jer asked.

Both healers nodded.

"Absolutely not," Ellie said with some vehemence. "This should be her choice. She's an adult, and far too much has already been taken from her. Taking her cubs is just cruel."

He looked over at Ellie with sympathy. He knew how much Ellie wanted a cub. She'd come to him for help with her appeal to the Healer's Guild, but he'd refused to take the case.

"If I thought there was even a chance she would survive, I'd say yes," Hyacinth replied. "But between her brain injury and recent suicide attempt, I believe her ability to make that decision is impaired."

"That's not even remotely true," Ellie spat, and her tail began thwapping again. "I may not be a healer, but Marsee is perfectly sane and managing far better than she has any right to. The thinking and reasoning parts of her brain were uninjured. You just gave her a full exam, which proved that. Even her reason for the suicide attempt was valid now that we've determined it was caused by untreated pain. Gods. I still hurt, and I went through far less than she did. She's more than aware of the risks of pregnancy and more than capable of making this decision if you inform her, and if she decides she wants to try anyway, that should be her choice."

"It's not just her we need to think about," Rowena said. "Even if she somehow managed to survive the jump back to Saber and the exertion of a heat, she won't be able to carry even one cub to term. If it doesn't kill her, it'll kill the cubs. She's just too small. I know you know how devastating that loss can be. Do you really want to put her through that?"

Ellie growled. "It's not my choice to make. It's hers. Besides, you're talking about more than just stopping a heat without telling her. You're talking about forcing her to become male, which she doesn't want, and remain this size for the rest of her life. Twenty years is a long time to figure out how to fix her so she could survive her growth spurt. What if you do, and then she finds out she lost her chance of having cubs decades before? That will devastate her more than making that decision now."

"Ellie, even if we somehow managed to restore her sense of pain, the odds of her surviving her growth spurt and bringing a cub to term are worse than you surviving a third heat," Hyacinth replied. "Printed organs don't grow fast enough, and with all her scaring, she'll need multiple surgeries to replace them, likely even before she hits her growth spurt. The only real chance she has to have a long life and genetic offspring is as a male."

Jer stared at the healers. "You didn't mention that before. What else have you been hiding?"

Hyacinth pursed her lips at the accusation. "I haven't been hiding anything. I just didn't go into detail as to why her loss of pain would make it impossible for her to survive her growth spurt. I didn't exactly have that chance when I informed her or you. You've been through it. Every scar is a potential failure point."

"How sure are you that she's going into heat?" Jer asked.

"Sure enough," Rowena replied. "but it's still early."

"Can you stop her heat without giving her an implant?" Marcus asked.

"We could try, but it might not work. Those options aren't as reliable as an implant."

"Will her growth be stopped if you treat it medically?"

"I honestly don't know. The medications we have are usually only given if someone's implant fails and there isn't one immediately available for replacement. We can't find any record of them being given to someone Marsee's age before. Granted, the same goes for the implant."

Jer rubbed at the back of his scruff, trying to decide. Ellie was glaring at him. Marcus and the two healers wore their masks. He was beginning to wonder if he would ever regain that calm. "I believe you're both right. It should be her choice, but I am also very worried about how she would react if she found out, both about the possibility of having been raped and the knowledge that she might be in heat. Treat her medically, but don't give her an implant. That needs to be her choice. Her complaint is mood swings. If she asks, you're treating her for that, nothing else. If there is a need for more, I would rather wait until the others are here if possible. She'll manage better if she has Little Flower and Hope to care for."

"I second that decision," Marcus said. "I think it's a fair compromise."

"This isn't right," Ellie growled.

"Perhaps, but I've made my decision, Ellie," he replied. "You will not inform her of anything that was discussed here. Is that understood?"

Ellie glared at him. "Perfectly, Senior Councilor, but when she finds out and claws you for this, don't say I didn't warn you." With another growl at both of them, Ellie stormed off.

He watched her leave and sighed.

"If it's easier, Councilor, I'm more than willing to take responsibility for this decision," Hyacinth replied.

He shook his head. "Thank you, but no. I'm well aware of the potential consequences of this decision, and I don't make any decisions I'm not willing to stand behind, even if she may never forgive me for it. I would rather she live and hate me for the rest of her life than die trying for the impossible."

Even at the detriment of my own family, he thought bitterly, and without another word, he, too, stood and left.

CHAPTER 67

Tamarin: Secrets

Tamarin signed off as Aris, Thatcher, and Tanner arrived for the night shift, but she wasn't ready to leave quite yet. Ellie hadn't returned, likely still working to gather the equipment Rowena needed, but techs had arrived with a new bed for Marsee and had just finished setting it up.

She stepped inside the room after Aris and carefully tried to wake Marsee. Outside of a murmur and twitch of her paw, Marsee slept on, exhausted from her lengthy swim earlier. Fully expecting to get clawed but not particularly worried about it, she gently lifted Marsee, purring softly to calm her if she did wake.

Marsee shifted in her arms and snuggled in, appearing far more cublike than the general she was destined to become.

Don't get attached. You know what's going to happen, Tamarin thought, knowing it was already far too late. It was hard not to. Even as injured and depressed as she was, her compassion, integrity, and humor shone through. It hurt watching Marsee struggle through her transition, unable to help, although they were all trying to find ways to work around their orders. She gave Marsee a gentle hug before carefully laying her down on the new bed.

The techs started the calibration program and left with the old bed, but she didn't bother looking up at the monitor. Instead, she stared down at Marsee and her scar-covered body, still absent of any sign of fur.

The poor child.

She still couldn't believe Marsee had survived, much less transitioned on her own. She was handling her trauma far better than any of them had expected, suicide attempt included. Even when people knew what was going on, they still lost far too many, overwhelmed by the effects of the transition and far too often struggling from trauma of their own.

But then she's the General, Tamarin thought. There was no question about that now, and that thought terrified her. *War is on the way. The question is, with whom, and will she be ready in time?*

"You alright, Tam?" Avery asked quietly.

She nodded. "I'll meet up with you in a bit. I want to make sure the bed is fully calibrated before heading out."

That was true, but not the entire truth. She knew Avery could sniff it out, but he let the lie slide. They all let the little ones slide. It was the only privacy they had.

"I'll meet you in the arena," Avery said as he stepped out.

"Yes, sir," she replied. It was expected. She might be off duty, but she still needed to train, and they had a lot to talk about.

She waited until Avery left before readjusting her attention back to Marsee. Rowena and Hyacinth had been hiding something. The question was, what? She took a deep breath and focused on Marsee. Her body was covered in scars, both the jagged streaks of her burns and the sharp lines of her incisions. To her nose, they stood out in stark contrast to the rest of Marsee's body. She dismissed one surface injury after another from her mind. She was nearly as good as Avery at this, but the sheer number of scars made it a challenge. Eventually, Marsee's broken hand and the mesh that surrounded several of the bones, along with the four new organs, appeared bright in her mind. There was still a great deal of inflammation, but everything there was healing, too, at least according to her nose.

She looked up at the monitor and waited impatiently for the calibration program to finish. When it was finally done, she ran a full scan on Marsee. If nothing else, they needed the baseline for the bed.

"Turning healer, are you?" Rowena asked.

She turned, surprised she hadn't heard the old healer swim up and wondered how long Rowena had been there watching but nodded. "Just earned my Journeyman's the other day," she replied. "It's a useful skill to have in the guard."

"That it is," Rowena replied, squinting slightly, but then followed up with a brilliant smile.

Tamarin couldn't pick up on any emotions through the shield or tell if Rowena was looking at her or the monitor behind her.

Rowena connected her tablet to the monitor so she could access it remotely and then, after squinting at her tablet for a moment, motioned down the hall. "Come. It's been decades since I checked that tail, and I want to hear all about your cubs."

Tamarin smiled and stepped out. "Those cubs are all grown up now. Robbie's a musician, and Jack's a pilot in the Ship's guild. He has three young cubs of his own. They're a rambunctious lot, but I've only met them once. Jack's currently stationed on Flyer, and this last year has been rather busy."

"Grandcubs! My, where has the time gone?"

"That's what happens when you stick your nose in a microscope and don't look up for a century," Tamarin teased.

Rowena snorted. "I see you haven't lost any of your snark."

She laughed. "Nope. That's the whole reason I was assigned to Avery's squad. He was the only one willing to put up with me after my mentor retired."

"I would have thought you'd have your own squad by now."

She shrugged. "Rank has never been important to me, but that may change soon. I'm hoping to transfer to New Hope as part of First Squad once the Hue-mans decide they want a permanent guard."

"I wondered if you might."

Rowena stopped at a door and hit the switch to open it, revealing a packed office full of stacked boxes and partially assembled equipment. "Basal, are you still in here?" she called out in Digger.

"Yes, ma'am," came a reply, and a young Digger rolled out from around the stack of boxes, didn't stop in time, and bumped into another stack, knocking it over with a large crash that just barely missed several pieces of equipment.

"Watch what you're doing, pup!" Rowena yelled. "That's expensive and delicate tech!"

"Sorry, Aunty," he said as he uncurled and started stacking the boxes back up. "No harm done, though. These are the boxes I've already unpacked."

"That's no excuse for not paying attention," she growled. "They could have damaged that other equipment, and you know there aren't replacements here!"

Basal curled back up in his shell under the onslaught of Rowena's anger.

Rowena sighed at the sight. "Go on. Get out of here before I decide to take a few pieces of that shell for myself. Find me something good for supper, and I might change my mind. Try not to break anything else while you do it, and don't come back here for an hour."

"Yes, ma'am," he replied from inside his shell and rolled out between them in a hurry.

Tamarin quickly moved out of the way as he barreled through the shield and bounced off the far wall before uncurling upside down and taking off in a fast paddle, using his claws to gain traction on the ceiling.

"Pups," Rowena muttered and shook her head. "That's my great great...great grand nephew. He's brilliant when it comes to maintaining and programming the tech, Level Four Journeyman already, but he's an absolute klutz otherwise. I'm pretty sure his mother sent him to me just to keep him from destroying her house. I have lost more equipment and experiments in the past year than in the entire past century combined." She shook her head again.

Tamarin chuckled. "I was always amazed at how much damage my two boys could do. Tiny whirlwinds of mass destruction. Thankfully, I could always send them to the arena when they started to get out of control."

"Hmm," Rowena grunted. "I might have to try that."

She helped Rowena through the shield, and once inside, she hit the door switch and privacy screen. As much as she hated it, she plastered her mask on and assumed the persona of a guard. "Alright, out with it, old healer. What are you hiding?"

Rowena snorted. "I'm surprised you didn't figure that out already, but then maybe you haven't been taught that yet."

"Taught what?" Tamarin pressed.

"Those weren't any old hormonal imbalances. Marsee's in heat or will be soon."

Tamarin sat down, stunned, and then blanched as she realized what it meant. "Ancient gods. That poor child. On top of everything else?"

"Exactly," Rowena replied as she shuffled over to a low seat and climbed in with a groan. "That's why we didn't tell her. I have no doubt that knowledge would put her over the edge, as unstable as she is right now. Jeran thinks it's his fault for biting her scruff to snap her out of her psychosis, and frankly, I'm willing to let him believe that. It's not like Marsee can make Rip any more dead than he already is."

"I wonder if that's what she won't tell us?"

"Probably, although I'm not sure she even realizes it."

"I'm sure her mother would have explained after what happened to Little Flower."

"Your mating cycle, sure, but not his. We have no real proof outside of the fact that the majority of her scars are to her sides."

"But she's not physically mature yet. Would her instinct even recognize it?"

Rowena snorted. "And you blame me for hiding things. Use that fur-brained noggin of yours. How could she be in heat if she *wasn't* physically mature?"

"But..."

"But nothing. Your guild isn't the only one keeping secrets."

Tamarin stared at Rowena. "I'm a guard. There should be no secrets from us, especially something like this."

Rowena snorted. "Everyone has secrets, child." She squinted at the stack of boxes on the desk next to her before tapping one on the bottom. "Lift the others, please."

Tamarin did, setting them on the floor beside the desk.

Rowena placed her thumb on the case to unlock it, revealing a large selection of medications.

"What's all this?"

"Mostly, a distraction, in case anyone looked," Rowena said. "Most of this will go to Hyacinth in case someone else needs it. Her pharmacy was severely lacking in off-species medications." Rowena pulled out a small vial, squinted at it, and then handed it to her, along with another one she pulled out.

"If anyone asks, you didn't get this from me. This is the most regulated substance on your planet, and you wouldn't believe the hoops I had to jump through to secure it. One injection of this and any Saber over the age of three would be in heat. It'll leave a bio-marker, which would be traced back to me if anyone looked."

"Three?!" Tamarin exclaimed. "Why do you even have this?"

"Research. Scan the code. I imagine you'll find the attached documentation very enlightening."

Tamarin did as ordered. An authorization screen came up. She placed her thumb on the tablet to authorize and frowned.

Authorization Denied!

"Denied?!" Tamarin said in surprise. "Who would deny access to the information sheet on a medication?"

Rowena grunted and held out her hand. "Well, that confirms a suspicion I had." Rowena used her authorization to access the information. "I'm guessing that might be logged somewhere, but I seriously doubt they'll care that a guard is accessing it, especially you. If anyone is notified, it'll be Nerissa or Marcus, and both know you've been involved in her care."

Tamarin nodded and then tilted her head at Rowena. "You have the rank, but why would you be researching this? That hasn't been your area of study."

"Of course it was. I've studied everything relating to your instincts, especially your mating instinct. I have yet to figure out why that remains unaffected by the transition."

Tamarin raised a brow. "But they are, or at least I always thought they were. I never had any loss of control during my heat, even if it was very enjoyable. Certainly, nothing like before I transitioned."

"Well, that probably had more to do with who you partnered with. Was it an open heat?"

"No, I went with another guard. We were nothing more than friends at the time, but he's retired from active duty due to an injury and had the time to help care for the cubs."

"If you decide to have another litter, I suggest an open mating. You'll find it's a very different experience, at least the ones I observed were."

Tamarin raised the other brow. "You are full of surprises today, old healer."

Rowena chuckled. "You don't live as long as I do without collecting a few. Now, what are you going to do about Jeran and Marsee? Nerissa and I are doing our best to deflect, but once Ammond gets here with that scanner, I'm not sure we're going to be able to keep your secret hidden any longer. Marsee's already starting to recover, and Jeran's on borrowed time."

"Watch and wait is all we can do right now," Tamarin replied. "I'm not sure Jeran is as close as it would appear. Neither Avery or I noticed anything when Marsee crashed. We were both surprised when Marcus appeared and pulled him out of there. He was terrified, but who wouldn't be in that situation? Besides, he's far too visible, and his death would do far more damage. There's no way for us to hide it here, not now anyway. Hopefully, he'll make it through the trial and back to Saber before he loses it completely."

"You know that's unlikely. You could bring them both into the guard."

She snorted. "After ten thousand years, do you honestly think Kendra will let the Council know what's going on? We had orders not to bring Marsee in before we left. Granted, we expected to be hiding psychosis, not a transition."

Rowena squinted at her and then tapped Tamarin on her forehead. "Don't forget. I know what's really going on. I've heard the stories. Her name can't be a coincidence."

Tamarin snorted again. "You honestly put weight in those old legends? I didn't think your species believed in that kind of thing."

"I *am* an old legend," Rowena replied. "And I forget nothing. The thing about being a scientist is that the more you know about how the universe works, the more mysterious it becomes. I've studied this illness for most of my life. The odds that I would live long enough to treat her are astronomical. It's a miracle Marsee even survived the transition. Her instinct was bigger than any I've ever scanned. She is going to be powerful and far sooner than you expect. Like I said, she's already starting to recover."

"Already?" Tamarin asked with a frown. "It hasn't even been a week."

Rowena knocked her on the head again, harder this time. "Were you even paying attention today? Her sense of pain is already returning. I give her four, maybe five standard days before the rest of her senses start to return. It's going to get very interesting around here. If Marcus even suspects her instinct is returning and taking control, he'll kill her before we can stop him. I tried my best to suggest that Marsee might have some odd side effects as she recovers, more so after you left."

"He'll be risking a war if he does. Both Wind Rider and Clear Seas have placed her under their protection."

Rowena blinked and scratched at a bare spot on her shell. "I've known Marcus since he was a cub. That won't stop him. He'll do what he thinks is right and claw anyone who gets in the way."

Tamarin nodded. That was her impression of Marcus, too, even if he played the loving uncle around Marsee. "I'm honestly surprised he's allowed Marsee to live this long, family or not."

"He has softened over the years. I thought for sure he was going to kill Ellie today."

"Ellie?! Why? Did she have an episode?"

Rowena shrugged. "I couldn't tell from where I was if her instinct was on or not, but she attacked Jeran when she thought he'd raped her. No one was hurt besides Ellie. Marcus broke her paw, stopping her, and Jeran said she could take a swipe at a later date if she wanted."

She snorted. "There goes ten credits. She's been doing remarkably well, not even a twang, but an outburst was expected. What time did it happen?"

"About five minutes after you left."

She opened her tablet and recorded the bet, then sent a coded message to her team informing them, not that they weren't keeping watch for issues anyway.

Rowena chuckled, but her laughter turned into a yawn. "Help me with this mess, and I'll share a few more secrets with you. I suppose someone should know before I die."

She spent the next hour helping Rowena set up the equipment as the old Healer gave her a mix of rapid-fire instructions and training from her seat before Rowena called it quits, claiming she was too tired to continue. Tamarin offered to help her back to wherever she was staying, only to be surprised when Rowena pointed her to an unpacked case.

"I'm far too old to waste time traveling back and forth to an apartment," Rowena said as Tamarin pulled out the case and found an inflatable mattress inside. As she was setting it up, there was a hesitant knock on the door. "That must be my klutz of a nephew. Right on time, at least. I hope he found something decent to eat."

Tamarin walked over and opened the door. Basal was outside, with a large bag in one hand. She heard the skittering of Rowena's live meal of crawlies inside and managed to keep the shudder off her face by plastering on her guard mask.

Basal swallowed hard at the sight of her and shuffled past, as far away from her as he could get and far more cautious than before.

She bid them a good night and left.

After a quick stop at the market for a meal of her own, one far less skittery, she made her way to the barracks and the private arena where her nose said Avery was still training. Unlike many of the other areas in the guard complex, this training hall and the apartments within were only accessible to members of her own species. No cameras were allowed inside, and a record of every access was sent to Kendra. Even still, they made regular sweeps of the building to ensure no one else had entered.

The two guards at the entrance nodded as she swam inside and made her way into the arena, where several squads were actively training. Avery, however, was waiting for her on the balcony. The smell of sweat and sand on his fur told her that he had already finished his training.

"What took so long?" he asked. "I was starting to get worried."

"I had a very interesting conversation with Rowena," she replied, not wanting to discuss it in public.

Avery picked up on her hesitation and motioned for her to follow him down to a nearby conference room. Once there, she flopped into a chair. Decades of training meant it was easy to stand guard for hours on end, but like all guards, they took whatever opportunity they could to rest.

He surprised her by not asking about Rowena. "What are your thoughts on Jeran?"

She shrugged. "I'm not sure what to make of him. He's as much of an anomaly as Marsee. Emotionally, he's a wreck, but no more than any parent would be in his situation. He was a jagged mess the entire way here, but I didn't notice anything wrong in Marsee's room outside of the fear he radiated, and there was more than enough blood to cause problems."

"Neither did I," he replied. "But he did admit to hearing his instinct and being non-verbal, and he wasn't lying about it either."

She nodded the point. "True. However, the circumstances have been extreme, and he was in control today when you tested him. I didn't even see the slightest flicker of a waiver, and he knew you had every right to kill him for his admission. Marsee claims she heard hers for over eight months, and he has far more training than she does. If he weren't on the Council, I'd bring him in."

"So would I," Avery said. "There was one brief flicker the moment he mentioned hearing his instinct. His claws came out, too."

"I wasn't looking at him then. I was examining the scans. That could be a normal reaction. He knows the consequences. I'm surprised he was even able to mention it to us."

"True. I wish I had seen Marsee before that day in the garden. It might give us some insight into his control."

"No, you don't. You would have killed her."

He shrugged. "I suppose you're right. Still, if she was able to hear her instinct for months, that would certainly explain Jeran's control. Clear Seas pulled me in again for questioning after he spoke with Marsee the other day. He believes she was never taught *how* to use her instinct. Certainly, her conversation with Marcus and her written testimony would lend to that hypothesis."

"Who is?" Tamarin asked. "I certainly wasn't. I didn't even know what that meant when I was brought in."

Avery flicked his ears back. "You weren't? My mother taught me when I was two, maybe three years old."

"No, at least I don't think so. I honestly don't remember much before I was brought in. I get bits and pieces every now and then." She shrugged. "Anyway, I didn't purposely try using my instinct until I joined the guard and, well, you know how that went."

He flicked an ear back as he considered. "So what did Rowena want?"

She pursed her lips and sighed. "They think Marsee's in heat. They're treating her for it but not telling her as they don't believe she'll handle it well. She also informed me that Marsee's already recovering and gives her another four or five standard days before her senses start to return. "

He frowned and scratched behind his ears. "I was afraid of that. I sent Kendra a coded message on Marsee's status, but I didn't get a response back before she jumped. I just hope what Rowena did will be enough to help Marsee until Kendra gets here."

"And if not? She's already tried to kill herself once. What's going to happen when her senses start going haywire on her? If she doesn't kill herself, then Marcus will, and she doesn't deserve that."

"None of the children we've had to kill deserved that." He let out a heavy sigh as he tapped his claws on the table, and then his expression hardened as he made a decision. "How committed are you to transferring to New Hope?"

She flicked an ear back in surprise at the sudden change in the conversation. They had already submitted their applications for transfer. "You know I am. They need our protection. That much is more obvious now than ever. Why?"

"Because if Kendra doesn't bring Marsee in and assuming Kendra doesn't kill me immediately..."

"You're going to disobey her orders?!" she inferred.

"They won't be my orders if Kendra's no longer my Senior."

She nodded the point and leaned back in her chair, considering. "It doesn't take a ten-thousand-year-old prophecy to see that we're on the verge of war, but you'll be walking a fine line. Marcus and Kendra could execute you for treason, as could I for even suggesting it."

"It wouldn't be the first time," he replied. "We're treading a fine line now as it is. We've all said more than we should. If you've got a better idea, I'm all for it."

She grunted in acknowledgment. "We're going to need our general, and the squad or two we'll have in New Hope won't be enough to win a war. If Kendra doesn't see that, then perhaps it's time for her to step down."

Avery raised a brow at her. "You aren't thinking of challenging her for Senior, are you?"

"If necessary," she replied.

"You're good, Tam, but you're not that good. Quinn's probably the only one who has a chance at beating her, but I don't know if he would challenge her over this."

"Then I guess I'd better get my tail over to the arena and pray Kendra's in a good mood and doesn't kill you when she arrives."

He squinted his eyes at her for the slight barb, but she could tell he wasn't annoyed. He was scared. He hid it well, though. "Just out of curiosity. What's the current bet?" he asked.

She chuckled. "The vast majority believe she'll put you on the pole for a month. My bet is that she'll have you cleaning out the waste rooms for the next decade. Granted, you did save Marsee's life yesterday, so that might work in your favor. Although I imagine she won't be happy that you allowed yourself to get clawed so badly in the process. That'll get you laps at the very least."

He snorted. "You got hurt, too."

"A scratch. She nearly gutted you."

"I know," he replied. "I wasn't expecting her to be so strong or fast. Not with her injuries." His humor vanished with both frustration at his lack of ability to handle the situation and a touch of confusion.

She shook her head at him. For all his skill, he was oblivious at times. "She's the General, Avery. She killed Rip while injured and without the use of a stunner, something neither of us could do, and she pinned her father without any training. What's one little Honor Guard with orders not to hurt her?"

"That was with her instinct. Besides, we don't know if she's the..."

"Don't lie to yourself, Avery," she said and stood to walk out. "Look what she did to save Stormy yesterday. She's going to be as strong, if not stronger than she was before, and you know it."

He sighed and leaned forward onto the table. "Gods. What a mess."

"You do tend to find yourself in the middle of them. And drag us along with you."

"Sorry. You know, she did die, briefly. I suppose we could all be wrong about the war. Maybe killing Rip ended it before it could start."

She snorted. "You know that's wishful thinking. All you have to do is sniff the Seniors to know that. Even Sammianna's worried. This is far bigger than Rip. Now, enough moping. I need to sharpen my claws. You up for a round in the sparring ring or do you need more time to recover from your injuries."

He rolled his eyes but stood to follow her out. "Like you'll land anything on me."

"Five credits says I do," she replied, tail curled with humor.

"Just five?" he replied. "You are scared."

"I was being nice," she replied. "Five hundred?"

He squinted his eyes at her at the challenge. Deal."

An hour later, she was five hundred credits richer, but Avery had landed more than a few strikes on her and 'killed' her several times in the process.

After treating their injuries and returning to her room and a shower, she flopped on her bunk and curled up to read the documentation Rowena had shared with her. Several additional documents had been sent to her while she trained. She started flipping through them and then pinned her ears back in surprise. It was all of Rowena's research, notes, and scribbles, every last little bit from over two hundred years of research on psychosis. It would take her months to dig through everything, but Rowena had highlighted several sections. She read through those first, and by the time she finished, she was pretty sure her ears couldn't go any further back from surprise.

"Secrets indeed!"

Yawning, she set her alarm and turned off the lights. She was almost asleep when a loud, ear-twitching noise woke her. Groaning, she grabbed her pillow and buried her head under it. Avery was snoring in the room next to her, and the walls did nothing to keep the sound out, and neither did her pillow.

"Gods! Just one night without snoring! Is that too much to ask?"

The gods sadly did not answer her prayer.

CHAPTER 68

Little Flower: Apprentice

The days ticked by with agonizing slowness, even though Little Flower managed to stay busy the entire time. In between preparing for the meeting and caring for Hope, when the others allowed her any time with her child, Ammond continued her physical therapy, which they did in the privacy of her tiny room.

He was as much of a taskmaster as her mother had been, if not more so, but there was a big difference. For one, she was finally seeing progress. She wasn't going to win any races against her daughter any time soon, but she was able to care for herself, by herself, and for the most part care for her daughter now. For another, Ammond was focusing on her goals, which now centered around caring for Hope and furthering her need for independence.

She learned that a large portion of the time spent in the clinic during the Saber's growth year was geared towards learning how to parent. When she expressed an interest in that, he started working through that information with her and, in the process, updating the guides with Hue-man-specific information that he gathered from the other women. Those conversations were hilarious and enlightening to everyone, and she started re-kindling friendships with the others, who, to her relief, weren't seeing her as a child anymore but as a new mother, struggling to figure out how to be a parent.

More importantly, she had a reason to work for it now. She needed to be strong for Marsee. Her nightmares had increased to the point where she could barely sleep, every one of them of Marsee being swallowed whole by the same amorphous swirling darkness or dragged down into the depths of the sea. She was terrified about what she would find when they arrived, that she would be too late. Even though she couldn't connect to the network, she still sent dozens of messages to Marsee, hoping that maybe they'd connect to a relay and a message would get through.

In addition to her therapy, she had Ammond teach her the basics of how to use a med scanner and treat basic injuries so she would be able to help Marsee when she was released from the Trauma Center. Ammond was hesitant about teaching her, though, as she wasn't part of the Healers Guild, so she joined. If she was required to become a Journeyman in order to legally care for her sister, then she would. Ammond agreed to mentor her as long as she didn't stop drawing and then buried her in homework. She found it absolutely fascinating, which honestly surprised her, as she'd never once considered a medical career and had loathed her science classes nearly as much as she'd hated learning Spanish.

Eight eternally long Earth days later, the ships finally arrived. Hope had been sedated again before they exited jump, and everything was packed up and ready to unload once they landed. It was nearly midnight when they arrived. She could see little as they approached the landing platform except for the dark sea lit up by a single moon that gave her pangs of homesickness, even though it was far larger than Earth's moon had been. After so long living in a desert, seeing so much water was astounding. From what little she could see, there was a faint outline of islands off in the distance, but other than that, everything was water.

The ship landed without incident on top of the platform. As it was so late, she decided to keep Hope sedated until it wore off on its own, as did most of the other mothers. Once they'd gathered their belongings from their rooms, they were led off the ship. The smell of salt air hit her the moment the door opened and reminded her of the few visits she'd taken to the ocean as a child. The air was cold and windy compared to their new world, but they weren't outside long.

They were one of the last off as they'd purposely let everyone else go ahead so that her slow pace wouldn't slow them down and followed the rest down a long ramp into a large terminal. The others were already being led off by platform workers to show them to their rooms. As the crowds thinned, they found Marcus and her father waiting for them, and she did her best to pick up her pace to meet them.

Her father dropped all semblance of the dignified Senior Councilor he was and ran to meet her, scooping her up in a hug that practically enveloped her in his copper fur. While he was careful of Hope sleeping in her carry sack, she could feel his body shaking with emotion and relief to see them safe.

"I can't believe how much better you're walking!" he signed after setting her down. Then, after looking at her mother for several moments, he tilted his head in Marcus's direction. "Marcus will show you to your rooms. I need to remain to handle the extradition of Damon into Water Sprite custody."

Her mother nodded, and they followed Marcus out of the terminal to a large bank of elevators, which he led them into and down several levels before exiting.

"The rest of your Council is in the other building, but I figured you'd all want rooms near each other," he said, "and this was the closest set of available rooms to the Trauma Center. I know it's smaller than you're used to, but it will be easier for Marsee once she's released, and it's more secure."

"I don't care where I sleep," Little Flower replied.

Henry and GrandFather had rooms on one side of the hallway, while she and her mother had separate rooms on the other.

"There are connecting doors between the suites if you want to unlock them. I'll bring you over to see Marsee as soon as you're ready. We'll need to go outside, so bring your masks," he informed them.

The door switches to her room had been lowered so she could easily reach them. When she entered, she found a fully human-sized room, complete with a single large bed, a table with four chairs, a crib for Hope, a small kitchenette, and a wall of cupboards and drawers to store their stuff. After being around the oversized Saber furniture, it felt tiny and odd. There was only one room outside of a fairly generic waste room, which thankfully had a proper toilet. Marcus showed her how the sleeping area could be closed off if she wanted and then left to give her privacy, but she left it open. It was an interior room, so there were no windows, but a beautiful mural and strategically placed lighting and plants more than made up for it. It was warm and comfortable and, more importantly, felt safe.

Grandfather and Henry dropped her bags off and left for their rooms.

On the bed was a package for her, which she quickly opened and smiled as she examined the purchases she'd made before she'd left.

She used the facilities, changed into her wetsuit, and then changed Hope. With some effort, she managed to put Hope back in the carry sack on her own, shoved the package and several diapers inside the sack with Hope, and grabbed her flippers and their masks.

Her grandfather and mother were already waiting for her when she left the room. They followed Marcus back down the hallway to the bank of elevators, which they took down to the bottom before putting their masks and flippers on. Her grandfather helped her with hers, as she couldn't put them on while carrying Hope, and then went through the static shield into the ocean beyond. She'd tried the shield out already in the pool back home, so she was prepared for the experience, but it was so very different from what she was used to. It was as close to weightless as she'd ever been.

Marcus handed her a drone and showed them how to use it. Relieved she wouldn't have to swim the entire way, as she was already exhausted from the long walk, they took off, followed by a pair of Water Sprite guards who were waiting for them outside.

They crossed a park dimly lit by scattered streetlights and the lights of their drones but saw no one else. It wasn't long before they arrived at the Trauma Center. Marcus led them inside, leaving their escort behind, where they hung up their drones and followed after him. With the flippers, she could keep up with the Sabers, but the Water Sprite healers they saw practically zoomed by. Even still, she was exhausted by the time they made it to Marsee's room, which was flanked by two guards, one Saber and one Water Sprite, as was every door they'd passed through. Marcus introduced them to every set of guards and gave them permission to enter at any time.

When they entered, Marsee was curled in a tight ball, wrapped around a pillow, sound asleep, but Ellie was still up and waiting for them.

Ellie stood and gave her mother a long hug. She heard the deep rumble of conversation before they pulled apart. Ellie turned to her. "She's been asleep for about an hour. She tried to stay awake for you and wants you to wake her, but be cautious when you do. She startles easily."

Her mother sat on the bed and gently stroked Marsee's face. "Marsee, we're here."

Marsee jerked awake with a ferocious snarl and stopped just short of clawing her mother in the face before she fully woke.

"Mama!" Marsee said, and then, seeing the rest of them, signed, "You're here! I'm so sorry, Mama! I didn't mean to swipe at you."

"Shh, it's okay," her mother signed back. "I scared you. That was my fault." Her mother hugged Marsee, but Little Flower shoved her aside, wanting her turn.

"Hey, Chenzie Butt, you'd better have a hug left for me. Mama, help me up!"

It was far too high for her to climb even before her injury. Her mother picked her up and handed her to Marsee, who held out her arms for her. She snuggled into her sister's arms and sighed, feeling safe and whole for the first time since the moment her sister had left. They both held each other for a long time. She could feel her sister shake and knew it wasn't from her purring. Marsee pulled away just enough to look down at Hope, who was still sleeping in the carry sack.

"They sedated her for the landing. She'll be asleep for hours," she explained to her sister, who gently caressed the top of Hope's head.

"I always thought Hope's fur was kind of skimpy, but now she has more fur than the both of us combined."

"That's okay. At least this way, I won't get hairballs caught in my throat while I'm sleeping," she teased.

Marsee chuckled. "I guess there are some benefits to not having fur."

"Yup, several. Now you don't have to worry about me pulling your tail fur while you sleep, either."

Her sister laughed and then frowned. "I don't think it's safe for us to sleep together anymore. I clawed Papa badly the other day when I was stuck in a night terror. I don't want to hurt you or Hope."

"You won't," Little Flower signed. "I figured you might have night terrors like I did, so I ordered something special for you, and it was waiting for me when I arrived."

She reached inside the carry sack, pulled out the small package, and handed it to her sister.

Marsee awkwardly opened the package and dumped the contents onto her lap.

"I had them make up some of the gloves you use for working with the archives but had them pad them extra thick and make a set for your back feet, too. This way, you'll be able to keep from scratching me while you sleep and can take them off in a hurry if you need to defend us from a creepy crawly."

"What's this, though?" Marsee asked, holding up an object with a buckle in the back.

She rubbed the back of her head and looked sheepish before answering. "It's a muzzle. It wraps around your nose and mouth so you can't accidentally bite me. Not that I think you'll harm me, but I want *you* to feel comfortable and safe around us. The buckle is a quick release, too."

Instead of being offended, as she'd feared when she ordered it. Marsee nearly crushed her in a hug. "Thank you! I felt horrible after hurting Papa but didn't know what to do." Marsee spoke to her in English, her voice a deep melodic baritone, with a thick accent unlike any she'd heard before, but beautiful nonetheless. She knew just how hard it was for the Sabers to speak her language, and Marsee had worked hard to become fluent for Hope.

"I hope it fits," she replied.

Marsee tried everything on and then tried to destroy her pillow, with little success.

The others watched but said nothing, although she could see the rough edges around her mother's mask.

"I can't even begin to tell you how good that makes me feel," Marsee told everyone after she was done with her test.

"Good, now everyone, go home and get some sleep. You too, Ellie. Now that I'm here, the night shift is officially mine."

"Are you sure?" Ellie asked.

"Positive. You can resume whacking her with your tail in the morning."

"Hey!" Marsee squawked. "I have enough bruises. I don't need more from Ellie."

Ellie chuckled but gathered her things and hugged Marsee before swimming out.

"Do you want me to watch Hope?" her grandfather asked.

"Nope, I'm all set," she replied. "Go on. You too, Mama." She gave her mother a pointed glare.

Her mother nodded and hugged both of them before leaving with GrandFather and Marcus.

She glared up at the only remaining person in the room, a large female Saber guard. "You too. Out."

"I have orders to remain in the room from your father," the guard replied.

"I don't care what his orders are. I'm a Councilor, too, and I declare this room my district. Marsee is under my protection as a resident of my district, and if you don't leave the room in five seconds, I'll have you arrested for trespassing. Out! You can guard from the hallway."

The guard stared her down, ears pinned back in astonishment, and said something to the two guards floating outside, who turned to peer in with equal astonishment. Behind her, Marsee snorted with laughter, and the tail wrapped around Little Flower's waist curled.

She continued to glare the guard down. "Five...four..."

The guard outside said something, and the one inside bolted for the door.

"And shut the door behind you," she added.

The expression of the guards outside shifted to amusement, but they did as ordered.

The moment the door shut, she turned back to Marsee with a grin over her tiny victory.

The cheerful mask Marsee had been wearing for her mother dropped. "Dark moons, Little Flower. I'm so scared!"

"I know, and you have every right to be, but I'm here now, and we'll get through this together. Now. Tell me as much or as little as you want."

Marsee pulled her in for another hug and held her tightly for a long time. She hugged back just as tightly and didn't say anything. Eventually, Marsee started talking, and they talked for hours before Marsee's exhaustion started winning the battle against her need to talk to someone who truly understood. Marsee climbed off the bed and helped her down so they could both use the hole of muck, and then after Marsee put on her safety gear, they curled up around each other like they usually slept. Both of them wrapped around Hope. It felt different without Marsee's fur, yet right in a way she couldn't explain. She gently traced along the lines of her sister's healed scars, both horrified by what had been done to her and deeply touched to know that it was thoughts of her and Hope that had kept her alive in the cave and what had allowed her to fight back against her instinct.

Within minutes, Marsee was sound asleep, but it took her a lot longer as she thought about everything her sister had told her and watched her child sleep, safely surrounded and protected by Marsee's mittened paws. With a smile, she drifted off into the first nightmare-free sleep she'd had in a very, very long time.

CHAPTER 69

Little Flower: Mother

Little Flower was awake before her sister, which was a fairly regular occurrence, but stayed snuggled in Marsee's warm, if no longer fury, embrace and watched as a healer, based on their badge, entered, carrying a large tray, and did a double-take to see her there and then the gear that Marsee was wearing.

"Marsee," Little Flower called out quietly.

Her sister groaned.

"Marsee, it's time to wake up."

Her sister grumbled and pulled her in tight for a hug, half asleep. but then her head shot up, and she looked down at her, wide-eyed and ears pinned back. "You're still in one piece!" her sister exclaimed, as if completely surprised that she hadn't harmed her in her sleep.

"Yup, you didn't even twitch last night," she replied. "At least not as far as I could tell."

Her sister took off the safety gear and then signed. "You'd have noticed. I usually wake up screaming or swiping at whoever walks in. That was the best sleep I've had since I left home. Oh, Rowena, this is my sister Little Flower and her cub Hope."

"Rowena? The brain specialist?" Little Flower asked.

"The one and only," Rowena replied, which Marsee translated for her. "It's nice to meet you finally, and I'm glad to see you're doing better."

"I am. Thank you. For everything."

Rowena nodded and shuffled forward, setting the tray on the table next to the bed. "I've brought breakfast for you. Congratulations, you've officially been upgraded to solid food as of this morning. I've brought you a random selection of what they had available in the kitchen so you can see if any of it tastes good or not, and a menu for future meals. I've circled the items you're allowed to eat. Avoid anything spicy or hot for at least another week. I'll be back for your therapy in an hour."

After the healer left, Marsee shifted her attention to stare at the tray of food.

Little Flower peered at it dubiously, not recognizing much of anything, and most of it looked unappealing. "Before you start eating that...um... lovely plate of chenzie poop disguised as food, will you help me down off the bed? I need to use the hole of muck."

Marsee did and then followed her. By the time they were back, Hope was starting to wake.

"Marsee!" Hope squealed when she saw her aunt, not the least bit confused by Marsee's lack of fur.

"Hey there! How's my favorite niece?" Marsee said and then tickled Hope. Hope squealed with laughter.

"Need poop!" Hope signed, so Marsee carried her over to the hole of muck so she could go.

"What a big girl! I'm so proud of you!" Marsee signed when Hope was done and then chased her back over.

She caught her and tickled her, making Hope giggle.

Marsee sat down beside her, panting hard. "I tire so easily now, and I'm convinced the Senior Healer has been turning up the gravity in the room every day."

There was a rumble from the hallway, and Marsee pinned her ears. "I knew it!"

She growled something back, and the sounds of their rumbling laughter returned as Marsee wilted.

"What is it?"

"Aris says the room isn't even up to full Saber gravity yet. Gods. I'm so weak."

"You'll improve quickly. I'm sure. You'll probably have a much easier time than me since you don't have to rebuild all of your muscles like I did."

"I hope so. Of course, that assumes I don't keep injuring them. I broke my tail the other day and didn't even know it." Marsee flicked her tail up.

"Well, I suppose it could be worse?" she replied.

"How?"

"You could have rolled over it with a rocking chair like Ellie did. That had to have hurt."

Marsee's tail spiraled in laughter, proving that no permanent harm had been done to it.

"Now, come on, let's try that chenzie poop and see if it tastes as bad as it smells."

Marsee didn't move from where she'd sat down. "You didn't bring any cookies with you by any chance?"

She shook her head. "I didn't, but I'll ask Mama. I think there were still some left on the ship. Go on. You won't know until you try, and besides, it can't be any worse than the stuff they made me eat at the Agency." Little Flower picked up Hope. "Come on, help us back up on the bed."

Marsee sighed but helped them up before climbing up herself, then dragged the table over so they could both reach it. Marsee grabbed a piece. "Here goes nothing," she said, tossed it in, and slowly chewed.

"It doesn't taste the same, but it's not horrible. That's an improvement, I guess."

Little Flower grabbed a piece of fruit for Hope and then one for herself but spit it out almost immediately. Hope made a horrible face and threw it across the room. "You know, I stand corrected. This is worse.

I'm not sure your taste buds are off. This food is disgusting, and that's being kind." She grabbed another piece of fruit that looked familiar and nearly gagged. "That was not what I thought it was at all."

They spent the next hour trying the various foods and only found a few that were even remotely edible.

"Do me a favor and swim to the market when you get a chance and find a vendor named Opal and buy out her booth for me. I don't know if you'll like them, but she has this creation I call fire sticks. They taste better than chocolate chip cookies."

"Gladly. Anything with that rating is worth trying. So, how long do you have to stay here?"

"I don't know. They're still trying to figure out everything that's wrong with me. I tried leaving once but never even made it down the hall before passing out."

"Well, if they don't need to monitor you the entire time, you should see if you can return to the suites with us. Even Ammond needs time to sleep. Oh, that reminds me, I joined the Healer's Guild."

"You *what*?!" Marsee exclaimed. "Why?"

"So I can help take care of you. That way, you won't have to spend the rest of your life stuck in the trauma center or have Mama follow you around everywhere. Plus, none of the healers really know anything about how to treat the kinds of trauma we've been through. I want to fix that. It's been surprisingly fun. Ammond's mentoring me."

"He is? I didn't think he'd take another protege after he turned down GrandFather. He's already retired once."

"I'm far more persistent than GrandFather," Little Flower said with a wicked grin.

"Fair. I thought for sure you'd stick with the Guild once you started drawing again. I never expected Healers."

"To be honest, neither did I. I hated everything to do with biology in school, but then Ammond's a far better teacher than any I ever had."

"Of course, I'm a better teacher," Ammond signed with a huff as he walked in. "I've been doing it for nearly eight of your lifetimes. Now move over so I can give Marsee a hug." Ammond nearly crushed Marsee, then picked up Hope and hugged her.

"What? I don't get one?" Little Flower pouted.

"Pah! Unruly apprentices don't deserve hugs," he grumbled, "but I'll give you a pass this one time since you said such nice things about me. Don't let it go to your head."

"I promise," Little Flower said with a laugh, then tilted her head at Ammond. "Wait a minute. I was talking in English. You can hear me and understand it?"

He grinned. "I wondered when you'd figure that out. I can't speak your language to save my life. Your words are impossible to say, but I can hear and mostly understand you. I agree with your father, though. I'm pretty sure you're just making up words half the time."

"We are," Little Flower replied.

He blinked at her, surprised.

"When we don't have a word for something, we make it up or borrow from other languages. So how is it that you can hear me?"

He tilted his head to show a pair of hearing aids. "I modified the hearing aids to lower your voices to a frequency I could hear easier."

"So why didn't you tell me so I could speak to you?" she asked.

"Because I wanted you to work on your hand dexterity," he replied.

"Moons' forsaken healers are all alike," she muttered, causing both of them to laugh.

He turned to Marsee. "I can't stay long. I need to rescue the Senior Healer from your mother and commandeer a room for my equipment so we can scan that lovely brain of yours, but I wanted to give you some good news."

"What's that?" Marsee asked, perking up.

"If we're not able to fix the issue with your ability to feel pain, we think we've found a way to at least make it so you don't die during your growth spurt," Ammond said.

"Oh, that?" Marsee sagged with disappointment. "Rowena already told me."

"Rowena? She's here?" Ammond asked, pinning his ears back in surprise.

"You didn't know?" Marsee asked.

He shook his head. "No. She hasn't left Digger in close to fifty years. She's been consulting on your case, but I never expected her to show up."

Marsee wiggled her paws and grinned. "She told me she was looking forward to getting her paws on your new brain scanner."

He laughed. "She would. I've been teasing her about it for months. I haven't seen a report from her, but I'm four days behind on everything and came straight here as soon as I woke up. Did she find anything?"

Marsee nodded. "They made me crawl up to one of the Earth delegation ships that they parked on the roof of the Trauma Center and scanned me there. Anyway, Rowena said it's not all gone, just the control hub, and apparently, I *am* feeling pain. Sort of. They think that's what the hollowness I'm feeling is, and why it's so much worse when I try to turn my instinct on. She said that was phantom pain. They've been able to manage it some. It's been a weird couple of days since she arrived. They've been running all sorts of experiments on me, trying to see if I can retrain my brain. I think I may have drained the Senior Healer of her shocks one day. I never felt a thing, but apparently, my brain did. She's trying to figure out how to make a brain scanner small enough for me to wear if I can't."

He grunted. "Knowing her, she's probably going to hold those test results ransom until I let her play with my scanner and then try to take it apart."

Marsee chuckled, but then her ears drooped. "So, the implant. I take it you want to give it to me now?"

He nodded. "The sooner you do it, the better. You'll still grow another foot or more over the next two decades, which could cause a lot of strain and injury. If nothing else, you'll be alive."

"If you give it to me now, would I be male or infertile?"

"We don't know. From what we've been able to determine, a few people each year choose not to go through with their growth spurt, so we know it's safe, but according to our records, none of them have any genetic offspring. We have no way of knowing if that's intentional."

"Thanks, Uncle Ammond. I'll think about it," Marsee said, putting on a cheerful face, which fell the moment he left. Marsee picked up Hope and hugged her, rocking slightly.

"What's wrong?" Little Flower asked. "I would think you'd be happy to find out you've got longer to live."

"I am. It's just that even if I did react to a female, no one would ever mate with me," Marsee said as she started to rock Hope and purr. Her ears were drooped, and her furless tail wrapped tightly around her and Hope.

Hope snuggled in and started sucking her thumb.

"Why not?" Little Flower asked.

"I wouldn't be big enough. The female would choose a bigger male," Marsee said.

"Not if you're the only one there."

"Maybe, but I doubt anyone would *choose* to mate with me either. They'll be afraid their cubs will be born with psychosis."

"Well, you could always adopt someone else's children," Little Flower replied.

"Who would want to partner with me?" Marsee said. "I'm broken, missing all my fur, and I would always look like a child. I might have the rights of an adult, but in-betweeners are still treated differently. It's hard to explain."

"I know how you feel there. I hate being so short sometimes. Still, I'm sure you could find someone willing to partner with you. Someone who knows how wonderful, special, and talented you are and who thinks you're perfect just the size you are. Someone who knows how good you are with children and whose children love you to the moons and back."

"Yeah, right, who's even going to give me that chance?" Marsee muttered.

"I would," she said with a grin.

"Yeah, but you're my sister," Marsee replied morosely. Her ears drooped even further.

"Exactly. Weren't you the one that says siblings often partner together to raise children? You could be my partner. Help me raise Hope. She needs a father, and I couldn't think of anyone better suited for that role than you."

Marsee looked up at her, jaw dropped and ears pinned back in astonishment.

Little Flower counted slowly to fourteen before Marsee found her voice.

"You would let me adopt Hope?! Why me? Surely someone of your own species would be better?"

"Because you've been more of a mother to Hope these past few months than I could ever be. You've certainly changed far more of her poopy diapers than I have. You're the one who burped her and soothed her gums when her teeth came in, taught her how to crawl, walk, run, use the bathroom, and even talk. She obviously loves you. Look how content she is right now. With everyone else, she won't stay for more than a quick hug, even with me, not unless she's sleeping. But it's more than that. I love you. You've been there for me every step of the way, caring for both of us without a moment's hesitation. I was a complete mess the moment you left, and I'll be perfectly honest. I don't have any interest in any of the others of my species, male or female, and I don't need a mate. After what happened to me, I doubt I'll ever trust anyone enough to mate with them anyway. If I want more cubs, I'll just have Mama whip me up a batch. What I need is a partner, someone who wants to raise lots of cubs with me, someone who makes me a better person, who can hold me together when I fall apart, just like I promise to do for them, for you."

Marsee continued to stare at her in wide-eyed, ears-back amazement. "You really feel that way about me?"

"I really do," she replied. "Marsee Bet Chenzira, will you marry me?"

Laura Napoli was born and raised in northern Vermont and continues to make the area her home. When not spending her time on the warm clicky box (computer), she is the caregiver to four heating cats who provide her with heat, massage, acu-paw-ture, and purr-therapy in exchange for pets and catnip treaties.

PUBLICATIONS

Book 1: The Tails of Little Flower
Book 2: The Pride of Little Flower
Book 3: The Whiskers of Hope
Book 4: The Paws of Hope
Book 5: Saber's Instinct

COMING SOON

Book 6: Saber's Guard

IMPORTANT IN-FUR-MATION

CHARACTER PURR-REFERENCE

SENSITIVITY IN-FUR-MATION

https://www.heatingcats.com